From the Pages of
Nana

Nana, very tall and very plump for her eighteen years, in the white tunic of a goddess, and with her beautiful golden hair floating over her shoulders, walked towards the foot-lights with calm self-possession, smiling at the crowd before her. Her lips parted, and she commenced her great song:

"When Venus takes an evening stroll—"

(page 17)

Everything betokened the damsel abandoned too quickly by her first genuine protector, and fallen back into the clutches of unscrupulous lovers; a most difficult debut miscarried, and trammelled with a loss of credit and threats of eviction.

(page 35)

"Only fancy, I intend to sleep a whole night—a whole night all to myself!"

(page 59)

The women avenged morality in emptying his coffers.

(page 101)

In her dress of soft white silk, light and crumpled like a chemise, with her touch of intoxication, which had taken the colour from her face and made her eyes look heavy, she seemed to be offering herself in a quiet, good-natured sort of way. The roses she had placed in her dress and hair were now all withered, and only the stalks remained. (page 115)

As she listened to the robin, whilst the boy pressed close against her, Nana recollected. Yes, it was in novels that she had seen all that. Once, in the days gone by, she would have given her heart to have seen the moon thus, to have heard the robin and to have had a little fellow full of love by her side. Oh, heaven! she could have cried, it all seemed to her so lovely and good! For certain she was born to live a virtuous life.   (page 169)

"Ah! they're getting on well, your respectable women! They even interfere with us now, and take our lovers!"   (page 212)

From that night their life entirely changed. For a "yes" or a "no" Fontan struck her. She, getting used to it, submitted. Occasionally she cried out or menaced him; but he forced her against the wall, and talked of strangling her, and that made her yield.   (page 234)

Then Nana became a woman of fashion, a marchioness of the streets frequented by the upper ten, living on the stupidity and the depravity of the male sex. It was a sudden and definitive start in a new career, a rapid rise in the celebrity of gallantry, in the full light of the follies of wealth and of the wasteful effronteries of beauty.   (page 294)

"All those people no longer amaze me. I know them too well. You should see them with the gloss off! No more respect! respect is done with! Filth below, filth up above, it's always filth and company. That's why I won't put up with any nonsense." (page 340)

"Do you think I shall go to heaven?"   (page 365)

A lewdness seemed to possess them, and inspire them with the delirious imaginations of the flesh. The old devout frights of their night of wakefulness had now turned into a thirst for bestiality, a mania for going on all fours, for grunting and biting. Then one day, as he was doing the woolly bear, she pushed him so roughly that he fell against a piece of furniture; and she broke out into an involuntary laugh as she saw a bump on his forehead. From that time, having already acquired a taste for it by her experiment on La Faloise, she treated him as an animal, goaded him and pursued him with kicks.   (page 422)

She dreamed, too, of something better; and she went off in a gorgeous costume to kiss Satin a last time—clean, solid, looking quite new, as though she had never been in use.   (page 433)

Nana

Émile Zola

Translated by Burton Rascoe

With an Introduction and Notes
by Luc Sante

George Stade
Consulting Editorial Director

BARNES & NOBLE CLASSICS
NEW YORK

𝕁𝔹

BARNES & NOBLE CLASSICS

NEW YORK

Published by Barnes & Noble Books
122 Fifth Avenue
New York, NY 10011

www.barnesandnoble.com/classics

Nana was first published in French in 1880. Burton Rascoe's English
translation first appeared in 1922.

Published in 2006 by Barnes & Noble Classics with new Introduction, Notes,
Biography, Chronology, Inspired By, Comments & Questions,
and For Further Reading.

Nana
ISBN-13: 978-1-59308-292-5
ISBN-10: 1-59308-292-4
LC Control Number 2005932871

Produced and published in conjunction with:
Fine Creative Media, Inc.
322 Eighth Avenue
New York, NY 10001

Michael J. Fine, President and Publisher

Printed in the United States of America

QM

1 3 5 7 9 10 8 6 4 2

FIRST PRINTING

Émile Zola

Émile Zola was born in Paris on April 2, 1840. In 1843 his family moved to Aix-en-Provence, where his father, Francesco, a civil engineer of Italian origin and meager means, had found work planning a new water-works system. Four years later, he contracted a fever and died, leaving his widow, Émilie, and Émile in acute financial peril. With the help of family and friends, Émile studied at the Collège Bourbon in Aix, where he became a close friend of the future painter Paul Cézanne. After he and his mother moved to Paris in 1858, he continued his studies, with the help of a scholarship, at the Lycée Saint-Louis. Though he had won academic awards at school in Aix, his performance at the Lycée was undistinguished. He failed the *baccalauréat* exam twice and could not continue his studies, instead sinking into a grim state of unemployment and poverty.

In 1862 Zola was hired by the publisher Hachette, and he rose quickly through the ranks of the advertising department to earn a decent living. At the same time, he began to write journalistic pieces and fiction. In the latter, he sought to truthfully depict life and not censor the experiences of brutality, sex, and poverty. His explicit autobiographical novel, *Claude's Confession* (1865), created such a scandal that the police searched his house for pornographic material. Zola left Hachette in 1866 to work as a freelance journalist, and he inflamed readers with his opinionated critiques of art and literature. In 1867 he published his first major work, *Thérèse Raquin*. In his preface to this novel about adultery and murder, Zola introduced the term "naturalist" to describe his uncompromisingly "clinical" portrayals of human behavior.

A year after his marriage in 1870 to a former seamstress, Gabrielle Alexandrine Meley, Zola began publishing a series of novels that was to occupy him for more than twenty years. Under the umbrella name *Les Rougon-Macquart*, the series details the fortunes of three branches of a French family during the Second Empire (1852–1870). Among the twenty volumes are several masterpieces, including *The Drunkard* (1877), *Germinal* (1885), *Earth* (1887), and *Nana* (1880). As Zola's fame grew, he often retired to his second home in the countryside, where he was surrounded by fellow writers and literary disciples. As he claimed in his aesthetic manifesto, *The Experimental Novel* (1880), he and his friends created groundbreaking narratives that proudly defied the conventions of Romantic fiction.

While Zola was at work on a new series, *The Three Cities*, France was shaken by a scandal in the highest ranks of the military. In 1894 a Jewish officer, Alfred Dreyfus, was convicted of leaking secret military information to a German military attaché. When it became clear that Dreyfus had been framed by French officials under a cloud of anti-Semitism, Zola wrote "J'Accuse"—an open letter excoriating the military and defending the wrongfully convicted officer. Then Zola himself was convicted of libeling the military and sentenced to prison; he fled to England but returned the next year for Dreyfus's second court martial. The subsequent years were relatively much quieter for Zola as he worked to finish a new series of novels, *The Four Gospels*.

In 1902 Émile Zola died from carbon monoxide poisoning that some said was planned by fanatics offended by his role in the Dreyfus Affair. At Zola's funeral, which was attended by some 50,000 people, Anatole France eulogized him as "a moment in the history of human conscience." Zola was buried at Montmartre Cemetery, but in 1908 his remains were moved to a place of honor in the Panthéon in Paris.

Table of Contents

The World of Émile Zola and Nana

1840 Émile Zola is born on April 2 in Paris, to Francesco Zola, an Italian civil engineer, and Émilie Zola, née Aubert.

1843 The Zolas move to Aix-en-Provence, where Francesco engineers and executes a plan to supply drinking water to the town.

1844 *Le Comte de Monte Cristo* (*The Count of Monte Cristo*), by Alexandre Dumas (*père*), is published.

1847 Francesco dies of illness brought on by work-related exposure to bad weather, leaving his wife and son in dire financial straits.

1848 The Revolution of February 24 leads to the fall of the July Monarchy and the establishment of the Second Republic. Louis-Napoléon Bonaparte is elected president.

1852 Émile enrolls at the Collège Bourbon in Aix, where he wins prizes in several subjects. He and fellow student and future painter Paul Cézanne form what will be a longstanding friendship. A love of the work of Alfred de Musset and Victor Hugo reflects Émile's early affinity for Romanticism. Louis-Napoléon becomes emperor as Napoléon III.

1853 Baron Georges Haussmann begins his large-scale redesign of Paris. The Crimean War begins.

1856 Gustave Flaubert's novel *Madame Bovary* is published.

1857 Charles Baudelaire's poetry collection *Les Fleurs du mal* (*The Flowers of Evil*) is published.

1858 When they can no longer afford to live independently in Aix, Émilie and Émile move to Paris, hoping for assistance from friends. Émile receives a bursary (scholarship) that allows him to begin school at the prestigious Lycée Saint-Louis.

1859 Émile fails the *baccalauréat*, the test required for university study. His limited options for employment lead to a two-year period of destitution that will deeply influence his writing. Living the bohemian life in Paris's Latin Quarter, he writes poems, many of which have not been recovered.

1862   Zola is hired as a clerk by the publisher Hachette and advances in the advertising department. In his free time, he reads contemporary fiction and writes journalistic pieces and fiction. Victor Hugo's *Les Misérables* (*The Miserable Ones*) is published.

1863   Édouard Manet's painting *Déjeuner sur l'herbe* (*Luncheon on the Grass*), which depicts a nude woman and a partially nude woman picnicking with two dressed men, is exhibited in the *Salon des Refusés* and creates a scandal.

1864   A book of Zola's short stories, *Les Contes à Ninon* (*Tales for Ninon*), is published. The author corresponds with the brothers Edmond and Jules de Goncourt, who publish the naturalistic novel *Germinie Lacerteux* (*Germinie*). The International Workingmen's Association is founded.

1865   Zola meets and sets up a household with his future wife, Gabrielle Alexandrine Meley, a working-class seamstress. He publishes a sexually explicit fictional memoir, *La Confession de Claude* (*Claude's Confession*), to considerable scandal and a great deal of publicity. A book that will substantially influence Zola's thinking, Claude Bernard's *Introduction à l'étude de la médecine expérimentale* (*An Introduction to the Study of Experimental Medicine*) is published. Zola later argues that the novelist, like the scientist, can bring the scientific method to his work, and that the novelist can experiment with as well as observe his characters.

1866   Zola meets Édouard Manet, whose portrait of Zola will eventually hang in the Musée d'Orsay in Paris. Zola resigns from Hachette and writes highly opinionated art and literary criticism for the newspaper *L'Événement. Mes Haines* (*My Hates*) and *Mon Salon*, two volumes of essays on art and literature, are published.

1867   Zola's compelling novel of murder, *Thérèse Raquin*, is published to many hostile reviews; in the book's pref-ace, Zola uses the term "naturalist" to describe a new form of writing that unites scientific observation and lit-erary depiction. The first International Exhibition of Paris opens.

1868 In the novel *Madeleine Férat*, published this year, Zola ex-plores the concept of heredity.

1869 Gustave Flaubert's *L'Éducation sentimentale (Sentimental Education)* is published. Zola writes a letter introducing himself to the author. Zola presents the master plan of *Les Rougon-Macquart*, his richly detailed twenty-novel portrait of a family, to his publisher.

1870 Meley and Zola marry. The Franco-Prussian War begins, which leads to the Siege of Paris and the fall of the Sec-ond Empire. During the 1870s, Zola will meet often with influential authors Flaubert, Edmond de Goncourt, and Ivan Turgenev.

1871 Zola returns to Paris and publishes *La Fortune des Rougon (The Fortune of the Rougons)*, the first of the Rougon-Macquart cycle; the novel enjoys only modest success. The Franco-Prussian War ends. Adolphe Thiers, presi-dent of France's newly formed Third Republic, sup-presses the Commune of Paris.

1872 Zola publishes *La Curée (The Kill)*, a novel about real estate dealings during the years when Paris was being re-designed.

1873 Zola publishes *Le Ventre de Paris (The Belly of Paris)*, a novel that takes place in the central food markets of Paris. Arthur Rimbaud's *Une Saison en enfer (A Season in Hell)* and Jules Verne's *Le Tour du monde en quatre-vingts jours (Around the World in Eighty Days)* are published. Napoleon III dies, and Patrice de MacMahon becomes president of the French republic, following the resigna-tion of Thiers.

1874 *La Conquête de Plassans (The Conquest of Plassans)*, the fourth novel of the Rougon-Macquart series, is pub-lished. The first Impressionist art exhibition is held.

1875 *La Faute de l'abbé Mouret (The Sin of Father Mouret)*, Zola's novel about a priest in love, is published and is a commercial success.

1876 Another novel in the Rougon-Macquart series, *Son Excellence Eugène Rougon* (*His Excellency Eugène Rougon*), is published.

1877 Zola's *L'Assommoir* (translated as *The Drinking Den, The Dram Shop,* and *The Drunkard*), an authentic portrait of working-class life and the effects of alcoholism, is denounced by the left and the right but meets with great commercial success. Now financially well-off, the Zolas move to the rue de Boulogne.

1878 *Une Page d'Amour* (*A Love Affair*), about the guilty passions of an adulterous couple, is published. The Zolas buy a cottage at Médan, near Paris.

1879 A theatrical production of *L'Assommoir* is a huge success. Jules Grévy, a moderate, is elected president of the Third Republic. Jules Guesde founds the French Socialist Workers Party.

1880 Zola has his greatest commercial success with his ninth Rougon-Macquart novel, *Nana.* His influential treatise on naturalism, *Le Roman Expérimental* (*The Experimental Novel*), is published. *Les Soirées de Médan* (*Evenings at Médan*), a collection of stories by Zola and fellow authors, is published. Zola's mother dies. Flaubert dies.

1882 Zola publishes the novel *Pot-Bouille* (*Restless House*).

1883 *Au Bonheur des dames* (*A Ladies' Paradise*), about how a new enterprise, the department store, affects smaller merchants, is published. Guy de Maupassant's *Une Vie* (*A Life*) is published.

1884 Zola's novel *La Joie de vivre* (*The Joy of Life*) is published. The Waldeck-Rousseau law legalizes labor unions. J.-K. Huysmans publishes *À rebours* (*Against the Grain*), an attack on naturalism.

1885 *Germinal,* thought by many to be Zola's greatest work, is published; it depicts the hard life of coal miners in northern France.

1886 *L'Oeuvre* (*The Masterpiece*) is published; the novel describes an Impressionist painter resembling Cézanne.

1887 The next Rougon-Macquart novel, *La Terre* (*Earth* or *The Soil*), is published.

1888 A "fairy tale" novel, *La Rêve* (*The Dream*), is published. While still married, Zola begins an affair with a young housekeeper, Jeanne Rozerot, that will continue until the end of his life.

1889 Rozerot gives birth to Zola's first child, Denise. Construction of the Eiffel Tower, begun in 1887, is completed.

1890 *La Bête Humaine* (*The Beast in Man*), considered by some to be Zola's most pessimistic book, is published.

1891 Jacques, Rozerot and Zola's second child, is born. Zola and his wife travel through the Pyrenees. *L'Argent* (*Money*) is published.

1892 *La Débâcle* (*The Debacle* or *The Collapse*), a war novel that also traces the rise of the Paris Commune, is published.

1893 Zola publishes *Le Docteur Pascal* (*Doctor Pascal*), the final Rougon-Macquart work.

1894 *Lourdes*, the first installment of Zola's idealistic trilogy *Les Trois Villes* (*The Three Cities*), is published. Sadi Carnot, president of the French republic, is assassinated, and Jean Casimir-Périer becomes president. Spurred by virulent anti-Semitism in the military, the public, and the press, the French government without clear justification convicts Alfred Dreyfus, an officer in the French army, of giving secret information to a German military attaché.

1896 *Rome*, the next book in the *Three Cities* trilogy, is published.

1897 Edmond Rostand's *Cyrano de Bergerac* debuts.

1898 *Paris*, the last book of the *Three Cities* trilogy, is published. New evidence leads to the reopening of the Dreyfus case, and Zola publishes his famous open letter in defense of Dreyfus, "J'Accuse," in the newspaper *L'Aurore*. He accuses the army of deception and cover-up; found guilty of libeling the army, he is fined 3,000 francs and sentenced to a year in prison. He flees to England.

1899 Zola returns to Paris. Dreyfus is reconvicted at a second court martial but is granted a presidential pardon. Zola publishes *Fécondité* (*Fecundity*), the first installment of a new series, *Les Quatre Évangiles* (*The Four Gospels*).

1901 *Travail* (*Labor*), the next in the *Four Gospels* series, is published.

1902 Zola dies, asphyxiated by carbon monoxide fumes resulting from a blocked chimney in his Paris apartment building. Many speculate that he was deliberately killed because of his involvement in the Dreyfus Affair. When he is buried at Montmartre Cemetery, his funeral is attended by 50,000 people.

1903 *Vérité* (*Truth*), the last of the *Four Gospels* novels that Zola completed, is published. The final volume, *Justice*, was not finished at the time of his death.

1906 Dreyfus is exonerated from any wrongdoing.

1908 In recognition of Zola's achievements, his remains are transferred to the Panthéon in Paris.

1937 *The Life of Émile Zola*, a film directed by William Dieterle, wins three Academy Awards.

Introduction

For about a hundred years, novelists were seized with the desire to replicate the entire world. Beginning with Honoré de Balzac in the early nineteenth century and ending rather less memorably in the first few decades of the twentieth century with the likes of Jules Romains and John Galsworthy, this tendency saw the production of sweeping multi-volume series in which societies were sectioned up into thematic units and teeming masses of characters were assigned sociologically appropriate fates by their godlike authors. Balzac, who set the tone and the challenge, composed his *Comédie humaine* of some ninety novels and novellas, grouped together primarily according to their settings: private life, provincial life, city life, country life, military life, and so on. Characters sometimes overlapped from one book to another, and stories embryonically suggested in one volume would be fully developed in another. Balzac's intention was to account for the entirety of life in France in his time, with all of its contrasts and variations. Although Balzac lived and wrote during a time of herculean production by writers of fiction, few followed his lead at first. While novelists all over Europe might comfortably issue two or three triple-decker epics a year, many ranging broadly in their focus all across the surface of their time, none was inclined toward Balzac's systematic chronicle of society, not even Dickens, who came the closest.

It was not until two decades after Balzac's death in 1850 that his heir presumptive announced himself. In 1871 Émile Zola published the first installment in what was to be a twenty-volume series of novels, *Les Rougon-Macquart,* an examination of the whole of French society through the lens of the family named in the collective title. Zola intended to go Balzac one better in the way of rigor. His chronicle would be founded on strict scientific principles derived from the work of Charles Darwin and his disciples. Mere realism was no longer sufficient; a methodical, experimental procedure was required, as firmly controlled and emotionally detached as the protocols that attended laboratory work. Each volume would depict one aspect of French life in all its breadth, would be meticulously researched, would be planned out to the last iota with nothing left to chance or inspiration. "Naturalism," as this style came to be known, was to be as pitiless and comprehensive as photography, with no concessions made to piety, aesthetics, or received ideas. And it did effectively challenge conventional thinking about the role of literature—in some cases about society itself—so that it came to be associated with political radicalism, and regarded in some quarters as nothing better than pornography. Even if the works that have held up the best after a century or more have done so despite their extraliterary claims, naturalism in its time was crucial in confronting readers with aspects of society they were inclined to avoid.

Émile Zola was born in Paris on April 2, 1840. His father, François, who was born Francesco Zolla in Venice, arrived in France right after the July Revolution of 1830, to make his mark and his fortune as an engineer. He was brilliant, and was unquestionably in the right place at the right time for the fulfillment of his talents and energies. The culmination of his enterprise was to be the construction of a system of canals and tunnels to bring drinking water to the city of Aix. Unfortunately, in early 1847, when the work was in its initial stages, he contracted pneumonia and died, at the age of fifty-one. His investment in the scheme was immediately parceled up among the other investors. His wife and child were left just enough money to send Émile to the local *collège*, where he spent a reasonably happy adolescence running around with his friends Louis Baille and Paul Cézanne, who was to become a great painter, although neither he nor Émile showed any particular promise at the time. After Émile's maternal grandmother died when he was an adolescent, the remainder of the family—he, his mother, and his grandfather—moved to Paris, where they lived in penury. Émile proceeded to become entranced by the wonders of the city to the detriment of his studies. After failing his oral examination—he never earned his secondary degree—he spent several years living the bohemian life in all its most traditional aspects: unheated garrets in miserable neighborhoods, lack of food and clothing, all-night debates with his companions on artistic and philosophical subjects. At his lowest ebb, he occupied a furnished room in a hotel otherwise populated by prostitutes, and threw in his lot with one of them, who pawned his last overcoat for him. This period was to prove significant when, almost two decades later, he set out to write *Nana*.

Finally, when he was nearly twenty-two, his luck began to turn. First he pulled a high number in the draft lottery, virtually exempting him from military service, and then a friend of his father's got him a job at the Hachette publishing house. It was a lowly position in the shipping department, but he was able to turn it to considerable advantage. He got to know many of the most important writers in France, running errands for them and otherwise ingratiating himself. Since the lineup included the two most fearsome critics in the country, Charles-Augustin Sainte-Beuve and Hippolyte Taine, he had obtained for himself a powerful set of connections for his future career. Now that he was solvent and adequately lodged, he did not disdain the lowlife among whom he had earlier been consigned, but methodically explored alleys and dives and concert saloons, sometimes in the company of his friend Cézanne, who could not force himself to become a full-time Parisian any more than he could remain in the countryside for longer than a few months at a stretch.

Zola began to publish: a collection of tales, a study of *Don Quixote*, an increasing number of newspaper and magazine contributions, both criticism and fiction, and eventually, in 1865, his first novel, *La Confession de Claude*. Around this same time, partly as a result of his friendship with Cézanne, he came to know and befriend a group of young painters who found themselves at odds with the prevailing aesthetic as dictated by the powers who controlled the Salon. Manet, Monet, Renoir, Pissarro, and Cézanne all had their works rejected by exhibition juries composed of the art establishment of the day, men like Jean-Léon Gérôme and Ernest Meissonier, neoclassical painters of battle scenes and overupholstered nudes. Zola became spokesman for the painters, writing numerous articles about them for the press and an entire short book about Manet, and he figures among the painters in two tableaux showing members of the group—the Impressionists, as yet unnamed—gathering together in studios. Nevertheless, his life remained precarious. Even as he was serializing his first major work, *Thérèse Raquin* (1867), he supported himself by setting type for a provincial newspaper, while Alexandrine Meley, his mistress—whom he later married—was still wrapping books at Hachette.

What initially made his name, oddly enough, was not his writing but the great portrait of him by Manet, exhibited in the 1868 Salon, in which he appeared as the very figure of dynamism and modernity—seated at his desk, fierce in his bicolored beard, talismanically backed by Chinese and Japanese prints and a copy of Manet's own scandalous nude *Olympia*. Meanwhile, Taine had written to him, "I believe that the future of the novel consists of the story of the will, struggling and winning its way through the chaos and upheavals of society" (Mitterand, *Album Zola*, p. 98; see "For Further Reading"). The notion did not fall on deaf ears. Zola had been reading Balzac, after all. In 1868 he signed a contract with the Lacroix publishing house for a cycle of ten novels, *The Story of a Family*, to be delivered at a rate of two volumes a year and annually compensated at 6,000 francs; eventually there would be twenty books, published over twenty-two years, at a steadily increasing rate of pay. Zola had been researching feverishly in libraries, particularly on the subject of heredity. He drew up a family tree in order to get a visual grip on his collective subject, carefully distributing the clan around all the major divisions of society, which he saw as consisting of four principal worlds—workers, tradespeople, bourgeoisie, and nobility—and "one world apart: whores, murderers, priests, artists" (Mitterand, p. 99).

He set to work at his usual feverish pace, but his rhythm was immediately thrown off by events. The regime of Napoleon III was weakening then, and republican forces—among whom

Zola figured—were increasing in strength, but their rise was countered by ever more repressive measures. Newspapers, including virtually all the ones to which Zola contributed, were suppressed for varying periods, while the most direct assault on the liberty of the press came when the journalist Victor Noir was shot and killed by a member of the Bonaparte family. Meanwhile, industrial strikes raged around the country. As is frequently the case when regimes find themselves imperiled, the panacea came in the form of war, in this case against the Prussians. In the summer of 1870, crowds gathered in the streets of Paris, shouting, "To Berlin!" By September, however, after its decisive defeat at Sedan, on France's eastern frontier, the empire had fallen and the emperor was a prisoner in Germany. From September 19 to January 28, Paris was besieged by the Prussians, a brutal war of attrition that saw numerous deaths from famine and disease. Zola first fled to the south, but he could not keep himself away from power and intrigue; besides, he was broke. So he traveled to Bordeaux, site of the provisional government, and tried for an official post, but the best he could obtain was a temporary handout. He returned to Paris in the spring of 1871, this time equipped with an assignment as parliamentary correspondent for a newspaper. Shortly thereafter, the government moved to Versailles, and an insurrection—which was to become the Commune—broke out in Paris. Zola blithely commuted between the two camps, which were at war with one another, eventually being suspected by each of sympathy for the other. He lived through the bloody repression at the end of May, when the forces of Versailles invaded the city, and tried, with little success, to urge clemency for various Communards sentenced to death or exile.

By the fall of 1871 and the winter of 1872, when the first two volumes of the Rougon-Macquart series finally appeared, a month apart, Zola's opinions had gotten him banned from the Parisian newspapers altogether—for the following four years his views on the passing scene would be reserved for the reading public of Marseilles—but he had become a much greater presence in the literary and artistic circles of the city; he now numbered among his friends Gustave Flaubert, Ivan Turgenev,

Stéphane Mallarmé, Alphonse Daudet, and the Goncourt brothers. The third volume, *Le Ventre de Paris* (1873; *The Belly of Paris*), made an impression for its meticulous documentation of the great produce market Les Halles, a place every Parisian knew but few among the reading public knew intimately. Although Zola was inspired by the painters, and wished to give an account of Paris that would match the immediacy and visceral power of one of the urban canvases of Monet or Degas, the book also marked the birth of an enduring archetype: the journalist-novelist, who painstakingly works up a subject from firsthand research, sometimes in the process issuing less a novel than an illustrated thesis.

The seventh installment, *L'Assommoir* (1877; *The Dram Shop* or *The Drunkard*) went even further, and can be considered both the first major work of naturalism and Zola's first authentic masterpiece. Based on firsthand observation as well as on research by sociologists, *L'Assommoir* depicts the lives in the Parisian slums of the poor, the disenfranchised, and the marginal, bound together by alcohol. Where previous literary treatments of poverty and dissolution in France had sentimentalized and moralized, *L'Assommoir* takes a nuanced view of its characters, who are rounded and memorable. *L'Assomoir* judges, but with sympathy and understanding, and it knows that blame for the worst of its characters' behavior can be directly attributed to the inequalities of capitalist society. As a result, Zola was branded a socialist and a communard, terms not taken lightly then, a mere six years after the defeat of the insurrection. That did not, however, keep the book from a resounding popular success. The attraction was, naturally, prurient. The book exuded sexuality, of a sort that its readership would view as primordial, and there were many ancillary pleasures, such as its use of French slang, called *argot*, which had been around since the Middle Ages but studiously avoided by upper-case Literature. The government banned the sale of the book in train stations, but that had little effect on its runaway success, which can best be viewed in the light of its spinoffs: a play that ran for 300 performances, popular songs, pipes in the shape of characters' heads, dishes printed with vignettes of major scenes.

One of the book's minor characters, who appeared near the end of the story, was a little girl named Anna Coupeau, known as Nana. The daughter of Gervaise Macquart, who already had three sons by a previous relationship, and an alcoholic laborer named Coupeau, she was predestined for a life of waste and a miserable end, it appeared. Three years later, in 1880, Zola brought out the ninth in his series, *Nana*, which told the remainder of the story of Anna Coupeau. Besides the sketch in *L'Assommoir*, the character had another source as well: Manet's 1876 painting, also entitled *Nana*, which shows a young actress in deshabille in her dressing room, turning away from applying her makeup to look directly at the viewer with an assured, slightly calculating gaze, as a stout older suitor in top hat and tails sits waiting on a couch, bisected by the edge of the frame. Zola assembled her character from a series of prominent actresses and courtesans of the day, used various bits of gossip to inform the plot, pursued his research by simply being who he was by then: a man of the world and an attendee at the theaters, receptions, salons, and restaurants of *le tout Paris*. The notoriety of his book exceeded even that of *L'Assommoir*—the first printing consisted of 55,000 copies, an outrageous figure for the time. It was immediately adapted for the stage and launched songs and caricatures and denunciations.

By that time, the Naturalist school had been formally constituted, with Zola presiding over a coterie of slightly younger writers, of whom Joris-Karl Huysmans and Guy de Maupassant became the most prominent. Besides writing a series of critical works—*Le Roman experimental* (*The Experimental Novel*), the bible of Naturalism, was published in 1880, and the following year saw the publication of no fewer than four volumes of critical essays—he was issuing novels in the Rougon-Macquart series at a clip of nearly one per year. *Pot-Bouille* (1882; *Restless House*), the tenth, took the facade off a fashionable apartment building, unraveling the tangled lives within. *Au Bonheur des dames* (1883; *Ladies' Delight* or *A Ladies' Paradise*), the eleventh, chronicled the life of a large department store. The thirteenth,

Germinal (1885), was an uncompromising exposition of the misery of coal miners, and it galvanized the European labor movement. The fifteenth, *La Terre* (1887; *Earth* or *The Soil*), was his chronicle of the peasantry; its relative frankness about sexuality and bodily functions was enough to cause some of the more delicate Naturalists to separate themselves from their master. *La Bête humaine* (1890; *The Human Beast* or *The Beast in Man*), the seventeenth, was inspired by Zola's turn at jury duty; it is a study of homicidal pathology, set against the background of the railroads. The nineteenth, *La Débâcle* (1892; *The Debacle* or *The Collapse*), his novel of war, was in its time the greatest success of the whole series.

His energy did not flag. After completing the Rougon-Macquart series he immediately embarked on *Les Trois Villes* (*The Three Cities*): *Lourdes* (1894), *Rome* (1896), and *Paris* (1898), the first two of which targeted the Catholic Church. Although Zola had at one point accepted an assignment from the right-wing newspaper *Le Figaro,* causing a flurry of denunciations by the socialist press, he was by then unambiguously identified with the left; it was a period of sharply polarized political divisions that extended into nearly every aspect of French life. Clearly, although he was the country's preeminent novelist and had been unopposed in that rank since the death of Flaubert in 1880, he would never be elected to the Académie Française. He had a broad base of popular support, but few allies at the top; although he was a rich man, his candor and moral resoluteness set him apart and made him anathema to the power brokers.

Thus it was that in 1898 he embarked upon the most significant episode of his life, which was only tangentially connected to literature. In 1894 Captain Alfred Dreyfus, a career officer, was accused of spying for the Germans, convicted, and sent to the penal colony on Devil's Island, off the coast of French Guiana. Very soon indications began to turn up that Dreyfus had been falsely accused, targeted because he was Jewish. The incriminating documents had, it appeared, been forged by a certain Major Esterhazy. Zola, who examined the evidence, became convinced of Esterhazy's guilt and Dreyfus's innocence.

After Esterhazy was cleared by the military of any wrongdoing, Zola wrote an open letter to the president, Félix Faure, published on the front page of the newspaper *L'Aurore* and given the resounding title "J'Accuse . . . !" Zola directly accused the government of conspiracy in having tried and sentenced Dreyfus on the basis of forged evidence while deliberately concealing the existence of exculpatory material. In response, the government accused Zola of libel; his trial featured a parade of superior officers who accused him, in effect, of treason. Zola was found guilty and sentenced to a year in jail. He appealed, but the appeal languished, and in the meantime he was constantly attacked by anti-Semites and the right (the overlap between those two designations was nearly one hundred percent). The attacks occurred in the press, although they undoubtedly would have been physical had Zola been sufficiently imprudent to show himself in public, and they consisted of every possible form of insult, one journalist taking it upon himself to besmirch the life and career of Zola's father and employing forged documents to make his case. When it appeared that Zola's appeal would fail, his friends counseled voluntary exile, and he went off, under a pseudonym and leaving his family behind, to voluntary exile in England. It was nearly a year later that the Cour de Cassation, the highest appeals court in France, finally reversed Dreyfus's conviction. Zola then returned, although his own sentence was never formally voided.

He had continued to write, by then engaged in a new series, *Les Quatre Evangiles* (*The Four Gospels*), consisting of *Fécondité* (1899; *Fecundity*), *Travail* (1901; *Work*), and *Vérité* (1903; *Truth*), the last bearing largely on the Dreyfus case; his death interrupted the final volume, *Justice.* In his last years he also became an accomplished photographer whose scenes of city and country life are valuable documents of their time and apt extensions of his documentary novels. He was only sixty-two in September 1902—although physically and psychologically much aged by his sufferings—when he died of carbon monoxide poisoning. A clogged chimney diverted fumes from the pellet stove into the bedroom as he and his wife slept; she recovered. Murder was alleged and investigated, but the matter

xxiv   *Introduction*

was never resolved. At his funeral a delegation of coal miners accompanied the casket, gravely intoning "Ger-mi-nal" in cadence, over and over again.

Zola's star has risen and fallen since his death. In the first half of the twentieth century he was one of the most widely read authors in the world, his name virtually synonymous with the struggle for social progress. He was translated into all languages and was a staple, especially, in the Soviet Union. His role in the Dreyfus affair doubly assured his stature—because of it he was even the subject of a Hollywood film, *The Life of Émile Zola* (1937), with Paul Muni in the part. But the 1930s were probably the peak of his posthumous career. After World War II, especially, his work acquired a reputation as turgid, well-meaning gruel. The New Left more or less consigned him to the dustbin of history, and litterateurs everywhere decided he was clumsy, laborious, didactic. It is true that even in his lifetime and among his supporters he was never considered a particularly subtle author, and his most fervent disciples would have found it hard to make a case for him as a prose stylist—a fatal deficiency in France, where style reigns supreme, where his older colleague Flaubert, the model of the stylist, sometimes hesitated for weeks over a choice of words.

Nana, however, shows how wrongheaded all such approaches were in regard to Zola, and effects a demonstration of his unparalleled strengths. Zola may not have parsed ambiguities or dealt in fugitive emotions—he did not work close up, with a single-hair brush, but on a large scale, with a palette knife (perhaps, actually, like his old friend Cézanne, he could be said to have worked with a brush in one hand and a knife in the other). The analogy to painting is not idly chosen, and it is not simply because of his close connection to the Impressionists, although in many ways he resembles less the starkly graphic Manet or the dreamily approximative Monet or even the dramatically essentialist Cézanne than he does Gustave Caillebotte, the Impressionist most devoted to depicting the flotsam and jetsam of urban life, which he framed as radically as with a camera lens. For that matter, while it has become a terrible cliché to say of a writer of the past that had he lived in our time, he would surely have become a filmmaker, with Zola it might actually be true.

Zola is at his best when staging crowd scenes and major conflicts. This is no small feat, especially when you consider how often great writers have avoided such things—in how many classic war novels, for example, the principal action is set off-stage or viewed through a narrow and subjective focus. And while most nineteenth-century novels begin and end with a major set piece—one to introduce the characters and set them in motion against the backdrop, the other to tie up loose ends and release us and the characters from our mutual contract—each of *Nana*'s chapters is a set piece. The chapters pass in succession, like so many acts of a tragedy: the theater, the dinner, the country house, the horse race. The chapters immediately call up a visual analogy: They are wide-screen affairs, like movies shot in Cinerama or like the panoramic photographs Zola himself took around 1900. Although in truth there are plenty of closeups and flurries of montaged action, we are given the illusion that the camera, as it were, takes in the whole scene, all at once and unmovingly, while characters pass across its unblinking aperture. Zola excels at directing his characters' points of view, listening to them talk while they take in the setting and the peripheral action surrounding them, and then following their gaze to some other characters some distance away. Upon being introduced by the commentary of the first set of characters, these become in their turn the focus of the author's attention for a while before passing the baton to yet more people in some other corner of the setting. This provides for a powerful spatial illusion.

Zola's method appears to all but eliminate the omniscient narrator—he is present at all times, of course, but Zola is so clever at inserting exposition into casual dialogue that it feels as though we are witnessing everything for ourselves without mediation. The direct authorial commentary, meanwhile, discreetly dissolves into the scene setting, since almost all of it is parenthetical, the most significant observations being either delivered by the characters in the course of apparently banal chitchat or else built into the fabric of the plot. The final chapter, for example, tells us everything we need to know about Zola's attitude toward the Franco-Prussian War, but it does so incidentally, in hubbub rising up from the street while our attention is focused on Nana's plight as she lies in bed in her hotel room. Like a great documentary painter (anyone from Bruegel to Courbet to Seurat) or filmmaker (perhaps Jean Renoir, who was the son of the Impressionist painter Auguste, an acquaintance of Zola's, and who made a spectacular silent adaptation of Nana in 1926), Zola unfolds for his audience the entire social fabric of his setting, in lavish detail, and conveys exactly what he thinks about it all while pretending to be no more than passively subjected to it, as if it were weather, and keeping his eye on a few central figures, as if their actions were not crucially interwoven with and wholly dependent upon their background.

The story of *Nana* is simplicity itself—thanks largely to the movies, it has become a thumping cliché in the intervening century and a quarter, although it wasn't yet one at the time. It is, classically, the story of the poor girl who uses her body to advance through society, nearly to the very top, before being finally betrayed by her fate, or her genes, or her hubris, or her lack of education, so that she falls back down, metaphorically or otherwise, to the muck of her origins. Meanwhile men of all shapes, sizes, ages, and stations have become besotted with her, all of them at some cost, whether to their money or their marriages or their dignity or their lives. Besides the obvious titillation factor, the story is so potent and durable because, like all the most mythopoetic stories (consider *Don Quixote* or *Moby-Dick*, for instance), its plot and its central metaphor are one and the same. Nana herself is a perfectly rounded, three-dimensional character, whose strength and generosity are as apparent by the end as her vanity and cruelty and selfishness, but she is also a metaphorical linchpin, the embodiment of the vapid decadence and dull hypocrisy of the Second Empire, whose fall she enacts in boudoir scale.

The Second Empire was a particularly ignoble passage in French history. Napoleon III was essentially a bounder who fancied himself a Caesar. Whereas his uncle, the first

Napoleon, had at least the excuse that he had helped put an end to the carnage of the Revolution in its final throes—as well as the less defensible proposition that he had subjugated the better part of Europe and North Africa in a psychopathic drive of murderous greed easily assimilated to the collective vanity of a nation—the "little Napoleon" (as Victor Hugo called him) had nothing but his name to boast of. France was by then something of a modern country—Paris, at least, was arguably the most modern city in the world—and yet it was subject to imperial whim and beset by an idiotic ruling class that did not even have the alibi of tradition to excuse its follies and delusions. Zola, writing ten years after the action depicted, describing a time when he was an impetuous young journalist and the friend and champion of the Impressionists, is not concerned with his own milieu but seeks to represent the elite, the people who shut down his newspapers and oppressed his readers—the class that was, in effect, still in charge of France after Sedan and the fall of the empire and the Commune and its bloody suppression, for all that they were now operating within an ostensibly republican frame, and that social laws were gradually ameliorating the lives of their subjects.

He brilliantly selects his characters to provide a cross section of the imperial bestiary without appearing schematic. There are the theater people, the prostitutes, the operators, the deadbeat aristocrats, the upright citizens who lose their minds in the presence of sex, the upwardly mobile courtesans, the church-intoxicated matrons, the cynical press hacks, and so on. All of these people are magnetized by Nana, loose meteorites who fall into her orbit, some coming into otherwise unlikely contact with others, the class order temporarily rearranged so that it becomes clear how little class standing has to do with any virtue but the mere possession of power. Nana's power is, of course, temporary and provisional, the result of a genetic freak in concert with an odd combination of innocence and guile, passivity and willpower. She can effect a kind of misrule for an interval, and then she will fade away or be crushed. Her type came into being with the creation of the middle class, which allowed the illusion of class mobility. The mobility of the courtesan is false advertising; not only can she ascend only briefly, but in the process she has forfeited her ties to any other class. The myth is that she will marry a rich man and perhaps outlive him and inherit his property, and such a creature is indeed evoked in the book, but Zola carefully keeps the apparition ambiguous—we are finally unsure whether the woman Nana sees actually corresponds to the story she seeks to illustrate. Nana's fate has an inevitability that comes with the job; consciously or not, we are aware from the first pages that we are about to witness the arc of a rocket.

Nana is a crepuscular novel. Its laughter is shrill, its lights are too bright, its frenzies are dangerous, its small moments of actual happiness are so obviously doomed they seem sadistically intended. An empire is about to fall, and although all things considered, that fall will only briefly reorganize society, the reader is aware before the end that the characters most likely to land on their feet are the very worst ones. All the amateurs, romantics, overreachers, and pretenders will be crushed. Zola's scientific affectations, whether the alleged detachment of Naturalism or the obsolete genetic blather that makes its way into the narration, barely intrude upon the reader; his misogynistic puffing—his invocations of Nana's poisonous effect on men—can be safely glided over, since it is clear he does not entirely believe it himself. Nana is too complicated a character to be useful as a moralistic blunt instrument, even if Zola seems unwilling to acknowledge this until the very end of the book. *Nana* is about power, and in that sense it is zoological, as well as cautionary. It is also a great illusion, an exhilarating work of total cinema, a whirlwind that does not let up, with a force undiminished by time or technological competition.

Luc Sante was born in Verviers, Belgium. He is the author of *Low Life, Evidence,* and *The Factory of Facts* and coeditor, with Melissa Holbrook Pierson, of *O.K. You Mugs: Writers on Movie Actors.* He is the recipient of a Whiting Writer's Award, a Guggenheim Fellowship, an Award in Literature from the

American Academy of Arts and Letters, and a Grammy (for album notes), and is a Fellow of the American Academy of Arts and Sciences. He is Visiting Professor of Writing and the History of Photography at Bard College. He lives with his wife and son in Ulster County, New York.

Nana

CHAPTER I

At nine o'clock the Variety Theatre was still almost empty. In the balcony and orchestra stalls a few persons waited, lost amidst the garnet-coloured velvet seats, in the faint light of the half extinguished gasalier.* The huge crimson curtain was enveloped in shadow, and not a sound came from the stage behind. The foot-lights were not yet lit up, and the seats of the musicians were unoccupied. High up, however, in the third gallery, close to the roof—displaying figures of naked women and children floating among clouds, to which the gas imparted a greenish tinge—were heard the sounds of shouts and laughter above a continual hum of conversation, and a crowd of men and women, all wearing the caps of the working classes, were seated in rows reaching almost to the gilded festoons of the ceiling. Now and again an attendant would appear, fussily conducting a lady and gentleman to their seats—the gentleman in evening dress, and the lady slim and slightly stooping, and glancing slowly over the house. Two young men suddenly appeared in the stalls close to the orchestra. They remained standing, looking round about them.

"What did I tell you, Hector?" exclaimed the elder—a tall fellow, with a slight, black moustache. "We have come too early. You might just as well have allowed me to finish my cigar."

An attendant passed by at this moment. "Oh! M. Fauchery," she said familiarly, "it will not begin for half an hour."

"Then why on earth do they say nine o'clock on the bills?" asked Hector, whose long, thin face assumed an expression of intense annoyance. "This very morning Clarisse, who is in the piece, assured me that the curtain would go up at nine, precisely."

---

*Type of chandelier used in the mid-nineteenth century in which the branches were capped by gas jets.

3

For a minute they relapsed into silence, as they raised their heads and gazed into the shadows of the boxes; but the green paper, with which the latter were lined, made them obscurer still. Below, the small boxes under the balcony disappeared in total darkness. In the balcony boxes only a very stout lady, leaning heavily on the velvet-covered balustrade was to be seen. To the right and the left, between high columns, the stage boxes, hung with drapery deeply fringed, remained empty. The body of the house, decorated in white and gold, relieved by pale green, seemed to disappear filled as it was with a misty haze arising from the subdued light emanating from the huge crystal gasalier.

"Did you succeed in securing a stage-box for Lucy?" asked Hector.

"Yes," replied the other, "but not without a deal of trouble. Oh! there is no danger of Lucy's coming too early—not she!" He stifled a yawn, and then, after a brief silence, resumed; "You are lucky, you who have never yet been present at a first night. 'The Blonde Venus' will be the success of the year. Every one has been speaking of the piece for six months past. Ah! my boy, such music—such 'go'! Bordenave, who knows what's what, kept it purposely for the time of the Exhibition."*

Hector listened religiously. At length he hazarded a question: "And Nana—the new star who is to play Venus—do you know her?"

"Oh, hang it! are you going to begin that too?" exclaimed Fauchery, gesticulating wildly. "Ever since this morning I have heard of nothing but Nana. I have met more than twenty fellows I know, and it has been Nana here and Nana there! Do you suppose I know every petticoat in Paris? Nana is one of Bordenave's inventions. She must be something choice!"

After this explosion he calmed down a little. But the emptiness of the house, the dim light that pervaded the whole, the opening and shutting of doors, and the hushed voices suggestive of a church, irritated him.

---

*The fourth major Exposition Universelle, or World's Fair, held in Paris in 1867, attracted 11 million visitors. This mention of the exposition establishes the date when the book starts.

"Confound it!" he said, suddenly. "I can't stand this, you know. I must go out. Perhaps we shall meet Bordenave below. He will give us some details."

In the marble paved vestibule, where the box-office was situated, they found the public beginning to arrive. Through the three open doors all the busy throng on the Boulevards could be seen enjoying the beautiful April evening. Carriages dashed up to the theatre, and the doors were slammed noisily. People entered by twos and threes, and, after stopping at the box-office, ascended the double staircase in the rear— the women walking slowly with a swinging gait. In the glare of the gas were pasted, on the naked walls of this hall, whose meagre decorations in the style of the Empire suggested the peristyle of a card-board temple, some enormous yellow posters, in which Nana's name appeared in huge black letters. Men were loitering in front of these bills as they read them, while others were standing about talking among themselves, and blocking up the doorways; whilst near the box-office a thick-set man, with a big, clean-shaved face, was roughly replying to some people who were in vain endeavouring to obtain seats.

"There's Bordenave!" said Fa_chery, as he and Hector descended the stairs.

But the manager had caught sight of him. "You are a nice fellow," he called out. "That is the way you write me a notice, is it? I opened the 'Figaro'* this morning—not a word."

"Wait a bit," replied Fauchery. "I must see your Nana before I can write about her. Besides, I made no promise!"

Then, to prevent further discussion, he presented his cousin, M. Hector de la Faloise, a young man who had come to complete his education in Paris. The manager weighed the young man at a glance; but Hector surveyed the manager with some little emotion. This then was Bordenave, the exhibitor of women, whom he treated in the style of a prison

---

*Important Parisian newspaper; founded in 1826 as a gossip sheet on the arts and published irregularly until 1854, when it began to appear weekly, it became a daily in 1866, and still exists today.

warder, and whose brain was ever hatching some fresh money-making scheme—a perfect cynic, always shouting, or spitting, or smacking his thighs, and possessing the coarse mind of a trooper! Hector was anxious to make a good impression on him.

"Your theatre—" he began, in clear, musical tones.

Bordenave interrupted him quietly, and said, with the coolness of a man who prefers to call things by their right names: "Say my brothel, rather."

Fauchery laughed approvingly, but La Faloise was shocked to a degree, and his meditated compliment stuck in his throat, as he endeavoured to look as though he appreciated the joke. The manager had rushed off to shake hands with a dramatic critic whose criticisms had great influence, and, when he returned, La Faloise had almost recovered himself. He feared lest he should be regarded as a provincial if he appeared too much disconcerted.

"I have been told," he began, wishing at any rate to say something, "that Nana has a delicious voice."

"She!" cried the manager, shrugging his shoulders—"she has no more voice than a squirt."

The young man hastened to add: "Besides, she is an excellent actress."

"She!—a regular lump! She never knows where to put her hands or her feet."

La Faloise coloured slightly. He was at a loss what to understand. He managed to stammer out: "On no account would I have missed this first night. I know that your theatre—"

"Say my brothel," interrupted Bordenave again, with the cool obstinacy of a man thoroughly convinced.

Meanwhile Fauchery had been calmly examining the women as they entered. He now came to his cousin's assistance, when he saw him doubtful whether to laugh or be angry. "Gratify Bordenave; call his theatre just what he desires, as it amuses him. And as for you, my dear fellow, you need not try to fool us. If your Nana can't sing and can't play, you will make a regular fiasco of it to-night. And that is just what I am expecting."

"A fiasco! a fiasco!" exclaimed the manager, whose face became purple with rage. "Is it necessary for a woman to know how to sing and act? Ah! my boy, you are much too stupid. Nana has something else, damn her! and something that will make up for anything she may lack. I scented it, and she has plenty of it, or I have only the nose of a fool! You will see, you will see—she has only to appear, and all the spectators will at once smack their lips." He raised his big hands, which trembled with enthusiasm, and then, lowering his voice, murmured to himself, "Yes, she will go far—ah! damn her! yes, she will go far. A skin—oh, such a skin!"

Then, in answer to Fauchery's questions, he condescended to give certain details, making use of such offensive language that he quite shocked Hector. He had become acquainted with Nana, and wished to bring her out; and it so happened that he was in want of a Venus. He never allowed a woman to hang on to him very long; he preferred to let the public have its share of her at once. But he had had a damnable time in his shop; the arrival of this great hulking girl had revolutionized everything. Rose Mignon, his star, a fine actress and an adorable singer, threatened daily to leave him in the lurch. Divining a rival in Nana she was furious. And the playbills—Deuce take it! what a row they had caused. However, he had decided to print the names of the two actresses in letters of equal size. They had better not badger him too much. When one of his little women, as he called them, Clarisse or Simone, did not do as she was told, he just kicked her behind. If he treated them differently they would never leave him any peace. He dealt in them, and he knew what they were worth, the hussies!

"Ah!" he exclaimed, interrupting himself. "There come Mignon and Steiner! They are always together. You know that Steiner begins to have had enough of Rose; so the husband sticks to him like a plaster lest he should escape."

The flaring gas jets running along the cornice of the theatre threw a sheet of vivid light over the footpath. Two small trees stood out clearly with their fresh green foliage, and a pillar was so brilliantly illuminated by the blaze of light that the bills posted upon it could be read at a distance as clearly as at mid-day; whilst, afar off, the dense darkness of the Boulevards* was studded with multitudinous lights, revealing the surging of an ever moving crowd. Many of the men did not enter the theatre at once, but loitered outside to finish their cigars and chat under the gaslight, which gave a livid pallor to their faces, and threw their shadows, short and black, upon the asphalt beneath. Mignon, a tall, stout fellow, with the square head of the Hercules of a travelling show, shouldered his way through the crowd, dragging on his arm the banker Steiner—a short man, with a big stomach and a round face fringed with a greyish beard.

"Well!" said Bordenave to the banker, "you saw her yesterday in my office."

"Ah! that was her, was it?" exclaimed Steiner. "I thought as much. Only, I was going out as she entered; I scarcely saw her."

Mignon listened with downcast eyes, all the time nervously twisting a large diamond ring on his little finger. He knew at once that they were talking of Nana. Then as Bordenave proceeded to give a description of his new star which caused the banker's eyes to sparkle, he decided to interfere.

"That'll do, my dear fellow; she's not worth looking at. The public will soon send her to the right about. Steiner, my boy, you know that my wife is expecting you in her dressing-room."

He tried to lead him away, but Steiner refused to leave Bordenave. The crowd at the box-office became more compact, the buzz of voices grew louder, and the name of Nana was repeated over and over again with a sing-song enunciation of its two syllables. The men, standing in front of the posters, read it out loud; others, as they passed, uttered it interrogatively, while the women, smiling and uneasy, repeated it softly with an air of surprise. No one knew Nana. Where on earth had Nana come from? And little jokes were passed about from ear to ear,

*Wide, straight streets cut through the heart of Paris in the urban reconfiguration carried out by Baron George-Eugène Haussmann between 1853 and 1870; the reference here is to the concentration of boulevards in the center of the Right Bank.

and little tales told. The very name sounded like a caress, and fell familiarly from the lips of every one. Its constant repetition amused the crowd and kept it in a good humour. A fever of curiosity took possession of everybody—that Parisian curiosity which is sometimes as violent as an attack of brain fever. All were eager to see Nana. One lady had the train of her dress torn, and a gentleman lost his hat.

"Ah! you ask me too much," cried Bordenave, whom twenty men were besieging with questions. "You will see her presently. I must be off, they are waiting for me."

He disappeared, radiant at having inflamed his public. Mignon shrugged his shoulders, and reminded Steiner that Rose was expecting him to show him her costume for the first act.

"Hallo! there's Lucy, over there, getting out of her carriage," said La Faloise to Fauchery.

It was in fact Lucy Stewart—a little, ugly woman of about forty, with a neck too long, a thin, drawn face, and thick lips, but so lively, so graceful, that she charmed every one. She was accompanied by Caroline Héquet and her mother. Caroline with her frigid beauty, the mother very stately, and looking as if she were stuffed.

"You are coming with us, of course," she said to Fauchery; "I have kept a place for you."

"So that I shall see nothing!—not if I know it!" he answered. "I have an orchestra stall; I prefer to be there."

Lucy fired up at once. Was he afraid to be seen with her? Then suddenly calming down, she jumped to another subject.

"Why did you never tell me that you knew Nana?"

"Nana! I never saw her!"

"Is that really true? I have been assured that you once slept with her."

But Mignon, who was in front, put his finger to his lips to signal to them to be silent. And when Lucy asked why, he pointed to a young man who had just passed, murmuring, "Nana's sweetheart."

They all stared after him. He was certainly very good-looking. Fauchery recognised him: his name was Daguenet, and he

had squandered a fortune of three hundred thousand francs*
on women, and now dabbled in stocks in order to make a little money with which he could treat them to an occasional
bouquet and dinner. Lucy thought he had very handsome
eyes.

"Ah! there's Blanche!" she exclaimed. "It was she who told
me that you had slept with Nana."

Blanche de Sivry, a heavy blonde, whose pretty face was getting too fat, arrived, accompanied by a slender, well-dressed
man with a most distinguished air.

"Count Xavier de Vandeuvres," whispered Fauchery to La
Faloise.

The count shook hands with the journalist, whilst a lively
discussion took place between Lucy and Blanche. They quite
blocked up the entry with their skirts covered with flounces,
one in pink and the other in blue, and Nana's name fell from
their lips so frequently that the crowd lingered to listen. The
count at length led Blanche away, but Nana's name did not
cease to resound from the four corners of the vestibule in
louder and more eager tones. Would they never begin? The
men pulled out their watches, late comers leaped from their
carriages before they really drew up, and the groups left the
pavement, whilst the passers-by, as they slowly crossed the
stream of light, stretched their necks to see what was going on
in the theatre. A street urchin who came up whistling, stood
for a moment before one of the posters at the door; then, in a
drunken voice shouted out, "Oh, my! Nana!" and reeled on his
way, dragging his old shoes along the asphalt. People laughed,
and several well-dressed gentlemen repeated, "Nana! Oh, my!
Nana!" The crush was tremendous. A quarrel broke out at the
box-office, the cries for Nana increased; one of those stupid
fits of brutal excitement common to crowds had taken possession of this mass of people. Suddenly, above this uproar, the
sound of a bell was heard. The rumour extended to the Boulevards that the curtain was about to rise, and there was more

---

*The French franc was equivalent to about 20 U.S. cents at the exchange rate
of the time.

pushing and struggling; every one wished to get in; the employés of the theatre were at their wits' end. Mignon, looking uneasy, seized hold of Steiner, who had not been to inspect the dress Rose was to wear. At the first tinkle of the bell, La Faloise pushed through the crowd, dragging Fauchery with him, fearing lest he should miss the overture. Lucy Stewart was irritated by all these demonstrations of eagerness. What vulgar persons to push ladies about! She remained to the last with Caroline Héquet and her mother. At length the vestibule was empty; outside, the Boulevards maintained their prolonged rumble.

"As if their pieces were always funny!" Lucy kept repeating as she ascended the stairs.

Fauchery and La Faloise stood in their places, examining the house, which was now very brilliant. The crystal gasalier blazed with prismatic hues, and the light was reflected from the ceiling on to the pit like a shower of gold. The garnet-coloured velvet of the seats appeared as though shot with lake, whilst the glitter of the gilding was softened by the decorations of pale green beneath the coarse paintings of the ceiling. The foot-lights blazed upon the crimson curtain, the richness of which suggested the most fabulous of palaces, and offered a melancholy contrast to the poverty of the frame, the crevices in which showed the plaster beneath the gilding. It was already excessively warm. In the orchestra the musicians were tuning their instruments, and the light trills of the flute, the stifled sighs of the horn, the singing notes of the violin, were drowned by the increasing hum of voices. All the spectators were talking together, pushing and squeezing each other in their endeavours to reach their seats; and the crush in the corridors was so great that it was with difficulty the doors gave ingress to the never-ceasing flow of people. Friends nodded to each other from a distance, and with the rustling of clothes came a procession of gay costumes and headdresses, broken now and again by a black dress suit or a dark overcoat. However, the seats were gradually filling; here and there appeared a bright coloured robe, and a head with a delicate profile displayed a chignon on which sparkled some valuable jewel. In one of the boxes a glimpse was caught of a woman's naked

shoulder, seemingly as white as ivory. Other women, calmly
waiting, fanned themselves languidly as they watched the surging crowd; while a group of young dandies standing in the orchestra stalls—all shirt front, and wearing gardenias in their
button-holes—gazed through their opera-glasses, which they
held with the tips of their daintily-gloved fingers.

Then the two cousins looked around in search of acquaintances. Mignon and Steiner sat side by side in a box, with their
arms resting on the velvet balustrade. Blanche de Sivry appeared to be alone in one of the stage-boxes. But La Faloise
watched more especially Daguenet, who had an orchestra stall
two rows in front of his. Next to him was seated a youngster,
some seventeen years old, just fresh from college, who opened
his cherub-like eyes wide with delight. Fauchery smiled as he
caught sight of him.

"Who is that lady in the balcony?" asked La Faloise, suddenly. "I mean the one who has a young girl in blue next her."

He directed his companion's glance to a woman whose stout
figure was tightly laced, and whose once blonde hair, now grey,
was dyed yellow, whilst her round puffed face, coloured with
rouge, almost disappeared beneath a shower of little baby
curls.

"That's Gaga," replied Fauchery simply; and, as the name
seemed to convey no information to his cousin, he added,
"Haven't you heard of Gaga? She was one of the beauties of the
first years of Louis Philippe's* reign. Now she is never seen
anywhere without her daughter."

La Faloise had no eyes for the young girl. Gaga, however, affected him strangely; he could not cease looking at her. He
thought her still very handsome, though he dared not say so.
At length the conductor of the orchestra gave the signal, and
the musicians struck the first note of the overture. People were
still coming in, and the noise and bustle increased. On special
occasions like this there were different parts of the house
where friends met with a smile; whilst the regular frequenters,

*King of France from 1830 to 1848.

thoroughly at their ease, exchanged bows right and left. All Paris was there—the Paris of letters, of finance, and of pleasure, many journalists, some few authors, and several speculators, more kept girls than respectable women—a company, in short, that was a most singular mixture, composed of every kind of genius, tainted with every description of vice, where the same weariness and the same fever seemed inscribed on every face. Fauchery, questioned by his cousin, pointed out to him the boxes of the various newspapers and clubs, and then the dramatic critics, one skinny and dried up, with thin and wicked-looking lips, but more especially a stout, good-natured-looking man, who leaned on the shoulder of his companion, an artless young person, over whom he watched with a kind, paternal eye. But he suddenly cut his descriptions short on seeing La Faloise bow to some people who occupied one of the centre boxes. He seemed surprised.

"What! you know Count Muffat de Beuville?" he asked.

"Oh, yes. I have known him for a long time," replied Hector. "The Muffats had an estate near ours. I very often call on them. The count is with his wife and her father, the Marquis de Chouard."

Delighted at his cousin's astonishment, and spurred on by vanity, La Faloise went into further details. The marquis was a state councillor, and the count had just been appointed chamberlain to the Empress. Fauchery raised his opera-glass and examined the countess—a dark, plump woman, with a lovely white skin, and beautiful black eyes.

"You must present me between the acts," he said at last. "I have already met the count, but I should like to go to their Tuesdays at home."

An energetic "Hush!" was heard from the upper gallery. The overture had commenced but people were still coming in. Whole rows of persons were compelled to rise to allow late comers to get to their seats, the doors of the boxes banged, and loud voices were heard quarrelling in the corridors. Still the buzz of conversation, similar to the noisy chattering of sparrows at sunset, never ceased. Everything was in the greatest confusion; it was a medley of moving heads and arms, the owners of which were either sitting down and seeking the most comfortable positions, or persisting in standing up to take a last look around. The cry, "Sit down! sit down!" came from obscure corners of the pit. Every one trembled with eagerness, for at last the famous Nana, of whom people had been talking for a week, was about to be seen! By degrees, however, the noise subsided, with an occasional swell from time to time. And in the midst of this faint murmur, of these expiring whispers, the orchestra burst forth in the gay little notes of a waltz, the saucy rhythm of which suggested the laugh raised by some over-free piece of buffoonery. The audience, fairly tickled, already began to smile; but the claque, seated in the front row of the pit, commenced to applaud vociferously. The curtain rose.

"Hallo!" said La Faloise, whose tongue still wagged. "There is a gentleman with Lucy," and he looked at the stage box to the right of the first tier, in the front of which sat Lucy and Caroline, while in the rear the dignified face of Caroline's mother was to be discerned, and also the profile of a tall light-haired young man, most irreproachably dressed.

"Look," repeated La Faloise with persistence, "there's a gentleman."

Fauchery slowly brought his opera-glass to bear on the box indicated; but he turned away immediately.

"Oh! it's only Labordette," he murmured in a careless tone of voice, as if the presence of that gentleman was the most natural as well as the most unimportant thing in the world.

Behind them some one cried, "Hush!" and they were driven to silence. Everybody was now perfectly still, and a regular sea of heads, upright and attentive, filled the house from the stalls to the amphitheatre. The first act of "The Blonde Venus" was laid in Olympus—a card-board Olympus, with clouds at the sides, and Jupiter's throne on the right. Iris and Ganymede first appeared, surrounded by a crowd of celestial assistants, who sang a chorus as they arranged the seats for the gods in council. Again the applause of the paid claque was heard, but the audience as yet was not inclined to respond. La Faloise, however, had applauded Clarisse Besnus, one of Bordenave's little women, who played the part of Iris, in pale blue, with a broad scarf of the seven colours fastened round her waist.

"You know she takes off her chemise to get into that costume," he said to Fauchery in a loud whisper. "We tried it on this morning, and the chemise showed under the arms and on the back."

But a slight tremor took possession of the audience on the appearance of Rose Mignon as Diana. Although she had neither the face nor the figure for the part, as she was thin and dark, with the adorable ugliness of a Parisian urchin, she seemed charming, intended as she might have been as a mockery of the character she personated. Her entrance song, consisting of words stupid enough to send you to sleep, and in which she complained of Mars, who was neglecting her for Venus, was sung in a bashful manner, but so full of smutty inuendoes, that the audience warmed up. Her husband and Steiner laughed aloud as they sat side by side. And the whole house burst into applause when Prullière, that especial favourite, appeared as Mars in the uniform of a general, adorned with a monstrous plume, and dragging a sword that reached to his shoulder. He had had enough of Diana; she expected too much. So she swore to watch him and be revenged. Their duo wound up with a ludicrous tyrolienne,* which Prullière sang in his funniest style, and in the voice of an angry tabby. He possessed the amusing conceit of a young actor in high favour, and swaggered about as he rolled his eyes in a way that elicited the shrill laughter of the women in the boxes. After that, however, the audience became as cool as before; the scenes which followed were dull in the extreme. Old Bosc, as an imbecile Jupiter, his head crushed under an enormous crown, succeeded only in raising a smile, as he quarrelled with Juno on account of their cook's wages. The procession of the gods Neptune, Pluto, Minerva, and all the others, almost spoilt everything. The spectators were becoming very impatient, an ominous murmur slowly arose, every one began to lose all in-

---

*A yodel, or a song marked by yodeling.

terest in the piece, and looked about the house rather than upon the stage. Lucy laughed with Labordette; the Count de Vandeuvres emerged a little from behind Blanche's broad shoulders; while Fauchery watched the Muffats from out of the corner of his eyes. The count looked very grave, as if he had not understood anything; and the countess, smiling vaguely, seemed wrapped in reverie. But suddenly the applause of the claque burst forth with the regularity of a discharge of musketry, and every eye became rivetted on the stage once more. Was it Nana at last—that Nana who had kept them waiting so long?

It was a deputation of mortals introduced by Ganymede and Iris, respectable citizens, all deceived husbands, come to lay before Jupiter a complaint against Venus, who inspired their wives with a great deal too much ardour. The chorus, which they sang in a simple and doleful manner, was now and again interrupted by the most significant pauses, and amused the audience immensely. A whisper went round the house: "The cuckolds' chorus, the cuckolds' chorus;" the name stuck to it, and it was encored. The get-up of the singers was very comic, their faces were in accordance with the part they played; there was one especially, a stout fellow with a face as round as a moon. Vulcan, however, appeared on the scene in a state of furious indignation, seeking his wife, who had disappeared from home three days before. The chorus struck up again, imploring Vulcan, the god of cuckolds, to help them. The part of Vulcan was played by Fontan, a comic actor gifted with a talent as spicy as it was original, who waddled about in the most ludicrous manner imaginable, in the costume of a village blacksmith, with a flaring red wig on his head, and his arms bare and tattooed all over with hearts pierced by arrows. A woman's voice exclaimed aloud, "Oh! isn't he ugly!" and every one laughed as they applauded. The next scene seemed interminable. Would Jupiter never get all the gods together that he might submit to them the deceived husbands' petition? and still no Nana! Did they mean to keep back Nana until the curtain fell? This long suspense ended by irritating the spectators, and they recommenced their murmurs.

"It's going from bad to worse," said Mignon, delighted, to Steiner. "A regular fiasco; see if it isn't!"

At this moment the clouds parted at the back of the stage, and Venus appeared. Nana, very tall and very plump for her eighteen years, in the white tunic of a goddess, and with her beautiful golden hair floating over her shoulders, walked towards the foot-lights with calm self-possession, smiling at the crowd before her. Her lips parted, and she commenced her great song:

"When Venus takes an evening stroll—"

At the second line, people exchanged glances of wonder. Was this a jest on the part of Bordenave, or a wager? Never had so false a voice and so poor a method been heard. The manager had spoken truly when he said that she had no more voice than a squirt. Nor did she know how to stand or move on the stage. She threw her arms forward and wriggled her body about in a manner that was considered scarcely proper and very ungraceful. The pit was beginning to murmur, in fact a few hisses were heard, when suddenly from the orchestra stalls a voice, resembling that of a young cock moulting, exclaimed aloud in a tone of intense conviction:

"She is stunning!"

The whole house looked to see who had uttered these words. It was the cherub, the youngster fresh from college, his lovely eyes strained wide open, his childish face all aglow with admiration of Nana. When he saw every one looking at him, he turned scarlet with shame at having unintentionally spoken so loud. Daguenet, who sat next him, looked at him with a smile, and the audience laughed aloud and thought no more of hissing, while the young gentlemen with white kid gloves also carried away by Nana's curves, applauded with vehemence.

"So she is!" they cried. "Bravo!"

Nana, seeing every one laughing, laughed also, and this redoubled the gaiety. She was funny, all the same, this beautiful girl; and as she laughed, a love of a dimple appeared on her chin. She waited, not in the least embarrassed, but on the con-

trary quite at her ease and thoroughly at home with the audience, looking as though she herself were saying with a wink of
her eye that she didn't possess a ha'porth of talent, but it
didn't matter, she had something better than that. And after
making a sign to the conductor, which meant, "Off you go, old
boy!" she commenced her second verse:

"At midnight, Venus passes by—"

It was still the same grating voice, but this time it tickled the
hearers in the right place, and succeeded now and again in
eliciting an approving murmur. Nana's smile was still on her
red lips, and shone in her large light blue eyes. At certain lines,
which were a trifle broad in meaning, her pink nostrils dilated
and the colour rose to her cheeks. She continued to wriggle
her body about, not knowing what else to do; but it was no
longer considered unbecoming; on the contrary, every opera-
glass was turned upon her. As she finished the verse her voice
failed her entirely, and she saw that she could not go on. Without being in the least disturbed, she jerked her hip in a manner which indicated its plumpness beneath her scanty tunic,
and, with her body bent forward, displaying her bare breast,
she extended her arms. Applause burst forth from all parts of
the house. She at once turned round, showing as she retired to
the back of the stage the nape of a neck, the red hair on which
looked like the fleece of an animal; and the applause became
deafening.

The end of the act elicited less enthusiasm. Vulcan wished
to slap his wife's face. The gods took council, and decided that
they had best investigate matters on the earth, before deciding
in favour of the deceived husbands. Diana, overhearing some
tender passages between Venus and Mars, swore that she
would not once let them out of her sight during the journey.
There was also a scene in which Cupid, acted by a little girl of
twelve, answered to every question, "Yes, mamma," "No,
mamma," in tearful tones and with her fingers in her nose.
Then Jupiter, with all the severity of an angry master, shut
Cupid in a dark closet, and bade him conjugate twenty times

the verb, "to love." The finale, a chorus very brilliantly rendered, met with more success. But, after the curtain had fallen, the claque in vain tried to obtain an encore; everybody rose and moved towards the doors. As the audience pushed their way through the rows of seats, they exchanged their impressions. One phrase was constantly heard: "It is simply idiotic!" A critic observed that the piece wanted a great deal of cutting down. But the piece, after all, mattered little. Nana was the chief topic of conversation. Fauchery and La Faloise, who were among the first to leave their seats, met Steiner and Mignon in the passage leading to the stalls. The atmosphere was stifling in this hole, which was low and narrow like some gallery in a mine, and was lighted here and there by flaring gas-jets. They stood for a moment at the foot of the staircase on the right, protected by the railing. The spectators from the upper part of the house tramped down with a great noise of heavy shoes, the procession of men in evening dress seemed as though it would never cease, and a box-opener endeavoured to prevent a chair on which she had piled coats and shawls from being swept away by the crowd.

"But I know her!" cried Steiner as soon as he saw Fauchery. "I have certainly seen her somewhere. At the Casino, I think; and she was so drunk that she got locked up."

"Well, I'm not quite sure," said the journalist. "I'm like you, I have certainly met her somewhere." He lowered his voice and added with a laugh, "At old Tricon's, I daresay."

"Of course, in some vile place!" exclaimed Mignon, who seemed exasperated. "It is disgusting to see the public welcome in such a way the first filthy wench that offers. Soon there will not be a respectable woman left on the stage. Yes, I shall have to forbid Rose playing any more."

Fauchery could not repress a smile. Meanwhile, the heavily-shod crowd continued to pour down the stairs, and a little man in a cap said, in a drawling voice: "Oh, my! she is plump! You could eat her!"

In the lobby, two young men, with their hair exquisitely curled, and looking very stylish with their stuck-up collars turned slightly down in front, were quarrelling. One kept say-

ing, "Vile! vile!" without giving any reason; whilst the other re-
taliated with, "Stunning! stunning!" equally disdaining to explain. La Faloise liked her immensely. He, however, only
ventured to observe that she would be much better if she cultivated her voice. Then Steiner, who had left off listening,
seemed to wake up with a start. They must wait, though. Perhaps in the next acts everything would come to grief. The audience, though very lenient so far, was not yet smitten with the
piece. Mignon swore no one would sit it through; and as
Fauchery and La Faloise left them to go into the saloon, he
took hold of Steiner's arm, and, pressing close up to his shoulder, whispered in his ear, "Old boy, come and see my wife's costume for the second act. It is the limit!"

Upstairs, the foyer was brilliantly illuminated by three crystal gasaliers. The two cousins paused for a moment. The glass
doors, standing wide open, showed them a wave of heads,
which two contending currents whirled about in a continual
eddy. They entered. Five or six groups of men, talking and gesticulating earnestly, stood their ground in spite of the crush,
while others were walking up and down in rows, now and again
turning sharply on their heels, which resounded on the waxed
boards. To the right and left, women, occupying the red velvet
seats placed between the jasper columns, watched the crowd as
it passed with a weary air, as if exhausted by the intense heat;
and behind them could be seen their chignons in the tall
glasses decorating the walls. At the end of the saloon, a man
with a very big belly was standing at the bar drinking a glass of
syrup.* Fauchery had gone out on to the balcony to get a
breath of fresh air. La Faloise who had been studying some
photographs of actresses placed in frames, which alternated
with the looking-glasses between the columns, ended by following him. The row of gas-jets in front of the theatre had just
been extinguished. It was dark and cool on the balcony, which
appeared to be vacant, with the exception of one solitary figure—that of a young man who, enveloped in shadow, leant

---

*Grenadine or a similar concoction, diluted with soda water.

against the stone balustrade in the recess on the right smoking a cigarette. Fauchery recognised Daguenet. They shook hands.

"Whatever are you doing there, old fellow?" asked the journalist. "Hiding in odd corners; you who, as a rule, never leave the stalls during a first night's performance."

"But I am smoking, as you see," answered Daguenet.

Then Fauchery, so as to embarrass him, said, "And the new star, what do you think of her? The remarks I have heard made about the house are rather disparaging."

"Oh!" murmured Daguenet, "by men with whom she would not have anything to do."

This was all the criticism he offered on Nana's talent. La Faloise, leaning forward, looked up and down the Boulevard. The windows of a hotel and a club opposite were brilliantly lighted, while on the pavement a compact mass of customers occupied the tables of the Café de Madrid. Nothwithstanding the lateness of the hour, the crowd was immense; everyone had to walk slowly. A stream of people continually flowed from the Passage Jouffroy, and persons were obliged to wait five minutes sometimes, before they could cross from one side of the road to the other, so great was the throng of vehicles.

"What animation! what noise!" La Faloise, who had not yet ceased to be astonished at Paris, kept repeating.

A bell rang, and the saloon rapidly emptied. Every one hurried along the passages. The curtain had risen, but a crowd still streamed in, much to the disgust of those of the audience who were already seated. The late comers hastened to their places with animated and attentive looks. La Faloise's first glance was for Gaga; but he was astonished to notice by her side the tall fellow with light hair, who, during the first act, had been in Lucy's stage-box.

"What did you say was the name of that gentleman?" he asked.

Fauchery did not see the person meant at once. "Ah! yes, Labordette," he said at last, in the same careless tone of voice as before.

The scenery of the second act was a surprise. It represented a low dancing establishment of the suburbs, called the "Boule

Noire," on a Shrove Tuesday. Some masqueraders, dressed in
grotesque costumes, sang a lively strain, the chorus of which
they accompanied by stamping their heels. The words and gestures being not over decorous and quite unexpected, amused
the audience immensely, and secured the honours of an encore. And it was into this place that the troop of gods, led
astray by Iris, who falsely claimed to know the earth, had come
to pursue their investigations. They were disguised so as to
preserve their incognito. Jupiter appeared as King Dagobert,*
with his breeches turned wrong side out, and a huge tin crown
on his head. Phœbus masqueraded as the Postillion of
Longjumeau,† and Minerva as a Norman wet nurse. Shouts of
laughter greeted Mars, who wore a preposterous costume, as a
Swiss admiral; but the mirth became scandalous when Neptune, dressed in a blouse and tall cap, with little curls glued to
his temples, dragged after him his slip-shod shoes, and said, in
an unctuous tone of voice: "Well! what next? When a fellow's
handsome, he must allow himself to be adored!" This elicited
a few "Oh! ohs!" while the ladies slightly raised their fans. Lucy,
in her stage-box, laughed so noisily that Caroline Héquet en-
treated her to be quiet. From this moment the piece was saved,
and was even a great success. This carnival of the gods, Olympus dragged through the mud, religion and poetry alike
scoffed at, struck the public as extremely witty. A fever of ir-
reverence took possession of this intellectual first night audience; ancient legends were trodden under foot, and antique
images were broken. Jupiter had a fine head, Mars was highly
successful. Royalty became a farce, and the army a jest. When
Jupiter, desperately smitten all of a sudden by the charms of a
little laundress, broke into a wild cancan, and Simone, who
played the part of the laundress, raised her foot on a level with
the nose of the master of the gods, calling him, in such a funny
manner, "My fat old boy!" a peal of mad laughter shook the
house. While the others danced, Phœbus treated Minerva to

*Seventh-century king of France; he was a quasi-mythic figure and the subject
of a popular song.

†Proverbial rural mail carrier.

some hot wine, and Neptune sat surrounded by some seven or eight women, who stuffed him with cakes. The audience snatched at the faintest allusions, obscenities were discovered where none were intended, and the most inoffensive words were invested with a totally different meaning by the exclamations of the occupants of the stalls. It was long since the theatre-going public had wallowed in such disgusting foolery, and it took its fill. The action of the piece, however, advanced in spite of all this by-play. Vulcan, dressed in the latest style, only all in yellow, and with yellow gloves and a glass in his eye, was there in pursuit of Venus, who at last arrived, dressed as a fish-woman, a handkerchief thrown over her head, her breasts protruding, and covered with huge gold ornaments. Nana was so white, and so plump, and so natural in this part of a person strong in the hips and the gift of the gab, that she at once gained the entire audience. Rose Mignon, a delicious baby, with a baby bonnet on her head, and in short muslin skirts, was quite forgotten, although she had just sung Diana's woes in a charming voice. The other, the big girl with her arms akimbo, who clucked like a hen, was so full of life and the power of woman, that the audience became fairly intoxicated.

After this no exception was taken at anything that Nana did. She was allowed to pose badly, to move badly, to sing every note false, and forget her part. She had only to turn to the audience and smile, to be treated with wild applause. Each time she gave her peculiar movement of the hips the occupants of the stalls brightened up, and the enthusiasm rose from gallery to gallery up to the very roof, so that when she led the dance her triumph was complete. She was in her element as, with arms akimbo, she dragged Venus through the mire. The music, too, seemed written for her voice of the gutter—a music of reed-pipes, a sort of reminiscence of a return from the fair of Saint Cloud,* with the sneezes of the clarionets† and the gambols of the flutes. Two concerted pieces were again en-

*Yearly fair; at the time, Saint-Cloud was a rustic suburb of Paris.
†Old spelling of "clarinet."

cored. The waltz of the overture, that waltz with the saucy rhythm, returned and whirled the gods round and round. Juno, as a farmer's wife, caught Jupiter flirting with the washerwoman, and spanked him. Diana surprising Venus in the act of arranging a meeting with Mars, hastened to inform Vulcan of the time and place, when the latter exclaimed—"I have my plan." The remainder of the act did not seem very clear. The gods' inquiry terminated in a final gallopade, after which Jupiter, in a great perspiration, all out of breath, and having lost his crown, proclaimed that the little women of the earth were delicious, and that the men alone were in the wrong. The curtain fell, and above the applause rose some voices shouting loudly, "All! All!" Then the curtain rose again, and the actors and actresses reappeared hand-in-hand. In their midst were Nana and Rose Mignon, bowing side by side. The applause was repeated, the claque surpassed their former efforts, and then the house slowly became half empty.

"I must go and pay my respects to Countess Muffat," said La Faloise.

"Very well," replied Fauchery; "and you can introduce me. We can go outside afterwards."

But it was not such an easy matter to reach the balcony boxes, as the crowd in the passages was almost impenetrable. To pass through the different groups, it was necessary to use one's elbows rather freely. Leaning against the wall, beneath a brass gas-bracket, the stout critic was giving his opinion of the piece to an attentive circle. People, as they passed, lingered and told their friends in a low voice who he was. It was rumoured that he had laughed during the whole act; however, he now showed himself very severe, and talked of good taste and morality. Farther on, the critic with the thin lips was most favourable, but his remarks had an unpleasant after-taste, like milk turned sour. Fauchery searched the different boxes with a glance through the small round windows in the doors. But the Count de Vandeuvres stopped him to ask him some questions. When he learnt that the two cousins intended paying their respects to the Muffats, he directed them to their box,

No. 7, which he had just left. Then he whispered in the journalist's ear:

"I say, old fellow, this Nana is surely the girl we met one night at the corner of the Rue de Provence."

"Why, of course! you are right," exclaimed Fauchery. "I was sure I had met her somewhere!"

La Faloise introduced his cousin to Count Muffat de Beuville, whose manner was cool in the extreme. But on hearing Fauchery's name, the countess looked up quickly and complimented him on his articles in the "Figaro" in a well-turned phrase. Leaning against the velvet-covered balustrade, she half turned towards him with a graceful movement of her shoulders. They talked for a few minutes, and the conversation fell upon the Exhibition.

"It will certainly be very fine," said the count, whose square face and regular features preserved a certain official gravity. "I visited the Champ de Mars* to-day and I returned filled with wonder."

"I am told, however, that it will not be ready in time," observed La Faloise. "Something has gone wrong—"

"It will be ready! The emperor insists upon it!" interrupted the count in his stern voice.

Fauchery told gaily how he had been almost lost in the aquarium, during its building one day when he had gone there in search of materials for an article. The countess smiled. She looked from time to time about the house, raising an arm with its long white glove reaching to the elbow, and fanning herself slowly. The seats were now mostly unoccupied; a few gentlemen who had remained in the stalls were reading the evening papers; and several women were receiving their friends much as if they were at home. There was now no sound above a well-bred whisper beneath the crystal gasalier, the brightness of which was dimmed by the fine dust raised by the stir at the end of the act. About the doors, some men lingered to inspect the

---

*Large military parade ground on the Left Bank, site of five Expositions Universelles (World's Fairs) and eventually of the Eiffel Tower, built for the exposition in 1889.

few women who remained seated; and for a minute they stood quite motionless, stretching their necks, and displaying their white shirt fronts.

"We shall expect to see you next Tuesday," said the countess to La Faloise.

And she extended her invitation to Fauchery, who thanked her with a low bow. The play was not alluded to, nor was the name of Nana pronounced. The count's manner was so icy and dignified, that one might have supposed him to be at a meeting of the Corps Législatif.* He took occasion to say, as if to explain their presence, that his father-in-law had an especial fondness for the theatre. The door of the box had remained open, and the Marquis de Chouard, who had gone out to leave room for the visitors, now stood tall and erect in the doorway, his pale, flabby face shaded by his broad-brimmed hat, as he followed with his dim eyes the women who passed. As soon as the countess had given her invitation, Fauchery retired, feeling that under the circumstances it would not be in good taste to discuss the play. La Faloise left the box the last. He had just noticed in Count de Vandeuvres's stage-box the fair-haired Labordette, quite at his ease, and conversing intimately with Blanche de Sivry.

"I say," said he, as he joined his cousin, "this Labordette appears to know all the women. He's with Blanche now."

"Know them all! Of course he does," answered Fauchery, coolly. "Why, wherever have you sprung from, young man?"

The passage was not nearly so crowded now. Fauchery was on the point of going down the stairs when Lucy Stewart called him. She was standing just outside the door of her box. The heat, she said, was intolerable inside; so, in company of Caroline Héquet and her mother, she blocked up the whole width of the passage, crunching burnt almonds. One of the box-openers was conversing with them in a maternal manner. Lucy began at once to pick a quarrel with the journalist. He was a nice fellow—he was in a precious hurry to go and see the other

*The legislature, at that time not elected but composed of members of the nobility.

women, but he couldn't even come and ask them to have a drink! Then, suddenly dropping the subject, she said lightly:

"I say, old fellow, I think Nana a big hit."

She wanted him to be in her box for the last act; but he escaped, promising to see them at the end of the piece. Outside, in front of the theatre, Fauchery and La Faloise lit their cigarettes. A small crowd blocked the pavement, formed of a part of the male portion of the audience, who had come down the steps to breathe the fresh night air, amidst the growing stillness of the Boulevard.

In the meanwhile Mignon had dragged Steiner to the Café des Variétés. Seeing Nana's success, he spoke of her enthusiastically, all the time watching the banker from out of the corner of his eye. He knew him; twice had he assisted him in deceiving Rose, and when the caprice was over, had brought him back to her, faithful and penitent. Inside the café the too numerous customers were squeezing round the marble tables, and some men, standing up, were drinking hastily; the large mirrors reflected this mass of heads *ad infinitum*, and increased inordinately the size of the narrow saloon with its three gasaliers, its mole-skin-covered seats, and its winding staircase draped with red. Steiner seated himself at a table in the outer room, which was quite open on to the Boulevard, the frontage having been removed a little too early for the season. As Fauchery and his cousin passed, the banker stopped them.

"Come and take a glass of beer with us," he said.

He himself, however, was absorbed with an idea which had just occurred to him; he wanted to have a bouquet thrown to Nana. At length he called one of the waiters, whom he familiarly named Augustus. Mignon, who was listening to all he said, looked at him so straight in the eyes that he became quite disconcerted as he faltered, "Two bouquets, Augustus, and give them to one of the attendants. One for each of the ladies, at the right moment, you understand."

At the other end of the room, with her head supported against the frame of a mirror, a girl, who could not have been more than eighteen, sat motionless before an empty glass, as though benumbed by a long and useless waiting. Beneath the

natural curls of her beautiful fair hair appeared the face of a
virgin with a pair of velvety eyes looking so gentle and honest.
She wore a dress of faded green silk, with a round hat which
had been knocked in by sundry blows. The chilly evening air
made her look quite white.

"Hallo! why, there's Satin," murmured Fauchery as he
caught sight of her.

La Faloise questioned him. Oh! she was nobody. Only a
wretched street-walker; but she was so foul-mouthed, it was
rare fun to make her talk. And the journalist raised his voice:
"Whatever are you doing there, Satin?"

"Wearing my guts out," she quietly replied, without moving.

The four men, highly delighted, burst out laughing. Mignon
assured the others that there was no need to hurry; it would
take at least twenty minutes to set up the scenery of the third
act. But the two cousins, who had finished their beer, wished to
return to the theatre; they felt cold. Then Mignon, left alone
with Steiner, leaned both elbows on the table, and, looking him
full in the face, said, "Well then, it's quite understood, we will
call on her, and I will introduce you. You know, it's quite between ourselves; my wife need not know anything about it."

Back in their places, Fauchery and La Faloise noticed in the
second tier of boxes a very pretty woman, very quietly dressed.
She was accompanied by a solemn-looking gentleman, the
head of a department at the Ministry of the Interior, whom La
Faloise knew from having met him at the Muffats'. As for
Fauchery, he said he believed she was called Madame Robert—
a worthy woman who had a lover, but never more than one,
and he was always a highly respectable person. As they turned
round, Daguenet smiled at them. Now that Nana had proved
a success, he no longer kept himself in the background; he
had just returned from wandering about the house and enjoying her triumph. The youngster, fresh from college, beside
him had not once quitted his seat, so overpowering was the
state of admiration into which the sight of Nana had plunged
him. So that, then, was woman! and he blushed deeply, and
kept taking off and putting on his gloves mechanically. At last,

as his neighbour had talked about Nana, he ventured to question him.

"Excuse me, sir," he said, "but this lady, who is playing—do you happen to know her?"

"Yes—a little—" murmured Daguenet in surprise, and with some hesitation.

"Then you know her address?"

The question came so abruptly, and so strangely, as addressed to him, that Daguenet felt like slapping the lad's face.

"I do not," he answered coldly, and turned his back.

The youngster understood that he had been guilty of some impropriety; he blushed all the more, and was mortified beyond expression.

The three knocks resounded throughout the house, and some of the attendants, their arms full of opera-cloaks and overcoats, were obstinately endeavouring to restore the various garments to their owners, who were hastening back to their seats. The claque applauded the scenery, which represented a grotto in Mount Etna,* hollowed out of a silver mine, with sides that glittered like newly coined crown pieces; at the back was Vulcan's forge, with all the tints of a sunset. In the second scene Diana arranged everything with the god, who was to pretend to go on a journey so as to leave the coast clear for Venus and Mars. Then scarcely was Diana left alone, than Venus arrived. A thrill ran through the audience. Nana was next to naked. She appeared in her nakedness with a calm audacity, confident in the all-powerfulness of her flesh. A slight gauze enveloped her; her round shoulders, her amazonian breasts, the rosy tips of which stood out straight and firm as lances, her broad hips swayed by the most voluptuous movements, her plump thighs, in fact, her whole body could be divined, nay, seen, white as the foam, beneath the transparent covering. It was Venus rising from the sea, with no other veil than her locks. And when Nana raised her arms, the glare of the footlights displayed to every gaze the golden hairs of her armpits.

---

*Active volcano in Sicily.

There was no applause. No one laughed now. The grave faces of the men were bent forward, their nostrils contracted, their mouths parched and irritated. A gentle breath, laden with an unknown menace, seemed to have passed over all. Out of this laughing girl there had suddenly emerged a woman, appalling all who beheld her, crowning all the follies of her sex, displaying to the world the hidden secrets of inordinate desire. Nana still preserved her smile, but it was the mocking one of a destroyer of men.

"The devil!" said Faucherey to La Faloise.

Mars, in the meantime, hurrying to the meeting, with his big hat and plume, found himself caught between the two goddesses. Then there ensued a scene in which Prullière played very ingeniously. Fondled by Diana, who wished to make a last attempt to bring him back into the right path before delivering him up to Vulcan's vengeance, cajoled by Venus, whom the presence of her rival stimulated, he abandoned himself to all these endearments with the happy expression of a donkey in a field of clover. The scene ended with a grand trio, and it was at this moment that an attendant entered Lucy Stewart's box, and threw two enormous bouquets of white lilac on to the stage. Every one applauded, and Nana and Rose Mignon curtsied their acknowledgments, whilst Prullière picked up the flowers. Some of the occupants of the stalls turned smilingly in the direction of the box occupied by Steiner and Mignon. The banker, all inflamed, moved his chin convulsively as though something had stuck in his throat. The acting which followed quite took the house by storm. Diana having gone off furious, Venus, seated on a bed of moss, at once called Mars to her side. Never before had so warm a scene of seduction been risked upon the stage. Nana, her arms around Prullière's neck, was slowly drawing him to her, when Fontan, grotesquely imitating the most awful fury, exaggerating the looks of an outraged husband who surprises his wife in the very act, appeared at the back of the grotto. In his hands he held his famous iron net; for a moment he poised it like a fisherman about to throw, then, by some ingenious device, Venus and Mars were ensnared, the net covered them, and held them fast in their guilty posture.

Then arose a murmur resembling one huge sigh. A few hands clapped, and every opera-glass was fixed on Venus. Little by little Nana had gained possession of the audience and now every man succumbed to her. The lust she inspired, similar to an animal in heat, had grown more and more till it filled the house. Now, her slightest movements fanned the desire; the raising of her little finger caused all the flesh beholding her to quiver. Backs were arched, vibrating as though the muscles, like so many fiddle-strings, were being played on by some invisible hand; on the napes of the outstretched necks the down fluttered beneath the warm and errant breath escaped from some women's lips. Fauchery beheld in front of him the youngster fresh from college start from his seat in his agitation. He had the curiosity to look at the Count de Vandeuvres, who was very pale, with tightly pressed lips—the stout Steiner, whose apoplectic face seemed bursting—Labordette examining through his eyeglass with the astonished look of a jockey admiring a thorough-bred mare—Daguenet, whose ears were flaming red, and trembling with enjoyment. Then, for an instant, he turned round, and was amazed at what he saw in the Muffats' box: behind the countess, who was looking pale and serious, the count had raised himself up, his mouth wide open, and his face blurred with red blotches; whilst, beside him, in the shadow, the troubled eyes of the Marquis de Chouard had become cat-like in appearance, full of phosphorescence and flecked with gold.

The heat was suffocating; even the hair weighed heavily on the perspiring heads. During the three hours that the piece had lasted, the foul breath had given the atmosphere an odour of human flesh. In the blaze of light the dust now appeared thicker, and seemed suspended, motionless, beneath the big crystal gasalier. The audience, tired and excited, seized with those drowsy, midnight desires which murmur their wishes in the depths of alcoves, vacillated, and was gradually becoming dazed. And Nana, facing this half-swooning crowd, these fifteen hundred persons, packed one above the other, and sinking with emotion and the nervous excitement of an approaching finale, remained victorious with her marble flesh, her sex alone strong enough to conquer them all and remain scathless.

The play was rapidly drawing to an end. In answer to Vulcan's triumphant calls, all Olympus defiled before the lovers, uttering cries of stupefaction or indulging in broad remarks. Jupiter said, "My son, I consider you are very foolish to call us to see this." Then there was a sudden change of feeling in favour of Venus. The deputation of cuckolds, again introduced by Iris, beseeched the master of the gods not to give heed to their petition, for since their wives passed their evenings at home they made their lives unbearable, so they preferred to be deceived and happy, which was the moral of the piece. Venus, therefore, was set free. Vulcan obtained a judicial separation. Mars made it up again with Diana. Jupiter, for the sake of peace and quietness at home, sent the little washerwoman into a constellation; and Cupid was at last released from his prison, where he had been making paper fowls, instead of conjugating the verb "to love." The curtain fell on an apotheosis, the deputation of cuckolds kneeling and singing a hymn of gratitude to Venus, smiling and exalted in her sovereign nudity.

The spectators had already risen from their seats, and were hastily making for the doors. The authors were named, and there was a double call in the midst of a thunder of applause. The cry, "Nana! Nana!" re-echoed again and again. Then, before the house was fairly empty, it became quite dark. The foot-lights were turned out, the lights of the gasalier were lowered, and long grey coverings were drawn over the gilding of the balconies; and the heat and the noise suddenly gave place to a death-like stillness, and an odour of dust and mildew. At the door of her box stood the Countess Muffat, wrapped in her furs and gazing into the darkness, as she waited for the crowd to pass away. In the passages the jostled attendants were fast losing their senses among the piles of cloaks and other garments. Fauchery and La Faloise had hurried to see the people come out. In the vestibule several gentlemen were waiting in a row, while down the double staircase descended two interminable and compact processions.

Steiner, led away by Mignon, was one of the first to leave. The Count de Vandeuvres went off with Blanche de Sivry on his arm. For a moment, Gaga and her daughter seemed embarrassed, but Labordette hastened to secure them a cab, and gallantly saw them into it. No one noticed Daguenet leave. As the youngster fresh from college, with his cheeks all aglow, bent upon waiting at the stage door, hastened to the Passage des Panoramas,* the gate of which he found closed, Satin, loitering on the pavement, came and grazed him lightly with her skirts; but he, quite broken-hearted, roughly declined her advances, and disappeared in the crowd, with tears of powerless longing in his eyes. Some of the spectators, lighting cigars, went off humming the song—"When Venus takes an evening stroll." Satin had returned to the Café des Variétés, where Augustus was allowing her to eat the lumps of sugar left by the customers. A stout man, who was greatly excited, having just quitted the theatre, at length took her off into the darkness of the now gradually hushed Boulevard.

The crowd still continued to pour down the double staircase. La Faloise was waiting for Clarisse, and Fauchery had promised to escort Lucy Stewart, with Caroline Héquet and her mother. They now arrived, monopolising a whole corner of the vestibule to themselves, and laughing loudly, just as the Muffats passed, looking very frigid. At that moment Bordenave, opening a little door, appeared, and obtained from Fauchery a distinct promise of a notice. He was covered with perspiration, his face as red as though he had had a sunstroke, and looking intoxicated with success.

"Your piece will run for two hundred nights at least," said La Faloise, obligingly. "All Paris will visit your theatre."

But Bordenave, his rage getting the better of him, indicated,

---

*Glassed-in shopping arcade, built in 1800 and the first public space in Paris to be illuminated by gas, in 1816.

with a rapid movement of his chin, the crowd that filled the vestibule—that mob of men with parched mouths and sparkling eyes, still inflamed with their passionate longing for Nana—and violently exclaimed:—

"Say my brothel, can't you? you pig-headed animal!"

CHAPTER II

The next morning at ten o'clock, Nana was still sleeping. She occupied, in the Boulevard Haussmann, the second storey of a large new house, the owner of which was content to let to single ladies, in order to get his plaster dried. A rich merchant from Moscow, who had come to spend a winter in Paris, had installed her there, paying two quarters' rent in advance. The rooms, too large for her, had never been completely furnished; and a gaudy luxury—gilded chairs and sideboards—contrasted with the rubbish of second-hand dealers—mahogany tables and zinc candelabra imitating Florentine bronze. Everything betokened the damsel abandoned too quickly by her first genuine protector, and fallen back into the clutches of unscrupulous lovers; a most difficult debut miscarried, and trammelled with a loss of credit and threats of eviction.

Nana was sleeping lying on her stomach, her bare arms entwining the pillow in which she buried her face, all pale with fatigue. The bedroom and dressing-room were the only two rooms to which a neighbouring upholsterer had really given his attention. By the aid of the faint streak of light gleaming between the curtains, one could distinguish the violet ebony furniture, the blue and grey hangings and chair coverings. In the warm, drowsy atmosphere of this bedchamber Nana suddenly awoke with a start, as though surprised to find the place beside her vacant. She looked at the other pillow placed next to her own, and which still showed the warm impression of a head in the midst of its frilling. Then, feeling with her hand, she pressed the knob of an electric bell, placed at the head of her bed.

"Has he gone, then?" she asked of the maid who appeared.

"Yes, madame. M. Paul left about ten minutes ago. As madame was tired, he would not wake her. But he requested me to tell madame that he would come to-morrow."

Whilst speaking, Zoé, the maid, had thrown open the shutters. The bright daylight inundated the room. Zoé was very dark, and wore a little frilled cap; her face, long and pointed like a dog's, was livid and scarred, with a flat nose, thick lips, and restless black eyes.

"To-morrow, to-morrow," repeated Nana, still only half awake, "is to-morrow his day, then?"

"Yes, madame. M. Paul always comes on Wednesdays."

"Ah! now I recollect!" exclaimed the young woman, sitting up in bed. "Everything is altered. I meant to tell him so this morning. He would meet the blackamoor, and then there would be no end of a row!"

"Madame did not warn me, how was I to know," murmured Zoé. "Next time madame alters her days, she will do well to tell me, so that I may act accordingly. So the old miser will no longer come on Tuesdays?"

It was thus between themselves, and without a smile, that they termed "old miser" and "blackamoor" the two paying gentlemen of the establishment, a tradesman of the Faubourg Saint-Denis, of a rather economical temperament, and a Wallachian,* a pretended count, whose money, always long in coming, had a most singular odour. Daguenet had secured for himself the morrows of the old miser; as the tradesman had to be at his shop by eight in the morning, the young man watched in Zoé's kitchen until he took his departure, and then jumped into the warm place he had just vacated, where he remained until ten o'clock, when he also went off to his business. Nana and he thought this arrangement very convenient.

"Never mind!" said she, "I will write to him this afternoon. And, if by chance he doesn't receive my letter, you must not let him in when he calls to-morrow."

Zoé walked softly about the room. She talked of the great success of the previous evening. "Madame had shown such talent, she sang so well! Ah! madame need not bother herself now about the future!"

---

*Native of Wallachia, a principality in southeastern Europe now incorporated into Romania.

Nana, her elbow buried in the pillow, only answered by nodding her head. Her chemise had slipped from her shoulders, over which fell her unkempt hair.

"No doubt," she murmured, musingly; "but how can we manage to wait? I shall have all sorts of annoyances to-day. By the way, has the landlord sent yet this morning?"

Then they both began to discuss ways and means. There were three quarters' rent owing, and the landlord threatened to put in an execution. Besides him, there was a host of other creditors, a job-master, a linen-draper, a dressmaker, a coal merchant, and several others, who came every day and installed themselves on a bench in the anteroom; the coal merchant, especially, made himself most obnoxious, he shouted on the stairs. But Nana's greatest worry was her little Louis, a child she had had when only sixteen, and whom she had placed out to nurse in a village near Rambouillet. The nurse demanded three hundred francs owing to her before she would give up Louis. Nana's maternal love had been aroused ever since her last visit to the child, and she was in despair at not being able to realize what had now become her most ardent wish, which was to pay the nurse, and place the child at Batignolles with her aunt, Madame Lerat, so that she could see him whenever she wished. The maid, at this point, hinted that she ought to have confided her troubles to the old miser.

"I know!" exclaimed Nana, "and I did tell him everything; but he replied that he had some very heavy bills to meet. He won't part with more than his thousand francs a month. As for the blackamoor, he's quite stumped just now; I think he's been losing at cards. And poor Mimi is really in want of money himself; a fall in stocks has cleared him out completely. He can't even bring me any flowers now."

She was speaking of Daguenet. On awaking in the morning she always felt in a confidential mood, and told Zoé everything. The maid, accustomed to such outpourings, listened with respectful sympathy. As madame deigned to talk to her of her affairs, she would take the liberty of giving her opinion. First of all, though, she could not help saying that she loved madame very much; it was for that reason that she had left

Madame Blanche, and God knew that Madame Blanche was doing all she could to get her to return to her! She was well known, and would never have any difficulty in obtaining a situation; but she would remain with madame, even though things were not very brilliant, because she believed madame had a great future before her. And she ended by giving her advice. When one was young, one did very foolish things. Now it was necessary to be very careful, for men only thought of amusing themselves. And there would be no end of them! If madame liked she would only have a word to say to quiet her creditors and procure the money she was in want of.

"All that does not give me three hundred francs," Nana kept repeating, as she passed her fingers through her hair. "I want three hundred francs to-day, at once. How stupid it is not knowing someone who would give three hundred francs."

And she tried to think of some means of obtaining the money. She was expecting Madame Lerat that very morning, and she would have liked so much to have sent her off at once to Rambouillet. Her inability to gratify her whim quite spoilt her triumph of the preceding night. To think that among all those men who had greeted her with such applause there was not one who would bring her fifteen louis!* Besides, she could not accept money in that way. Oh, how miserable she was! And then she thought of her baby: his blue eyes were like an angel's; he could just lisp "Mamma" in such a funny tone of voice that it almost made her die with laughing!

Just then the electric bell of the outer door sounded, with its rapid and trembling vibration. After going to see who was there, Zoé returned, and whispered confidentially:

"It is a woman."

She had already seen this woman at least twenty times, only she pretended never to recognise her, and to ignore the nature of her dealings with ladies down in their luck.

"She told me her name—Madame Tricon."

---

*Gold coin, also called a Napoléon, that was worth 20 francs.

"Old Tricon!" exclaimed Nana. "Why, I forgot all about her! I will see her."

Zoé ushered in a tall old lady, wearing long curls, and looking like a countess frequently visiting her solicitor. Then she retired, disappeared without noise, with the snake-like movement with which she left a room when a gentleman called. She might just as well, however, have remained where she was. Old Madame Tricon did not even sit down. She only uttered a few short words.

"I have somebody for you to-day. Are you willing?"

"Yes. How much?"

"Twenty louis."

"And at what time?"

"At three o'clock. Then, that's settled?"

"Yes, that's settled."

Madame Tricon immediately began to talk of the weather; it was very dry, and good for walking. She had still to call on four or five persons; and off she went, after consulting a little notebook. Nana, left alone, felt a weight lifted off her mind. A slight shiver passed across her back; she slowly drew the warm clothes over her, with the indolence of a chilly cat. Little by little her eyes closed; she smiled at the idea of prettily dressing little Louis on the morrow; then, in the sleep which at length overtook her, her feverish dream of the night, a prolonged thunder of applause, returned like a thorough-bass, and lulled her weariness. At twelve o'clock, when Zoé showed Madame Lerat into the room, Nana was still sleeping. But the noise awoke her, and she at once said:

"Ah! it's you. You will go to Rambouillet to-day?"

"I came for that," replied the aunt. "There is a train at twenty past twelve. I have time to catch it."

"No, I shall only have the money this afternoon," said the young woman, stretching herself, her breasts rising as she did so. "You will have some lunch, and then we will see."

Zoé whispered, as she brought her a dressing-gown, "Madame, the hairdresser is there."

But Nana would not retire into her dressing-room. She called out:

"Come in, Francis."

A gentleman, very stylishly dressed, pushed open the door. He bowed. Just at that moment Nana was getting out of bed, her legs quite bare. Without hurrying herself, she held out her arms, so that Zoé could pass the sleeves of the dressing-gown on to them; and Francis, quite at his ease, waited in a dignified manner, and without looking away. Then, when she had seated herself, and he had passed the comb through her hair, he spoke:

"Madame has, perhaps, not yet read the papers? There is a very good article in the 'Figaro.'"

As he had the paper with him, Madame Lerat put on her spectacles, and read the article out loud, standing in front of the window. She drew up to her full trooper-like stature, her nostrils contracted each time she came to an adjective exceptionally gallant. It was a notice of Fauchery's, written directly after leaving the theatre—two very warm columns, full of witty but unkind remarks, so far as regarded the actress, and of a brutish admiration for the woman.

"Excellent! excellent!" kept repeating Francis.

Nana didn't care a button for the chaff about her voice! He was a nice fellow, that Fauchery; all the same, she'd pay him out for his pleasant little ways! After reading the article a second time, Madame Lerat abruptly declared that all the men had the devil in the calves of their legs; and she refused to explain further, satisfied with having made this racy allusion, which she alone was able to understand. Meanwhile Francis had finished fastening up Nana's hair. He bowed and said,

"I shall have my eye on the evening papers. The same time as usual, I suppose—at half-past five?"

"Bring me a pot of pomatum* and a pound of burnt almonds from Boissier's!" Nana called after him across the drawing-room, just as he was shutting the door.

Then the two women, left alone, remembered that they had not kissed each other, so they cordially embraced one another

---

*Variant of "pomade," a hair-dressing ointment.

on the cheek. The article had rather excited them. Nana, until then only half awake, again felt all the fever of her triumph. Ah! Rose Mignon must have spent a very pleasant morning! As her aunt had not been to the theatre, because, as she said, all emotion upset her stomach, she began to relate the events of the evening, the recital intoxicating her as though Paris itself had crumbled beneath the applause. Then, suddenly interrupting herself, she asked, with a laugh, if anyone would ever have expected as much in the days when she dragged her blackguard little person about the Rue de la Goutte d'Or. Madame Lerat shook her head. No, no; no one could ever have foreseen it. She spoke in her turn in a grave tone of voice, and calling her her daughter. For wasn't she her second mother, now that the real one had gone to join the papa and the grandma. Nana, greatly affected, was on the point of shedding tears. But Madame Lerat said that by-gones were by-gones, and very filthy by-gones too! things that should not be touched upon every day in the week. For a long while she had given up seeing her niece, for the other members of the family accused her of going to the bad in her company. As if, great heavens! such a thing were possible! She did not want to know her niece's secrets; she was sure that the latter had always led a respectable life. And now she was satisfied with finding her in a good position, and seeing that she entertained a motherly feeling for her son. In this world, after all, there was nothing to beat honesty and work.

"Who is the father of your baby?" she asked, suddenly interrupting her sermon, her eyes lighted up with intense curiosity.

Nana, surprised, hesitated for a second. "A gentleman," she replied.

"Ah!" resumed the aunt, "I was told it was a mason who used to beat you. Well, you can tell me all about it some other day; you know that I can be trusted! Be easy, I will take as great care of him as though he was the son of a prince."

She had given up her artificial flower-making business and retired on her savings—six hundred francs a year—hoarded up sou by sou. Nana promised to take some nice rooms for her, besides which she would allow her one hundred francs a month. When she heard this the aunt quite forgot herself in her delight, and impressed upon her niece that she should squeeze them whilst she had the chance. She was alluding to the men. Then they kissed each other again. But Nana, in the midst of her joy, and just as she had once more begun to talk of little Louis, seemed to get sad at some sudden recollection.

"What a nuisance it is: I have to go out at three o'clock!" she murmured. "It's an awful bore!"

At that moment Zoé came to say that the lunch was ready. They went into the dining-room, where they found an elderly lady already seated at the table. She had not taken her bonnet off, and was dressed in a dark gown of no precise colour, but something between puce and goose droppings. Nana did not seem surprised at seeing her there. She merely asked her why she had not gone into the bedroom.

"I heard voices," answered the old lady. "I thought you were engaged."

Madame Maloir, who had a respectable appearance and distinguished ways, acted as Nana's old lady friend. She entertained her and accompanied her about. At first, Madame Lerat's presence seemed to make her uneasy; but when she learnt that the stranger was only the aunt, she looked at her in quite a pleasant sort of a way, and smiled faintly. However, Nana, who said her stomach had gone right down into her heels, started on some radishes, which she devoured without any bread. Madame Lerat, becoming very ceremonious, declined the radishes, saying they produced wind. Then, when Zoé brought in some cutlets, Nana played with the meat, and ended by merely sucking the bone. Now and again she cast a glance in the direction of her old friend's bonnet.

"Is that the new bonnet I gave you?" she eventually asked.

"Yes, I have altered it to suit me," murmured Madame Maloir, with her mouth full.

The bonnet looked frightful with the big feather she had stuck in it. Madame Maloir had a mania for re-making up all her bonnets: she alone knew what suited her, and in a minute she would utterly spoil the most elegant article. Nana, who had bought her the bonnet so as not to feel ashamed every time she went out with her, began to get angry.

"Well! you might at least take it off!" she cried.

"No, thank you," the old lady replied most politely, "It does not trouble me. I can eat very well with it on."

After the cutlets came some cauliflower and the remains of a cold chicken. But Nana turned up her nose at each dish put upon the table, and left her food untouched on her plate. After smelling everything and hesitating what to take, she finished her lunch with some jam. The dessert lasted some time, and Zoé did not remove the cloth before serving the coffee; the ladies merely pushed away their plates. They talked of the great success achieved at the theatre the previous evening. Nana was making cigarettes, which she smoked as she leant back in her chair; and Zoé, having remained in the room, standing up against the sideboard swinging her arms about, at length began relating the story of her life. She said that she was the daughter of a midwife, who had got into trouble. First of all she obtained a situation at a dentist's, then with an agent for an insurance company, but she did not like it; and then she mentioned, with a touch of pride in her voice, the names of the different ladies with whom she had lived as lady's-maid. Zoé spoke of these ladies as though they owed her everything. For certain, more than one of them would have got into a nice mess had it not been for her. For instance, one day that Madame Blanche was with M. Octave, the old gentleman unexpectedly arrived. What did Zoé do? She pretended to fall down as she passed through the drawing-room; the old gentleman hastened to help her, and then rushed off to the kitchen to get her a glass of water, while M. Octave got clear away.

"Ah! that was capital!" exclaimed Nana, who had listened with a tender interest and a sort of obsequious admiration.

"As for me, I have met with many misfortunes," commenced Madame Lerat. And drawing her chair close to Madame Maloir, she related to her various incidents of her private life. They were both sucking lumps of sugar which they had previously dipped in their coffee. But Madame Maloir listened to the secrets of others without ever letting out a word about herself. It was said that she lived on a mysterious pension, in a room into which she never allowed any one to enter.

All of a sudden Nana flew into a passion. "Aunt!" she cried, "don't play with the knives. You know that it always upsets me."

Without thinking of what she was doing, Madame Lerat had crossed two of the knives on the table. All the same the young woman pretended she was not superstitious. For instance, spilling salt never affected her, neither did anything happening on a Friday; but crossed knives was more than she could stand, they had never misled her. For certain, something disagreeable would happen to her. She yawned, and in a tone of vexation, said, "Already two o'clock. I shall have to go out. What a nuisance!" The two old women exchanged a glance. Then all three shook their heads without speaking. True, it was not always amusing to have to go out. Nana was again leaning back in her chair, and smoking another cigarette, whilst the others discreetly kept their lips tight, and put on their most philosophical looks.

"While you are gone, we will have a game at bézique,"* said Madame Maloir, after a short silence. "Does madame know the game?"

Of course Madame Lerat did, and played it better than any one. It was not necessary to disturb Zoé, who had left the room; a corner of the table was all they wanted, so they turned the cloth up over the dirty plates. But, just as Madame Maloir had got the cards out of a drawer of the sideboard, Nana said she would be very good if, before commencing the game, she would write a letter for her. It bothered her to write, and besides, she was not very sure of her spelling, whilst her old friend wrote letters so well. She ran and fetched from her bedroom some beautiful note-paper. A common three sou† inkbottle was lying about, with a rusty old pen. The letter was for Daguenet. Madame Maloir commenced in her beautiful round hand, "My darling little man," and then she proceeded to tell him not to come on the morrow, because "it could not

*Card game resembling pinochle, but played with a larger deck.
†Coin equivalent to 5 centimes, or the twentieth part of a franc.

be," but "far or near, every moment in the day, she was thinking of him."

"And I will end with a thousand kisses," murmured Madame Maloir.

Madame Lerat had approved each phrase with a nod of her head. Her eyes sparkled: she had a weakness for being mixed up in love affairs. So she could not resist adding something of her own.

"A thousand kisses on your beautiful eyes," she cooed, with a tender look.

"Yes, that's it: 'A thousand kisses on your beautiful eyes!'" repeated Nana, whilst a sanctimonious expression overspread the features of the two old women.

They rang for Zoé, for her to give the letter to a commissionnaire.* She was just then talking with a messenger from the theatre who had brought madame a communication from the stage-manager, which should have been sent to her in the morning. Nana had the man in, and asked him to leave the letter at Daguenet's on his way back. Then she began to question him. Oh! M. Bordenave was very pleased; all the seats were booked for a week at least; madame had no idea of the number of persons who had inquired for her address since the morning. When the messenger had left, Nana said that she would not be away more than half an hour at the most. If any visitors called, Zoé was to ask them to wait. As she spoke, the electric bell of the outer door sounded. It was one of the creditors, the job-master; he had taken a seat on the bench of the anteroom. Oh! he might wait and twirl his thumbs until night-time; they were not going to disturb themselves for him.

"I must pull myself together," said Nana lazily, again stretching herself and yawning. "I ought to be there by now."

All the same she did not move. She watched the game, in which her aunt had just scored a hundred aces. Her chin in her hand, she was becoming interested; but she suddenly started on hearing three o'clock strike.

---

*Messenger.

"Damn it!" she roughly exclaimed.

Then Madame Maloir, who was counting the tens, said to her in a gentle, encouraging voice, "My child, you would do better to get your business over at once."

"Yes, be quick over it," added Madame Lerat, as she shuffled the cards. "I shall be able to leave by the half-past four train, if you are here with the money by four o'clock."

"Oh! it won't take long," she muttered in reply.

In ten minutes Zoé had helped her to put on a dress and bonnet. She didn't care if she looked untidy. Just as she was about to go off, there was another ring at the bell. This time it was the coal merchant. Well! he could keep the job-master company; they might entertain each other. To avoid a row, however, she passed through the kitchen, and went out by the servants' staircase. She often went that way; all she had to do was to keep her skirts from touching the ground.

"When one is a good mother, the rest is of no consequence," sententiously observed Madame Maloir, now left alone with Madame Lerat.

"I mark eighty kings," replied the latter, who had a great weakness for cards. And they both became more and more wrapped up in the game.

The table had not been cleared. A mixed odour pervaded the room—the fumes of the lunch and the smoke of the cigarettes. The two ladies returned to their lumps of sugar soaked in coffee. For twenty minutes they played as they sipped, when, the bell having rung a third time, Zoé bounced into the room, and jostled them in a most familiar manner.

"I say!" she exclaimed, "there's another ring. You won't be able to remain in here. If many more people are coming, I shall want every room in the place. Now, then, up you get! up you get!"

Madame Maloir wanted to finish the game; but Zoé having made a feint of gathering up the cards, she decided to remove them carefully, without disturbing anything, whilst Madame Lerat secured the brandy bottle, some glasses, and the sugar, and they both hastened into the kitchen, where they placed their things on an end of the table between some dirty cloths that were drying and a large bowl full of greasy water.

"I'm three hundred and forty. It's your play."

"I lead hearts."

When Zoé returned, she found them once more deep in the game. After a short silence, and as Madame Lerat gathered up the cards and shuffled them, Madame Maloir asked:

"Who was it?"

"Oh! no one," answered the maid, carelessly, "only a youngster. I ought to have sent him about his business; but he is so pretty, without a hair on his face, and with blue eyes and such a girlish figure, that I told him he could wait. He has an enormous bouquet in his hand, and he won't leave go of it. He deserves to be whipped, a brat who ought still to be at college!"

Madame Lerat got up to fetch hot water to concoct some grog; the sugar and coffee had made her thirsty. Zoé murmured that, all the same, she could manage some as well. Her mouth had a bitter taste like gall.

"Well, and where have you put him?" resumed Madame Maloir.

"Why, in the little spare room that isn't furnished. It just holds one of madame's trunks and a table. That's where I put such youngsters."

And she was sweetening her grog with several lumps of sugar, when another ring at the bell made her jump. Hang it all! wasn't she to be allowed to have a drink in peace, now? If what they had already had was only the beginning of it, it promised to be lively. However, she hastened to see who was there. Then, when she returned, seeing Madame Maloir's questioning look, "Only a bouquet," she observed.

They all three drank, after nodding to each other. The bell rang again twice, as Zoé, at last, cleared the table, carrying the dirty plates to the sink one by one. But all this ringing was for nothing of any consequence. She kept the occupants of the kitchen well informed. Twice she came and repeated her disdainful phrase—"Only a bouquet."

However, the ladies had a good laugh between two of the deals, as she told them of the looks of the creditors in the anteroom when the flowers were brought. Madame would find her bouquets on her dressing-table. What a pity it was that they cost so much, and that one couldn't even raise ten sous on them! Well, there was a good deal of money wasted in the world.

"For myself," said Madame Maloir, "I should be satisfied if I had every day what the men spend on the flowers they give the women in Paris."

"I daresay, you are not at all hard to please," murmured Madame Lerat. "If I had only the money spent on the wire alone. My dear, sixty queens."

It was ten minutes to four. Zoé was surprised—could not understand at all how madame could remain out so long. Generally, when madame found herself obliged to go out in the afternoon, she got it over in less than no time. But Madame Maloir observed that one was not always able to do as one would wish. One certainly met with many obstacles in life, declared Madame Lerat. The best thing to do was to wait. If her niece was late it was because she had been detained, was it not? Besides, they had nothing to complain of. It was very comfortable in the kitchen. And, as she had no more hearts in her hand, Madame Lerat played diamonds. The electric bell was again set in motion. When Zoé reappeared her face was quite radiant.

"Fatty Steiner! girls," said she in a whisper, as soon as she got her head in at the door. "I put him in the parlour."

Then Madame Maloir talked of the banker to Madame Lerat, who did not know any of that class of gentlemen. Was he going to chuck up Rose Mignon? Zoé wagged her head; she knew many things. But she was again obliged to go and answer the bell.

"Well! this beats everything!" she murmured on returning. "It's the blackamoor! It was no use, though I told him again and again that madame was out; he has gone and made himself comfortable in the bedroom. We did not expect him till this evening."

At a quarter past four Nana was still absent. What could she be doing? It was most absurd of her. Then two more bouquets were brought. Zoé, not knowing what to do with herself, looked to see if there was any more coffee. Yes, the ladies would willingly finish the coffee, it would wake them up again. They were falling asleep, settled in their chairs, and continuously drawing cards from the pack with the same movement of their arms. The half past struck. Something, surely, must have happened to madame, they whispered to each other.

All of a sudden, Madame Maloir, forgetting herself, exclaimed in a loud voice—"Double bézique! Five hundred!"

"Hold your row! will you?" cried Zoé, angrily. "What will all those gentlemen think?"

And in the silence which reigned, with the exception of a slight murmur, caused by the disputes of the two old women, was heard the sound of hastily approaching footsteps on the servants' staircase. It was Nana at last. Before she opened the door one could hear her panting. She entered looking very red, and very abrupt in manner. Her skirt, the strings of which had probably broken, had dragged over the stairs, and the flounces had soaked in a regular pool—some filth that had flowed from the first floor, where the cook was a perfect slut.

"Here you are at last! well, it's fortunate!" said Madame Lerat, with a nasty look about her mouth, and still put out by Madame Maloir's double bézique. "You can flatter yourself that you know how to keep people waiting!"

"Madame is really very foolish!" added Zoé.

Nana, already out of temper, became exasperated by these reproaches. Was that the way to receive her after all the unpleasantness she had gone through?

"Mind your own business, can't you?" she cried.

"Hush! madame, there are some people here," said the maid.

So, lowering her voice, the young woman faltered, all out of breath, "Do you think I've been amusing myself? I thought I should never have been able to get away. I should have liked to have seen you in my place. I was boiling. I was on the point of using my fists. And then, not a cab to be got to come back in. Fortunately it's close by. All the same, I ran as fast as I could."

"Have you the money?" asked the aunt.

"What a question!" replied Nana.

She had seated herself in a chair close to the grate, her legs almost too tired to bear her, and, before she had even recovered her breath, she felt inside the body of her dress and drew forth an envelope, in which were four bank-notes of one hundred francs each. One could see the notes by a large tear she had made in the envelope with her finger so as to make sure of what it contained. The three women around her looked fixedly at the envelope of common paper, all crumpled and dirtied, in her little gloved hands. It was too late; Madame Lerat should not go to Rambouillet till the next day. Nana began to give her various instructions.

"Madame, there are some people waiting," repeated the maid.

But she again flew into a passion. The people could wait. She would attend to them by-and-by, when she had settled what she was about. Then, as her aunt put out her hand to take the money, "Oh! no, not all," said she. "Three hundred francs for the nurse, fifty francs for your journey and expenses, that makes three hundred and fifty. I shall keep fifty francs."

The great difficulty was to get change. There were not ten francs in the place. They did not ask Madame Maloir, who was listening with an uninterested look, for she never had with her more than the six sous necessary for an omnibus. At length Zoé left them, saying that she would go and look in her trunk, and she shortly returned with a hundred francs, all in five franc pieces. They counted them on the corner of the table. Madame Lerat went off at once, promising to fetch little Louis on the morrow.

"You say there are some people waiting?" resumed Nana, still sitting down, resting.

"Yes, madame, three persons."

And Zoé named the banker first. Nana pouted her lip. Did that Steiner think she was going to stand any of his nonsense, just because he had had a bouquet thrown to her on the previous evening?

"Besides," she declared, "I've had enough for to-day. I shall not receive any one. Go and say that you no longer expect me."

"Madame will reflect—madame will receive M. Steiner," murmured Zoé, without stirring, looking very grave and annoyed to find her mistress on the point of behaving very foolishly. Then she spoke of the Wallachian, who must be beginning to find time hang very heavily on his hands all alone in the bedroom. But Nana got into a rage and became more obstinate. No, she would see no one! Why was she ever bothered with a fellow who would stick to her to that extent?

"Kick 'em all out! I'm going to have a game at bézique with Madame Maloir. I like that much better."

The ringing of the bell interrupted her. This was too much! How many more of them would come to bother her? She forbade Zoé to open the door. The latter, without listening to what she said, left the kitchen. When she returned, she stated in a peremptory tone of voice, as she handed two cards to her mistress: "I told the gentlemen that madame would see them. They are in the drawing-room."

Nana jumped up from her seat in a regular fury, but the names of the Marquis de Chouard and Count Muffat de Beuville, on the cards, calmed her. She remained an instant wrapped in thought.

"Who are they?" she asked at length. "Do you know them?"

"I know the old one," replied Zoé, discreetly; and as her mistress continued to question her with her eyes, she quietly added, "I have seen him at a certain place."

This statement seemed to determine the young woman. She reluctantly left the kitchen, that warm refuge where one could gossip and take one's ease, with the smell of the coffee warming on the embers of the charcoal. She left behind her Madame Maloir, who was now cutting the cards and telling her own fortune. She had continued to keep her bonnet on, only, to be more at her ease, she had untied the strings and thrown the ends back over her shoulders. In the dressing-room, where Zoé rapidly helped her to change her things, Nana avenged herself for the worries she had to put up with by uttering in a low voice the most abominable oaths against men in general. These foul expressions grieved the maid, for she saw with regret that her mistress was a long time in getting free of the evil effects of her early surroundings. She even ventured to beg of her to be calm.

"Oh, pooh!" replied Nana, coarsely; "they are a set of pigs, and they like it."

Nevertheless, she put on what she styled her princess look, and was moving towards the drawing-room, when Zoé stopped her, and, of her own accord, hastened to usher into the dressing-room the Marquis de Chouard and Count Muffat. It would be much better that way.

"Gentlemen," said the young woman with studied politeness, "I regret that you have had to wait."

The two men bowed and sat down. An embroidered blind subdued the light admitted into the room, which was the most elegantly furnished one of the set: it was hung with light drapery, and contained a handsome marble dressing-table, a large cheval-glass, with an inlaid frame, a reclining-chair, and several easy-chairs covered in blue satin. On the dressing-table were placed the bouquets of roses, lilac and hyacinths, quite a pyramid of flowers, emitting a strong and penetrating perfume; whilst in the moist atmosphere, with the insipid smell rising from the dirty water, an odour more pronounced could now and again be discerned, emanating from a few sprigs of dry patchouli broken up into small pieces at the bottom of a cup. And cuddling herself up, drawing round her the unfastened dressing-gown she had slipped on, Nana appeared as though she had been surprised at her toilet, her skin scarcely dried, looking smiling though startled in the midst of her laces.

"Madame," gravely said Count Muffat, "excuse our taking you thus by storm. We have called respecting a collection. This gentleman and myself are members of the poor relief committee for this district."

The Marquis de Chouard gallantly hastened to add, "When we heard that a great actress lived in this house, we at once determined to call and personally plead the cause of our poor. Talent is ever allied to a generous heart."

Nana made a great show of modesty. She acknowledged their remarks by slightly nodding her head, reflecting furiously, however, all the time. It must have been the old one who had brought the other; his eyes looked so wicked. Yet, the other one too was to be mistrusted, his temples seemed curiously swollen; he might have managed to come alone. No doubt, they had heard about her from the concierge, and each had called on his own account.

"Certainly, gentlemen, you were quite right to come," said she, most pleasantly. But the sound of the bell made her start. What! another visitor, and that Zoé who would persist in letting them in! "I am only too happy to be able to give," she continued. In reality, she felt extremely flattered.

"Ah! madame," resumed the marquis, "if you but knew the extent of the misery! Our district contains more than three thousand poor, and yet it is one of the richest. You can have no idea of the amount of distress prevailing—children without food, women lying ill, deprived of all necessities, dying of cold."

"Poor people!" cried Nana deeply affected.

Her pity was so great that tears filled her beautiful eyes. In an impulsive moment she leant forward, forgetting any longer to study her movements, and her open dressing-gown displayed all her neck, whilst her bended knees indicated, beneath the flimsy material, the roundness of her form. A slight tinge of colour illumined the ghastly pallor of the marquis's cheeks, and Count Muffat, who was on the point of speaking, lowered his eyes. It was decidedly too warm in that small room, it was heavy and close like a hot-house. The roses were drooping, and the smell of the patchouli in the cup was intoxicating.

"One would like to be very rich on such occasions," added Nana. "However one does what one can. Believe me, gentlemen, had I only known—"

She was on the point of saying something foolish under the influence of her emotion; but she recovered herself, and left the phrase unfinished. For a moment she remained perplexed, not recollecting where she had put the fifty francs when she took her dress off; but at length she recollected, they must be on a corner of her dressing-table under a pomatum-pot turned upside down. As she rose from her seat the bell sounded again, violently this time. Good! another one! Would

it never cease? The count and the marquis had also risen, and
the ears of the latter seemed to turn in the direction of the
door; no doubt he knew what the frequent rings at the bell
meant. Muffat glanced at him; then each looked on the
ground; no doubt they were in each other's way. But they soon
regained their composure, the one looking proud and strong,
his head well covered with his dark brown hair, the other
straightening his bony shoulders, over which fell his meagre
crown of rare white hairs.

"Really, gentlemen," said Nana, laughing, as she brought
the ten big silver coins, "I'm afraid I shall burden you. Remember it is for the poor."

And an adorable little dimple appeared in her chin. She
had assumed her "hail fellow well met" air, and stood in an easy
posture, holding out her hand full of silver—offering it to the
two men, as though saying, "Come, who'll take?" The count
was the more active, he took the money; but one coin remained in the young woman's hand, and, to remove it, his fingers were obliged to come in contact with her skin—a skin so
warm and soft that touching it sent a thrill through his frame.
Nana, greatly amused, continued laughing.

"There, gentlemen," she resumed. "Next time I hope to give
more."

Having no pretext for remaining longer, they bowed and
moved towards the door. But, as they were about to leave the
room, the bell sounded again. The marquis could not repress
a faint smile, whilst a shadow passed over the count's grave
face. Nana detained them a few seconds, to allow Zoé time to
find some out-of-the-way corner for the new comer. She did
not like people to meet one another when calling on her. This
time, the place must be quite full. She was agreeably surprised,
however, to find the drawing-room empty. Had Zoé, then, put
them into the cupboards?

"Good-day, gentlemen," she said, as she stood in the open
doorway.

She enveloped them in her smile and her clear glance.
Count Muffat bowed low, disconcerted in spite of his great experience of the world, longing for a breath of fresh air, dizzy

from his contact with that room, and carrying away with him
an odour of woman and flowers which nearly stifled him. And,
behind him, the Marquis de Chouard, certain of not being observed, dared to wink at Nana, his face, for the moment, all distorted, and his tongue between his lips. When the young
woman re-entered the dressing-room, where Zoé awaited her
with some letters and visiting-cards, she laughed louder than
ever, and exclaimed:

"Well, there go a couple of sharks! They wheedled my fifty
francs out of me!"

But she was not annoyed; it amused her to think that men
should ask her for money. All the same, they were a couple of
pigs; she hadn't a sou left. The sight of the cards and the letters brought back her bad temper. The letters might be tolerated; they came from gentlemen who, after applauding her at
the theatre, now hastened to make their declarations. As for
the visitors, they might go to the devil! Zoé had put some
everywhere; and she remarked that the suite of rooms was very
convenient, for each one opened on to the passage. It was not
the same at Madame Blanche's, where you always had to pass
through the drawing-room; and Madame Blanche had had a
great deal of unpleasantness on that account.

"You must send them all to the right about," resumed Nana,
following her original idea. "Begin with the blackamoor."

"I sent him off a long time ago, madame," said Zoé with a
smile. "He merely wished to tell madame that he couldn't
come to-night."

What great joy! Nana clapped her hands. He wasn't coming—what luck! Then she would be free! She sighed with relief, as though she had been pardoned when about to endure
the most abominable of punishments. Her first thought was
for Daguenet—that poor duck whom she had just put off till
the Thursday! Quick, Madame Maloir must write another letter! But Zoé said that, as usual, Madame Maloir had gone off
without letting any one know. Then Nana, after speaking of
sending some one, began to hesitate. She was very tired. A
whole night for sleep—it would be so nice! The idea of such a

treat at length proved irresistible. She might, just for once, stand herself that.

"I shall go to bed at once on returning from the theatre," she murmured, in a greedy sort of way, "and you must let me sleep till twelve o'clock." Then, raising her voice, she added, "Now, then, look alive! shove 'em all on to the staircase!"

Zoé didn't stir. She would never permit herself openly to give advice to madame, only she arranged matters in such a way as to enable madame to profit by her vast experience, when she saw that madame was about to do something foolish.

"M. Steiner also?" she briefly asked.

"Certainly," replied Nana. "He before the others."

The maid still waited, to give madame time to reflect. Wouldn't madame be proud to do her rival, Rose Mignon, out of such a rich gentleman—one so well known in all the theatres?

"Look sharp, my dear," resumed Nana, who understood perfectly, "and tell him that he plagues me." But she suddenly altered her mind. On the morrow she might want him; so, winking her eye, she laughingly added, "After all, if I want to hook him, the best thing is chuck him out."

Zoé seemed very much struck with the remark. She gazed on her mistress with a look of admiration, then went and sent Steiner about his business without hesitation. Nana waited a few minutes to give her time to sweep the place, as she termed it. One had never before heard of such an assault! She looked into the drawing-room; it was empty—the dining-room also; but as she continued her inspection, quite reassured, and certain she would not come across any one, she suddenly found herself in the company of a very little fellow, on opening the door of a spare room. He was seated on the top of a trunk, very quiet and looking very good, with an enormous bouquet on his knees.

"Oh, heavens!" she exclaimed. "There is still one in here!"

On seeing her the little fellow jumped to the floor, his face as red as a poppy, and he did not seem to know what to do with his bouquet, which he passed from one hand to the other, almost strangled by emotion. His youth, his embarrassment, the comical figure he cut with his flowers, touched Nana, who burst out laughing. What! children as well? Now men came to her when they had scarcely left off their swaddling clothes. She became quite easy, familiar, maternal, even, in her way; and, slapping her thighs, asked him, for a bit of fun,

"Have you then come to be whipped, baby?"

"Yes," replied the youngster, in low and entreating accents.

This reply amused her all the more. He was seventeen years old, his name was George Hugon. He was at the Variety Theatre on the previous evening, and he had come to see her.

"Are those flowers for me?"

"Yes."

"Give them to me, then, you little booby!"

But, as she took the bouquet, he seized her hands, with the gluttony of his happy age. She had to strike him to make him leave go. There was a young monkey who went it hot! She quite blushed and smiled as she scolded him. Then she sent him away, giving him permission to come again. He staggered; he could scarcely find the door. Nana returned to her dressing-room, where Francis appeared almost immediately to do her hair for the evening. She never dressed before then. Seated before the looking-glass, lowering her head beneath the skilful fingers of the hair-dresser, she remained silent and pensive, when Zoé entered, saying,

"Madame, there is one who will not go away."

"Very well, then, let him stop," she calmly replied.

"Besides, as fast as some go others come."

"Never mind, tell them to wait. When they get very hungry they will go off!"

She had again altered her mind. It now delighted her to keep the men waiting. A sudden idea perfected her amusement. She escaped from Francis's hands, and ran and bolted the door. Now they could come and fill the other rooms as much as they liked, they wouldn't be able to pierce the walls, she supposed! Zoé could go in and out by the little door that led into the kitchen. However, the electric bell kept on as lively as ever. Every five minutes the sound came again, sharp and clear, with the regularity of a well-oiled machine; and Nana

counted the tinklings by way of distraction. But a sudden recollection burst upon her.

"And my burnt almonds, what about them?" she cried.

Francis also was forgetting the burnt almonds. He withdrew
a packet from the pocket of his frockcoat, with the discreet
manner of a man of the world offering a present to a lady
friend. However, each time his account was settled he did not
forget to include the burnt almonds in the bill. Nana put the
bag between her knees and commenced to munch, moving
her head now and again, according to the gentle pushes of the
hair-dresser.

"The deuce!" she murmured, after a short silence, "there's
a regular band of them." Three times successively had the bell
sounded. It scarcely ceased ringing. Some of the rings were
very modest ones, they seemed to falter with the nervousness
of a first avowal; others were very bold, vibrating beneath the
touch of some rough hand; whilst others, still, were very hurried, and passed away in a moment. They produced an inces-
sant peal, as Zoé said, sufficient to disturb the whole
neighbourhood, all this crowd of men pushing in turn the
ivory knob of the electric bell. It was too bad of that joker Bordenave. He had really given the address to too many persons—
nearly all the previous night's audience seemed to be calling.

"By the way, Francis," said Nana, "have you five louis?"

He took a step backwards, scrutinized the head-dress, then
quietly replied, "Five louis? well, that depends."

"Oh! you know," she returned, "if you want securities—"

And, without finishing the sentence, she nodded in the direction of the adjoining rooms. Francis lent the five louis. Zoé,
in her moments of respite, came and prepared everything for
her mistress's toilet. Soon she had to come and dress her,
whilst the hair-dresser waited, wishing to give a few finishing
touches to his work. But the sound of the bell constantly called
away the maid, who left her mistress with her stays half un-
laced, or with only one stocking on. She got quite bewildered
in spite of her experience. After having put men everywhere,
even in the smallest corners, she was at length obliged to put
three or four together, a proceeding which was altogether

against her principles. Well, so much the worse if they ate each other, it would give more room! And Nana, safely bolted in, laughed at them, saying that she could hear them puffing and blowing. They must have a very queer look, all with their tongues hanging out, like a lot of puppies sitting on their haunches in a ring. It was the success of the previous evening continuing; this pack of men had followed on her trail.

"I hope they won't break anything," she murmured. She was commencing to get uneasy, under the influence of the hot breaths which percolated through the cracks. But Zoé ushered in Labordette, and the young woman uttered a cry of relief. He had called to tell her of an account he had settled for her at the office of the justice of the peace. She didn't listen to him, but kept repeating, "I shall take you with me. We will dine together. Then you shall see me to the Variety Theatre. I don't go on till half-past nine."

That dear Labordette, he had just dropped in at the right time. He never asked for anything! He was merely the ladies' friend, and interested himself in their little affairs. For instance, on coming in, he had sent all the creditors to the right about. Those worthy people, however, had not wished to be paid; on the contrary, if they persisted in waiting, it was merely to compliment madame, and personally to offer her their services after her great success.

"Let's be off," said Nana, who was now dressed.

Just then Zoé hastened into the room crying, "I cannot answer the bell again, madame. There's a regular crowd coming up the stairs."

A crowd on the stairs! Even Francis laughed, in spite of the coolness he affected, as he gathered up his combs. Nana, seizing hold of Labordette's arm, dragged him into the kitchen; and, free at length of the men, she hurried away thoroughly happy, knowing that she could be alone with him, no matter where, without any fear of his making a fool of himself.

"You must bring me home again," she said, as they went down the back stairs. "Then I shall be safe. Only fancy, I intend to sleep a whole night—a whole night all to myself! Just a whim of mine, old fellow!"

CHAPTER III

Countess Sabine, as Madame Muffat de Beuville was called to distinguish her from the count's mother who had died the year before, received every Tuesday, at her house in the Rue de Miromesnil at the corner of the Rue de Penthièvre. It was a large square building, and had been occupied by the Muffat family for more than a hundred years past. The frontage, overlooking the street, was high and dark, and as quiet and melancholy-looking as a convent, with immense shutters which were nearly always closed; at the rear, in a little damp garden, some trees had grown up in their search for sunshine, so tall and lank that their branches could be seen overtopping the roof. On this particular Tuesday evening, towards ten o'clock, there were scarcely a dozen persons assembled in the drawing-room. When she was only expecting intimate friends the countess never threw open either the parlour or dining-room. One was more comfortable and could gather round the fire and chat. The drawing-room, moreover, was very large and very high; four windows looked on to the garden, the dampness of which could be more especially felt on this showery April evening, in spite of the substantial logs burning in the fireplace. The sun never shone there. In the day-time a greenish light only very imperfectly illuminated the apartment; but at night-time, when the lamps and the chandelier were lit, it merely looked solemn, with the massive mahogany furniture in the style of the First Empire, and the hangings and chair-coverings in yellow velvet ornamented with satin-like designs. On entering the room one found oneself in an atmosphere of cold dignity, of ancient customs and of a past age, exhaling an odour of godliness. However, on the side of the fireplace, facing the arm-chair in which the count's mother died—a square chair with stiff straight woodwork and hard cushions—the Countess Sabine was reclining in a low easy-chair, covered with crimson silk, the padding of which had the softness of eider-down. It was the only modern article of furniture in the room, the gratification of a fancy which seemed like a blasphemy amidst the surrounding austerity.

"So," the young woman was saying, "we are to have the Shah of Persia."

They were talking of the great personages who were coming to Paris on account of the Exhibition. Several ladies were seated in a semicircle round the fire. Madame du Joncquoy, whose brother, a diplomatist, had fulfilled a mission in the East, was giving some details respecting the Court of that potentate.

"Are you unwell, my dear?" asked Madame Chantereau, the wife of an iron-founder, seeing the countess shudder slightly and turn pale.

"Oh, no, not at all," replied the latter, with a smile. "I felt rather cold. This room takes such a long time to get warm!" and she looked along the walls, and up to the ceiling. Her daughter, Estelle, a young girl of sixteen, skinny and insignificant-looking, got up from the stool on which she was sitting, and came and silently replaced on the top of the fire one of the logs which had rolled off. Madame de Chezelles, one of Sabine's convent friends, but five years younger than she, exclaimed:

"Well! I should like to have a drawing-room like yours! You, at least, are able to receive. In modern houses the rooms are no bigger than boxes. If I was in your place—"

She spoke thoughtlessly, with animated gestures, explaining that she would change the hangings, the seats, everything; then she would give balls to which all Paris would long to be invited. Behind her, her husband, a judge, listened with a grave face. It was said that she deceived him, and openly, too; but every one forgave her, and received her all the same, because, so the report ran, she was mad.

"Oh, Léonide!" Countess Sabine, with her faint smile, contented herself with murmuring. A slight shrug of the shoulders completed her thought. It was not after having lived in it seventeen years that she would think of altering her drawing-room. Now, it would remain the same as her mother-in-law had wished it should be during her life-time. Then, resuming the conversation, she observed, "I have been told that we shall also have the King of Prussia and the Emperor of Russia."

"Yes, it is announced that there will be great festivities," said Madame du Joncquoy.

The banker Steiner, recently introduced into the house by Léonide de Chezelles, who knew every one, was conversing seated on a sofa between two windows. He was questioning a deputy,* from whom he was cunningly trying to extract some news relative to a stock exchange affair of which he had an inkling; whilst Count Muffat, standing in front of them, was listening in silence, looking blacker than ever. Four or five young men formed another group near the door, surrounding Count Xavier de Vandeuvres, who, in a hushed voice, was relating to them some adventure, rather improper, no doubt, for they were all making great efforts to smother their laughter. All alone, in the middle of the room, a stout man, the head of a department at the Ministry of the Interior, was ponderously seated in an arm-chair, asleep with his eyes open. But one of the young men having seemed to throw doubt on Vandeuvres's story, the latter raised his voice, and exclaimed:

"You are too sceptical, Foucarmont; you will spoil all your pleasures."

And with a laugh he moved towards the ladies. The last of a great race, effeminate and intelligent, he was then devouring a fortune with the rage of an appetite that nothing could appease. His racing-stable, one of the most celebrated of Paris, cost him an enormous sum; his losings at the Imperial Club amounted each month to a most unpleasant number of louis; his mistresses every year, good or bad, relieved him of a farm and several acres of meadow or forest land, making quite a hole in his vast estates in Picardy.

"You do well to call others sceptical, you who believe in nothing," said Léonide, making room for him beside her. "It is you who spoil your pleasures."

"Exactly," he replied. "I want others to profit by my experience."

---

*Member of the legislature.

But he was made to stop. He was scandalizing M. Venot. Then, some of the ladies moving, disclosed to view, on a sort of sofa-chair, a little man of sixty, with bad teeth and a cunning smile. He was installed there just as though he were at home, listening to every one and never uttering a word. With a gesture he notified that he was not scandalized. Vandeuvres assumed his most dignified look, and gravely added, "M. Venot knows very well that I believe that which I ought to believe."

It was an act of religious faith. Léonide herself appeared satisfied. The young men at the end of the room no longer laughed. It was a strait-laced place, and they did not amuse themselves much there. A coldness had passed over all. In the midst of the silence arose the sound of Steiner's snuffling voice, the deputy's discretion having ended by putting the banker in a rage. For a few minutes Countess Sabine looked into the fire, then she renewed the conversation.

"I saw the King of Prussia last year, at Baden. He is still full of vigour for his years."

"Count Bismarck* will accompany him," said Madame Du Joncquoy. "Do you know the count? I lunched with him at my brother's, oh! a long time ago, when he was representing Prussia at Paris. I cannot understand such a man achieving the great success he has."

"Why?" asked Madame Chantereau.

"Well! I scarcely know how to tell you. He does not please me. He has a brutish look, and is ill-mannered. Besides, for myself, I think him stupid."

Then everyone talked about Count Bismarck. The opinions were very divided. Vandeuvres knew him, and asserted that he was a hard drinker and a good player. But, at the height of the discussion, the door opened and Hector de la Faloise appeared. Fauchery, who accompanied him, approached the countess, and bowing, said, "Madame I did not forget your gracious invitation."

She greeted him with a smile and a kind word. The journal-

---

*Otto von Bismarck (1815–1898), unifier of Germany, future chancellor of the German Reich, and a foe of France.

ist, after shaking hands with the count, stood for a moment like a fish out of water, in the midst of the company of whom he only recognised Steiner. Vandeuvres, having turned round, came and greeted him; and, happy at the meeting, and seized with a desire to be communicative, Fauchery at once drew him aside, saying in a low voice:

"It's for to-morrow; are you going?"

"Of course!"

"At midnight at her place."

"I know, I know. I'm going with Blanche."

He wished to escape to rejoin the ladies and give another argument in Count Bismarck's favour. But Fauchery detained him.

"You will never guess what invitation she has asked me to deliver."

And he slightly nodded his head in the direction of Count Muffat, who at that moment was discussing the budget with the deputy and Steiner.

"It can't be!" said Vandeuvres, amazed, but at the same time highly amused.

"On my honour! I had to swear I would bring him. I have called partly on that account."

They both had a quiet laugh, and then Vandeuvres, hastening to rejoin the ladies, exclaimed,

"I assure you, on the contrary, that Count Bismarck is very witty. For instance, he made one night, in my hearing, a most delightful pun—"

La Faloise, however, having overheard the few rapid words exchanged in a low voice between the two friends, looked at Fauchery, hoping for an explanation which came not. Whom were they talking of? What was going to take place the next day at midnight? He stuck to his cousin wherever he went. The latter had gone and sat down. Countess Sabine especially interested him. She had often been talked about in his presence. He knew that, married when she was only seventeen, she would then be thirty-four, and that ever since her marriage she had led a sort of cloistered existence between her husband and her mother-in-law. In society, some said she was as cold as a devotee, but others pitied her as they recalled her merry laughter, her big, sparkling eyes, in the days before she was shut up in that old house. Fauchery examined her and hesitated. One of his friends, a captain who had been recently killed in Mexico,* had imparted to him after dinner, on the eve of his departure, one of those brutal secrets which the most discreet men let out at certain moments. But Fauchery's recollection of the matter was very vague; they had both dined well that evening, and he had his doubts as he watched the countess, dressed in black, with her quiet smile, in the middle of that old-fashioned drawing-room. A lamp placed behind her detached her sharp profile, that of a plump brunette, of which the lips alone, slightly thick, had a sort of imperious sensuality.

"What's the matter with them and their Bismarck!" murmured La Faloise, who always pretended to be very much bored when in society. "It's awfully slow here. It was a queer idea of yours to want to come!"

All at once Fauchery questioned him, "I say, the countess, has she got any lover?"

"Oh! no, my dear fellow; oh! no," he stammered, visibly upset, and quite forgetting his off-hand style. "Wherever do you think you are?" Then he became aware that his indignation was not quite the thing for a man of the world like himself, so, leaning back on the sofa, he added, "Well! I say no; but really I'm not sure of anything. There's a fellow over there, that Foucarmont, who's always to be found about the place. One has seen stranger things than that, that's certain. For myself, I don't care a hang. Anyhow, if the countess does amuse herself in that way, she must be very cunning, for no one has ever found it out; she is never talked about."

Then, without Fauchery taking the trouble to question him further, he related all he knew respecting the Muffats. He spoke in a very low voice in the midst of the tittle-tattle of the ladies gathered round the fire; and one would have thought, seeing them in their white ties and gloves, that they were discussing

---

*That is, he was in the retinue of Maximilian, the Austrian archduke chosen by Napoleon III to be emperor of Mexico; Maximilian was deposed and executed by a popular insurrection in 1867.

some serious matter in the most select words. Mamma Muffat, whom La Faloise had known intimately, was an insupportable old woman, always mixed up with priests. As for Muffat, the tardy son of a general, made count by Napoleon I., he naturally found himself in favour after December 2nd.* He also was not very gay; but he was considered to be a very worthy and honest man. With that he possessed opinions belonging to another world, and had such a high idea of his post at court, of his dignities and of his virtues, that he carried his head like the holy sacrament. It was Mamma Muffat who had given him that beautiful education—confession every day, no youth, no sprees of any kind. He was most religious; he had frequent fits of faith of great violence, similar to attacks of brain fever. Then, to finish his portrait with a last detail, La Faloise whispered a word in his cousin's ear.

"It's not possible!" said the latter.

"On my honour, I was assured of it! He had it still when he married."

Fauchery laughed as he glanced at the count, whose face, surrounded with whiskers and without moustache, looked squarer and harder than ever as he quoted figures and totals to Steiner, who disputed them.

"Well, he looks like one of that sort," he murmured. "A fine present he made to his wife! Ah, poor little thing! how he must have bored her! I bet she doesn't know anything at all!"

Just then Countess Sabine spoke to him, but he was so interested and amused with what he had been told about the count that he did not hear her. She repeated her question.

"M. Fauchery, have you not written an article on Count Bismarck? You have spoken to him, have you not?"

He rose from his seat quickly, and joined the ladies, trying to compose his features, at the same time, however, finding a reply with ease.

"Really, madame, I must at once own that I wrote that article by the aid of some of his biographies published in Germany. I have never seen Count Bismarck."

---

*The coup d'état by which Napoleon III seized the throne of France occurred on December 2, 1851.

He remained next to the countess, and whilst talking with
her he continued his reflections. She did not look her age; one
would have thought her twenty-eight years old at most; her
eyes, which her long lashes shaded with a blue shadow, especially retained a sparkle of youth. Brought up by parents living
apart, spending one month with the Marquis de Chouard and
the next with the Marchioness, she married when very young,
shortly after her mother's death, incited thereto, no doubt, by
her father, in whose way she was. He was a terrible man, the
marquis, and strange stories were beginning to circulate about
him, in spite of his great show of piety! Fauchery asked if he
would have the honour of seeing him. Certainly, her father
would come, though very late; he had so much work to attend
to! The journalist, who thought he knew where the old man
spent his evenings, preserved his gravity; but a mark he noticed
on the countess's left cheek near her mouth, surprised him
greatly. Nana had the same—exactly. It was funny. On the
mark were some little curly hairs, only the hairs on Nana were
light, whilst those on the other were as black as jet. But, no
matter, this woman hadn't a lover.

"I always had a wish to know Queen Augusta," said she. "I
have heard that she is so good and so pious. Do you think that
she will accompany the king?"

"It is said that she will not, madame," he replied.

She had no lover—that was evident to all. It was sufficient to
see her there, beside her daughter, so inert and so unnatural
on her stool. The sepulchral drawing-room, with its church-
like odour, told sufficiently under what an iron hand, in what
a rigid existence, she passed her life. There was nothing of
hers in that antiquated abode, blackened with damp. It was
Muffat who domineered and who governed, with his bigoted
education, his penances, and his fasts. But the sight of the little old man with bad teeth and cunning smile, whom Fauchery
noticed just then in the easy-chair behind the ladies, appeared
to him a more forcible argument still. He knew the fellow,
Théophile Venot, an ex-attorney who had had the speciality of
ecclesiastical causes. Having retired with a very handsome fortune, he now led a rather mysterious existence, was received

everywhere, treated with great respect, and even slightly feared, as though he represented a great power—an occult one which, so to say, could be felt about him. Besides that, he affected great humility; he was a church-warden at the Madeleine, and had merely taken a situation as adjunct to the mayor of the ninth arrondissement to occupy his leisure, so he said. The countess was well protected, and no mistake! there was nothing to be done in that quarter.

"You are right; one is bored to death here," said Fauchery to his cousin, when he had succeeded in escaping from the ladies. "We'll be off."

But Steiner, whom Count Muffat and the deputy had just left, came towards him looking furious, all in a perspiration, and grumbling in a low voice. "Confound them! they can keep their information to themselves if they want to. I shall find plenty of others who will speak." Then, pushing the journalist into a corner, he said in a victorious tone of voice, "Well! it's for to-morrow. I shall be there, my buck!"

"Ah!" murmured Fauchery, surprised.

"You didn't know? Oh! I had an awful job to find her at home! Besides that, Mignon stuck to me wherever I went."

"But they are going, the Mignons."

"Yes; so she told me. Well, she at length received me, and invited me. At midnight precisely, after the theatre." The banker looked beaming with delight. He winked his eye, and added, giving to each word a peculiar significance, "And you, did it come off?"

"What do you mean?" asked Fauchery, who affected not to understand. "She wished to thank me for my article, so she came to call on me."

"Yes, yes. You are lucky, you fellows; you are rewarded. By the way, who is it who pays to-morrow?"

The journalist opened his arms, as though to declare that no one had been able to find out. Here Vandeuvres called to Steiner, who knew Count Bismarck. Madame du Joncquoy was almost convinced. She ended by saying:

"He made a bad impression on my mind; I think he looks

wicked. However, I am willing to believe he has plenty of wit. That will explain his great successes."

"No doubt," said the banker—a Frankfort Jew, with a ghastly smile.

This time, however, La Faloise plucked up courage to question his cousin, and following him closely, whispered in his ear, "So there's to be a supper at some woman's to-morrow night? At whose place is it, eh? at whose place?"

Fauchery signalled to him that some one was listening; they must observe the proprieties. Again the door had opened, and an old lady entered, followed by a youth, whom the journalist recognised as the youngster fresh from college, who, on the first night of the "Blonde Venus," had uttered the famous "Isn't she stunning!" which was still talked about. The lady's arrival caused quite a commotion in the drawing-room. Countess Sabine hastily rose from her chair to meet her. She took hold of her hands, and called her her dear Madame Hugon. Seeing his cousin watch this scene rather curiously, La Faloise, with the view of impressing him, explained it in a few words. Madame Hugon was a notary's widow, and had retired to a place called Les Fondettes, an estate which had long belonged to her family, and which was situated near Orleans. She had kept up a small establishment in Paris, in a house belonging to her in the Rue de Richelieu, and was now passing a few weeks there for the purpose of arranging everything for her younger son, who was studying for the bar. She had been the Marchioness de Chouard's great friend, and had been present at the countess's birth. The latter had often spent months with her, up to the time of her marriage with the count, and they were still very intimate together.

"I have brought George to see you," Madame Hugon was saying to Sabine. "I fancy you will find him grown!"

The youth, with his bright eyes and fair curls, looking like a girl dressed up as a boy, greeted the countess, not at all bashfully, and recalled to her recollection a game at battledore and shuttle-cock* that they had played together, two years before, at Les Fondettes.

---

*Game resembling badminton.

"Is Philip not in Paris?" asked Count Muffat.

"Oh, no!" replied the old lady. "He is still with the garrison at Bourges."

She had seated herself, and talked with pride of her elder son, a big fellow, who, after enlisting in a hasty moment, had rapidly attained the rank of lieutenant. All the ladies surrounded her with a respectful sympathy. The conversation became nicer and more agreeable; and Fauchery, seeing there that worthy Madame Hugon, with her white hair, and her maternal face lighted up with such a sweet smile, thought himself highly ridiculous for having for a moment suspected Countess Sabine. However, the big crimson silk easy-chair, in which the countess had re-seated herself, attracted his attention. He thought it looked too loud, and altogether out of place, in that smoky old drawing-room. For certain, it was not the count who had introduced such a means of gratifying a voluptuous indolence. One might have thought it a sort of experiment, the commencement of a desire and of an enjoyment. Then his thoughts went dreamily back to the past, returning, in spite of himself, to that story told one evening in a private room at a restaurant. He had sought to become acquainted with the Muffat family, prompted by a sensual curiosity; for, since his friend had been killed in Mexico, who knew what might happen? it was for him to see. There was probably nothing in it after all. The thought of it, however, disturbed and attracted him, and all the vice in his nature was awakened. The big easy-chair had a tumbled look and a curve in the back which now rather amused him.

"Well! shall we go?" asked La Faloise, with the intention of asking, when they got outside, the name of the woman who was to give the supper.

"In a little while," replied Fauchery.

And he no longer hurried himself, but took as a pretext for staying the invitation with which he had been charged, and which it was not at all easy to deliver. The ladies were talking of a young girl who had recently become a nun. The ceremony, which was a very touching one, had affected all fashionable Paris for three days past. She was the eldest daughter of the

Baroness de Fougeray, and had joined the Carmelites, having an irresistible calling to do so. Madame Chantereau, the cousin in a remote degree of the Fougerays, was relating that the baroness had been obliged to take to her bed on the following day, being so overcome by her emotion.

"I had a capital place," said Léonide. "I thought it all very curious."

Madame Hugon, however, pitied the poor mother. What anguish to lose her daughter! "I have been accused of being a devotee," said she, with simple frankness. "That does not prevent me thinking children who persist in such a suicide very cruel."

"Yes, it is a terrible thing," murmured the countess, with a slight shiver, as she cuddled closer into her chair before the fire.

Then the ladies entered into a long discussion on the subject. But their voices were subdued, and only occasionally did a faint laugh interrupt the solemnity of the conversation. The two lamps on the mantlepiece, covered with rose-coloured shades, shed but a feeble light over them; and there being only three other lamps, which were placed at a distance on different pieces of furniture, the vast room was in a pleasant shadow. Steiner began to feel bored. He related to Fauchery an adventure of that little Madame de Chezelles, whom he familiarly called Léonide. A regular hussy, said he, as he lowered his voice behind the ladies' chairs. Fauchery watched her in her dress of pale blue satin, as she sat on a corner of her chair, looking as slim and as impudent as a boy, and he ended by feeling surprised at seeing her there. They knew better how to behave themselves at Caroline Héquet's, whose establishment had just been placed on a substantial footing by her mother. It was quite a subject for an article. What an extraordinary world was the Parisian one! The strictest drawing-rooms were becoming invaded. That silent Théophile Venot, who contented himself with smiling and showing his bad teeth, was evidently a bequest of the defunct countess, just the same as the elderly ladies, Madame Chantereau, Madame du Joncquoy, and four or five old gentlemen who remained immovable in their corners. Count Muffat brought some government officials, who affected that correctness of bearing which was the fashion of the Tuileries.* Amongst others, the head of the department remained seated by himself in the middle of the room, with his clean shaven face and dull-looking eyes, and so tightly buttoned up in his coat that he seemed as though he dare not move. Nearly all the young men, and some persons of lofty style, had been introduced by the Marquis de Chouard, who had kept up his connection with the legitimists, after having joined the Empire and become a member of the Council of State. There remained Léonide de Chezelles, Steiner, a most ambiguous lot, which was relieved by Madame Hugon with the serenity of an amiable old woman; and Fauchery, who still had his article in his mind, called them Countess Sabine's set.

"On another occasion," continued Steiner, speaking very low, "Léonide made her tenor come to Montauban. She was living at the Château de Beaurecueil, two leagues from there, and every day she came in a carriage and pair to see him at the Hotel du Lion-d'Or, where he was staying. The carriage waited at the door, and Léonide remained in the hotel for hours, whilst a crowd assembled and admired the horses."

The conversation ceased, and a rather solemn interval succeeded. Two young men were whispering, but they soon left off, and nothing was heard but Count Muffat's faint footsteps as he walked across the room. The lamps seemed to be burning low, the fire was going out, and a deep shadow almost hid from sight the old friends of the family, as they sat in the chairs they had occupied there for forty years past. It was as though, between a couple of sentences, the guests had felt the count's mother return with her grand, icy cold look. Countess Sabine, however, soon resumed:

"At any rate there was a report to that effect. The young man, it seems, died, and that will explain why the poor child

---

*Royal palace as of 1564; abandoned by royalty after the construction of Versailles, then the center of power during the Revolution; later the official residence of both Napoleons; partly burned in 1871, in the final week of the Commune, and finally demolished in 1882.

took the veil. It is said, also, that M. de Fougeray would never have given his consent to the marriage."

"There are a great many other things said, too," giddily exclaimed Léonide.

She laughed, at the same time refusing to explain herself. Sabine, affected by this gaiety, carried her handkerchief to her mouth. And this laughter, in the solemnity of the vast apartment, had a ring which struck Fauchery; it sounded like the breaking of glass. Without a doubt something was cracked there. Then the ladies all started off talking at once. Madame du Joncquoy protested; Madame Chantereau knew that a marriage had been contemplated, but that nothing further had taken place. Even the gentlemen ventured to give their views. For some minutes there was quite a confusion of opinions, in which the different elements of the room—the Bonapartists and the legitimists, mixed with the worldly sceptics—elbowed each other, and spoke at the same time. Estelle had rung for more wood for the fire, and the footman had wound up the lamps; it was quite like an awaking. Fauchery was smiling, as though perfectly at his ease.

"Why, of course! they espouse God, when they cannot marry their cousin," said Vandeuvres between his teeth, thoroughly bored with the subject, as he went and joined Fauchery. "My boy, have you ever seen a woman beloved become a nun?" He did not wait for a reply, he had had enough of it; and in a low voice he added, "I say, how many shall we be to-morrow? There will be the Mignons, Steiner, you, Blanche, and myself. Who else?"

"Caroline, I think, Simone, Gaga for certain. One never knows exactly, you know. On such occasions, one expects about twenty and thirty turn up."

Vandeuvres, who was looking at the ladies, turned to another subject. "She must have been very good looking, Madame du Joncquoy, fifteen years ago. That poor Estelle seems to have grown longer than ever. What a plank she'll be to put in a bed!" But he interrupted himself, and returned to the question of the supper. "The nuisance in that sort of things is that one always meets the same women. We ought to have some new ones. Try and discover one. Wait! I have an idea! I'll go and ask that stout man to bring the girl he was lugging about at the Variety Theatre the other evening."

He was speaking of the head of the department, who was dozing in the middle of the room. Fauchery amused himself by watching the delicate negotiation from a distance. Vandeuvres seated himself beside the stout man, who continued to look very dignified. For a short time they both seemed to discuss, with all the seriousness it merited, the weighty question of the moment, which was what real reason a young girl could have for becoming a nun. Then the count returned, saying,

"It isn't possible. He swears that she is virtuous. She would be sure to refuse. Yet, I would have bet that I had seen her at Laure's."

"What! you go to Laure's!" murmured Fauchery with a laugh. "You venture to risk your person in such places! I thought it was only we poor devils who did that!"

"Oh! dear boy, one must see everything." Then they both chuckled, and their eyes sparkled as they gave each other different details about the dining place in the Rue des Martyrs, where fat Laure Piédefer, for three francs a head, provided dinner for ladies who were down in their luck. It was a dirty hole! All the little women kissed Laure on the mouth. Then, as the countess looked in their direction, having overheard a word or two, they moved away together, both very lively and highly amused. They had not noticed George Hugon standing near them, listening, and blushing so hard that from his neck to his ears he became quite red. The baby was full of a mixture of shame and rapture. Since his mother had left him alone in the drawing-room, he had hovered round about Madame de Chezelles, the only woman whom he thought at all up to anything, and yet Nana could give her a lot!

"Last night," Madame Hugon was saying, "George took me to the theatre. Yes, to the Variety, where I had certainly not been for ten years or more. The child adores music. As for myself, it did not amuse me much, but he seemed so happy! They bring out most peculiar pieces now-a-days. I must admit, however, that I have no great taste for music."

"What! madame, you do not care for music!" exclaimed Madame du Joncquoy, raising her eyes to heaven. "Is it possible that everybody does not like music?"

The exclamation was general. No one offered a remark in reference to the piece produced at the Variety Theatre, and of which the worthy Madame Hugon had not understood anything; the other ladies knew about it, but would say nothing. They at once went in for sentiment, and a refined and ecstatic admiration of the great masters. Madame du Joncquoy only cared for Weber, Madame Chantereau preferred the Italians. The sound of the ladies' voices became soft and languid; one might have thought the group gathered round the fire to be a party at church, discreetly and faintly intoning a canticle in some little chapel.

"Let's see," murmured Vandeuvres, leading Fauchery into the middle of the room, "we must, somehow or other, discover a new woman for to-morrow. Suppose we ask Steiner?"

"Oh! Steiner," said the journalist, "never gets hold of a woman until all Paris has had enough of her."

Vandeuvres, however, looked about him. "Wait," he resumed, "I met Foucarmont with some fair charmer the other day. I will go and ask him to bring her."

And he beckoned to Foucarmont. They rapidly exchanged a few words; but there seemed to be some difficulty, for they both cautiously picked their way over the ladies' skirts and joined another young man, with whom they continued their conference in the recess of a window. Fauchery, left alone, decided to join the group by the fire just as Madame du Joncquoy was stating that she could never hear Weber's music without at once seeming to see lakes, forests, and the sun rising over landscapes bathed in dew; but a hand touched his shoulder, whilst a voice said behind him,

"It's not at all kind of you."

"What isn't?" he asked, turning round and recognising La Faloise.

"That supper, to-morrow night—you might at least have got me invited."

Fauchery was just about to reply, when Vandeuvres returned

and said to him, "It seems the girl has nothing to do with Fou-carmont, she belongs to that other gentleman over there. She won't be able to come. What a bore! But, all the same, I've hooked Foucarmont. He will try and bring Louise of the Palais-Royal Theatre."

"M. de Vandeuvres," asked Madame Chantereau, raising her voice, "is it not true that Wagner's music was hissed on Sunday?"

"Oh! atrociously, madame," he replied, advancing with his exquisite politeness. Then, as the ladies did not detain him, he moved away and continued in an undertone in the journalist's ear, "I shall go and hook some more. All these young fellows must know some little women."

Then he was seen, pleasantly smiling the while, to go up to the different men and talk with them in all parts of the room. He mingled with the various groups, dropped a few words here and there, and then withdrew, winking his eyes and making other signs. It was as though he was, in his easy way, giving out a watchword. His words were passed from one to another, and appointments were made; whilst the ladies' sentimental disser-tations on music drowned the agitated buzz caused by all these alluring attempts.

"No, don't mention your Germans," repeated Madame Chantereau. "Song is gaiety, is light. Have you heard Patti* in 'Il Barbiere'?"†

"Delicious!" murmured Léonide, who could only strum opera-bouffe airs on her piano.

Countess Sabine now rang for tea, which was served in the drawing-room when the visitors on a Tuesday were not numer-ous. Whilst having a small table cleared by a footman, the count-ess followed Count de Vandeuvres with her eyes. She preserved that vague smile which showed a little the whiteness of her teeth; and, as the count passed near her, she questioned him.

"Whatever are you plotting, M. de Vandeuvres?"

*Adelina Patti (1843–1919), an Italian soprano.

†*Il Barbiere di Siviglia* (1816; *The Barber of Seville*), an opera by Gioacchino Rossini.

"I, madame?" he calmly replied, "I am not plotting anything."

"Ah! You seemed to be so very busy. See, you must make
yourself useful."

She placed an album in his hands and asked him to put it
on the piano. But he found means of informing Fauchery on
the quiet that Tatan Néné, who had the best neck and shoulders of the season, would be there, and also Maria Blond, who
had just made her first appearance at the Folies-Dramatiques
Theatre. La Faloise, however, kept stopping him at almost
every step, expecting an invitation. He ended by offering himself. Vandeuvres engaged him at once; only, he made him
promise to bring Clarisse, and as La Faloise affected to be
scrupulous, he quieted him by saying, "But I invite you! That is
quite sufficient."

Nevertheless La Faloise would very much have liked to have
known the name of the woman at whose house the supper was
to take place, but the countess had recalled Vandeuvres, and
was questioning him as to the way tea was made in England. He
was often there, attending the races in which his horses ran.
According to him, only the Russians knew how to make tea;
and he mentioned their recipe. Then, as though he had been
thinking very much whilst speaking, he interrupted himself to
ask, "By the way, and the marquis? Were we not to have seen
him?"

"Why, yes; my father certainly promised," replied the countess. "I am beginning to feel uneasy. His work must have detained him."

Vandeuvres smiled discreetly. He also seemed to have a doubt
as to the nature of the work on which the Marquis de Chouard
was engaged. He had thought of a charming person whom the
marquis sometimes took into the country. Perhaps they might
be able to get her for the supper. However, Fauchery thought
the time had come for acquainting Count Muffat with the invitation he had for him. It was getting late.

"Do you seriously mean it?" asked Vandeuvres, who thought
it was a joke.

"Most seriously. If I don't ask him, she will scratch my eyes out. It's a whim of hers, you know."

"Then I'll help you, my boy."

The clock struck eleven. The countess and her daughter served the tea. As there were scarcely any but intimate friends, the cups and plates of biscuits and cake were familiarly handed round. The ladies remained in their chairs before the fire, sipping their tea, and crunching the biscuits which they held between the tips of their fingers. From music the conversation dwindled to tradesmen. There was no one like Boissier for sweets, and Catherine for ices; Madame Chantereau, however, preferred Latinville. The talk slackened, a weariness seemed to seize upon every one. Steiner had resumed his attack on the deputy, whom he blockaded in the corner of a sofa. M. Venot, whose teeth had probably been destroyed by sweetmeats, was rapidly devouring some hard cakes, making a little noise like a mouse; whilst the head of the department, his nose in his cup, never seemed to have had enough. And the countess, without the least hurry, moved from one to another, not pressing them, but standing a few seconds looking at the men in a sort of silent interrogative manner, then smiling and passing on. The heat of the fire had given quite a colour to her face, and she seemed to be the sister of her daughter, who looked so skinny and awkward beside her. As she drew near to Fauchery, who was conversing with her husband and Vandeuvres, she noticed that they left off talking. She did not stop, but, passing further on, offered George Hugon the cup of tea she was carrying.

"It is a lady who desires your company at supper," gaily resumed the journalist, addressing Count Muffat.

The latter, whose countenance had retained its dark look all the evening, seemed greatly surprised. What lady could they mean?

"Why, Nana!" said Vandeuvres, so as to have it out at once.

The count became still more serious. He scarcely moved his eyelids, whilst a pain, like a twitch of neuralgia, passed over his face. "But I do not know the lady." he murmured.

"Oh! come now! Why you went and called on her," observed Vandeuvres.

"What! I called on her. Ah! yes, the other day, for the poor relief committee. I had forgotten all about it. All the same, I do not know her. I cannot accept."

He assumed his most dignified air, to let them understand that he considered their joke in very bad taste. The place of a man of his rank was not at the table of such a woman. Vandeuvres protested: it was merely a supper given to some actresses; talent excused everything. But without listening to him any more than to Fauchery, who began to tell him of a dinner at which a prince, the son of a queen, had sat next to a woman who used to sing at music-halls, the count gave a most decided refusal. He even, in spite of his great politeness, accompanied it with a gesture of annoyance.

George and La Faloise, standing up drinking their tea in front of each other, had overheard the few words that had been exchanged so near them. "Halloo! so it's to be at Nana's," murmured La Faloise. "I might have known it!"

George said nothing, but he became very red in the face, his fair hair was all ruffled, his blue eyes were shining like candles. The vice with which he had mixed during the last few days inflamed and excited him. At last then, he was about to meet with all that he had dreamed of. "The nuisance is, I don't know the address," resumed La Faloise.

"Boulevard Haussmann, between the Rue de l'Arcade and the Rue Pasquier, on the third floor," said George, all in a breath; and as the other looked at him with astonishment, he added, becoming redder still in the face, and bursting with conceit and confusion, "I am going; she invited me this morning."

Just at this moment there was a great commotion in the drawing-room. Vandeuvres and Fauchery were therefore unable to press the count any further. The Marquis de Chouard had arrived, and every one hastened to greet him. He seemed to move along very painfully, his legs almost giving way beneath him; and he at length stood still in the middle of the room, his face ashy pale, and his eyes blinking, as though he had just come out of some very dark place and was quite blinded by the light of the lamps.

"I had quite given up expecting to see you, father," said the countess. "I should have been quite uneasy until I heard from you to-morrow."

He looked at her without replying, like a man who does not understand. His nose, which appeared very big on his clean-shaven face, looked like an enormous gathering; whilst his under-lip drooped. Madame Hugon, full of kindliness, seeing him so depressed, pitied him.

"You work too much. You ought to rest. At our age we should leave work to the younger ones."

"Work, ah! yes, work," he at length stammered out. "Always plenty of work."

He was becoming himself again. He straightened his bent frame, passing his hand in a way familiar with him over his white hair, the scanty locks of which were brushed behind his ears.

"What is it you work at so late?" asked Madame du Joncquoy. "I thought you were at the reception held by the Minister of Finance?"

But the countess interposed, "My father had to study some parliamentary bill."

"Yes, a parliamentary bill," said he, "a bill, exactly. I shut myself in. It was in respect to factories. I wish them to be closed on Sundays. It is really shameful that the government does not display more energy in the matter. The churches are now scarcely frequented; it will all end in a great catastrophe."

Vandeuvres glanced at Fauchery. They were both behind the Marquis, and they kept near him. When Vandeuvres was able to take him on one side, to ask him about the charming person whom he was in the habit of taking into the country, the old man affected great surprise. Perhaps they had seen him with Baroness Decker, at whose house at Viroflay he sometimes spent a few days. Vandeuvres, for revenge, asked him suddenly, "I say, wherever have you been? Your elbow is all covered with cobwebs and plaster."

"My elbow," he murmured, slightly troubled. "Why, so it is! A little dirt. I must have got that somehow as I came here."

Several persons were leaving. It was close upon midnight.

Two footmen silently removed the empty cups and the plates of cake. The ladies were still sitting in front of the fire, though in a smaller circle than before, conversing more freely in the languor of the end of an evening. Even the room itself seemed overcome with drowsiness, and heavy shadows lingered about the walls. Then Fauchery talked of retiring. However, his eyes once more sought Countess Sabine. Having seen to her guests, she was now resting in her accustomed seat, saying nothing, her glance fixed on a log that was gradually burning away, and her face so white and impenetrable, that his doubts returned to him. The little black hairs on the mark she had near the corner of her mouth seemed quite golden in the firelight—exactly the same as Nana's even to the colour. He could not resist whispering to Vandeuvres about it. It was really quite true, he had never noticed it before; and they continued the parallel between Nana and the countess. They discovered a vague resemblance about the chin and the mouth; but the eyes were not at all alike. There Nana looked thoroughly kindhearted and good-natured; whilst the countess was altogether doubtful—one would have said a cat asleep, with her claws hidden away, and her paws only slightly agitated with a nervous tremble.

"All the same she's a fine woman," declared Fauchery.

Vandeuvres seemed to unrobe her with a glance. "Yes, all the same," said he. "But, you know, I have great doubts as to her thighs. She hasn't any worth speaking of, I'll bet!"

He stopped as Fauchery sharply nudged his elbow, and directed his attention to Estelle, who was seated on her stool in front of them. They had raised their voices without noticing her, and she had most likely overheard them. However, she remained upright and immovable, with her skinny neck of a girl growing too fast, and on which not the smallest hair had turned. So they moved away a few steps, and Vandeuvres expressed his opinion that the countess was a most virtuous woman.

At this moment, the ladies seated round the fire having raised their voices, Madame du Joncquoy was heard to say, "I have admitted that Count Bismarck may possess some wit.

However, if you pretend he has genius—" They had once more returned to their first subject of conversation.

"What! Bismarck again!" murmured Fauchery. "Well, this time I will indeed be off."

"Wait a minute" said Vandeuvres. "We must have a final 'no' from the count."

Count Muffat was conversing with his father-in-law and a few serious-looking men. Vandeuvres took him to one side, and repeated the invitation more pressingly, saying that he himself was going to the supper. A man could go anywhere. No one would think of seeing harm where, at the most, there was only a little curiosity. The count listened to these arguments with downcast eyes and immovable features. Vandeuvres noticed that he seemed to hesitate, when the Marquis de Chouard joined them, with a look of interrogation on his face; and when the latter was made acquainted with the subject under discussion, when Fauchery invited him also, he glanced furtively at his son-in-law. There was a moment of silence and embarrassment; but they encouraged each other, and they would no doubt have ended by accepting, if Count Muffat had not noticed that M. Venot was watching him fixedly. The little old man no longer smiled, his face bore a cadaverous expression, his eyes were sharp and piercing like gimlets.

"No," replied the count at once, in such a decided tone of voice that there was nothing more to be said.

Then the marquis declined more sternly still. He talked of morality. The upper classes ought to set an example. Fauchery smiled, and shook hands with Vandeuvres. He would not wait for him, but went off at once, as he had to look in at the office of his paper.

"At Nana's at midnight, don't forget."

La Faloise was leaving also, and Steiner had just taken leave of the countess. Other men were following them, and the same words were whispered on all sides, each one repeating, "At Nana's at midnight," as he put on his overcoat in the anteroom. George, who was waiting for his mother, stood in the doorway, and gave them all the correct address—the third floor, the door on the left hand side. Before retiring, Fauchery gave one last look round. Vandeuvres had resumed his place in the midst of the ladies, and was jesting with Léonide de Chezelles. Count Muffat and the Marquis de Chouard were joining in the conversation, whilst worthy Madame Hugon was going to sleep with her eyes open. Behind the ladies' petticoats, M. Venot, making himself scarce again, had recovered his smile, and in the big, solemn room the clock slowly struck midnight.

"What! what!" Madame du Joncquoy was exclaiming, "you think that Count Bismarck will declare war against us, and that he will beat us? Oh! that's too much!"

They were, in fact, all laughing at Madame Chantereau, who had just made the statement, which she had heard in Alsace, where her husband owned a factory.

"The Emperor is watching, thank goodness," said Count Muffat, with official solemnity.

These were the last words that Fauchery heard. He closed the door, after looking once more at Countess Sabine. She was calmly conversing with the head of the department, and seemed interested in the talk of the stout man. Most certainly he must have been mistaken, there was no flaw. It was a pity.

"Well, aren't you coming?" called La Faloise to him from the hall.

And outside, on the pavement, as they bid each other good night, they both again repeated, "To-morrow, at Nana's."

CHAPTER IV

Ever since the morning, Zoé had given up the entire apartment to a person who had arrived from Brébant's with quite a staff of waiters and other assistants. Brébant was to furnish everything—the supper, the glass and crockery, the table-linen, flowers, and even seats and stools. Nana would not have found a dozen napkins if she had ransacked all her cupboards, and, not having as yet had time to set herself up in everything since her new start in life, disdaining to go to a restaurant, she had preferred to make the restaurant come to her. It was more the thing. She wished to celebrate her great success as an actress by a supper which would be the talk of every one. As the dining-room was too small, they had set up the table in the drawing-room—a table on which places for twenty-five had been laid rather close together.

"Is everything ready?" asked Nana, on returning home at midnight.

"Oh! I don't know," roughly replied Zoé, who seemed altogether out of sorts. "Thank goodness! I have nothing to do with it. They are smashing everything in the kitchen and all over the place! With all that, I've had another row. The other two have been again. Upon my word, I chucked them out of the place."

She was speaking of madame's two ex-gentlemen—the tradesman and the Wallachian—whom Nana had decided to dismiss; for, being now certain as to the future, she wished to turn over a new leaf, as she called it.

"What an abominable nuisance they are!" she murmured. "If they come again, threaten them with the commissary of police."

Then she called Daguenet and George, who had remained in the anteroom, hanging up their overcoats. They had met at the stage-door in the Passage des Panoramas, and she had brought them in her cab. As no one else had then arrived, she called to them to come into the dressing-room whilst Zoé got her ready. In haste, and without changing her things, she had her hair done up, and placed some white roses in it and some others in her dress. The dressing-room was all encumbered with the furniture of the drawing-room, which had been placed there—a lot of little round tables, sofas, and arm-chairs, one on the top of the other—and she was quite ready, when her skirt caught on one of the castors and tore. Then, in her fury; she swore and cursed. Such accidents only happened to her. She tugged at her dress with rage, and pulled it off. It was made of a soft white silk, so simple, so supple, and so fine, that it enveloped her like a long chemise. But, not finding another dress to her taste, she put it on again at once, almost crying, and saying she would look like a rag-picker. Daguenet and George fastened up the tear with pins, whilst Zoé tidied her hair once more. All three busied themselves round about her, the youngster especially, who was on his knees on the floor, his hands buried in her skirt. She at length became calmer, when Daguenet assured her it could not be more than a quarter past midnight, for she had so hurried the last act of the "Blonde Venus," scamping the cues, and skipping entire verses.

"It was, anyhow, quite good enough for all those fools," said she. "Did you notice? they were a rum-looking lot to-night! Zoé, my girl, you will have to wait here. Don't go to bed, as I may perhaps want you. By jingo! just in time. Here's some one."

She hastened out of the room, leaving George on the floor, his coat tails sweeping the carpet. He blushed as he noticed Daguenet watching him. However, they had begun to feel a certain affection for each other. They re-arranged their neckties in front of the big looking-glass, and gave one another a brush, to get rid of the white powder that hung about their clothes from their contact with Nana.

"It's just like sugar," murmured George, with a laugh of a greedy baby.

A footman, hired for the night, ushered the guests into the parlour—a narrow room, in which four easy-chairs only had been left, so as to leave more space for the people. From the drawing-room close by could be heard a noise of crockery and plate being moved about; whilst a bright light shone under the door. Nana, on entering, found Clarisse Besnus, whom La Faloise had brought, already seated in one of the chairs.

"What! you are the first!" said Nana, who treated her familiarly since her own success.

"Well! it's his fault," replied Clarisse. "He is always afraid of being too late. If I had listened to him, I should not even have waited to take my wig and my make-up off."

The young man, who met Nana for the first time, bowed and complimented her, spoke of his cousin, and sought to hide his confusion under an excess of politeness. But Nana, without listening to him, without even knowing who he was, shook his hand, and hastened to receive Rose Mignon. She became, at once, most ladylike.

"Ah! dear madame, how kind of you! I longed so much to have you with us!"

"It is I who am charmed, I assure you," said Rose, equally amiable.

"Pray sit down. Do you require anything?"

"No, thank you. Ah! I have forgotten my fan in my pelisse.* See, Steiner, in the right hand pocket."

Steiner and Mignon had entered behind Rose. The banker went out and returned with the fan; whilst Mignon fraternally embraced Nana, and made Rose kiss her too. Were they not all of the same family, they of the theatre? Then he winked his eye, as though to encourage Steiner; but the latter, disconcerted by Rose's fixed look, did not venture to do more than kiss Nana's hand. Just then the Count de Vandeuvres arrived with Blanche de Sivry. There was a great deal of bowing and curtseying. Nana most ceremoniously led Blanche to a chair. Vandeuvres laughingly related that Fauchery was having a row below, because the concierge would not allow Lucy Stewart's carriage to enter the courtyard. They could hear Lucy Stewart in the anteroom speaking of the concierge as a dirty black-guard. But when the footman opened the door, she advanced graceful and smiling, pronounced her name herself, and took

---

*Cloak made of or lined with fur.

hold of both Nana's hands, saying she loved her as soon as ever she saw her, and that she thought she had a wonderful talent. Nana, all proud of her position as mistress of the house, but greatly confused, murmured her thanks. She seemed, too, to be rather pre-occupied ever since Fauchery's arrival. As soon as she was able to get near him, she asked in a low voice. "Will he come?"

"No, he declined," roughly replied the journalist, taken un-awares, although he had prepared a long rigmarole to explain Count Muffat's refusal. He at once saw his stupidity as he no-ticed how the young woman paled, and he tried to modify what he had said. "He was not able to come; he has to take the countess to-night to the ball at the Ministry of the Interior."

"All right," murmured Nana, who suspected he had not troubled himself in the matter, "I'll make you smart for that, my boy."

"Look here!" he returned, indignant at the menace, "I don't care for such errands. Another time give them to Labordette."

They were both quite angry and turned their backs on each other. At that moment Mignon pushed Steiner up against Nana. When she was alone he said to her in a low voice, with the good-natured cynicism of a pal wishing to oblige a friend, "You know, he's dying for love of you. Only, he's afraid of my wife. You'll protect him, won't you?"

Nana pretended not to understand. She smiled, and looked at Rose, her husband, and the banker; then she said to the lat-ter, "M. Steiner, you will sit next to me."

But sounds of laughter were heard coming from the ante-room, there were whisperings, and then quite a hubbub of gay voices all speaking at once, as though a whole convent full of girls had been let loose there. Suddenly Labordette appeared, dragging five women behind him—his school, as Lucy Stewart maliciously termed them. There was Gaga, looking very majes-tic in a blue velvet dress that was a great deal too tight for her, Caroline Héquet, always in black Flemish silk trimmed with Chantilly lace, then Léa de Horn, most slovenly dressed as usual, plump Tatan Néné, a jolly fair girl with the breast of a wet-nurse, whom every one made fun of, and finally little

Maria Blond, a girl of fifteen, as thin and as wicked as a street-arab, and who was becoming quite the fashion ever since her first appearance at the Folies-Dramatiques Theatre. Labordette had brought them all in the same cab; and they were still laughing at the recollection of how they had been squeezed together, with Maria Blond on the others' knees. But they composed themselves, shaking hands and bowing all round, like the most respectable people. Gaga acted quite childishly; and even stuttered in her attempts to behave well. Tatan Néné, however, who had been told coming along that six naked blacks would wait on them during Nana's supper, became very uneasy at not seeing them. Labordette called her a goose, and told her to hold her tongue.

"And Bordenave?" inquired Faucho.

"Oh! I am really quite upset," cried Nana, "he will not be able to join us."

"Yes," said Rose Mignon, "his foot caught in a trap-door and he has sprained his ankle most abominably. If you had only heard him swear, with his leg all tied up and stretched out on a chair!"

Then, they all expressed their regret. No one ever gave a good supper without Bordenave. However, they must try to do without him. And they were already talking of something else, when the sound of a loud voice reached them—

"What next! what next! so that's the way I'm buried and forgotten!"

There was a shout, and all the heads were turned in the direction of the door. It was Bordenave—enormous in size and very red, his leg stretched out straight—who appeared leaning on Simone Cabiroche's shoulder. For the time being, Simone was the lady of his affections. The child, who had received a good education, being able to play the piano and speak English, was fair and very pretty, but so delicate that she quite bent beneath Bordenave's heavy weight, though smiling and submissive all the time. He stood still for a few seconds, conscious that they made quite a picture.

"Well! what do you say? just see how I love you," he continued. "The truth is, I was afraid I should feel deuced dull, so I said to myself, 'I shall go.' " But he interrupted himself with an oath, "Damnation!"

Simone had made a step rather too quickly, and his foot had touched the ground. He abused and shook her. She, without ceasing her smile, held down her pretty face like an animal that is afraid of being beaten, supporting him with all the strength of a plump little blonde. However, in the midst of his exclamation, the others hastened to assist him. Nana and Rose Mignon wheeled forward an arm-chair, into which Bordenave allowed himself to be placed, whilst the other women slipped another chair beneath his injured leg; and all the actresses, who were there, kissed him as a matter of course. He groaned, he sighed.

"Confound it! confound it! Anyhow, the stomach's all right, as you'll soon see."

Other guests had arrived, and one could scarcely move about in the room. The noise of the plate and the crockery had ceased; but now the sound of a quarrel came from the drawing-room, where the head-waiter was speaking in a furious tone of voice. Nana was becoming very impatient, for, not expecting any one else, she was surprised the supper was not served. She had sent George off to see what the waiters were about, when, to her great surprise, some more people, both men and women, entered the room. These last comers she did not know at all. Then, scarcely knowing what to think, she questioned Bordenave, Mignon, Labordette. But they were not acquainted with them either. When she spoke to the Count de Vandeuvres, he suddenly recollected; they were the young men that he had got hold of at Count Muffat's. Nana thanked him. It was all right, all right. Only they would have to sit very close together; and she asked Labordette to have seven more places laid. He had scarcely left the room, when the footman ushered in three more persons. Oh! this time it was becoming too ridiculous; there would never be room for every one. Nana, who was beginning to lose her temper, said in her grandest style that it was scarcely proper. But, seeing two more arrive, she burst out laughing, she thought it altogether too funny. So much the worse! they would have to make room for

each other the best way they could. They were all standing up
except Gaga and Rose Mignon, and Bordenave who monopo-
lized to himself two of the four chairs. There was a regular
hum of voices, they talked low and now and again suppressed
some slight yawns.

"I say, my child," observed Bordenave, "supposing we adjourn to supper. We have our full number, have we not?"

"Oh! yes, to be sure we have our full number!" she replied,
laughing.

She looked about her. But she suddenly became serious, as
though surprised at not seeing some one there. There was
doubtless still one guest missing, of whom she had not spoken.
They must wait. A few minutes later they noticed in their midst
a tall gentleman with a noble-looking countenance and a
handsome white beard. And the strange thing was that no one
had seen him enter the room; he must have got into the parlour from the bedroom by a door that was left ajar. Only some
whispering broke the silence. Count de Vandeuvres evidently
knew the gentleman, for they had very discreetly shaken each
other by the hand, but he only answered the women's questions with a smile. Then Caroline Héquet, in a low voice, bet
he was an English nobleman who was returning to London on
the morrow to be married; she knew him well, in fact only too
well. This story went the round of the ladies, only Maria Blond
pretended, on her side, that he was a German ambassador, and
to prove it said that he was most intimately acquainted with
one of her lady friends. The men, in a few words, rapidly
judged him. He looked like a person of means. Perhaps he
stood the supper. It was probable. It appeared like it. Well!
what did it matter so long as the supper was good? At all events,
every one remained in doubt; they were already forgetting the
presence of the old gentleman with the white beard, when the
head-waiter opened the drawing-room door.

"Madame is served."

Nana took Steiner's arm, without seeming to notice a movement on the part of the old gentleman, who therefore walked
behind her, all by himself. Besides, it was out of the question
to go in in couples. The men and women all entered anyhow,

pleasantly joking on the want of ceremony, like so many worthy tradespeople. A long table stretched from one end of the large room to the other, and yet this table was too small, for the plates on it all touched. Four candelabra, with ten candles each, lighted it up; there was one especially in plated metal, with sheaves of flowers on either side. It was the luxury of a restaurant—plates and dishes without initials or crests, but with gold lines round them, plate worn and tarnished by constant washings, glasses that were almost all odd ones and of the commonest patterns. It was like a house-warming given too soon, in the midst of a sudden accession to fortune, and before anything had been put straight. A gasalier was wanting; the candles of the candelabra, being very tall, could only be snuffed with difficulty, and shed a yellow and feeble light over the dessert dishes, the centrepieces, and the glass plates in which the fruit, the cakes, and the preserves were alternated symmetrically.

"You know," said Nana, "you must all seat yourselves as you like. It's more amusing."

She was standing up at the middle of the table. The old gentleman, whom no one knew, had placed himself on her right, whilst she kept Steiner on her left. Some of the guests were already seating themselves, when a storm of oaths issued from the parlour. It was Bordenave who had been forgotten, and who had the greatest difficulty in the world in getting up from his two chairs, bawling away, shouting for that jade Simone, gone off with the others. The women, full of pity, hastened to him. Bordenave soon appeared, supported, almost carried, by Caroline, Clarisse, Tatan Néné, and Maria Blond, and it was quite an affair to place him comfortably.

"In the middle of the table, opposite Nana!" they all cried. "Bordenave in the middle! He shall preside!"

Then the ladies seated him in the place indicated; but he required a second chair for his leg. Two of the women raised the injured limb and carefully placed it out straight. It didn't matter, he would only have to eat sideways.

"Confound it all!" he groaned; "it's a deuced tight fit! Ah, my little darlings! you must look well after papa."

He had Rose Mignon on his right hand and Lucy Stewart on his left. They promised to take every care of him. The others now all hastened to seat themselves. The Count de Vandeuvres placed himself between Lucy and Clarisse, and Fauchery between Rose Mignon and Caroline Héquet. On the other side of the table Hector de la Faloise had hurriedly taken the seat next to Gaga, in spite of Clarisse, who sat facing them; whilst Mignon, who stuck as close as possible to Steiner, was only separated from him by Blanche, having Tatan Néné on his left. Then came Labordette, whilst at the ends of the table were several young men and some women, Simone, Léa de Horn, Maria Blond, all jumbled up together, without the least order. It was there that Daguenet and George Hugon sympathised with each other more and more as they smilingly watched Nana. There was a good deal of chaffing, however, as two persons had been unable to find seats. The men offered their knees. Clarisse, who could not move her elbows, told Vandeuvres that he would have to feed her. That Bordenave, he occupied such a lot of room with his two chairs! There was a final effort, another squeeze, and every one was at last seated; but as Mignon exclaimed, they were packed like herrings in a barrel.

"Asparagus soup—Deslignac* soup," murmured the waiters, as they handed round the plates behind the guests.

Bordenave was advising every one to take the Deslignac soup, when a shout of protestation and anger rose. The door had a once more opened, and three late comers, a woman and two men, had entered the room. Oh, no! it was too much; it would never do! Nana, however, without leaving her chair, shaded her eyes, and tried to see if she knew them. The woman was Louise Violaine but she had never seen the men before.

"My dear," said Vandeuvres, "this gentleman, M. de Foucarmont, whom I invited, is a friend of mine and a naval officer."

Foucarmont, bowing in an easy sort of way, added, "And I ventured to bring one of my friends."

"Oh! quite right, quite right," said Nana, "pray be seated.

---

*Clear soup with a chicken base.

Come, Clarisse, move a little this way. You have lots of room over there. There, now, with a little good will."

They all squeezed together closer than ever, and Foucarmont and Louise managed to get a tiny corner of the table for themselves; but the friend had to sit at some distance from his plate, and eat by passing his arms between his neighbours' shoulders. The waiters removed the soup plates, and truffled rabbit formed the next course. Bordenave created quite a row by stating that he had had the idea of bringing Prullière, Fontan, and old Bosc. Nana became most dignified at once. She said sharply that she would have received them in a way that they would not have liked. If she had wanted her comrades she was quite capable of asking them herself. No, no; she would have none of that sort. Old Bosc was always drunk, Prullière was a good deal too conceited; and as for Fontan, he made himself quite unbearable in society, with his loud voice and his stupidity. Then, you see, such wretched strollers as they were always out of place with gentlemen.

"Yes, yes; it's quite true," declared Mignon.

All these gentlemen seated round the table looked very stylish in their dress suits, and with their pale faces, which their fast way of living rendered all the more refined. The old gentleman was very deliberate in his movements, and smiled serenely, as though he were presiding at a congress of diplomatists. Vandeuvres was so exquisitely polite to the ladies on either side of him, that one might have thought him at Countess Muffat's. That very morning Nana had said to her aunt that one could not hope for better sort of men, all noble or else rich—in fact, men who were quite the fashion; and as for the ladies, they behaved themselves very well. A few—Blanche, Léa, Louise—had come with low-neck dresses. Gaga alone displayed more, perhaps, than she ought, especially as at her age she had far better have shown nothing at all. Now that they had all managed to seat themselves, the laughter and chaffing ceased. George could not help thinking that he had assisted at much livelier meals at the houses of the middle-class citizens of Orleans. There was hardly any conversation. The men, not knowing one another, merely stared, and the women kept very quiet. That was what most astonished George. He thought them very slow—he had expected that there would have been a great deal of kissing at once.

They were serving the next course, consisting of Rhine carp and venison cooked in the English style, when Blanche said, out loud, "Lucy, my dear, I met your Ollivier on Sunday. How tall he has grown!"

"Well, you know! he is eighteen years old," replied Lucy. "It doesn't make me look any the younger. He went back to school yesterday."

Her son Ollivier, of whom she spoke with pride, was a student at the naval school. Then they started talking of the children. All the ladies became very tender-hearted. Nana told them how happy she was; her baby, her little Louis, was now at her aunt's, who brought him to see her every morning at eleven o'clock, and she took him into bed with her, where he played with Lulu, her terrier. It would make you laugh to see them get under the clothes right down to the bottom of the bed. No one had any idea how sharp little Louis had already become.

"Oh! yesterday, I had such a day of it!" related Rose Mignon in her turn. "Only fancy, I went and fetched Charles and Henri from their school, and in the evening they insisted on going to the theatre. They jumped for joy and clapped their little hands: 'We shall see mamma act! we shall see mamma act!' Oh! they were quite delighted!"

Mignon smiled complacently, his eyes wet with tears of paternal love. "And during the performance," he continued, "they were so funny, looking as serious as men, devouring Rose with their eyes, and asking me why their mamma hadn't any clothes on her legs."

Every one round the table burst out laughing. Mignon triumphed, flattered in his paternal pride. He adored the little ones, his only anxiety was to increase their fortune by administering, with all the skill of a faithful steward, the money which Rose earned at the theatre and elsewhere. At the time they married, when he was leader of the band at the music-hall where she was engaged to sing, they loved each other passionately. Now they remained merely good friends. It was all arranged between them. She worked as hard as she could, with all her talent and with all her beauty; he had given up his violin the better to watch over her successes as an actress and a woman. One could never have found a more comfortable or united couple.

"How old is the eldest?" asked Vandeuvres.

"Henri is nine years old," replied Mignon. "Oh! but he's so strong!"

Then he chaffed Steiner, who did not care for children, and told him with quiet audacity that if he were a father he would not squander his fortune so stupidly. Whilst talking, he kept eyeing the banker across Blanche's shoulders, to see how he was getting on with Nana. But, for some minutes past, Rose and Fauchery, who had been speaking very close to each other, had made him rather anxious. He hoped Rose was not going to waste her time with such stupidity. If she were he would make it his business to prevent it. And with his well-shaped hands, which sported a diamond ring on the little finger, he finished cutting up his venison steak. The conversation about children, however, continued. La Faloise, rendered quite bashful by Gaga's proximity, began to ask her for news of her daughter, whom he had had the pleasure of seeing with her at the Variety Theatre. Lili was very well, but she was still quite a tomboy! He was quite astounded when he heard that she was almost nineteen years old. Gaga at once became in his eyes far more imposing. And as he tried to find out why she had not brought Lili with her—

"Oh, no! never, never!" she said, highly indignant. "Only three months ago she insisted on leaving school. I wished to marry her at once. But she loves me so much, I was obliged to have her with me, ah! quite against my wish, I assure you."

Her blue eyelids, with the lashes all burnt away, blinked as she spoke of settling the young lady in life. If, at her age, she had never been able to put a sou on one side—always working, obliging the men still, especially very young ones, whose grandmother she might have been—it was really because a good marriage was worth far more. She leaned towards La

Faloise, who turned quite red beneath the enormous naked
and plastered shoulder with which she almost crushed him.

"You know," she murmured, "if she makes a mistake, it won't
be my fault. But girls are so peculiar when they are young!"

There was a good deal of commotion going on round the
table. The waiters hurried about. The next course, consisting
of fattened pullets, fillets of sole and stewed liver, made its appearance. The head-waiter, who, in the way of wine, had up till
then only offered Meursault, now sent round some Chambertin and some Léoville. In the slight hubbub occasioned by
the changing of the plates, George, more surprised than ever,
asked Daguenet if all the ladies had children; and he, amused
by the questions, gave him a few particulars.

Lucy Stewart was the daughter of a porter of English origin
employed on the Northern Railway; she was thirty-nine years
old, with the head of a horse, but nevertheless a most adorable
person, frightfully consumptive yet never dying—the greatest
swell of all the women there, and who could count amongst
her conquests three princes and a duke. Caroline Héquet, who
was born at Bordeaux, was the daughter of a clerk in humble
circumstances, who died of shame. She had the good luck to
possess a mother who was a strong-minded woman, and who,
after cursing her and indulging in a year's reflection, suddenly
restored her to her place in the maternal affections, with the
object of watching over her fortunes. The daughter, who was
twenty-five years old, and of a very cold nature, enjoyed the
reputation of being one of the prettiest women in the market,
at the price that never varied. The mother, a very orderly
woman, kept the books with the utmost accuracy as to profit
and loss, and managed the entire establishment from the small
apartment she occupied two floors above, and where she had
set up a dressmaking business for the production of her
daughter's elegant costumes and underclothing. As for
Blanche de Sivry, whose real name was Jacqueline Baudu, she
came from a village near Amiens. She was magnificently
shaped but was very stupid and a great liar, pretending her
grandfather was a general and not owning to her thirty-two

years. She was very much in vogue with the Russians, on account of her corpulence.

Then Daguenet rapidly added a few details about the others. Clarisse Besnus was brought from Saint-Aubin-sur-Mer to Paris by a lady as nursery-maid, and was debauched by the husband, who started her in her new career. Simone Cabiroche, the daughter of a furniture dealer of the Faubourg Saint-Antoine, was educated at a high-class school with the object of becoming a governess; and Maria Blond, and Louise Violaine, and Léa de Horn, had all been driven on to the streets, without counting Tatan Néné, who had tended cattle until twenty years old, in the beggarly Champagne. George listened, watching the women as he did so, and feeling quite dazed and excited by such a cynical undressing coarsely muttered into his ear; whilst, behind him, the waiters kept repeating in a respectful tone of voice, "Fattened pullet—fillet of sole."

"My boy," said Daguenet, giving him the benefit of his experience, "don't take any fish, it's not advisable to do so so late at night as this; and stick to the Léoville, it is less treacherous."

The atmosphere was becoming quite impregnated with the heat from the candles and the fumes of the dishes and of everything else on the table, around which thirty-eight persons were almost suffocating; and the waiters, becoming careless, were scurrying about over the carpet, which was already grease-stained in several places. The supper, however, still continued a rather quiet affair. The ladies trifled with their food, leaving half of it on their plates. Tatan Néné alone ate greedily of everything. At that late hour of the night there were nothing but nervous appetites, the caprices of disordered stomachs. Seated beside Nana the old gentleman declined all the dishes offered him. He had merely taken a spoonful of soup; and he silently looked about him in front of his empty plate. There was a good deal of discreet yawning. Now and again some of the guests quite closed their eyes, whilst the faces of others became really cadaverous-looking. It was most awfully slow, as Vandeuvres said. Suppers of that sort, to be amusing, should not be too select. Otherwise, if all were on their good behaviour, and everything was highly respectable, one might just as well go and feed in good society, where one could not be more bored. If it hadn't been for Bordenave, who continued his shouting, every one would have gone to sleep. The lazy beast, his leg carefully stretched out, put on the airs of a sultan, as he allowed his neighbours, Lucy and Rose, to wait on him. They did nothing but look after him and pamper him, and see that his glass and his plate were constantly filled; but all that did not prevent him complaining.

"Who will cut up my meat for me? I can't do it myself, the table is a mile away."

Every moment Simone continued going and standing behind him, and cutting up his meat and his bread. All the women interested themselves in what he had to eat. They called back the waiters and had his plate filled again and again. Then Simone having wiped his mouth, whilst Rose and Lucy changed his plate and knife and fork, he thought it all very nice; and, deigning at last to show his pleasure, he said, "There! You are right, my girl. A woman is made for nothing else."

Every one began to wake up a bit, and the conversation became more general. Some orange sherbet had just been served round. The hot roast was a truffled fillet of beef, and the cold roast a galantine of guinea-fowl with jelly. Nana, who was quite put out by the want of animation among her guests, now commenced to talk very loud.

"You know that the Prince of Scotland has already had a stage-box booked for him to see the 'Blonde Venus,' when he comes for the Exhibition."

"I hope all the princes will come and see it," said Bordenave, with his mouth full.

"The Shah of Persia is expected on Sunday," observed Lucy Stewart.

Then Rose Mignon talked of the Shah's diamonds. He wore a tunic which was quite covered with precious stones, it was a marvel, a blazing star, and was worth millions; and all the ladies, with pale faces and eyes glaring with covetousness, stretched their necks as they mentioned the other kings and emperors who were expected. They were all thinking of some caprice of royalty, of a fortune made in a night.

"I say, my dear," asked Caroline Héquet, leaning towards Vandeuvres, "how old is the Emperor of Russia?"

"Oh! he's no age," replied the count, laughing. "You've no chance in that quarter, I assure you."

Nana pretended to be very much offended. The conversation was becoming too coarse, many protested by a murmur; but Blanche started giving some information about the King of Italy, whom she had seen once at Milan. He was not very handsome, but that did not prevent him from being very successful with the women; and she seemed quite disappointed when Fauchery stated that Victor-Emmanuel would not be able to come. Louise Violaine and Léa preferred the Emperor of Austria. All of a sudden little Maria Blond was heard to say, "What a dry old stick the King of Prussia is! I was at Baden last year. I was constantly meeting him with Count Bismarck."

"Ah! Bismarck," interrupted Simone. "I used to know him. He is a charming fellow."

"That's just what I was saying yesterday," exclaimed Vandeuvres, "and no one would believe me."

And just the same as at Countess Sabine's, they talked for a long while about Count Bismarck. Vandeuvres repeated the same phrases he had used before. For a moment one seemed to be again in the Muffats' drawing-room; the women, only, were changed. In just the same way, too, the conversation turned on music. Then, Foucarmont having dropped a word about the taking of the veil which all Paris was talking of, Nana became interested and insisted on hearing all about Mademoiselle de Fougeray. Oh! poor little thing, to go and bury herself alive in that way! However, it was her own wish! The women round the table were all deeply affected. George, tired of hearing the same things over again, was questioning Daguenet respecting Nana's private habits, when the conversation fatally returned to Count Bismarck. Tatan Néné, leaning towards Labordette and whispering in his ear, asked him who was that Bismarck, whom she had never heard of. Then, Labordette coolly told her some of the most awful lies imaginable:

Bismarck fed on raw meat; whenever he encountered a woman near his stronghold, he carried her off on his back; though only forty years old, he had already had thirty-two children.

"Only forty years old, and thirty-two children!" exclaimed Tatan Néné, quite astounded, but convinced. "He must be awfully worn out for his age." Then as every one burst into a laugh, she saw it was at her, so she hastened to add: "How stupid you are! How am I to know when you are only joking?"

Gaga, however, had continued talking of the Exhibition. Like all the other ladies, she was rejoicing and making her preparations. It would be a good season, with all the provincials and the foreigners rushing to Paris. Then, perhaps, after the Exhibition, if everything went well, she could retire to Juvisy, to a little house she had had her eye upon for a long time.

"What would you?" said she to La Faloise, "one never has any prospects. If one were only loved!"

Gaga was going in for a little tenderness, because she had felt the young man's knee touch her own. He was very red in the face. She, lisping all the while, weighed him with a glance. A little gentleman, not very wealthy; but, then, she was no longer hard to please. La Faloise obtained her address.

"Look," murmured Vandeuvres to Clarisse, "I fancy that Gaga is robbing you of your Hector."

"Oh! I don't care a fig!" replied the actress. "The fellow's a fool. I have already turned him out of my place three times. But, you know, when youngsters go in for the old ones, it disgusts me."

She interrupted herself to draw his attention, with a slight nod, to Blanche, who, ever since the early part of the supper, had been leaning in a very uncomfortable position, looking very proud, but wishing to display her shoulders to the distinguished old gentleman, who was seated only three places from her.

"You are being abandoned also, my boy," resumed Clarisse.

Vandeuvres smiled shrewdly, with a gesture of indifference. He, certainly, wouldn't stand in the way of poor Blanche making a conquest. He was far more interested in the exhibition Steiner was making of himself. The banker was well known for his numerous love affairs. The terrible German Jew, the great hatcher of businesses whose hands founded millions, became quite a fool whenever he had a hankering after a woman; and he wanted them all. One could never appear at a theatre but he secured her, no matter at what price. The most incredible amounts were mentioned. Twice during his life had his furious appetite for the fair sex ruined him. As Vandeuvres said, the women avenged morality in emptying his coffers. A grand transaction in shares of the saltworks of the Landes having restored him his position on the Bourse,* the Mignons, for six weeks past, had been having a rare nibble at the profits. But now bets were freely made that it wouldn't be the Mignons who would finish them, for Nana was showing her white teeth. Once again Steiner was hooked, and so securely that, seated beside Nana, he looked quite dumbfounded, eating without the least appetite, his under lip hanging down, and his face a mass of blotches. She had only to fix a sum. Yet she did not hurry herself, but played with him, blowing little laughs into his hairy ear, and amusing herself with the sight of the spasms which now and again passed over his fat face. It would be quite time enough to land him, if really that uncivil beast Count Muffat was going to play at being Joseph.†

"Léoville or Chambertin?"‡ murmured a waiter, thrusting his head in between Nana and Steiner, just as the latter was whispering to the young woman.

"Eh! what!" he stammered, quite bewildered. "What you like, I don't care."

Vandeuvres nudged Lucy Stewart, who was noted for saying unpleasant things, and having a most fiendish temper whenever put out about anything; and Mignon's behaviour all the evening had quite exasperated her.

"You know he would even go and hold the candle," said she to the count. "He hopes to do the same as he did with young

*The Paris stock exchange.

†That is, being the complaisant consort; after the husband of Mary, whose son Jesus Christ was, according to Christian belief, fathered by God.

‡The choice is between a Bordeaux wine and a Burgundy.

Jonquier. You recollect Jonquier, who was with Rose, and who took a fancy to tall Laure. Mignon went and arranged everything with Laure for Jonquier, and then he brought him back, arm-in-arm, to Rose, like a husband who had been allowed to go on a spree. But this time it won't do. Nana is not one to return the men who are lent her."

"Whatever is Mignon looking at his wife in that angry way for?" asked Vandeuvres.

He leant forward a little, and noticed that Rose was getting very sweet on Fauchery. That explained to him why his neighbour had spoken in such a spiteful manner. He resumed with a laugh, "The devil! are you jealous?"

"Jealous!" repeated Lucy, furious. "Ah, well! if Rose wants Léon, I give him to her freely. He isn't worth much! One bouquet a week, and that not always! Look you, my boy, all those theatre-girls are the same. Rose wept with rage when she read Léon's article on Nana, I know it for certain. So, you see, she also must have an article, and she's earning it. As for me, I'll kick Léon out of my place, you bet!" She stopped to tell a waiter standing behind her with his two bottles, "Léoville," then, lowering her voice, she resumed, "I'm not going to kick up a fuss, it's not my way; but she's a dirty hussy all the same. If I were her husband, I'd lead her a fine dance. Oh! this won't bring her any luck. She doesn't know my Fauchery, a dirty fellow, he too, who sticks to a woman simply to improve his position in the world. They're a fine lot!"

Vandeuvres tried to calm her. Bordenave, abandoned by Rose and by Lucy, was fast losing his temper, and kept calling out that every one was letting papa die of hunger and thirst. This caused a happy diversion. The supper was becoming interminable; almost every one had left off eating, but the champagne, that many of the guests had been drinking ever since the soup, was gradually animating them with a nervous intoxication. They began to be more free in their behaviour; the women put their elbows on the table, now all in disorder, the men, to breathe more at ease, leant back in their chairs, and the black coats mingled in still closer proximity with the gay-coloured dresses, whilst naked shoulders, turned sideways to the light, had a gloss like silk. It was a great deal too warm, the light from the candles became yellower still, and the atmosphere was loaded with the fumes rising from the table. Now and then, when a head bent forward beneath a shower of curls, the flash from some diamond ornament illuminated the high chignon. The increasing merriment inflamed all, putting laughter into the eyes and displaying pearl white teeth in smiles, whilst the reflection of the candelabra caused the glasses of champagne to sparkle again. Broad jokes were uttered aloud, and every one was gesticulating in the midst of unanswered questions and remarks sent from one end of the room to the other. But the waiters made the most noise of all, as though thinking themselves in their restaurant—pushing up against each other as they served the ices and dessert, giving vent to guttural exclamations the while.

"My children!" shouted Bordenave, "don't forget that we have a performance to-morrow. Take care! beware of the champagne!"

"Oh," said Foucarmont, "I have drunk of every kind of wine made in the world—some of the most extraordinary liquids, alcohols capable of killing a man right off. Well! they never affected me in the least. I can't get drunk. I've tried, but I can't."

He looked very pale and cool, as he leant back in his chair and continued drinking.

"All the same," murmured Louise Violaine, "leave off, you've had enough. It will be very amusing if I have to nurse you for the rest of the night."

A slight intoxication coloured Lucy Stewart's cheeks with a consumptive-looking flush, whilst Rose Mignon, her eyes moist with a desire to cry, had become quite tender-hearted. Tatan Néné, dizzy with having eaten too much, laughed vaguely at her own stupidity. The others, Blanche, Caroline, Simone, Maria, were all talking together, telling each other their private affairs—a dispute with a coachman, a contemplated trip into the country, and some complicated stories of lovers stolen and returned; but a young man near George, having tried to kiss Léa de Horn, received a slap with an, "I say, you! just leave me alone!" full of the most virtuous indignation; and George, who was very drunk and excited by the sight of Nana, hesitated before putting into execution an idea he had been nursing, which was to crawl under the table, and curl himself up at her feet like a little dog. No one would have seen him, and he would have kept very quiet. Then, Daguenet having, at Léa's desire, told the young man to behave himself, George, all of a sudden, felt quite sad, as though he had just been scolded himself; it was stupid, it was dull, there was nothing left worth living for. Daguenet, however, joked with him, and made him drink a tumblerful of water, asking him at the same time what he would do if he found himself alone with a woman, as three glasses of champagne were too much for him.

"For instance," resumed Foucarmont, "in Havana they make a spirit out of some wild berry; it's just like swallowing fire. Well! one night I drank nearly two pints of it, and it had no effect on me whatever. But I can tell you more than that; another time, when on the coast of Coromandel, some savages brought us a mixture that tasted like pepper and vitriol, and it had no effect on me. I can't get drunk."

For some little time past he had taken an aversion to La Faloise who was sitting in front of him. He kept sneering and saying most unpleasant things. La Faloise, who was becoming rather light-headed, moved about a good deal, keeping at the same time as close as possible to Gaga. But a great anxiety increased his restlessness—some one had taken his handkerchief; he kept asking for it in a drunken obstinate mood, questioning his neighbours, and stooping down to look under their chairs and amongst their feet. Then, as Gaga tried to quiet him: "It's absurd," he murmured, "there are my initials and my crest in the corner. It may compromise me."

"I say, M. Falamoise, Lamafoise, Mafaloise!" cried Foucarmont, who thought it very witty to thus disfigure the young man's name.

But La Faloise got angry. He stutteringly spoke of his ancestors. He threatened to pitch a decanter at Foucarmont's head. Count de Vandeuvres had to interfere and assure him that Foucarmont was very funny. Indeed, every one laughed. That upset the bewildered young man's determination, so he quietly sat down; and he went on eating as obediently as a child, when his cousin told him to do so in an angry tone of voice. Gaga kept him close to her again; only, every now and then, he glanced furtively and anxiously at the others, in search of his handkerchief. Then, Foucarmont, in his witty mood, attacked Labordette, right across the table. Louise Violaine tried to make him keep quiet, because, said she, whenever he got quarrelsome like that with others, it always ended badly for her. He thought it very funny to call Labordette "madame;" it seemed to amuse him immensely, for he kept on doing so, whilst Labordette coolly shrugged his shoulders, saying each time, "Keep quiet, my boy; don't be a fool."

But as Foucarmont continued, and even became insulting, without any one knowing why, Labordette left off answering him, and addressed himself to the Count de Vandeuvres. "Have the goodness to make your friend keep quiet, sir. I do not wish to lose my temper."

He had fought in two duels—he was admitted and welcomed everywhere; so there was a general rising against Foucarmont. Every one was amused, thinking him very funny; but that was no reason for upsetting the harmony of the evening. Vandeuvres, whose fine face wore a dark look, insisted on his restoring Labordette his sex. The other men, Mignon, Steiner, Bordenave, all very far gone, interfered also, shouting so as to drown his voice; and the old gentleman, who was quite forgotten in his seat beside Nana, alone preserved his distinguished look, his quiet, weary smile, as he watched with his pale eyes the tumult around him.

"My little duck, suppose we have our coffee here," said Bordenave. "We are all very comfortable."

Nana did not answer at once. Ever since the commencement of the supper, she had not seemed to be in her own home. She felt quite lost among all these people, who almost stunned her with their loud talk and their calls for the waiters, and who were all thoroughly at their ease, as though in a restaurant. She, too, began to forget her duties as mistress of the house, occupying herself solely with stout old Steiner, who was almost bursting with apoplexy beside her. She listened to

him, shaking her head the while, and laughing in the provoking way of a plump blonde. The champagne she had drunk
had heightened her colour and moistened her lips, and given
an extra sparkle to her eyes; and the banker offered more at
every cajoling movement of her shoulders, at each slight
though voluptuous heaving of her neck when she turned her
head. He noticed, near her ear, a dainty little spot, a velvety
skin which almost drove him mad. Now and then Nana recollected her guests, and tried to do the amiable, to show that she
knew how to entertain. Towards the end of the supper she became quite tipsy. That vexed her very much. Champagne always got into her head at once. Then an idea seized upon her
that thoroughly exasperated her. It was a dirty trick the other
women were playing her, by behaving badly in her rooms. Oh!
she saw through it well enough! Lucy winked her eye to stimu-
late Foucarmont against Labordette; whilst Rose, Caroline,
and the others excited the gentlemen. Now, the row they
kicked up was so great that it was impossible to hear oneself
speak—just to show that they could all do as they liked when
supping at Nana's. Well! they would see. Though she was tipsy,
she was still the best looking and the best behaved of the lot.

"My little duck," repeated Bordenave, "tell them to serve the
coffee in here. I should prefer it, on account of my leg."

But Nana roughly jumped up from her seat, murmuring to
Steiner and the old gentleman, who were lost in astonishment,
"It serves me right; it will teach me not to invite such a low set
another time." Then, pointing to the dining-room door, she
added aloud, "You know, if you want any coffee, there's some
in there."

Every one rose from the table, and hurried towards the
dining-room, without noticing Nana's anger. And soon no one
was left in the drawing-room but Bordenave, who was holding
on to the walls and advancing cautiously, swearing all the
time against those confounded women, who didn't care a
damn for papa, now that their bellies were full. Behind him,
the waiters were already removing the cloth, under the directions of their chief, who shouted out his orders. They hurried themselves, shoving up against one another, making the

table disappear like the scenery of a fairy play on the signal of the head scene-shifter. The ladies and gentlemen were to return to the drawing-room after taking their coffee.

"Thank goodness! it isn't so warm in here," said Gaga, with a slight shiver, as she entered the dining-room.

The window had been left open. Two lamps lighted up the table, on which the coffee was served with some liqueurs. There were no chairs, so they all took their coffee standing; whilst the noise caused by the waiters in the next room increased. Nana had disappeared; but no one was troubled about her absence. They got on very well without her, helping themselves, searching in the sideboard drawers for the spoons they wanted. Several groups were formed—those who had been separated during the supper rejoining one another, and exchanging looks, significant smiles, or a few words which summed up the situation.

"I say, Augustus," said Rose Mignon, "ought not M. Fauchery to come and lunch with us one of these days?"

Mignon, who was playing with his watch chain, looked at the journalist severely for a second. Rose, he thought, was mad. As a good manager, he would put a stop to all such waste. For an article, well and good; but after that no admittance. However, as he knew that his wife would sometimes have her own way, and that he made a rule of paternally allowing her to commit a folly whenever he could not prevent it, he replied in his most amiable manner, "Certainly, I shall be delighted. Why not come to-morrow, then, M. Fauchery?"

Lucy Stewart, who was conversing with Steiner and Blanche, overheard the invitation. She raised her voice, and said to the banker, "Is it a mania they've all got? One of them has even stolen my puppy. Really, now, is it my fault if you've discarded her?"

Rose turned her head. Her face was very pale as she looked fixedly at Steiner, slowly sipping her coffee the while, and all the repressed anger she felt at her abandonment gleamed in her eyes like a flame of fire. She understood the matter better than Mignon. It was absurd to try and repeat the Jonquier experiment. That sort of things did not come off twice. Well, so much the worse! she would have Fauchery. She had felt a hankering for him ever since the supper, and if Mignon didn't like it, it would teach him to act differently another time.

"You are not going to fight, I hope?" Vandeuvres came and said to Lucy Stewart.

"Oh, no! never you fear. Only she had better keep quiet, or I'll give her a piece of my mind"; and, calling to Fauchery in a haughty tone of voice, Lucy added, "Young 'un, I've got your slippers at home. I'll have 'em left to-morrow with your concierge."

He tried to jest about it, but she moved away from him with the air of a queen. Clarisse, who was leaning against the wall so as the more conveniently to drink a glass of kirsch, shrugged her shoulders. What a fuss to make about a man! Wasn't it the custom, whenever two women found themselves together with their lovers, for each to try and get hold of the other's? It was quite a settled thing. If she had chosen, she might have scratched out Gaga's eyes, all on account of Hector. But, pooh! she didn't care a button. Then, as La Faloise passed near her she contented herself with saying to him, "Listen! you seem to like them very far advanced. You are not satisfied with their being ripe, you want them rotten!"

La Faloise appeared very much put out. He continued uneasy. Seeing Clarisse scoffing at him he suspected her. "No humbug," he murmured, "you have taken my handkerchief. Give me my handkerchief."

"What a nuisance he is with his handkerchief!" she cried. "Look here, you idiot; what should I have taken it for?"

"Why," said he, mistrustfully, "to send it to my relations, so as to compromise me."

All this while Foucarmont was going in strongly for the liqueurs. He continued to sneer as he watched Labordette, who was drinking his coffee surrounded by the women, and he kept uttering a number of unconnected phrases, much in this style: "The son of a horse-dealer, others said the bastard offspring of a countess—no means, and yet always twenty-five louis in his pocket—the servant of all the girls of easy virtue— a fellow who never went to bed."

"No, never! never!" he repeated, growing angry. "I can't help it; I must really slap his face."

He tossed off a glass of chartreuse. Chartreuse never upset him; not that much, said he, and he clacked his thumb-nail between his teeth. But all of a sudden, just as he was advancing towards Labordette, he turned ghastly pale, and fell all in a heap in front of the sideboard. He was dead drunk. Louise Violaine was in an awful way. She had said that it would end badly; now she would be the rest of the night nursing him. But Gaga reassured her. She examined the officer with the eye of an experienced woman, and declared that there was no cause for alarm. The gentleman would sleep like that for twelve or fifteen hours without the least accident; so they removed Foucarmont.

"Hallo! wherever has Nana got to?" asked Vandeuvres.

Yes, as a matter of fact, she had disappeared on leaving the supper table. They now began to think of her; every one made inquiries. Steiner suddenly became most anxious, questioned Vandeuvres with respect to the old gentleman, who had also disappeared; but the count calmed his fears. He had just seen the old gentleman off. He was a distinguished foreigner, whose name it was unnecessary to mention. He was very rich, and was satisfied with paying for the suppers. Then, every one again forgetting Nana, Vandeuvres noticed Daguenet's head at the door, signalling to him to come; and in the bedroom, he found the mistress of the house seated quite rigid, with her lips all white, whilst Daguenet and George were standing watching her with looks of consternation.

"What's the matter with you?" he asked, surprised.

She did not reply, nor did she even turn her head. He repeated his question.

"I don't intend to be made a fool of in my own place!" she at length exclaimed. "That's what's the matter."

Then she uttered everything that came readily to her tongue. Yes, yes, she wasn't an idiot; she could see what it all meant. They had all made a fool of her during supper. They had said the most beastly things, just to show that they didn't care a curse for her. A parcel of strumpets, who were not fit to clean her boots. She wouldn't worry herself for them another time, just to be treated in that scurvy way afterwards! She didn't know what it was kept her from kicking the whole dirty lot out of the place; and, her rage choking her, she sobbed aloud.

"Come, my girl, you're drunk," said Vandeuvres in a most affectionate manner. "You must be reasonable."

No, she refused beforehand; she would remain there. "I may be drunk, it's very possible; but I intend to be respected."

For a quarter of an hour past, Daguenet and George had been vainly entreating her to return to the dining-room; but she was obstinate. Her guests might do what they liked; she had too great a contempt for them to return amongst them. Never, never! They might cut her up into pieces, but she would remain in her room.

"I ought to have expected it," she resumed. "It's that strumpet Rose who organised the plot; and it's no doubt she who prevented that respectable lady I invited from coming."

She was speaking of Madame Robert. Vandeuvres assured her, on his word of honour, that Madame Robert had of her own free will declined the invitation. He listened and discussed without laughing, used to such scenes, and knowing how to deal with women when they were in that state; but the moment he tried to take hold of Nana's hands, to raise her from her chair and lead her away, she struggled with increased fury. No one would ever make her believe, for instance, that Fauchery had not dissuaded Count Muffat from coming. He was a regular serpent, that Fauchery, a most envious fellow, a man who was capable of sticking to a woman until he had destroyed her happiness; for she knew very well the count had taken a fancy to her. She might have had him.

"He, my dear—never!" exclaimed Vandeuvres, forgetting himself and laughing.

"But why not?" asked she, serious, and slightly sobered.

"Because he's mixed up with the priests, and if he only touched you with the tip of his finger, he would go and confess it on the morrow. Now listen to a good piece of advice. Don't let the other one escape."

For a moment she reflected in silence. Then she rose, and went and bathed her eyes. Yet, when they again tried to get her into the dining-room, she furiously declined to go. Vandeuvres left the room with a smile, without insisting any more; and directly he was gone, she had a fit of tenderness, throwing herself into Daguenet's arms, and saying,

"Ah! my Mimi, there is no one like you. I love you, as you know! I love you so much! It would be too good if we could always live together. Oh! why are women such unhappy creatures?"

Then noticing George, who had turned very red on seeing them embrace each other, she kissed him also. Mimi could not be jealous of a baby. She wished Paul and George always to get on well together, because it would be so nice to remain like that, all three knowing that they loved one another so much. But a peculiar noise disturbed them. Some one was snoring in the room. Then, looking about, they discovered Bordenave, who, after drinking his coffee, had apparently made himself comfortable there. He was asleep on two chairs, his head resting on the edge of the bed, and his leg stretched straight out. Nana thought he looked so comic, with his mouth wide open and his nose moving at each snore, that she quite shook with laughter. She left the room, followed by Daguenet and George, and, passing through the dining-room, entered the drawing-room, laughing more than ever.

"Oh, my dear!" cried she, almost throwing herself into Rose's arms, "you have no idea—come and see."

All the women were obliged to go with her. She caressingly seized hold of their hands, and dragged them away, in so genuine a transport of gaiety, that they laughed before knowing why. They all disappeared, and then returned after having remained for a minute, with bated breath, around Bordenave, majestically stretched out. And then their laughter burst forth afresh, when one of them called for silence, Bordenave could be plainly heard snoring in the distance.

It was nearly four o'clock. In the dining-room a card-table had been placed, around which Vandeuvres, Steiner, Mignon, and Labordette hastened to seat themselves. Lucy and Caroline stood behind them betting; whilst Blanche, feeling very drowsy and dissatisfied with her evening, kept asking Vandeuvres every five minutes if they would not soon be going. In the drawing-room others were trying to dance. Daguenet was kindly assisting at the piano, as Nana said she wouldn't have any strumming, and Mimi could play as many waltzes and polkas as any one could wish. But the dancing flagged; many of the women were reclining on the sofas, chatting among themselves. All on a sudden there was a frightful uproar. Eleven young men, who had just arrived together, were laughing very loudly in the anteroom, and pushing their way towards the drawing-room door. They had just left the ball at the Ministry of the Interior, and were all in evening dress and bedecked with various unknown decorations. Nana, annoyed at the noise they made, called the waiters, who were still in the kitchen, and ordered them to chuck the gentlemen out, swearing that she had never seen them before. Fauchery, Labordette, Daguenet, and the other men hastened forward to insure the respect due to the lady of the house. Angry words were uttered, fists were shaken. Another minute, and there would have been a general punching of heads. However, a little fair-haired fellow, with a most sickly appearance, kept on repeating, "Come now, Nana; the other night, at Peters's, in the big red room. You surely must recollect! You invited us."

The other night, at Peters's? She did not remember it at all. First of all, what night? And when the little fair-haired fellow told her the day, Wednesday, she recollected that she had supped at Peters's on the Wednesday, but she had invited no one, of that she was almost certain.

"But yet, my girl, if you did invite them," murmured Labordette who began to have doubts on the subject, "you were perhaps a little bit on."

Then Nana laughed. It was possible, she couldn't say. However, as the gentlemen were there, they had better come in. And so it was settled. Many of the new comers found friends of theirs amongst those in the drawing-room, and the squabble ended in a general hand-shaking. The little fair-haired fellow with the sickly appearance bore one of the greatest names of

France. Besides, they announced that several others were following them; and, true enough, the door opened every minute to admit men with white kid gloves and in their most official get-up. They all came from the ball at the Ministry of the Interior. Fauchery jokingly inquired if the minister himself would not soon arrive; but Nana, very much annoyed, replied that the minister visited people who were certainly not as good as she. What she did not mention was a hope she entertained—that of seeing Count Muffat enter in the midst of all the others. He might have altered his mind; and, as she conversed with Rose, she kept watching the door.

Five o'clock struck. The dancing had ceased. The players alone stuck to their cards. Labordette had given up his seat, and the women had gone back into the drawing-room. The somnolence that accompanies a prolonged dissipation hung heavily over all in the dull light of the lamps, the charred wicks of which gave a reddish hue to the globes. The women had reached that maudlin state when they feel the desire to relate their own histories. Blanche de Sivry talked of her grandfather the general, whilst Clarisse invented quite a romance about a duke who had seduced her at her uncle's, where he had come to hunt the wild boar; and each, with her back turned, kept shrugging her shoulders, and asking if it was possible to tell such crammers. As for Lucy Stewart, she quietly avowed her humble origin, and talked freely of the days of her youth, when her father, the porter on the Northern Railway, used to treat her to an apple turnover on a Sunday.

"Oh! I must tell you!" suddenly exclaimed little Maria Blond. "There's a gentleman living opposite to me, a Russian, in short a man who's awfully rich. Well, yesterday I received a basket of fruit—oh! such a basket of fruit!—some enormous peaches, grapes as big as that, something really extraordinary at this time of the year. And in the middle of all, six bank notes of a thousand francs each. It was the Russian. Of course I sent all back again, but I was rather sorry to do so, because of the fruit!"

The other women looked at each other trying not to smile. Little Maria Blond possessed rare cheek for her age. As if that sort of adventures happened to such hussies as she! They all felt a great contempt for each other. Many were furiously jealous of Lucy on account of her three princes. Ever since Lucy had taken to riding on horseback of a morning in the Bois de Boulogne, which had been the starting-point of her great success, they had all been seized with a violent mania for learning to ride.

The day was about to break. Nana no longer watched the door, having lost all hope. Every one was bored to death. Rose Mignon had refused to sing the "Slipper," and was curled up on the sofa, where she was whispering with Fauchery, whilst waiting for Mignon, who had already won about fifty louis from Vandeuvres. A stout, distinguished-looking gentleman, wearing a decoration, had, it is true, just recited "Abraham's Sacrifice," in Alsatian patois,* spiced with a certain amount of profanity; only, as no one understood more than a word or two, the recitation fell very flat.

Nobody knew what to be at to infuse some gaiety into the proceedings, to finish the night in a sufficiently wild manner. For an instant Labordette had the idea of secretly denouncing the women to La Faloise, who kept prowling round each to see if she hadn't his handkerchief stowed away in her bosom. However as some bottles of champagne remained on the side-board, the young men started drinking again. They called to each other, they tried to excite one another; but an invincibly mournful drunkenness, of a stupidity to make one weep, overcame them all. Then the little fair-haired fellow, he who bore one of the greatest names of France, quite at a loss what to do, in despair at not being able to think of something funny, had a sudden idea; he took up a bottle of champagne and emptied the contents into the piano. All the others writhed with laughter.

"Hallo!" said Tatan Néné, who had watched him with astonishment, "why does he pour champagne into the piano?"

"What! my girl, don't you know that?" replied Labordette,

---

*In Alsace, an eastern province of France, the local language has a strong infusion of German.

seriously. "There is nothing so good as champagne for pianos. It improves the tone."

"Ah! really," murmured Tatan Néné, thoroughly convinced.

And as every one laughed, she got into a temper. How was she to know? They were always telling her wrong. Things were decidedly going from bad to worse. The night seemed likely to end in an unpleasant kind of manner. In a corner of the room, Maria Blond was having a row with Léa de Horn, whom she accused of receiving men who were not sufficiently rich; and they had come to oaths, as they abused each other's looks. Lucy, who was ugly, quieted them. Looks were nothing; the thing was to have a good figure. Farther off, on a sofa, an attaché to an embassy had passed his arm round Simone's waist, and was trying to kiss her on the neck; but Simone, quite tired out, and very sulky, pushed him away each time, saying, "Don't bother me!" and hitting him on the head with her fan. Besides, the other women would not allow anybody to touch them. Who did they take them for? Gaga, however, who had caught hold of La Faloise, kept him by her, almost on her knees; whilst Clarisse, shaking with the nervous laugh of a woman being tickled, was disappearing between two gentlemen. Around the piano the little game continued, in a fit of stupidity. There was a good deal of pushing; each one wanted to empty his bottle into it. It was simple and neat.

"Here! old fellow, take a drink. The devil! isn't he thirsty, the poor piano! Look out there! here's another; we mustn't lose a drop."

Nana, who had her back turned towards them, did not see what they were after. She had evidently made up her mind to do the best she could with stout old Steiner, who was seated beside her. So much the worse! It was all that Muffat's fault, for he had not been willing. In her dress of soft white silk, light and crumpled like a chemise, with her touch of intoxication, which had taken the colour from her face and made her eyes look heavy, she seemed to be offering herself in a quiet, good-natured sort of way. The roses she had placed in her dress and hair were now all withered, and only the stalks remained. Suddenly Steiner withdrew his hand from off her dress, where he

had just encountered the pins placed by George. A few drops
of blood issued from his fingers. One fell on the dress and
stained it.

"Now it is signed," said Nana seriously.

The day had dawned. An awfully sad and dubious sort of
light entered by the windows. Then the breaking-up began—a
leave-taking full of uneasiness and ill-nature. Caroline Héquet,
annoyed at having wasted her night, said it was time for those
to go who did not wish to assist at some very strange things.
Rose made a face like that of a respectable woman who had
been compromised. It was always the same with those hussies.
They never knew how to behave themselves; they were always
most disgusting from the first. And Mignon having quite
stumped Vandeuvres, the couple went off, without troubling
themselves about Steiner, though not until they had again invited Fauchery for the morrow. Lucy, then, refused to let the
journalist see her home, and told him out loud to go with his
dirty actress. Rose, who heard her, turned round, and answered with "Filthy hag!" muttered between her teeth; but
Mignon, well versed in women's quarrels, paternally pushed
his wife outside, and told her to dry up. Behind them, Lucy, all
alone, descended the staircase like a queen. Then it was La
Faloise, feeling quite ill and sobbing like a child, who was led
away by Gaga, whilst he called for Clarisse, long ago gone off
with her two gentlemen. Simone also had disappeared. There
still remained Tatan, Léa, and Maria; but Labordette obligingly offered to take charge of them.

"I don't feel at all sleepy!" said Nana, "Do let us do something.

She looked at the sky through the window panes—a sky of a
livid colour, and over which floated sooty black clouds. It was
six o'clock. Facing her, on the other side of the Boulevard
Haussman, the houses were still hushed in sleep, their damp
roofs standing out in the dim light; while a party of scavengers
were passing along the deserted pavement, on which their
wooden shoes resounded. In the presence of this mournful
awakening of a gay city, Nana was seized with the emotion of a

young girl, with an intense longing for the country, for an idyllic existence, for something pure and peaceful.

"Oh! I'll tell you what," said she, going up to Steiner, "you must take me to the Bois de Boulogne, and we will have some milk."

She clapped her hands with a childish joy, and ran to throw a pelisse over her shoulders, without waiting for any answer from the banker, who naturally consented, though inwardly annoyed, and dreaming of something very different. The only persons left in the drawing-room were the young men who had come in a body; but, having drained everything, even the glasses, into the piano, they were talking of leaving, when one of them triumphantly appeared, holding in his hand a last bottle, which he had discovered in the kitchen.

"Wait! wait!" cried he, "a bottle of chartreuse! There now, he wanted some chartreuse, that will bring him to again. And now, boys, let's be off. We're a set of idiots."

Nana had to wake up Zoé, who had fallen asleep on a chair in the dressing-room. The gas was still burning. Zoé shivered as she helped her mistress to don her hat and pelisse.

"Well, it's all over; I've done as you wished," said Nana, in a most familiar manner, relieved at having at length made up her mind. "You were right, it may as well be the banker as another."

The maid was sullen and still drowsy. She grunted that madame should have come to that decision on the first night. Then, as she followed her into the bedroom, she asked what she was to do with the two who were there. Bordenave had not left off snoring. George, who had slyly come and buried his head in a pillow, had ended by falling asleep, breathing as gently as a cherub. Nana told the girl to let them sleep. But all her tenderness returned on seeing Daguenet enter the room; he had been waiting for her in the kitchen—he looked very sad.

"Come now, my Mimi, be reasonable," said she, taking him in her arms, and hugging him with all manner of fondling ways. "Nothing is altered, you know it is my Mimi alone whom I adore—don't you now? I was obliged to do it. I swear to you, we shall be all the happier. Come to-morrow, we will settle the hours for seeing each other. Now, quick, kiss me as much as you love me—oh! more, more than that!"

And, tearing herself away from him, she rejoined Steiner, thoroughly happy and full of her fad of going to drink some new milk. In the room, now almost deserted, Count de Vandeuvres remained with the distinguished-looking gentleman who had recited "Abraham's Sacrifice"; they were both seated at the card-table, no longer knowing what they were doing, and not noticing that it was broad daylight; whilst Blanche had curled herself up on the sofa, and tried to sleep.

"Ah! Blanche shall go too!" cried Nana. "We are going to drink some milk, my dear. Come quick, you can return here for Vandeuvres."

Blanche lazily roused herself. This time the banker's bloated face turned pale with annoyance at the idea of being accompanied by that fat girl, who would be in his way. But the two women were already leading him off, and repeating:

"You know, we must see the cows milked."

CHAPTER V

The "Blonde Venus" was being performed for the thirty-fourth time at the Variety Theatre. The first act had just ended. Simone, got up as a washerwoman, was in the green-room, standing before a mirror placed between the two doors that opened on to the passage leading to the dressing-rooms. She was all alone, and, lighted by the naked flames of the gas-jets on either side, was occupied in improving her make-up by passing a finger under her eyes.

"Do you know if he's arrived yet?" asked Prullière, who entered in his costume of a Swiss admiral, with his long sword, his high boots, and his immense plume.

"Whom do you mean?" said Simone, without disturbing herself, and laughing at the glass so as to see her lips.

"The prince."

"I don't know, I'm going down. Ah! so he's coming. He comes, then, every day!"

Prullière walked up to the fire-place, which faced the mirror, and in which a coke fire was burning; two gas-jets were flaring away on either side. He raised his eyes and looked at the clock and the barometer, placed to the right and the left, and accompanied by gilded sphinxes in the style of the Empire. Then he buried himself in a vast high-backed arm-chair, the green velvet of which, worn and soiled by four generations of actors, had here and there turned to a yellowish hue, and he remained there immovable, his eyes vaguely gazing into space, in the weary and resigned attitude of actors accustomed to the "waits" between their cues. Old Bosc had just made his appearance, coughing and shuffling his feet, and wrapped in an old yellow box-coat, which had slipped off one shoulder and displayed King Dagobert's laminated golden cassock. For an instant, after having placed his crown on the piano, without saying a word, he angrily stamped his feet, looking all the while, however, a thoroughly good-natured fellow, with his hands slightly shaking from an over-abuse of alcohol, whilst a

119

long white beard gave a venerable appearance to his inflamed tippling-looking face. Then, as the silence was broken by a shower of rain and hail striking against the panes of the large square window which looked on to the court-yard, he made a gesture of disgust.

"What beastly weather!" he grunted.

Neither Simone nor Prullière moved. On the walls four or five pictures, landscapes, and a portrait of Vernet the actor, were gradually turning yellow through the beat of the gas. On the shaft of a column a bust of Potier, one of the old glories of the Variety Theatre, looked on with its empty eyes. But there suddenly arose the sounds of a voice. It was Fontan, in his second act dress, that of a stylish young man, clothed all in yellow, and with yellow gloves on his hands.

"I say!" he cried, gesticulating, "don't you know?—it's my saint's-day to-day."

"Is it now, really?" asked Simone, going up to him with a smile, as though attracted by his long nose and his big comical mouth. "Were you, then, christened Achilles?"

"Exactly! And I'm going to tell Madame Bron to bring up some champagne, after the second act."

For a moment past a bell had been heard tingling in the distance. The prolonged sound died away and then returned; and, when the bell finally left off ringing, a cry resounded which went up and down the staircase and was lost in the passages: "The overture's on for the second act! The overture's on for the second act!" This cry at length approached the green-room, and a pale little man passed before the doors shouting at the top of his shrill voice: "The overture's on for the second act!"

"The deuce! champagne!" said Prullière, without seeming to have noticed the row. "You are going it fine."

"Were I you, I'd have it sent in from the café," slowly observed old Bosc, who had seated himself on a bench covered with green velvet, his head resting against the wall.

But Simone said they ought not to forget Madame Bron's little profit. She clapped her hands, delighted, devouring Fontan with her eyes, whilst his goat-like face kept moving with a continual play of the eyes, nose, and mouth. "Oh! that Fontan!" she murmured; "there is nobody like him, there is nobody like him!"

The two doors were wide open, showing the passage leading to the dressing-rooms; and along the yellow wall, vividly lighted up by an unseen gas-lamp, shadows were rapidly passing of men in various costumes, women, half-naked, wrapped in shawls, all the chorus of the second act, with the masqueraders of the "Boule Noire"; and from the end of the passage one could hear the sound of their feet stamping on the five wooden steps which led on to the stage. As tall Clarisse rapidly passed by, Simone called to her; but she answered that she would be back in a minute. And, in fact, she returned shortly afterwards, shivering in the thin tunic and sash which formed Iris's costume.

"By Jove!" said she, "it isn't very warm; and I've been and left my fur-cloak in my dressing-room!" Then, standing before the fire, warming her legs, the tights covering which showed the colour of the flesh beneath, she continued, "The prince has arrived."

"Ah!" exclaimed the others inquisitively.

"Yes; I went to ascertain; I wanted to see. He is in the first stage-box on the right, the same as on Thursday. Well! it's the third time he's been in a week. Isn't she lucky, Nana? I had bet that he wouldn't come again."

Simone opened her mouth, but her words were drowned by a fresh cry, which burst out close to the green-room. The shrill voice of the old call-boy shouted along the passage, "The curtain is going up!"

"Three times! Well, it's becoming something surprising," said Simone, as soon as she could be heard. "You know, he won't go to her place; he takes her to his. And it seems it costs him a pretty penny."

"Why, of course! one must pay for one's enjoyments!" maliciously observed Prullière, rising to glance into the glass at his well-formed figure, which created such havoc among the occupants of the boxes.

"The curtain's rising! the curtain's rising!" repeated the old call-boy in the distance, as he hurried along the different passages.

Then Fontan, who knew what had taken place the first time between the prince and Nana, related the story to the two women who were squeezing up against him, and laughed very loud each time he stooped to give them certain details. Old Bosc, full of indifference, hadn't moved. Such tales as that didn't interest him. He was stroking a big tortoise-shell cat curled up asleep on the bench; and he ended by taking it in his arms with the tender simplicity of a crazy king. The cat arched its back; then, after sniffing a considerable while at his long white beard, disgusted, apparently, by the smell of the gum, it returned to the bench, where, curling itself up, it soon fell asleep. Bosc remained solemn and thoughtful.

"All the same, if I were you, I would have the champagne from the café; it will be much better," said he suddenly to Fontan, as the latter finished his story.

"The curtain's up!" drawlingly exclaimed the old call-boy in a cracked tone of voice. "The curtain's up! the curtain's up!"

The cry lasted for an instant, and then died away. There was a sound of scurrying footsteps; then the sudden opening of the door at the end of the passage admitted a blast of music, a distant hubbub, and the door closed again with a dull thud. Once more a heavy quiet reigned in the green-room, as though it were a hundred miles away from the crowded audience that was applauding vociferously. Simone and Clarisse were still talking of Nana. She never hurried herself!—only the night before she missed her entrance cue. But they stopped speaking as a tall girl thrust her head in at the door, then, seeing she had made a mistake, hurried off to the end of the passage. It was Satin, wearing a bonnet and veil, and looking like a lady out visiting. "A pretty piece of goods!" murmured Prullière, who had constantly been in the habit of seeing her for a year past at the Café des Variétés. And Simone related how Nana, having come across Satin, an old school-fellow of hers, had taken a great fancy to her, and was bothering Bordenave to bring her out.

"Hallo! good evening," said Fontan, shaking hands with Fauchery and Mignon who just then entered.

Even old Bosc held out a finger, whilst the two women embraced Mignon.

"Is there a good house to-night?" inquired Fauchery.

"Oh! superb!" answered Prullière. "You should see how they're all taking it in!"

"I say, my children," remarked Mignon, "it's time for you to go on, isn't it?"

"Yes, shortly." They did not appear till the fourth scene. Bosc alone rose, with the instinct of an old veteran of the boards who scents his cue from afar. And at that moment the old call-boy appeared at the door. "Monsieur Bosc! Mademoiselle Simone!" he cried.

Simone quickly threw a fur cloak over her shoulders, and hastened out. Bosc, without hurrying himself, fetched his crown and banged it on his head. Then, dragging his mantle after him, he went off, unsteady on his legs, grunting, and with the annoyed look of a man who has been disturbed.

"You said some very kind things in your last article," remarked Fontan to Fauchery. "Only why did you state that comedians are vain?"

"Yes, young 'un, why did you say that?" exclaimed Mignon, bringing his enormous hands down on the journalist's slender shoulders so roughly that the latter sank beneath the shock.

Prullière and Clarisse with difficulty refrained from laughing. For some time past the members of the company had been highly amused by a comedy that was being performed behind the scenes. Mignon, rendered furious by his wife's infatuation, disgusted at seeing that Fauchery never contributed towards their expenses anything more than a questionable publicity, had conceived the brilliant idea of avenging himself by overwhelming the journalist with various proofs of his friendship. Every evening, when he met him behind the scenes, he quite belaboured him with blows, as though carried away by an excess of affection; and Fauchery, looking most puny beside this colossus, was obliged to submit, smiling the while in a constrained manner, so as not to quarrel with Rose's husband.

"Ah! my fine fellow, so you insult Fontan!" resumed Mignon, continuing the farce. "Attention! One, two, and full in the chest!"

He had struck out and hit the young man so severe a blow that the latter remained for an instant very pale and quite speechless. But, with a wink of her eye, Clarisse drew the others' attention to Rose Mignon, who was standing in the doorway. Rose had seen all that had passed. She went straight up to the journalist, as though unaware of her husband's presence, and standing on tiptoe, her arms bare, and in her baby costume, she offered her forehead to him with a childish pout.

"Good evening, baby," said Faucherly, familiarly kissing her.

That was his reward. Mignon pretended not to notice the embrace; every one kissed his wife at the theatre. But he laughed as he cast a rapid glance at the journalist. The latter would certainly pay dearly for Rose's temerity. The door of the passage opened and shut, admitting the sound of tempestuous applause into the green-room. Simone had returned after going through her scene.

"Oh! old Bosc made such a hit!" cried she. "The prince was wriggling with laughter, and he applauded just like the others as though he had been paid to do so. I say, do you know the tall gentleman who is sitting beside the prince, in the stage-box? A handsome man, looking most dignified, and he's got such lovely whiskers."

"It's Count Muffat," replied Faucherly. "I know that the day before yesterday, at the Empress's, the prince invited him to dinner for this evening. He probably prevailed upon him to come here afterwards."

"Count Muffat! why we know his father-in-law, don't we, Augustus?" asked Rose of Mignon. "You know the Marquis de Chouard, at whose house I went to sing? He is also here to-night. I noticed him at the back of a box. He's an old—"

Prullière, who had just placed the hat with the enormous plume on his head, turned round and called to her, "Hi! Rose, look sharp!"

She hurried after him, without finishing her sentence. At this moment the doorkeeper of the theatre, Madame Bron, passed by, carrying an enormous bouquet. Simone jokingly asked if it was for her; but the old woman, without answering, indicated with her chin the door of Nana's dressing-room at the end of the passage. That Nana! how they covered her with flowers. Then, as she returned, Madame Bron handed a letter to Clarisse, who muttered an oath beneath her breath. Again that confounded La Faloise! there was a fellow who wouldn't leave her alone! And when she heard that the gentleman was waiting in the doorkeeper's room, she exclaimed, "Tell him I'll come down when the act is over. I mean to smack his face."

Fontan rushed forward, shouting, "Madame Bron, listen— now listen, Madame Bron. After the act bring up six bottles of champagne."

But the old call-boy reappeared, quite out of breath, repeating in a singsong voice, "Every one on the stage! every one on the stage! Be quick, M. Fontan! Be quick! be quick!"

"Yes, yes, I'm going, old Barillot," replied Fontan, quite bewildered; and, running after Madame Bron, he continued, "Now you understand? Six bottles of champagne, in the greenroom, after the act. It's my saint's-day; I'm going to stand treat."

Simone and Clarisse had gone off, making a great noise with their skirts. When they had all left, and the door at the end of the passage was once more closed, one could hear in the silence of the green-room the sound of a fresh shower striking against the window panes. Barillot, a little pale old man, who had been call-boy at the theatre for thirty years past, went familiarly up to Mignon and offered him his snuff-box. This pinch of snuff offered and accepted procured him a minute's rest in his continual running up and down the stairs and passages. There was still, to be sure, Madame Nana, as he called her; but she only did as she chose, and never cared a fig for the fines. When she chose to miss her cue, she missed it. He stopped suddenly, murmuring in astonishment:

"Why! here she is; she's actually ready! She must know that the prince is there."

Nana had, indeed, appeared in the passage, dressed as a fisherwoman, her arms and face all white, excepting two dabs of colour under her eyes. She did not enter the green-room, but simply nodded to Mignon and Fauchery.

"Good-day, how are you?"

Mignon alone shook the hand she held out; and Nana continued on her way in queenly style, followed by her dresser, who, as she trod close on her heels, bent down to give a finishing touch to the folds of her skirt. Then, behind the dresser, bringing up the rear of the procession, came Satin, trying to look very lady-like, and really feeling bored to death.

"And Steiner?" suddenly queried Mignon.

"Monsieur Steiner left yesterday for the Loiret," said Barillot, who was returning to the stage. "I believe he is going to purchase a country residence there."

"Ah! yes, I know; an estate for Nana."

Mignon became very grave. That Steiner had once promised Rose a mansion! Well, it was of no use quarrelling with anybody; it was an opportunity which he had lost, and which he must regain. Full of thought, but still quite master of himself, Mignon walked up and down from the fire-place to the mirror. There were only he and Fauchery left in the green-room. The journalist, feeling tired, had just stretched himself out in the easy-chair; and he kept very quiet, his eyes half closed, beneath the glances which the other gave him as he passed to and fro. When they were alone, Mignon disdained to pommel him. What would have been the use? as no one would have been there to enjoy the fun. He cared too little about the matter to find any amusement for himself in playing the bantering husband. Fauchery, thankful for this short respite, was languidly stretching his legs out before the fire, as his eyes wandered from the barometer to the clock. Mignon interrupted his walk for a moment, and stood before the bust of Potier, which he looked at without seeing. Then he went and placed himself at the window opening on to the dark court-yard beneath. It had left off raining, and a profound silence had succeeded, whilst the atmosphere had become closer through the heat of the coke fire and the flaring of the gas-jets. Not a sound could be heard from the stage. The staircase and the passages were as still as the tomb. It was the hushed peacefulness occasioned by the end of an act, when all the company are on the stage joining in the deafening uproar of some finale, whilst the empty green-room is under the influence of asphyxia.

"Oh! the strumpets!" suddenly exclaimed Bordenave, in a hoarse voice.

He had only just arrived, and he was already bellowing at two of his chorus-girls, who had almost fallen down on the stage through playing the fool. When he saw Mignon and Fauchery he called them to him to show them something: the prince had just requested permission to compliment Nana in her dressing-room, between the acts. But as he was taking them on to the stage, the stage-manager passed.

"Just fine those hussies, Fernande and Maria!" shouted Bordenave, furiously. Then calming himself, and trying to look dignified like a father and a nobleman, after passing his handkerchief over his face, he added, "I will go and receive His Highness."

The curtain fell amidst thunders of applause. Immediately there was a regular stampede in the semi-obscurity of the stage, no longer under the glare of the foot-lights; the actors and the supers were hastening to reach their dressing-rooms, whilst the carpenters were rapidly changing the scenery. Simone and Clarisse, however, remained at the back of the stage, whispering together. During the last scene, between two of their lines, they had just arranged a little affair. Clarisse, after thinking the matter over, preferred not to see La Faloise, who no longer wished to leave her to go with Gaga. It would be better for Simone quietly to explain to him that it was not the thing to stick to a woman to that extent. In short, she was to send him about his business.

Then Simone, dressed as a washerwoman in a comic opera, with her fur cape thrown over her shoulders, descended the narrow winding staircase, with its greasy stairs and its damp walls, which led to the doorkeeper's room. This room, situated between the actors' and manager's staircases, shut in on the right and the left by some glass partitioning, was like a huge

transparent lantern, inside which two gas-jets were flaring
high. A set of pigeon-holes was crammed full of letters and
newspapers. On the table bouquets of flowers were lying beside forgotten dirty plates and an old bodice, the button-holes
of which the doorkeeper was occupied in mending. And, in
the midst of all this disorder, similar to the confusion of a
lumber-room, some fashionable gentlemen, stylishly dressed
and wearing light kid gloves, occupied the four old rush-
bottomed chairs, with patient and submissive looks, and
quickly turning their heads each time Madame Bron returned
from the interior of the theatre with answers for them. She had
just handed a note to a young man, who hastened to open it
beneath the gas-jet in the hall, and who turned slightly pale as
his eyes encountered this classic phrase, which he had so often
read before in the same place, "Not to-night, ducky; I'm engaged." La Faloise was on one of the chairs at the end of the
room, between the table and stove. He seemed ready to pass
the evening there, looking rather anxious though, and keeping his long legs under his chair because a litter of little black
kittens were gambolling around him, whilst the mother sat
staring at him with her yellow eyes.

"What! you here, Mademoiselle Simone? Whatever do you
want?" asked the doorkeeper.

Simone wished La Faloise to be sent out to her; but Madame
Bron could not see to this at once. In a sort of deep cupboard,
under the stairs, she kept a little bar where the supers came to
drink between the acts, and as she then had four or five big fellows there, still dressed as masqueraders at the "Boule Noire,"
all of them in a great hurry and clamouring for drink, she was
a little bit flurried. By the aid of the gas that was blazing away
in the cupboard, one could distinguish a table covered with a
sheet of tin, and several shelves stocked with partly emptied
bottles. When the door of this coal-hole was opened there issued from it a violent stench of alcohol, which mingled with
the smell of burnt fat that always pervaded the room, and the
strong perfume of the bouquets left on the table.

"So," resumed the doorkeeper, when she had finished serving the supers, "it's the little dark fellow over there that you want to speak to?"

"No, don't be absurd!" said Simone. "It's the thin one sitting beside the stove—the one your cat's snuffing the trousers of."

And she led La Faloise into the hall, whilst the other gentlemen, though half suffocating, appeared as resigned as ever, and the supers stood drinking on the stairs, indulging among themselves in a good deal of noisy drunken horse-play. Upstairs, Bordenave was yelling at the scene-shifters, who were still engaged in changing the scenery. They were such a time; it was done on purpose; the prince would receive some of it on his head.

"Now then! shove away—all together!" exclaimed the chief of the gang.

At length the drop scene at the back was raised, and the stage was free. Mignon, who had been watching for Fauchery, seized this opportunity of continuing his delicate attentions. He caught him up in his strong arms, crying out, "Take care! that pole almost fell on you."

And he carried him off, and even shook him before placing him on the ground again. Fauchery turned pale as the workmen roared with laughter, his lips quivered, and he was on the point of giving vent to his passion, whilst Mignon went on in a most good-natured sort of way, slapping him affectionately on the shoulder almost hard enough to double him up, and saying each time, "You know I am very anxious about your health! By Jove! I should be in a fine way if any accident happened to you!"

But a whisper passed from mouth to mouth, "The prince! the prince!" And every one looked towards the little door that gave access to the auditorium. At first one could only see Bordenave's round back and his butcher's neck, as he puffed and blowed and bent himself double in a series of obsequious bows. Then appeared the prince, tall and strong, wearing a fair beard, his complexion of a deep rose colour, and looking altogether like a solid man about town, whose well-shaped figure was discernible beneath an irreproachably fitting overcoat. He was followed by Count Muffat and the Marquis de Chouard.

The corner of the theatre where they were was very dark, and they almost disappeared among the big ever-moving shadows. To speak to this son of a queen, the future inheritor of a throne, Bordenave had adopted the tones of a lion-tamer's voice trembling with a pretended emotion. He kept saying:

"If your Highness will kindly follow me— Will Your Highness deign to pass this way? Your Highness, please to take care—"

The prince did not hurry himself in the least; on the contrary, he waited and watched the scene-shifters with a good deal of interest. A float had just been lowered from the flies, and the row of flaring gas-jets, encompassed in wire net-work, shed a brilliant light upon the stage. Muffat, never having been behind the scenes of a theatre before, was especially lost in astonishment, and was seized with an unpleasant sensation, a vague repugnance mixed with fear. He looked up towards the flies, where other floats, the gas-lights of which were turned down, appeared like so many constellations of little blue stars in all the chaos of the light wooden frame-work, and the ropes and pulleys of different sizes, of the hanging-stages, and the back-drops spread out aloft, looking like immense cloths hung out to dry.

"Let go!" suddenly exclaimed the head scene-shifter.

And the prince himself was obliged to warn the count. One of the drop-scenes was being lowered. They were placing the scenery of the third act—the grotto in Mount Etna. Some men were fixing poles in openings made for the purpose in the flooring; others fetched the frames, which were leaning against the walls, and fastened them to the poles with strong cords. At the back of the stage a lamp-lighter was lighting a number of red lamps, to produce the reflection of Vulcan's fiery forge. There seemed to be great confusion and hustling about, yet the least movements were regulated; whilst, amidst all this hurry, the prompter walked slowly up and down to stretch his legs.

"Your Highness overwhelms me," Bordenave was saying, still continuing to bow. "The theatre is not large; we do the best we can. Now, if Your Highness will deign to follow me—"

Count Muffat had already moved off in the direction of the

passage leading to the dressing-rooms. The rather sharp incline of the stage surprised him, and his uneasiness was to a great extent caused by these boards, which seemed to move beneath his feet. Through the open trap-doors he could see the gas-lights burning beneath. It was quite an underground world, with deep and obscure abysses, from which arose the sound of men's voices, and the musty smell peculiar to cellars. But, as he passed along, a slight incident detained him. Two little women, dressed for the third act, were conversing together before the peep-hole of the curtain. One of them, leaning forward and widening the opening with her fingers, so as to see better, was looking round the house.

"I see him," she suddenly exclaimed. "Oh! what a mug!"

Bordenave, awfully scandalized, only restrained himself with difficulty from kicking her behind; but the prince smiled, looking delighted and excited at having overheard the words, whilst he gazed tenderly on the little woman, who didn't care a fig for His Highness. She laughed impudently. However, Bordenave at length induced the prince to follow him. Count Muffat, all in a perspiration, removed his hat. What inconvenienced him most was the closeness of the atmosphere, which had become overheated and, so to say, thick, and in which hovered a very strong smell—that odour of behind the scenes, stinking of gas, the glue of the scenery, the mouldy dirt in out-of-the-way corners, and the unwashed bodies of the female supers. In the passage the oppressiveness increased. The stench of dirty water, the perfume of scented soaps, escaped from the dressing-rooms, mingled now and again with the poisonous exhalations of foul breaths. As he passed, the count rapidly glanced up the staircase, struck by the sudden flood of light and warmth which descended upon him. From above came sounds of people washing, laughing, and calling to one another, a great noise of opening and shutting of doors, emitting feminine odours, the musk of the make-up mixed with the smell of perspiring heads of yellowy-red hair. He did not linger, but hastened his footsteps, almost flying under the emotion caused by this sudden glimpse of a world hitherto unknown to him.

"Well, a theatre is a curious place, is it not?" observed the

Marquis de Chouard, with the delighted manner of a man finding himself once more at home.

But Bordenave had at length reached Nana's dressing-room at the end of the passage. He coolly turned the door handle; then, standing aside, said, "If Your Highness will please to enter."

There was a cry of a woman taken by surprise, and one saw Nana, naked to the waist, run and hide herself behind a curtain, whilst her dresser, who had been occupied in drying her, was left standing with the towel in her hands.

"Oh! how stupid it is to enter a room like that!" exclaimed Nana from her hiding-place. "Don't come in; you see very well you cannot come in!"

Bordenave seemed put out by this bashfulness. "Don't run away, my dear; there is not the slightest necessity for doing so," said he. "His Highness is here. Come, don't be a child." And, as she refused to appear, being slightly startled still, though, nevertheless, already beginning to laugh, he added, in a grumpy, paternal tone of voice, "Why, bless me! these gentlemen know very well what a woman's like. They won't eat you."

"But that is not certain," gallantly observed the prince.

Every one laughed, courtier-like, in a most exaggerated manner. A most witty remark, thoroughly Parisian, according to Bordenave. Nana no longer answered. The curtain shook; no doubt she was making up her mind to appear. Then Count Muffat, who had become very red in the face, looked about him. It was a square room, very low in the ceiling, and hung throughout with some light West Indian material. A curtain of the same stuff, hanging on a brass rod, completely shut off one end of the chamber. Two large windows looked out on to the courtyard of the theatre, at a distance of only a few feet from a leprous-looking wall, on to which, in the darkness of the night, the panes of glass reflected a series of yellow squares. A big cheval-glass* stood opposite a marble dressing-table, which was covered with innumerable glass bottles and pots containing

---

*Full-length mirror that pivots within a frame.

hair oils, scents, face powders, and all the ingredients necessary for making up. Approaching the mirror, the count caught sight of his own red face, with beads of perspiration resting on his forehead. He lowered his eyes, and proceeded to place himself before the dressing-table, on which a basin full of soapy water, some wet sponges, and various little ivory implements scattered about seemed to absorb his mind for a while. The same dizzy feeling he had experienced on the occasion of his visit to Nana, in the Boulevard Haussmann, again seized hold of him. He seemed to sink deeper into the thick carpet beneath his feet; the gas-jets burning on either side of the dressing-table and the cheval-glass were like the hissing flames of a furnace surrounding his temples. One minute, fearful of fainting away under the influence of all the feminine odour, full of warmth, and rendered ten times more pronounced by the lowness of the ceiling, which he encountered for the second time, he seated himself on the edge of the well-padded sofa that occupied the space between the two windows. But he rose up again almost immediately, and returned to the dressing-table, no longer to examine anything, but with a vague expression in his eyes, and thinking of a bouquet of tuberoses which had been allowed to fade in his room a long time ago, their powerful smell having nearly killed him. When tuberoses decay they emit a kind of human odour.

"Do be quick!" whispered Bordenave, passing his head behind the curtain.

The prince, meanwhile, was complaisantly listening to the Marquis de Chouard, who, having taken up a hare's foot from the dressing-table, was explaining how actresses put on the powder with it. Satin, sitting in a corner, with her virgin-like face, was staring at the gentlemen; whilst the dresser, Madame Jules, was preparing the tunic and tights composing Venus's costume. Madame Jules no longer had an age; her face had much the appearance of parchment, and her features were immovable, like those of old maids whom no one has ever known to have been young. She had dried up in the heated atmosphere of the dressing-rooms, in the midst of the most celebrated legs and breasts of Paris. She always wore a faded black dress, and over her flat and sexless bosom a forest of pins were stuck next to the heart.

"You must excuse me, gentlemen," said Nana, drawing aside the curtain. "I was taken by surprise."

Every one turned towards her. She had not dressed herself at all, but had merely buttoned up a little cambric chemisette, which only half hid her bosom. When the gentlemen surprised her, she had but partly undressed herself, having rapidly doffed her fisher-woman's costume, and the end of her chemise could be seen protruding through the opening in her drawers. With bare arms and shoulders and firm projecting breasts, in her adorable freshness of a plump young blonde, she continued to hold the curtain with one hand, as though ready to draw it again should the least thing occur to scare her.

"Yes, I was taken by surprise. I shall never dare—" stammered she, pretending to be very much confused, blushing down to her neck, and smiling in an embarrassed sort of way.

"Oh! nonsense!" exclaimed Bordenave; "you look very well as you are!"

She risked a few more of her hesitating, ingenuous ways, quivering the while as though she was being tickled, and repeating, "His Highness honours me too much. I beg His Highness to excuse me for receiving him in such a condition—"

"It is I, madame, who am obtrusive," said the prince; "but I could not resist the desire of coming to compliment you."

Then, in order to get to her dressing-table, she quietly walked in her drawers through the midst of the gentlemen, who all made way for her. Around her substantial hips her drawers looked like a balloon, as, with chest expanded, she continued to greet her visitors with her sly smile. Suddenly she appeared to recognise Count Muffat, and she shook hands with him as a friend. Then she scolded him for not having come to her supper. His Highness deigned to chaff Muffat, who stuttered out an explanation, trembling at the idea of having held in his hot hand for a second those tiny fingers, that were as cool as the water they had just been washed in. The count had dined well at the prince's, who was a great eater and a splendid drinker. They were both, in fact, slightly tipsy, although they did not show it. To hide his confusion Muffat was only able to make a remark about the heat.

"How very warm it is in here," said he. "However do you manage to exist in such a temperature, madame?"

And the conversation was about to start from that, when the sound of loud voices was heard at the door. Bordenave slid aside a little board that closed a convent-like peep-hole. It was Fontan, who was accompanied by Prullière and Bosc, all three carrying bottles of champagne under their arms, and with their hands full of glasses. He knocked, he shouted that it was his saint's-day and that he was standing champagne. Nana, with a look, consulted the prince. Why, of course! His Highness did not wish to be in anyone's way, he would be only too delighted! But without waiting for the permission, Fontan entered the room, saying:

"I'm not ill-bred; I stand champagne—"

But he suddenly caught sight of the prince, whom he did not know was there. He stopped short, and putting on a ludicrously solemn look, he said:

"King Dagobert is outside, and requests the honour of drinking with Your Royal Highness."

The prince having smiled, everyone thought it very witty. The dressing-room, however, was too small for all these people. They were obliged to huddle up together, Satin and Madame Jules at the end of the room, against the curtain, and the gentlemen close to each other around Nana, who was half-naked. The three actors were still in their second act costumes. While Prullière took off his Swiss admiral's hat, the immense plume of which would have touched the ceiling, Bosc, in his purple cassock and his tin crown, steadied himself on his drunken legs, and greeted the prince like a monarch receiving the son of a powerful neighbour. The wine was poured out and they clinked glasses.

"I drink to Your Highness!" said old Bosc, right royally.

"To the army!" added Prullière.

"To Venus!" shouted Fontan.

The prince complaisantly balanced his glass in his hand. He

waited, and then bowed thrice, murmuring, "Madame—admiral—sire."

And he swallowed the wine at a draught. Count Muffat and the Marquis de Chouard had done the same. There was no more jesting now, they were all at court. This theatrical world was making them forget the real one, with a serious farce performed beneath the hot glare of the gas. Nana, forgetting that she was in her drawers and displaying the tail of her chemise, acted the grand lady, Queen Venus, opening her private apartments to the great personages of the state. To every sentence she uttered she added the words "royal highness," which she accompanied with curtsies, and she treated those masqueraders, Bosc and Prullière, in the style of a queen accompanied by her prime minister. And no one smiled at the strange mixture, of a real prince, heir to a throne, who was drinking a stroller's champagne, quite at his ease in this carnival of the gods, in this masquerade of royalty, in the midst of a crowd composed of dressers and strumpets, players and exhibitors of women. Bordenave, carried away by the scene, was thinking of the money he would make if His Highness would only consent to appear like that in the second act of the "Blonde Venus."

"I say!" he exclaimed, becoming very familiar. "I'll have all my little women down."

But Nana objected, though she was beginning to forget herself. Fontan attracted her with his grotesque face. She kept close to his side, looking tenderly at him like a pregnant woman with a longing for something the reverse of nice; suddenly she addressed him most familiarly:

"Come, pour out, you big ninny!"

Fontan filled the glasses again, and they drank, repeating the same toasts.

"His Highness!"

"The army!"

"Venus!"

But Nana motioned for silence. She held her glass high above her head, and said, "No, no, we must drink to Fontan! It's Fontan's saint's-day. To Fontan! Fontan!"

Then they clinked glasses a third time, and they all exclaimed "Fontan." The prince, who had noticed the young woman devour the actor with her eyes, bowed to him.

"M. Fontan," said he, with true politeness, "I drink to your successes."

Meanwhile His Highness's overcoat was rubbing against the marble dressing-table behind him. It was like being in the depths of an alcove, or a narrow bath-room, with this vapour from the basin and the sponges, the strong perfume from the scents mixed with the slightly sourish intoxicating odour of the champagne. The prince and Count Muffat, between whom Nana now found herself, were obliged to hold up their hands so as not to touch her hips or her bosom each time they moved. And Madame Jules, without the least sign of perspiration, was waiting, standing as erect as a post; whilst Satin, with all her vice, astonished at seeing a prince and gentlemen in evening-dress join in a lot of mummers in running after a naked woman, thought to herself that fashionable people were not so very virtuous after all.

Old Barillot now came along the passage tingling his bell. When he appeared at the dressing-room door and saw the three actors still in their second act costumes, he was almost dumb-foundered.

"Oh! gentlemen, gentlemen," he stammered out, "do be quick. The bell has just rung in the foyer."

"Never mind!" said Bordenave, coolly; "the audience can wait."

Nevertheless, as the bottles were empty, the actors went up to dress, after again bowing. Bosc, having soaked his beard with champagne, had taken it off, and beneath the venerable appendage the drunkard had suddenly reappeared, with the diseased and purple face of an old actor who had taken to drink. He was heard at the foot of the stair-case saying to Fontan, in his hoarse voice, in allusion to the prince:

"Now, didn't I astonish him?"

His Highness, the count, and the marquis still remained with Nana. Bordenave had gone off with Barillot, after ordering him not to have the curtain raised without first warning madame.

"Excuse me, gentlemen," said Nana, as she proceeded to make up her face and arms again with more than ordinary care on account of the nudity of the third act. The prince seated himself on the sofa with the Marquis de Chouard. Only Count Muffat remained standing. The couple of glasses of champagne, taken in that suffocating atmosphere, had increased their intoxication. Satin, seeing the gentlemen shut in with her friend, had discreetly retired behind the curtain, and there she waited, seated on a trunk, tired of doing nothing; whilst Madame Jules quietly moved about the room, without a word, and without looking either to the right or to the left.

"You sang your rondeau marvellously well," observed the prince.

Then the conversation was established, but only in short phrases, broken by numerous pauses. Nana could not always be answering. After spreading some cold cream over her face and arms with her hand, she laid on the white paint with the corner of a towel. For an instant she ceased looking at herself in the glass, and smiled as she glanced at the prince, without, however, laying down the towel and the paint.

"Your Highness is spoiling me," she murmured.

The making-up was a most complicated business, which the Marquis de Chouard followed with extreme delight. He, also, ventured an observation.

"Could not the orchestra," he asked, "accompany you more softly? It drowns your voice, and that is an unpardonable crime."

This time Nana did not turn round. She had taken the hare's foot, and was passing it very lightly and carefully over her face, leaning so forward over the dressing-table as to cause the rounded portion of her white drawers to swell out, the corner of her chemise still protruding. To show that she was sensible of the old gentleman's compliment, she slightly moved her hips. A pause ensued. Madame Jules had observed a rent in the drawers. She took one of the pins stuck over her heart, and remained kneeling for a moment on the ground, occupied about Nana's leg; whilst the young woman, without appearing to know that she was there, was covering herself with powder, being careful, however, not to lay any on the upper part of her cheeks. When the prince remarked that, if she came to sing in London, all England would want to applaud her, she laughed pleasantly, and turned herself round for a second, her left cheek very white in the midst of a cloud of powder. Then she suddenly became very serious: she was about to put on the rouge. Once more, standing with her face close to the glass, she dipped her finger in a pot, and applied the rouge under her eyes, spreading it gently up to the temples. The gentlemen maintained a respectful silence.

Count Muffat had scarcely said a word: he was immersed in thoughts of his youth. The room he had when a child had been very cold. Later on, when sixteen years old, he used to kiss his mother every night, and would then feel, even in his sleep, the icy coldness of her embrace. One day, as he passed a half-closed door, he caught a glimpse of a maid-servant washing herself; and that was the only reminiscence that had troubled him from the age of puberty to the day of his marriage. Then he had encountered in his wife a strict observance of conjugal duties; he himself experienced a sort of devout repugnance. He grew up, he grew old, ignorant of the ways of the flesh, bent to rigid religious practices, having regulated his life according to precepts and laws; and suddenly he found himself deposited in this actress's dressing-room, in company of this almost naked girl. He who had never even seen Countess Muffat put on her garters was now assisting at the most secret details of a woman's toilet, in the midst of that fascinating and powerful odour, surrounded by all those pots and basins. His whole being revolted; the slow possession that Nana had taken of him for some little time past terrified him, as it recalled to his mind the pious stories he had read in his childhood of persons possessed by devils. He believed in the devil. In his confused state of mind, Nana, with her smiles and her body full of vice, was the devil in person. But he would be strong; he would know how to defend himself.

"Then that is settled," the prince was saying, as he took his ease on the sofa. "Next year you come to London, and you will receive such a welcome that you will never return to France.

Ah! my dear count, you do not value your pretty women sufficiently. We shall take them all from you."

"He will not miss them," maliciously murmured the Marquis de Chouard, who threw off his mask on such occasions as the present. "The count is virtue itself."

Hearing the count's virtue spoken of, Nana looked at him in so peculiar a manner that Muffat felt greatly annoyed. Then he was surprised at having given way to the feeling, and became angry with himself. Why should the fact of his being virtuous embarrass him in the presence of that girl? He could have beaten her. But Nana, reaching over for a hair pencil, let it fall; and as she stooped to pick it up, he hastened to anticipate her. Their breaths mingled, and Venus's golden locks fell over his hands. It was a pleasure alloyed with remorse—one of those pleasures of Catholics whom the fear of hell is perpetually goading when in sin.

Just then old Barillot's voice was heard outside. "Madame, may I give the signal? The audience is becoming very impatient."

"Presently," replied Nana, without hurrying herself.

She had dipped the hair pencil into a pot of black; then, her nose almost touching the looking-glass, her left eye closed, she delicately painted the lashes. Muffat stood behind her, looking on. He saw her in the glass, with her plump shoulders and her neck drowned in a roseate shadow; and he could not, in spite of his efforts, withdraw his gaze from that face rendered so provoking by the closed eye, and full of dimples, as though transported with desires. When she shut her right eye, and applied the pencil, he felt that he belonged to her wholly.

"Madame," again cried the panting voice of the old call-boy, "they are stamping their feet; they will end by smashing the seats. May I give the signal?"

"Oh! damn 'em!" said Nana angrily. "Give the signal; I don't care! If I'm not ready, well! they'll have to wait for me." Suddenly calming herself, she turned towards the gentlemen, and added with a smile, "It's true; one can't even have a few minutes' quiet conversation."

She had now finished her face and arms. She added, with

her finger, two broad streaks of carmine to her lips. Count Muffat felt more agitated still, bewitched by the perversion of the powders and the pigments, seized with an inordinate desire for that painted beauty, with her mouth too red and her face too white, her eyes enlarged, ardent and circled with black, as though wounded by love. However, Nana passed behind the curtain for a moment to get into Venus's tights, after taking off her drawers. Then, without the least shame, she doffed her chemisette, and held out her arms to Madame Jules, who slipped on the short sleeves of the tunic.

"Now, let me dress you quick, as they are making a disturbance!" murmured the old woman.

The prince, with half closed eyes, examined the symmetry of her neck and chest with the eye of a connoisseur, whilst the Marquis de Chouard wagged his head involuntarily. Muffat, in order that he might see no more, gazed down at the carpet. Venus was now ready, as that gauze drapery was all that she wore over her shoulders. Madame Jules hovered round her, looking like an old woman carved out of wood, with clear, expressionless eyes, and every now and then she kept taking pins from the inexhaustible cushion over her heart to pin Venus's tunic, passing her bony hands over those next to naked rolls of fat, without their awakening in her mind a single recollection, and with the greatest indifference for her sex.

"There!" said the young woman, as she gave a last look at herself in the glass.

Bordenave came back, very anxious, saying that the third act had commenced.

"Well! I am ready," resumed she. "What a fuss to make! I always have to wait for the others."

The gentlemen left the dressing-room, but they did not say good-bye, the prince having a desire to witness the third act from the wings. Left alone, Nana looked about her with surprise.

"Wherever has she got to?" asked she.

She was seeking Satin. When she at length found her behind the curtain, sitting waiting on the trunk, Satin quietly said, "I certainly didn't intend to be in your way there, with all

those men!" And she added that she would now go off. But
Nana stopped her. She must be cracked to think of such a
thing, when Bordenave had consented to engage her! They
could settle the matter after the performance. Satin hesitated.
It was altogether such a queer place, nothing like anything she
had been used to. In spite of all this, however, she remained.

As the prince descended the little wooden staircase, a
strange noise, a mixture of stifled oaths and stampings of feet
as of men struggling, reached him from the other side of the
theatre. It was caused by an occurrence that quite scared the
actors and actresses awaiting their cues. For some little while
Mignon had been amusing himself again by overwhelming
Fauchery with delicate attentions. He had just imagined a little
game, which consisted in every now and then snapping his fingers close to the journalistic nose, to keep the flies off, as he
said. This little business naturally amused the onlookers immensely. But suddenly, Mignon, carried away by his success,
taking a greater interest in the performance, gave the journalist what was really a blow, and a good hard blow too. This time
he had gone too far. Fauchery could not, in the presence of
the others, smilingly receive such a punch on the nose. And
the two men, putting an end to the comedy, their faces livid
and full of hate, had sprung at each others' throats. They
rolled about the stage, behind one of the side-scenes, calling
each other the vilest names imaginable.

"M. Bordenave! M. Bordenave!" cried the terrified stage-
manager, panting for breath.

Bordenave followed him, after having begged to be excused
by the prince. When he recognised Fauchery and Mignon on
the ground, he made a gesture implying that he was very much
put out. Really, they chose a nice time, with His Highness on
the other side of the scenery, and all the audience, who could
overhear them! To complete his annoyance, Rose Mignon arrived, all out of breath, and at the moment she had to go on
the stage. Vulcan gave her her cue, but Rose remained as
though petrified, as she caught sight of her husband and her
lover lying at her feet, strangling each other, struggling together, their hair all in disorder, their clothes covered with

dust. She was unable to pass them, and one of the scene-
shifters only just succeeded in catching hold of Fauchery's hat
as it was rolling into view of the audience. Vulcan, who had
meanwhile interpolated a string of gag to amuse the audience,
again gave Rose her cue. But she stood watching the two men,
without moving.

"Don't look at them!" angrily whispered Bordenave behind
her. "Go on! go on! It's nothing to do with you! You're missing
your cue!"

And, pushed forward by him, Rose stepped over the prostrate bodies, and found herself before the audience in the
glare of the footlights. She had not understood why they were
on the ground fighting together. All in a tremble, and with a
buzzing in her ears, she walked towards the conductor with the
bewitching smile of an amorous Diana, and gave the first line
of her duo in so warm a voice, that she received quite an ova-
tion. But she could still hear the two men pommelling each
other at the side. They had now rolled to within a few steps of
the footlights. Fortunately the noise of the band prevented the
sound of the blows reaching the audience.

"Damnation!" exclaimed Bordenave, exasperated, when he
had at length succeeded in separating the pair, "couldn't you
go and fight it out in your own place? You know very well I
don't like this sort of thing. You, Mignon, you will do me the
pleasure of remaining here, on the prompt side; and you,
Fauchery, I'll kick you out of the theatre if you dare to leave
the o.p.* side. Now, that's understood, eh? Prompt side and
o.p. side, or else I'll forbid Rose to bring you here again."

When he returned to the prince, the latter asked what had
been the matter. "Oh! nothing at all," he calmly murmured.

Nana, wrapped in a fur cloak, stood talking to the gentlemen while she waited for her cue. As Count Muffat advanced
to obtain a view of the stage between two side scenes, he understood from a sign of the stage-manager that he must tread
softly. All was quiet up above. In the wings, which were most

---

*Side of the stage farthest from the prompter's box.

brilliantly lighted up, a few persons were standing talking in whispers, or moving off on tiptoe. The gas-man was at his post, close to the complicated collection of taps; a fireman, leaning against one of the supports, was stretching his neck trying to get a glimpse of the performance; whilst the man who manœuvred the curtain was waiting on his seat up aloft, with a resigned look on his countenance, quite ignoring the piece and merely listening for the bell which directed his movements. And, in the midst of this stifling atmosphere and the faint noise caused by the light footsteps and the low whispers, the sound of the voices of the actors on the stage seemed strange and hushed, and surprisingly out of tune. Then, farther off, beyond the din of the orchestra, there was the audience breathing as with one immense respiration, which now and again swelled as it broke out in murmurs, laughter, and applause. One could feel the public without seeing it, even when it was silent.

"There is something open," said Nana suddenly, drawing her fur cloak closer around her. "Look and see, Barillot. I'm sure some one has opened a window. Really, the place will be the death of me!"

Barillot swore that he had shut everything himself. Perhaps there was a broken window somewhere. Actors were always complaining of draughts. In the oppressive heat of the gas, one of those currents of cold air, productive of inflammation of the lungs, as Fontan said, might frequently be felt.

"I should like to see you have to stand here with hardly anything on you," continued Nana, who was getting angry.

"Hush!" muttered Bordenave.

On the stage, Rose had thrown so much expression into a phrase of her duo that the applause quite drowned the music. Nana left off talking, and looked very serious. On the count advancing too far along one of the wings, Barillot stopped him, saying that he might be seen. He caught sight of the reverse of the side-scenes slantwise, with the backs of the frames consolidated by a thick layer of old posters, and a portion of the further drop, representing the silver cavern of Mount Etna, with Vulcan's forge in the background. The floats that had been lowered cast a glare of light on the daubs of metallic paint representing the silver. Some red and blue glass judiciously intermingled imitated the flames of a furnace; whilst midway up the stage a number of flaring gas-jets running along the floor lit up a row of black rocks. And behind these, reclining on a gently sloping boulder, surrounded by all the lights, which looked like so many Chinese lanterns among the grass on a day of illuminations, old Madame Drouard who played Juno, and was half blinded by the glitter, drowsily awaited the moment to make her appearance.

Just then there was a slight commotion. Simone, who was listening to a story of Clarisse's, exclaimed, "Halloa! there's old Tricon!"

It was, indeed, old Tricon, with her long curls and her air of a countess consulting her solicitor. As soon as she caught sight of Nana, she went straight up to her.

"No," said the latter, after a rapid exchange of words. "Not this time."

The old lady looked very solemn. Prullière shook hands with her, as he passed by. Two little chorus girls gazed on her with emotion. For a moment she seemed to hesitate; then she beckoned to Simone, and another rapid exchange of words took place.

"Yes," said Simone, at last. "In half an hour."

But, as she went up to her dressing-room, Madame Bron, who was again distributing some letters, handed her one. Bordenave, in a low tone of voice, began abusing the doorkeeper for having let old Tricon into the theatre. That woman in the place when His Highness was there! it was disgusting! Madame Bron, who had been thirty years in the theatre, replied in a surly tone of voice: How was she to know? Madame Tricon transacted business with all the ladies. M. Bordenave had seen her there dozens of times without ever saying a word; and whilst the manager muttered a string of oaths, old Tricon coolly examined the prince, staring him straight in the face, like a woman who weighs a man with a glance. A smile lighted up her yellow countenance. Then she slowly retired in the midst of the little women, who respectfully made way for her to pass.

"As soon as possible; now don't forget," said she, turning towards Simone.

Simone seemed very much worried. The letter was from a young man whom she had promised to meet that evening. She gave Madame Bron a note she had hastily scribbled, "Not tonight, ducky; I'm engaged." But she remained very anxious; the young man might wait for her all the same. As she was not in the third act, she wished to get away at once, so she asked Clarisse to go and see. The latter had nothing to do until almost the end of the piece. She went down stairs, whilst Simone returned for a minute to the dressing-room they shared together. There was no one in Madame Bron's little bar below but a super, dressed in a red and gold costume, who personated Pluto. The door-keeper's little business had evidently gone well, for the recess under the stairs was quite damp from the rinsings of the glasses. Clarisse gathered up the skirts of her robe, which dragged on the greasy steps; but she prudently stopped when she got to where the staircase turned, and, stretching out her neck, took a peep into the room.

She was well inspired, for that idiot La Faloise was still waiting there, on the same chair, between the table and the stove! He had pretended to go off when Simone had spoken to him, and returned directly after. The room, too, was still full of gentlemen in evening dress, with light kid gloves, and looking submissive and patient. They were all waiting, gravely eyeing one another. On the table there only remained the dirty plates, Madame Bron having just distributed the last bouquets; a rose alone, fallen from one of them, was lying half faded, close to the old cat, who had curled herself up and gone to sleep, whilst the kittens were madly careering between the gentlemen's legs. For a moment Clarisse thought of having La Faloise turned out. The fool didn't like animals; that showed what sort of a person he was. He kept his arms close to his sides for fear of touching the old cat, asleep on the table by him.

"Take care! he'll catch you," said Pluto, a funny fellow, as he went upstairs wiping his lips with the back of his hand.

Then Clarisse gave up the idea of having a row with La Faloise. She had seen Madame Bron hand Simone's letter to the young man, who went and read it under the gas-jet in the passage: "Not to-night, ducky; I'm engaged"; and, no doubt used to the phrase, he quietly went off. He, at least, knew how to behave! He wasn't like the others, who obstinately sat waiting there on Madame Bron's old worn-out cane chairs, in that lantern-like glass box, which was as hot as an oven, and which didn't smell particularly nice. What dirty beasts men were! Clarisse returned upstairs, thoroughly disgusted. She passed at the back of the stage, and ran up the three flights of stairs leading to her dressing-room to let Simone know that the young man had gone off. At the wings, the prince had drawn Nana on one side and was conversing with her. He had remained with her all the time, glancing tenderly at her with his half closed eyes. Nana, without looking at him, smilingly said "yes," with a nod of her head. But suddenly Count Muffat obeyed an invincible feeling within him. He quitted Bordenave, who was giving him some information respecting the manœuvring of the windlasses and the drums, and advanced to interrupt their conversation. Nana raised her eyes and smiled at him, the same as she smiled at His Highness. She was, however, listening all the while for her cue.

"The third act is the shortest, I think," said the prince, whom the count's presence embarrassed.

She did not answer. Her face changed in a moment, and she was entirely occupied with her business. She rapidly let the fur cloak slip from off her shoulders, and Madame Jules, standing behind her, received it in her arms; and, after passing her hands over her hair as though to smooth it, she advanced on the stage in an almost nude state.

"Hush! hush!" whispered Bordenave.

The count and the prince remained lost in surprise. In the midst of the silence there arose a profound sigh, the distant murmur of a vast crowd. Every night the same effect was produced as Venus appeared in her goddess-like nudity. Then Muffat, wishing to see, looked through a hole in the scenery. Beyond the dazzling semi-circle formed by the foot-lights, the

house wore a sombre look, as though filled with a reddish
coloured smoke; and on that neutral background, over which
the rows of faces seemed to cast a confused pallor, Nana stood
out all in white, looking taller, and quite hiding the boxes from
the first tier to the amphitheatre. He could see her bent back
and her opened arms, whilst on a level with her feet was the
old prompter's head, looking as though it was severed from his
body, and wearing a poor and honest expression. At certain
lines of Nana's song, an undulating movement seemed to start
from her neck, to descend to her waist, and then expire at the
trailing edge of her flimsy tunic. When she had uttered her last
note, in the midst of a tempest of applause, she bowed, the
gauze drapery waving about her, and her hair reaching to her
hips as she did so. Seeing her thus, bent forward and with her
haunches expanded, move backwards towards the hole
through which he was watching her, the count became very
pale, and turned away. The stage disappeared, and all he saw
was the wrong side of the scenery, the medley of posters pasted
in all sorts of ways. Amidst the gas-jets, behind the row of rocks,
the other Olympian gods and goddesses had joined Madame
Drouard who was still dozing. They were awaiting the end of
the act; Bosc and Fontan seated on the ground, their chins
buried in their knees, Prullière yawning and stretching himself
before making his last appearance of the evening, all of them
looking worn out, with bloodshot eyes, and impatient to get
home to bed.

Just then, Fauchery, who had been wandering about on the
o.p. side, since Bordenave had forbidden him to appear on the
prompt one, got hold of the count, for want of some one better, and offered to show him the dressing-rooms. Muffat,
whom an increasing indolence left without any will of his own,
ended by following the journalist, after looking about for the
Marquis de Chouard, who was no longer there. He felt, at the
same time, a relief and a slight uneasiness on leaving the wings,
from whence he could hear Nana's voice. Fauchery had already preceded him up the staircase, which was shut off on the
first and second floors by little wooden doors. It was one of
those staircases that are generally met with in houses of evil

reputation—such as Count Muffat had occasionally come across in his rounds as member of the poor relief committee—with bare, tumble-down, yellow walls, steps all worn with the constant traffic of feet, and an iron rail highly polished by the hands that rubbed along it. On each landing, on a level with the floor, was a low window, looking like the air-hole of a cellar; and, in lanterns fixed against the walls, jets of gas were blazing, crudely lighting up all this wretchedness, whilst emitting a heat that ascended and accumulated beneath the narrow ceilings of the landing-places.

As the count reached the foot of the stairs, he again felt a scorching breath at the back of his neck, that feminine odour coming from the dressing-rooms above, in a flood of light and noise; and now, at every step he mounted, the musky smell of the face powders, the tartness of the toilet-vinegars, heated him and stupefied him all the more. On the first landing two passages branched off with a sharp turn, and on to these several doors, painted yellow and bearing large white numbers, opened, giving to the place very much the appearance of an hotel of suspicious character. Several of the tiles composing the flooring were missing, and left so many holes. The count ventured along one of the passages, and glancing into a room, the door of which was only half closed, he beheld a wretched den, looking not unlike a barber's shanty in some low neighbourhood, and furnished with two chairs, a looking-glass, and a dressing-table containing a drawer, blackened by the grease and scurf from the combs. A big fellow, covered with perspiration, and his shoulders steaming, was changing his underlinen; whilst in a similar room, situated close by, a woman, ready to leave, was putting on her gloves, with her hair all damp and uncurled, as though she had just come out of a bath.

Fauchery here called to the count, and the latter reached the second storey just as a furiously uttered oath issued from the passage on the right. Mathilde, a smutty little thing, who personated virtuous persecuted damsels, had just broken her basin, the soapy water from which ran out on to the landing. A door was closed violently. Two women in their stays jumped across the passage; another, holding the tail of her chemise between her teeth, suddenly appeared, and as hastily made off. Then were heard a great deal of laughing, the sound of a quarrel, a song commenced and almost immediately interrupted. Through the cracks in the walls and the doors of the passage, one caught glimpses of nudity, rosy skins and white underlinen. Two girls, who were very merry, were showing one another the different marks on their bodies; a third, very young, almost a child, had lifted up her skirts, and was mending her drawers; whilst the dressers, seeing the two men, gently closed the curtains out of decency.

It was the jostling at the end of the performance, the great washing off of white paint and rouge, the resumption of everyday dress in the midst of a cloud of face powder, an increase of the human odour which issued through the slamming doors. Arrived on the third storey, Muffat abandoned himself to the intoxication which was taking possession of him. The dressing-room of the female supers was there: twenty women heaped together, a confusion of soaps and bottles of lavender water, resembling the common room of a house of ill-fame in the suburbs. As he passed, he heard behind a closed door a great noise of washing, a storm in a basin. And he was moving on to the top storey, when he had the curiosity to look through a peep-hole left open in a door; the room was unoccupied, and all he could see by the light of the flaring gas was a familiar utensil forgotten amidst a pile of skirts thrown on the floor. This was the last vision he carried away with him. Up above, on the fourth storey, he felt as though he would choke. All the odours, all the heat congregated there. The yellow ceiling had a roasted appearance; a gas-lamp was burning in a sort of ruddy mist. For a moment he clung to the iron railing, which had the cool feeling of living flesh, and, closing his eyes, he drew a long breath, seeming by doing so to inhale all that pertained to the female sex he was still unacquainted with, although he was, as it were, enveloped by it.

"Come on," cried Fauchery, who had disappeared a moment before; "someone wants you."

He was in Clarisse's and Simone's dressing-room—a long
sort of attic under the slates, badly constructed, with innumerable angles. Two deep openings in the roof admitted the
light. But, at that time of night, flames of gas illuminated the
room, hung with wall-paper, rose-coloured flowers on a green
trellis-work, costing a farthing a yard. Side by side two
wooden shelves, deal-boards covered with oil-cloth, blackened by the dirty water constantly spilt upon it, served as
dressing-tables; beneath them were scattered some zinc cans
very much the worse for wear, two or three pails full of slops,
and several coarse yellow earthenware jugs. There were, in
fact, an infinity of things more or less damaged or dirtied by
use—chipped basins, horn combs with half the teeth broken
off, all, indeed, which the haste and carelessness of two
women, who dress and wash in common, leave untidily about
them in a place that they only momentarily occupy, and the
dirt and disorder of which no longer affects them when once
they are out of it.

"Come on," repeated Fauchery, with that comradeship
which men affect when in company with damsels of easy virtue;
"Clarisse wants to kiss you."

Muffat at length entered the room, but he was greatly surprised to find the Marquis de Chouard seated on a chair between the two dressing-tables. The marquis had retired there.
He kept his feet wide apart because one of the pails leaked,
making a big pool of soapy water on the floor. He appeared to
be very much at his ease, evidently knowing the best places,
and looking quite young again in that oppressive bath-room atmosphere, in the presence of that quiet feminine wantonness,
which the unclean surroundings rendered the more natural
and, so to say, excusable.

"Are you going with the old boy?" asked Simone of Clarisse,
in a whisper.

"Never! not if I know it!" answered the latter out loud.

The dresser, a very ugly and very familiar young girl, who
was helping Simone to put on her cloak, burst out laughing.
They all three incited one another, murmuring words which
redoubled their merriment.

"Come, Clarisse; kiss the gentleman," said Fauchery. "You know he can afford it." And turning towards the count, he added, "You'll see, she's very nice; she's going to kiss you."

But Clarisse had had enough of the men. She spoke vehemently of the beasts who were waiting below in the door-keeper's room. Besides, she was in a hurry to get down, they would make her miss her cue in the last scene. Then, as Fauchery stood in front of the door to detain her, she kissed Muffat's whiskers, saying:

"It's not because it's you, anyhow! it's merely because Fauchery bothers me!" And she hastened away.

The count felt very uneasy in the presence of his father-in-law. He became very red in the face. When in Nana's dressing-room, surrounded by all the luxury of mirrors and hangings, he had not experienced the acrid excitation of the shameful misery of that garret, full of the two women's indelicacy. The marquis, however, had gone off after Simone, who seemed in a great hurry, whispering in her ear, whilst she kept shaking her head. Fauchery followed them laughing. Then the count found himself left alone with the dresser, who was rinsing out the basins. So he also went off and descended the staircase, his legs scarcely able to bear his weight, startling women in their petticoats, and causing doors to be hastily closed as he passed. But in the midst of this hurry-skurry of girls across the four storeys, the only thing he distinctly saw was a cat—the big tortoise-shell cat who, in that furnace poisoned with musk, crawled down the stairs rubbing its back against the rails of the balustrade, with its tail erect.

"Well!" exclaimed a woman's hoarse voice, "I thought they were going to keep us to-night! They're always having calls!"

It was the end; the curtain had just gone down. There was a rush up the staircase, which resounded with exclamations of all kinds; everyone was in a violent hurry to get dressed and go home. As Count Muffat reached the foot of the stairs he saw Nana and the prince walking slowly along the passage. Stopping suddenly, the young woman smiled and said in a low tone of voice:

"Very well, then; in a few minutes."

The prince returned to the stage, where Bordenave awaited him. Then, finding himself alone with Nana, Muffat gave way to an impulse of rage and desire and hastened after her, and, just as she reached her dressing-room, he kissed her roughly on the back of the neck, where the little golden curls hung between her shoulders. It was as though he was returning the kiss he had received upstairs. Nana, in a fury, raised her arm, but, when she recognised the count, she smiled.

"Oh! you frightened me," was all she said.

And her smile was adorable, confused and submissive, as if she had despaired of that kiss and was happy at having received it. But she could not respond to it, neither then nor on the morrow. They must wait. Even if she had not been obliged to do so, she would have made him wait. Her look said all these things. At length she resumed:

"You know, I am a landowner now. Yes, I have purchased a small estate near Orleans, in a part of the country where you go sometimes. Baby told me so—little George Hugon; you know him, do you not? Come and see me there."

The timid count, frightened at his own rude outburst, ashamed of what he had done, bowed ceremoniously and promised to avail himself of her invitation. Then he went off to rejoin the prince, walking as though in a dream, and as he passed the green-room he heard Satin exclaim:

"You are a dirty old beast! Leave me alone!"

It was the Marquis de Chouard, who, for want of some one better had pitched upon Satin. The latter thought she had decidedly had enough of those fashionable people. Nana had, it is true, presented her to Bordenave; but it had bored her too much to remain all the while with her mouth shut, for fear of saying something stupid, and she wanted to make up for the waste of time, the more especially as she had run against an old flame of hers in the wings, the super who personated Pluto, a pastry-cook who had already given her a whole week of love and blows. She was waiting for him, and felt greatly annoyed with the marquis for addressing her as though she was one of the women of the theatre. So she ended by saying in a very dignified tone of voice:

"My husband will be here directly, and then you will see!"

The actors, with their overcoats on, and looking very fatigued, now began to leave one by one. Groups of men and
women went down the little winding staircase, casting shadows
of old knocked-about hats and ragged shawls on the wall, with
the ghastliness of strollers who have wiped off their rouge. On
the stage, where all the gas-jets were being turned out, the
prince was listening to an anecdote of Bordenave's. He was
waiting for Nana. When she at length appeared, the stage was
in darkness, and the fireman was going round with a lantern
giving a last look to everything. To save His Highness from having to go through the Passage des Panoramas, Bordenave had
the doors opened of the corridor leading from near the doorkeeper's room to the vestibule of the theatre, and several of
the women scurried along there, delighted at escaping from
the men who were waiting for them outside the stage-door.
They pushed against each other, squeezing their way through,
glancing back every instant, and holding their breath until
they found themselves outside; whilst Fontan, Bosc, and Prullière moved slowly off home, joking amongst themselves about
the ladies' protectors—solemn-looking gentlemen, who were
walking up and down the Galerie des Variétés near the stage-
door, at the same time that the damsels themselves were hastening along the Boulevards in the company of the chosen
ones of their hearts. But Clarisse was especially cunning. She
determined to beware of La Faloise. And, in fact, he was still in
the doorkeeper's room with the other gentlemen who obstinately stuck to Madame Bron's chairs. They were all watching
and listening intently; so, keeping close to a friend, she passed
rapidly before them. The gentlemen blinked their eyes, bewildered by the rapid succession of skirts whirling round at the
foot of the narrow stair-case, and quite despondent, after having waited so long for the ladies, at seeing them all disappear
like that without being able to recognise a single one. The litter of black kittens were asleep on the oil-cloth, cuddled up
against their mother, who, with a look of intense happiness,
had separated her legs to receive them; whilst the big tortoise-
shell cat, seated at the other end of the table with its tail

stretched out, watched with its yellow eyes the women hurrying away.

"If His Highness will pass through here," said Bordenave, at the foot of the stairs, as he pointed to the corridor.

A few women were still there pushing past each other. The prince followed Nana, and Muffat and the marquis came after them. It was a long passage situated between the theatre and the next house, in fact, a sort of narrow alley covered with a sloping roof, in which were two or three sky-lights. A dampness hung about the walls, and the footsteps resounded over the pavement the same as in a tunnel. It was full of the disorder of a garret. There was a carpenter's bench, on which the door-keeper's husband occasionally planed a piece of scenery, and quite a collection of wooden barriers used of an evening to regulate the pressure of the crowd. Nana was obliged to hold up her skirts as she passed a water-tap which, not being properly turned off, was inundating the place. On reaching the vestibule everyone bowed. And when Bordenave was left alone, he summed up his opinion of the prince with a shrug of the shoulders, full of a disdainful philosophy.

"He's a bit of a muff, all the same," said he, without explaining himself further to Fauchery, whom Rose Mignon was taking home with her husband with the intention of making them good friends again.

Muffat found himself alone on the footpath outside. His Highness had quietly placed Nana in his carriage and driven off. The marquis, in a very excited state, had followed Satin and her super, contenting himself with keeping close to those two embodiments of vice, with the vague hope of their taking compassion on him. Then Muffat, his head as hot as a furnace, decided to go home on foot. All combat within him had ceased. A new era of life had drowned all his ideas and his beliefs of forty years' standing. As he walked along the Boulevards the noise caused by the belated vehicles seemed to deafen him with the sound of Nana's name, whilst in the gas-lamps a naked vision, Nana's supple arms and her white shoulders, appeared to dance before his eyes, and he felt that he was wholly hers; he would have abjured all, have sold everything he possessed, to have had her with him but for one short hour that very night. It was his youth that was at length awakening within him, the gluttonous puberty of an adolescent that had suddenly become inflamed in the midst of his jesuitical coldness and his dignity of mature age.

CHAPTER VI

Count Muffat, accompanied by his wife and daughter, had arrived the previous evening at Les Fondettes, where Madame Hugon, who was alone with her son George, had invited them to come and spend a week. The house, built towards the end of the seventeenth century, was erected in the middle of an immense square enclosure, without a single ornament; but the garden contained some magnificent trees, and a series of playing fountains, supplied by neighbouring springs. On the road from Orleans to Paris it appeared like a flood of verdure, a bouquet of trees, breaking the monotony of that flat country, where cultivated fields could be seen as far as the horizon.

At eleven o'clock, when the second sounding of the bell had gathered every one round the luncheon table, Madame Hugon, with her kind, maternal smile, kissed Sabine on both cheeks, saying:

"You know that when in the country I always do so. Having you here makes me feel twenty years younger. Did you sleep well in your old room?" Then, without waiting for an answer, she turned toward Estelle, adding, "And this little one no doubt slept soundly all night? Come and kiss me, my child."

They had sat down in the vast dining-room, the windows of which looked on to the ornamental garden; but they only occupied one end of the big table, so as to be more together. Sabine was very merry, recalling the events of her childhood which this visit had awakened: months passed at Les Fondettes, long walks, a fall into one of the fountains one summer's evening, an old romance of chivalry discovered on the top of some cupboard and read in winter, seated before a blazing fire of vine-cuttings; and George, who had not seen the countess for some months past, noticed a peculiar look about her, with something changed in the expression of her face; whilst that stick, Estelle, on the contrary, seemed more a nonentity than ever, still more awkward and dumb. As they were eating some boiled eggs and some cutlets done very plainly, Madame Hugon began to complain, as only the mistress of a household can, of the outrageous prices the butchers were charging for their meat. She had to have everything from Orleans, and they never sent her the pieces she ordered. Besides, if her guests fared badly it was their own fault; they came too late in the season.

"It is most foolish," said she. "I have been expecting you ever since last June, and now we are in the middle of September. As you see, it is no longer so nice out of doors."

With a gesture, she indicated the trees on the lawn, the leaves of which were commencing to turn yellow. It was a cloudy day, a kind of bluey mist obscured the horizon in a melancholy peacefulness.

"Oh! I am expecting some people," continued she; "it will be more lively. First, there are two gentlemen whom George has invited, M. Fauchery and M. Daguenet. You know them, do you not? Then M. de Vandeuvres, who has promised to come these five years past. This year, perhaps, he will really do so."

"Ah, well!" said the countess, laughing, "we have not much to expect if we have only M. de Vandeuvres to look forward to! He is too busy."

"And Philippe!" queried Muffat.

"Philippe has asked for leave," replied the old lady, "but you will probably have left Les Fondettes before he arrives."

The coffee had just been served, and the conversation had turned to Paris, when Steiner was mentioned. On hearing the name, Madame Hugon uttered a faint cry.

"By the way," said she, "M. Steiner is that stout gentleman I met at your house one evening, is he not? a banker, I think. He is a terrible man. He has bought an actress a small estate about a league from here, on the other side of the Choue, near Gumières! Every one in the neighbourhood is scandalized. Did you know of it, my friend?"

"Not at all," replied Muffat. "Ah! so Steiner has bought an estate near here?"

On hearing his mother approach this subject, George buried his nose in his cup; but, surprised at the count's answer, he raised his head again, and looked Muffat full in the face. Why had he lied so deliberately? The count having, on his side, noticed the young man's movement, glanced at him with suspicion. Madame Hugon gave some further particulars. The estate was called La Mignotte. To reach it you had to follow the course of the Choue as far as Gumières, where there was a bridge, and that made the road a good two miles longer; otherwise you had to wade across the stream, and risk falling in.

"And what is the actress's name?" asked the countess.

"Ah! I had heard it mentioned," murmured the old lady. "George, you were there this morning, when the gardener was talking——"

George made a pretence of trying to recollect. Muffat waited, turning a teaspoon between his fingers meanwhile. Then the countess, addressing him, said, "Is not M. Steiner living with that singer of the Variety Theatre, that Nana?"

"Nana; yes, that is the name. A most abandoned woman!" exclaimed Madame Hugon, who was losing her temper. "And they are expecting her at La Mignotte. I have heard all about it from the gardener. George, did not the gardener say they expected her this evening?"

The count started slightly with surprise. But George hastily replied, "Oh, mamma! the gardener spoke without knowing. Only a little while ago the coachman was saying something quite different. No one is expected at La Mignotte until the day after to-morrow."

He tried to talk in a natural manner, and watched the count from out of the corner of his eye, to see the effect of his words. Muffat, with a reassured look, was again turning the spoon between his fingers. The countess, gazing vaguely on the bluey horizon, seemed to be miles away from the conversation, as she followed, with the shadow of a smile, a secret thought suddenly awakened within her; whilst Estelle, erect on her chair, had listened to all that had been said about Nana without a change on her pale virgin face.

"Well! really now," murmured Madame Hugon, after a pause, her good nature triumphing, "it is wrong of me to feel angry. Every one must live. If we should ever meet this person in our walks, the only thing to do is not to take any notice of her."

And, as they rose from the table, she again scolded Countess Sabine for having been so long in coming to see her; but the countess excused herself, saying the delay was all her husband's fault. Twice when they had been ready to start, with their trunks all packed, he had put off their departure, saying that some very important matters required his presence in Paris; then he had suddenly given orders for starting, just as the journey seemed definitely abandoned. Then the old lady related that George had in the same way announced to her his coming on two separate occasions, but had not made his appearance at either time, and that he had suddenly arrived at Les Fondettes two days before when she was no longer expecting him. They had now entered the garden. The two men, looking very important, were walking on either side of the ladies, and listening to them in silence.

"All the same," said Madame Hugon, as she kissed her son's fair hair, "it is very kind of Zizi to come and bury himself in the country with his old mother. Dear Zizi! he does not forget me!"

During the afternoon, she became very uneasy. George, who directly after lunch had complained of pains in the head, appeared to be gradually overcome by a most violent headache. Towards four o'clock he said he would go upstairs to bed, it was the best remedy; when he had had a good sleep till morning he would be all right again. His mother persisted in putting him to bed herself. But, as she left the room, he ran and locked the door after her, pretending that he did so that no one might come and disturb him; and he called out, "Good night, mother dear!" in a most loving tone of voice, and promised to sleep soundly through the night. He did not go back to bed, however, but with a bright complexion and sparkling eyes he noiselessly dressed himself again, then, seating himself in a chair, he patiently waited. When the dinner bell rang he watched for Count Muffat, whom he saw enter the drawing-room. Ten minutes later, certain of not being seen, he nimbly escaped from the house by the window of his room, and slid down a water pipe to the ground. He found himself in the midst of a shrubbery, and was soon outside the grounds; and, with an empty stomach, and a heart thumping with emotion, he ran across country in the direction of the Choue. Darkness was setting in, and a fine rain had commenced to fall.

It was indeed that evening that Nana was expected at La Mignotte. Ever since the month of May, when Steiner had bought her her country residence, she was every now and then seized with such a longing to go and inhabit it, that she would burst into tears; but each time Bordenave refused her the smallest holiday, putting her off until September, on the pretext that he could not possibly replace her by an under-study, even for one night, during the time of the Exhibition. Towards the end of August, he began to talk of October. Nana, furious, declared that she would be at La Mignotte by the 15th of September, and, to show that she meant what she said, she invited a number of people, in Bordenave's presence, to go and stay there with her. One afternoon as Muffat, whose advances she artfully resisted, was passionately imploring her to be less cruel, she at length promised to be kind when she was in the country; and, to him also, she named the 15th as the date of her arrival there. Then, on the 12th, she was seized with a desire to start off at once, alone with Zoé. Perhaps Bordenave, knowing that she wanted to go, would find some means of detaining her. It amused her to think of leaving him in the lurch by merely sending him a doctor's certificate. When once the idea of being the first to arrive at La Mignotte, of living there two whole days without any one knowing of it, had seized hold of her, she made Zoé hurry the packing of the trunks and then pushed her into a cab, where, quite overcome, she kissed her and begged her pardon. It was only when she reached the railway station that she thought of sending a note to Steiner to inform him of her departure. She asked him to wait till the day after the morrow before joining her, if he wished to find her well and loving. Then, jumping to another idea, she wrote a second letter, in which she begged her aunt to bring little Louis to her at once. It would do baby so much good! and they would be so happy playing together under the trees! In the train, from Paris to Orleans, she could speak of nothing else, with her eyes full of tears, and mixing up together the flowers, the birds, and her child, in a sudden outburst of maternal affection.

La Mignotte was distant more than three leagues from Orleans. Nana lost an hour in securing a vehicle to take her there—an immense dilapidated open carriage, which rolled slowly along with a great jingling of old iron. She at once attacked the driver, a little taciturn old man, whom she belaboured with questions. Had he often passed by La Mignotte? So, it was behind that hill? There were probably plenty of trees there, were there not? And could the house be seen from a distance? The little old fellow only answered with grunts. Nana jumped about impatiently in the vehicle; whilst Zoé, annoyed at having had to leave Paris in such a hurry, remained stiff and sulky. The horse having suddenly stopped, the young woman thought they had arrived. She leant over towards the driver, asking:

"Is this the place?"

For all answer the coachman whipped up his horse, which painfully commenced ascending a hill. Nana was enchanted with the large expanse of country beneath the grey overcast sky.

"Oh! Look, Zoé, what a lot of grass! Is that corn, do you think? Heavens! how lovely!"

"It is very plain that madame has never been in the country," the maid ended by saying in a surly tone of voice. "I had only too much of the country when I was at the dentist's, who had a house at Bougival. It's very chilly, too, this evening. Besides, the air is damp about here."

They were passing beneath some trees. Nana sniffed at the scent of the leaves like a young dog. Suddenly, on the road taking a turn, she caught sight of the corner of a house amidst the trees. Perhaps that was it; so she recommenced questioning the driver, who again said "No" with a shake of the head. Then, as they descended the hill on the other side, he contented himself with pointing his whip, murmuring:

"There it is over there."

She jumped up and looked ahead. "Where? where?" cried

she, very pale and not distinguishing anything. At length she noticed a bit of a wall. Then she sang and jumped for joy, like a woman quite overcome by a powerful emotion.

"Zoé, I see it, I see it! Look, on the other side. Oh! on the roof there's a sort of little terrace with some bricks. Over there there's a conservatory! Oh! but it's an enormous place. Oh! I am so pleased! Look, Zoé, look!"

The carriage had stopped in front of the iron gates. A little side door was opened, and the gardener, a tall thin fellow, appeared holding his cap in his hand. Nana tried to look dignified, for the driver already seemed to be laughing inwardly, though his lips were tightly compressed together. She restrained herself from running, and listened to the gardener, a very talkative one by the way, who begged madame to excuse the place being a little untidy, as he had only received her letter that very morning; but, in spite of her efforts, she seemed to be lifted from the earth, and walked so fast that Zoé could not keep up with her. At the end of the path she stopped for an instant to take a look at the house. It was a large building in the Italian style, flanked by a smaller structure, and had been erected by a rich Englishman who had resided for two years at Naples; he had, however, soon taken a dislike to it.

"I will show madame over the premises," said the gardener.

But Nana, who was some distance ahead, called to him not to trouble himself, she would look at everything by herself, she preferred that; and, without taking off her bonnet, she ran about the rooms, calling to Zoé, giving her opinion about everything, and filling with her shouts and her laughter the vacuum of that house which had remained uninhabited for so many long months. First, there was the hall; it was rather damp, but that did not matter, no one would have to sleep there. Then the drawing-room, which was splendid with its large windows opening on to the lawn; only, the red-covered furniture was frightful, she would have it altered. As for the dining-room, it was simply magnificent. And what parties one could give at Paris if one only had a dining-room of that size! As she was going up to the first floor she recollected that she had not seen the kitchen; she went down again, uttering all kinds of exclamations, and Zoé had to admire the beauty of the sink and the magnitude of the fire-place, which was large enough to roast a sheep. When she had gone up-stairs again, her bedroom especially enraptured her—it had been hung with pale rose-coloured cretonne, style of Louis XVI., by an upholsterer from Orleans. Well, one ought to sleep well in there, it was quite a school-girls' nest! There were also four or five other bed-rooms for guests, and some magnificent attics, which would be very useful for the trunks. Zoé, looking very sulky, just glanced coldly into each room, and kept a long way behind madame. She watched her disappear at the top of the steep ladder which led to the roof. Thank you for nothing! she didn't want to break her legs. But the sound of a voice reached her from afar off, as though coming down a chimney.

"Zoé! Zoé! where are you? come up here! Oh, you've no idea—it's like fairy-land!"

Zoé ascended the ladder, grumbling the while. She saw madame on the roof, leaning against the brick balustrade, and looking down upon the valley which extended into the distance. The horizon was immense, but it was half hidden by a grey mist, whilst a high wind drove away the fine drops of rain. Nana was obliged to hold her bonnet with both hands to prevent it blowing off, and her skirts flapped about like the snapping of a flag.

"Ah! no indeed!" said Zoé, bringing her head in at once. "Madame will be blown away. What awful weather!"

Madame did not hear. With her head bent forward, she was examining the grounds beneath her. There were seven or eight acres, all walled in. Then the view of the kitchen garden quite fascinated her. She hurried inside again, and rushed past the maid on the stairs, exclaiming:

"It's full of cabbages! Oh! cabbages as big as that! And lettuce, and sorrel, and onions, and everything! Come quick!"

The rain was falling faster. She opened her white silk parasol, and ran along the paths.

"Madame will be ill!" cried Zoé, who quietly remained standing beneath the verandah.

But madame wished to see everything. Each fresh discovery

brought more exclamations. "Zoé, here's some spinach! Come
and see! Oh! artichokes!—they do look funny. They flower
then, do they? I say! whatever's this? I don't know it at all.
Come and see, Zoé; perhaps you know?"

But the maid did not stir. Madame must really be mad. It
was now pouring in torrents. The little white silk parasol already looked quite black, and did not cover madame, whose
skirt was sopping. But this did not worry her. In spite of the
rain she inspected both the kitchen and fruit gardens, stopping at each tree, and leaning over each bed of vegetables.
Then she ran and gave a look down the well, raised a frame to
see what was underneath, and became quite absorbed in the
contemplation of an enormous pumpkin. Her business was to
go along every path, to take immediate possession of all these
things, of which she used to dream when she dragged her
work-girl's shoes along the streets of Paris. The rain fell faster
still, but she did not notice it, and only regretted that the night
was coming on apace. She could no longer see plainly, so she
felt with her hands whenever she had a doubt. All of a sudden,
in the twilight, she discovered some strawberries. Then her
childhood seemed to return to her.

"Strawberries! strawberries! There are some, I feel them!
Zoé, a plate! Come and gather some strawberries."

And Nana, who had stooped down in the mud, let go of her
parasol, and received the full force of the shower. With her
hands all wet, she gathered the strawberries among the leaves.
Zoé, however, did not bring the plate. As the young woman got
up, she had a fright. She thought she had noticed something
move.

"An animal!" she cried; but astonishment rooted her to the
centre of the path. It was a man, and she had recognised him.

"Why! it's baby! Whatever are you doing there, baby?"

"I've come, of course!" replied George.

She remained lost in surprise. "Did you then hear from the
gardener of my arrival? Oh! the child! He is soaked!"

"Ah! I must tell you. It began to rain after I started, and then
I didn't want to go round by Gumières, and in crossing the
Choue, I slipped and fell into a confounded pool."

Nana at once forgot the strawberries. She was all trembling, and full of pity. That poor Zizi* in a pool of water! She dragged him towards the house. She talked of making up a big fire.

"You know," he murmured, stopping her in the darkness, "I was hiding, because I was afraid of being scolded like at Paris, when I came to see you without being expected."

She began to laugh without answering, and kissed him on the forehead. Until that day she had treated him like a child, not thinking seriously of his declarations, and amusing herself with him as with a youngster of no consequence. She made a great deal of fuss so that he should be comfortable. She insisted on the fire lighted in her bed-room. They would be more cozy there. The sight of George did not surprise Zoé, used to all sorts of meetings; but the gardener, who brought up some wood, was struck dumb on seeing the gentleman dripping with water, to whom he was certain he had not opened the door. He was sent away, as nothing more was required. A lamp lighted the room, whilst the fire burst into a bright blaze.

"He will never become dry, he will catch cold," said Nana, seeing George shiver.

And not another pair of trousers in the house! She was on the point of calling the gardener, when an idea struck her. Zoé, who had been unpacking the trunks in the dressing-room, brought madame some clean clothes for her to change—a chemise, some petticoats, and a dressing-gown.

"But that's capital!" exclaimed the young woman, "Zizi can put on these. Eh! you don't mind putting on my things? When your own clothes are dry you can put them on again, and then hurry back home, so as not to be scolded by your mamma. Be quick, and I will go and change my things in the dressing-room."

When, ten minutes later, she reappeared in a dressing-gown, she clasped her hands in rapture.

"Oh, the love! how pretty he looks as a woman!"

He had merely put on a long night-dress, an embroidered

*This endearment is also baby talk for "penis."

pair of drawers, and a cambric dressing-gown trimmed with lace. In those clothes he looked like a girl, with his fair arms uncovered, and his light hair, still wet, hanging down his neck.

"He is really as slim as I am!" said Nana, taking hold of him round the waist. "Zoé, come and see how well they fit him. Eh! don't they look as though they were made for him? all except the body part, which is too broad. He hasn't as much as I have, poor Zizi."

"There certainly is a slight difference," murmured George, smiling.

All three were highly amused. Nana buttoned the dressing-gown all down the front so that he should look decent. She turned him about like a doll, gave him little taps, and made the skirt swell out behind. And she questioned him, asking him if he was comfortable, and if he was warm enough. Oh, yes! he was all right. Nothing was warmer than a woman's night-dress; if he had had his way he would always have worn one. He rolled himself about in it, pleased with the soft touch of the linen, with that loose garment that smelt so nice, and which to him seemed slightly impregnated with the warmth of Nana's body. Zoé had taken his wet clothes down to the kitchen, so as to dry them as quickly as possible before a large wood fire. Then George, stretched out in an easy chair, dared to make an avowal.

"I say, aren't you going to have anything to eat to-night? I'm famishing. I haven't had any dinner."

Nana was very angry. What a great stupid he was to run away from his mamma with an empty stomach, just to go and throw himself into a pool of water! But she also felt rather hungry. Of course they must have something to eat, only they would have to do the best they could. And they improvised the funniest dinner ever heard of, on a little table drawn up before the fire. Zoé ran over to the gardener, who had made some cabbage soup in case madame did not dine at Orleans. Madame had forgotten to mention in her letter what she required to be got ready. Fortunately the cellar was well-stocked. They had, there-fore, some cabbage soup, with a piece of bacon. Then, looking in her bag, Nana produced all sorts of things which she had taken the precaution to provide: a little goose liver pasty, a packet of sweets, some oranges. They both ate like ogres, with the appetite of youth, and, like comrades, without ceremony. Nana called George "my dear," she thought it more familiar and loving. For dessert they devoured a pot of jam, discovered on the top shelf of a cupboard, both eating in turn with the same spoon so as not to disturb Zoé.

"Ah, my dear!" said Nana, as she pushed the little table on one side, "for ten years I haven't dined so well."

It was getting late, however, and she wished to send the youngster home so as not to bring him into trouble. He kept repeating that he had plenty of time; besides, the clothes were not drying well—Zoé declared that they would take at least an hour longer, and as she was every minute falling asleep, being tired out by the journey, they sent her off to bed. Then they were left alone in the silent house. It was a calm, pleasant night. The fire was burning low, and the heat was rather stifling in the big room, the bed of which Zoé had made before leaving. Nana, feeling too warm, rose to open the window for a minute. But she uttered a faint cry.

"Heavens! how lovely it is! Look, my dear."

George joined her, and, as though the window-rail was not long enough for two, he put his arm round Nana's waist and rested his head on her shoulder. The weather had suddenly changed, the sky was perfectly clear and studded with stars, whilst a full moon lit up the country with a sheet of gold. A sovereign peacefulness hung over all, the valley widened and opened on to the immensity of the plain, where the trees cast shadows that looked like islands in the motionless lake of light. And Nana was deeply moved and felt like a child again. She was sure she had dreamt of such nights at an epoch of her life which she could no longer recall. All that she had seen since she left the train, this vast expanse of fields, this grass that smelt so nice, this house, these vegetables, all these upset her to such an extent, that it seemed as though she had left Paris fully twenty years before. Her existence of the previous day was already far away. She felt as she had never previously felt. George, all this while, was slyly kissing her on the neck, which increased her perturbation. With a hesitating hand she repelled him as one would a child when wearied by its caresses, and she repeated that it was time for him to go home. He did not say "no," by-and-by, he would leave by-and-by. But a bird began to sing, then stopped. It was a robin, in an elder bush under the window.

"Wait a minute," murmured George, "the lamp-light frightens him, I will put it out." And, when he came back, again placing his arm around Nana's waist, he added, "We can light it again directly."

Then, as she listened to the robin, whilst the boy pressed close against her, Nana recollected. Yes, it was in novels that she had seen all that. Once, in the days gone by, she would have given her heart to have seen the moon thus, to have heard the robin and to have had a little fellow full of love by her side. Oh, heaven! she could have cried, it all seemed to her so lovely and good! For certain she was born to live a virtuous life. She again repelled George, who was becoming bolder.

"No, leave me, I won't. It would be very wrong at your age. Listen, I will be your mamma."

She had become quite bashful; her face was flushing scarlet. Yet no one could see her. The room behind them was full of the darkness of night, whilst as far as the eye could reach the countryside unfolded the silence and immobility of its solitude. Never before had she felt such shame. Little by little her strength seemed to leave her in spite of her constraint and her struggles. That disguise, that woman's night-dress and that dressing-gown, made her laugh still. It was like a girl friend teasing her.

"Oh! it is wrong, it is wrong," murmured she, after a last effort; and she fell like a virgin into the child's arms, in the face of the beautiful night. The house was hushed in sleep.

On the morrow, when the luncheon bell rang at Les Fondettes, the table in the dining-room was no longer too large. A first vehicle had brought Fauchery and Daguenet, and after them came the Count de Vandeuvres, who had arrived by a later train. George made his appearance the last, looking rather pale and heavy about the eyes. In answer to all inquiries he replied that he was much better, although still upset by the violence of the attack. Madame Hugon, who looked into his face with an anxious smile, passed her hand through his hair, which was badly combed that morning, whilst he drew back as though embarrassed by the caress. During luncheon, she affectionately scolded Vandeuvres, whom she said she had been expecting for five years past.

"Well, here you are at last! How did you manage it?"

Vandeuvres thought best to treat the matter as a joke. He related that he had lost an enormous sum of money the previous evening at his club; so he had started off with the idea of settling down in the provinces.

"Yes, really now, if you can only find me an heiress somewhere in the neighbourhood. There must be some very charming ladies about here."

The old lady was thanking both Daguenet and Fauchery for having so kindly accepted her son's invitation, when she experienced another pleasant surprise on seeing the Marquis de Chouard, who had just arrived in a third vehicle, enter the room.

"Ah!" she exclaimed, "it must be a general meeting this morning. You have all arranged to assemble here. Whatever has happened? For years past I have never been able to get you to come, and now you all arrive together. Oh! but I am not complaining."

Another place was laid at the table. Fauchery found himself seated beside Countess Sabine, who surprised him with her liveliness—she whom he had seen looking so languid, in the austere drawing-room of the Rue Miromesnil. Daguenet, seated on Estelle's left, seemed uncomfortable at being so close to the silent, lanky girl, whose sharp elbows were his horror. Muffat and de Chouard exchanged a sly glance. Vandeuvres continued to joke about his contemplated marriage.

"Respecting ladies," Madame Hugon ended by saying to him, "I have a new neighbour whom you probably know"; and she mentioned Nana.

Vandeuvres affected the utmost astonishment. "What! Nana's country-house is near here?"

Fauchery and Daguenet also pretended to be surprised. The Marquis de Chouard devoured the breast of a chicken, without appearing to understand. Not one of the men had smiled.

"Without doubt," resumed the old lady; "and what is more, this person arrived last night at La Mignotte, as I had expected. I heard of it this morning from the gardener."

On receiving this information, none of the gentlemen could hide their genuine astonishment. They all looked up. What! Nana had arrived! And they were not expecting her till the morrow; they had thought they were before her! George, alone, did not raise his eyes, but looked at his tumbler in a wearied sort of way. Ever since the beginning of the meal he had seemed asleep with his eyes open, and a vague smile hovered about his lips.

"Do you still suffer, Zizi?" inquired his mother, who scarcely moved her eyes from him.

He started, and blushing, answered that he was quite well again; but he still preserved the look of a girl who had been dancing too much.

"What is the matter with your neck?" suddenly asked Madame Hugon, in a frightened tone of voice. "It is all red."

He became confused, and could scarcely stammer out a reply. He didn't know; he hadn't anything the matter with his neck. Then, pulling up his shirt collar, he added, "Ah! yes, some insect stung me."

The Marquis de Chouard cast a sidelong glance at the red mark. Muffat also looked at George. Luncheon was drawing to an end, and they began to arrange some excursions in the neighbourhood. Fauchery became more and more affected by Countess Sabine's gaiety. As he passed a plate of fruit to her their hands touched, and she looked at him for a second with so deep a gaze that his thoughts again reverted to that confidence of which he was the recipient on a night of intoxication. Then she no longer appeared the same. There was something that was more pronounced about her. Her grey silk dress, made loose at the shoulders, gave a sort of ease to her refined and sensitive elegance.

On leaving the table, Daguenet remained behind with

Fauchery, to make some rather facetious and coarse remarks about Estelle. "A pretty broomstick to shove into a fellow's arms." However, he became serious when the journalist mentioned the amount of her dowry: four hundred thousand francs.

"And the mother?" inquired Fauchery. "She's a fine woman, isn't she?"

"Oh! she as much as you like! But there's no chance, my boy!"

"Bah! one never knows without trying!"

No one was going out that day, as it was still very showery. George had hastily disappeared and locked himself in his room. The gentlemen avoided coming to an explanation among themselves, though they individually knew very well what reasons had brought them together. Vandeuvres, who had lost heavily at play, had indeed entertained the idea of spending some time in the country, and counted on the proximity of a female friend to reconcile him to his voluntary exile. Fauchery, taking advantage of the holiday allowed him by Rose, who just then was very much occupied, proposed to make an arrangement with Nana for a second article, in the event of a country life bringing their hearts together again. Daguenet, who had been sulky ever since Steiner appeared on the scene, thought of making it up again, and of picking up a few crumbs of love, should occasion offer. As for the Marquis de Chouard, he bided his time. But among all these men on the track of Venus, only half free of her paint, Muffat was the most ardent, the most tormented with new sensations of desire, of fear, and of anger, which contended in his agitated person. He had a distinct promise. Nana was expecting him. Why, then, had she left Paris two days earlier? He determined to go to La Mignotte that very night, after the dinner.

That evening, as the count left the grounds, George followed him. He parted from him on the road to Gumières, and, wading across the Choue, arrived at Nana's all out of breath, his eyes filled with tears of rage. Ah! he understood. That old fellow who was on the road had an appointment with her. Nana, astonished at this display of jealousy, uneasy at the turn things were taking, folded her arms around him, and consoled him as well as she could. No; he was mistaken. She was not expecting any one. If the gentleman was coming it was not her fault. Zizi was a great stupid to put himself out so much about nothing at all! She swore by her child that she loved no one but her George, and she kissed him, and wiped away his tears.

"Listen, you will see that everything is for you," said she, when he had become calmer. "Steiner has arrived, he is upstairs. You know, my darling, I can't send him away."

"Yes, I know; I don't mind him," murmured the youngster.

"Well, I have put him in the room at the end of the passage, pretending that I was not well. He is unpacking his portmanteau. As no one saw you come in, run up quick and hide yourself in my room, and wait for me."

George jumped up and put his arms round her. It was true, then, she did love him a little! So it would be yesterday over again? They would turn out the lamp, and remain together till daylight dispelled the darkness. Then, hearing a bell ring, he noiselessly hurried away. Upstairs, in the bed-room, he at once took off his shoes so as not to make any noise. Then he hid himself, crouched upon the floor, behind a curtain, and waited like a good boy.

When Count Muffat appeared, Nana felt a slight awkwardness, having scarcely regained her composure after the scene with George. She had promised the count, and she would have liked to have kept her promise, because he seemed a man who meant business. But, really, who could ever have foreseen all that had occurred the previous day? The journey, this house that she had never known before, the youngster who had arrived soaking wet; and how nice it had all seemed to her, and how pleasant a continuance of it would be! So much the worse for the gentleman! For three months past she had dallied with him, playing the respectable woman, so as to inflame him all the more. Well! he would have to wait a bit longer. He could hook it if it didn't please him. She would rather chuck up everything than be unfaithful to George.

The count had seated himself in the ceremonious way of a country neighbour making a call. His hands alone trembled slightly. In his sanguineous constitution, still in a state of virginity, inordinate desire, scourged by Nana's skilful tactics, was at length producing frightful ravages. That grave-looking man, that chamberlain who traversed with such a dignified step the gilded saloons of the Tuileries, would, at night-time, bite the bolster on his bed and sob aloud, carried away by his exasperation, and ever invoking the same sensual vision. But this time he was determined to end his suffering. Along the road, in the peaceful twilight, he had thought of gratifying his passion by force; and directly they had exchanged a few words, he tried to take Nana in his arms.

"No, no, mind what you are doing," said she simply, without getting angry, and smiling at him all the time.

At length he caught her, his teeth firmly clenched; then, as she struggled, he became brutal, and coarsely told her why he had come. She, still smiling, though embarrassed, held his hands. She spoke to him lovingly, so as to make her refusal seem less harsh.

"Come, my darling, keep quiet. Really, I cannot. Steiner is upstairs."

But he was mad; never before had she seen a man in such a state. She began to feel frightened. She placed her hand over his mouth to hush the cries he uttered, and, lowering her voice, she begged him to keep quiet, to let her go. Steiner was descending the stairs. Her position had become ridiculous! When Steiner entered the room, he heard Nana, who was comfortably stretched out in an easy chair, saying,

"As for myself, I adore the country."

Turning her head, she interrupted herself, and added, "Darling, this is Count Muffat, who noticed the lights as he was passing by, and has just called in to bid us welcome."

The two men shook hands. Muffat stood an instant without speaking, his face in shadow. Steiner seemed sulky. They talked of Paris; business was very bad, and some most abominable things had occured on the Bourse. At the end of a quarter of an hour, Muffat took his leave. And as the young woman accompanied him to the door, he asked, without obtaining it, an appointment for the following evening. Steiner, almost immediately, went off to bed, grumbling against the ailments that were always affecting the female sex. At last, the two old fellows were got rid of! When Nana was at length able to rejoin George, she found him still patiently waiting behind his curtain. The room was in darkness. He had drawn her down on the floor beside him, and they played together, rolling about like children, stopping every now and then, and smothering their laughter with kisses, whenever their feet knocked against any of the furniture. Afar off, on the Gumières road, Count Muffat was walking slowly along, holding his hat in his hand, and cooling his heated brow in the fresh night air.

Then, the following days, their life was adorable. In the youngster's company, Nana seemed once more a girl of fifteen. Beneath the child's caresses, the flower of love bloomed again, in spite of her knowledge of man, and the loathing it caused her. She found herself constantly blushing, she experienced an emotion that made her shiver, an inclination to laugh and cry, in short all the feelings of an awakened virginity added to desires of which she was ashamed. She had never felt thus before. The country filled her with tenderness. When a young child, she had for a long time desired to live in a meadow with a goat, because one day, on the slope of the fortifications, she had seen a goat bleating, fastened to a stake. Now, this estate, all this land belonged to her, swelled her with an overflowing emotion, so much were her wildest dreams more than realised. She again experienced all the sensations of a child; and at night-time, when dizzy from a day spent in the open air, intoxicated with the odour of the trees and flowers, she went upstairs to rejoin her Zizi, hidden behind the curtain, it seemed to her like a freak of a school-girl home for the holidays, a love passage with a cousin whom she was evidently to marry. She trembled at the least sound, as though afraid of being caught by her parents; she tasted all the delicious embarrassments, all the voluptuous fears of a first fault.

At this time, Nana indulged in the fancies of a sentimental girl. She would look at the moon for hours. One night, she insisted on going down into the garden with George, when all the household was asleep; and they wandered about under the trees, their arms round each other's waists, then they lay down on the grass and got thoroughly soaked with the dew. Another time, in the bed-room, after a rather long pause, Nana sobbed on the youngster's neck, murmuring she was afraid she was going to die. She often sang in a low voice a ballad of Madame Lerat's, full of flowers and birds, becoming affected even to tears, and interrupting herself to clasp George in a passionate embrace and cause him to utter vows of eternal love. In short, she behaved very foolishly as she herself would often admit, when, becoming comrades again, they both smoked cigarettes seated on the edge of the bedstead, their heels knocking against the wood-work.

But what caused the young woman's heart completely to melt was the arrival of little Louis. Her attack of maternal love bordered on madness. She carried her son into the sunshine to see him sprawl about; she rolled with him over the grass, after dressing him like a prince. She at once insisted that he should sleep near her, in the next room, where Madame Lerat, very much smitten with the country, commenced to snore as soon as she was lying on her back. And little Louis did not in the least interfere with her love for Zizi; on the contrary. She said that she had two children; she confounded them in the same caprice of affection. During the night, on more than ten occasions, she quitted Zizi to go and see if little Louis was breathing all right; but when she returned she cuddled her Zizi with the remains of her maternal caresses. She acted the mamma towards him; whilst he, vicious youngster! liking very much to be little in the arms of that big girl, let her nurse him like a baby being rocked to sleep. It was so nice that, charmed with this existence, she seriously proposed to him that they should never again leave the country. They would send every one away, and live alone together—he, she, and the baby. And they built a thousand castles in the air until daybreak, without hearing Madame Lerat, who, tired out with gathering wild flowers, snored loud enough to waken the whole household.

This fine life lasted for nearly a week. Count Muffat came every night, and went back home with swollen features and hot, feverish hands. One night he was not even admitted,

Steiner having been obliged to go to Paris. He was told that madame was very unwell. Each day Nana revolted more and more at the idea of being unfaithful to George, so young and so innocent, and who had put his faith in her! She would have considered herself the most worthless of women. Besides, it would have disgusted her too much. Zoé, who assisted at this adventure with silent disdain, thought that madame was becoming cracked.

All on a sudden, on the sixth day, a band of visitors broke in upon this idyllic existence. Nana had invited a number of people, thinking that no one would come. So she was very much astounded and very much vexed, one afternoon, on seeing an omnibus full of men and women draw up in front of the iron gates of La Mignotte.

"Here we are!" cried Mignon, the first to alight from the vehicle, from which he extricated his sons, Henri and Charles.

Labordette appeared next, and immediately assisted a number of ladies to descend—Lucy Stewart, Caroline Héquet, Tatan Néné, Maria Blond. Nana was hoping that that was the end, when La Faloise jumped out, to receive into his trembling arms Gaga and her daughter Amélie. That made eleven persons. It was difficult to find room for them all. At La Mignotte there were five guest chambers, one of which was occupied by Madame Lerat and little Louis. The largest bedroom was given to the Gaga and La Faloise family, and it was decided that Amélie should sleep on a camp-bedstead in the dressing-room adjoining. Mignon and his two sons had the third bedroom; Labordette the fourth. There still remained one, which was turned into a dormitory, with four beds for Lucy, Caroline, Tatan, and Maria. As for Steiner, he would have to sleep on the sofa in the drawing-room. After the lapse of an hour, when everything was settled, Nana, who first of all had felt furious, was delighted at doing the honours of her country abode. The ladies complimented her on La Mignotte—a most enchanting place, my dear! Then they brought her a puff of Paris air, the little scandals of the week. They all spoke at once, with sundry little taps, and exclamations, and bursts of laughter. And Bordenave! by the way, what had he said of her little escapade?

Why nothing much. After bellowing out that he would have her brought back by the gendarmes, when the evening came he merely filled her place with the understudy; and she, little Violaine, had scored a great success in the "Blonde Venus." This piece of news made Nana serious. It was only four o'clock. They began to talk of going for a stroll.

"You don't know," said Nana, "I was about to get some potatoes when you arrived."

So they all wanted to go and pick up potatoes, without even changing their clothes. They made quite a party. The gardener and two lads were already in the field, at the extreme end of the estate. The ladies knelt down on the ground, feeling in the earth with their fingers covered with rings, crying out every time they discovered a potato of any size. They thought it all so amusing! But Tatan Néné was in her element. She had picked up so many in her younger days, that she so far forgot herself as to give the others the benefit of her experience and to ridicule their awkwardness. The gentlemen took it more coolly. Mignon, looking a very worthy man, profited by his stay in the country to complete his sons' education. He talked to them of Parmentier, the introducer of the potato into France. In the evening the dinner was madly gay. Every one had an enormous appetite. Nana, very far gone, had a row with her butler, who had been at the Bishop of Orleans'. The ladies smoked with their coffee. Sounds of feasting and revelry issued through the windows, and were lost in the distance, in the serenity of the night; whilst between the hedges the belated peasants turned their heads and looked at the house blazing with light.

"What a nuisance it is you are all going away again the day after to-morrow," observed Nana. "We must arrange some excursion whilst you are here."

So it was settled that on the morrow, a Sunday, they should all go and visit the ruins of the ancient abbey of Chamont, which was situated about seven miles off. Five carriages were to come from Orleans to take the party after luncheon, and bring them back to dine at La Mignotte, towards seven o'clock in the evening. It would be delightful.

That night, as usual, Count Muffat ascended the hill to ring the bell at the iron gates. But the lights in the windows, the loud laughter surprised him. Recognising Mignon's voice he understood it all, and went away enraged by this new obstacle, driven to extremities, determined to use violence. George, who entered by a little side-door of which he had a key, quietly ascended to Nana's bed-room, keeping close to the walls. Only he had to wait for her until past midnight. She came at last, very tipsy, and more maternal even than on the other nights. When she drank it made her so loving that there was rather too much of it. Thus, she insisted on George's accompanying her to the abbey of Chamont. He resisted, afraid of being seen: if he was noticed in a carriage with her it would cause a frightful scandal. But she burst into tears, seized with the noisy despair of a discarded woman, and he consoled her, and faithfully promised to be one of the party.

"Then you do really love me?" she stuttered. "Say that you love me a lot. Tell me, my own darling, if I died, would you be very unhappy?"

At Les Fondettes, Nana's proximity upset the whole household. Every morning, during luncheon, worthy Madame Hugon talked in spite of herself about that woman, relating all that her gardener had told her, experiencing that kind of witchery exercised by gay women over the most respectable ladies. She, usually so tolerant, felt indignant and exasperated, with the vague presentiment of some misfortune, which alarmed her at eventide, as though she had known of the presence in the neighbourhood of a wild beast escaped from some menagerie. And she squabbled with her guests, accusing them all of wandering round about La Mignotte. Count de Vandeuvres had been seen laughing on the high road with a lady wearing a large quantity of hair; but he defended himself, swore that it wasn't Nana, for indeed it was Lucy who accompanied him for the purpose of telling him how she had just sent her third prince to the right about. The Marquis de Chouard went also for long walks every day; but he began to talk at once of his doctor's directions. As for Daguenet and Fauchery, Madame Hugon treated them very unjustly. The first, espe-

cially, never went outside the grounds of Les Fondettes, having
abandoned his intention of seeking to renew his intimate acquaintance with Nana, and making himself respectfully assidu-
ous towards Estelle. Fauchery also remained with the Muffat
ladies. On one occasion only he had come across Mignon in a
lane, his hands full of flowers, and giving a lesson in botany to
his sons. The two men had shaken hands and talked of Rose.
She was very well; each of them had received a letter from her
that very morning, in which she told them to take advantage of
the country air as long as they could. Of all her guests, therefore, the old lady only spared Count Muffat and George. The
count, who pretended he had some very important business to
attend to at Orleans, could not be running after girls; and as
for George, the poor child was beginning to cause her the
greatest anxiety, for every evening he was seized with the most
violent headaches, which forced him to go to bed before it was
really dark.

Fauchery had elected himself Countess Sabine's cavalier in
waiting, whilst the count disappeared regularly every afternoon. Whenever they went about the grounds he carried her
parasol and her campstool. Besides, he amused her with his
journalistic gossip, and soon established between them one of
those sudden intimacies which country life countenances. She
appeared to surrender at once, awakened to a second youth in
the society of this young man, whose noisy, scoffing ways
seemed incapable of compromising her. And sometimes, when
they found themselves alone for a second behind some hedge,
their eyes would seek each other's; they would stop in the
midst of a laugh, abruptly serious, with a languishing look as
though they had divined and understood each other.

On the Friday it had been necessary to lay another place at
lunch. M. Théophile Venot, whom Madame Hugon recollected having invited at the Muffats' the previous winter, had
just arrived. He put on his most agreeable look, and affected
the indifferent air of an insignificant person without appearing to notice the uneasy deference with which he was treated.
When he had succeeded in making himself forgotten, and
while crunching some little pieces of sugar during dessert, he

watched Daguenet, who was handing some strawberries to Estelle, and listened to Fauchery, one of whose anecdotes seemed to amuse the countess very much. The moment anyone looked at him he smiled in his quiet way.

On leaving the table, M. Venot took the count's arm and led him into the grounds. It was known that he exercised a great influence over the count, ever since his mother's death. Most singular stories were current as to the ex-attorney's domination over the household. Fauchery, whose plans were no doubt considerably interfered with by his arrival, related to George and Daguenet the origin of his fortune—a big lawsuit with which the Jesuits had once intrusted him; and, according to him, this little old fellow, who was a terrible man in spite of his pleasant looks, had now a finger in every clerical pie. The two young fellows began to laugh, for they thought the old man looked a bit of an idiot. The idea of an unknown Venot, of a gigantic Venot, acting for the clergy, seemed to them most comical. But they ceased talking as Count Muffat, still with the old gentleman at his side, returned looking very pale, and with his eyes red as though he had been weeping.

"They have, for certain, been talking of hell," murmured Fauchery jeeringly.

Countess Sabine, who had overheard him, slowly turned her head, and their eyes met, with one of those prolonged looks with which they prudently sounded each other, before running any risk.

Usually, after luncheon, every one adjourned to the end of the flower garden, to a terrace which overlooked the plain. The Sunday afternoon was deliciously mild. Towards ten o'clock in the morning it looked like rain; but the sky, without becoming perfectly clear, had so to say blended into a milky kind of mist, and a sort of luminous dust, all golden with sunshine. Then Madame Hugon suggested that they should go out by the little door of the terrace, and take a stroll in the direction of Gumières, as far as the Choue; she liked walking, being still very active in spite of her sixty years. Every one, moreover, stated that they would rather not have the carriage. They arrived thus, rather disbanded, at the wooden bridge thrown across the stream. Fauchery and Daguenet were in front with the Muffat ladies; the count and the marquis came next, on either side of Madame Hugon; whilst Vandeuvres, looking very stylish, and dreadfully bored at wandering along that high road, brought up the rear, smoking a cigar. M. Venot, slackening or hastening his footsteps, went smilingly from one group to another, as though to hear everything.

"And poor George is at Orleans!" Madame Hugon was saying. "He wished to consult old Doctor Tavernier, who no longer goes out, about his headaches. Yes, you were none of you up; he started before seven this morning. It will be a slight diversion for him, anyhow." But she interrupted herself to remark, "Dear me! why are they waiting on the bridge?"

Truly enough the ladies, and Daguenet and Fauchery, were standing at the foot of the bridge, with hesitating looks, as though some obstacle caused them uneasiness. The way seemed free, however.

"Straight on!" cried the count.

They did not move, but remained watching something that was coming and which the others could not see. There was a turn in the road which was bordered on either side by poplars. However, a rumbling noise, gradually increasing, now reached the entire party; there was a sound of wheels, mixed with laughter, and the cracking of whips, and suddenly five carriages appeared, following one after the other, almost crowded enough to break the axle-trees, and enlivened with a mixture of light blue and rose colour dresses.

"Whatever is all this?" asked Madame Hugon in surprise. Then she guessed, she seemed to divine; and indignant at such an invasion crossing her path, she murmured, "Oh, that woman! Walk on, do walk on. Pretend not to—"

But it was too late. The five carriages, which were taking Nana and her guests to the ruins at Chamont, were already close to the little wooden bridge. Fauchery, Daguenet, and the Muffat ladies had to step back, whilst Madame Hugon and the others stopped also, at various distances along the road. It was a superb procession. The laughing in the carriages had ceased; some faces turned round with curiosity. Each party looked at the other, amidst a silence that was only broken by the regular trot of the horses. In the first carriage, Maria Blond and Tatan Néné, reclining like duchesses, their skirts blown out over the wheels, looked disdainfully at the respectable ladies on foot. In the next was Gaga, who almost occupied an entire seat to herself, quite burying La Faloise, of whom only the anxious nose could be seen. Then came Caroline Héquet with Labordette, Lucy Stewart with Mignon and his sons, and at the end of all, accompanied by Steiner, was Nana, who had on the little seat in front of her that poor love of a Zizi, with his knees touching hers.

"It is the last one, is it not?" quietly inquired the countess of Fauchery, affecting not to recognise Nana.

The wheels of Nana's carriage almost grazed her, but she did not move back an inch. The two women had exchanged a searching look—one of those scrutinising glances lasting but a second, yet complete and definite. As for the men, they behaved admirably. Fauchery and Daguenet, perfectly impassive, recognised no one. The marquis, anxious, and afraid of some practical joke on the part of the girls, had plucked a blade of grass, which he was twirling between his fingers. Vandeuvres alone, being at some little distance from the others, just moved his eyelids by way of recognising Lucy, who smiled at him as she passed.

"Take care!" murmured M. Venot, standing behind Count Muffat.

The latter, greatly agitated, followed with his eyes, that vision of Nana, flying away from him. His wife had turned slowly round and was examining him. Then he looked on the ground, as though to lose sight of the galloping horses, who were carrying off his flesh and his heart. His agony almost made him cry aloud. He had understood all on seeing George lost amongst Nana's skirts. A child! It broke his heart to think that she should have preferred a child to himself! He did not mind about Steiner, but a child!

Madame Hugon, however, had not recognised George at first. On passing over the bridge he would have jumped into the stream, had not Nana's knees held him. So, white as snow and cold as ice, he sat immovable, looking at no one. Perhaps they would not see him.

"Ah! good heavens!" suddenly exclaimed the old lady, "it is George who is with her."

The carriages had passed in the midst of that uneasiness felt by persons who knew each other, and who yet did not bow. This delicate encounter, so rapid in reality, had seemed to last an eternity. And, now, the wheels were gaily carrying away into the sunny country those vehicles full of girls, with the wind blowing in their faces. Ribbons were flying about, the laughter commenced again, and jokes passed from one to another; whilst some stood up and gazed back at those highly respectable people, who had remained stationary at the side of the road, looking very much put out. Nana, as she glanced round, could see them hesitate, then retrace their steps without crossing the bridge at all. Madame Hugon was leaning on Count Muffat's arm, silent, and so sad that no one dared console her.

"I say," cried Nana to Lucy, who was leaning out of the carriage in front of hers, "did you notice Fauchery, my dear? Didn't he look a dirty rip? He shall smart for it. And Paul, a chap to whom I have been so kind—not the least sign. Really, they are polite!"

Then she had a frightful quarrel with Steiner, who considered that the gentlemen had behaved admirably. So they were not even worth the raising of a hat? The first blackguard they met might insult them? Thanks, he also was a nice fellow, he was; it only wanted that. One should always bow to a woman.

"Who was the tall one?" called out Lucy, in the midst of the noise caused by the wheels.

"Countess Muffat," answered Steiner.

"There now! I thought as much!" exclaimed Nana. "Well, my boy, in spite of her being a countess, I can tell you she's not worth much. Yes, yes, not worth much. You know I've an eye for that sort of thing, I have. Now, I know her as if I had made her, your countess. Will you bet that that viper Fauchery isn't her lover? I tell you that he is her lover! One can easily see that, between women."

Steiner shrugged his shoulders. Ever since the previous evening his bad temper had been on the increase. He had received some letters which would oblige him to leave on the following morning. Then, too, it wasn't very amusing to come to the country just to sleep on the drawing-room sofa.

"And this poor baby!" resumed Nana, suddenly become tender-hearted, as she caught sight of George, who was sitting pale and erect, and scarce able to breathe.

"Do you think that mamma recognised me?" he at length stammered forth.

"Oh! most decidedly. She cried out. But it's all my fault. He didn't want to come, and I made him. Listen to me, Zizi; shall I write to your mamma? She looks a very kind woman. I will tell her that I never saw you before, and that it was Steiner who brought you to me to-day for the first time."

"No, no, don't write," said George, anxiously. "I will arrange all myself. And, if they make a fuss, I'll come away and never go back again."

But he continued very dejected and absorbed in reflection, trying to invent some lies for the evening. The five vehicles continued along the straight and interminable level road, bordered on either side by some very fine trees. The country around was enveloped in a kind of silvery grey vapour. The ladies continued to pass remarks from one carriage to another, from behind the backs of the coachmen, who laughed to themselves at the strange company they were driving; now and again one of the women would stand up to obtain a better view, and, becoming interested, would remain in that position, leaning against her neighbour's shoulder, until a sudden jerk of the vehicle brought her to her seat again. Caroline Héquet was having some very important conversation with Labordette; they both came to the conclusion that Nana would be wanting to part with her country house in less than three months, and Caroline instructed Labordette to acquire it for her, under the rose, for a very moderate sum. In the carriage preceding them, La Faloise, very spooney, and unable to reach Gaga's apoplectic neck, was depositing kisses on that part of her dress which, almost bursting with the tightness of the fit, covered her backbone; whilst Amélie, sitting bolt upright on the little seat in front, sick of being there with empty arms watching her mother being kissed, kept telling them to leave off. In the next carriage, Mignon, with the view of surprising Lucy, made his sons recite one of La Fontaine's fables—Henri especially was prodigious, he could say it right off without a single mistake. But Maria Blond, at the head of the procession, was beginning to feel awfully bored, tired of poking fun at that fool of a Tatan Néné, who believed her when she said that the Paris dairymen made their eggs out of gum and saffron. It was too far, would they never arrive? And the question, passed from carriage to carriage, at length reached Nana, who, after consulting her coachman, stood up and called to the others:

"In about a quarter of an hour. You see that church over there, behind the trees—" Then, after a slight pause, she resumed: "You don't know, it seems that the owner of the Château de Chamont is an old flame of the time of the first Napoleon. And oh! such a fast one, so Joseph told me, and he heard it when he was at the bishop's. She used to lead a life such as one couldn't lead now. However, she has become awfully religious."

"What's her name?" asked Lucy.

"Madame d'Anglars."

"Irma d'Anglars!—I knew her!" cried Gaga.

From each vehicle there issued a string of exclamations, which were lost in the more rapid trot of the horses. Heads were stretched out to catch a glimpse of Gaga. Maria Blond and Tatan Néné turned round and knelt on the seat, holding on to the closed hood at the back of the carriage, and questions were asked, and malicious observations, tempered with a secret admiration, were made. Gaga had known her, that filled them all with respect for this far away past.

"I was very young, then," resumed Gaga. "All the same, I recollect I used to see her pass. It was said that she was something disgusting at home, but in her carriage she was magnificent! And the most incredible stories circulated—such filthy goings-on that it's a marvel she ever lived through them. It doesn't surprise me that she has a château. She could clear a man out

as easy as breathe on him. Ah! Irma d'Anglars is still among
the living! Well, my little friends, she must be about ninety
now."

On hearing this, the ladies all became very serious. Ninety
years old! There wasn't one of them, as Lucy said, who had a
chance of living to that age. They were all roarers. Nana, too,
declared that she didn't want to make old bones; it was funnier
not to. They had now almost reached their destination, and
their conversation was interrupted by the drivers cracking
their whips as they urged on the tired horses. Yet, in the midst
of the noise, Lucy, jumping to another subject, continued talking, and pressed Nana to leave with the others on the morrow.
The Exhibition was about to close, and the ladies were anxious
to get back to Paris, where the season so far had surpassed
their wildest hopes. But Nana was obstinate. She detested
Paris, she wouldn't go back there for a long time to come.

"Eh, ducky! we'll stay where we are?" said she, squeezing
George's knees, notwithstanding Steiner's presence.

The carriages suddenly stopped, and the party, very much
surprised, alighted in a desert-looking place at the foot of a
hill. One of the drivers had to point out to them with his whip
the ruins of the ancient abbey of Chamont, almost hidden by
the trees. It was a great deception. The ladies were disgusted.
All they could see were a few heaps of rubbish, over-grown with
brambles, and a half tumble-down tower. Really it was ridiculous to come two leagues to see that. The driver then pointed
out to them the chateau, the park belonging to which was
close to the abbey, and he told them they could reach it by following a little path that skirted the walls. They could take a
look round whilst the carriages waited for them in the village.
It was a most delightful walk. The party agreed to try it.

"The deuce! Irma must be very well off!" said Gaga, stopping in front of some iron railings at one of the corners of the
park.

They all gazed in silence at the handsome trees and shrubs
on the other side of the railings. Then they continued along
the narrow path, following the walls of the park, every now and
then raising their eyes to admire the trees, the branches of

which spread out overhead in an impenetrable green canopy. After three minutes' walk they came to some more iron railings, which enabled them to see an extensive lawn, over which two venerable oak trees cast a welcome shade; and three minutes' further walking brought them to some more railings, which exhibited to them an immense avenue, a passage of darkness, at the end of which the sun looked like a bright star. An admiration, at first silent, gradually burst forth into exclamations. They had, at the outset, indulged themselves in chaff, feeling rather envious, however, all the time; but this, decidedly, was too much for them. What a wonder she was, that Irma! Such things as this gave one a grand idea of woman! The trees still continued as plentiful as ever, and at every few steps there were patches of ivy trailing over the wall, with the tops of summer-houses just visible, and screens of poplars succeeding to compact groups of elms and aspens. Would it never come to an end! The ladies, tired of continually following this wall, without catching a glimpse, at every opening, of anything except masses of foliage, were anxious to see the château. They clutched the railings with both hands, pressing their faces against the iron. A feeling of respect took possession of them, while thus kept at a distance, and dreaming of the château hidden in this immensity of trees. After walking quickly for some time, they began to feel really fatigued. Yet there were no signs of the wall coming to an end. At every turn of the path ladies, despairing of ever reaching the end, talked of going back; but the more the length of the walk tired them, the more respectful they became, impressed as they were at every step by the calm and regal majesty of the domain.

"It's positively sickening!" muttered Caroline Héquet between her teeth.

Nana checked her with a shrug of the shoulders. For some little while she had not said a word, but walked along, looking slightly pale and very serious. Suddenly, at another turn, they found themselves close to the village; the wall abruptly terminated, and the château appeared at the end of a spacious courtyard. They all stopped, lost in admiration of the lofty grandeur of the broad entrance-steps, of the twenty windows that studded the facade, of the extent of the three wings, the brick walls of which were framed with stone-work. Henri IV. had inhabited that historic building, in which his bedroom still existed, with its enormous bed hung with Genoa velvet. Nana, deeply affected, sighed like a child.

"My goodness!" murmured she very softly to herself.

But a violent emotion seized upon all. Gaga, on a sudden, stated that it was Irma in person who was standing in front of the church. She recognised her perfectly; always upright, the minx, in spite of her age, and just the same eyes when she assumed her grand air. Vespers were just over. For an instant madame stood within the porch. She wore a silk dress of the colour of faded leaves, and looked very tall and simple, with the venerable countenance of an old marchioness who had escaped the horrors of the Revolution. In her right hand a bulky prayer-book shone in the sunshine; and she slowly traversed the open space before the church, followed by a footman in livery, who walked at a respectful distance behind her. The congregation was streaming out; all the Chamont folks bowed low as she passed them; an old man kissed her hand; a woman fell on her knees before her. She was a mighty queen, loaded with years and honours. She ascended the steps of her château and disappeared.

"That's what one comes to when one is careful," said Mignon, in a convinced manner, while looking at his sons as though giving them a lesson.

Then every one said something. Labordette thought her wonderfully preserved; Maria Blond called her an offensive name; whilst Lucy became quite angry, saying that one should ever respect old age—in short, they all agreed that she was something stupendous, and then rejoined the carriages. From Chamont to La Mignotte, Nana did not utter a word. She turned round twice to take a look at the château. Lulled by the noise of the wheels, she no longer felt Steiner by her side; she no longer beheld George seated in front of her. A vision rose from out of the twilight—madame still passing slowly along, with the majesty of a mighty queen, loaded with years and honours.

That evening George returned to Les Fondettes in time for dinner. Nana, more and more absent-minded and peculiar, had sent him home to ask his mamma's forgiveness. It was indispensable, said she severely, seized with a sudden respect for family duties. She even made him promise not to return to her that night. She was tired, and he would only be doing his duty in showing obedience. George, very much bored by this moral lesson, appeared before his mother with a heavy heart, and hanging down his head. Luckily for him, his brother Philippe had arrived—a big soldier and a very lively fellow. This dispelled the storm that was impending. Madame Hugon contented herself with looking at him with her eyes full of tears; whilst Philippe, informed of what had occurred, threatened to bring him back by the ears if he ever returned to that woman. George, greatly relieved, slyly thought of a plan by which he might escape the next afternoon towards two o'clock, and arrange about his meetings with Nana.

During dinner, the guests at Les Fondettes seemed labouring under a certain embarrassment. Vandeuvres had announced his departure; he wished to take Lucy back to Paris, amused at the idea of carrying off this woman, whom he had known for ten years past without having felt the slightest desire for her person before. The Marquis de Chouard, his nose buried in his plate, was thinking of Gaga's young lady; he recollected having nursed her on his knee. How quickly children grew up! She was really becoming quite a plump little thing. Count Muffat, his face very red, remained absorbed in reflection. He continually glanced at George. When dinner was over he went and shut himself in his room, complaining of a slight touch of fever. M. Venot had hastened after him; and upstairs there was quite a scene between them. The count had flung himself on the bed and was stifling his nervous sobs in the pillow, whilst M. Venot, in a mild tone of voice, called him his brother, and exhorted him to implore the divine mercy. He heard not, he had a rattling in his throat. All on a sudden, he jumped from the bed, and stammered,

"I am going—I can no longer resist—"

"Very well," said the old man, "I will go with you."

As they went out, two shadows were disappearing in the depths of a side-walk. Every night, Fauchery and Countess Sabine now let Daguenet help Estelle make the tea. On the high road, the count walked at such a pace, that his companion was obliged to run to keep up with him. Though short of breath, the old man did not cease offering him the best possible arguments against succumbing to the temptations of the flesh. The other never opened his mouth, but hurried onwards in the darkness. When he reached La Mignotte, however, he said,

"I can fight no more—leave me."

"Then, God's will be done," murmured M. Venot. "He takes all means to assure his triumph. Your sin will become one of his weapons."

At La Mignotte, a good deal of quarrelling went on during the repast. Nana had received a letter from Bordenave, in which he advised her to take plenty of rest, but in a way that showed he did not care a pin about her: little Violaine was called twice before the curtain every night. And, as Mignon again pressed her to leave with them all on the morrow, Nana, exasperated, declared that she was not in want of advice from any one. Besides, whilst at table, she had behaved in a most ridiculously strait-laced manner. Madame Lerat, having made use of a rather objectionable word, she cried out—hang it all! she would allow nobody, not even her aunt, to utter filthy expressions in her presence. Then influenced by an idiotic attack of respectability, she bored everyone with her goody-goody sentiments, with her ideas of giving little Louis a religious education, and a whole course of good behaviour for herself. As they all laughed, she made use of some very profound words, wagging her head like a worthy woman thoroughly convinced, saying that order alone led to fortune, and that she didn't want to die on a dung heap. The other women, having had enough of it, protested. Was it possible! some one must have changed Nana! But she, immovable in her seat, relapsed into her reverie, her eyes gazing into space, and conjuring up a vision of a Nana very rich and very much bowed to.

When Muffat arrived, they were all just going up to bed.

Labordette noticed him in the garden, and, understanding his object, rendered him the service of getting Steiner out of the way, and of leading him by the hand along the dark passage to the door of Nana's room. Labordette, for this sort of jobs, had a most gentlemanly way, was very dexterous, and seemed delighted at conducing to another's happiness. Nana showed no surprise, but merely felt bored by Muffat's persistence. However, one must have an eye for business during life! It was stupid to love, it led to nothing. Besides, she had scruples on account of Zizi's youth: she had really behaved disgracefully. Well! she would return to the right path, and go for the old fellow.

"Zoé," said she to the maid who was only too delighted to leave the country, "pack the trunks the first thing to-morrow morning. We are going back to Paris."

And she allowed Muffat to remain, though it caused her no pleasure.

CHAPTER VII

Three months later, one night in December, Count Muffat was walking up and down the Passage des Panoramas. It was a very mild evening. A shower had just driven a crowd of people into the Passage. There was quite a mob, and it was a slow and difficult task to pass along between the shops on either side. Beneath the glass roof, brightened by the reflection, there was a most fierce illumination, consisting of an endless string of lights—white globes, red and blue lamps, rows of flaring gas-jets, and monstrous watches and fans formed of flames of fire—burning without any protection whatsoever; and the medley of colours in the various shop windows—the gold of the jewellers, the crystal vases of the confectioners, the pale silks of the milliners—blazed behind the spotless plate-glass, in the strong light cast by the reflectors; whilst among the chaos of gaudily painted signs, an enormous red glove in the distance looked like a bleeding hand, cut off and fixed to a yellow cuff.

Count Muffat had strolled leisurely as far as the Boulevard. He cast a glance on the pavement, then slowly retraced his footsteps, keeping close to the shops. A damp and warm air filled the narrow thoroughfare with a kind of luminous vapour. Along the flagstones, wet from the drippings of umbrellas, footsteps reverberated continuously, without the sound of a single voice. The passers-by, elbowing the count at each turn, gazed at his impassive face, rendered paler than usual by the glare of the gas. So, to escape from their curiosity, he went and stood in front of a stationer's shop, where he inspected, apparently with profound attention, a display of glass paperweights, containing coloured representations of landscapes and flowers.

But in reality he saw nothing. He was thinking of Nana. Why had she lied to him again? That morning she had written to tell him not to come to her in the evening, pretending that little Louis was ill, and that she would stay with him all night at her aunt's. But he, being suspicious, had called at her house, and had learned from the concierge that madame had just gone off to her theatre. It surprised him, for he knew that she had no part in the new piece. Why, then, that lie, and what could she be doing at the Variety Theatre that evening?

Pushed against by some passer-by, the count, without knowing he did so, quitted the paper-weights, and found himself in front of a window full of miscellaneous articles, and looking in his absorbed way at a quantity of pocket-books and cigar-cases, all which had the same little blue swallow painted on one of the corners. Nana was certainly altered. In the early days, after her return from the country, she used to send him mad when she kissed him on the face and whiskers, with the little playful ways of a kitten, swearing that he was her ducky darling, the only little man whom she adored. He no longer feared George, who was kept by his mother at Les Fondettes. There remained fat old Steiner, whose place he supposed he had taken, but he had never dared to ask a question on the subject. He knew that Steiner was in a great mess about money matters, and on the point of being declared a defaulter at the Bourse, and that his only chance was a rise in the shares of the Salt Works of the Landes. If he ever met him at Nana's she would always explain, in a reasonable sort of way, that she had not the heart to send him off like a dog, after all he had spent upon her. Besides, for three months past, he, the count, had lived in the midst of a sort of a sensual whirlpool, outside of which he understood nothing very clearly but the necessity of possessing Nana. This late awakening of his flesh was like the gluttony of a child, which leaves no room for either vanity or jealousy. Only a precise sensation could strike him: Nana was not as nice as at first, she no longer kissed him on the beard. This caused him some anxiety, and, as a man ignorant of the ways of women, he asked himself what she could have to reproach him with. Yet, he fancied that he satisfied all her desires; and his thoughts returned to the letter of the morning, to that complicated lie, told for the simple object of spending the evening at her theatre. Jostled again by the crowd, he had crossed the Passage, and was racking his brain at the entrance to a restaurant, his eyes fixed on some plucked larks and a fine salmon, which were displayed in the window.

At length he seemed to tear himself from this spectacle. He pulled himself together, and, raising his eyes, noticed that it was close upon nine o'clock. Nana would soon be coming out, and he would insist upon knowing the truth; and he walked about, recalling to mind the evenings already spent in that place, when he used to call for her at the stage door of the theatre. He knew all the shops. He recognised their odours in the atmosphere laden with the stench of gas, the strong smell of Russian leather, the fragrance of vanilla which came from the basement of a dealer in chocolate, the whiffs of musk issuing from the open doors of the perfumers; and he no longer dared stop in front of the pale faces of the shop-women, who placidly surveyed him as an old acquaintance. One minute he appeared to study the row of little round windows above the shops, in the midst of the different signs, as though he saw them for the first time. Then he went again as far as the Boulevard, and stood there a little while. The rain now only came down in very fine drops, which, falling cold upon his hands, calmed him. Now his thoughts wandered to his wife, who was at a château near Mâcon, with her friend Madame de Chezelles, who had been very unwell ever since the autumn. The vehicles on the Boulevard rolled along in a river of mud. The country must be unbearable in such weather. But, this anxiety suddenly returning, he plunged once more into the stifling heat of the Passage, and walked with rapid strides past the loungers. The idea had just occurred to him that, if Nana had any doubts about his coming, she might make off by the Galerie Montmartre.

From that moment the count watched at the stage-door itself. He did not like waiting in that bit of a lobby, where he was afraid of being recognised. It was at the junction of the Galerie des Variétés and of the Galerie Saint-Marc,[1] a nasty corner, with some obscure shops—a cobbler who never had any customers, dealers in musty furniture, a smoky reading-room in a state of somnolence, with its shaded lamps shedding a green light at night. Hereabouts one could always see gentlemen stylishly dressed, patiently wandering about amongst all that usually encumbers a stage-door—drunken scene-shifters, and painted hussies in gaudy rags. A single gas-jet, in an unwashed globe, lighted up the entrance. One moment Muffat had the idea of questioning Madame Bron, but then he feared that, should Nana hear of his being there, she might leave by the Boulevard. He resumed his walk, resolved to wait until he was turned out when the man shut the gates, as had already happened to him on two occasions.

The thought of going back alone filled his heart with anguish. Each time that any dressed-up girls, or men in dirty garments, came out and looked at him, he went and stood in front of the reading-room, where, between a couple of posters in the window, he always beheld the same sight—a little old man, sitting upright and alone at the immense table, in the green light of a lamp, reading a green newspaper which he held in his green hands. But a few minutes before ten o'clock, another gentleman—a tall handsome man, fair, and wearing well-fitting gloves, began also to wander about outside the theatre. Then every time they met, they mistrustfully gave each other a sidelong glance. The count walked as far as the junction of the two galleries, which was decorated with a tall mirror; and, seeing himself in it looking so solemn-faced, and with such a correct gait, he was seized with shame, mixed with fear.

Ten o'clock struck. Muffat suddenly remembered that it was easy enough for him to see if Nana was in her dressing-room. He went up the three steps, passed through the little hall besmeared with a coat of yellow paint, and reached the courtyard by a door that was only latched. At that hour the courtyard, narrow and damp like a well, with its foul-smelling closets, its water-tap, the kitchen-stove, and the plants with which the doorkeeper lumbered it, was bathed in a black mist; but the two walls which rose up, studded with windows, were ablaze with light. Below were the property-room and the firemen's station, on the left the manager's rooms, on the right and up above the dressing-rooms. On the sides of this well they looked like so many oven doors opening into darkness. The count had at once noticed a light in the window of the dressing-room on the first floor; and, feeling relieved and happy, he stood there in the greasy mud, looking up in the air, and inhaling the unsavoury stench at this back of an old Parisian house. Large drops were running down from a cracked water pipe. A ray of gaslight, from Madame Bron's window, gave a yellow tinge to a bit of the moss-covered pavement, to the foot of a wall eaten away by the water from a sink, and to a heap of rubbish on which innumerable old pails and cracked pots and pans had been thrown together, with a saucepan in which a scraggy spindle-tree was vainly endeavouring to grow. There was heard the sound of a window opening, and the count hastened away.

Nana would certainly be coming out directly. He returned to the window of the reading-room. In the deep shadow, broken only by a faint glimmer like that of a night-light, the little old man could still be seen there with his face buried in his paper. Then the count walked about again, strolling rather farther off. He crossed the main gallery, and followed the Galerie des Variétés as far as the Galerie Feydeau, cold and deserted, and plunged in a lugubrious obscurity; and then he returned, and, passing before the theatre, ventured along the Galerie Saint-Marc as far as the Galerie Montmartre, where he watched a machine cutting up sugar in a grocer's shop. But on his third turn, the fear that Nana might go off behind his back made him lose all self-respect. He went and stood with the fair gentleman right opposite the stage-door, and they both exchanged a glance of fraternal humility, lighted up with a remnant of mistrust as to a possible rivalry. Some scene-shifters who came out to smoke their pipes during one of the acts shoved up against them, without either of them daring to complain. Three big girls, with tangled hair and dirty dresses, appeared in the doorway, eating apples and spitting out the cores; and the two men hung down their heads, and submitted to the effrontery of their stares and the coarseness of their remarks, consenting to be dirtied and bespattered by these hussies, who amused themselves by jostling against them as they roughly played together.

Just then Nana came down the three steps. She turned deadly pale as she caught sight of Muffat.

"Ah! it's you," she stammered.

The jeering girls became frightened when they recognised her; and they stood still in a row, erect and serious, like servants caught by their mistress when doing wrong. The tall fair gentleman had moved a little distance off, sad and reassured at the same time.

"Well! give me your arm," resumed Nana abruptly.

They walked slowly away. The count, who had prepared a number of questions, could find nothing to say. It was she who, in a rapid tone of voice, related a long rigmarole—she had stayed at her aunt's till eight o'clock; then, seeing that little Louis was a great deal better, she had had the idea of coming to the theatre for a short time.

"For anything particular?" asked he.

"Yes, a new piece," she replied, after a slight hesitation. "They wanted to have my opinion."

He knew that she lied. But the warmth of her arm, leaning heavily on his, left him without strength to say a word. His anger and his annoyance at having had to wait for her so long had disappeared; his sole anxiety was to keep her, now that he had her with him. On the morrow he would try and find out what she had been about in her dressing-room. Nana, still hesitating, and visibly a prey to the inward struggle of a person trying to regain her composure and to decide on a course of action, stopped, on turning the corner of the Galerie des Variétés, in front of a fan-maker's window.

"Look! isn't it lovely?" she murmured, "the mother-of-pearl one trimmed with feathers." Then, in a careless tone of voice, she added, "So, you are coming home with me?"

"Why, of course," said Muffat, astonished, "as your child is better."

She regretted her long-winded story. Perhaps little Louis had had another attack, and she talked of returning to Batignolles: but as he offered to go too, she let the subject drop. One minute she boiled with rage, like a woman who finds herself caught and who is obliged to show herself submissive and gentle. However, she became resigned to her fate, and resolved to gain time; if she could only get rid of the count by midnight, all would go as she wished.

"Ah! yes; you are a bachelor to-night," she resumed. "Your wife does not return till to-morrow morning, does she?"

"No," replied Muffat, slightly annoyed at hearing her speak of the countess in that familiar way. But she continued to question him, asking the time of the arrival of the train, and wishing to know whether he intended going to the station to meet his wife. She had again slackened her footsteps, as though very much interested in the contents of the shop windows.

"Oh! Look there!" she exclaimed, stopping in front of a jeweller's, "what a funny bracelet!"

She loved the Passage des Panoramas. Ever since her girlhood she had had a passion for the glitter of Paris gew-gaws, counterfeit jewellery, gilded zinc, and imitation leather. Whenever she passed through it she could not drag herself away from the shops, just the same as when she used to run about the streets, lingering opposite the sweets of a confectioner's, listening to the playing of an organ next door, smitten above all by the bad taste of the articles that seemed marvels of cheapness—housewives contained in monstrous walnut shells, rag-pickers' baskets full of toothpicks, Vendome columns and Luxor obelisks* holding thermometers. But that night she was too much upset, she looked without seeing. It bothered her immensely not to have her evening to herself, and, in her secret revolt, she felt a longing to do something foolish. A fat lot of use it was to have men well off! She had just run through the prince and Steiner, indulging all her childish caprices, without in the least knowing where the money had gone to. Her rooms in the Boulevard Haussmann were not even now completely furnished; the drawing-room alone, all in crimson satin, but too full and too lavishly decorated, had a certain effect. At this

---

*That is, cheap Parisian souvenirs. The Vendôme column is a pillar surmounted by a statue of Napoleon I that was erected in 1810, pulled down by the Commune in 1871, and rebuilt after the Commune's suppression. The obelisk was seized by Napoleon from the ancient Egyptian city of Luxor and mounted in the Place de la Concorde in 1836.

time, too, her creditors were dunning her more than ever before, when she was quite without means, and this surprised her immensely, for she looked upon herself as a model of economy. For a month past, that old thief Steiner could only find a thousand francs with the greatest difficulty on occasions when she threatened to kick him out of the place if he did not bring the money. As for Muffat, he was a fool; he had no idea of what a man should give a woman like her, so she could not blame him for his stinginess.

Ah! she would have sent the whole of them to the right about if she had not all day kept repeating to herself a number of wise maxims! One must be reasonable, Zoé was in the habit of saying to her every morning, and she herself had ever present to her mind a sacred recollection, the royal vision of Chamont, constantly invoked and embellished. And that was why, in spite of a tremor of suppressed rage, she walked submissively along, leaning on the count's arm, going from one shop window to another in the midst of the now less frequent passers-by. Outside, the foot-pavement was gradually drying, a cool breeze entered the Passage, sending before it the hot air collected beneath the glass roof, and creating quite a commotion among the coloured lamps, the rows of gas-jets, and the monstrous fan flaming away like fire-works. A waiter was turning out the lights at the door of the restaurant, whilst in the empty and brilliantly illuminated shops, the immovable shop-women seemed sleeping with their eyes open.

"Oh! the love!" exclaimed Nana, glancing in at the last window, and returning a few steps to admire a porcelain greyhound, which was raising its paw over a nest hidden among some roses.

They at length quitted the Passage, and she would not take a cab. It was very nice out of doors, said she; besides, there was no occasion to hurry, it would be delightful to walk home. Then, when they had got as far as the Café Anglais, she longed to have some oysters, saying that she had eaten nothing since the morning, on account of little Louis's illness. Muffat did not like to disappoint her. As yet, he had not ventured much about with her in public, so he asked for a private room, and hurried along the corridor. She followed him slowly, like a woman thoroughly acquainted with the establishment, and they were just on the point of entering an apartment of which a waiter had opened the door, when a man suddenly rushed out of an adjoining room, from which issued a regular tempest of shouts and laughter. It was Daguenet.

"Hallo! Nana!" cried he.

The count quickly vanished inside his room, leaving the door ajar. But, as his broad back disappeared, Daguenet winked his eye, and added jokingly:

"The deuce! you are getting on; you take them from the Tuileries now!"

Nana smiled, and placed her finger on her lips to make him hold his tongue. She saw that he was a bit on, but was happy all the same at meeting him, still keeping a little corner in her heart for him, in spite of his shabby behaviour in not recognizing her when he was in the company of ladies.

"What are you doing now?" she inquired in a friendly way.

"I am turning over a new leaf. In fact, I am seriously thinking of getting married."

She shrugged her shoulders with a look of pity. But he, continuing his joking tone, said that it was not a life worth living just to earn on the Bourse barely sufficient to pay for the bouquets he gave to his lady friends, in order that they should not think him mean. His three hundred thousand francs had only lasted him eighteen months. He intended to be more practical. He would marry a big dowry and die a prefect like his father. Nana continued to smile incredulously. She nodded her head in the direction of the room he had just left.

"Whom are you with?"

"Oh! quite a party," said he, forgetting his projects in a burst of intoxication. "Just fancy, Léa is relating her journey in Egypt. It's awfully funny! There's a certain story of a bath—"

And he related the story. Nana complaisantly waited to hear it. They had ended by leaning against the walls of the corridor, one in front of the other. Jets of gas were flaring beneath the low ceiling, a vague odour of cookery hung about the folds of the hangings. Now and then, in order to hear themselves above the occasionally increasing noise, they were obliged to put their faces close together. Every few seconds, a waiter laden with dishes, finding the way blocked up, was forced to disturb the pair. But they, without interrupting themselves, squeezed close up against the walls, calmly conversing together amidst the din caused by the customers, and the interruptions of the servants.

"Look there," whispered the young man, pointing to the door of the room Muffat had entered.

They both watched. The door shook softly, as though moved by some gentle breeze; then it slowly closed, without the least sound. They exchanged a silent laugh. The count must cut a funny figure, all alone there by himself.

"By the way," asked she, "have you read the article Fauchery has written about me?"

"Yes, the 'Golden Fly,'" replied Daguenet. "I did not speak of it, as I though you might not like it."

"Not like it, why? It's a very long article."

She felt flattered by being written about in the "Figaro." Without the explanations of Francis, her hairdresser, who had brought her the paper, she would not have known that she was the person alluded to. Daguenet watched her from out the corner of his eye, with a sneer on his face. Well, as she was pleased, every one else ought to be.

"By your leave!" cried a waiter, as he passed between them, holding in both hands a magnum of champagne in ice.

Nana moved a step in the direction of the room where Muffat awaited her.

"Well! good-bye," said Daguenet. "Go back to your cuckold."

"Why do you call him a cuckold?" she inquired, standing still again.

"Because he is a cuckold, of course!"

Very much interested, she returned to him, and, leaning up against the wall as before, merely said, "Ah!"

"What, didn't you know it? His wife has succumbed to Fauchery, my dear. It probably first took place when they were staying together in the country. Fauchery left me just now as I was coming here, and I fancy they have arranged a meeting at

his place for to-night. They have invented some journey, I believe."

For some minutes Nana remained dumb with emotion. "I
thought as much!" said she at length, slapping her thighs. "I
guessed it the first time I saw her, you recollect, when we
passed them on that country road. Is it possible, a respectable
woman to deceive her husband, and with such a dirty blackguard as Fauchery! He'll teach her some fine things."

"Oh!" murmured Daguenet maliciously, "this isn't her first
trial by a long way. She knows perhaps as much as he does."

"Really? Well, they're a nice lot! it's too abominable!" she
exclaimed, indignantly.

"By your leave!" cried another waiter, passing between them,
laden with several more bottles of wine.

Daguenet walked with her towards her room, and then held
her for a moment by the hand. He assumed his crystal-toned
voice—a voice that sounded like a harmonica, and which was
the cause of his great success among the ladies.

"Good-bye, darling. You know I love you always."

She released herself; and smiling on him, her voice
drowned by a thunder of cries and bravos which shook the
door of the room in which the party was being held, she said:

"Don't be a fool; that's all over now. But, all the same, come
and see me one of these days. We can have a long chat." Then,
becoming very serious, she added, in the highly indignant
tone of a most respectable woman, "Ah! he's a cuckold. Well!
my boy, that's a confounded nuisance. I've always felt the greatest disgust for a cuckold."

When she at length entered the room, she found Muffat,
with pale face and trembling hands, resignedly sitting on a
narrow sofa. He did not utter a single reproach. She, dreadfully excited, was divided between feelings of pity and contempt. The poor man, who was so shamefully deceived by a
wicked woman! She had a longing to put her arms round his
neck, and to console him. But yet it was only just; he was such
a fool with women, it would be a lesson for him. Her pity, however, got the better of her. She did not send him off, after having her oysters, as she had intended doing. They remained a

quarter of an hour longer at the Café Anglais, and then went home together to the Boulevard Haussmann. It was eleven o'clock; by midnight she would easily discover some pleasant means of getting rid of him.

When she was in the anteroom she prudently gave Zoé some instructions.

"You must watch for him, and when he comes tell him not to make any noise, if the other one is still with me."

"But where shall I put him, madame?"

"Keep him in the kitchen; that will be the safest."

Muffat was taking off his overcoat in the bedroom. A big fire was burning in the grate. It was the same room, with its violet ebony furniture, its hangings and chair coverings of figured damask, large blue flowers on a grey ground. On two occasions Nana had thought of having it altered—the first time she wished it to be all in black velvet, the second in white satin, with rose-coloured ribbons; but as soon as Steiner consented, she squandered the money she obtained from him to pay for it. All she had added was a tiger skin in front of the fire-place, and a crystal lamp that hung from the ceiling.

"I'm not at all sleepy; I'm not going to bed yet," said Nana, as soon as they had shut themselves in.

The count obeyed her with the submission of a man who is no longer afraid of being seen. His sole anxiety was not to anger her.

"As you please," he murmured.

However, he took off his boots, before sitting down in front of the fire. One of Nana's delights was to undress herself opposite her wardrobe, which had a glass door in which she could see herself full length. She would remove everything, and would then become lost in self-contemplation. A passion which she had for her own person—a rapturous admiration of her satin-like skin and the suppleness of her form—would root her there, serious and attentive, absorbed in a love of herself. The hairdresser would at times enter the room and find her thus occupied, without her even turning her head. Then Count Muffat would fly into a passion, and she would be greatly surprised. What was the matter with him? It wasn't for the benefit of others that she did it; it was for her own.

That night she had lighted all the candles, and, as she was about to let her last garment drop from her shoulders, she stood still, pre-occupied for a moment, having a question at the tip of her tongue.

"Have you read the article in the 'Figaro'? The paper is there, on the table." The recollection of Daguenet's sneering laugh had returned to her; she was filled with a doubt. If that Fauchery had been slandering her, she would have her revenge. "They say that it refers to me," she resumed, affecting an air of indifference. "Well, what do you think, ducky?"

And slipping off her chemise she remained naked, waiting until Muffat had finished reading. Muffat read slowly. Fauchery's article, entitled the "Golden Fly," was the story of a girl born from four or five generations of drunkards, her blood tainted by a long succession of misery and drink, which, in her, had transformed itself into a nervous decay of her sex. She had sprouted on the pavement of one of the Paris suburbs; and, tall, handsome, of superb flesh, the same as a plant growing on a dunghill, she avenged the rogues and vagabonds from whom she sprung. With her, the putrefaction that was left to ferment among the people, rose and polluted the aristocracy. She became, without herself wishing it, one of nature's instruments, a ferment of destruction, corrupting and disorganizing Paris. It was at the end of the article that the comparison with the fly occurred—a fly of the colour of the sun, which had flown from out some filth—a fly that gathered death on the carrion left by the roadside, and that, buzzing and dancing, and emitting a sparkle of precious stones, poisoned men by merely touching them in their palaces which it entered by the windows.[2]

Muffat raised his head and looked fixedly into the fire.

"Well, what do you think of it?" asked Nana.

But he did not answer. He appeared inclined to read the article over again. A cold shudder passed from his head to his shoulders. The article was written in a most diabolical style, with capering phrases, an excess of unexpected words and strange comparisons. However, he remained very much struck by it; it had abruptly aroused in him all that which, for some months past, he had not cared to disturb.

Then he raised his eyes. Nana was absorbed in her admiration of herself. She had bent her neck and was looking attentively in the glass at a little brown mole on her side, and she touched it with the tip of her finger, making it stand out more by slightly leaning back, thinking, no doubt, that it looked droll and pretty. Then she amused herself by studying other parts of her body with the vicious curiosity of her childhood. It always surprised her thus to see herself; she appeared amazed and fascinated like a young girl on first discovering her puberty. After slowly spreading out her arms to develop her plump Venus-like frame, she ended by swinging herself from right to left, her knees wide apart, her body bent back over her loins, with the continual quivering movement of an almeh dancing the stomach dance.

Muffat watched her. She frightened him. The newspaper had fallen from his hands. In that moment of clear understanding, he despised himself. It was true. In three months she had corrupted his life, he already felt tainted to his very marrow by an abomination which he would never himself have dreamt of. At that hour everything was beginning to fester within him. For an instant he was conscious of the results of sin, he beheld the disorganization wrought by this ferment, himself poisoned, his family destroyed, a corner of society cracking and tumbling into ruins. And, not being able to withdraw his gaze, he watched Nana fixedly, and sought to add to his disgust.

Nana was not moving now. With an arm passed behind her neck, and one hand clasped in the other, she was leaning back her head, with her elbows wide apart. He caught sight obliquely of her half-closed eyes, her slightly opened mouth, her face covered with a bewitching smile, her firm amazonian breasts with their sturdy muscles quivering beneath the satin of her skin, and behind her her loose yellow hair covering her back with a mane like a lioness. Muffat followed this delicate profile, these flakes of rosy flesh disappearing in a golden shadow, these curves which the light of the candles caused to shine like silk. He thought of his old horror of woman, the monster of Scripture,* lecherous and bestial. Nana was covered all over with a reddish down which gave to her skin the appearance of velvet; whilst, in her flanks and mare-like thighs, in the thick rolls of flesh which veiled her sex with their troubled shadow, there was something of the beast. It was the golden insect, unconscious of its power, but yet destroying the world with its smell alone. Muffat still continued to look, so completely possessed by the sight that, having for a moment lowered his eyelids and withdrawn his gaze, the animal reappeared in the depths of the darkness, enlarged, terrible, and with its posture exaggerated. And it would remain there, before his eyes in his very flesh, as it were, for evermore.

Nana was now rolling herself up. A tremor of endearment seemed to have passed through her limbs. With moistened eyes she tried to become smaller, as though to feel herself all the better. Then she unclasped her hands behind her neck, and let them slip slowly down to her breasts, which she pressed in a nervous embrace. And, satiated, melting into a caress of her whole body, she fondlingly rubbed her cheeks, right and left, against her shoulders. Her rapacious mouth breathed desire upon her. She pouted her lips and kissed herself longingly close to her arm-pit, smiling the while at that other Nana who was also kissing herself in the looking-glass.

Then Muffat uttered a low and prolonged sigh. This self-enjoyment exasperated him. All his reason was abruptly swept away as though by a gale of wind. He seized Nana round the waist, and, in an outburst of brutal passion, flung her on to the carpet.

"Let me be," cried she—"you have hurt me!"

He was conscious of his defeat. He knew that she was stupid, ribald and deceitful, and he desired her all the same, even poisonous though she might be.

"Oh! it's ridiculous!" said she, in a fury, when she had regained her feet.

However, she became calmer. He would soon be going off.

---

*The Whore of Babylon (Revelation 17:3–18).

After putting on a night-dress trimmed with lace, she sat down on the rug before the fire. It was her favourite place. As she again questioned him respecting Fauchery's article, Muffat gave vague answers, anxious to avoid a scene. Then she lapsed into a long silence, thinking of some means of getting rid of the count.

She wanted to do it pleasantly, for she was a good-natured girl, and was sorry to pain others, and more especially him, because he was a cuckold—a circumstance that had led to making her feel more kindly disposed towards him.

"So it's to-morrow morning," she at length observed, "that you are expecting your wife?"

Muffat had thrown himself into an easy-chair. He looked drowsy and tired. He nodded his head. Nana watched him seriously, racking her brain the while. Still seated on the rug, amidst the rumpled lace, she was nursing one of her bare feet between her hands, and kept turning it about mechanically.

"How long have you been married?" asked she.

"Nineteen years," replied the count.

"Ah! And your wife, is she nice? Do you get on well together?"

He did not answer. Then, in an embarrassed sort of way, he said, "You know, I have asked you never to speak of such matters."

"Really! And why, pray?" she cried, already beginning to lose her temper. "I sha'n't eat your wife by speaking of her, that's very certain. My dear fellow, all women are alike."

Here she paused, afraid of saying too much. Only, she assumed a superior sort of an air, as she thought herself exceedingly kind. The poor man, one ought not to be too hard on him. Besides, a merry idea had just occurred to her. She smiled as she critically examined him. She resumed,

"I say, I haven't told you the report that Fauchery has spread about you—he's a regular viper! I've no ill-feeling against him, because his article might be true; but, all the same, he's a regular viper." And laughing boisterously, and letting go of her foot, she crawled along the rug and leant her bosom against the count's knees. "Only fancy, he swears you were a perfect innocent when you married your wife! Do you understand? Is it true?"

She looked him straight in the face, and placing her hands on his shoulders, she shook him to make him confess.

"Of course it is," he at length replied in a solemn tone of voice.

Then she again rolled herself at his feet in a wild fit of laughter, stuttering and slapping his legs.

"No, it's not possible. Such a thing could only happen to you. You're a phenomenon. But, my poor ducky, you must have looked foolish! When a man knows nothing it's always so funny! By Jove, I should have liked to have seen you! And did it go off all right? Tell me, oh! come now, tell me all about it."

She pressed him with questions, asking everything, insisting on having details. And she laughed so heartily, with such sudden outbursts as made her roll about in her night-dress—which one moment slipped from her shoulders, and the next curled itself up under her, and displayed her skin shining like gold in front of the blazing fire—that the count, little by little, gave her the history of his wedding-night. He no longer felt any repugnance, and ended by thinking it great fun to explain. He merely chose his words, through a remnant of shame. The young woman, very excited, questioned him about the countess. She was beautifully made, but a regular icicle, so he pretended.

"Oh! you've no cause for jealousy," he despicably murmured.

Nana had left off laughing, and had resumed her seat, her back to the fire, and her chin resting on her knees, round which she had clasped her hands.

"My dear fellow, it's the greatest mistake out for a man to appear a ninny to his wife on the first night," declared she, in a grave tone of voice.

"Why?" asked the count, in surprise.

"Because," replied she, slowly, like a professor.

She was lecturing, she wagged her head. However, she deigned to explain herself.

"You see, I know all about it. Well! my boy, women don't like simpletons. They say nothing, on account of their modesty, you know; but you may be quite sure they think a great deal, and, sooner or later, when they haven't had what they expected, they seek for it elsewhere. There, now you know as much as I do."

He did not seem to understand, so she was more circumstantial. She became quite maternal, and gave him this lesson in a friendly way, out of the kindness of her heart. Ever since she had heard that he was a cuckold, the knowledge of this circumstance worried her. She had a hankering to discuss the matter with him.

"Well, really! I've been talking of things that don't concern me. What I say is simply because I want every one to be happy. We're merely having a chat, aren't we? Come, now, you must answer me truly."

But she interrupted herself to change her position. The fire was so fierce.

"By Jove! isn't it hot? My back's quite cooked. Wait a moment, I'll cook my stomach a bit now; it's good for the spasms!"

And when she had turned herself round, with her legs doubled under her, she resumed, "You and your wife don't occupy the same room, do you?"

"No, I assure you," replied Muffat, afraid not to answer.

"And you think that she's a regular stick?"

He affirmatively bowed his head.

"And that's why you come to me? Answer me! I sha'n't be angry."

He bowed his head again.

"Very well!" concluded she, "I thought as much. Ah! poor fellow! You know my aunt, Madame Lerat? Next time she comes get her to tell you the story of the green-grocer who lives in her street. Just fancy, the green-grocer—Drat it! the fire is hot; I must turn round again. I'll cook my left side this time."

As she presented her hip to the flames, a funny idea seized hold of her, and she joked herself in a jolly sort of way, delighted at seeing how plump and rosy she looked in the reflection of the fire.

"I say! I'm just like a goose. Yes! that's it—a goose roasting. I turn, I turn. Really, I'm cooking in my own juice."

Again she laughed aloud, when suddenly there was a sound of voices and of closing doors. Muffat, surprised, interrogated her with a look. She at once became serious, and there was an anxious expression on her face. It was no doubt Zoé's cat, a confounded beast that was always breaking everything. Half past twelve. Whatever had she been thinking of, wasting her time in working for her cuckold's happiness? Now that the other one was there she must get rid of him, and quickly, too.

"What were you saying?" asked the count complaisantly, delighted at finding her so amiable.

But in her desire to send him off, her humour quickly changed. She was coarse, and no longer minced her words.

"Ah! yes, the green-grocer and his wife. Well! my boy, they never got on together, not a bit! She, you know, expected all sorts of things; but he was a ninny. And so it went on till it ended like this—he, thinking her a stick, went with a lot of strumpets, and got more than he bargained for; whilst she, on her side, consoled herself with some fellows who knew a trifle more than her simpleton of a husband. And it always ends like that when you don't understand each other. I know it does!"

Muffat paled, understanding at last her allusions, and wished to make her leave off. But she intended to have her say.

"No, hold your row! If you were not all a set of fools, you would be just as nice with your wives as you are with us; and if your wives were not a lot of geese, they would take the same trouble to keep you to themselves that we take to hook you. But you all give yourselves such confounded airs. There, my boy; put that in your pipe and smoke it.

"Do not talk about respectable women," said he, severely. "You do not know anything about them."

On hearing this, Nana rose on her knees.

"I don't know anything about them! But they're not even clean, your respectable women! No, they're not even clean! I defy you to find one who would dare to show herself as I am here. Really, you make me laugh, with your respectable women! Don't drive me too hard; don't force me to say things that I should regret afterwards."

For sole rejoinder, the count muttered a foul word between his teeth. Nana, in her turn, became deadly pale. She looked at him for a few seconds without speaking. Then, in a clear voice, she asked,

"What would you do if your wife deceived you?"

He made a menacing gesture.

"Well! and I, supposing I deceived you?"

"Oh! you," he murmured, shrugging his shoulders.

Nana was certainly not unfeeling. Ever since the first words, she had been resisting a desire to tell him of his cuckoldom to his face. She would have liked to have confessed him quietly. But he exasperated her; she must put an end to it.

"Therefore, my boy," she resumed, "I don't know what the devil you're doing here. You've done nothing but pester me for the last two hours. So go and join your wife, who's consoling herself with Fauchery. Yes, I know what I'm saying; in the Rue Taitbout, at the corner of the Rue de Provence. I give you the address, you see." Then, seeing Muffat rise on his feet, staggering like an ox that had just received a stunning blow, she added triumphantly, "Ah! they're getting on well, your respectable women! They even interfere with us now, and take our lovers!"

But she was unable to continue. In a terrible passion he threw her full length on the floor, and raising his heel, was about to crush her face to silence her. For the moment she had an awful fright; but he, blinded, and as though mad, left her, and rushed helplessly about the room. Then the choking silence he maintained, the sight of the internal struggle which shook his frame, brought tears to her eyes. She felt a mortal regret; and curling herself up before the fire, so as to cook her right side, she undertook to console him.

"I assure you, darling, I thought you knew of it. Otherwise, I would certainly not have spoken. Then, after all, perhaps it isn't true. I'm not sure of anything. I merely heard it—people talk about it; but that proves nothing, does it? Ah! really now, you're very stupid to be put out about it. If I was a man, I wouldn't care a tinker's curse for any woman! Women, my boy, high or low, are all the same—all loose fish; it's six of one and half-a-dozen of the other."

She went in for abusing women in general, so as to make the blow less hard to bear; but he did not listen to her, he did not hear her. Whilst stamping about, he had somehow or other managed to get on his boots and his overcoat. For a moment longer he wandered about the room; then, with a last rush, as though he had only just discovered the door, he disappeared. Nana felt very much put out.

"Well! ta ta!" she continued aloud, though all alone. "He's polite, he is, when he's being spoken to! And I, who was sweating away to make it up again with him! Anyhow, I was the first to hold out my hand. I made quite enough excuses, I think! Besides, he shouldn't have stopped here annoying me!" However, she remained displeased with herself, scratching her legs with both hands; but she at length muttered consolingly,

"Oh! dash it! It isn't my fault that he's a cuckold!"

And, roasted on all sides, as hot as a quail just removed from the spit, she jumped into bed, after ringing for Zoé to usher in the other one, who was waiting in the kitchen.

Outside, Muffat continued to hurry on. Another shower had just fallen. He slipped along the greasy pavement. As he mechanically looked up in the air he saw large black clouds floating rapidly across the moon. At that hour the Boulevard Haussmann was almost deserted. He passed by the scaffoldings of the new Opera-house, keeping in the shadow and stammering disconnected sentences. The girl lied. She had cruelly invented that to annoy him. He ought to have crushed her head when he had it beneath his heel. It was too shameful. He would never touch her nor see her again; if he did, he would indeed be a cur. And he drew a long breath of relief at his deliverance. Ah! that stupid naked monster, cooking like a goose, drivelling about all that he had respected for forty years past! The clouds had cleared away from the moon, which now lighted up the empty street. He was seized with fear and burst into sobs, suddenly giving way to despair, as though he had been precipitated into illimitable space.

"Oh! heaven!" he stammered, "all is over, there is nothing more."

Along the Boulevards a few belated pedestrians were hurrying home. The count tried to compose himself. The girl's story kept perplexing his heated brain; he wished to examine it calmly. That very morning the countess was to return from Madame de Chezelles's château. There was nothing to have prevented her returning on the previous evening, and passing the night with that man. He now recalled certain things that had occurred during their stay at Les Fondettes. One night he had found Sabine wandering about among the trees, and she was so agitated that for some time she was unable to answer him. That man was there, then. Why should she not be with him now? The more he thought of it, the more it seemed to him possible. He ended by thinking it only natural, and even inevitable. Whilst he had been taking off his coat at a harlot's his wife had been disrobing herself in a lover's bedchamber; there was nothing more simple or more logical. And, as he reasoned thus, he forced himself to keep cool. He experienced the sensation of a fall into the follies of the flesh, which, spreading and gaining on him, swept the world away from around him. Phantoms, created by his heated imagination, pursued him. Nana undressed, abruptly evoked Sabine, undressed also. At this vision, which gave the two women a like parentage of wantonness and the same inordinate desires, he stumbled. A cab passing along the road nearly crushed him; some women, coming out of a café, pushed up against him, laughing coarsely. Then, again giving way to tears, in spite of his efforts, and not wishing to sob aloud before the passers-by, he turned down a dark, empty street, the Rue Rossini, where he cried like a child as he moved past the silent houses.

"All is over," he kept saying in a hollow voice. "There is nothing more, nothing more."

His tears so mastered him that he leant against a door, burying his wet face in his hands. A sound of footsteps chased him away. He felt such shame and such fear that he fled from everyone, with the cautious tread of a night prowler. Whenever anybody passed him on the pavement he tried to assume a careless gait, as though he imagined that his history could be read in the movement of his shoulders. He had turned down the Rue de la Grange-Batelière and reached the Faubourg Montmartre, but the bright lights caused him to retrace his footsteps, and for close upon an hour he wandered thus about the neighbourhood, choosing always the darkest turnings. He had, no doubt, a goal to which his feet instinctively conducted him, patiently and by a most circuitous road. At length, at the turn of a street, he raised his eyes. He had arrived. It was the corner of the Rue Taitbout and of the Rue de Provence. He had, in the painful disorder of his brain, taken an hour to reach it, while he might have done so in five minutes. One morning, in the previous month, he recollected having called on Fauchery to thank him for having mentioned his name in the description of a ball at the Tuileries. The apartment was on the first floor, with little square windows half hidden by the colossal sign-board of the shop. The last window on the left was divided by a streak of brilliant light, the ray of a lamp passing between the partly closed curtains. And, with his eyes fixed on that bright line, he stood absorbed, awaiting something.

The moon had disappeared in an inky sky, from which a drizzling, icy rain fell. Two o'clock struck at the church of the Trinity. The Rue de Provence and the Rue Taitbout, with their lighted gas-lamps, disappeared in the distance in a yellow vapour. Muffat did not stir. That was the room. He recollected it well, hung in crimson, and with a Louis XIII. bedstead at the back of the apartment. The lamp was probably to the right, on the mantel-piece. No doubt they were in bed, for not a shadow passed the immovable line of light; and he, still watching, arranged a plan. He would ring, and hastening upstairs in spite of the door-keeper, would burst into the room and fall upon them in bed, without even giving them time to disengage their arms. The knowledge that he had no weapon arrested him for a moment. Then he decided that he would strangle them. He turned his plan over in his head, he perfected it, always awaiting something, some sign, to make him certain. Had the shadow of a woman's form appeared at that moment, he would have rung the bell; but the thought that he was perhaps

mistaken froze him. What would he be able to say? His doubts
returned to him. His wife could not be with that man. The idea
was monstrous and impossible; but still he stayed on, overcome
by degrees by numbness, succumbing to weakness, in that long
vigil, to which the fixity of his look imparted a sense of hallu-
cination.

The shower increased. Two police officers drew near, and he
was obliged to leave the door-post against which he had sought
shelter. When they had disappeared down the Rue de
Provence he returned, wet and shivering. The bright line still
showed across the window. This time he was going away, when
a shadow passed. The movement was so rapid that he thought
he might be mistaken, but one after another other shadows
passed, and there seemed quite a commotion in the room. Rivetted again to the pavement opposite, he experienced an insupportable sensation of burning in the stomach. Profiles or
arms and legs came and went. An enormous hand, bearing the
silhouette of a water-can, glided by. He distinguished nothing
clearly, yet he thought he recognised a woman's head of hair;
and he argued within himself, it was like Sabine's head-dress,
only the back of the neck seemed broader than hers. But at
that hour he was incapable of determining, he could not tell.
His stomach caused him so much suffering that he pressed up
against a door, like a shivering outcast, to obtain relief in the
agony of this frightful uncertainty. Then as, in spite of all, he
could not take his eyes from off that window, his anger melted
into the imagination of a moralist. He saw himself a deputy. He
was speaking in the Chamber, inveighing against debauchery,
prophesying catastrophes, and he repeated the arguments in
Fauchery's article on the poisonous fly, and declared that society could no longer exist with the manners and customs of the
Second Empire. This did him some good. The shadows had
now disappeared. No doubt they had gone back to bed. He,
ever on the watch, still waited.

Three o'clock struck, then four o'clock. He could not tear
himself away. Each time a shower came down he squeezed up
against the door-post, the rain beating on his legs. No one
passed by now. Occasionally his eyes closed, as though burnt by

the ray of light, on which, with obstinate folly, he persistently fixed them. Twice again did the shadows reappear, going through the same movements, carrying the same gigantic water-can; and each time afterwards all became still as before, whilst the lamp continued to glimmer discreetly. These shadows increased his doubts. Besides, a sudden idea had just appeased him, in deferring the hour of action. He had merely to wait till the woman came out. He would easily recognise Sabine. Nothing could be simpler, there would be no scandal, and he would no longer be in doubt. All he had to do was to remain there. Of all the confused feelings that had hitherto agitated him, he no longer experienced anything but a morbid desire to know. Having nothing to do, however, standing up against that door, soon made him feel drowsy. To keep himself awake, he tried to calculate the time it would be necessary for him to wait. Sabine was to have arrived at the station at about nine o'clock. That gave him almost four and a half hours. He was full of patience. He would never have moved again, finding a charm in fancying that his night vigil would be an eternal one.

Suddenly, the ray of light disappeared. This very simple occurrence was an unexpected catastrophe for him, something disagreeable and annoying. They had evidently turned out the lamp, and were going to sleep. At such an hour it was only natural. But he felt irritated, because that window, being now in darkness, no longer interested him. He watched it for a quarter of an hour longer, then it tired him, so he left the doorway and took a few steps along the pavement. Until five o'clock, he walked to and fro, occasionally raising his eyes. The window remained in the same dormant state; and at times he would ask himself whether he had not dreamed that he had seen shadows cross those panes. A great fatigue overwhelmed him, which made him forget what he was waiting for at that street-corner, stumbling over the paving-stones, awaking with starts and the cold shiver of a man who no longer knows where he is. What was the good of his bothering himself about the matter? As the people had gone to sleep, all he had to do was to leave them in peace. Why should he mix himself up in their affairs? It was very dark, no one would know of his having waited there; and then all feeling in him, even his curiosity, fled, carried away in a desire to have done with it all, and to seek some solace elsewhere. The cold increased, the street became unbearable. Twice he moved away, then returned slowly, but only to move away again, farther off. It was over, there was nothing more. He went in the direction of the Boulevards, and did not return.

He wandered silently through the streets. He walked slowly, always with the same step, and keeping close to the wall. His heels resounded on the pavement; he beheld nothing but his shadow, which turned at each lamp-post, becoming larger and smaller. That amused him, mechanically occupying him. Afterwards, he could never recall through what streets he had gone; he seemed to have dragged himself along for hours in a circle. One single recollection remained, and that very clearly. He had found himself, he could not tell how, with his face pressed against the iron railings that closed the Passage des Panoramas, clasping the bars in his hands. He was not shaking them, he was merely trying to see into the Passage, under the influence of an emotion, with which his heart was bursting. But he could distinguish nothing; darkness reigned in the deserted gallery, whilst the wind which entered by the Rue Saint-Marc blew the dampness of a cellar into his face. And a strange infatuation kept him there. Then, awakening as though from a dream, he was filled with surprise, and asked himself what he was seeking at that hour, pressed against those railings with such a force, that the bars had left their marks upon his face. And he resumed his tramp in despair, his heart filled with a great sadness, as if betrayed and alone for evermore in all that darkness.

Day at length broke, and to the winter night there succeeded that dull light which looks so melancholy on the muddy pavement of Paris. Muffat had returned into the large new roads that were being made around the scaffoldings of the new Opera-house.* Soaked by the showers, broken up by the

*The Opéra de Paris, designed by Charles Garnier, construction on which was begun in 1862 but not completed until 1875.

heavy carts, the chalky soil had become changed into a miry lake. And, without looking where he placed his feet, he continued walking on, slipping, and with difficulty keeping his legs. The awakening of Paris, the gangs of scavengers and the early groups of workmen, brought him a fresh worry as the day advanced. He was stared at with surprise, with his wild appearance, his muddy clothes, and his hat soaked with the rain. For a long time he sought refuge against the palings, among the scaffolding. In his empty head one idea alone remained, which was that he was very miserable.

Then his thoughts turned to God. The sudden idea of divine assistance, of a superhuman consolation, surprised him, like something extraordinary and unexpected. It awakened in his mind the picture of M. Venot. He beheld his plump little person, his decayed teeth. For certain, M. Venot, whom for months past he had been grieving by not going near him, would be very happy were he now to knock at his door, and weep on his breast. At other times God had always been merciful to him. At the least sorrow, or the smallest obstacle encountered in life, he would enter a church, and, kneeling, would humble himself before the Supreme Being, and he would come out fortified by prayer, ready to enjoy the sweets of life, with the sole desire for the salvation of his soul; but now, he could only pray by fits and starts, just when a fear of hell seized upon him. He had given way to a great indolence. Nana interfered with his duties, and the thought of God surprised him. Why had he not thought of the Almighty in the first instance, during that frightful crisis in which his weak humanity succumbed?

Then, with feeble footsteps, he sought a church. He could remember nothing. The early hour seemed to alter the streets. As he turned the corner of the Rue de la Chassée d'Antin, however, he caught sight of the church of the Trinity in the distance, its steeple seen very indistinctly in the fog. The white statues overlooking the naked garden appeared like so many shining Venuses among the faded yellow leaves of a park. Beneath the porch he paused a moment to take breath, fatigued by the ascent of the high flight of steps. Then he entered. The church was very cold, the great stove having been extinguished the previous evening, and the tall arches were filled with a fine mist, which had filtered in through the apertures of the glass windows. A shadow hung over the lower part. Not a soul was there beyond a beadle, who, in the midst of that semi-darkness, dragged his feet over the stones in the sullenness of the awaking hour. Muffat, after knocking up against a number of chairs, feeling lost, his heart fit to burst, had fallen on his knees against the railings of a little side chapel, close to a holy-water font. He had clasped his hands, trying to find a prayer in which he could pour forth his very soul, but his lips alone muttered words. His mind was elsewhere—outside, following the streets, without repose, as though beneath the lash of some implacable necessity; and he repeated: "O Lord help me! O God, do not abandon your creature, who abandons himself to your justice! O merciful Father, I adore you; will you let me perish beneath the blows of your enemies!" Nothing seemed to answer. The shadow and the cold hung about his shoulders. The noise of the beadle walking in the distance continued, and prevented him from praying. He heard nought but that irritating sound in the deserted church, which had not even then been swept, nor had the early mass been performed. Then, holding on to a chair, he raised himself, with a cracking of his knees. God had not yet arrived. Why should he go and weep on M. Venot's breast? That man could do nothing.

And he mechanically returned to Nana's. Outside, having slipped, he felt tears come to his eyes, not with anger against fate, but simply because he felt weak and ill. He was really too tired; he had been out too long in the rain, he felt the cold too much. It froze him to think of going back to his dismal home in the Rue Miromesnil. At Nana's the street-door was not open, he had to wait till the concierge appeared. As he went up-stairs he smiled, already feeling the pleasant warmth of that nest, where he would at length be able to stretch himself and sleep.

When Zoé let him in, she made a gesture of amazement and uneasiness. Madame, having been seized by a violent headache, hadn't closed her eyes all night. However, she would go and see whether she had fallen asleep or not; and she glided into the bed-room, whilst he sank down on a chair in the drawing-room. But Nana appeared almost instantly. She had jumped out of bed, scarcely taking time to put on a petticoat, and entered with bare feet, her hair hanging about her shoulders, her night dress rumpled and torn, in the disorder of a night of love.

"What! you here again!" cried she, red with passion. Under the influence of her rage, she was hastening to put him out herself; but seeing him in such a state, so utterly helpless, she was once more moved to pity. "Well! you're in a nice mess, my poor fellow!" she resumed in a more pleasant tone of voice. "What is the matter with you? Ah! you've been watching them, you've been having a fine time of it!"

He said nothing; he looked like a stunned ox. Yet she understood that he had not been able to obtain any proof, as she added, just to bring him to himself again:

"You see, I was mistaken. Your wife is all right, on my word she is! Now, my boy, you must go home and get to bed. You are in want of sleep."

He did not stir.

"Come, be off; I can't keep you here. You don't, I suppose, want to stop at this time of day?"

"Yes, let us go to sleep," he muttered.

She repressed a violent gesture. She was fast losing patience. Was he going crazy?

"Come, be off," said she a second time.

"No."

Then, thoroughly exasperated, she broke out in revolt.

"But it's disgusting! Understand me, I've had a great deal too much of you. Go and find your wife, who's making a cuckold of you. Yes, she's making a cuckold of you—it's I who tell you so, now. There! have you got what you wanted? Will you leave me or not?"

Muffat's eyes filled with tears. He clasped his hands.

"Let us go to sleep."

Nana scarcely knew what she did, choking as she was with nervous sobs. It was too much! Did all these matters concern her? She had certainly taken all possible precaution in telling him, so as not to hurt his feelings, and now she was to pay for the broken glass! Oh, no! if you please! She was good-natured, but not to that extent.

"Damnation! I've had enough of it all!" swore she, striking the furniture with her clenched fists. "Ah, well! I who took so much care to keep faithful. Why, my fine fellow! I could be as rich as ever to-morrow, if I only said a word."

He raised his head in surprise. He had never given the money question a thought. If she would express a desire, he would gratify it at once. His whole fortune was hers.

"No, it's too late," replied she, furiously. "I like the men who give without being asked. No, were you to offer me a million for one embrace, I would refuse you. It's all over, I have something better there. Be off, or I will no longer answer for myself. I shall do something dreadful."

And she advanced towards him, menacingly; but in the midst of this exasperation of a kind-hearted girl pushed to extremes, and convinced of her right and of her superiority over the worthy people who pestered her, the door suddenly opened and Steiner appeared. This was the last straw. She uttered a terrible cry.

"Hallo! here's the other one now!"

Steiner, bewildered by the noise of her voice, stood still. Muffat's unexpected presence annoyed him, for he was afraid of an explanation, from which he had kept aloof for three months past. Blinking his eyes, he twisted himself about in an uneasy sort of way, and avoided looking at the count; and he breathed hard, with the red and distorted features of a man who has rushed about Paris to bring some good news, and who finds he has fallen into a catastrophe.

"What do you want—you, eh?" asked Nana, roughly, speaking familiarly to him, in spite of the count's presence.

"I—I—," he stammered, "I have brought you—you know what."

"What's that?"

He hesitated. Two days before she had told him not to show himself there again without bringing a thousand francs, which she required to pay a bill. For two days he had been seeking the money, and he had just succeeded in completing the sum that very morning.

"The thousand francs," he ended by saying, as he withdrew an envelope from his pocket.

Nana had forgotten all about them.

"The thousand francs!" cried she. "Do I ask for charity? Look! see what I do with your thousand francs!"

And seizing the envelope, she threw it in his face. Like a prudent Jew he picked it up, though painfully. He glanced at the young woman in a stupefied fashion. Muffat exchanged a look of despair with him, whilst Nana placed her hands on her hips in order to shout the louder.

"I say now, have you nearly finished insulting me? As for you, my boy, I'm glad you've also come; for now, look here, I can have a clean sweep. Now then! out you go!" Then, as they did not seem to hurry themselves, but stood as though paralysed, she went on: "What! you say I'm foolish? That's possible! but you've plagued me too much; and, drat it all! I've had enough of a fashionable existence! If I bust up, it's my lookout.

"One—two—you refuse to go? Well! look here then, I've got a friend."

With a sudden movement she threw the bedroom door wide open. Then the two men beheld Fontan in the middle of the tumbled bed. He had not expected to be exhibited thus, with his dusky person spread out like a goat in the midst of the crumpled lace, his legs showing under the flying tail of his night shirt. He was not, however, by any means embarrassed, used as he was to the surprises of the stage. After the first shock was over, he was able to make a face which insured him the honours of war. He did the rabbit, as he called it, thrusting out his mouth, curling his nose, and moving all the muscles of his face at the same time. His head, resembling that of a libidinous faun, exuded vice through every pore. It was Fontan whom Nana, seized by that mad infatuation of women for the hideous grimaces of ugly comic actors, had been fetching nightly, for a week past, from the Variety Theatre.

"There!" said she, pointing to him with a tragic gesture.

Muffat, who was prepared for almost anything, indignantly resented the affront.

"Strumpet!" he stammered.

But Nana, already in the bedroom, returned to have the last word.

"Strumpet, indeed! Then what about your wife?"

And, turning on her heel, she loudly banged the door after her and bolted it. The two men, left alone, looked at each other in silence. Zoé then entered the room. She did not hurry them off, but talked very sensibly to them. Like a reasonable being, she thought madame had behaved very foolishly. However, she took her part. Her mania for that wretched stroller wouldn't last long. All they had to do was to wait till she had got over it. They then withdrew. They had not uttered a word. Outside on the pavement, moved by a sort of fraternal feeling, they silently shook hands; and, turning their backs on each other, and dragging their legs along, they went off in opposite directions.

When Muffat at length returned to his house in the Rue Miromesnil, his wife had just arrived there. They both met on the broad staircase, the sombre walls of which diffused an icy chill around. Raising their eyes, they beheld each other. The count was still in his muddy clothes, and his face had the frightful pallor of a man returning from a surfeit of vice. The countess, blear-eyed, with her hair all dishevelled, and looking thoroughly exhausted by a night passed in the train, seemed scarcely able to keep awake.

CHAPTER VIII

I t was in the Rue Véron, at Montmartre, in a little apartment on the fourth floor. Nana and Fontan had invited a few friends to partake of their Twelfth Night cake.* They had only got settled three days before, and intended having a house-warming.

Everything had been done hastily, in the first ardour of their honeymoon, without any fixed intention of their living together. On the morrow of her grand brawl, when she had so energetically sent the count and the banker about their business, Nana felt that she had got herself into a fine mess. She saw her position at a glance. The creditors would invade her anteroom, interfere in her love affairs, and talk of selling her up if she was not reasonable. There would be endless quarrels and constant worries, just to keep a few sticks of furniture from their grasp. She preferred to let all go. Besides, she was sick of her apartment in the Boulevard Haussmann. It was unbearable with its great gilded rooms. In her infatuation for Fontan, her dream of her girlhood returned to her—of the days when she was apprenticed to the artificial flower-maker, and longed for nothing more than a pretty bright little room, with a wardrobe of violet ebony with a glass door, and a bed hung with blue rep.† In two days she sold everything that she could safely remove—nick-nacks, jewels, and the like—and disappeared with about ten thousand francs, without saying a word to the landlord—a perfect header, and not a trace remaining behind. That accomplished, there was no fear of having any men dangling about her petticoats. Fontan was very nice. He didn't say "no," he let her do as she liked—in fact, he behaved altogether like a regular chum. He possessed about seven thousand

---

*January 6, the twelfth and final night of Christmas. In many countries on that date a cake is served in which a single bean has been baked; whoever gets the slice with the bean is assured of good luck in the coming year.

†A ribbed or corded fabric.

francs, and agreed to put them with Nana's ten thousand, although he had the reputation of being miserly. That seemed to them something solid to start housekeeping on. And they commenced thus, each taking what he or she required out of the common fund, furnishing the two rooms in the Rue Véron, and sharing everything alike. At the beginning this kind of life was simply delicious.

On Twelfth Night, Madame Lerat was the first to arrive, with little Louis. As Fontan had not returned, she ventured to express her fears, for she trembled to see her niece renouncing fortune.

"Oh! aunt, I love him so much!" cried Nana, pressing her hands prettily across her breast.

These words produced an extraordinary effect on Madame Lerat. Her eyes moistened.

"That's right," said she in a convincing manner; "love before everything."

And she praised the prettiness of the rooms. Nana showed her everything in the bedroom and the dining-room, and even in the kitchen. Well! they were not large, but they had been newly painted and papered; and the sun shone there so brilliantly. Then Madame Lerat kept the young woman in the bedroom, whilst little Louis went and installed himself in the kitchen, behind the charwoman, in order to see her put a chicken down to roast. If she ventured to make any remarks, it was because Zoé had been to see her only a short time before. Zoé was so devoted to madame that she bravely remained at the breach. Madame would pay her some time or other—she had no anxiety on that score. And in the downfall of the establishment of the Boulevard Haussmann, she coped with the creditors, operating a masterly retreat, saving waifs from the wreck, and telling every one that madame was travelling, but without ever giving an address; and for fear, too, of being followed, she denied herself the pleasure of calling on madame. However, that very morning she had hastened to Madame Lerat, because there was something new in the wind. The day before several creditors had called—the upholsterer, the coal merchant, the milliner—and they had offered to give time, proposing even to advance a considerable sum of money to madame, if madame would return to her apartment, and consent to act like a sensible being. The aunt repeated Zoé's very words. There was no doubt some gentleman at the bottom of all that.

"Never!" declared Nana indignantly. "Well! they're a dirty lot—those tradespeople! Do they think that I'm going to sell myself, just for the sake of seeing their bills paid? Listen to me now, I'd sooner die of hunger than deceive Fontan."

"That's just what I answered," said Madame Lerat. "I told her that you would only obey the dictates of your heart."

Nana, however, was very annoyed to hear that La Mignotte had been sold, and that Labordette had purchased it for a most ridiculous sum for Caroline Héquet. That put her in a rage against the clique. They were nothing better than street-walkers, in spite of their grand airs. Ah, yes! by Jove! she was worth more than the whole lot of them!

"They may laugh," she wound up by saying. "Money will never give them real happiness. And then, look you, aunt, I no longer know even whether these people are in existence. I am too happy to give them a thought."

Just then Madame Maloir entered, with one of those extraordinary bonnets which she alone had the science of making. It was quite a happy meeting. Madame Maloir explained that greatness intimidated her, but that now she would call occasionally to have a game at bézique. For the second time they went over the apartments; and in the kitchen, in the presence of the charwoman who was basting the chicken, Nana talked of how economical she was going to be, saying that a servant would cost too much and that she intended to do the housework herself, whilst little Louis greedily watched the chicken roasting. But there was a sound of voices. It was Fontan, with Bosc and Prullière. The dinner could be served at once, and the soup was already on the table, when Nana, for the third time, showed her guests over the rooms.

"Ah, children! how comfortable you must be here!" Bosc kept saying, simply to please the friends who stood him a dinner, for in reality the question of the nest, as he called it, did not affect him in the least. In the bedroom he seemed scarcely able to find sufficient words to express his admiration. Usually he alluded to women as being no better than animals, and the idea that a man could embarrass himself with one of the dirty hussies raised in him the only indignation of which he was capable, in the drunken disdain with which he enveloped the world.

"Ah! the lucky ones!" he continued, blinking his eyes, "they've done it all on the sly. Well! really, you're right. It'll be charming, and we'll come and see you—I'm blowed if we won't!"

But as little Louis just then galloped in, riding on a broom-handle, Prullière said, with a malicious giggle:

"What! you've already got that big baby?"

They all thought it very funny. Madame Lerat and Madame Maloir nearly split their sides with laughing. Nana, far from feeling offended, smiled in a loving sort of way, saying that unfortunately it was not the case; she would have liked it to have been so for the little one's sake and her own, but perhaps they would have one all the same. Fontan, acting the kind-hearted man, took little Louis in his arms, playing with him, and stuttering:

"All the same, you love your papa; don't you? Call me papa, you little monkey!"

"Papa—papa!" lisped the child.

Everyone caressed and fondled him. Bosc, taking no real interest in the matter, moved that they should go to dinner—that was the only thing worth living for. Nana asked to be allowed to have little Louis beside her. The meal was a very merry one. Bosc, however, did not get on very well on account of the child's proximity to him, and his time was taken up in defending his plate from the youngster's attacks. Madame Lerat disturbed him also. She became very tender, and whispered in his ear most mysterious things—stories of gentlemen very well off who still followed her about, and on two separate occasions he was obliged to move his knee, for she kept pushing hers against it, looking at him most lovingly the while. Prullière behaved most shamefully to Madame Maloir, not helping her to a single thing. He was occupied solely with Nana, greatly annoyed at seeing her with Fontan. The turtle doves, too, were becoming a nuisance, kissing each other at every moment. In spite of all the usages, they had persisted in sitting side by side.

"Do leave off and eat your dinners!" Bosc kept on saying, with his mouth full. "You will have plenty of time to cuddle each other afterwards. Wait till we have gone."

But Nana could not restrain herself. She was all wrapped up in her love, as rosy as a virgin, and full of endearing smiles and glances. With her eyes fixed on Fontan, she called him all the pretty names she could think of—ducky, darling, cherub, and whenever he handed her anything, the water or the salt, she leant forward and kissed him on whatever part of his head her lips encountered—on his eyes, his nose, or his ears; then, if the others scolded her, she retired again to her seat with most wary tactics, and the humility and suppleness of a cat that had just been whipped, though at the same time slyly taking hold of his hand beneath the table, to kiss it again at the first opportunity. She must touch some part of him. Fontan assumed an important air, and condescendingly allowed himself to be adored. His big nose quivered with a sensual joy; his goatish physiognomy, his ugliness suggestive of some ridiculous monster, seemed to expand beneath the devout adoration of that superb girl, so plump and white. Occasionally he would return her kiss, like a man who, though having the best of it, still wishes to act nicely.

"Look here, you two, you are really unbearable!" exclaimed Prullière at length. "Get out of there, you!"

And he turned Fontan out of his seat, changing the plates and glasses, and took the place beside Nana. This called forth no end of exclamations, outbursts of applause, and some rather indecent remarks. Fontan pretended to be in despair, and assumed his comical look of Vulcan crying for Venus. Prullière at once made himself very attentive; but Nana, whose foot he tried to touch under the table, gave him a kick to force him to leave off. No, she would certainly not have anything to do with him. The month before she had been slightly smitten with his handsome head, but now she detested him. If he pinched her again when pretending to pick up his napkin, she would throw her glass in his face.

But everything went off well. They naturally talked of the Variety Theatre. That rogue, Bordenave, would never die, it seemed. His foul diseases had broken out again, and he was in such a state that one could scarcely touch him with a pair of tongs. The day before he had done nothing but blackguard Simone all through the rehearsal. Nobody would weep for him over-much! Nana said that if he dared to offer her another part she would send him to the devil. Besides, she didn't think she would go upon the stage again; she preferred being at home to being at the theatre. Fontan, who was not in the new piece, nor yet in the one they were rehearsing, also exaggerated the sweets of liberty, and the felicity of spending his evenings with his little darling, his legs stretched out before the fire. And the others called them lucky creatures, pretending to envy their happiness.

They had cut the Twelfth Night cake. The bean had fallen to Madame Lerat, who at once put it in Bosc's glass. Then they all shouted: "The king drinks! the king drinks!" Nana took advantage of this outburst of gaiety to put her arms round Fontan's neck and kiss him, and whisper in his ear. But Prullière, with the vexed laugh of a handsome fellow who finds his good looks are not appreciated, cried out that it was not fair. Little Louis had been put to sleep on two chairs; and the party did not break up till one in the morning, the guests calling out "good-night" as they descended the stairs.

And for three weeks the life of the two lovers was sweet indeed. Nana thought herself back again at the commencement of her career, when her first silk dress had caused her so much pleasure. She went out but little, affecting solitude and simplicity. One morning early, when going to buy some fish at the Rochefoucauld market, she was astonished to find herself face to face with Francis, the hairdresser. He was dressed with his habitual correctness, fine clean linen, and an irreproachable overcoat; and she was ashamed at being seen by him in the street in a dirty morning gown, her hair all in disorder, and with a pair of old shoes upon her feet. But he had the tact to be even more exaggerated in his politeness. He did not ask a question, but pretended to think that madame had been abroad. Ah! madame had broken a great many hearts by going away! It was a loss for all the world. The young woman, however, seized with a curiosity which ended by dispelling her first embarrassment, could not refrain from questioning him. As the crowd kept jostling against them, she drew him into a doorway, and stood in front of him, with her little basket in her hand. What was being said about her little escapade? Well! really, the ladies at whose houses he called said this and that; in short, it had caused quite a commotion and was undoubtedly a tremendous success. And Steiner? M. Steiner had fallen very low; he would end badly, unless he succeeded in some fresh speculation. And Daguenet? Oh! he was doing very well; M. Daguenet was settling down. Nana, excited by her reminiscences, was on the point of asking some fresh question, but she felt a restraint in uttering Muffat's name. Then Francis smilingly alluded to him. As for the count, it was shocking to see him, he had suffered so much after madame's departure; he looked like the ghost of some unburied corpse, as he wandered about the various places that madame used to frequent. However, M. Mignon, having come across him, had taken him home. This news made Nana laugh, but in a constrained manner.

"Ah! so he's with Rose now," said she. "Well, you know, Francis, I don't care a hang! The old hypocrite! He's got into such habits, he can't even abstain from them for a few days! And he swore that he would never have anything to do with any woman after me!" Though outwardly calm, she was in reality greatly enraged. "It's my leavings," she resumed. "Rose has treated herself to a queer fish! Oh! I see it all; she wanted to have her revenge for my carrying off that old beast Steiner from her. She's done a smart thing in taking a man into her house that I turned out of mine!"

"M. Mignon tells a different story," said the hairdresser. "According to him, it was the count who turned you out—yes, and in a rather unpleasant way, too, with a kick behind."

On hearing this, Nana became deadly pale.

"Eh? what?" exclaimed she. "A kick behind? Well, that's too much, that is! Why, my boy, it was I who chucked him downstairs, the cuckold! for he is a cuckold, as I daresay you know— his countess has no end of lovers, even that filthy Fauchery. And that Mignon, who walks the streets for his monkey-faced wife, whom no one will touch, because she's so skinny! What a beastly world! what a beastly world!" She was choking. She stopped to take breath. "Ah! so they say that? Well, my little Francis, I'll just go and seek them out. Shall we go together, at once? Yes, I'll go, and we'll see if they'll have the cheek to talk then about kicks behind. Kicks! why I have never submitted to be kicked by any one. And I'll never be beaten, either; because, look you, I'd kill the man who laid a finger on me."

But she gradually quieted down. After all, they could say what they liked. She thought no more of them than of the mud on her shoes. It would defile her to pay the least attention to such people. She had her conscience, and that was enough for her. And Francis became more familiar, seeing her expose her inmost feelings as she stood there in her dirty old gown, and he ventured to give her some advice. She was foolish to sacrifice everything simply for an infatuation; infatuations spoilt life. She listened to him, holding down her head, whilst he spoke in a sad tone of voice, like a connoisseur who grieved to see so lovely a girl throw herself away in such a manner.

"That's my business," she ended by saying. "But thanks all the same, old fellow."

She squeezed his hand, which was always a trifle greasy, in spite of his perfect get-up; then she left him and went to buy her fish. During the day the story of the kick behind occupied her a great deal. She even spoke of it to Fontan, again affecting the style of a strong-minded woman who would not submit to an insult from any one. Fontan, like the superior being he was, declared that all those grand gentlemen were muffs, and that they should despise them. And from that moment Nana was filled with a real disdain.

It happened that evening that they went to the Bouffes Theatre to see a little woman, whom Fontan knew, make her first appearance in a part of ten lines. It was nearly one o'clock in the morning when they at last got back to Montmartre on foot. In the Rue de la Chaussée d'Antin they had stopped to buy a cake, a mocha; and they ate it in bed, because the night was cold, and it was not worth while lighting a fire. Sitting up in bed, side by side, with the clothes well over them, and the pillows piled up behind, they talked of the little woman as they supped. Nana thought her ugly and quite without go. Fontan, who slept on the outside of the bed, passed the slices of cake, which stood on the night-table between a box of matches and the candle. But they ended by quarrelling.

"Oh! is it possible to talk so?" cried Nana. "Her eyes are like gimlet holes, and her hair is the colour of tow."

"Shut up!" replied Fontan. "She has beautiful hair, and her eyes are full of fire. It's funny that you women always pull each other to pieces!" He seemed greatly annoyed. "There, that's enough!" he said at length, in a rough tone of voice. "You know I don't like wrangling. We'll go to sleep, or there'll be a row."

And he blew out the candle. Nana was furious, and continued talking. She was not going to be spoken to like that; she was in the habit of being respected. As he no longer answered, she was obliged to leave off; but she could not go to sleep—she kept turning over and turning over.

"Damn it all! have you finished moving about?" he asked suddenly, jumping up in a sitting posture.

"It's not my fault if there are crumbs in the bed," said she sharply.

And there were indeed crumbs in the bed. She even felt them under her legs, they were all about her. The smallest crumb irritated her, and made her scratch herself till her flesh bled. Besides, when one eats anything in bed, one should always shake the clothes afterwards. Fontan, in a towering rage, lit the candle. They both got out; and in their night-dresses, and with their feet bare, they uncovered the bed and swept the crumbs away with their hands. He, who was shivering all the time, hastily got back into bed, and told her to go to the devil, because she asked him to wipe his feet. Then she returned to her place; but she had scarcely lain down again before she recommenced her dance. There were still some crumbs left.

"Of course! I knew it," said she. "You brought them back again on your feet. I can't go to sleep like this! I tell you I can't!"

And she rose in bed, as though about to step over him. Then, unable to stand it any longer, and wishing to go to sleep, Fontan thrust out his arm and slapped her. The blow was given with such force that Nana at once found herself lying down in bed again, with her head on the pillow. She lay still as though stunned.

"Oh!" said she simply, sighing like a child.

He threatened her with another smack if she moved again. Then, blowing out the candle, he turned on his back, and soon began to snore. She buried her face in her pillow to smother her sobs. It was cowardly to take advantage of her inferior strength. But she was dreadfully frightened, Fontan's usually funny face had looked so terrible. And her anger disappeared, as though the smack had appeased it. She respected him; she squeezed up against the wall to leave him all the room. With her cheek tingling, her eyes full of tears, she even ended by falling asleep in such a delicious dejection of spirits, in such a wearied state of submission, that she no longer felt the crumbs. In the morning, when she awoke, she had her arms round Fontan, holding him very tightly. He would never do it again, would he now? She loved him too much. Still it was even nice to be beaten by him.

From that night their life entirely changed. For a "yes" or a "no" Fontan struck her. She, getting used to it, submitted. Occasionally she cried out or menaced him; but he forced her against the wall, and talked of strangling her, and that made her yield. More frequently she fell on to a chair and sobbed for five minutes. Then she forgot all about it, becoming very gay, and singing and laughing and skipping about the room. The worst was that Fontan now disappeared all day and never came home before midnight; he frequented the cafés where he was likely to meet his friends. Nana tremblingly and caressingly submitted to everything, not daring to utter a reproach for fear of never seeing him again. But some days, when she had neither Madame Maloir nor her aunt with little Louis to help her pass away the time, she felt very wretched indeed. Therefore, one Sunday, when she had gone to the Rochefoucauld market to purchase some pigeons, she was delighted to come across Satin, who was buying a bunch of radishes. Ever since the evening when the prince had partaken of Fontan's champagne, they had lost sight of each other.

"What! it's you! you live in this neighbourhood?" asked Satin, amazed at seeing her out of doors in her slippers at that time of day. "Ah! my poor girl, you must be down in your luck!"

Nana frowned at her to make her leave off, because there were some other women there, women in dressing-gowns, and who did not appear to have any underclothes on, whose hair was all dishevelled and whose faces were smothered with powder. Every morning all the loose women of the neighbourhood, having scarcely got rid of the men picked up the night before, came to make their purchases, dragging their old shoes over the pavement, their eyes heavy with want of sleep, and in the bad temper caused by the fatigue of a night of dissipation. Down every street leading to the market they could be seen coming, all looking very pale, some quite young girls most seductive in appearance, others regular old hags, both fat and flabby, not minding in the least to be seen thus outside their business hours; whilst the passers-by might turn to look at them without even one of them deigning to smile, for they were all in too much of a hurry for that, and went about their errands with the disdainful airs of thrifty women who have no dealings with men whatever. Just as Satin was paying for her bunch of radishes, a young man, some clerk who was late, called to her as he passed, "Good-morning, darling." She at once drew herself up with the dignity of an offended queen, saying,

"What's the matter with that pig there?"

Then she thought she knew him. Three days before, as she was returning from the Boulevards about midnight, she had spoken to him for about half-an-hour at the corner of the Rue

Labruyère before he would make up his mind. But the recollection only annoyed her the more.

"What fools men are to call out such things in the daytime," she resumed. "When one goes out on one's private business, one ought to be respected."

Nana had at length selected her pigeons, though she had doubts as to their freshness. Then Satin wanted to show her where she lived; it was close by in the Rue Rochefoucauld. And, as soon as they were alone together, Nana related the story of her love for Fontan. When she reached her door, the little one stood with her radishes under her arm, interested by the final particulars given by the other, who was lying in her turn, saying that she had sent Count Muffat out of her place with a kick behind.

"Oh! that was grand, very grand!" observed Satin. "A kick behind—oh, splendid! And he didn't dare say a word, did he? Men are such cowards! I should have liked to have been there to have seen his mug. My dear, you were right. Drat their money! I, when I've a fancy, I'd die for it. Well, you'll come and see me, won't you? The door on the left. Knock three times, for there are always a lot of people who come to bother me."

After that day, whenever Nana felt dull, she went to see Satin. She was always certain of finding her in, for the little one never went out before six in the evening. Satin had two rooms, which a chemist had furnished for her so that she should be safe from the police; but, in less than thirteen months, she had broken the furniture, destroyed the seats of the chairs, soiled the curtains, and got everything into such a state of dirt and disorder that the rooms looked as though they were occupied by a troop of mad tabbies. The mornings when she herself, quite disgusted, started cleaning, legs of chairs and shreds of curtains remained in her hands, so hard was the battle she had to fight with the filth. On those days everything looked dirtier still and it was impossible to enter the rooms, for all manner of things were piled up in the doorways. At length she ended by neglecting her home altogether.

In the lamp-light the wardrobe with its mirror, the clock, and what remained of the curtains, looked sufficiently well to

satisfy the men who came to see her. Besides, for six months
past, her landlord had been threatening to turn her out; so
why should she trouble herself by looking after the place? and
for him, perhaps; not if she knew it! And whenever she got up
in a bad temper she shouted out, "Gee up! gee up!" giving formidable kicks on the sides of the wardrobe and the chest of
drawers, which were cracking all over.

Nana nearly always found her in bed. Even the days when
Satin went out on her errands, she was always so tired on her
return that she would fall asleep again on the edge of the bed.
During the daytime she merely dragged herself about, dozing
on the chairs, and never rousing from this state of languor till
the evening when the gas-lamps were lit. And Nana always felt
very comfortable there, sitting doing nothing in the midst of
the untidy bed, of the basins full of dirty water, placed on the
floor, and of the muddy skirts, cast off the night before, soiling
the chairs on which they had been carelessly thrown. She
would cackle and talk of her private affairs without ceasing,
whilst Satin, in her shift and sprawling on the bed with her feet
in the air, listened to her, and smoked cigarettes. Sometimes
on the afternoons, when they had troubles which they wanted
to forget, as they said, they treated each other to absinthe.
Then, without going downstairs, or even putting on a petticoat, Satin would call over the balusters for what she wanted,
to the concierge's little girl, a youngster of ten, who looked at
the lady's naked legs when she brought up the absinthe in a
glass. All the conversation of the two women had reference to
men's abominable ways. Nana was quite unendurable with her
Fontan; she could not utter ten words without alluding to
something he had said or done. But Satin good-naturedly listened to these eternal stories of watchings at the window, of
quarrels about a burned stew, and of reconciliations in bed
after hours of sulking. Through a hankering always to talk
about him, Nana ended by recounting all the blows that he
gave her. Only the previous week he had blackened her eye,
and the evening before, not being able to find his slippers, he
had given her a blow which had sent her reeling against the
night-table. And the other expressed no surprise, quietly puff-

ing her cigarette, and only interrupting Nana to say that for her part she always ducked, with the result of sending the gentleman and his blow to the other end of the room.

They both became deeply interested in these stories of beatings, feeling happy and diverted by the constant repetition of the same stupid incidents, and yielding over again to the warm and sluggish lassitude occasioned by the infamous thrashings of which they spoke. It was the enjoyment of discussing Fontan's blows, of always talking about him, even to describing his way of taking off his boots, that brought Nana there every day, the more especially as Satin invariably sympathised with her. She told in return of things that happened to her which were even worse—of a pastry cook who would leave her on the ground for dead, and whom all the same she loved more than ever. Then came the days when Nana cried, and declared that she could not put up with it any longer. Satin accompanied her to her door, and waited an hour in the street to see if Fontan didn't murder her; and, on the morrow, the two women enjoyed the afternoon, discussing the reconciliation, preferring, however, though without saying so, the days when there was a good row on because that impassioned them the more.

They became inseparable. Yet, Satin never went to Nana's, Fontan having declared that he would not have any strumpets in his place. They would walk out together, and it was thus that one day Satin took her to call on a woman, who turned out to be the Madame Robert whom Nana often thought about with a certain respect ever since she had declined to come to her supper. Madame Robert lived in the Rue Mosnier, one of the new and quiet streets near the Place de l'Europe, not containing a single shop, and the handsome houses of which, with their tiny suites of apartments, are entirely occupied by ladies. It was five o'clock; down the silent thoroughfare, amidst the aristocratic quietude of the tall white houses, the broughams of stock-jobbers and merchants awaited, whilst men hurried along the foot pavements, raising their eyes to the windows, where women in dressing-gowns seemed to be watching for them. Nana at first would not go upstairs, saying stiffly that she was not acquainted with the lady; but Satin insisted. One could always take a friend with one. She was merely paying a visit of politeness. Madame Robert, whom she had met the day before in a restaurant, had behaved very nicely to her, and had made her promise to come and see her. So Nana at length gave in. Upstairs, a little servant, half asleep, said that her mistress was out. However, she ushered them into the drawing-room, and left them there.

"By Jove! how handsome!" murmured Satin.

It was furnished in the severe style of the middle classes, and the hangings were of sombre hue, whilst the whole had that appearance of gentility usually to be seen in the surroundings of the Parisian shopkeeper who has retired on a fortune. Nana, drawing her own conclusions from all this, began to make a few broad remarks; but Satin got angry, and answered for Madame Robert's virtue. She was always to be met in company with grave elderly gentlemen, with whom she walked arm-in-arm. Just now she had a retired chocolate manufacturer, who was of a most serious turn of mind. He was so delighted with the genteel appearance of the establishment, that, whenever he visited there, he always made the servant announce him, and addressed Madame Robert as his child.

"But look, that's she!" said Satin, pointing to a photograph placed in front of the clock.

Nana studied the portrait for a minute. It represented a very dark woman, with a long face, and lips smiling discreetly. One would at once have said, a lady of fashion, but more reserved.

"It's funny," murmured she, at length, "I've certainly seen that face somewhere. Where, I no longer recollect; but it could not have been in a respectable place. Oh! no, it was decidedly not in a respectable place;" and she added, turning towards her friend, "So she made you promise to come and see her. What does she want with you?"

"What does she want with me? Why, to have a chat, no doubt; to be a little while together. It's mere politeness."

Nana looked at Satin straight in the eyes, then she slightly smacked her tongue. Well, it didn't matter to her. However, as the lady was a long time in coming, she declared that she would not wait any further, and they both went away.

On the morrow, Fontan having told Nana that he would not be home to dinner, she started off early to find Satin, in order to treat her to a feast at a restaurant. The selection of the restaurant was a weighty affair. Satin suggested various places, all of which Nana thought abominable. At last she induced her to try Laure's. It was an ordinary in the Rue des Martyrs, where the charge for dinner was three francs a-head. Tired of waiting until the time when it began, and not knowing how to occupy themselves in the streets, they went to Laure's fully twenty minutes too soon. The three rooms were still empty. They seated themselves at a table in the room where Laure Piedefer sat throned behind a high counter. Laure was a person about fifty years old, of a most massive figure, which was kept in shape by the aid of tightly laced stays and waist-bands. A number of women quickly began to arrive, and, standing on tip-toe, and leaning over the piles of little salvers filled with lumps of sugar, they kissed Laure on the mouth with tender familiarity; whilst the fat monster, with moist eyes, tried to divide her attentions, so as not to occasion any jealousies. The maid who waited on the guests, unlike her mistress, was tall and scraggy, with an emaciated look about her, and black eyelids, beneath which her eyes were lighted up with a sombre fire.

The three rooms rapidly filled. There were about a hundred customers, disseminated according to the hazard of the tables, most of them about forty years old, enormous in size, overloaded with flesh, and with faces bloated by vice; and mingling with this assemblage of turgid breasts and stomachs, were a few slim, pretty girls, looking still ingenuous in spite of their brazen gestures—beginners, picked up at low dancing establishments, and brought by some of the customers to Laure's, where the multitude of big, flabby women, thrown quite into a flutter by the sight of their youth, jostled one another, and formed a court around them, like a crowd of anxious old boys, while treating them to all sorts of dainties. As for the men, they were few in number—ten or fifteen at the most—and they all looked very humble amidst the overwhelming shoal of skirts, with the exception of four fellows, who had merely come to see the show, and who joked about it very much at their ease.

"It's very good, their stew, isn't it?" asked Satin.

Nana nodded her head with an air of satisfaction. It was a solid dinner, such as used to be given in country hotels—vol-au-vent, stewed fowl and rice, haricot beans with gravy, and iced vanilla cream. The ladies went in especially for the stewed fowl and rice, almost bursting in their stays, and slowly wiping their lips. At first, Nana was afraid of meeting some of her old acquaintances, who might have asked her stupid questions—but she grew more easy as she noticed no one she knew amongst that very mixed crowd, in which faded dresses and weather-beaten bonnets were to be seen side by side with the most elegant costumes in the fraternity of the same corruption. For a minute she was interested in a young man, with short, curly hair, and an impudent-looking face, who kept a whole table of women, bursting with fat, and bent on satisfying his every whim, in a breathless state of anxiety. But on the young man laughing, his breasts rose.

"Why, it's a woman!" Nana exclaimed, with a smothered cry.

Satin, who was stuffing herself with fowl, raised her head, and then whispered,

"Ah! yes, I know her; she's quite the go! They're all after her."

Nana pouted with disgust. She couldn't understand that. Yet she said, in her reasonable sort of way, that it was no use arguing about tastes and colours, for one never knew what one might like some day; and she ate her ice cream with a philosophical air, perfectly aware of the sensation Satin was causing among the neighbouring tables with her big, blue, virgin-like eyes. She more especially noticed a large, fair-haired person seated near her, who was making herself most amiable. She gave such glances, and edged up so close, that Nana was on the point of interfering.

But just at that moment a woman entered the room, who caused her a great surprise. She had recognised Madame Robert. The latter, with her pretty look of a little brown mouse, nodded familiarly to the tall, scraggy maid, and then went and leaned against Laure's counter, and they both kissed each other a long time. Nana thought this caress rather peculiar on the part of so lady-like a woman, the more especially as Madame Robert no longer had her modest look, but the contrary. She glanced about the room, as she conversed in a low tone of voice. Laure had just sat down again, once more throning herself with the majesty of an old idol of vice, with face worn and polished by the kisses of the faithful; and, from above the plates of viands, she reigned over her connection of big, bloated women, bulkier than even the most enormous of them, and enjoying the fortune that had rewarded forty years of labour.

Madame Robert, however, had caught sight of Satin. So leaving Laure, she hastened to her, and was most amiable, saying she regretted extremely having been out on the previous day; and as Satin, quite charmed, insisted on making room for her at the table, she declared that she had dined. She had merely come to look about. As she talked, standing up behind her new friend, she leant on her shoulders, and, in a smiling, wheedling way, kept saying,

"Well, when shall I see you? Do you happen to be free—"

Nana, unfortunately, was unable to hear more. The conversation annoyed her, and she was burning to give that respectable woman a bit of her mind; but the sight of a troop of people just arrived paralysed her. It consisted of some very stylish women, in gorgeous dresses and diamonds. Displaying their hundreds of francs' worth of precious stones on their persons, and seized with an inclination to visit the old haunt, they had come in a party to Laure's, whom they treated most familiarly, to dine there at three francs a head, amidst the jealous astonishment of the other poor, mud-bedabbled women. When they entered, with loud voices and clear, ringing laughter, bringing, as it were, a ray of sunshine from the outside, Nana quickly turned her head, greatly annoyed at seeing Lucy Stewart and Maria Blond amongst them. For close upon five minutes, during the whole time these ladies were conversing with Laure, before passing into the next room, she kept her face bent down, pretending to be very busy in rolling some bread crumbs over the cloth. Then, when she was at length able to turn round, she was aghast at seeing that the chair next to her was empty. Satin had disappeared.

"Whatever has become of her?" she unconsciously exclaimed aloud.

The big, fair-haired woman, who had been so attentive to Satin, laughed ill-humouredly; and as Nana, irritated by the laugh, gave her a menacing look, she said softly, in a drawling tone of voice,

"It's certainly not I who've run away with her, it's the other one."

And Nana, understanding that she would only get laughed at, held her tongue. She even remained seated a short time longer, not wishing to show her annoyance. From the other room she could hear the voice of Lucy Stewart, who was standing treat to a whole table of girls, who had come from the dancing places of Montmartre and La Chapelle. It was very warm. The maid was removing piles of dirty plates, smelling strongly of the stewed fowl and rice, whilst the four gentlemen had ended by standing some strong wine to several different parties of women, in hope of making them drunk, and of hearing something smutty. What exasperated Nana was having to pay for Satin's dinner. She was a nice hussy to allow herself to be well stuffed, and then to go off with the first who asked her, without even saying "Thank you!" It was, it is true, only three francs, but she thought it hard, all the same. It was such a dirty trick to play. She paid, however, banging her six francs down before Laure, whom she despised then more than the mud in the gutter.

In the Rue des Martyrs Nana's rancour increased. She certainly wouldn't go and run after Satin—she wouldn't go near such a vile creature! But all the same her evening was spoilt, and she returned slowly towards Montmartre, feeling frightfully enraged with Madame Robert. That one certainly had a famous cheek to pretend she was a respectable woman. She was respectable enough for a dust-bin! Now she recollected perfectly of having seen her at the "Butterfly," a foul dancing-place in the Rue des Poissonniers, where she used to sell herself for thirty sous. And she got hold of government officials by her modest ways, and she refused suppers, to which she had been honoured by an invitation, just to pretend that she was a virtuous person! Ah! she should have some virtue given her! It was always such prudes as she who got hold of the most shocking diseases, in ignoble holes that no one else knew of.

However, Nana, while thinking of all these things, had at length arrived home in the Rue Véron. She was amazed to see a light in the windows. Fontan, having been left directly after dinner by the friend who had invited him, had come home in a very bad humour. He listened in a cold way to the explanations she hastened to give in her fear of being knocked about and her bewilderment at seeing him there when she had not expected him before one in the morning; she lied, for though she admitted spending six francs, she said she had been with Madame Maloir. He remained wrapt in his dignity, and handed her a letter, which he had coolly opened although addressed to her. It was a letter from George, who was still kept at Les Fondettes, and who gave vent to his feelings every week in several pages of the most impassioned language. Nana was delighted when anyone wrote to her, expecially letters full of vows of love. She read them to everyone. Fontan was acquainted with George's style, and appreciated it. But that night she so feared a row that she affected the greatest indifference; she glanced through the letter in a sulky sort of way, and then threw it on one side. Fontan was beating the tattoo on a window pane, not wanting to go to bed so early, and not knowing what to do to while away the evening. Suddenly he turned round.

"Suppose we write an answer to the youngster at once," said he.

It was usually he who wrote; he had a much finer style. And then he was pleased when Nana, full of admiration for his letter, which he would read out aloud, would kiss him and exclaim that only he could find such pretty things to say. And all that ended by exciting them, and they adored each other.

"As you like," she replied. "I will make some tea. We can go to bed afterwards."

Then Fontan made himself comfortable at the table, with a

great display of pen, ink, and paper. He rounded his arms, and thrust out his chin.

"My heart," he began, reading out loud.

And he worked away for more than an hour, reflecting occasionally about a sentence, his head buried in his hands, and laughing to himself whenever he thought of some expression exceptionally tender. Nana had already taken two cups of tea in silence. At length he read the letter as they read on the stage, just making a few gestures. He wrote, on five sides of paper, about the "delicious hours passed at La Mignotte, the memory of which would remain like subtile perfumes," he swore "an eternal fidelity to that springtide of love," and ended in declaring that his sole desire was "to recommence that happiness, if happiness can commence again."

"You know," he explained, "I say all that out of politeness. As it's only for fun—well! I think it'll do!"

He was delighted with himself. But Nana, still dreading a row, was foolish enough not to throw her arms round his neck and utter words of admiration. She thought the letter would do very well, but that was all. Then he was very much put out. If his letter did not please her she could write another one; and, instead of embracing each other, as they usually did after a great many protestations of love, they remained very cold on either side of the table. She had, however, poured him out a cup of tea.

"What muck!" he cried, as he wetted his lips with it. "You have been putting salt into it!" Nana unhappily shrugged her shoulders. He became furious. "Ah! everything's going wrong this evening!"

And the quarrel started from that. It was only ten by the clock, so it was a way of killing time. He worked himself up, he flung all sorts of accusations at her, full of insults, without giving her time to answer them. She was dirty, she was idiotic, she had led a fine life! Then he raved about the money. Was he in the habit of spending six francs when he dined out? He had his dinners paid for, otherwise he would have taken pot-luck at home. And all for that old procuress Maloir, too—an old hag whom he would pitch downstairs if she dared show herself there again! Ah well! they would go far if every day they chucked six francs into the street in that style!

"First of all," cried he, "I must have your accounts! Come, give me the money; let me see how we stand now!"

All his miserly instincts were awakened. Nana, subdued and terrified, hastened to fetch the money that was left from the drawer, and laid it before him. Until then the key had been left in the lock and they had each taken what they needed.

"What!" said he, after counting, "there are scarcely seven thousand francs remaining out of seventeen thousand, and we have only been living together for three months. It isn't possible."

He rushed from his seat and turned out the drawer by the light of the lamp. But there were really only six thousand eight hundred and a few odd francs. Then the row became a regular storm.

"Ten thousand francs in three months!" he bellowed. "Damnation! what have you done with them, eh? Answer me! It all goes to your old hag of an aunt, eh? or else you've been treating yourself—that's very clear. Answer me at once!"

"Ah! you get in a passion instantly!" said Nana. "It's very easy to make up the account. You forget all the furniture; then I am obliged to buy a lot of linen. Money soon goes when there is everything to buy."

But though he demanded explanations, he would not listen to them.

"Yes, it goes a great deal too quickly," resumed he in a calmer tone of voice; "and look here, young woman, I've had enough of this share and share alike business. These seven thousand francs, you know, are mine. Well! now I've got them, I intend to stick to them. As you're so wasteful as all that, I'll take care I'm not ruined. One has a right to one's own"; and he magisterially put the money in his pocket, whilst Nana looked at him in amazement. Then he complaisantly continued, "You understand, I'm not such a fool as to keep aunts and children who are not mine. It pleased you to spend your money, and that was your business; but mine is sacred! When you cook a leg of mutton, I'll pay half. Every night we'll settle up!"

On hearing this, Nana revolted. She could not restrain a cry, "I say, that's disgusting! You had your share of my ten thousand francs!"

But he did not waste more time in discussion. Leaning across the table, he gave her a slap in the face with all his might, exclaiming, "Say that again!"

She did so, in spite of the slap, and then he fell upon her with kicks and blows. He soon put her into such a state that she ended, as usual, by undressing herself and going sobbing to bed. He puffed and blowed, and was also about to get into bed, when he noticed the letter he had written for George lying on the table. Then he folded it up with care, and turning towards the bed, said menacingly,

"The letter will do very well. I will post it myself, because I don't intend to put up with any caprices. And don't whine, for it annoys me."

Nana, who was weeping bitterly, held her breath. When he got into bed, she felt as though choking, and throwing herself on his breast, sobbed aloud. Their battles always ended thus. She trembled at the thought of losing him. She felt a mean want of knowing he was all her own, in spite of everything. He twice pushed her away with a haughty gesture; but the warm embrace of the supplicating woman, with her large tearful eyes, resembling those of some faithful animal, kindled a flame of desire within him. And he acted the good prince, without, however, stooping to make any advances. He let himself be caressed, and, so to say, taken by force, in the style of a man whose forgiveness is worth winning. Then he was seized with anxiety. He feared that Nana had only been acting a little comedy to get possession of the cash again. He had blown out the candle, when he thought it necessary to assert once more his authority.

"You know, my girl, I meant what I said. I intend to keep the money."

Nana, who was going to sleep with her arms round his neck, said sublimely, "Yes, never fear; I will work."

But from that evening their life together became worse than ever. From one end of the week to the other the sound of slaps could be heard, just like the tick-tick of a pendulum which seemed to regulate their existence. Nana, through being beaten so frequently, became as supple as fine linen; and it made her skin so delicate, and so soft to the touch—her complexion so pink and white, so clear to the eye—that she was more beautiful than ever. And that was why Prullière was for ever dangling about her skirts, calling when he knew Fontan would not be there, and pushing her into corners and trying to kiss her; but she, at once becoming highly indignant, struggled and blushed with shame. She thought it disgusting of him to wish to deceive his friend. Then Prullière sneered with vexation. Really, she was becoming precious stupid! How could she stick to such a monkey? for Fontan was indeed a monkey, with his big nose for ever on the move—a disgusting pig! and a fellow, too, who was always knocking her about!

"That may be, but I love him as he is," she replied one day, in the cool way of a woman owning to some most revolting taste.

Bosc contented himself with dining there as often as possible. He shrugged his shoulders behind Prullière; a handsome fellow, but not serious. He had often assisted at rows in the house. During dessert, when Fontan slapped Nana, he would continue chewing in a matter-of-fact way, thinking it the most natural thing in the world. By the way of paying for his dinners, he always pretended to be in raptures at the sight of their happiness. He proclaimed himself a philosopher; he had renounced everything, even glory. Prullière and Fontan, leaning back in their chairs, would sometimes forget themselves after the table had been cleared, and fall to relating their successes up to two o'clock in the morning, with their stage voices and gestures; whilst he, wrapt in thought, and only occasionally giving a little sniff of disdain, would silently finish the bottle of brandy. What was left of Talma? Nothing. Then they had better shut up, and not make such fools of themselves!

One night he found Nana in tears. She removed her bodice

and showed him her back and arms covered with bruises. He looked at the skin, without being tempted to take advantage of the situation, as that fool Prullière would have been. Then he sententiously observed,

"My child, wherever there are women, there are slaps. It was Napoleon who said that, I think. Bathe yourself with salt water. Salt water is excellent for such trifles. Take my word for it, you will receive a great many more; and do not complain, so long as there is nothing broken. You know, I shall invite myself to dinner; I noticed a leg of mutton."

But Madame Lerat was not gifted with similar philosophy. Each time Nana showed her a fresh bruise on her white skin, she complained loudly. Her niece was being murdered; it could not last. The truth was, Fontan had turned Madame Lerat out, and said that he would not have her in the place again; and, ever since that day, if she happened to be there when he returned home, she was obliged to take her departure by way of the kitchen, which humiliated her immensely. And so she never ceased abusing that unmannerly person. With the airs of a most well-bred woman, to whom no one could teach anything pertaining to a polite education, she reproached him with having been shockingly badly brought up.

"Oh! one can see that at a glance," she would say to Nana. "He has no idea of even the slightest propriety. His mother must have been a very low woman. Don't deny it, he shows it only too plainly! I do not say it on my own account, although a person of my age has a right to a certain respect; but you, really now, how do you manage to put up with his bad manners? for, without flattering myself, I always taught you how to behave yourself, and in your own home you received the very best advice. We were all very respectable in our family, were we not?"

Nana did not protest, she listened with her head bowed down.

"Then," continued the aunt, "you have only been acquainted with well-to-do people. We were just talking about it last night at home with Zoé. She can't understand either why you put up with all this. 'How,' said she, 'can madame, who

could do just as she pleased with the count'—for between ourselves you appear to have treated him as though he were a donkey—'how can madame allow herself to be massacred by that
ugly clown?' I added that slaps might even be borne, but that
I would never have submitted to such a want of respect. In
short, he has nothing whatever in his favour. I wouldn't have
his portrait in my room on any account. And you are ruining
yourself for such a sorry bird as he is; yes, you are ruining yourself, my darling. You are going about in want of everything,
when there are so many others, and far richer ones too, and
gentlemen connected with the government. But that's
enough! it's not I who ought to tell you all this. However, were
I in your place, the very next time he treated me ill, I'd leave
him to himself, with a 'Sir, whom do you take me for?' said in
your grand style, you know, which would show him you were
not going to be made a fool of any longer."

Then Nana burst into tears, and sobbed: "Oh! aunt, I love
him."

The truth was Madame Lerat was feeling very anxious, seeing that it was only with the greatest difficulty that her niece
managed to give her a twenty sous piece at distant intervals, to
pay for little Louis's board. Of course she would do her utmost,
she would keep the child all the same, and wait for better
times; but the idea that it was Fontan who was the cause why
she, the child and its mother were not rolling in wealth enraged her to such a pitch, that she denied the existence of
love. Accordingly she concluded with these harsh words:

"Listen; one day when he has skinned you alive, you will
come and knock at my door, and I will let you in."

The want of funds soon became Nana's great care. The
seven thousand francs Fontan had taken had quite disappeared. No doubt he had put them in some safe place, and she
did not dare question him; for she was very timid with that
sorry bird, as Madame Lerat styled him. She trembled lest he
should think her capable of sticking to him for the sake of his
money. He had promised to give something towards the housekeeping expenses, and he started by giving three francs every
morning; but he expected all sorts of things for his money. He

wanted everything for his three francs—butter, meat, early fruit, and vegetables; and if she hazarded an observation—if she insinuated that it was impossible to purchase all in the market for three twenty sous pieces—he fumed, he called her a good-for-nothing, an extravagant hussy, a stupid fool whom the market people robbed, and invariably wound up by threatening to get his meals elsewhere. Then after the expiration of a month, on some mornings he would forget to leave the three francs on the top of the chest of drawers. She ventured to ask him for them timidly, in a round-about way; but this had occasioned such quarrels—he made her life so miserable on the first pretext he could get hold of—that she preferred no longer to count on him. Whenever he had not left the money, and found all the same a good dinner ready for him, he was as gay as a lark, and most amiable, embracing Nana and waltzing about the room with the chairs. And this made her so happy that she reached the point of wishing not to find anything on the drawers, in spite of the difficulty she had in making both ends meet. One morning even she returned him his three francs, telling him a long rigmarole about having some money left from the previous day. As he had given nothing for two days he hesitated for a moment, fearing a lesson. But she looked at him with her eyes overflowing with love, she embraced him with a complete abandonment of her whole person; and he put the money back into his pocket, with the slight convulsive trepidation of a miser recovering an amount that had been in danger. From that day he ceased to trouble himself, never asking where the money came from, looking very black when there were only potatoes, and laughing fit to dislocate his jaws on beholding a turkey or a leg of mutton; without prejudice, however, to sundry cuffs with which he favoured Nana, even in his happiest moments, just to keep his hand in training.

Nana had therefore found means of supplying everything. On certain days the house was glutted with food. Bosc feasted there so sumptuously twice a week that he suffered from indigestion. One evening as Madame Lerat was leaving, angry at seeing before the fire an abundant dinner of which she was not to partake, she could not resist bluntly asking who it was who paid for it. Nana, taken by surprise, no longer knew what she was about and began to cry.

"Well! it's a nice state of things," said the aunt, who understood.

Nana had resigned herself for the sake of peace and quietness in her home. It was partly, too, the fault of old Tricon, whom she had met in the Rue de Laval one day when Fontan had gone off in a fury because there had been nothing but salt cod for dinner. So she had said "yes" to old Tricon, who happened to be in a difficulty. After that, as Fontan never came home before six in the evening, she was able to dispose of her afternoons, and often brought back as much as forty or sixty francs, and sometimes more. She might have made as much as ten and fifteen louis had she been entirely free; but still she was very glad to get enough to keep things going. At night-time she forgot all, when Bosc was almost bursting with food, and Fontan, with his elbows on the table, let her kiss his eyes with the self-satisfied air of a man who is loved for himself alone.

Then, whilst adoring her darling, her dear love, with a passion all the more blinding as it was she who now paid for all, Nana reverted again to the depravity of her early days. She walked the streets as she did when a young girl in quest of a five francs piece. One Sunday, at the Rochefoucauld market, she made it up with Satin, after flying at her and bullying her on account of Madame Robert. But Satin merely replied that when one did not like a thing, one had no right to seek to disgust others with it; and Nana, who was by no means narrow-minded, yielded to the philosophical idea that one never knows how one may end, and forgave her. And her curiosity being awakened, she even questioned her in regard to some details of vice, amazed at learning something fresh at her age, after all she knew. She laughed, and thought it very funny, yet feeling all the time a slight repugnance, for at heart she was rather conservative in her habits. She often went to Laure's when Fontan dined out. She was amused with the stories she heard there, with the loves and the jealousies which had so much interest for the other customers, though they never caused them to lose a mouthful. However she was never mixed up with them, as she said. Stout Laure, with her maternal affection, often invited her to spend a few days at her villa at Asnières—a country house where there were rooms for seven ladies. She declined—she was afraid; but Satin having declared to her that she was mistaken, that gentlemen from Paris would swing them and play at different games in the garden with them, she promised to come later on, as soon as she was able to get away.

At that time Nana was very worried, and was not much inclined for a spree. She was greatly in want of money. When old Tricon had nothing for her, and that occurred only too often, she did not know whom to go to. Then she would wander about with Satin all over Paris, amidst that degrading vice which prowls along the muddy by-streets, beneath the dim glimmer of the gas lamps. Nana returned to the low dancing places of the barriers, where she had first learned to hop about with her dirty skirts. She once more beheld the dark corners of the outer Boulevards, the posts against which men used to kiss her when only fifteen years old, whilst her father was seeking her to give her a hiding. They both hastened along, visiting all the balls and the cafés of a locality, crawling up stairs wet with saliva and spilt beer; or else they walked slowly, following street after street, and standing up every now and then in the doorways. Satin, who had first appeared in the Quartier Latin, took Nana there, to Bullier's, and to the cafés of the Boulevard Saint-Michel. But it was vacation time, and the quarter was almost deserted; so they returned to the principal Boulevards. It was there that they met with most luck. From the heights of Montmartre to the plateau where the Observatory was situated, they thus rambled about the entire city. Rainy nights when their shoes would become trodden down at heel, warm nights which made their clothes adhere to their skin, long waits and endless wanderings, jostlings and quarrels, brutal abuse from a passer-by enticed into some obscure lodging, down the dirty stairs of which he retired swearing.

The summer was drawing to a close—a stormy summer, with

sultry nights. They would start off together after dinner, about nine o'clock. Along the pavements of the Rue Notre-Dame de Lorette, two lines of women, keeping close to the shops, holding up their skirts, their noses pointing to the ground, might be seen hastening towards the Boulevards, without bestowing a glance on the displays in the windows, and looking as though they had some most important business on hand. It was the famished onslaught of the Bréda quarter, which commenced with the first glimmer of the gas-light. Nana and Satin passed close to the church, and always went along the Rue le Peletier. Then, at a hundred yards from the Café Riche, having reached the exercising ground, they would let fall the trains of their dresses, which until that moment they had carefully held in their hands; and after then, regardless of the dust, sweeping the pavement and swinging their bodies, they would walk slowly along, moving slower still whenever they came into the flood of light of some large café. Holding their heads high, laughing loudly, and looking back after the men who turned to glance at them, they were in their element. Their whitened faces, spotted with the red of their lips and the black of their eye-lashes, assumed in the shadow the disturbing charm of some imitation Eastern bazaar held in the open street. Until twelve o'clock, in spite of the jostling of the crowd, they promenaded gaily along, merely muttering "stupid fool!" now and again behind the backs of the awkward fellows whose heels caught in their flounces. They exchanged familiar nods with the café waiters, lingered sometimes to talk at the tables, accepting drinks which they swallowed slowly, like persons happy at having the chance to sit down, while waiting till the people came out of the theatres. But, as the night advanced, if they had not made one or two trips to the Rue la Rochefoucauld, their pursuit became more eager—they no longer picked and chose. Beneath the trees of the now gloomy and almost deserted Boulevards, ferocious bargains were made, and occasionally the sound of oaths and blows would be heard; whilst fathers of families, with their wives and daughters, used to such encounters, would pass sedately by without hastening their footsteps.

Then, after having made the tour ten times from the Opera to the Gymnase Theatre, finding that the men avoided them, and hurried along all the faster in the increasing obscurity, Nana and Satin would adjourn to the Rue du Faubourg-Montmartre. There, up till two o'clock in the morning, the lights of the restaurants, of the beer saloons, and of the pork-butchers, blazed away, whilst quite a swarm of women hung about the doors of the cafés; it was the last bright and animated corner of nocturnal Paris, the last open market for the contracts of a night, where business was overtly transacted among the various groups, from one end of the street to the other, the same as in the spacious hall of some public building. And on the nights when they returned home unsuccessful, they wrangled with each other. The Rue Notre-Dame de Lorette appeared dark and deserted, with only the occasional shadow of some woman dragging herself along; it was the tardy return of the poor girls of the neighbourhood, exasperated by an evening of forced idleness, and pertinaciously striving for better luck as they argued in a hoarse voice with some drunkard who had lost his way, and whom they detained at the corner of the Rue Bréda or the Rue Fontaine.

However, they occasionally had some very good windfalls—louis given them by well-dressed gentlemen, who put their decorations in their pockets as they accompanied them. Satin especially scented them from afar. On wet nights, when dank Paris emitted the unsavoury smell of a vast alcove seldom cleansed, she knew that the dampness of the atmosphere, the fetidness of the low haunts, excited the men. And she watched for those that were the best off; she could see it in their pale eyes. It was like a stroke of carnal madness passing over the city. It is true that she was at times rather frightened, for she knew that the most gentlemanly-looking men were generally the most filthy-minded. All the polish vanished and the brute appeared beneath, exacting in his monstrous tastes and refined in his perversion. So Satin, therefore, had no respect for the great people in their carriages, but would say that their coachmen were far nicer, for they treated women as they should be treated, and did not half kill them with ideas worthy of hell.

This fall of well-to-do people into the crapulence of vice still astonished Nana, who had reserved certain prejudices of which
Satin relieved her. When seriously discussing the subject she
would ask, Was there, then, no virtue? From the highest to the
lowest, all seemed to grovel in vice. Well! there were some
pretty doings in Paris from nine in the evening till three in the
morning; and then she would laugh aloud and exclaim that if
one were only able to look into all the rooms, one would witness some very queer things—the lower classes going in for a
regular treat, and here and there not a few of the upper classes
poking their noses even more than the others into the beastly
goings-on. She was completing her education.

One night, on calling for Satin, she recognised the Marquis
de Chouard coming down the stairs, leaning heavily on the
balustrade, his legs yielding beneath him, and his face ghastly
pale. She took out her handkerchief and pretended to blow
her nose; then, when she found Satin surrounded by the accustomed filth, the room not having been touched for more
than a week past, basins and other utensils lying about on all
sides, the bed in a most dirty condition, she expressed her astonishment that her friend should know the marquis. Ah, yes!
she knew him; in fact, he had been an awful nuisance when she
and her pastrycook were living together! Now, he came from
time to time; but he pestered her immensely. He sniffed about
in every dirty place he could find, even in her slippers.

"Yes, my dear, in my slippers. Oh! he's a filthy beast! He's always wanting things—"

What most troubled Nana was the sincerity of these low de-
baucheries. She recalled to mind her comedies of pleasure,
during the days of her fast life; whilst she saw the girls about
her losing their health at it day by day. Then Satin frightened
her terribly with the police. She was full of stories about them.
Once she used to keep up an acquaintance with one of the in-
spectors of public morals, so as to insure being left alone; on
two occasions he had prevented her name from being entered
in their books, and now she trembled, for she knew what to expect if they caught her a third time. It was shocking to hear
her. The police arrested as many women as they possibly could,

in order to get bribes, they seized all they came across, and silenced you with a slap in the mouth if you cried out, for they were certain of being upheld and rewarded, even though there happened to be a respectable girl among the number. In the summer they would start off, twelve or fifteen together, and make a round-up on the Boulevards, surrounding one of the footpaths, and securing as many as thirty women in an evening. Satin, however, knew their favourite spots. As soon as ever she caught a glimpse of a policeman, away she bolted, amidst the wild flight of the long trains, through the crowd. There was a dread of the law, a terror of the Préfecture of Police so great that many remained as though paralysed at the doors of the cafés, in spite of the advancing policemen, who swept the road before them. But Satin most dreaded being informed against; her pastry cook had been mean enough to threaten to denounce her when he left her. Yes, some men lived on their mistresses by those means, without counting the dirty women who would betray you through jealousy, if you were better looking than they.

Nana listened to all these stories which greatly increased her fears. She had always trembled at the name of the law—that unknown power, that vengance of men which could suppress her, without anyone in the world defending her. The prison of Saint-Lazare appeared to her like a tomb, an enormous black hole, in which women were buried alive, after having had their hair cut off. She would say to herself that she had only to give up Fontan to find no end of protectors; and Satin might tell her hundreds of times of certain lists of women, accompanied by their photographs, that the policemen had to consult, and be careful never to interfere with the originals. She was nevertheless dreadfully frightened, she was always seeing herself jostled and dragged off to be inspected on the morrow; and the idea of the inspection filled her with agony and shame, she who had so often thrown her chemise over the house-tops.

It so happened that one night towards the end of September, as she was walking with Satin along the Boulevard Poissonnière, the latter suddenly started off at full gallop. And as she asked her why she did so:

"The police!" panted her friend. "Hurry up! hurry up!"

There was a headlong rush through the crowd; skirts were torn in their flight—there were blows and cries, a woman fell to the ground. The mob laughingly looked on at the brutal onslaught of the police, who rapidly contracted their circle. Nana, however, had soon lost sight of Satin. She felt her legs failing her; she was on the point of being caught, when a man, taking her arm in his, led her off in the face of the infuriated policemen. It was Prullière, who had just at that moment recognised her. Without speaking, he turned with her down the Rue Rougemont, which was almost deserted, where she was able to take breath; but she felt so faint, that he had to support her. She did not even thank him.

"Well," said he at length, "you had better come round to my place and rest yourself a bit."

He lived close by, in the Rue Bergère. But she pulled herself together at once.

"No, I won't."

"But everyone does," he roughly resumed. "Why won't you?"

"Because—"

To her mind that said everything. She loved Fontan too much to deceive him with a friend. The others did not count, as it was from necessity and not pleasure that she listened to them. In the face of such stupid obstinacy, Prullière behaved with the meanness of a handsome man wounded in his pride.

"Well! please yourself," said he. "Only I'm not going your way, my dear. Get out of the mess by yourself."

And he walked off. All her fright came back again; she returned to Montmartre by a most roundabout way, keeping close to the shops, and turning pale every time a man came near her.

It was on the morrow that Nana, still feeling the shock of her terrors of the night before, suddenly found herself face to face with Labordette, in a quiet little street at Batignolles, as she was on her way to her aunt's. At first they both seemed rather uneasy. He, though always most obliging, had some business which he kept to himself. However, he was the first to regain his composure, and express his pleasure at the meeting.

Really, every one was still amazed at Nana's total eclipse. She was inquired after everywhere, her old friends were all pining away. And, becoming paternal, he preached her a little sermon.

"Now, frankly, my dear, between ourselves, you are making a fool of yourself. One can understand a bit of infatuation, but not being reduced to the point you are, to be eaten up to that extent and then only to pocket kicks and blows! Are you going in for the prize of virtue?"

She listened to him in an embarrassed manner. But when he spoke to her of Rose, who was triumphing with her conquest of Count Muffat, her eyes sparkled. She murmured:

"Oh! if I choose—"

He at once offered his mediation, in his obliging way. But she refused. Then, he attacked her on another subject. He told her that Bordenave was going to bring out a new piece by Fauchery, in which there was a capital part that would suit her splendidly.

"What! a new piece with a part that would suit me!" she exclaimed in amazement; "but *he* is in it, and he never told me!"

She did not name Fontan. Besides, she became calm again almost directly. She would never return to the stage. No doubt Labordette was not convinced, for he insisted with a smile.

"You know you have nothing to fear with me. I will prepare Muffat, you will return to the theatre, and then I will lead him to you like a lamb."

"No!" said she energetically.

And she left him. Her heroism caused her to bemoan her fate. A cad of a man would not have sacrificed himself like that without trumpeting it abroad. Yet one thing struck her: Labordette had given her exactly the same advice as Francis. That evening, when Fontan returned home she questioned him about Fauchery's piece. He had been back at the Variety Theatre for two months past. Why had he not told her about the part?

"What part?" asked he in his cross voice. "Do you happen to mean the part of the grand lady? Really now, do you then think yourself a genius? But, my girl, you could no more play that part than fly. Upon my word, you make me laugh!"

Her feelings were dreadfully hurt. All night he chaffed her, calling her Mademoiselle Mars. And the more he ridiculed her, the more she stood up for herself, feeling a strange pleasure in that heroic defence of her whim, which, in her own eyes, made her appear very great and very loving. Ever since she had been consorting with other men, for the purpose of feeding him, she loved him the more, in spite of all the fatigue and the loathing which this existence caused her. He became her vice, for which she paid, and which, beneath the sting of the blows, she could not do without. He, seeing her as loving and obedient as an animal, ended by abusing his power. She irritated his nerves. He became seized with a ferocious hatred to such an extent, that he lost sight altogether of his own interests. Whenever Bosc made an observation on the subject, he exclaimed, exasperated without any one knowing why, that he did not care a curse for her or her good dinners, and that he would turn her out of the place, just for the sake of spending the seven thousand francs on another woman. And that was indeed the end of their intimacy.

One night Nana, on coming home about eleven o'clock, found the door bolted on the inside. She knocked a first time, no answer; a second time, still no answer. Yet she could see a light under the door, and Fontan was walking about inside. She knocked again and again without ceasing, and calling to him angrily. At length Fontan said in a slow, thick voice:

"Go to the devil!"

She knocked with both her fists.

"Go to the devil!"

She knocked louder, almost enough to break the panel.

"Go to the devil!"

And for a quarter of an hour the same words answered her like a jeering echo of the blows she hammered on the door. Then, seeing that she did not tire, he suddenly opened it, and standing on the threshold, with his arms crossed, said in the same cold brutal tone of voice:

"Damnation! have you nearly done? What is it you want? You

had better let us go to sleep! You can see very well that I am not alone."

And true enough he was not alone. Nana caught a glimpse of the little woman of the Bouffes Theatre, already in her nightdress, with her curly hair that looked like tow, and her eyes like gimlet holes, who was enjoying the fun in the midst of the furniture that Nana had paid for. Fontan stepped out on to the landing, looking terrible, and opening his big fingers said:

"Be off, or I'll strangle you!"

Then Nana burst into nervous sobs. She was frightened and ran off. This time it was she who was turned out. In her anger she suddenly thought of Muffat, and of how she had treated him; but really it was not for Fontan to avenge him.

Outside, her first idea was to go and sleep with Satin, if no one else was with her. She met her outside her house, she having been also chucked out, but by her landlord, who had put a padlock on her door, against all legal right, as the furniture was hers. Satin cursed and swore, and talked of having him up before the commissary of police. However, as midnight was striking, the first thing to do was to obtain a bed somewhere. And Satin, thinking it best not to make the policeman acquainted with the state of her affairs, ended by taking Nana to a lady who kept a licensed lodging-house in the Rue de Laval. They obtained a small back room on the first floor overlooking the courtyard.

"I might have gone to Madame Robert's," said Satin. "There is always room there for me; but I couldn't have taken you. She's becoming most ridiculously jealous. The other night she beat me."

When they had fastened themselves in, Nana, who up till then had not unbosomed herself, burst into tears, and related again and again the dirty trick that Fontan had played her. She listened complaisantly, consoled her, and became even more indignant than she, abusing the men heartily.

"Oh, the pigs! oh, the pigs! You should have nothing more to do with such pigs!"

Then she helped Nana to undress. She hovered around her

like a gentle and obliging little woman, and kept saying, coaxingly,

"Let's get into bed quickly, my dear. We shall be much better there. Ah! how silly you are to be worried! I tell you that they're a foul set! Don't think of them any more. You know I love you very much. Now leave off crying—do, for your little darling's sake."

And in bed she at once took Nana in her arms, so as to calm her. She would not hear Fontan's name mentioned again. Each time that it came to her friend's lips she stopped it with a kiss, prettily pouting with anger, her hair all loose, and looking childishly beautiful, and full of tenderness. Then, little by little, in this sweet embrace, Nana dried her tears. She was touched; she returned Satin's caresses. When two o'clock struck the light was still burning. Both were laughing gently, and uttering words of love.

But suddenly a great noise was heard in the house. Satin, half naked, jumped out of bed and listened.

"The police!" said she, pale with fear. "Ah! damn it! we've no luck. We're done for!"

She had told of the searches the policemen made in the hotels and lodging-houses fully twenty times, and yet, when they went to the Rue de Laval that night they had neither of them given the matter a thought. At the word police, Nana lost her wits entirely. She jumped out of bed, and, running across the room, opened the window, with the wild look of a mad woman about to jump out. But, fortunately, the little courtyard was covered in with glass, and over this was a wire net-work on a level with the window. She did not hesitate, but, stepping on to the sill, disappeared in the darkness, her chemise blowing about her, and her bare legs exposed to the keen night air.

"Stay here," cried Satin, terrified. "You will kill yourself."

Then, as they were knocking at the door, she good-naturedly closed the window, and threw her friend's clothes into the bottom of a cupboard. She had already resigned herself to her fate, saying to herself that after all, if they did put her on their list, she would no more have occasion for that stupid fright.

She pretended to be sound asleep, yawned, parleyed, and ended by opening the door to a big fellow with a dirty beard, who said:

"Show your hands. You've no needle marks on your fingers. You don't work. Come, dress yourself."

"But I'm not a needle-woman, I'm a burnisher," declared Satin boldly.

But all the same, she quietly dressed herself, for she knew that it was no use arguing. Cries were heard about the house. One girl held on to the door, refusing to move. Another, who was in bed with her lover, and for whom he became responsible, acted the part of the grossly insulted respectable woman, and threatened to take proceedings against the Prefect of Police. For nearly an hour there was a noise of heavy boots on the stairs, of doors shaken by violent blows, of piercing shrieks ending in sobs, of women's skirts grazing the walls—all the abrupt awakening and the terrified departure of a flock of women, brutally collared by three policemen, under the charge of a little, fair-haired, and very polite commissary of police. Then a great silence reigned throughout the house.

No one had betrayed her. Nana was saved. She crept back into the room, shivering and almost dead with fright. Her bare feet were bleeding from the scratches caused by the wire. For a long while she remained, listening, seated on the edge of the bed. Towards morning, however, she fell asleep; but at eight o'clock, when she awoke, she quickly left the house, and hastened to her aunt's. When Madame Lerat, who happened to be just taking her breakfast with Zoé, saw her at that early hour, dressed in such a slovenly way, and with a scared look about her face, she understood it at once.

"Ah! and so it's happened, has it?" she exclaimed. "I told you he would even want the skin of your body. Well, come in, you're always welcome here."

Zoé had risen, and murmured, with respectful familiarity, "At length madame is restored to us. I was expecting madame."

But Madame Lerat wished Nana to kiss little Louis at once, because, said she, the child's happiness consisted in his

mother's good sense. Little Louis was still sleeping, looking
sickly through lack of blood; and when Nana leant over his
white, scrofulous* face, all her troubles of the last few months
returned to her, and seemed to stick in her throat and almost
strangle her.

"Oh! my poor little one, my poor little one!" she stuttered,
in a last outburst of sobs.

---

*Suffering from tuberculosis of the lymphatic glands.

CHAPTER IX

They were rehearsing the "Little Duchess" at the Variety Theatre. The first act had just been gone through, and they were about to commence the second. In two old arm-chairs placed close to the footlights, Fauchery and Bordenave were arguing together; whilst the prompter, old Cossard, a little hunchback, was seated on a rush-bottomed chair, a pencil between his lips, turning over the leaves of the manuscript.

"Well! what are you all waiting for?" suddenly exclaimed Bordenave, thumping furiously on the boards with his heavy walking-stick. "Barillot, why don't you begin?"

"It's M. Bosc—he's disappeared," replied Barillot, who was acting as assistant stage-manager.

Then there was quite a storm of shouts. Every one called Bosc. Bordenave cursed and swore.

"Damn it all! it's always the same. One may ring and call—they're always where they oughtn't to be; and then they grumble when they're kept after four o'clock."

Bosc, however, arrived with a serene coolness.

"Eh? what? who wants me? Ah! it's time for my entrance! Then why didn't you say so. Good! Simone, give me my cue, 'There are the guests arriving,' and I enter. How am I to enter?"

"Why, through the door, of course," shouted Fauchery, losing patience.

"Yes, but where is the door?"

This time Bordenave attacked Barillot, cursing and swearing again, and banging his stick on the boards sufficient to split them.

"Damn it all! I said a chair was to be placed there to represent the door. Every day I have to repeat the same thing. Barillot! where's Barillot? There's another! they all bolt off!"

Barillot, however, bowing beneath the tempest, came and placed the chair without saying a word; and the rehearsal continued. Simone, with her bonnet on, and enveloped in her fur cloak, assumed the airs of a servant arranging some furniture. She interrupted herself to say,

"You know, I'm not very warm, so I shall keep my hands in my muff." Then changing her voice, she greeted Bosc with a faint cry, and said, "Why! it's the count. You are the first, sir, and madame will be very pleased."

Bosc had on a muddy pair of trousers, a big drab overcoat, and an immense muffler rolled round his neck. With his hands in his pockets, and an old hat on his head, he said in a hollow voice, without any acting but merely dragging himself along,

"Do not disturb your mistress, Isabella; I wish to give her a surprise."

The rehearsal went on. Bordenave, scowling, and buried in his arm-chair, listened with an air of fatigue. Fauchery, nervous and constantly changing his position, was seized every minute with a desire to interrupt, which, however, he repressed. But he heard whispering behind him in the dark and empty house.

"Is she there?" he asked, leaning towards Bordenave.

The latter nodded his head. Before accepting the part of Géraldine which he had offered her, Nana had wished to see the piece; for she hesitated before agreeing to act the part of a gay woman. What she longed for was to appear on the stage as a lady. She was half hidden in the shadow of a box with Labordette, who was exerting himself with Bordenave for her. Fauchery glanced round at her, and then again gave all his attention to the rehearsal.

Only the front of the stage was lighted up. A large jet of gas issuing from a pipe erected at the junction of the footlights, and the glare of which was disseminated by means of a powerful reflector, looked like a great yellow eye in the semi-obscurity, where it blazed with a sort of dubious sadness. Against the slender gas-pipe stood Cossard, holding up the manuscript close to the light, which vividly exposed the outline of his hump. Then more in the shadow were Fauchery and Bordenave. In the midst of the enormous structure, this light, which illumined the distance of a few yards only, looked like the glimmer of a lantern fixed to a post at some railway station, the actors appearing like so many strange phantoms, with their shadows dancing before them. The rest of the stage, full of a kind of fine dust similar to that which hangs about houses in the course of demolition, resembled a gigantic nave undergoing repair, with its ladders, its frame-works, and its side-scenes, the faded paint on which imitated heaps of rubbish; and the drop-scenes suspended up aloft had an appearance of frippery hanging to the beams of some vast rag warehouse, whilst a ray of sunshine, which had penetrated through some window, intersected the darkness above like a bar of gold.

At the back of the stage some of the actors were conversing together while waiting for their cues. They had gradually raised their voices.

"I say there! will you keep quiet?" yelled Bordenave, who sprung from his chair in a rage. "I can't hear a word. Go outside if you want to talk; we're working. Barillot, if any one talks again, I'll fine the whole lot!"

They held their tongues for a short time. They formed a little group, seated on a bench and some rustic chairs in a bit of a garden—the first scene for the evening which was placed there, ready to be fixed. Fontan and Prullière were listening to Rose Mignon, who had just received a splendid offer from the manager of the Folies-Dramatiques Theatre. But a voice called out,

"The duchess! Saint-Firmin! Now then, the duchess and Saint-Firmin!"

Prullière did not recollect till the second call that he was Saint-Firmin. Rose, who played the part of the Duchess Hélène, was waiting for him to make their entrance. Slowly dragging his feet over the vacant, sonorous boards, old Bosc returned to sit down. Then Clarisse offered him half the bench.

"What does he yell about like that for?" asked she, speaking of Bordenave. "It will be getting unbearable soon. He can't bring out a new piece now without giving vent to his feelings in that way."

Bosc shrugged his shoulders; he was above all those shindies. Fontan whispered:

"He smells a failure. I think it's a most idiotic piece." Then, returning to Rose's story, he said to Clarisse, "Do you believe it, eh? Three hundred francs a night, and a hundred performances guaranteed. Why not a country house into the bargain? If his wife was offered three hundred francs, Mignon would chuck up Bordenave, and without warning too!"

Clarisse believed in the truth of the offer. Fontan was always running his comrades down! But Simone interrupted them. She was shivering. All well buttoned up and with scarves round their necks, looked up at the sunbeam which shone without descending into the mournful coldness that hung about the stage. Outside it was freezing beneath a clear November sky.

"And there's no fire in the green-room!" said Simone. "It's disgusting; he's becoming beastly miserly! I've a good mind to go home, I don't want to be ill."

"Silence there!" cried Bordenave again, in a voice of thunder.

Then for a few minutes nothing was heard but the confused voices of the actors. They scarcely indicated the gestures, and spoke in a quiet voice so as not to tire themselves. However, when they intended to score a point, they glanced at the auditorium. It appeared to them like an enormous hole in which floated a vague shadow, similar to a fine dust confined in a big loft without windows. The house, which was in darkness except for the feeble light transmitted from the stage, seemed wrapped in a troubled and melancholy sleep. The paintings on the ceiling were veiled in obscurity. From the top to the bottom of the stage-boxes, on the right and left, hung immense breadths of coarse grey linen to protect the hangings; and strips of the same material were thrown over the velvet of the balustrades, girdling the balconies with a double winding-sheet, staining, as it were, the gloom with their pale tint. In the general discolouration one could only distinguish the darker recesses of the boxes, which indicated the different storeys, and the breaks caused by the seats, the red velvet of which had a blackish look. The great crystal gasalier, lowered almost to the ground, filled the stalls with its pendants, and gave one the idea of a removal, of a departure of the public on a journey from which it would never return.

Rose, in her part of the little duchess lost at the house of some fast woman, just then advanced towards the footlights. She raised her hands and pouted adorably to that dark, empty house, which was as sad as though it were in mourning.

"Good heavens! what curious people!" said she, accentuating the phrase, certain of the effect.

At the back of the box in which she was seated, Nana, wrapped in a large shawl, was listening to the piece and devouring Rose with her eyes. She turned to Labordette and asked him in a low voice,

"You're sure he's coming?"

"Quite sure. No doubt he will come with Mignon, as a pretext. As soon as he arrives you must go up into Mathilde's dressing-room, and I will bring him there to you."

They were talking to Count Muffat. It was an interview on neutral ground, arranged by Labordette. He had had a serious talk with Bordenave, whom two successive failures had brought to a very low ebb. And Bordenave had hastened to lend his theatre and offer a part to Nana, wishing to get on good terms with the count, with the view of borrowing some money of him.

"And the part of Géraldine, what do you think of it?" resumed Labordette.

But Nana neither answered nor moved. After the first act, in which the author made the Duke de Beaurivage deceive his wife with the fair Géraldine, an operatic star, came the second act, where the Duchess Hélène went to the actress's on the night of a masked ball, to learn by what magic power such creatures conquered and retained the husbands of better women. It was a cousin, the handsome Oscar de Saint-Firmin, who introduced her there, hoping to seduce her. And, to her great surprise, as a first lesson she heard Géraldine abusing the duke in the language of a navvie, whilst the latter seemed to be delighted; this sight drew from her the cry, "Ah, well! if that's the way the men must be spoken to!" This was about the only scene Géraldine had in the act. As for the duchess, she was soon punished for her curiousity. An old beau, the Baron de Tardiveau, took her for one of the gay women and attacked her vigorously, whilst, on the other side, Beaurivage made it up with Géraldine, who was reclining in an easy chair, and kissed her. As the part of the latter was not filled up, old Cossard had risen to read it, and he accentuated certain passages in spite of himself, and acted in Bosc's arms. They had reached this scene, the rehearsal dragged on tediously, when suddenly Fauchery jumped up from his chair. He had restrained himself till then, but his nerves had at length got the better of him.

"That isn't it!" he exclaimed.

The actors paused, their arms dangling beside them. Fontan, screwing up his nose, asked in a sneering way:

"What? What isn't it?"

"You're all wrong! it's not that at all, not that at all!" resumed Fauchery, who marched about the stage gesticulating, and went through the scene. "Look here, Fontan, you must understand Tardiveau's excitement; you lean forward like this, with this gesture, to seize hold of the duchess. And you, Rose, it's then that you pass, quickly, like this, but not too soon, not till you hear the kiss—" He interrupted himself, and called to Cossard, in the heat of his explanations: "Géraldine, give the kiss—loud! so that it can be well heard!"

Old Cossard turned towards Bosc, and smacked his lips vigorously.

"Good! that's the kiss," said Fauchery jubilantly. "Give the kiss once more. Now you see, Rose, I've had time to pass, and then I utter a faint cry—'Ah! she has kissed him!' But, for that, Tardiveau must follow you towards the back of the stage. Do you hear, Fontan? you must follow her to the back of the stage. Now, try it over again, and all together!"

The actors went through the scene a second time, but Fontan played his part with such ill-will, that it was worse than ever. Twice again Fauchery gave his directions, acting the mimic each time with more warmth. They all listened to him in a mournful way, looked at one another for an instant, as though he had asked them to walk on their heads, and then awkwardly tried again, to stop almost directly with the rigidity of puppets whose strings have just been broken.

"No, it's too much for me; I can't understand it," Fontan ended by saying in his insolent tone of voice.

During all this while, Bordenave had not opened his lips. Buried in the depths of his arm-chair, one could only see by the pale light of the gas-jet the top of his hat, which he had pulled over his eyes, and his immense stomach, in front of which was his walking-stick, abandoned between his legs; and one would have thought him asleep. Suddenly he rose up.

"My young friend, it's absurd," said he to Fauchery, in a quiet tone of voice.

"How! absurd!" exclaimed the author, turning very pale. "You are absurd yourself, my boy!"

Bordenave at once flew into a passion. He repeated the word absurd, and seeking for something stronger, substituted imbecile and idiotic. It would be hissed, they would never be allowed to finish the act; and as Fauchery, exasperated though not particularly offended by his abuse, which occurred each time they rehearsed a new piece together, roundly called him a brute, Bordenave lost all control over himself. He twirled his stick in his hand, and breathing like a mad bull, exclaimed:

"Damnation! go to the deuce. There's another quarter of an hour wasted in stupidity—yes, stupidity. There's not the least particle of common sense in it. And yet it's so simple! You, Fontan, you're not to budge. You, Rose, you make a little movement like this, you know, but no more, and then you come forward. Now try it that way, off you go; Cossard, give the kiss."

The scene went no better. The confusion became greater. Then Bordenave also began to mimic with the gracefulness of an elephant, whilst Fauchery stood by sneering and shrugging his shoulders, in a pitying sort of way. Then Fontan mixed himself up in it, and even Bosc ventured to give his advice. Rose, quite tired out, had finished by sitting down on the chair which indicated the door. No one any longer knew what they were about. To crown the confusion, Simone, thinking she heard her cue, made her entrance too soon, in the midst of the disorder. This so enraged Bordenave, that whirling his stick round in a terrible manner, it alighted with great force on her posterior. He often struck the women, who had been his mistresses, during rehearsals. She rushed off, pursued by this furious cry:

"Take that home with you, and damn it all! I'll shut up the show if I'm bothered any more!"

Fauchery had pressed his hat down on his head, and pretended to leave the theatre; but he remained standing at the back of the stage, and came forward again when he saw Bordenave return to his arm-chair in a frightful state of perspiration. He resumed his own seat. They remained a short time side by side, without stirring, whilst complete silence reigned throughout the house. The actors waited nearly two minutes. They all seemed to be in a state of the greatest dejection, as though they had just gone through a most fatiguing task.

"Well! continue," said Bordenave at length in his ordinary tone of voice, and perfectly calm.

"Yes, continue," repeated Fauchery. "We will arrange the scene to-morrow."

And they stretched themselves out, and the rehearsal resumed its course of tediousness and supreme indifference. During the row between the manager and the author, Fontan and the others had had a most enjoyable time at the back, seated on the bench and the rustic chairs. They had laughed quietly among themselves, with numerous grunts and witty remarks; but when Simone returned with her whack behind, and her voice broken by sobs, they went in for tragedy, saying that in her place they would have strangled the old pig. She wiped her eyes, nodding her head the while. It was all over; she would leave him, more especially as Steiner, the day before, had offered to provide for her. Clarisse was lost in astonishment—the banker was without a sou; but Prullière laughed and reminded her of how the confounded Jew had advertised himself by means of Rose, when he had been working the shares of the Salt Works of the Landes. Just then he had another project—a tunnel under the Bosphorus. Simone listened very much interested. As for Clarisse, she had been in an awful rage for a week past. That beast La Faloise, whom she had flung into Gaga's venerable arms, had just inherited the property of a very rich uncle! She had no luck; she was always warming the house for the next tenant. Then that brute Bordenave had only given her a wretched part of fifty lines, when she could very well have played Géraldine! She was longing for the part, and had great hopes that Nana would refuse it.

"Well! and I?" said Prullière indignantly; "I haven't two hundred lines. I wished to decline the part. It's an insult to ask me to play that Saint-Firmin; it's as bad as being shelved. And what a piece, my friends! You know, it'll be an awful fiasco."

Here Simone, who had been talking with old Barillot, returned and said, all out of breath, "I say, Nana's here!"

"Whereabouts?" asked Clarisse, rising quickly from her seat to see.

The news passed rapidly from one to the other. Every one leant forward to have a look. For an instant the rehearsal was interrupted; but Bordenave suddenly roused himself, and yelled,

"Well! what's the matter? Finish the act, can't you? And keep quiet you over there; the row you kick up is intolerable!"

Nana was still watching the piece from her box. Labordette had twice addressed her; but she had impatiently pushed him with her elbow to make him leave off. The second act was just about ending, when two figures appeared at the back of the stage. As they walked down to the front, on the tips of their toes, so as not to make any noise, Nana recognised Mignon and Count Muffat, who nodded in silence to Bordenave.

"Ah! there they are," murmured she with a sigh of relief.

Rose Mignon gave the last cue. Then Bordenave said that they must go through the second act again, before touching the third one; and, leaving the rehearsal, he greeted the count with most exaggerated politeness, whilst Fauchery pretended to be wholly engaged with the actors around him.

Mignon whistled quietly to himself, with his hands behind his back, and looking tenderly at his wife, who seemed rather nervous.

"Well! shall we go up?" asked Labordette of Nana. "I will make you comfortable in the room, and then come back for him."

Nana left the box at once. She had to feel her way along the passage which led to the boxes and stalls; but Bordenave guessed she was there, as she was hurrying along in the dark, and he caught her up at the end of the corridor which passed behind the stage—a narrow place where the gas was kept burning night and day. There, so as to get the matter settled quickly, he at once attacked her about the part of Géraldine.

"Eh! what a part! what go there is in it! It is exactly suited to you. Come to-morrow to rehearsal."

Nana kept very cool. She wished to see the third act.

"Oh! the third act is superb! The duchess plays at being a fast woman in her own home, which disgusts Beaurivage and gives him a lesson. And then there's a very funny imbroglio. Tardiveau arrives, and thinking he is at some dancer's—"

"And what does Géraldine do in all that?" interrupted Nana.

"Géraldine?" repeated Bordenave slightly embarrassed. "She has a scene, not very long, but a capital one. The part is a splendid one for you, I tell you! Come and sign an agreement now."

For a few seconds she looked him straight in the face, and then replied, "We'll talk it over by-and-by."

And she joined Labordette, who was waiting for her on the stairs. Every one in the theatre had recognised her. They were all whispering together. Her return quite scandalised Prullière, and Clarisse was very uneasy about the part she was longing for. As for Fontan, he pretended supreme indifference. It was not for him to abuse a woman he had loved. In his heart—in his old infatuation now turned to hatred—he entertained a ferocious grudge against her on account of her devotion to him, of her beauty, and of that dual existence which he had severed through the perversion of his monster-like inclinations.

However, when Labordette returned and went up to the count, Rose Mignon, already put on her guard from the knowledge of Nana's presence, suddenly understood what was going on. Muffat bored her immensely but the thought of being thrown over in that fashion was too much for her. She broke the silence she usually maintained with her husband on those matters, and said to him bluntly,

"You see what is going on? Well! I give you my word that if she tries on the Steiner dodge again, I will scratch her eyes out!"

Mignon, calm and serene, shrugged his shoulders with the air of a man who sees everything.

"Be quiet, will you!" he murmured. "Just oblige me by holding your tongue!"

He knew what he was about. He had got pretty well all he could out of Muffat. He felt that on a sign from Nana the count was ready to lie down and be her footstool. It was impossible to fight with such a passion as his; and so, knowing what men are, his only thought was to get the most he could out of the situation. He must wait and see how things went. And he waited.

"Rose, it's your scene!" cried Bordenave. "The second act over again."

"Go!" resumed Mignon. "Leave me to manage this."

Then in his bantering way he amused himself by complimenting Fauchery on his piece. It was a capital play, only why was his grand lady so extremely virtuous? It was not natural. And he jeeringly asked who was the original of the Duke de Beaurivage—the fool whom Géraldine did what she liked with. Fauchery, far from being annoyed, began to smile; but Bordenave, glancing in the direction of Muffat, seemed annoyed, and that made Mignon serious again, and set him thinking.

"Damn it all! are we ever going to begin?" yelled the manager. "Look sharp, Barillot! Eh? Bosc isn't there? Does he think he's going to make a fool of me any longer?"

But at that moment Bosc quietly appeared and took his place. The rehearsal recommenced just as Labordette went off

with the count. The latter trembled at the thought of seeing
Nana again. After their rupture he had felt himself alone in
the world, he had allowed himself to be led to Rose, not knowing how to employ his time, and thinking he was merely suffering from the alteration in his habits. Besides, in the state of
stupor in which he then was, he wished to be ignorant of everything, forbidding himself to seek Nana, and avoiding an explanation with the countess. It seemed to him that he owed
that oblivion to his dignity. But there was a secret power at
work, and Nana slowly reconquered him by his recollections,
by the weaknesses of his flesh, and by new feelings, exclusive,
tender, and almost paternal. The abominable scene in which
he had taken part was forgotten; he no longer beheld Fontan,
he no longer heard Nana ordering him out as she twitted him
with his wife's adultery. They were mere words which passed by
as soon as they were uttered, whilst in his heart there remained
a sting the pangs of which almost suffocated him. His thoughts
at times became quite childish, he accused himself, imagining
that she would not have deceived him had he really loved her.
His agony became intolerable, and he was most unhappy. It
was like the smart of an old wound, no longer that blind and
impatient desire putting up with anything, but a jealous love of
that woman, a need of her alone, of her hair, of her mouth, of
her body, that haunted him. Whenever he recalled the sound
of her voice a tremor ran through his limbs. He longed for her
with the exigencies of a miser and infinite delicacy. And this
love had seized upon him so grievously, that, at the first words
Labordette uttered when sounding him respecting an interview, he threw himself into his arms by an irresistible movement, ashamed afterwards of having given way in a manner so
ridiculous for a man of his rank. But Labordette knew how to
see and forget. He gave another proof of his tact in leaving the
count at the foot of the stairs, with these simple words quickly
uttered:

"On the second floor, turn to the right, the door is only
pushed to."

Muffat found himself alone in this silent corner of the
building. As he passed by the green-room he noticed, through

the open doors, the dilapidation of the vast apartment, which, in the daylight, appeared in a disgraceful state through dirt and constant wear and tear. But what surprised him, on his leaving the noise and semi-obscurity of the stage, were the bright clear light, the intense quietude of that staircase, which he had seen one night smoky with gas and sonorous with the rush of women skurrying about from floor to floor. One could tell the dressing-rooms were unoccupied, the passages deserted, for there was not a soul, not a sound, whilst through the small square windows, on a level with the stairs, entered the pale November sun, in the yellow rays of which an infinitesimal dust disported itself, whilst a death-like peacefulness hung over all. He felt happy in this silence and calm. He mounted the stairs slowly, trying not to get out of breath; his heart bounded against his breast, and he was seized with the fear of acting like a child, with sighs and tears. Then, when he reached the first landing, he leant against the wall, certain of not being seen, and, holding his handkerchief to his mouth, he looked at the warped steps, at the iron hand-rail shining from the constant friction, at the soiled walls, at all that wretchedness which gave the place the look of some low brothel displayed in all its bareness at that drowsy hour of the afternoon when the girls are sleeping. When he arrived at the second landing he had to step over a big tortoise-shell cat curled up asleep on the top stair. With its eyes half closed, this cat watched all alone over the house, always in a state of somnolency from the cool and stuffy odours left behind there every night by the women.

In the passage on the right, the door of the dressing-room was, as Labordette had said, only pushed to. Nana was waiting there. That little slut of a Mathilde kept her dressing-room in a slovenly state; there were cracked pots scattered all about, a dirty wash-hand basin, and a chair stained with rouge, as though some one had been bleeding on the rush seat. The paper which covered the walls and the ceiling was splashed all over with soapy water. There was such a stench there, such a smell of lavender turned musty, that Nana opened the window. She stood there for a minute, breathing the fresh air, and leaning out to catch a glimpse of Madame Bron, whom she heard vigorously sweeping the green flagstones on the shady side of the narrow courtyard. A canary, in a cage hung up against a shutter, was uttering some piercing roulades. One could not hear the sounds of the vehicles on the Boulevard or in the neighbouring streets, all was as peaceful as in the country, though the sun but seldom penetrated there. On raising her eyes, Nana saw the little buildings and the shining glass roofs of the galleries of the Passage; then, farther off, in front of her, the high houses of the Rue Vivienne, the backs of which were so devoid of life that they seemed empty. Terraces rose one above another. On a roof a photographer had perched an enormous cage of blue glass. It looked very gay. Nana was becoming absorbed in contemplating the scene, when she thought she heard a knock at the door. She turned round and called out:

"Come in!"

On seeing the count enter she closed the window. The day was cold, and it was not necessary that curious Madame Bron should overhear them. They looked at one another gravely. Then, as he stood very stiff and speechless, she laughed, and said:

"Well! so there you are, you big booby!"

His emotion was so strong that he seemed frozen. He called her madame, and said how happy he was to see her again. So, to bring matters to the point that she desired, she became more familiar still.

"Now don't stand on your dignity. As you wished to see me, it was not for us to look at each other like a couple of china dogs, I suppose! We've both been wrong. As for me, I forgive you!"

And it was agreed that they would not refer to the subject again. He nodded his approval. He was becoming calmer but, as yet, could find nothing to say out of the tumultuous flow of words which rushed to his lips. Surprised at his coldness, she played her trump card.

"Well, now, you're reasonable," she resumed, with a slight

smile. "As we've made our peace, let's shake hands and remain good friends for the future."

"How good friends?" murmured he, becoming suddenly anxious.

"Yes, perhaps it's stupid of me, but I was desirous of your esteem. At present we've explained matters, and if we ever meet each other anywhere, we, at least, won't look like a couple of fools—"

He seemed on the point of interrupting her.

"Let me finish what I have to say. No man—do you hear?— no man has ever had anything to reproach me with. Well, it vexed me to begin with you. We all have our honour, my pet."

"But that's not it!" he exclaimed, violently. "Sit down and listen to me."

And, as though he feared she might go away, he pushed her on to the only chair. He walked about, his agitation increasing. The little dressing-room, close and full of sunshine, had a moist, warm atmosphere, and not a sound from outside reached it, except the canary's piercing roulades, which, in the pauses, seemed like the distant trills of a flute.

"Listen," said he, standing before her, "I have come to take you back. Yes, I want to begin again. You know it well, so why do you talk to me like this? Tell me—you consent?"

She held down her head, and was scratching with her nail the red coloured rush seat, which appeared to be bleeding beneath her; and, seeing him so anxious, she did not hurry herself. At length she raised her face, now become serious, while to her eyes she had managed to give an expression of sadness.

"Oh! impossible, little man. Never again will I live with you."

"Why?" stuttered he, as a twinge of intense suffering passed over his countenance.

"Why? well!—because—it's impossible, that's all. I don't wish it."

He looked at her ardently for a few seconds longer. Then, bending his legs, he knelt on the floor. She looked annoyed and contented herself by adding.

"Oh! don't be a child!"

But he was already behaving as one. Fallen at her feet, he

had seized her round the waist, which he squeezed tightly, with his face between her knees, which he was pressing against his breast. When he felt her thus, when he felt again the velvet-like texture of her limbs beneath the thin material of her dress, his frame shook convulsively; and shivering with fever, and distracted, he pressed harder against her, as though he wished to become a part of her. The old chair creaked. Sighs of desire were stifled beneath the low ceiling, in the atmosphere rendered foul by stale perfumes.

"Well! and what next?" said Nana, letting him do as he pleased. "All this will not help you, when I tell you it's not possible. Dear me! how young you are!"

He became quieter, but he remained on the ground. He did not let go of her, and he said, in a voice broken by sobs,

"At least, listen to what I came to offer you. I have already seen a mansion near the Parc Monceau. I would realise all your desires. To have you all my own I would give my fortune. Yes! that would be the only condition—all my own, you understand me! and if you consent to be mine alone, oh! I should wish you to be the most admired, and also the richest—carriages, diamonds, dresses—"

Nana proudly shook her head at each offer. Then as he continued, as he talked of settling money on her, not knowing what more to lay at her feet, she seemed to lose patience.

"Come, have you finished mauling me about? I'm good-natured, I let you do it for a minute, because you seemed so upset; but there now, that's enough, isn't it? Let me get up; you're tiring me."

She shook him off. When she rose, she said: "No, no, no—I won't."

Then he regained his feet painfully, and having no strength left, he dropped on to the chair, leaning against the back, his face buried in his hands. Nana in her turn, walked about. For a moment she looked at the stained wall-paper, the greasy dressing-table, all over that dirty hole, bathed in the pale sunlight. Then stopping in front of the count, she spoke without the slightest emotion.

"It's funny how rich people suppose they can have every-

thing for their money. Well! but if I won't? I don't care a pin
for your presents. You might give me all Paris, and I would say
'no,' and always 'no.' It isn't very clean in here, as you see.
Well! I should think it lovely, if it pleased me to live here with
you; whereas one pines away in your palaces, if one's heart isn't
there. Ah! money! my poor fellow, I have some somewhere!
But let me tell you, I dance on money! more, I spit upon it!"

And she assumed a look of disgust. Then, she went in for
sentiment, and added in a melancholy tone of voice:

"I know of something that is worth more than money. Ah! if
any one gave me what I desire."

He slowly raised his head, his eyes sparkled with hope.

"Oh! you can't give it me," she resumed; "it's not in your
power to do so, and that is why I speak of it to you. Well, this is
only between ourselves—I wish for the part of the grand lady,
in their new piece."

"What grand lady?" murmured he in surprise.

"Their Duchess Hélène, of course! If they think I'm going
to play Géraldine, they're very much mistaken! A part of no
consequence at all—one scene, and not much in that! Besides,
it's not only that. I've had enough of gay women.* Always gay
women; one would think I've nothing in me but gay women.
It's become annoying in the long run, for I can see clear
enough, they fancy I'm ill-bred. Ah, well! my friend, they make
a slight mistake! When I choose to be the grand lady, I do it as
well as any one! Just look at this!"

And she retreated to the window, then advanced carrying
her head high, measuring her steps with the circumspect air of
a fat old hen, hesitating to dirty her feet. He watched her with
his eyes still full of tears, stupefied by this sudden bit of comedy traversing his anguish. She walked about for a while to
show all her by-play, smiling delicately, blinking her eye-lids,
swaying her skirts; then stopping in front of him, she said:

"Well! I think that's good enough, isn't it?"

---

*Unmarried and presumably loose women, whether actresses, dancers,
artists' models, courtesans, or prostitutes.

"Oh! quite," he stammered, with a choking sensation in his throat, and his glance still dim.

"I told you I could do the grand lady! I tried it at home, and there's not one of them that has my little air of a duchess who doesn't care a hang for the men. Did you notice, when I passed in front of you, how I quizzed you? That air only comes with the blood. And then I want to play the part of a respectable woman. It has been my dream; it is making me quite unhappy. I must have the part, do you hear? I must have it!"

She spoke in a harsh tone of voice. She had become serious now, and was greatly affected, suffering from her stupid desire. Muffat, not yet recovered from the blow of her refusals, waited without understanding. There was a short silence, which was not disturbed by the least sound.

"Do you know," she resumed, without any more beating about the bush; "you must get that part given to me."

He was astounded. Then with a gesture of despair, he said, "But it is not possible! You said yourself that I had no power to do so."

She interrupted him with a shrug of her shoulders.

"You've only to go downstairs and say to Bordenave that you want the part. Pray don't be so simple! Bordenave is in want of money. Well! you can lend him some, as you've such a lot to throw out of the window." And as he still argued against it, she grew angry. "Very well, I understand; you're afraid Rose won't like it. I didn't speak to you of her when you were sobbing on the ground. I should have had too much to say about her. Yes, when a man swears to a woman that he will love her for ever, he shouldn't go the next day and make up to the first one he meets. Oh! the wound is here; I sha'n't forget it! Besides, my friend, it's not so pleasant after all to take the Mignons' leavings! Before you went and made a fool of yourself down at my knees, you would have done better to have broken off entirely with that dirty set!"

He kept protesting, and ended at last by being able to say a few words. "But I don't care a button for Rose; I will cast her off at once."

Nana appeared to be satisfied on that point. She resumed:

"Then what is it that bothers you? Bordenave's the master. You'll tell me that besides Bordenave there's Fauchery."

She spoke slower now. She was arriving at the delicate part of the matter. Muffat, his eyes fixed on the ground, said nothing. He had remained in a voluntary ignorance respecting Fauchery's assiduities for the countess, gradually quieting his suspicions, and hoping that he had been mistaken on that frightful night passed by him in a doorway of the Rue Taitbout. But he entertained a certain repugnance and a secret anger against the man.

"Well—what! Fauchery isn't the devil!" repeated Nana, feeling her way, wishing to find out how things were between the husband and the lover. "It's easy enough to get over Fauchery. He is at bottom a very decent fellow, I assure you. Well! it's understood; you'll tell him it's for me."

The mere idea of such an undertaking was revolting to the count.

"No, no, never!" cried he.

She waited. This phrase came to her lips, "Fauchery can refuse you nothing"; but she felt that it would be rather too strong an argument to use. Only she smiled, and her smile, which was a peculiar one, seemed to speak the words. Muffat, glancing up at her face, lowered his gaze again, and looked pale and embarrassed.

"Ah! you're not at all obliging," murmured she at length.

"I cannot!" said he in a voice full of agony. "Everything you wish; but not that, my love—oh! I pray you!"

So she did not waste any more time in arguing. With her little hands she bent back his head; then stooping forward, she pressed her lips to his in one long embrace. A thrill passed through his frame. He started beneath her; his eyes were closed, his reason gone. And she raised him from his seat.

"Go," said she, simply.

He walked, he moved towards the door; but as he was about to leave the room, she took him once more in her arms, and, looking up at him meekly and coaxingly, she rubbed her cat-like chin against his waistcoat.

"Where is the mansion?" asked she, in a very low voice, in

the confused and laughing way of a child returning to some good things it would not at first look at.

"In the Avenue de Villiers."

"And are there any carriages?"

"Yes."

"And lace, and diamonds?"

"Yes."

"Oh! how kind you are, my ducky! You know, just now, it was because I was jealous; and this time, I swear to you, sha'n't be like the first, for now you know what a woman requires. You give me everything, don't you? Then I sha'n't want to have any-thing to do with any one else. Look! they're only for you now!—that, and that, and that!"

When she had pushed him outside, after stimulating him with a shower of kisses on his face and hands, she stood a mo-ment to take breath. Good heavens! what a stench there was in the dressing-room of that untidy Mathilde! It was warm in there, just like a room in the south of France with the winter sun shining upon it; but, really, it smelt too much of stale lavender water, and of other things not very clean. Nana opened the window. She looked out as before, and examined the glass roof of the Passage to pass the time away.

Muffat staggered down stairs with a buzzing in his ears. What was he to say? how could he enter into this matter, which was none of his business? As he reached the stage he heard sounds of quarrelling. They were finishing the second act. Prullière was in a fury because Fauchery had wished to strike out one of his speeches.

"Strike them all out then," cried he, "I would rather you did that! What! I haven't two hundred lines, and now some of those are to be taken away! No, I've had enough of it; I throw up my part."

He pulled out of his pocket a crumpled little memorandum and turned it over in his trembling hands, as though about to throw it on to Cossard's knees. His injured vanity convulsed his pale face, his lips being tightly compressed, and his eyes on fire, without his being able to conceal that internal revolution.

He, Prullière, the idol of the public, to perform a part of two hundred lines!

"Why not make me bring in letters on a salver?" resumed he, bitterly.

"Come, Prullière, do be pleasant," said Bordenave, who humoured him on account of his influence on the people in the boxes. "Don't begin your complaints again. We will find you some good effects. Eh, Fauchery? you'll introduce some effects for him. In the third act we could even lengthen one of the scenes."

"Then," declared the actor, "I must have the word at the end. You certainly owe me that."

Fauchery's silence appeared to give consent, and Prullière put his part back in his pocket, still excited and discontented all the same. Bosc and Fontan, during the discussion, had assumed looks of supreme indifference. Every one for himself. It did not concern them, they took no interest in it; and all the actors surrounded Fauchery, questioning him and fishing for compliments, whilst Mignon listened to Prullière's final complaints, without losing sight of Count Muffat, whose return he had been watching for. The count remained in shadow at the back of the stage, hesitating to advance into the midst of the quarrel; but Bordenave catching sight of him, hastened to where he stood.

"Aren't they a set of grumblers?" murmured he. "You've no idea, count, what trouble I have with those people. They're all more vain one than the other, and so disobliging and spiteful—always slandering other people, and only too delighted if I make myself ill in keeping them to their business. But excuse me, I'm losing my temper."

He stopped, and silence ensued between them. Muffat was seeking a way of leading up to the subject that occupied his mind; but failing in his endeavour, he ended by abruptly saying, so as to get it over the sooner,

"Nana wants to play the part of the duchess."

Bordenave started violently as he exclaimed, "Pooh! that's absurd!" Then glancing at the count, he saw him looking so pale, so agitated, that he regained his composure at once. "The deuce!" he added simply.

And there was again silence between them. As for himself, he did not care a fig. It would perhaps be funny to have that fat Nana to play the part of the duchess. Besides, he would thus have a strong hold on Muffat. So his decision was soon formed. He turned round and called,

"Fauchery!"

The count made a slight gesture to stop him. Fauchery did not hear. Fontan had got him up against the proscenium wall, and was giving him his ideas of the part of Tardiveau. The actor thought he should make up as a Marseillais, with the southern accent, which he kept imitating. He made whole speeches that way; was that the proper rendering of the part? He seemed only to be giving his own ideas, and which he himself had doubts about. But Fauchery, keeping very cool in the matter, and offering numerous objections, Fontan became annoyed at once. Very well! As the correct reading of the part had entirely escaped him, it would be far better for every one that he should not play it.

"Fauchery!" Bordenave again called.

Then the young man hurried away, glad of the opportunity of escaping from the actor, who felt highly indignant at being left in so abrupt a manner.

"Don't let us remain here," resumed Bordenave. "Come, gentlemen."

To be out of the way of indiscreet ears, he took them to the property room behind the stage. Mignon watched them go off, greatly surprised. A few steps descended to the room, which was square, with a couple of windows looking on to the courtyard. The ceiling was low, and the dirty window panes only admitted that dim light usually met with in cellars. In pigeon-holes placed about the room was a collection of all sorts of things—the turn-out of a second-hand dealer of the Rue de Lappe* selling off, an odd medley of plates, of cups in

*Street of pawn shops in what was then the Jewish quarter of Paris.

gilded pasteboard, of old red umbrellas, of Italian pitchers, of
clocks of every shape and size, of trays and inkstands, of fire-
arms and squirts—the whole heaped anyhow, chipped, broken, unrecognisable, and covered with a layer of dust an inch
thick; and an unbearable stench of old iron and rags and of
damp pasteboard arose from the piles formed of the remains
of the pieces produced during a period of fifty years.

"Come in here," said Bordenave. "We shall at least be by
ourselves."

The count, very much embarrassed, moved on a few steps,
to leave the manager to arrange matters by himself. Fauchery
could not make it all out.

"What's up?" he asked.

"Well, it's just this," said Bordenave at length. "An idea has
occurred to us—now, don't jump, it's very serious. What do
you think of Nana playing the part of the duchess?"

At first the author was quite bewildered, then he burst out,

"Oh, no! you can't mean it—it must be a joke. Every one
would laugh at it."

"Well! it's something to get people to laugh! Think it over,
dear boy. The count is very much smitten with the idea."

Muffat, to conceal his emotion, had taken an object that he
did not seem to recognise from amidst the dust on a shelf. It
was an egg-cup, the foot of which had been mended with plaster. He kept it in his hand without knowing he did so, and
advanced towards the others to murmur:

"Yes, yes, it would be capital."

Fauchery turned round upon him, with an impatient gesture. The count had nothing to do with his piece; and he exclaimed in a decided tone of voice:

"Never! Nana as the gay woman as much as you like, but as
the grand lady, not if I know it!"

"You do not judge her fairly, I assure you," resumed Muffat,
becoming bolder. "Only just now, she was showing me how well
she could play the grand lady."

"Where?" inquired Fauchery, whose astonishment increased.

"Upstairs, in one of the dressing-rooms. Well! she did it

splendidly. Oh! such distinction! She can give such glances, too, you know, in passing—this way."

And with the egg-cup in his hand, he tried to imitate Nana, forgetting himself in the force of his desire to convince the two other men. Fauchery watched him in amazement. He understood, and his anger vanished. The count, who felt his glance upon him, in which there was derision and pity combined, blushed slightly and stopped.

"Well! it may be so," murmured the author, obligingly. "She would perhaps do it very well, only the part is already given. We cannot take it away from Rose."

"Oh! if that's all," said Bordenave, "I will undertake to manage that."

But then, seeing them both against him, understanding that Bordenave had some hidden motive for acting as he did, the young man, not wishing to give way, declined again, but with increased energy, and in a manner not to admit of any further discussion.

"No, I say! and no, and always no! Even if the part was not filled up I would never give it to her—there, is that clear enough for you? And now let me be, I don't want to damn my own piece."

After this there was an embarrassed silence. Bordenave, thinking himself in the way, withdrew some distance off. The count stood with his head bowed down. He raised it with an effort, and said, in a broken voice,

"My dear fellow, if I ask you to do it as a special favour to myself?"

"I cannot, I cannot," repeated Fauchery, struggling.

Muffat's voice became harsher.

"I beg of you—I wish it!"

And he looked him straight in the eyes. Beneath that black look, in which he read a menace, the young man suddenly gave way, stammering confusedly,

"Well, after all, do as you wish—I don't care. Ah! you are unfair. You will see—you will see—"

The embarrassment then became greater. Fauchery had leant up against some shelves, and was nervously stamping on the floor with his foot. Muffat appeared to be examining the egg-cup very attentively, as he continued to turn it round between his fingers.

"It's an egg-cup," Bordenave obligingly came and said.

"Why! yes, it's an egg-cup," repeated the count.

"Excuse me, you're all covered with dust," continued the manager, as he replaced the article on a shelf. "You see, it would be impossible to be dusting here every day—one would always be at it. The consequence is it's not very clean. What a mixture, isn't it? Well, believe me if you like, it represents a lot of money. Look here—and here."

He led Muffat, in the greenish light that came from the courtyard, in front of all the shelves, naming the different articles, wishing to interest him in his rag merchant's inventory, as he called it. Then, when they had worked their way round to where Fauchery stood, he said, in an easy tone of voice,

"Listen! As we are now agreed, we'll settle this matter at once. Ah! there is Mignon."

For a little while past Mignon had been hanging about in the passage. At the first words Bordenave uttered, suggesting an alteration in their agreement, he flew into a passion. It was disgraceful. They wanted to ruin his wife's prospects. He would go to law about it. Bordenave, however, remained very calm, and reasoned with him. He did not think the part worthy of Rose—he preferred to reserve her for an operetta, which would come on after the "Little Duchess"; but as the husband still complained, he abruptly offered to annul the agreement, and spoke of the proposals which the management of the Folies-Dramatiques Theatre had made the singer. Then Mignon, for a moment worsted, affected a great disdain for money, without, however, denying the existence of the offers in question. They had engaged his wife to play the part of the Duchess Hélène, and she would play it, even though it cost him his fortune. It was a question of dignity, of honour. Once engaged on this ground, the discussion became interminable. The manager always reverted to this argument: as the Folies-Dramatiques people offered Rose three hundred francs a night—one hundred performances guaranteed—whilst she

only received one hundred and fifty from him, his letting her
go meant a profit of fifteen thousand francs for her. The husband, on his side, did not depart from his standpoint—that of
art. What would be said if the part was taken away from his
wife? that she was not equal to it, and had been replaced. That
would do her a great injury, and would lower her artistic standard considerably. No, no, never! glory before wealth! Then,
all on a sudden, he hinted at a compromise. According to the
agreement, if Rose threw up her engagement she forfeited ten
thousand francs. Well, if they gave her that sum she would go
to the Folies-Dramatiques Theatre. Bordenave could scarcely
believe his ears, whilst Mignon, who had not taken his eyes off
the count quietly waited.

"Then that settles everything," murmured Muffat with relief. "We are all agreed."

"Ah, no! by Jove! it would be too idiotic!" exclaimed Bordenave, carried away by his business instincts. "Ten thousand
francs to get rid of Rose! you must think me a fool!"

But the count kept signalling to him to agree to the pro-
posal. He, however, still hesitated. At length, grumbling, regretting the ten thousand francs, though they were not to
come out of his pocket, he curtly resumed,

"After all, I'm willing. I shall at least be rid of you."

For a quarter of an hour past, Fontan had been listening in
the courtyard. Very curious to know what was going on, he had
gone and posted himself there. When he had heard all there
was to learn, he returned indoors, and gave himself the treat
of informing Rose. Ah, well! they were having a fine talk about
her; she was done for. Rose rushed to the property room. They
all remained silent. She looked at the four men. Muffat bowed
his head; Fauchery answered her inquiring gaze with a despairing shrug of his shoulders. As for Mignon, he was discussing the terms of the agreement with Bordenave.

"What's up?" asked she in a sharp tone of voice.

"Nothing," said her husband. "It's only Bordenave who's
going to give ten thousand francs for the return of your part."

She was very pale and trembling as she stood there with
clinched fists. For a moment she looked him straight in the

eyes in a revolt of her whole being—she who ordinarily quietly submitted to him in all business matters, the making of agreements with her managers and her lovers. She only found these few words to say, which struck him full in the face like the lash of a whip,

"Ah, really! you are too much a coward!"

And then she left them. Mignon, greatly alarmed, hastened after her. What was the matter? was she mad? He explained to her in a whisper that ten thousand francs from one side and fifteen thousand francs from the other made twenty-five thousand francs. A magnificent stroke of business! Anyhow, it was certain that Muffat was going to leave her; therefore it was quite evident they ought to congratulate themselves on having succeeded in plucking that last feather from his wing. But Rose was so enraged she would not answer. Then Mignon left her with disdain to her woman's vexation. He said to Bordenave, who was returning to the stage with Fauchery and Muffat,

"We will sign the agreement to-morrow morning. Have the money ready."

Nana, informed by Labordette of what had taken place, arrived triumphant. She affected the style of a respectable woman, with most distinguished ways, just to astonish every one and to prove to those idiots that, when she liked, not one of them could come up to her; but she almost forgot herself. Rose, as soon as she saw her, flew at her, stammering in a choking voice,

"Ah! I shall see you again. We must have it out, do you hear?"

Taken off her guard by this sudden attack, Nana was on the point of putting her fists on her hips and abusing the other roundly. She restrained herself, however, and exaggerating the fluty tone of her voice, making the gesture of a marchioness on the point of treading on a piece of orange peel, she said,

"Eh? what? You must be crazy, my dear!"

And she continued her airs, whilst Rose went off followed by Mignon, who scarcely knew her. Clarisse, to her great delight, had just had the part of Géraldine given to her by Bordenave. Fauchery moodily stamped about, without being able to make up his mind to leave the theatre. His piece would be damned; he was wondering how he could save it. But Nana went and seized hold of him by the wrists, and asked him if he thought her so very dreadful. She would not damn his piece; and she made him laugh, and let him understand that she might be of assistance to him with Muffat. If her memory failed her, she would make use of the prompter; they would pack the house. Besides, he was mistaken in her; he would see how she would carry all before her. Then it was settled that the author should slightly alter the part of the duchess, so as to give more to Prullière. The latter was delighted. In the general joy that Nana seemed naturally to bring with her, Fontan alone remained indifferent. Standing up, full in the yellow glare of the gas-jets, he showed himself off, displaying his sharp goat-like profile, and affecting an easy posture. Nana coolly went up to him, and holding out her hand, said,

"Are you quite well?"

"Yes, pretty well. And you?"

"I'm very well, thanks."

That was all. It seemed as though they had left each other only the night before at the door of the theatre. The actors, during all this time, had been waiting; but Bordenave at length said they would not rehearse the third act that day. Punctual for a wonder, old Bosc went off grumbling; they were always keeping them without any necessity, they made them waste entire afternoons. Everyone went away. Below, arrived on the pavement, they blinked their eyes, blinded by the bright daylight, with the bewilderment of people who have spent three hours quarrelling in the depths of a cellar, with a constant strain upon their nerves. The count, feeling dizzy and overwrought, got into a cab with Nana, whilst Labordette went off consoling Fauchery.

A month later, the first performance of the "Little Duchess" was a great disaster for Nana. She was atrociously bad in it. She made pretensions to high-class comedy which filled the audience with merriment. No one hissed, they were all too much amused. Seated in one of the stage-boxes, Rose Mignon greeted each appearance of her rival with a shrill burst of

laughter, thus setting off the whole house. It was a first revenge. And when, at night-time, Nana found herself alone with
the count, who was very much cut up, she said to him furiously,

"What a dead set they made against me! It's all jealousy! Ah!
if they knew how little I care for it! I can do without them all
now! I'll bet a hundred louis that I'll make all those who
laughed lick the ground at my feet! Yes, I'll teach your Paris
what it is to be a grand lady!"

CHAPTER X

Then Nana became a woman of fashion, a marchioness of the streets frequented by the upper ten, living on the stupidity and the depravity of the male sex. It was a sudden and definitive start in a new career, a rapid rise in the celebrity of gallantry, in the full light of the follies of wealth and of the wasteful effronteries of beauty. She reigned at once among all that was most costly. Her photographs were in all the windows, her name was mentioned in the newspapers. When she passed along the Boulevards in her carriage, the crowd turned to look at her, and uttered her name with the emotion of a people saluting its sovereign; whilst she, quite at her ease, reclined in her wavy costumes, and smiled gaily beneath the shower of little golden curls which half hid the blue circle round her eyes and the carmine on her lips. And the marvel was that this big girl, who was so awkward on the stage, so ludicrous the moment she tried to act the respectable woman, charmed every one about town without an effort. Adorned with a deshabille as artful and exquisitely elegant as it was ostensibly unintentional, she combined the suppleness of the adder with the nervous distinction of a thorough-bred cat, like an aristocracy of vice, superb and rebellious, treading Paris under foot in the manner of an all-powerful mistress. She set the fashion, and great ladies followed it.

Nana's mansion was in the Avenue de Villiers, at the corner of the Rue Cardinet, in that quarter of luxury which had sprung up in the midst of the empty expanse, formerly the plain of Monceau. Erected by a young painter intoxicated by a first success, and who had been forced to sell it when the plaster was scarcely dry, it was built in the renaissance style, with the air of a palace, a certain fantastical internal arrangement, and modern conveniences within a space rather restricted for such a display of originality. Count Muffat had purchased the place furnished, full of a host of knick-knacks, of beautiful Eastern hangings, of old credences, and big arm-chairs of the time of Louis XIII.; and Nana had thus fallen into a stock of the choicest artistic furniture selected from the productions of centuries. But as the studio which occupied the centre of the building could be of no use to her, she had pulled the different floors to pieces, leaving on the ground floor a conservatory, a drawing-room, and a dining-room, and arranging a parlour on the first floor close to her bed-room and dressing-room. She surprised the architect by the ideas she gave him, showing herself at once at home in all the refinements of luxury, like the Paris street-girl who has the instinct of elegance. In short, she did not spoil the mansion over much—she even added to the richness of its furniture—with the exception of a few traces of tender stupidity and gaudy splendour, typical of the former artificial flower-maker who had dreamily gazed into the shop windows of the Passages.

A carpet was laid up the steps in the courtyard beneath the grand verandah; and from the vestibule there came an odour of violets, a warm atmosphere confined by heavy hangings. A yellow and rose-coloured glass window, of the paleness of flesh, lighted the wide staircase, at the foot of which stood the figure of a negro, in sculptured wood, holding a silver salver full of visiting cards. Four women in white marble, with bare breasts, supported some elegant lamps, whilst bronzes and Chinese vases filled with flowers, sofas covered with the products of ancient Persian looms, and easy-chairs with old tapestries furnished the vestibule, adorned the landings, turning the one on the first floor into a kind of ante-room, in which men's coats and hats were always to be seen lying about. The carpets deadened all sound, and such a peacefulness hung about that one might have imagined oneself entering a chapel traversed by some pious tremor, and the silence of which hid a mystery behind the closed doors.

Nana only opened the drawing-room, which was in the Louis XVI. style, and rather overdone, on gala-nights when she entertained persons from the Tuileries, or distinguished foreigners. Usually, she was only downstairs at meal times, feeling, moreover, rather lost on the days when she lunched alone in the lofty dining-room, which was decorated with Gobelin tapestry, and a monumental credence, and enlivened with old china, and marvellous specimens of ancient silver ware. She would return upstairs as soon as the meal was over; for she lived, so to say, in the three rooms on the first floor—the bedroom, the dressing-room and the parlour. She had twice changed the decorations of the bedroom: the first time she had had it hung in mauve satin, the second in white lace on blue silk; but she was not satisfied, she thought it looked dull, and tried to think of some improvement, but without success. Over the well-padded bedstead, which was as low as a sofa, there was twenty thousand francs worth of Venetian lace. The furniture was in blue and white lacquer, inlaid with fillets of silver; whilst white bearskins were everywhere spread in such profusion, that they covered the carpet. This was one of Nana's caprices, she having been unable to get rid of the habit of sitting down on the floor to take her stockings off. Next to the bed-room, the parlour offered an amusing medley, and a most artistic one. Against the pale rose-coloured silk hangings—a faded Turkey rose, stitched with gold—stood out a multitude of objects of all countries, and of all styles—Italian cabinets, Spanish and Portuguese coffers, Chinese pagodas, a Japanese screen of the most precious workmanship, then china and bronzes, embroidered silks, and the finest tapestries; whilst easy-chairs as big as beds, and sofas as deep as alcoves, gave to the whole the lazy, drowsy appearance of a seraglio. The room preserved a tone of old gold, blended with green and red, without anything indicating too much the abode of a gay woman, excepting perhaps the voluptuousness of the seats: two small porcelain figures, a woman in her chemise catching fleas, and another perfectly naked walking on her hands, with her legs in the air, alone sufficed to sully the apartment with a stain of eccentric stupidity. And by a door almost always open, one caught sight of the dressing-room, all in marble and mirrors, with the white basin of its bath, its silver bowls and ewers, its furnishings of crystal and ivory. A closed curtain maintained a faint light, and gave the room a sleepy look, as though oppressed with an odour of violets, that exciting perfume of

Nana's, with which the whole house and even the courtyard was penetrated.

The great matter was to secure servants for the establishment. Nana still had Zoé, that girl who was so devoted to her fortune, and who for months past, confident in her instinct, had been quietly awaiting this new start in life. Now, Zoé triumphed—mistress of the household, and feathering her own nest, yet looking after madame's interests as honestly as possible. But a lady's maid was not sufficient. A butler, a coachman, a concierge, a cook, were required; besides which, it was necessary to furnish the stables. Then Labordette made himself very useful, in undertaking any commissions that bothered the count. He bargained for the horses, went to the coachbuilders, and assisted the young woman, who was continually met with on his arm at the different dealers, in her selections. Labordette even engaged the servants—Charles, a tall coachman who had been in the service of the Duke de Corbreuse; Julien, a little butler with curly hair and always smiling; and a married couple, of whom the woman, Victorine, was cook, while the man, François, acted as concierge and footman. The latter, with powdered hair and knee breeches, and wearing Nana's livery, light blue and silver lace, received the visitors in the vestibule. Everything was done in princely style.

By the second month all was in working order. The expenses were at the rate of three hundred thousand francs a year. There were eight horses in the stables, and five carriages in the coach-houses. There was one especially—a landau with silver ornaments—which for a time occupied all Paris. And Nana, in the midst of this fortune, gradually settled down. She had left the theatre after the second performance of the "Little Duchess," leaving Bordenave to struggle as best he could against threatened bankruptcy, in spite of the count's money. All the same, she bitterly felt her failure. It added to the lesson Fontan had given her—a dirty trick for which she held all the men responsible. She now considered herself proof against all fads and infatuations; but her thoughts of vengeance did not remain for long in her flighty brain. What did remain there, however, outside her moments of anger, was an ever keen ap-

petite for squandering money, a natural disdain for the man
who paid, a perpetual caprice for devouring and destroying, a
pride in the ruin of her lovers.

Nana commenced by putting the count on a satisfactory
footing. She settled clearly the programme of their relations.
He gave twelve thousand francs a month, without counting
presents, and only asked in return an absolute fidelity. She
swore to be faithful; but she insisted on being treated with deference, on enjoying entire liberty as mistress of the household,
and on having all her wishes respected. For instance, she
would receive her friends every day; he himself should only
come at stated hours—in short, he should trust her implicitly
in everything. And when he hesitated, seized by a jealous anxiety, she became very dignified, threatening to return him
everything, or else swearing fidelity on the head of her little
Louis. That ought to be sufficient. There could be no love
where there was no esteem. At the end of the first month, Muffat respected her.

But she desired and she obtained more. She soon influenced him in a good-natured sort of way. When he arrived in
a moody state of mind, she enlivened him, then advised him,
after confessing him. Little by little she busied herself with his
family cares—his wife, his daughter, all matters connected with
his heart and his money; and she did so in a very reasonable
manner, full of justice and honesty. Once only did she let herself be carried away by passion—the day when he told her that
he thought Daguenet was about to ask him for his daughter's
hand. Ever since the count had been openly protecting Nana,
Daguenet had thought it a clever move to break off all connection with her, to treat her as a hussy, and to swear to deliver
his future father-in-law from the creature's clutches. So she
abused her old friend Mimi in a fine way. He was a dissipated
rascal who had squandered his fortune with the most abominable women. Now, he had no decency about him. He did not
exactly make them give him money, but he profited by what
others gave them, merely going himself to the expense of an
occasional bouquet or dinner; and as the count seemed to excuse these weaknesses, she told him coarsely that she had been

Daguenet's mistress, and furnished him with some salacious details. Muffat became very pale, and did not again speak of the young man. It would teach the latter to be ungrateful.

The mansion, however, was scarcely furnished, when Nana, one night that she had been most energetically swearing ever-lasting fidelity to Muffat, retained Count Xavier de Vandeu-vres, who, for a fortnight past, had been paying court to her most assiduously, by means of visits and flowers. She gave way not through any infatuation, but rather to prove to herself that she was at liberty to do as she pleased. The interested motive came afterwards, when Vandeuvres, on the morrow, helped her to settle an account, that she would rather not mention to the other one. She would be able to get out of him about eight or ten thousand francs a month, which would be very useful by way of pocket money. He was just then finishing up his fortune in a violent fit of fever. His horses and Lucy had cost him three farms, and Nana was about to devour his last château, near Amiens, in a single mouthful. He seemed in a hurry to sweep off everything—even to the remains of the old castle, built by a Vandeuvres in the reign of Philip Augustus*—with a mad-dening appetite for ruins, and thinking it a fine thing to leave the last gold bezants† of his coat-of-arms in the hands of that girl whom all Paris desired. He also accepted Nana's condi-tions—entire liberty and love at fixed times—without even being so passionately simple as to exact oaths. Muffat sus-pected nothing. As for Vandeuvres, he knew perfectly all that was going on; but he never made the slightest allusion. He af-fected ignorance, with the cunning smile of a sceptical man about town who does not expect impossibilities, so long as he has his own particular time, and that Paris knows it.

Then Nana's establishment was indeed complete. Nothing was wanting, either in the stables, the kitchen, or the bedroom. Zoé, who had the general management, found means of es-cape out of the most difficult entanglements. There was a kind

---

*King of France from 1180 to 1223.

†In heraldry, circular figures representing coins.

of machinery in everything, as at a theatre. All was regulated as in a government office, and it worked with such precision, that for some months there was no hitch—nothing got out of gear. Only madame gave Zoé an immense deal of trouble, through her imprudence, her fads, and her foolish bravados. So the maid ended by being less careful, seeing that she made a far larger profit when anything had gone wrong—whenever madame had committed some new piece of stupidity that needed being set right. Then it rained presents, and she hooked louis in the troubled waters.

One morning, when Muffat was still in the bed-room, Zoé ushered a gentleman, all in a tremble, into the dressing-room, where Nana was changing her under-garments.

"Why! Zizi!" said the young woman, in amazement.

It was indeed George. But seeing her in her chemise, with her golden hair hanging over her naked shoulders, he seized hold of her, put his arms round her neck, and smothered her with kisses. She struggled, greatly frightened, saying, in a suppressed voice,

"Leave off—do, he's in there! It's stupid of you! And you, Zoé, are you mad? Take him away! Keep him downstairs; I'll try and come there."

Zoé had to push him before her. Downstairs in the dining-room, when Nana was able to rejoin them, she scolded them both. Zoé bit her lips, and went off looking very vexed, saying that she thought to have gratified madame in doing as she did. George looked at Nana with so much pleasure at seeing her again, that his beautiful eyes filled with tears. Now the evil days had gone by, his mother thought he had got over his infatuation, and had allowed him to leave Les Fondettes; but on reaching the Paris terminus, he had hastened in a cab to kiss his darling sweetheart as quickly as possible. He talked of living by her side for the future, the same as in the country, when he used to wait with bare feet in the bed-room at La Mignotte; and, as he told his story, he thrust out his fingers, through a longing to touch her after that year of cruel separation. He seized hold of her hands, felt up the wide sleeves of her dressing-gown, even as high as her shoulders.

"You still love your baby?" he asked, in his child-like voice.

"Of course I do!" replied Nana, who abruptly disengaged herself; "but you arrive here without a word of warning. You know, my little boy, I'm not free. You must be good."

George, who alighted from his cab dazzled by a long desire on the point of being satisfied, had not bestowed a glance on the place he entered. But now he was conscious of a great change around him. He examined the rich dining-room, with its lofty gilded ceiling, its Gobelin tapestry, and its sideboard shining with silver plate.

"Ah, yes!" said he sadly.

And she gave him to understand that he must never call in the morning. The afternoon, if he liked, between four and six o'clock, which was the time when she received company. Then, as he gazed at her with a supplicating look of interrogation, but without asking for anything, she kissed him on the forehead, in a very kind good-natured way.

"Be very good, and I will do my best," she murmured.

But the truth was she no longer felt as she did in regard to him. She thought George very nice, she would have liked to have had him for a companion, but nothing more. However, when he came every day at four o'clock, he seemed so sad, that she often again yielded, permitted him to hide in her cupboards, and continually to pick up the crumbs of her beauty. In time, he scarcely ever left the house, where he was as much at home as the little dog Bijou, both of them among the mistress's skirts, having a little of her, even when she was with another, and catching windfalls of sugar and caresses, in the hours of weary solitude.

No doubt Madame Hugon heard of her boy's new fall into the power of that bad woman, for she hurried to Paris and sought the assistance of her other son, Lieutenant Philippe, who was then in garrison at Vincennes. George, who had been hiding from the elder brother, was seized with despair, fearing the employment of force; and as he could keep nothing to himself, in the nervous expansion of his tender-heartedness,

he soon talked to Nana, continually, of his big brother—a
strong fellow who would dare anything.

"You see," he explained, "mamma will not come here herself, but she can very well send my brother. I'm sure she will
send Philippe to fetch me."

The first time he mentioned this, Nana was greatly offended. She said sharply,

"I should just like to see him do it! In spite of his being a
lieutenant, François will very quickly send him to the right
about!"

Then, the youngster constantly alluding to his brother, she
ended by thinking a little of Philippe. When a week had gone
by, she knew him from the hair of his head to the tips of his
toes—very tall, very strong, lively and rather rough; and with
all that, some more minute details, certain hairs on his arm, a
mole on his shoulder. So that one day, full of the image of this
man, whom she was to send off a little quicker than he came,
she exclaimed,

"I say, Zizi, it doesn't seem as if your brother was coming. He
must be a coward!"

On the morrow, as George was alone with Nana, François
came and asked if madame would receive Lieutenant Philippe
Hugon. The youngster turned quite pale, and murmured,

"I was expecting it; mamma spoke to me this morning."

And he implored the young woman to send word that she
was engaged. But she had already risen and said, greatly incensed,

"Why, pray? he'll think I'm afraid. Ah, well! we'll have a
good laugh. François, let the gentleman wait a quarter of an
hour in the drawing-room, and then bring him to me."

She did not sit down again but walked feverishly about,
going from the looking-glass over the mantlepiece to a Venetian mirror hanging above a little Italian casket, and each time
she gave a glance or essayed a smile, whilst George, lying on a
sofa without an atom of strength left in him, trembled at the
idea of the scene which was preparing. As she walked about
she kept uttering short phrases:

"It will calm the fellow to keep him waiting a quarter of an hour. And then, if he thinks he's come to a nobody's, the drawing-room will astonish him. Yes, yes, take a good look at everything, my friend; it's all genuine. It'll teach you to respect the mistress. It's the only thing men can understand—respect. Is the quarter of an hour gone yet? No, scarcely ten minutes. Oh! we've plenty of time."

She could not keep still. When the quarter was up she sent George away, after making him swear not to listen at the doors, for it would look very bad if the servants were to see him. As he went into the bed-room, Zizi ventured to say in a choking voice,

"You know, it's my brother—"

"Don't be afraid," said she with dignity; "if he's polite, I'll be polite."

François ushered in Philippe Hugon, who was attired in an overcoat. At first George moved across the bed-room on the tips of his toes, so as not to listen, as the young woman had told him; but, hearing the voices, he stopped, hesitating, and so full of anguish that his legs yielded beneath him. He was fancying all manner of things—catastrophes, slaps, something abominable that would sever him for ever from Nana; so much so that he could not resist retracing his footsteps and putting his ear to the key-hole. He heard very indistinctly, as the thickness of the hangings deadened the sound. Yet he was able to catch a few words uttered by Philippe, harsh phrases in which occurred such expressions as "child, family, honour." In his anxiety to hear what his darling would reply, his heart beat wildly, almost stunning him with its confused hum. No doubt she would retaliate with a "stupid fool!" or a "go to the deuce, I'm in my own house!" But nothing came from her, not even the sound of breathing; it seemed as though Nana was dead in there. Soon, too, his brother's voice became softer. He could no longer understand anything, when suddenly a strange noise completed his amazement. It was Nana sobbing. For an instant contrary feelings struggled within him. He felt impelled to run away—to rush in at Philippe. But just at that moment

Zoé entered the bed-room, and he withdrew from the door, ashamed at having been caught.

She quietly put some linen away in a cupboard, whilst he, dumb and immovable, and a prey to uncertainty, pressed his forehead against a window-pane. After a short silence, she asked:

"Is it your brother who's with madame?"

"Yes," replied he, in a choking voice.

"And are you uneasy about it, Monsieur George?" she inquired after another silence.

"Yes," he repeated with the same painful difficulty.

Zoé did not hurry herself. She folded up some lace, and then said slowly,

"You should not be. Madame will settle everything all right."

And that was all. They did not speak again; but she did not leave the room. For another quarter of an hour she moved about, without noticing the exasperation of the youth, who grew pale with constraint and doubt. He gave side glances in the direction of the drawing-room. What could they be doing all that while? Perhaps Nana was still crying. The ruffian must have slapped her. So when Zoé at length went off, he ran back to the door, and again held his ear to the key-hole; and he was quite bewildered, his brain in a whirl, for he heard a sudden burst of gaiety, tender voices whispering, and the smothered laughter of a woman being tickled. But almost immediately Nana conducted Philippe to the staircase, with an interchange of cordial and familiar expressions. When George at length ventured into the parlour, the young woman was standing in front of the mirror, looking at herself.

"Well?" he asked, scarcely able to say a word.

"Well, what?" said she, without turning round. Then she negligently added, "What were you saying? He's a very nice fellow, your brother!"

"Then it's all settled?"

"Of course, it's settled. Really! what's the matter with you? Did you think we were going to fight?"

But still George did not understand. "I thought I heard—" he stammered out. "Have you not been crying?"

"Crying? I?" she exclaimed, looking him straight in the face. "You were dreaming! Whatever did you think I had to cry about?"

And the youngster got still more confused when she scolded him for having been disobedient and listened at the key-hole, spying upon her. As she continued cross with him, he resumed, very submissively and coaxingly, wishing to know,

"Then my brother?"

"Your brother saw at once where he was. You see I might have been some low common girl, and then he would have been right to interfere, on account of your age and the family honour. Oh! I understand those feelings. But a glance was sufficient for him; he behaved like a man of the world. So don't be uneasy—it's all over; he will ease your mother's mind." And she continued with a laugh, "Besides, you'll see your brother here. I've invited him, and he'll come."

"Ah! he's coming again," said the youngster, turning pale.

He said nothing more, and they no longer talked of Philippe. She was dressing to go out, and he watched her with his big sad eyes. No doubt he was pleased that matter had been arranged, for he would have preferred death to not seeing Nana again; but in his heart there was a silent anguish, a deep pain, which he had never felt before, and which he did not dare to mention. He never knew how Philippe had quieted their mother's anxiety. Three days later she returned to Les Fondettes, seeming quite satisfied. That same night, at Nana's, he started when François announced the lieutenant. The latter gaily chaffed him, treated him as a boy whose escapade he had winked at, as it was of no consequence. George, feeling sick at heart, not daring to move, blushed like a girl at the least word. He had lived but little with Philippe, who was ten years older than he. He feared him as a father, from whom one hides one's little adventures with women; and he felt an uneasy shame on seeing him so free with Nana, laughing very loud, full of health, and thoroughly enjoying himself. However, as his brother soon called every day, George began to get used to his presence. Nana was radiant with joy. It was a last change of residence in the full fling of a courtesan's life—a house-warming insolently given in a mansion overflowing with men and furniture.

One afternoon, when the two Hugons were there, Count Muffat called outside his regular hours; but Zoé having told him that madame was with some friends, he went away again, without seeing her, in the discreet style of a gallant gentleman. When he came back in the evening, Nana received him in the cold, angry way of an insulted woman.

"Sir," said she, "I have given you no reason for insulting me. Understand that when I am at home you are to enter like every one else!"

The count stood with his mouth wide open. "But, my dear—" he attempted to explain.

"Because I had visitors perhaps! Yes, there were some men here. And what, pray, do you think I do with them? It causes a woman to be talked about, affecting those airs of a discreet lover, and I do not wish to be talked about!"

He had great difficulty in obtaining forgiveness. At heart he was delighted. It was by similar scenes to this that she kept him obedient and convinced of her fidelity. For some time past she had made him submit to George's presence—a youngster who amused her, so she said. She got him to dine with Philippe, and the count was very amiable. On leaving the table, he took the young man on one side, and asked him for news of his mother. From that time the Hugons, Vandeuvres, and Muffat, openly belonged to the establishment, where they met together as intimate friends. It was more convenient. Muffat alone still discreetly timed his visits so as not to call too often, and invariably affected the ceremonious air of a stranger. At night-time, when Nana, seated on the floor on her bear-skins, pulled off her stockings, he talked in a friendly way of the other gentlemen, of Philippe especially, who was loyalty itself.

"That's true, they're all very nice," said Nana, still seated on the ground and changing her chemise. "Only, you know, they see who I am. Should they for a moment forget themselves, I would have them turned out of the house at once!"

Yet, in the midst of her luxury, in the midst of that court,

Nana was bored to death. She had men with her every minute of the night, and money everywhere, even in the drawers of her dressing-table amongst her combs and brushes; but that no longer satisfied her, she felt a void somewhere, a vacancy that made her yawn. Her life rolled on unoccupied, bringing each day the same monotonous hours. The morrow did not exist for her. She lived like a bird, sure of eating, ready to sleep on the first branch she came across. This certainty of being fed left her stretched out the whole day, without an effort, asleep in the midst of that idleness and that convent-like submission, as though quite hemmed in in her profession of courtesan. Going out only in a carriage, she began to lose the use of her legs. She returned to the amusements of her childhood, kissing Bijou from morning to night, killing time with the silliest pleasures in her unique expectation of the man whom she put up with in a complaisant and weary sort of way; and, in the midst of this abandonment of herself, the only anxiety she had was for her beauty. She was continually examining, washing, and perfuming herself all over, with the pride of being able to appear naked before anyone and at any moment, without feeling ashamed.

Nana rose every morning at ten o'clock. Bijou, the Scotch terrier, woke her by licking her face; and then she would play with him for five minutes, as he jumped about over her arms and legs, and even onto the count. Bijou was the first of whom he was jealous. It was not proper that an animal should thrust his nose under the bed-clothes in that way. Towards eleven o'clock, Francis came to do up her hair, preparatory to the complicated head-dress of the evening. At lunch, as she detested eating alone, she generally had Madame Maloir, who arrived in the morning from no one knew where, with her extraordinary bonnets, and returned at night to the mystery of her life without anybody troubling themselves about it. But the worst time was the two or three hours between luncheon and the evening toilet. Ordinarily she proposed a game at bézique to her old friend; sometimes she read the "Figaro," the theatrical and fashionable news in which interested her; she even occasionally opened a book, for she prided herself on her taste for literature. Her toilet occupied her until nearly five o'clock. Then only she seemed to awake from her long somnolence, going out in her carriage or receiving a host of men at home, often dining-out, going to bed very late, and rising the next morning with the same fatigue, and beginning a fresh day to pass it in a similar manner.

Her great diversion was to go to Batignolles to see her little Louis at her aunt's. For fifteen days together she would forget him entirely. Then she would be seized with a rage to see him, and hurry there on foot, full of the modesty and tenderness of a good mother, bringing all sorts of presents, as though for an invalid—snuff for the aunt, oranges and sweeties for the child; or else she would call in her laudau on her return from the Bois, attired in such loud dresses that they would upset the whole street. Ever since her niece had become such a grand lady, Madame Lerat had been puffed up with vanity. She called but rarely at the Avenue de Villiers, pretending that it was not her place; but she triumphed in her own street, happy when the young woman arrived in dresses costing four or five thousand francs, and occupied all the morrow in showing her presents, and quoting figures which amazed her neighbours. Generally, Nana reserved Sunday for her family, and on that day, if Muffat asked her to go anywhere, she refused, smiling like a young house-wife. It was not possible, she was going to dine with her aunt, she was going to see her baby. With all that, poor little Louis was always ill. He was nearly three years old, and was getting quite a big fellow; but he had had an attack of eczema on the back of his neck, and now he had deposits in his ears, which made them fear a caries of the bones of the cranium. When she saw him looking so pale, with his poor blood, and his soft flesh spotted with yellow, she became very serious, and above all she was greatly surprised. What could be the matter with the love for him to sicken like that? She, his mother, was always so well!

The days when her child did not engage her attention, Nana relapsed into the noisy monotony of her existence—drives in the Bois, first nights at theatres, dinners and suppers

at the Maison Dorée or the Café Anglais; then all the public re-
sorts, all the sights where the crowds flocked—Mabille,* reviews, races. But she still retained that empty feeling of stupid
idleness, which gave her pains in her inside. In spite of the
constant infatuations in which her heart indulged, she would
stretch her arms the moment she was alone, with a gesture of
immense fatigue. Solitude made her sad at once, for she found
herself again with the empty feeling, and the tedium of her
own society. Very gay by profession and by nature, she would
then become lugubrious, and would constantly sum up her life
in this cry, between two yawns,

"Oh! how men bore me!"

One afternoon, as she was returning home from a concert,
Nana noticed a woman passing along the Rue Montmartre,
with boots trodden down at heel, dirty skirts, and a bonnet that
had evidently been frequently soaked with rain. All of a sudden, she recognised her.

"Stop, Charles!" cried she to the coachman, and then called,
"Satin! Satin!"

The passers-by turned their heads; the whole street looked
on. Satin drew near, and dirtied herself still more against the
wheels of the carriage.

"Jump in, my girl," said Nana coolly, not caring a straw for
what the world would say.

And thus she picked her up and took her off, disgustingly
filthy as she was, in the light blue landau, and by the side of her
pearl grey silk dress trimmed with Chantilly lace; whilst every
one smiled at the highly dignified air of the coachman.

From that time Nana had a passion which occupied her.
Satin became her vice. Installed in the mansion of the Avenue
de Villiers, cleaned and clothed, for three days she gave her experiences of Saint-Lazare—all the troubles she had had with
the nuns, and those dirty policemen who had put her on their

*The Jardin Mabille, an open-air dance hall off the Champs-Elysées, opened
in 1844 and was immensely popular; the name became a byword for licen-
tiousness. It is associated with the birth of the cancan, the high-kick dance
whose participants wore nothing under their skirts.

list. Nana became very indignant, consoled her, and swore to get her out of the mess, even though she had to see the minister of police herself. For the moment, however, there was no hurry; they would certainly not come and seek her there. And afternoons full of tenderness commenced between the two women—caressing words were heard, and kisses broken with suppressed laughter. It was the little game, interrupted by the arrival of the policemen at the Rue de Laval, which had started again in the way of joke. Then one night it became serious. Nana, who was so disgusted at Laure's, now began to understand. She was quite upset and greatly enraged; the more so as, on the morning of the fourth day, Satin disappeared. No one had seen her go out. She had bolted with her new dress, seized with a longing for the open air, with a nostalgia for her favourite pavements.

That day there was such a storm in the house that all the servants hung down their heads without daring to say a word. Nana had almost beaten François for not having stood in front of the door. She tried, however, to restrain herself, and referred to Satin as a dirty strumpet. It would teach her not to pick such filth out of the gutter another time. That afternoon madame shut herself in, and Zoé heard her sobbing. Then in the evening she suddenly ordered her carriage and drove to Laure's. The idea had occurred to her that she might find Satin at the dining-place of the Rue des Martyrs. It was not to get her back again, but merely to slap her face. And it happened that Satin was dining at one of the little tables with Madame Robert. Seeing Nana, she laughed. The latter, struck to the heart, did not create a disturbance; but on the contrary kept very quiet and amiable. She stood champagne, and made a number of women tipsy, and then carried off Satin, while Madame Robert had left the room for a moment; but when she had got her in the carriage, she bit her, and threatened to kill her if she ran away again.

And then the same thing kept continually occurring. Twenty times Nana, tragical in her fury of a deceived woman, hastened after the hussy, who flew off simply for a fad, bored with the comfort of the grand establishment. She talked of smacking Madame Robert's face; one day she even had the idea of a duel, there was one too many. Now, whenever she went to dine at Laure's, she put on her diamonds, and was sometimes accompanied by Louis Violaine, Maria Blond, or Tatan Néné, all looking very gorgeous, and, beneath the yellow gas-light, in the smell of eatables which pervaded the three rooms, these ladies displayed their luxury in very questionable company, delighted at astonishing the girls of the neighbourhood, whom they carried off with them when the meal was over. On those days, Laure, laced-up and shining, kissed all her customers with a more maternal air than ever. Satin, however, in the midst of all this, preserved her calmness, with her blue eyes and her pure virgin-like face; bitten, beaten, pulled about by the two women, she merely said that it was funny, and that they would have done far better to have come to some understanding with each other. It was no use slapping her; she could not cut herself in two in spite of her wish to please every one. At last Nana carried the day, having bestowed on Satin the most love and presents; and, by way of revenge, Madame Robert wrote some most abominable anonymous letters to her rival's lovers.

For some little time past, Count Muffat had seemed uneasy. One morning, in a very agitated state, he placed under Nana's eyes an anonymous letter, in which she saw, in the first few lines, that she was accused of being unfaithful to the count with Vandeuvres and the two Hugons.

"It's false! it's false!" she exclaimed energetically, with an extraordinary accent of truthfulness.

"You swear it?" asked Muffat, already relieved.

"Oh! on what you like—on my child's head!"

But the letter was long. Afterwards it went on to recount her connection with Satin in the most ignoble terms. When she reached the end she smiled.

"Now I know where it comes from," said she, simply.

And as Muffat wished for a denial of the latter part, she resumed coolly, "That, my dear, is a thing which does not concern you. What can it matter to you?"

She did not deny it. His words showed his disgust. Then she

shrugged her shoulders. Where did he spring from? That sort of thing happened everywhere, and she named her friends; she even swore that ladies in the best positions were no strangers to it. In short, to hear her, there was nothing more common or more natural. What was not true, was not true; he had seen, just before, how indignant she was about Vandeuvres and the two Hugons. Ah! had that been true he would have done right in strangling her. But what was the use of telling him a lie about a matter of no consequence? And she kept repeating,

"Come now, what can it matter to you?"

Then as he continued to complain, she silenced him, saying in a rough voice,

"Well, my friend, if it doesn't please you, you have a very simple remedy. The doors are all open. You must either take me as I am, or leave me alone!"

He bowed his head. In his heart he was pleased with the young woman's protestations. She, seeing her power, no longer hesitated employing it; and from that time Satin was openly installed as part of the establishment, on the same footing as the gentlemen. Vandeuvres had not required the anonymous letter to understand what was going on. He joked about it, and had little quarrels of jealousy with Satin; whilst Philippe and George treated her as a comrade, shaking hands with her and saying some very equivocal things.

Nana had an adventure. One night, having been abandoned by the hussy, she had gone to dine in the Rue des Martyrs, without being able to come across her. While she was eating alone, Daguenet made his appearance. Though he had settled down, he came there occasionally—his old vices getting the better of him—trusting not to meet any of his friends in those dark corners of Parisian abomination. Consequently, Nana's presence seemed rather to put him out at first; but he was not the man to beat a retreat. He advanced smiling. He asked if madame would permit him to dine at her table. Seeing him inclined to joke, Nana put on her grand cold air, and sharply replied,

"Seat yourself wherever you please, sir. We are in a public place."

Commenced in this style, the conversation became very funny; but when the dessert was served, Nana, feeling bored, and burning to triumph, put her elbows on the table, and then resumed her old familiar way.

"Well, and your marriage, my boy; how is it getting on?"

"Not very well," admitted Daguenet.

As a matter of fact, when about to venture to ask for the young lady's hand, he had encountered such a coldness on the count's part that he had prudently abstained from doing so. It seemed to him that it was all up. Nana looked him straight in the face with her bright eyes, her chin in her hand, an ironic smile on her lips.

"Ah! so I'm a hussy!" she resumed slowly. "Ah! so you must deliver the future father-in-law from my clutches. Well, really! for an intelligent fellow, you're a damned fool! What! you go and say a lot of nasty things to a man who adores me and who tells me everything! Listen; your marriage will come off if I choose, my boy."

For a few minutes he had been of the same opinion; a project of complete submission was forming in his mind. However, he continued to joke, not wishing to let the matter become a serious one; and after putting on his gloves, he asked her, in the most correct manner, for the hand of Mademoiselle Estelle de Beuville. She ended by laughing, as though being tickled. Oh! that Mimi! it was impossible to be angry with him. Daguenet's great successes with the ladies were due to the softness of his voice—a voice of a musical purity and suppleness, which had caused him to be nicknamed among the gay women Velvet Mouth. All yielded beneath the sonorous caress with which he enveloped them. He knew his power, so he lulled her with an endless string of words, telling her all sorts of stupid stories. When they quitted the table she was quite rosy, trembling on his arm, reconquered. As the day was very fine, she dismissed her carriage, and accompanied him on foot as far as his lodging; then naturally she went in with him. Two hours later she said, as she was putting on her things again,

"So, Mimi, you want this marriage to come off?"

"Well," he murmured, "it's the best thing I can do. You know I'm quite stumped."

After a short silence she resumed, "All right, I'm willing; I'll help you. You know she's as dry as a faggot; but never mind, as you're all agreeable. Oh! I'm obliging; I'll settle it for you." Then, bursting out laughing, her bosom still uncovered, she added, "Only what will you give me?"

He had seized hold of her, and was kissing her shoulders in a transport of gratitude. She, very gay, quivering, struggled and threw herself back.

"Ah! I know," she exclaimed, excited by this play. "Listen! This is what I must have for my commission. On your wedding-day you must bring me the handsel* of your innocence, you understand!"

"That's it! that's it!" said he, laughing even more than she did. The bargain amused them. They thought it very funny.

It so happened that on the morrow there was a dinner party at Nana's, that is, the usual Thursday gathering—Muffat, Vandeuvres, the two Hugons, and Satin. The count arrived early. He was in want of eighty thousand francs to rid the young woman of two or three debts, and to present her with a set of sapphires for which she had a great longing. As he had already eaten considerably into his fortune, he wished to meet with a money-lender, not yet daring to sell a portion of his estates. So, by Nana's advice, he had applied to Labordette; but the latter, considering it too big a matter for himself, had desired to speak of it to the hairdresser, Francis, who was always willing to be useful to his customers. The count placed himself in the hands of these gentlemen, merely requesting that his name should not be mentioned. They both agreed to keep his acceptance for one hundred thousand francs in their possession, and they excused themselves for the twenty thousand francs of interest by railing against the swindling usurers, to whom, as

*Gift given on an auspicious occasion, or the first payment made to a new business.

they said, they had been forced to apply. When Muffat was ushered in, Francis was just finishing Nana's head-dress. Labordette was also in the dressing-room, in his familiar fashion of a
friend of no consequence. On seeing the count he discreetly
placed a heavy bundle of bank-notes among the powders and
the pomades, and the bill was accepted on a corner of the marble dressing-table. Nana wished Labordette to remain to dinner, but he declined, as he was showing a rich foreigner about
Paris. However, Muffat having taken him on one side to beg
him to go to Becker's, the jeweller, and bring him back the set
of sapphires, which he wished to have as a surprise for the
young woman that very night, Labordette willingly undertook
the commission. Half an hour later, Julien privately handed
the count the case of jewels.

During dinner Nana was very nervous. The sight of the
eighty thousand francs had upset her. To think that all that
money was going to be paid away to tradespeople! It annoyed
her immensely. As soon as the soup was served in that superb
dining-room, illuminated with the reflection of the silver plate
and the crystal ware, she became sentimental, and began to
praise the joys of poverty. The men were in evening dress. She
herself, wore a dress of embroidered white satin, whilst Satin,
more modest, and in black silk, had merely a golden heart—a
present from her darling friend—at her throat; and behind
the guests Julien and François waited, assisted by Zoé, all three
looking very dignified.

"I certainly amused myself a great deal more when I was
without a sou," Nana kept repeating.

She had Muffat on her right and Vandeuvres on her left but
she scarcely looked at them, being entirely occupied with
Satin, enthroned in front of her between Philippe and George.

"Eh, my love?" she said at each phrase. "Didn't we use to
laugh at that time, when we went to old mother Josse's school,
in the Rue Polonceau?"

They were then serving the roast. The two women launched
forth into recollections of their young days. They every now
and then had a longing for gossip, a sudden desire to stir up
all the mud of their youth; and it was invariably when men

were present, as though yielding to a mania for making them acquainted with the dungheap whence they sprouted. The gentlemen turned pale, and glanced about in an embarrassed manner. The two Hugons tried to laugh, whilst Vandeuvres nervously twirled his beard, and Muffat looked more solemn than ever.

"Do you remember Victor?" asked Nana. "He was a depraved youngster; he used to take little girls into the cellars!"

"I remember," replied Satin. "And I remember, too, the big courtyard at your place. There was a doorkeeper with a broom—"

"Mother Boche; she is dead."

"And I can still see your shop. Your mother was awfully stout. One night when we were playing, your father came home drunk, oh! so drunk!"

At this moment Vandeuvres essayed a diversion, by interrupting the ladies in the midst of their reminiscences.

"I say, my dear, I should like some more truffles—they are excellent. I had some yesterday at the Duke de Corbreuse's, which were not to be compared to these."

"Julien, hand the truffles!" said Nana roughly. Then she resumed. "Ah, yes! papa was very foolish. What a tumble-down! Ah! if you had only seen it—a regular plunge, such misery! I can well say that I have tasted of all sorts, and it's a miracle I didn't leave my carcass there, the same as papa and mamma."

This time Muffat, who had been nervously playing with a knife, ventured to interfere.

"It is not a very amusing subject you are talking about."

"Eh? what? not amusing?" exclaimed she, crushing him with a look. "I don't suppose it is amusing! You should have sent us some bread, my dear. Oh! as you know I'm a true-hearted girl, I say what I think. Mamma was a washerwoman, papa used to get drunk, and he died from it. There! if that doesn't suit you, if you're ashamed of my family—"

They all protested. What was she thinking of? They respected her family. But she continued:

"If you're ashamed of my family, well, leave me; for I'm not one of those women who disown their father and mother. You must take me with them, do you hear?"

They took her—they accepted the father and the mother, the past, everything she wished. With their eyes fixed on the table-cloth, they all four now made themselves small, whilst she kept them beneath her muddy old shoes, of the Rue de la Goutte d'Or, with the passion of her all-powerful will. And she was slow to lay down her arms. They might bring her no end of fortunes, build her innumerable palaces, still she would ever regret the time when she used to chew apples with the peel on. It was a fraud, that idiotic money! it was only invented for tradespeople. Then her outburst ended in a sentimental longing for a simple way of living, with one's heart in one's hand, in the midst of a universal benevolence.

But at that moment she caught sight of Julien standing with his arms hanging by his sides, and doing nothing.

"Well! what? Pour out the champagne," said she. "Why are you looking at me like a silly gander?"

During the row the servants had not even smiled. They seemed not to hear, becoming more majestic the more madame forgot herself. Julien poured out the champagne without flinching. Unfortunately, François, who was handing round the fruit, held the dish too much on one side, and the apples, the pears, the grapes, rolled all over the table.

"Stupid fool!" cried Nana.

The footman made the mistake of trying to explain that the fruit was not placed securely on the dish. Zoé had disturbed it in removing some oranges.

"Then," said Nana, "Zoé's a fool."

"But, madame—" murmured the maid, very much hurt.

At this madame rose, and with a gesture of royal authority said curtly, "That's enough, I think! Leave the room, all of you! We no longer require you."

This execution calmed her. She at once became very quiet and very amiable. The dessert passed off most pleasantly; and gentlemen were greatly amused at having to help themselves. But Satin, who had peeled a pear, went to eat it standing up behind her darling, leaning against her shoulders, and whisper-

ing things in her ear which made them both laugh very much;
then she wished to share her last piece of pear, and held it out
to Nana between her teeth, and their lips touched as they finished the fruit in a kiss. This produced a comical protest from
the gentlemen. Philippe called to them not to stand on ceremony. Vandeuvres asked if they would like him to leave the
room. George went and took hold of Satin round the waist and
led her back to her seat.

"How silly you are!" said Nana, "you make the little darling
blush. Never mind, my love, don't take any notice of them.
That's our business." And, turning towards Muffat, who was
looking on in his solemn way, she added, "Isn't it, dear?"

"Yes, certainly," murmured he, slowly nodding his head.

There were no more protests. In the midst of these gentlemen, of these great names, these ancient integrities, the two
women, seated in front of each other, exchanging tender
glances, imposed themselves, and reigned with the cool abuse
of their sex and their avowed contempt for man. They applauded.

The coffee was served upstairs in the parlour. Two lamps
lighted up with their feeble light the rose-colour hangings, the
lacquer and old gold knick-knacks. There was at this hour of
the night, in the midst of the caskets, the bronzes, the china a
discreet glimmer which illumined the gold and ivory incrusta-
tions, shone on the gloss of some carved wand, and watered a
panel with a silky reflex. The afternoon fire had burnt low, it
was very warm, a debilitating heat was confined by the heavy
curtains and hangings. And in this room, all full of Nana's private life, where her gloves, a handkerchief, an open book, lay
scattered about, one met her free from all ceremony, with her
odour of violets, her jolly-girl kind of disorder, creating a
charming effect amongst all that wealth; whilst the easy-chairs
as big as beds, and the sofas as deep as alcoves, seemed to invite to somnolence, forgetful of the flight of time, to sweet
words whispered in the shadows of their corners.

Satin went and stretched herself out on a sofa near the fire-
place. She lit a cigarette; but Vandeuvres amused himself with
pretending to be awfully jealous of her, and threatened to chal-

lenge her if she again turned Nana from her duties. Philippe and George joined in, teased her, and pinched her so hard, that she ended by crying out,

"Darling! darling! do make them leave off! They're annoying me again."

"Come, leave her alone," said Nana seriously. "You know I won't have her teased; and you, my deary, why do you always go with them, when you know they are so foolish?"

Satin, very red in the face, and putting out her tongue, went into the dressing-room, the open door of which showed the pale marble lighted up by the subdued flame of a gas-jet enclosed in a ground-glass globe. Then Nana conversed with the four men, with the charm pertaining to the mistress of a household. She had been reading during the day a novel that had created a great sensation—the history of a courtesan; and she was disgusted. She said that it was all false, showing, besides, an indignant repugnance for such filthy literature, which had the pretension of being true to nature, as though one could describe everything, as though a novel ought not to be written just to while away a pleasant hour! Regarding books and plays, Nana had very fixed opinions. She wished for noble and tender works—things to set her thinking and to elevate her soul. Then the conversation having turned on the troubles that were agitating Paris—on the incendiary newspaper articles, the attempts at riot following the calls to arms enunciated every night at public meetings—she vented her wrath on the Republicans. Whatever did they want, those dirty fellows who never washed themselves? Wasn't every one happy? Hadn't the Emperor done everything for the people? A lot of swine, these people! She knew them—she could speak of them; and forgetting the respect she had just exacted at the dinner-table for her little world of the Rue de la Goutte d'Or, she assailed her relations and friends of bygone days with all the disgust and the horror of a woman arrived at the top of the tree. It so happened that very afternoon she had read in the "Figaro" the report of a public meeting written in a most comical style, and the recollection of which still made her laugh, on account of the slang words used, and the description of a disgusting drunkard who had been turned out.

"Oh! those drunkards!" said she with an air of repugnance. "No, really now, their Republic would be a great misfortune for every one. Ah! may God preserve the Emperor as long as possible!"[3]

"God will hear you, my dear," solemnly replied Muffat. "But never fear—the Emperor is strong."

He liked to see that she had such good feelings. They were both of the same opinion in politics. Vandeuvres and Lieutenant Hugon were also full of jokes about the "roughs"—braying asses who bolted at the sight of a bayonet. George that night remained pale and gloomy.

"What's the matter with the baby?" asked Nana, noticing how quiet he was.

"Nothing, I'm listening," murmured he.

But he was suffering. On leaving the dining-room he had overheard Philippe joking with the young woman, and now it was Philippe and not he who was seated beside her. His chest heaved and seemed ready to burst, without his knowing why. He could not bear them to be together. He had such wicked thoughts that a lump rose in his throat, and he felt ashamed in spite of his anguish. He, who laughed about Satin, who had endured Steiner, then Muffat, then all the others, revolted, and became enraged at the idea that Philippe might one day become that woman's lover.

"Here! take Bijou," said she to console him, passing him the little dog, which was sleeping on her lap. And George became quite lively again, holding something belonging to her—that animal full of the warmth of her knees.

The conversation had fallen on a run of bad luck Vandeuvres had had the night before at the Cercle Impérial. Muffat, who was no player, expressed his surprise; but Vandeuvres, smiling, alluded to his approaching ruin, of which Paris already had begun to talk. It did not matter much how the end came, the thing was to end well. For some time past Nana had noticed he was nervous, with wrinkles at the corners of his mouth, and a vacillating look in his bright eyes. He retained his aristocratic haughtiness, the refined elegance of his impoverished race; and, as yet, it was only a slight vertigo at times, beneath that cranium emptied by women and play. One night that he passed with her he had frightened her with some atrocious idea. He was thinking of shutting himself up in his stable with his horses and setting fire to the place, when he had reached the end of his tether. At this time his only hope was in a horse named Lusignan, which was in training for the Grand Prize of Paris. He lived on this horse, which sustained his damaged credit. Every time Nana wanted money, he put her off till the month of June, if Lusignan won.

"Bah!" said she, jokingly, "he can afford to lose, as he is going to clear every one out at the races."

He merely replied with a mysterious little smile, then added lightly, "By the way, I have taken the liberty of naming a filly of mine, only an outsider, after you. Nana, Nana; it sounds very well. You are not annoyed?"

"Annoyed—why?" said she, in reality greatly delighted.

The conversation continued. They were talking of an execution shortly to take place, and which the young woman wanted to see, when Satin appeared at the dressing-room door, and called Nana in a supplicating voice. The latter rose at once and left the gentlemen, who were taking their ease, puffing their cigars, and discussing a very grave question, as to how far a murderer in a chronic state of alcoholism is responsible for his actions. In the dressing-room Zoé was seated on a chair, crying bitterly, whilst Satin was vainly endeavouring to console her.

"What's the matter?" asked Nana, in surprise.

"Oh, darling! speak to her," said Satin. "For the last twenty minutes I've been trying to reason with her. She's crying because you called her a fool."

"Yes, madame—it's very hard—it's very hard—" stuttered Zoé, almost choked by a fresh fit of sobbing.

This sight moved the young woman. She said some kind words; and as the other did not become calmer, she sat down before her, and put her arm round her waist, with a gesture of affectionate familiarity.

"But, you silly girl! I said 'fool' just the same as I should have said something else! I didn't mean it! I was in a passion. There! I was wrong. Now do leave off crying."

"I love madame so much," stammered Zoé. "After all that I have done for madame."

Then Nana kissed the maid. After which, wishing to show that she was not angry, she gave her a dress that she had worn only three times. Their quarrels always ended in presents. Zoé wiped her eyes with her handkerchief, and before carrying the dress off on her arm, she said that they were all very sad down in the kitchen, that Julien and Francois had not been able to eat any dinner, as madame's anger had taken away all their appetite. And madame sent them a louis as a pledge of reconciliation. She could not bear to see any one unhappy.

Nana returned to the drawing-room, happy at having put an end to the tiff, which was causing her some anxiety for the morrow, when Satin whispered quickly in her ear. She complained, she threatened to go away, if those men teased her again; and she insisted on her darling sending them all off that night. It would be a lesson for them. And then it would be so nice to be alone together! Nana, again becoming anxious, swore that it was not possible. Then the other spoke harshly to her, like a passionate child insisting on having her way.

"I insist on it, do you hear? Send them away, or else I'll go!" And she returned into the drawing-room, and lay down on a sofa, away from the others and near a window, where she remained quite silent and as though dead, waiting with her large eyes fixed on Nana.

The gentlemen were drawing their conclusions against the new theories of the writers on criminal law; with that wonderful proposition as to irresponsibility in certain pathological cases, there threatened to be no more criminals, but only invalids. The young woman, who kept nodding her approval, was trying to think of a means of getting rid of the count. The others would soon be going, but he would be sure to remain behind. And so it happened, when Philippe rose to leave, George followed him at once, his only anxiety was not to leave his brother behind him. Vandeuvres remained a few minutes longer; he sounded the ground; he waited to see if by chance some matter did not oblige Muffat to leave him in possession, but when he saw him evidently making himself comfortable for the rest of the evening, he did not persist, but took his leave like a man of tact. But as he moved towards the door he noticed Satin, with her fixed look; and understanding no doubt, and rather amused, he went and shook her hand.

"Well, we're not angry, are we?" murmured he. "Forgive me. On my word, you're the best of us after all!"

Satin disdained to reply. She did not take her eyes off Nana and the count, who were now left to themselves. Being no longer under any restraint, Muffat had gone and seated himself beside the young woman, and had taken hold of her fingers, which he was kissing. Then she, to create a diversion, asked him if his daughter Estelle was better. The night before he had complained that the child seemed very melancholy; he could never spend a happy day in his own home, with his wife always out and his daughter wrapped up in an icy silence. Nana was always full of good advice respecting these family matters. And as Muffat, his mind and his body upset, began again giving way to his lamentations,

"Why don't you get her married?" asked she, recollecting her promise.

And she at once ventured to speak of Daguenet. But, at the mention of the name, the count showed his disgust. Never, after what she had told him! She pretended to be greatly surprised, then burst out laughing, and putting her arms round his neck, said,

"Oh! how can you be so jealous? Do be reasonable. He had been talking to you against me, and I was furious. To-day I am really sorry—" But over Muffat's shoulder she encountered Satin's fixed gaze. Feeling uneasy, she let go of him, and continued in a serious tone, "My friend, this marriage must take place; I don't wish to prevent your daughter's happiness. He's really a very nice young man, you couldn't find a better one."

And she launched forth into unbounded praise of Daguenet. The count had taken hold of her hands again; he no longer said, "no," he would see, they could talk of it another

time. Then as he spoke of going to bed, she lowered her voice
and made objections. It was impossible, she was not well; if he
loved her a little he would not insist. However, he was obstinate, he would not leave, and she was already giving in when
she again encountered Satin's fixed look. Then she became in-
flexible. No, it could not be. The count, much affected, and
looking far from well, had risen and was seeking his hat. But at
the door he recollected the set of sapphires, the case containing which he felt in his pocket. He had intended hiding it at
the bottom of the bed, so that her legs might come in contact
with it when she first got in; it was a big child's surprise, which
he had been planning ever since dinner. And, in his confusion,
in his anguish at being thus dismissed, he abruptly handed her
the jewels.

"What is it?" asked she. "Why! sapphires. Ah! yes, that set we
saw. How kind of you! But, I say, darling, do you think it's the
same one? It looked better in the window!"

Those were all the thanks he had; she let him go. He had
just caught sight of Satin waiting in silence on the sofa. Then
he looked at the two women; and, no longer persisting, he submissively went off. The house door was scarcely closed when
Satin seized hold of Nana round the waist, and danced and
sang. Then, running to the window, she exclaimed:

"Let's see what a fool he looks outside!"

In the shadow of the curtains, the two women leant on the
iron rail. One o'clock struck. The Avenue de Villiers, now deserted, stretched far in the distance, with its double row of gas-
lamps, in the midst of that damp darkness of March, swept by
great gusts of wind full of rain. Patches of unoccupied ground
appeared as masses of shadow; houses in course of construction displayed their tall scaffoldings beneath the black sky. And
a mad fit of laughter seized the two girls as they caught sight of
Muffat's round back moving along the wet pavement, with the
mournful reflection of his shadow, across that icy, empty plain
of a new Paris. But Nana made Satin leave off.

"Take care—the police!"

Then they smothered their laughter, watching with a dumb
fear two black figures walking in step on the other side of the

Avenue. Nana, in all her luxury—in her royalty of a woman whom every one obeyed—had preserved a dread of the police, not liking to hear them spoken of any more than she did death. She felt uneasy whenever she saw a policeman look up at her house. One never knew what to expect from such people. They might very well take them for some low gay women, if they heard them laughing at that time of the night. Satin tremblingly pressed close up against Nana. Yet they remained there, interested by the approach of a light dancing in the midst of the puddles on the pavement. It was the lantern of an old female rag-picker who was searching the gutters. Satin recognised her.

"Why!" said she, "it's Queen Pomaré with her wicker cashmere!"

And whilst the wind beat the fine rain in their faces, she told her darling Queen Pomaré's history. Oh! she was a superb woman once, and drove all Paris mad with her beauty. She had such go, such cheek, used the men like animals, and often had grand personages weeping on her stairs! Now, she had taken to drink, the women of the neighbourhood amused themselves by giving her absinthe; and in the streets the urchins followed her, throwing stones—in short, a regular smash-up—a queen fallen into the mire! Nana listened, feeling very cold.

"You'll just see," added Satin.

She whistled like a man. The rag-picker, who was under the window, raised her head and showed herself in the yellow light of her lantern. There appeared in that bundle of rags, beneath a big handkerchief in tatters, a scarred, bluish face, with the toothless aperture of the mouth and the flaming loopholes of the eyes; and Nana, in front of this frightful old age of a courtesan drowned in alcohol, beheld in the darkness the vision of Chamont—that Irma d'Anglars, the retired prostitute loaded with years and with honours, ascending the steps of her château, surrounded by a prostrate crowd of villagers. Then as Satin whistled again, amused at the old hag who could not see her, she murmured in an altered tone of voice,

"Leave off—the police again! Let's go away, quick, my darling."

The sound of footsteps returned. They closed the window. On turning round, Nana, shivering and with her hair all wet, on beholding the room, remained, as it were, struck with astonishment, as though she had never seen it before and had entered some unknown place. She found the atmosphere so warm, so perfumed, that she experienced a pleasant surprise. The wealth piled up around the ancient furniture, the gold and silk stuffs, the ivory, the bronzes, all seemed reposing in the rosy light of the lamps; whilst from the now hushed house there arose the sensation of a great luxury—the solemnity of the grand drawing-room, the comfortable amplitude of the dining-room, the peacefulness of the vast staircase, with the softness of the seats and carpets. It was like an abrupt expansion of herself, of her requirements of domination and enjoyment, of her wish to possess everything merely to destroy it. Never before had she felt so strongly the power of her sex. She glanced slowly around her, and then said with an air of grave philosophy,

"Well! all the same, one is right in availing oneself of every opportunity when one is young!"

But Satin was already rolling about on the bear-skins of the bed-room and calling her.

"Come quick! come quick!"

Nana undressed herself in the dressing-room. To be ready quicker, she took her thick light hair in both hands, and shook it over the silver basin, whilst a shower of long hair-pins fell from it, ringing a chime on the shining metal.

CHAPTER XI

On that Sunday, beneath the cloudy sky of one of the first warm days of June, the race for the Grand Prize of Paris was to be run in the Bois de Boulogne. In the morning the sun had risen enveloped in a reddish mist; but towards eleven o'clock, at the moment when the first vehicles reached the Longchamps racecourse, a wind from the south swept the clouds before it. Long flakes of greyish vapour passed slowly away, whilst patches of dark blue sky gradually showed larger and larger from one end of the horizon to the other. And in the bursts of sunshine which kept appearing through the breaks in the clouds, everything sparkled abruptly—the green turf, which was little by little being covered by a crowd of vehicles, and of persons on horseback and on foot; the course still free, with the judge's stand, the winning-post, and the starting-place; then opposite, in the middle of the enclosure, the five symmetrical stands, with their storeys of brick and wood. Bathed in the midday light, the vast plain extended beyond, bordered by little trees, and confined in the west by the wooded hills of Saint-Cloud and Suresnes, which were crowned by the sharp outline of Mont Valérien.

Nana, as excited as if the race for the Grand Prize was to decide her own fortune, wished to have a place as near as possible to the winning-post. She arrived very early, one of the first, in her silver-mounted landau, to which were harnessed four magnificent white horses, a present from Count Muffat. When she appeared, with two postillions on the near side horses, and two grooms seated immovably behind the carriage, there was quite a rush on the part of the crowd, the same as at the passage of a queen. She wore the colours of the Vandeuvres stable, blue and white, intermingled in a most extraordinary costume. The little body and the tunic, in blue silk, were very tight fitting, and raised behind in an enormous puff which gave all the more prominence to the tightness in front; the skirt and sleeves were in white satin, as well as a sash that

passed over the shoulder, and the whole was trimmed with silver braid which sparkled in the sunshine. Whilst, the more to
resemble a jockey, she had placed a flat blue cap, ornamented
with a feather, on the top of her chignon, from which a long
switch of her golden hair hung down the middle of her back
like an enormous yellow tail.

Twelve o'clock struck. There were still three hours to wait
for the race for the Grand Prize. As soon as the landau had
taken up its position, Nana put herself at her ease, as though
at home. She had amused herself by bringing Bijou and little
Louis. The dog, asleep amongst her skirts, was shivering in
spite of the heat, whilst the child, dressed up in ribbons and
lace, remained as though dumb, and had become so pale from
the force of the wind that he looked like a wax figure. The
young woman, without troubling herself about her neighbours, talked very loud with Philippe and George Hugon,
seated opposite to her amidst such a pile of bouquets, white
roses and blue forget-me-nots, that they were invisible below
the shoulders.

"So," she was saying, "as he was becoming quite unbearable
I showed him the door; and for the last two days he hasn't been
near me."

She was speaking of Muffat, only she did not tell the two
young men the real cause of the quarrel. One night he had
found a man's hat in her room; it had merely been a stupid
fancy of hers, a mere nobody she had picked up just to enliven
her.

"You don't know how peculiar he's becoming," she continued, amused at the details she was giving. "He's a regular bigot.
For instance, he says his prayers every night. Oh! it's quite true.
He thinks I don't notice it, as I go to bed first so as not to be in
his way; but I have my eye on him. He mutters, he makes the
sign of the cross as he turns round to step over me to get to
the inside of the bed."

"How artful!" murmured Philippe. "Does he do it before
and after them?"

She laughed aloud.

"Yes, that's it; before and after. When I doze off, I can hear

him muttering again. But what annoys me is that we can't have
the least dispute without his immediately talking of the priests.
Now, I've always been religious. Oh! laugh as much as you like,
it won't prevent me believing what I believe. Only, he's too
bad; he sobs, he talks of his remorse. For instance, the day before yesterday, after our row, he had quite an attack; I began to
feel very anxious—" But she interrupted herself to say, "Look,
there are the Mignons. Why, they've brought the children.
Aren't they dressed up, those youngsters?"

The Mignons were in a very quiet coloured landau, with the
substantial air of people who had made their fortune. Rose, in
a grey silk dress, trimmed with little cerise puffs and bows, was
smiling, pleased at the evident delight of Henri and Charles,
sitting on the front seat, in their rather too ample collegian
uniforms. But when the landau had taken up its position, and
she caught sight of Nana, triumphing in the midst of her bouquets, with her four horses, her postillions and her grooms in
livery, she bit her lips, and sitting bolt upright, turned away her
head. Mignon, on the contrary, looking very well and lively,
waved his hand. It was one of his principles always to keep out
of women's quarrels.

"By the way," resumed Nana, "do you know a little old fellow,
very tidy in his appearance, and with very bad teeth? A Monsieur Venot. He called on me this morning."

"Monsieur Venot!" echoed George in amazement. "It can't
be! He's a Jesuit."

"Precisely, I soon found that out. Oh! you've no idea what
we talked about! It was so funny! He spoke of the count, and
of his disunited family, the happiness of which he implored me
to restore. He was very polite, too, and smiling all the time.
Then I told him I should be only too pleased to do as he
wished; and in the end I promised to make the count return to
his wife. You know, it's not a joke; for I shall be delighted to see
the whole lot of them happy! Besides, it will give me a rest, for
there are days when he is really too tiresome!"

Her weariness of the last few months escaped her in that cry
from her heart. With all that, too, the count appeared to be in
great straits for money. He was careworn; the bill he had given

to Labordette was coming due, and he did not see his way to meet it.

"Why, there is the countess over there," said George, who had been glancing along the stands.

"Where?" exclaimed Nana. "What eyes he has, that baby! Hold my parasol, Philippe."

But George, with a quick movement, forestalled his brother, and was quite delighted at holding the blue silk parasol, with silver fringe. Nana looked through an enormous field-glass.

"Ah, yes! I see her," said she at length. "In the stand to the right, close to a pillar, is she not? She is in mauve, with her daughter in white beside her. Why! there's Daguenet going up to them."

Then Philippe talked of Daguenet's approaching marriage with that stick Estelle. It was a settled thing; they were publishing the banns. The countess objected at first, but the count, so it was said, had insisted. Nana smiled.

"I know, I know," murmured she. "So much the better, Paul. He's a nice fellow—he deserves it"; and leaning towards little Louis, she added, "Well, are you amusing yourself? How serious the child looks!"

The child, without a smile, watched the crowd about him, looking very old, and as though full of sad reflections on what he saw. Bijou, driven from the skirts of the young woman, who was always moving about, had gone to shiver against the little one.

The space around was rapidly filling up. Vehicles of all sorts continuously arrived in a compact, interminable line. There were enormous omnibuses, like the "Pauline" which had started from the Boulevard des Italiens with its fifty passengers and which took up a position near the stands. Then there were dog-carts, victorias, and most elegant landaus, which mingled with old tumble-down cabs dragged by the most wretched horses; and four-in-hands and stage-coaches, with their owners seated on the top, and the servants inside taking care of the hampers of champagne; and light traps of every description, some driven tandem fashion, and accompanied by a jingling of bells. Now and again a gentleman on horseback passed, or a crowd of persons on foot rushed in amongst the vehicles. The rumbling noise which accompanied the latter all along the winding turnings of the Bois de Boulogne ceased as they drove on to the grass. Nothing was heard but the murmur of the ever-increasing crowd, shouts and calls and cracking of whips, which resounded in the open air. And each time the sun appeared from out the clouds scattered by the wind, a blaze of golden light lit up the mounted harnesses and the varnished panels, and brought out the brilliant colours of the costumes; whilst in that flood of sunshine the coachmen on their high seats were conspicuous with their long whips.

Labordette was alighting from an open carriage in which Gaga, Clarisse, and Blanche de Sivry had reserved him a place. As he was hastening to cross the course and enter the enclosure, Nana got George to call him. Then when he came up,

"What's my price?" she asked with a laugh.

She was speaking of Nana, the filly—that Nana which had been ignominiously defeated in the race for the Diana Prize, and which, even in the months just past—April and May—had not even been placed in the races for the Des Cars Prize and the Grand Poule des Produits, both of which had fallen to Lusignan, the other thoroughbred of the Vandeuvres stable. Lusignan had at once become chief favourite, and had latterly been freely taken at two to one.

"Still at fifty," replied Labordette.

"The devil! then I'm not worth much," resumed Nana, who was amused at the joke. "Then I sha'n't back myself. No, I'll be hanged if I do! I won't put a single louis on myself."

Labordette, who was in a great hurry, was starting off again; but she called him back. She wanted a piece of advice. He who knew a number of trainers and jockeys, had the best information respecting the different stables. Twenty times already his tips had come off. He was nicknamed the king of the sporting prophets.

"Come now, which horses ought I to back?" asked the young woman. "At what price is the English one?"

"Spirit? at three to one; Valerio II. also at three to one. Then the others—Cosinus at twenty-five, Hasard at forty, Boum at thirty, Pichenette at thirty-five, Frangipane at ten."

"No, I won't back the English horse. I'm patriotic. Well, what do you say? Shall it be Valerio II.? The Duke de Corbreuse looked quite beaming just now. Well, no! I'd rather not. Fifty louis on Lusignan—what do you say?"

Labordette looked at her in a peculiar manner. She leant forward and questioned him in a low voice, for she knew that Vandeuvres instructed him to bet for him with the bookmakers, so as to be more free in his own betting. If he had learnt anything, he might as well tell her; but Labordette, without explaining why, advised her to trust to his instinct. He would lay out her fifty louis as he thought best, and she should not regret it.

"All the horses you like," he cried gaily, as he went off, "but not Nana—she's a jade!"*

They all laughed madly in the carriage. The young men thought it very funny, whilst little Louis, without understanding, raised his pale eyes to his mother, the loud accents of whose voice surprised him. Labordette, however, was still unable to get off. Rose Mignon had beckoned him, and she gave him some instructions which he wrote down in his note-book; then Clarisse and Gaga called him back, as they wished to modify their bets; they had heard different things in the crowd, and would no longer back Valerio II., but went in for Lusignan; he, quite impassible, made notes of what they required. At length he got away, and was seen to disappear between two of the stands on the other side of the course.

Carriages still continued to arrive. They now comprised five rows along the barrier bordering the course, and formed quite a dense mass streaked here and there by the light hue of the white horses. Then beyond, there were numerous other isolated vehicles, looking as though they had stuck in the grass, a medley of wheels and of teams in every possible position, side by side, slantwise, crosswise, and head to head; and horsemen trotted across the plots of grass that were still comparatively

---

*Worn-out or worthless horse.

free, whilst foot-passengers appeared in black groups continually on the move. Overtopping this kind of fair-ground, amidst the strangely mixed crowd, rose the grey refreshment tents, to which the sunshine imparted a white appearance. But the greatest crush, an ever-moving sea of hats, was around the bookmakers, who were standing up in open vehicles, gesticulating like quack dentists, with their betting lists stuck up on boards beside them.

"All the same, it's awfully stupid not to know what horse one's backing," Nana was saying. "I must venture a few louis myself."

She stood up to select a book-maker whose face should take her fancy. But she forgot her intention as she caught sight of a crowd of acquaintances around her. Besides the Mignons, and Gaga, and Clarisse and Blanche, there were on the right, and the left, and behind, in the midst of the mass of vehicles which had now quite shut in her landau, Tatan Néné with Maria Blond in a victoria, Caroline Héquet with her mother and two gentlemen in a calash, Louise Violaine, all alone, and driving a little basket chaise* bedecked with orange and green ribbons, the colour of the Méchain stable, Léa de Horn on the box seat of a stage-coach, with a crowd of young men who were making a great noise. Farther off, Lucy Stewart, in a very simple black silk dress, was looking most distinguished beside a young man wearing the uniform of a midshipman, in a carriage of most aristocratic appearance. But what really astounded Nana was to see Simone arrive in a trap that Steiner was driving tandem fashion, with a tiger sitting bolt upright behind,† his arms folded, and quite immovable; she was resplendent, all in white satin striped with yellow, and sparkling with

---

*Carriage of various types. *Landau:* carriage with a two-part top; *victoria:* low carriage for two passengers, with a high seat for the coachman; *calash:* light, low-wheeled carriage with a folding top; *basket chaise:* lightweight, two-wheeled carriage.

†Simone arrived in a light, two-wheeled carriage with springs (a trap) that Steiner was driving with the horses one behind the other (in tandem fashion). The "tiger" sitting bolt upright behind was a liveried groom or footman.

diamonds from her waist to her bonnet, whilst the banker, with a long whip, urged on the two horses, the first a little chestnut, which trotted like a mouse, and the other, a tall bay, a stepper which raised its legs very high.

"By Jove!" said Nana, "that old thief Steiner must have made another haul at the Bourse! Doesn't Simone look smart? It's too much, he'll get copped one of these days."

But, all the same, she exchanged a bow with them from a distance. She kept waving her hand, smiling, and turning about, forgetting no one so as to be seen by all. And she continued talking.

"But it's her son that Lucy is dragging about with her! He looks very nice in his uniform. That's why she's trying to be so grand! You know that she's afraid of him, and pretends she's an actress. Poor young man, all the same! He doesn't seem to have an idea of the truth."

"Pooh!" murmured Philippe, laughing, "whenever she chooses she will find him a country heiress."

Nana left off talking. She had just caught sight of old Tricon, in the thick of the vehicles. Having come in a cab from which she could see nothing, the old lady had quietly mounted the driver's seat. And there, standing up to the full height of her tall figure, with her noble-looking face and long curls, she commanded a full view of the crowd, and seemed to be reigning over her women people. They all discreetly smiled to her. She, as a superior being, pretended not to know them. She was not there to work, she came to see the races for pleasure, for she was an inveterate gambler, and was mad about horses.

"Look! there's that idiot La Faloise!" said George suddenly.

It was a surprise to all of them. Nana no longer recognised her La Faloise. Since he had inherited his uncle's fortune, he had become an extraordinarily fashionable young man. With his collar slightly turned down in front, dressed in a light coloured suit, which fitted tightly to his bony shoulders, and with his hair curled, he affected a jog-trot of weariness, a feeble tone of voice, slang words, and phrases which he never took the trouble to finish.

"But he looks very well!" declared Nana, fascinated.

Gaga and Clarisse called La Faloise, throwing themselves at his head, so to say, trying to hook him again. But he left them at once, with an air of pity, mingled with disdain. Nana attracted him, and hastening to her, he stood on the step of the carriage; and as she chaffed him about Gaga, he murmured:

"Oh, no! no more of the old guard! It's no use their trying! Besides, you know, you're now my Juliet—"

He placed his hand on his heart. Nana laughed immensely at that abrupt declaration before everyone. But she resumed:

"There, that'll do. You're making me forget that I want to bet. George, you see that book-maker over there, the fat red one, with curly hair? He has the head of a dirty rascal, which takes my fancy. You go and bet with him. Well, what shall I back?"

"I'm no patriot!—oh, no!" stuttered La Faloise; "all my money is on the English horse. What a lark if he wins! All the French will go mad!"

Nana thought his language disgraceful. Then they discussed the merits of the different horses. La Faloise, to make everyone think that he was a judge of horse-flesh, pretended they were all sorry animals. Baron Verdier's Frangipane, was by Truth out of Lenore; It was a big bay, and might have had a chance if it had not been lamed during training. As for Valerio II., from the Corbreuse stable, it was not in condition, it had had the gripes in April; oh! they were keeping that dark, but he was sure of it, on his word of honour! And he ended by recommending Hasard, a horse belonging to the Méchain stable, the worst beast of the lot, and which no one would look at. The deuce! Hasard showed superb form, and such a style! There was an animal that would surprise everyone!

"No," said Nana. "I shall bet ten louis on Lusignan, and five on Boum."

On hearing this, La Faloise burst out again.

"But, my dear, Boum is simply awful! don't back him. Even Gase, the owner, won't. And Lusignan, he's not in it!—all rubbish! By Lamb out of Princess—just think of it! Not the ghost of a chance for anything by Lamb out of Princess! All too short in the legs!"

He was almost choking. Philippe observed that notwith-standing all that, Lusignan had carried off the Des Cars Prize and the Grande Poule des Produits. But the other was ready for him. What did that prove? Nothing at all. On the contrary, they should beware; and, besides, Gresham was to ride Lusig-nan, so what was the use of arguing? Gresham had no luck, he never won.

And the discussion, which started from Nana's landau, seemed to spread from one end of the race-ground to the other. Screeching voices were heard. The passion for gambling passed over all, giving a flush to the faces, and putting confu-sion into the gestures; whilst the book-makers were furiously calling out the prices, and inscribing the bets made. Only the small fry of the betting fraternity were there, the big bets were being made inside the enclosure. It was the greediness of the smaller gamblers risking their five francs, displaying their ea-gerness for a possible gain of a few louis. In short, the big bat-tle was expected to be between Spirit and Lusignan. Some Englishmen, easily recognisable by their appearance, were walking about amongst the different groups as though at home, with flushed faces, and already triumphing. Bramah, a horse of Lord Reading, had won the Grand Prize the previous year—a defeat for which all French hearts were still bleeding. This year it would be a regular disaster if France was beaten again, so that all the women were dreadfully excited on ac-count of national pride. The Vandeuvres stable became the rampart of the honour of France. They all backed Lusignan, they upheld him, they cheered him to the echo. Gaga, Blanche, Caroline, and the others all put their money on him. Lucy did not do so, because her son was with her; but it was said that Rose Mignon had commissioned Labordette to back him to the extent of two hundred louis. Only old Tricon, seated beside her driver, awaited the last moment, very cool in the midst of the wrangling, predominating over the increasing uproar, in which the names of the different horses were con-tinually repeated in the sprightly remarks of the Parisians, and the guttural exclamations of the Englishmen. She listened and took notes in a majestic manner.

"And Nana?" said George. "Is no one backing her?"

No, no one was backing her; she was not even mentioned. The outsider of the Vandeuvres stable was eclipsed by Lusignan's popularity. But La Faloise raised his arms in the air and exclaimed,

"An inspiration! I shall put a louis on Nana."

"Bravo! I'll put two," said George.

"And I three," added Philippe.

And they kept increasing their amount, pleasantly paying their court, quoting figures as though they were bidding for Nana at an auction. La Faloise talked of covering her with gold. Besides, everyone ought to back her for something. They would go and canvass among those willing to bet. But as the three young men hastened off to carry out their design, Nana called to them,

"Remember, I'll have nothing to do with her! Not on any account! George, ten louis on Lusignan and five on Valerio II."

They rushed away. She, greatly amused, watched them glide amongst the wheels, stoop beneath the horses' heads, and beat all about the place. As soon as they recognised any one in a carriage, they hurried to them and lauded the filly to the skies. And great bursts of laughter passed over the crowd as now and again they looked back and triumphantly held up their fingers to show the number of louis that had been bet; whilst the young woman, standing up in her carriage, waved her parasol. However, they did not meet with much success. A few men allowed themselves to be persuaded. Steiner, for instance, who felt strangely moved at the sight of Nana, risked three louis; but the women all most emphatically refused. Thank you; they did not want a certain loss! Besides, they were not in a hurry to add to the success of a beast of a girl who put them all in the shade with her four white horses, her postillions, and her air of devouring every one. Gage and Clarisse stiffly asked La Faloise if he thought them a couple of fools. When George boldly presented himself at the Mignons' carriage, Rose, highly incensed, turned away her head without answering. One must be a dirty baggage to allow one's name to be given to a horse!

Mignon, on the contrary, followed the young man, looking greatly amused, and saying that women always brought luck.

"Well?" asked Nana, when the young men returned after a long visit to the book-makers.

"You're at forty," said La Faloise.

"How at forty?" cried she in amazement. "I was at fifty. What has happened?"

Labordette just then returned. They were clearing the course, and the ringing of a bell announced the first race. And in the uproar that this occasioned, she questioned him respecting the sudden rise in price; but he answered evasively. No doubt there had been a few inquiries about the filly. She was obliged to be contented with that explanation. Besides, Labordette, who appeared to have something on his mind, told her that Vandeuvres intended coming if he could possibly get away for a time.

The race ended almost unnoticed in the waiting for the big event, when a cloud burst over the course. For some little while the sun had disappeared, and a dull light darkened the crowd. The wind rose, and the rain came down, first in big drops and then in torrents. There was a momentary confusion; shouts and jokes and oaths were heard on all sides, whilst the people on foot scrambled under cover in the refreshment tents. In the carriages the women tried to shelter themselves, holding their parasols with both hands, and the bewildered footmen hastened to raise the hoods. But the shower ceased almost immediately; the sun reappeared with dazzling splendour, shining amidst the last fine drops of rain. A long strip of blue appeared in the place of the cloud as the wind carried it over the Bois. And the sky became quite bright, raising the laughter of the women, who no longer feared for their elegant costumes; whilst the flood of golden sunshine, in the midst of the snorting of the horses and the helter-skelter and agitation of the soaked crowd shaking off the wet, lit up the ground all sparkling with drops of crystal.

"Oh! poor little Louis!" said Nana. "Are you very wet, my cherub?"

The child, without a word, let her wipe his hands with her

pocket-handkerchief. She then wiped Bijou, who was trembling more than ever. It was nothing, only a few spots on the white satin of her dress, but she didn't care. The bouquets, freshened up, glittered like snow; and she, feeling so happy, smelt one of them, wetting her lips as though in dew.

The shower, however, had had the effect of suddenly filling the stands. Nana looked at them through her field-glass. At that distance one could only distinguish a compact and mixed mass, piled up on the different tiers, a dark background broken by the pale faces. The sun filtered in through the corners of the roof, curtailing the seated crowd with angles of light, and giving a washed-out appearance to the costumes of the women. But Nana was most amused by the ladies whom the shower had driven from the rows of chairs placed on the gravel at the foot of the stands. As admission to the enclosure was rigorously denied to all gay women, Nana made the most spiteful remarks about the respectable members of her sex, who she considered were shockingly badly dressed and looked highly ridiculous.

A murmur ran through the crowd. The Empress was entering the little stand in the centre, a pavilion in the form of a Swiss cottage, the large balcony of which was furnished with red arm-chairs.

"Why, there he is!" said George. "I did not think he was on duty this week."

Count Muffat's stiff, solemn figure had appeared behind the Empress. Then the young men began to joke, regretting Satin was not there to go and give him a knock in the stomach. But Nana, looking through her field-glass, caught sight of the head of the Prince of Scotland in the imperial stand.

"Look! there's Charles!" she cried. She thought he was fatter. In eighteen months he seemed to have become broader. And she gave some details. Oh! he was a devilish strong fellow.

Round about her, the other women in their carriages were whispering that the count had given her up. It was quite a story. The Tuileries had become scandalized at the chamberlain's behaviour since he had been going about with her openly, so, to preserve his place, he had put an end to his con-

nection with her. La Faloise impudently repeated the story to
the young woman, again offering himself and calling her "his
Juliet." But she had a hearty laugh, and said:

"It's absurd. You don't know him. I've only to whistle to him,
and he'll throw everything up for me."

For a few minutes she had been watching Countess Sabine
and Estelle. Daguenet was still with them. Fauchery, who had
just arrived, disturbed everyone in order to get to them, and
he also remained there, smiling. Then she continued, disdainfully pointing to the stands,

"Besides, you know, all those people no longer amaze me. I
know them too well. You should see them with the gloss off! No
more respect! respect is done with! Filth below, filth up above,
it's always filth and company. That's why I won't put up with
any nonsense."

And she made an extended gesture which included all—
from the grooms leading the horses on to the course to the
sovereign herself, who was conversing with Charles, a prince,
but a dirty fellow all the same.

"Bravo, Nana! she's capital, Nana!" exclaimed La Faloise enthusiastically.

The sounds of the bell were lost in the wind. The races continued. The race for the Ispahan Prize had just been won by
Berlingot, a horse belonging to the Méchain stable. Nana
called to Labordette to ask him for news of her fifty louis. He
laughed, and refused to tell her which horses he had backed,
so as not to change the luck, he said. Her money was well invested, as she would see by-and-by. And as she told him of her
two bets—ten louis on Lusignan and five on Valerio II.—he
shrugged his shoulders with an air of saying that women would
make fools of themselves, in spite of everything. This surprised
her a great deal; she could no longer understand anything.

At this moment the animation increased around. Lun-
cheons were spread in the open air to help to pass the time
until the race for the Grand Prize was run. Everyone ate, and
drank still more, anywhere—on the grass, on the high seats of
the stage-coaches and the drags, in the victorias, the
broughams, and the landaus. There was a general spread of

cold meats, an unpacking of hampers of champagne, which the footmen brought from under box seats. The corks flew out with feeble detonations, which were carried away by the wind; jokes were bandied about; the sound of breaking glasses introduced cracked notes into the nervous gaiety. Gaga and Clarisse were making quite a meal with Blanche, devouring sandwiches on a cloth which they had spread over their knees. Louise Violaine had alighted from her basket chaise and joined Caroline Héquet; and on the grass, at their feet, some gentlemen had set up an imitation bar, where Tatan, Maria, Simone, and the others came to drink; whilst close by, up aloft, there was quite a band on a stage-coach with Léa de Horn, all emptying bottles as fast as they could, and getting quite tipsy in the sunshine, shouting and gesticulating above the crowd. But soon everyone pressed round Nana's landau. She was standing up filling glasses of champagne for the men who came to shake hands with her. One of the footmen, François, handed up the bottle, whilst La Faloise, imitating the voice of a mountebank, called out,

"Walk up, gentlemen. It's all for nothing. There's some for everyone."

"Do be quiet, my dear fellow," Nana ended by saying. "We look like a lot of buffoons."

She thought him very funny, however, and was immensely amused. One moment she had the idea of sending George with a glass of champagne to Rose Mignon, who pretended she did not drink. Henri and Charles looked bored to death. The youngsters would have liked some champagne; but George, being afraid of a row, drank the wine himself. Then Nana recollected little Louis, whom she had forgotten behind her. Perhaps he was thirsty; and she got him to take a few drops of wine, which made him cough frightfully.

"Walk up, walk up, gentlemen," repeated La Faloise. "It doesn't cost two sous, it doesn't cost one sou. We give it for nothing."

But Nana interrupted him, exclaiming: "Look! there's Bordenave over there! Call him, oh! please run and fetch him!"

It was indeed Bordenave, who was walking about with his

hands behind his back, and a hat that looked rusty in the sunshine, and a greasy frock-coat, all whitened at the seams; a Bordenave disfigured by bankruptcy, but still as furious as ever, displaying his misery amongst the world of fashion, with the cheek of a man ever ready to violate fortune.

"The devil! what style!" said he, when Nana, like the good-natured girl she was, held out her hand to him. Then, after tossing off a glass of champagne, he uttered this remark full of deep regret, "Ah! if I was only a woman! But, damn it all! it doesn't matter! Will you return to the stage? I've an idea. I'll take the Gaiety Theatre, and between us we will carry Paris by storm. What do you say? You at least owe me that."

And he remained standing, grumbling to himself, though happy at seeing her again; for, as he said, that confounded Nana was balm to his heart, merely by living before him. She was his daughter, his very blood.

The circle increased. Now, La Faloise was pouring out, whilst Philippe and George went in search of more friends. Slowly but surely everyone was attracted to the spot. Nana had a laugh and a witty remark for everyone. The different bands of drinkers drew nearer, all the champagne scattered about, came towards her, there was soon but one crowd, but one uproar, around her landau; and she reigned among the glasses held towards her, with her yellow hair flying in the breeze, and her snow white face bathed with sunshine. Then, to crown all, and to finally settle the other women, who were enraged at her triumph, she filled her glass and raised it on high, in her old posture of Venus victorious.

But some one was touching her on the back, and on turning round, she was surprised to see Mignon on the seat. She disappeared for a moment and seated herself beside him, for he had something important to say to her. Mignon was in the habit of saying everywhere, that his wife was ridiculous to have a grudge against Nana; he considered it stupid and useless.

"This is what's the matter, my dear," murmured he. "Be careful not to make Rose too wild. You understand, I prefer to put you on your guard. Yes, she has a weapon; and as she has never forgiven you the 'Little Duchess' affair—"

"A weapon?" interrupted Nana, "what the deuce do I care?"

"Listen, it's a letter that she must have found in Fauchery's pocket—a letter written to that wretch Fauchery by Countess Sabine. And on my word, it's all there, in black and white. So Rose intends to send the letter to the count, to be avenged on you and him."

"What the deuce do I care?" repeated Nana. "It's awfully funny, though. Ah! so it's true about Fauchery. Well! so much the better, she annoyed me immensely. What a joke it'll be."

"But no, I don't want it to be done," hastily resumed Mignon. "It would make such a scandal! Besides, it would be of no use to us—"

He stopped, afraid of saying too much. She exclaimed that she was certainly not going to pull a respectable woman out of the mire; but as he persisted she looked him full in the face. No doubt he was afraid of seeing Fauchery back in his family circle, if the countess were exposed. That was just what Rose wished, at the same time desiring vengeance, for she still entertained a tender feeling for the journalist. And Nana became thoughtful. She was thinking of M. Venot's visit, and was forming a plan whilst Mignon was trying to convince her.

"Well, suppose Rose sends the letter; there'll be a great scandal, won't there? You will be mixed up in it, everyone will say it's your fault. Then the count will at once separate from his wife—"

"Why so?" asked she. "On the contrary—"

But in her turn she interrupted herself. There was no need for her to think out aloud. At last, she pretended to enter into Mignon's views, so as to get rid of him; and, as he advised her to give in a bit to Rose—to pay her a little visit, for instance, there, before everyone—she replied that she would see, that she would think about it.

A sudden uproar caused her to stand up again. On the course some horses passed like a flash of lightning. It was the race for the City of Paris Prize, which fell to Cornemuse. Now the race for the Grand Prize was about to be run. The fever increased; anxiety seized on the crowd, which stamped and swayed in an endeavour to make the time pass more quickly;

and at that last moment a surprise bewildered the betting-
men—the continual rise in the price of Nana, the outsider of
the Vandeuvres stable. Gentlemen returned every minute with
a fresh quotation—Nana was at thirty, Nana was at twenty-five,
then at twenty, then at fifteen. No one understood what it
meant. A filly beaten on every race-course, a filly which, that
very morning, could not find a backer at fifty! What could be
the meaning of that sudden craze? Some laughed, and talked
of the clean sweep made of all those idiots who were allowing
themselves to be taken in; others, serious and anxious, were
sure there was something up. All sorts of stories were recalled,
of the robberies countenanced on the race-course; but this
time the great name of Vandeuvres silenced all accusations,
and the sceptics found most believers when they prophesied
that Nana would come in a good last.

"Who rides Nana?" asked La Faloise.

Just then the real Nana reappeared. Then the gentlemen,
bursting into exaggerated laughter, gave an indecent meaning
to the question. Nana bowed.

"It's Price," she replied.

And the discussion recommenced. Price was an English
celebrity unknown in France. Why had Vandeuvres engaged
this jockey, when Gresham generally rode Nana? Besides,
everyone was surprised to see him trust Lusignan to that Gresham, who, as La Faloise said, never came in first. But all these
remarks were lost in the jokes, and the contradictions, and the
extraordinary hubbub of various opinions. To pass the time
everyone returned to the bottles of champagne. Then a whisper passed round, the groups made way, and Vandeuvres appeared. Nana pretended to be cross.

"Well! you're nice, not to come till this time! I, who've been
longing to see the enclosure."

"Come then," said he, "there is still time. You can have a
look round. I just happen to have a lady's ticket."

And he led her off on his arm, she delighted at seeing the
jealous looks with which Lucy, Caroline, and the other women
watched her. The two Hugons and La Faloise, remaining in the

landau, continued to do the honours of her champagne. She called to them that she would be back directly.

But Vandeuvres, having caught sight of Labordette, beckoned to him, and a few brief words passed between them.

"Have you picked up everything?"

"Yes."

"For how much?"

"Fifteen hundred louis, a little everywhere."

As Nana, full of curiosity, was listening, they said no more. Vandeuvres was very nervous, and his clear eyes seemed lighted up with little flames of fire, the same as on the night when he frightened her by talking of burning himself in his stable with his horses. As they crossed the course, she lowered her voice, and said,

"I say, just tell me this. Why has the price of your filly gone up? It's creating quite a sensation!"

He started, and exclaimed, "Ah! so everyone's talking of it. What a set they are, those betting-men! When I've a favourite they all jump at it, and there's nothing left for me. Then, when an outsider's inquired after, they clamour and cry out as though they were being fleeced."

"Well, you know, you must put me on my guard, for I've been betting," she resumed. "Has she a chance?"

A sudden rage overpowered him, without any apparent reason. "Eh! have the goodness not to badger me any more. Every horse has a chance. The price has gone up, of course, because some people have been backing her! Who I don't know. I'd rather leave you if you're going to continue your idiotic questions."

This way of speaking was neither in accordance with his usual temper or habits. She felt more surprised than hurt. He, too, felt ashamed of himself; and, as she stiffly requested him to be more polite, he apologised. For some little time past he had been subject to these sudden fits of temper. No one belonging to the gallant world of Paris ignored that on that day he was playing his last cards. If his horses did not win, if they lost him the considerable sums for which he had backed them, it would be not only a disaster, but a regular collapse; the scaf-

folding of his credit, the grand appearances which his under-
mined existence, destroyed by disorders and debts, preserved,
would tumble and noise his ruin abroad. And Nana, as everyone also knew, was the man-destroyer who had finished him,
who had been the last to attack that already damaged fortune,
and had cleared off all that remained. The maddest caprices
imaginable were related—gold thrown to the winds, an excursion to Baden, where she had not even left him the money to
pay the hotel bill, a handful of diamonds flung into the fire
one night of intoxication, to see if they would burn like coal.
Little by little, with her big limbs and her noisy vulgar laughter, she had taken complete possession of that heir, so impoverished and so cunning, of an ancient race. At that hour he
was risking his all, overpowered by a taste for what was vile and
idiotic, that he had even lost the strength of his scepticism.
Eight days before she had made him promise her a château on
the Normandy coast, between Havre and Trouville; and he
made it a point of honour to keep his word. Only, she preyed
on his nerves; he thought her so stupid that he could have
beaten her.

The gatekeeper had permitted them to enter the enclosure,
not daring to stop the woman on the count's arm. Nana, full
of pride on at length placing her foot on that forbidden spot,
studied her poses, and walked slowly along in front of the
ladies seated at the foot of the stands. On ten rows of chairs
there was a deep mass of elegant costumes, blending their gay
colours in the open air. Chairs were turned round; friends had
formed into groups just as they chanced to meet, the same as
in some public garden, with children playing around; and,
higher up, the tiers of the stands were filled to overflowing,
whilst the delicate framework cast its shadows over the light-
coloured garments. Nana stared at the ladies. She made a
point of looking fixedly at Countess Sabine. Then as she
passed in front of the imperial pavilion, the sight of Muffat,
standing up near the Empress, in all his official dignity,
amused her immensely.

"Oh! how stupid he looks!" said she out loud to Vandeuvres.

She wished to see everything. This bit of a park, with its

lawns and its groups of trees, did not strike her as very inter-
esting. A refreshment contractor had set up a large bar near
the railings. Beneath an immense circular thatched roof, a
crowd of men were shouting and gesticulating. This was the
betting ring. Close by were some empty horse-boxes; and to
her disappointment she merely beheld the horse of a gen-
darme. Then there was the paddock, a little more than a hundred yards round, where a stable lad was walking Valerio II.,
well covered up. And that was all! with the exception of a number of men on the gravel paths, wearing their orange-coloured
tickets in their button-holes, and a continual promenade of
people in the open galleries of the stands, which interested her
for a moment; but, really! it wasn't worth while being upset, because one was kept out of there.

Daguenet and Fauchery, who were passing, bowed to her.
She beckoned to them, so they were obliged to draw near; and
she launched out into abuse of the enclosure. Then interrupting herself, she exclaimed,

"Hallo! there's the Marquis de Chouard; how old he's looking! He's doing for himself, the old rogue! Is he still as unruly
as ever?"

Then Daguenet related the old fellow's last prank—a story
of the day before, which had not then got about. After hovering around for months, he had just given Gaga, it was said,
thirty thousand francs for her daughter Amélie.

"Well! it's abominable!" exclaimed Nana indignantly. "It's a
fine thing to have daughters! But, now I think of it! it must
have been Lili that I saw over there in a brougham with a lady.
I thought I knew the face. The old fellow must have brought
her out."

Vandeuvres was not listening, but stood by impatiently and
anxious to get rid of her. However, Fauchery having said that if
she had not seen the bookmakers she had not seen anything,
the count was obliged to take her to these, in spite of his visible reluctance. This time she was satisfied; it was really very curious.

In an open space composed of a series of grass plots bordered by young chestnut trees, and shaded by tender green

leaves, a compact line of bookmakers, forming a vast circle, as though at a fair, awaited those desirous of betting. In order to overlook the crowd, they were standing on wooden benches. They had posted up their betting lists against the trees; whilst, with an eye ever on the watch, they at the least sign made notes of bets so rapidly that some of the spectators gazed at them with open mouths and without comprehending. All was confusion, odds were shouted out, and exclamations greeted the unexpected changes in the prices; and now and again, increasing the hub-bub, scouts running at full speed would arrive and call out at the top of their voices the news of a start or a finish, which would raise a long murmur midst all that fever for gambling beneath the shining sun.

"How funny they are," murmured Nana, highly amused. "Their faces all look as though they were turned inside out. You see that big one there? Well, I shouldn't care to meet him by myself in the middle of a wood."

But Vandeuvres pointed out to her a bookmaker, an assistant in a draper's shop, who had made three millions in two years. Slim, delicate-looking, and fair, he was treated by everyone with the greatest respect. He was spoken to smilingly, and people stood by to look at him.

They were at last about to leave, when Vandeuvres nodded to another bookmaker, who thereupon ventured to call to him. He was one of his old coachmen—an enormous fellow with shoulders like an ox, and a very red face. Now that he was tempting fortune on the race-course, with a capital of doubtful origin, the count gave him a helping hand, commissioning him with his secret betting, and always treating him as a servant from whom one has nothing to hide. In spite of this protection, the fellow had lost some very heavy sums one after another, and he also was playing his last card on that day, his eyes all blood-shot, and himself on the verge of a fit of apoplexy.

"Well, Maréchal," asked Vandeuvres, in a low voice, "how much have you against?"

"Five thousand louis, sir," replied the bookmaker, also

speaking low. "That's good, isn't it? I must admit that I've lowered the price. I've laid the odds at three to one."

Vandeuvres looked greatly annoyed. "No, no; I won't have it. Put it back at two to one at once. I will never tell you anything again, Maréchal."

"Oh, but what can that matter to you now, sir?" resumed the other, with the humble smile of a confederate. "I had to attract the people so as to place your two thousand louis."

Then Vandeuvres made him give over; but, as he went away, Maréchal, recollecting something, regretted that he had not questioned him respecting his filly's rise in price. He was in a pretty mess if the filly had a chance, for he had taken two hundred louis about her, laying fifty to one against.

Nana could not make anything out of the words whispered by the count, but she did not dare question him again. He seemed more nervous than ever, and abruptly placed her under the care of Labordette, whom they found waiting at the entrance to the weighing place.

"You must take her back," said he. "I have something to attend to. Good-bye."

And he went inside. It was a narrow apartment, with a low ceiling, and almost filled with a big weighing machine. It was like the room where luggage is weighed at a small suburban station. Nana was again greatly disappointed. She had figured to herself a very vast affair—a monumental apparatus for weighing the horses. What! they only weighed the jockeys! Then there was no need to make such a fuss about it. Seated in the scales, a jockey, looking an awful fool, with his saddle and harness on his knees, was waiting till a stout man in an overcoat had taken his weight; whilst a stable lad, at the door, held the horse, Cosinus, around which the crowd gathered, silent and wrapped in thought.

They were clearing the course. Labordette hurried Nana, but he returned a few steps to show her a little fellow talking to Vandeuvres apart from the others.

"Look, there's Price," said he.

"Ah! yes, he rides me," she murmured with a laugh.

She thought him very ugly. To her all the jockeys looked like fools, no doubt, said she, because they were not allowed to grow. That one, a man of forty, had the appearance of an old, dried-up child, with a long, thin face, looking hard and death-like and full of wrinkles. His body was so knotty, so reduced, that the blue jacket with white sleeves seemed to cover a piece of wood.

"No," she resumed as they moved away, "you know he isn't my fancy."

A mob still crowded the course, the wet trodden grass of which looked almost black. The crowd pressed in front of the boards, placed very high up on iron posts, which exhibited the numbers of the starters, and with raised heads, greeted up-roariously each number that an electric wire, communicating with the weighing place, made appear. Some gentlemen were ticking their racing cards; Pichenette having been scratched by his owner, caused a slight commotion. Nana, however, simply passed by on Labordette's arm. The bell was ringing persist-ently for the course to be cleared.

"Ah! my friends," said she as she re-entered her landau, "it's all humbug, their enclosure."

Everyone about her applauded her return. "Bravo, Nana! Nana is restored to us!" How stupid they were! Did they think her one to give them the slip? She returned at the right time. Attention! it was going to begin. And the champagne was for-gotten, everyone left off drinking. But Nana was surprised to find Gaga in her carriage, with Bijou and little Louis on her knees. Gaga had come there for the sake of being near La Faloise, though she pretended that she had done so because she so longed to kiss the baby. She adored children.

"Ah! by the way, and Lili?" asked Nana. "It's she, is it not, in that old fellow's brougham over there? I've just been told something that isn't very creditable."

Gaga assumed a most grieved expression of countenance.

"My dear, it has made me quite ill," said she woefully. "I cried so much yesterday, I was obliged to keep my bed all day, and even this morning I was afraid I should not be able to come. Well, you know what my notion was. I did not wish her to do as she has done; I had her brought up in a convent, and intended getting her well married. And she always had the best advice, and was constantly looked after. Well, my dear! she would have her own way. Oh! we had such a scene—bitter tears, unpleasant words, until it ended by my slapping her face. She felt so dull, she would try the change. Then when she took it into her head to say, 'It's not you, anyhow, who have the right to prevent me,' I said to her, 'You're a wretch, you dishonour us, be off!' And so off she went, but I consented to make the best arrangement I could for her. However, there's my last hope gone; and I had been planning, ah! such grand things!"

The sounds of a quarrel caused them to stand up. It was George who was defending Vandeuvres against several vague rumours that were passing from group to group.

"How absurd to say that he no longer believes in his horse!" exclaimed the young man. "Only yesterday, at the club, he backed Lusignan to the extent of a thousand louis."

"Yes, I was there," added Philippe. "And he didn't back Nana for a single louis. If Nana's got to ten to one, it's not owing to him. It's ridiculous to give people credit for so much calculation. Besides, what interest could he have in behaving so?"

Labordette listened in a quiet sort of way, and, shrugging his shoulders, observed,

"Let them say what they like, they must talk of something. The count has just laid another five hundred louis at least on Lusignan, and if he's backed Nana for a hundred it's merely because an owner must show some faith in his horses."

"What the devil can it matter to us?" yelled La Faloise, waving his arms. "Spirit will win. France is nowhere! Bravo, England!"

A tremor passed slowly through the crowd, whilst a fresh peal of the bell announced the arrival of the horses at the starting-place. Then Nana, to obtain a better view, stood up on one of the seats of her landau, treading on the bouquets of forget-me-nots and roses. With a glance round, she took in the vast horizon. At this last moment, when the excitement was at fever heat, she beheld first of all the empty course, enclosed by its grey barriers, along which policemen were stationed at inter-

vals, and the broad band of muddy grass before her became
greener and greener in the distance, until it merged into a soft
velvety carpet. Then, as she lowered her eyes and gazed
around in her immediate vicinity, she saw an ever-moving
crowd standing on tip-toe or clambering on to the vehicles, excited and animated by the same passion, with the horses neigh-
ing, the refreshment tents shaking in the wind, and riders
urging on their steeds in the midst of the foot passengers hastening to the barriers; whilst, when she looked at the stands on
the other side of the course, the people seemed smaller, the
mass of heads appeared merely a medley of colours filling the
paths, the benches, and the terraces, beneath the dull sky.

And she could see the plain beyond. Behind the ivy-covered
windmill, to the right, there was a background of meadows, intersected with plantations; in front, as far as the Seine, which
flowed at the foot of the hill, park-like avenues, along which interminable rows of immovable vehicles were waiting, crossed
each other; then on the left, towards Boulogne, the country
spreading out again, opened into a view of the bluey heights of
Meudon, intercepted only by a row of pawlonias, the rosy tufts
of which, without a single leaf, formed a sheet of vivid crimson.
People still continued to arrive, numbers were hastening from
over there looking like so many ants as they wended their way
along a narrow path which crossed the fields; whilst far off, in
the direction of Paris, the spectators who did not pay, a host
who camped out in the wood, formed a long black moving line
under the trees on the outskirts of the Bois.

But suddenly a feeling of gaiety excited the hundred thousand souls who covered that bit of a field with a commotion of
insects disporting themselves beneath the vast sky. The sun,
which had been hidden for the last quarter of an hour, reappeared and shone in a flood of light, and everything sparkled
once more. The women's parasols looked like innumerable
shields of gold above the crowd. Everyone applauded the sun,
gay laughter saluted it, and arms were thrust out to draw aside
the clouds.

At this moment a police officer appeared walking alone
along the centre of the now deserted course. Higher up, to-

wards the left, a man could be seen holding a red flag in his hand.

"That's the starter, the Baron de Mauriac," replied Labordette to a question of Nana's.

Among the men surrounding the young woman, and who pressed even on to the steps of her landau, there arose a hubbub of exclamations, of sentences left unfinished, in the flush of first impressions. Philippe and George, Bordenave, La Faloise could not keep quiet.

"Don't push!"—"Let me see!"—"Ah! the judge is entering his box."—"Did you say it was M. de Souvigny?"—"I say, he must have good eyes to decide a close contest from such a place!"—"Do be quiet, they're hoisting the flag."—"Here they come—look out!"—"The first one is Cosinus."

A red and yellow flag waved in the air from the top of the starting-post. The horses arrived one by one, led by stable lads, the jockeys in the saddle, their arms hanging down, and looking mere bright specks in the sunshine. After Cosinus, Hasard and Boum appeared. Then a murmur greeted Spirit, a tall, handsome bay, whose harsh colours, lemon and black, had a Britannic sadness. Valerio II. met with a grand reception. He was a lively little animal, and the colours were pale green, edged with pink. Vandeuvres's two horses were a long time making their appearance. At length, the blue and white colours were seen following Frangipane; but Lusignan, a very dark bay of irreproachable form, was almost forgotten in the surprise created by Nana's appearance. No one had ever before seen her thus. The sunshine gave to the chestnut filly the golden hue of a fair-haired girl. She glittered in the light like a new louis, with her deep chest, her graceful head and neck and shoulders, and her long, nervous, delicate back.

"Why! she has hair the colour of mine!" exclaimed Nana, delighted. "I feel quite proud of her!"

They all climbed on to the landau. Bordenave almost trod on little Louis, whom his mother had forgotten. He caught hold of him, grumbling in a paternal manner, and, lifting him on to his shoulder, he murmured,

"Poor young 'un, he must see too. Wait a minute and I'll

show you your mamma. There! over there—look at the gee-
gee."

And as Bijou was scratching his legs he lifted him up also,
whilst Nana, delighted with the animal that bore her name,
glanced at the other women to see how they took it. They were
all madly jealous. At this moment old Tricon, on her cab, immovable until then, waved her hands, and shouted some instructions to a bookmaker over the crowd. Her instinct
prompted her. She backed Nana.

La Faloise was making an unbearable row, however. He was
quite smitten with Frangipane. "I've an inspiration," he cried.
"Just look at Frangipane. See what go there is in him! I take
Frangipane at eight to one. Who'll bet?"

"Do be quiet," Labordette ended by saying. "You'll only regret it all by-and-by."

"Frangipane's a jade," declared Philippe. "He is already wet
with perspiration. Look! they're going to canter."

The horses had turned to the right, and they started on
their preliminary canter, passing in front of the grand stand in
a disordered crowd. Then the excited remarks broke out
again; every one spoke at the same time.

"Lusignan is in good condition, but he is too long in the
back."

—"You know, not a farthing on Valerio II. He is nervous; he
holds his head too high—it's a bad sign."—"Hallo! it's Burne
who is riding Spirit."—"I tell you he has no shoulder. A good
shoulder means everything."—"No, Spirit is decidedly too
quiet."—"Listen, I saw Nana after the race for the Grande
Poule des Produits. She was soaking her coat as though dead,
and breathing fit to burst. Twenty louis she isn't placed!"—
"Enough! enough! what a confounded nuisance he is with his
Frangipane! It's too late; they're going to start."

La Faloise, almost crying, was struggling to get to a bookmaker. The others had to reason with him. All the necks were
stretched out. But the first start was not a good one; the starter,
who in the distance looked like a thin black stick, had not lowered his red flag. The horses returned to the post after a short
gallop. There were two other false starts. At length the starter,

getting the horses all well together, sent them off with a skill that won admiration on all sides.

"Magnificent start!"—"No, it is chance!"—"Never mind, they're off!"

The noise died away in the anxiety which filled every breast. Now, the betting ceased; the game was being played on the immense course. Complete silence reigned at last, as though all breathing was suspended. Faces were raised, white and trembling. At the start Hasard and Cosinus had made the running, leading all the others. Valerio II. followed close behind them; the rest came on in a confused mass. When they passed in front of the stands, shaking the earth, and with the sudden gust of wind caused by their immense speed, the group had stretched out to fully forty lengths. Frangipane was last. Nana was a little behind Lusignan and Spirit.

"The deuce!" murmured Labordette; "the English one is picking his way well through them!"

Everyone in the landau had something to say—some exclamation to utter. All stood upon tiptoe, and watched intently the bright colours of the jockeys borne along in the sunshine. As they ascended the incline, Valerio II. took the lead. Cosinus and Hasard were losing ground, whilst Lusignan and Spirit, neck and neck, were still followed closely by Nana.

"Damn it! the English horse has won, that's quite plain," said Bordenave. "Lusignan is tiring, and Valerio II. can't stay."

"Well! it is disgusting if the English horse wins!" exclaimed Philippe, in a burst of patriotic grief.

A feeling of anguish gradually overwhelmed that mob of people. Another defeat! And a wish of extraordinary ardour, amounting almost to a prayer, for Lusignan's success was inwardly expressed by all; whilst they abused Spirit and his funereal-looking jockey. The crowd, scattered over the grass, broke up into bands who were running with all their might. Horsemen galloped swiftly over the ground. And Nana, turning slowly round, beheld at her feet that surging mob of men and animals—that sea of heads looking as though dashed about and carried along the course by the vortex of the race, streaking the bright horizon of the jockeys. She watched the fast-stepping legs, which, as the distance increased, assumed the slenderness of hairs. Now, at the farthest limit of the circle, she saw them sideways, looking so small and slight against the green background of the Bois. Then suddenly they disappeared behind a large cluster of trees close to the course.

"Don't despair!" cried George, still full of hope. "It's not over yet. The English horse is caught."

But La Faloise, again overcome by his disdain for the national cause, became quite scandalous in his applause of Spirit. Bravo! it served them right! France was in need of the lesson! Spirit first, and Frangipane second! it would aggravate his fatherland! Labordette, whom he thoroughly exasperated, seriously threatened to throw him out of the carriage.

"We'll see how long they take," quietly observed Bordenave, who, with little Louis on his shoulder, had pulled out his watch.

One by one the horses reappeared from behind the clump of trees. Then the crowd uttered a long murmur of amazement. Valerio II. still had the lead, but Spirit was gaining on him, and Lusignan, who was next, had given way, whilst another horse was taking his place. The spectators could not understand it at first; they mixed up the colours. Exclamations arose on all sides.

"But it is Nana!"—"Nana? absurd! I tell you Lusignan still keeps his place."—"Yes, it is, though, it is Nana! It is easy to recognise her by her golden colour."—"There! look at her now! She seems all on fire."—"Bravo, Nana! there's an artful minx for you!"—"Bah! it's nothing. She's only making the running for Lusignan."

For some seconds that was the general opinion. But the filly slowly continued to gain ground in a continued effort. Then an immense emotion seized upon all. The horses in the rear no longer excited the smallest interest. A last struggle began between Spirit, Nana, Lusignan, and Valerio II. Their names were on the lips of everyone, their progress or their falling off was proclaimed in short disconnected sentences. And Nana, who had climbed on to the coachman's seat, as though lifted up by some invisible power, was all pale and trembling, and so deeply moved that she could not say a word. Labordette, close beside her, was once more smiling.

"Well, the English horse is in difficulties," said Philippe, joyfully. "He is not going so well."

"Anyhow, Lusignan is done for," cried La Faloise. "Valerio II. leads the way. Look! there they are, the whole four of them, close together."

The same words came from every throat: "What a rate they're going at! Oh! what a frightful rate!"

Nana now beheld the group coming towards her like a flash of lightning. You could feel their approach, and almost their breathing, a distant roar which grew louder and louder every second. The whole crowd impetuously rushed to the barriers, and, preceding the horses, a heavy clamour escaped from every chest, coming nearer and nearer, with a sound like the ocean breaking on the shore. It was the final outburst of brutal passion aroused by a colossal venture, a hundred thousand spectators with one fixed idea, burning with the same hankering for luck, following with their eyes those animals whose gallop carried off millions. They shoved and trampled on one another, with clinched fists and open mouths, each one for himself, and urging on his favourite with his voice and gestures. And the cry of this vast multitude, which was like the roar of some savage beast, became more and more distinct.

"Here they come!—here they come!—here they come!"

But Nana continued to gain ground; now Valerio II. was distanced, and she led with Spirit by two or three necks. The rumbling noise resembling thunder increased. As they came on, a tempest of oaths greeted them from the landau.

"Gee up, Lusignan! you big coward, you sorry beast!"—"Look at the English one! isn't he grand? Go it, old fellow, go it!"—"And that Valerio, it's disgusting!"—"Ah! the carrion! my ten louis are nowhere now!"—"There's only Nana in it! Bravo, Nana! bravo, little slut!"

And Nana, on the coachman's box, was swinging her hips and thighs, without knowing she did so, as though she herself was running. She kept protruding her body, under the notion that it helped the filly along; and each time she did so she sighed wearily, and said, in a low, painful tone of voice,

"Go it—go it—go it."

A grand sight was then beheld. Price, erect in the stirrups, his whip raised, flogged Nana with an iron arm. That old, dried-up child, that long figure, usually looking so hard and dead, seemed shooting sparks of fire; and, in a burst of furious audacity, of triumphant will, he instilled some of his own spirit into the filly. He kept her up, he carried her along, covered with foam, and with eyes all bloody. The cluster of horses passed like a flash of lightning, sweeping the air, taking away the breath of all who saw them; whilst the judge, on the look-out, calmly awaited. Then there arose an immense cheer. With a final effort Price had lifted Nana to the post, beating Spirit by a head.

The clamour that burst forth was like the roar of the rising tide. "Nana! Nana! Nana!" The cry rolled and grew with the violence of a tempest, gradually filling the air, from the innermost recesses of the Bois to Mount Valérien, from the meadows of Longchamps to the plain of Boulogne. Around Nana's landau a mad enthusiasm was displayed. "Long Live Nana! Long Live France! Down with England!" The women waved their parasols. Some men sprung into the air, and turned round vociferating; others, laughing nervously, flung up their hats. And on the other side of the course the crowd in the enclosure responded. An agitation passed through the stands, without one being able to discern anything distinctly, beyond a commotion of the air (like the invisible flame of a brazier) above that living heap of little chaotic figures, twisting their arms about, with black specks indicating their eyes and open mouths. The cry continued unceasingly, growing in intensity, caught up in the distance by the people camping beneath the trees, to spread again and increase itself with the emotion of the imperial stand, where the Empress joined in the applause. "Nana! Nana! Nana!" The shout rose beneath the glorious sun, which stimulated the delirium of the crowd with a shower of gold.

Then Nana, standing on the box-seat of her landau,

stretched to her full height, thought it was she that they were applauding. For an instant she stood immovable in the aston-ishment of her triumph, watching the course invaded by a host so compact, by such a sea of black hats, that the grass could no longer be seen. Then, when all that mob had taken up its po-sition, leaving a narrow passage to the entrance of the course, acclaiming Nana again as she retired with Price, broken in ap-pearance, lifeless, and as though empty, the young woman vio-lently slapped her thighs, forgetting everything as she gave vent to her triumph in the coarsest language.

"Ah! damn it all! it's me, though. Ah! damn it all! what luck!"

And not knowing how to show the joy that was overwhelm-ing her, she seized hold of and kissed little Louis, whom she had just caught sight of on Bordenave's shoulder.

"Three minutes and fourteen seconds," said the latter, put-ting his watch back into his pocket.

Nana still listened to her name with which the whole plain resounded. It was her people who applauded her, whilst, in a straight line with the sun, she throned over them, with her hair shining like a star, and her blue and white dress of the colour of the heavens. Labordette, before hastening away, told her that she had won two thousand louis, for he had placed her fifty louis on Nana at forty to one. But the money affected her less than that unexpected victory, the splendour of which made her queen of Paris. The other women had all lost. Rose Mignon, in a fit of passion, had broken her parasol; and Caro-line Héquet, and Clarisse, and Simone, and even Lucy Stewart, in spite of her son's presence, all swore in an undertone, exas-perated by that big girl's luck; whilst old Tricon, who had crossed herself both at the start and the finish of the race, tow-ered above them to the full height of her tall body, delighted at her discernment, and like an experienced matron canoniz-ing Nana.

Around the landau, however, the rush of men increased. The band had uttered the most ferocious yells. George, almost choked, continued to shout by himself in a broken voice. As the champagne ran short, Philippe, taking the two grooms with him, hastened off to the refreshment tents. And Nana's court grew larger and larger; her triumph determined the laggards. The movement which had made her landau the central object ended in an apotheosis—Queen Venus surrounded by her delirious subjects. Behind her, Bordenave was muttering oaths with the tender feelings of a father. Steiner himself, reconquered, had left Simone, and was hanging on to one of the carriage steps. When the champagne arrived, when she raised her glass full of wine, the applause was so deafening—the cries of "Nana! Nana! Nana!" were so loud—that the amazed multitude looked around, expecting to see the filly; and one no longer knew whether it was the animal or the woman who most filled the men's hearts.

Mignon hastened to her, in spite of Rose's black looks. The confounded girl put him quite beside himself; he must embrace her. Then after he had kissed her on both cheeks, he said paternally,

"What bothers me is that Rose will now, for certain, send the letter. She's in such a rage."

"So much the better! That's just what I want!" said Nana, forgetting herself. But seeing him lost in astonishment at her words, she hastened to add, "No, no, whatever am I saying? Really, I no longer know what I say! I'm tipsy."

And indeed, she was intoxicated with joy and with the sunshine, as with her glass raised on high, she applauded herself.

"To Nana! to Nana!" cried she, in the midst of a still greater increase of uproar, laughter and cheers, which little by little, gained the entire race-course.

The races were drawing to a close; they were now running for the Vaublanc Prize. Vehicles were departing one by one. Vandeuvres's name was frequently uttered in the midst of squabbles. Now, it was clear. For two years past, Vandeuvres had been preparing for this exploit by always instructing Gresham to pull Nana; and he had only produced Lusignan to make the running for the filly. The losers lost their tempers, whilst the winners shrugged their shoulders. What next? it was all right. An owner could manage his stable as he chose. There had been much queerer things done than that! The greater number of people considered Vandeuvres very smart, to have secured through his friends all he could possibly get on Nana, which had explained the sudden rise in her price; they talked of two thousand louis, at an average of thirty to one, which meant a gain of twelve hundred thousand francs, a sum so large that it commanded respect, and excused everything.

But other rumours, very grave ones, which were whispered about, came from the enclosure. The men who returned from there brought details. Voices were raised as they related the particulars of a frightful scandal—that poor Vandeuvres was done for. He had spoilt his superb hit by a piece of arrant stupidity, an idiotic robbery, in commissioning Maréchal, a bookmaker, whose affairs were in a very queer state, to place on his account two thousand louis against Lusignan, just for the sake of getting back his thousand and odd louis, which he had openly bet on the horse, a mere nothing; and that was the fatal crack in the midst of his already tottering fortunes. The bookmaker, warned that the favourite would not win, had made about sixty thousand francs by the horse; only, Labordette, not having received exact and detailed instructions, had gone and placed with him two hundred louis on Nana, which he, in his ignorance of what was going to be done, continued to lay at fifty to one against. Done out of one hundred thousand francs by the filly, with a clear loss of forty thousand, Maréchal, who felt everything giving way beneath him, had suddenly understood all on seeing Labordette and the count conversing together after the race in front of the weighing place; and with the fury of an old coachman, and the rough manner of a man who has been robbed, he had just created a frightful disturbance before every one, telling the story in most atrocious language, and gathering a mob around him. It was added that the stewards were about to inquire into the matter.

Nana, whom Philippe and George were quietly informing of what had happened, kept making reflections, without, however, ceasing to laugh and to drink. It was, after all, very likely, she recollected certain things, and then, that Maréchal was a horrid fellow. Yet she still doubted, when Labordette appeared. He was very pale.

"Well?" queried she, in a low voice.

"It's all up with him!" he replied, simply.

And he shrugged his shoulders. He had acted like a child, this Vandeuvres! She made a gesture of being bored.

That night, at Mabille, Nana met with a colossal success. When she arrived, towards ten o'clock, the uproar was already formidable. This classic night of folly gathered together all the gallant youth of the capital, an aristocratic company indulging in horse-play and a stupidity worthy of lackeys. There was quite a crush beneath the garlands of flaring gas-jets, a mass of dress suits, of extravagant costumes; women with bare shoulders in old dresses only fit for soiling, walked round and yelled, stimulated by drinking on a gigantic scale. At thirty paces one could no longer hear the brass instruments of the orchestra. No one danced. Idiotic remarks, repeated no one knew why, circulated among the groups. They all exerted themselves, but without succeeding in being funny. Seven women, shut up in the cloak-room, cried to be delivered. A shallot, picked up and sold by auction, fetched two louis. Just then Nana arrived, still dressed in the blue and white costume that she wore at the races. The shallot was presented to her in the midst of a thunder of applause. They seized hold of her in spite of her struggles, and three gentlemen carried her in triumph into the garden, across the ruined lawns and the damaged beds of flowers and shrubs, and as the orchestra was in the way, they took it by assault, and smashed the chairs and desks. A paternal police organized the riot.

It was not till the Tuesday that Nana felt quite recovered from the emotions of her victory. She was talking that morning with Madame Lerat, come to give her news of little Louis, who had been unwell ever since his outing. She was highly interested in an event which at that moment was occupying Paris. Vandeuvres, warned off all the race-courses, his name withdrawn the same night from the list of members of the Cercle Impérial, had on the morrow set fire to his stable, and had been burned with his horses.

"He told me he would," the young woman was saying. "Ah! the young fellow was a regular madman. It gave me such a fright last night when I heard of it! You see he might very well have murdered me one night; and, besides, oughtn't he to have told me about his horse? I should, at least, have made my fortune! He said to Labordette that if I was let into the secret I would at once tell my hairdresser, and a host of other men. How very polite! Ah, no! really, I can't regret him much."

After thinking the matter over, she had become furious. At that moment Labordette entered the room. He had been collecting her winnings for her, and brought her about forty thousand francs. That only added to her ill-humour, for she ought to have won a million. Labordette, who pretended to be very innocent in the matter, boldly forsook Vandeuvres altogether. Those ancient families were all done for; they always came to grief in a ridiculous manner.

"Oh, no!" said Nana; "it is not ridiculous to set oneself afire like that in a stable. I think he ended grandly. Oh! you know, I'm not defending his affair with Mérachal. Now, that was ridiculous. When I think that Blanche had the idiocy to pretend that I was the cause of it all! I said to her, 'Did I tell him to steal?' I suppose one may ask a man for money without driving him to commit a crime. If he had said to me, 'I've nothing more,' I should have rejoined, 'Very well, we'd better part.' And that would have been the end of it."

"No doubt," observed the aunt gravely. "When men become obstinate, it is so much the worse for them!"

"But as for the closing scene—oh! it was indeed grand!" resumed Nana. "It seems that it was terrible; the thought of it makes my flesh creep. He got everybody out of the way, and shut himself inside, with some petroleum. And it blazed away—ah! it must have been a sight! Just fancy, a big place like that nearly all of wood, and full of hay and straw! The flames, they say, rose nearly as high as steeples. The best part was the horses, who didn't want to be roasted. They were heard kicking and flinging themselves against the doors, and uttering cries like human beings. Some of the people there nearly died from fright."

Labordette gave a low whistle of incredulity. He did not believe in Vandeuvres's death. One person swore that he had seen him get out through a window. He had set fire to his stable in a fit of madness, only as soon as it began to get warm, it probably brought him to his senses again. A man who behaved so stupidly with women, so empty-headed, was not capable of dying in such a grand style.

Nana's illusions were dispelled as she listened to him; and she merely made this remark,

"Oh! the wretch! it was such a grand ending!"

CHAPTER XII

It was nearly one o'clock in the morning, and Nana and the count, in the big bed hung with Venetian lace, were not yet asleep. He had returned that evening, after sulking for three days. The room, which was only feebly lighted by a lamp, was wrapped in silence, and felt warm and moist with an odor of love; whilst the white lacquer furniture, inlaid with silver, was only vaguely visible. A drawn curtain half hid the bed in a flood of shadow. There was a sigh, and then the sound of a kiss broke the silence; and Nana, gliding from under the clothes, remained seated for an instance on the edge of the bed, with her legs bare. The count, his head fallen back on the pillow, continued in the shadow.

"Darling, do you believe in God?" she asked, after a moment of reflection, with a grave look on her face, and filled with a religious terror on leaving her lover's arms.

Ever since the morning she had complained of an uneasiness, and all her stupid ideas, as she called them, ideas of death and hell, had been secretly tormenting her. On some nights, childish frights and the most horrible fancies seized upon her, with her eyes open. She resumed,

"Do you think I shall go to heaven?"

And she shivered, whilst the count, surprised at these singular questions at such a time, felt all his religious remorse awakened within him. But, with her night-dress slipped from her shoulders, her hair hanging loose about her, she fell upon his chest, sobbing and clinging to him.

"I'm afraid to die—I'm afraid to die."

He had all the difficulty in the world to get free from her. He himself was afraid of succumbing to the attack of madness from which that woman, pressed to his body in the contagious fear of the invisible, was suffering; and he reasoned with her. She was in very good health, all she had to do was to conduct herself well, to merit pardon hereafter. But she shook her head. No doubt she never did harm to anyone; she even always wore a medal of the Virgin, which she showed him hanging to a red ribbon between her breasts; only it was settled beforehand, all women, who, without being married, had anything to do with men, went to hell. Fragments of her catechism were returning to her. Ah! if one only knew for certain; but there, one knew nothing, no one ever returned with news, and, really, it would be stupid to put oneself out if the priests were only talking nonsense. Yet she devoutly kissed her medal, which was all warm from its contact with her body, as a conjuration against death, the thought of which filled her with an icy terror.

Muffat had to go with her into the dressing-room; she trembled at being alone for a minute, even with the door open. When he had got into bed again, she wandered about the room looking into all the corners, and starting at the least sound. As she came to a mirror, she stopped before it as in the old days, lost in the contemplation of her nudity. But the sight only increased her fear. She ended by leisurely feeling the bones of her face with both her hands.

"How ugly one looks when one's dead!" said she slowly.

And she drew in her cheeks, opened wide her eyes, and dropped her jaw to see how she would look. Then, with her features thus distorted, she turned to the count and said,

"Just look, my head will be so small,"

Then he grew angry. "You are mad; come to bed."

He could picture her in a grave, with the emaciation of a century; and, joining his hands, he muttered a prayer. For some time past religion had regained possession of him, his attacks of faith, every day, had the violence of apoplectic fits, and left him without the least strength. His fingers snapped, and he continually repeated these words: "My God—my God—my God." It was the cry of his impotence, the cry of his sin, against which he was powerless to resist, in spite of the certainty of his damnation. When Nana returned to the bed she found him lying under the clothes with a haggard look on his face, his nails digging into his chest, and his eyes gazing upwards as though seeking for heaven. And she burst out crying again; they embraced each other, their teeth chattering without their knowing it, both being oppressed by the same absurd nightmare. They had once before passed a similar night, only this time they were utterly idiotic, as Nana herself declared when she had got over her fright. A suspicion caused her to skilfully question the count; perhaps Rose Mignon had sent the famous letter. But it wasn't that, it was merely his nerves, nothing more, for he was still without proofs of his cuckoldom.

Two days later, after a fresh disappearance, Muffat called one morning, a time at which he had never come before. He was livid, his eyes were red with weeping, and his whole frame was still shaking from a great internal struggle. But Zoé herself, utterly scared, did not notice his agitation. She ran to meet him, and cried,

"Oh, sir! be quick! Madame very nearly died last night."

And, as he asked for particulars, she added, "Oh! something incredible, sir! A miscarriage!"

Nana was three months *enceinte*. For a long time she had thought she was merely unwell; Dr. Boutarel himself had doubts. Then, when he was able to say for certain, she was so vexed that she did everything she could to hide her condition. It seemed to her a most ridiculous mishap, something which lowered her in her own estimation, and about which everyone would have chaffed her. What a wretched joke! she had no luck, really! It was just her misfortune to be caught when she thought she was quite safe. And she experienced a constant surprise, as though disturbed in her sex. What! one got children even when one did not want them, and had another object in view? Nature exasperated her—that grave maternity which rose in the midst of her pleasures, that new life quickening when she was sowing so many deaths around her. Ought not one to be able to dispose of oneself as one liked without all that fuss? Now, who did the brat spring from? She could not for the soul of her tell. No one had asked for it, it was in everybody's way, and it would not meet with much happiness in life, that was quite certain!

Zoé gave the story of the catastrophe.

"Madame was seized with colics towards four o'clock. When I went into the dressing-room, not having seen her for some time, I found her lying on the ground in a swoon. Yes, sir, on

the ground, in a pool of blood, as though she had been murdered. Then, you know, I understood what had happened. I
was furious: madame ought to have told me of her mishap. M.
George happened to be here. He helped me to raise her, but
when I told him she had had a miscarriage, he became unwell
also. Really! I've been in an awful stew ever since yesterday!"

And indeed the house seemed topsy-turvy. All the servants
were continually running about the rooms and up and down
stairs. George had passed the night on a chair in the drawing-
room. It was he who had told the news to madame's friends
who had called in the evening at the time when madame usually received. He was very pale, and he related the story full of
astonishment and emotion. Steiner, La Faloise, Philippe, and
several others had called. At his first words they uttered exclamations. It could not be! it must be a joke! Then they became
very serious. They glanced at the bed-room door, looking very
much put out, shaking their heads, no longer thinking it a
funny matter. Up to midnight a dozen gentlemen had conversed in undertones in front of the fire-place, all of them
friends, and each one wondering if he were the father. They
seemed to be apologising to one another, with the confused
looks of awkward people. Then they assumed their airs again.
It was nothing to do with them; it was her fault entirely. She
was a scorcher, that Nana! One would never have expected
such a joke from her! And they went off one by one, on tiptoe,
the same as in the chamber of death, where one must never
laugh.

"But you had better go up all the same, sir," said Zoé to Muffat. "Madame is much better; she will see you. We are expecting the doctor, who promised to call again this morning."

The maid had persuaded George to go home to obtain
some sleep. Upstairs in the drawing-room there was only Satin,
reclining on a sofa, smoking a cigarette, and gazing at the ceiling. Since the accident, in the midst of the distraction of the
household, she had displayed a cold rage, shrugging her
shoulders, and saying most ferocious things. So as Zoé passed
before her, telling Muffat that her mistress's sufferings had
been very great;

"It serves her right; it will be a lesson for her!" she sharply exclaimed.

They turned around in surprise. Satin had not moved. Her eyes were still fixed on the ceiling; her cigarette was held nervously between her lips.

"Well, you haven't much feeling, you haven't!" said Zoé.

But Satin, sitting up on the couch, looked furiously at the count, and flung her former words in his face:

"It serves her right; it will be a lesson for her!"

And she laid herself down again, slowly puffing the smoke from her mouth, as though uninterested and determined not to mix herself up in anything. No, it was too absurd!

Zoé ushered the count into the bed-room. A smell of ether hung about in the midst of a lukewarm silence, which the rare vehicles of the Avenue de Villiers scarcely broke with a dull rumbling sound. Nana, looking very white on the pillow, was not asleep; her eyes were wide open and thoughtful. She smiled, without moving, on catching sight of the count.

"Ah, ducky!" murmured she slowly. "I thought I should never see you again."

Then when he bent forward to kiss her on her hair, she was moved, and spoke to him of the child, in good faith, as though he had been the father.

"I did not dare to tell you. I felt so happy! Oh! I had all sorts of dreams—I wanted it to be worthy of you. And now, it's all over. Well, perhaps it's best so. I don't want to saddle you with any encumbrance."

He, surprised at that paternity, stammered out a few sentences. He had taken a chair and seated himself beside the bed, one arm lying on the clothes. Then the young woman noticed his agitated countenance, his bloodshot eyes, the feverish trembling of his lips.

"What's the matter with you?" asked she. "Are you ill also?"

"No," he answered painfully.

She gave him a penetrating look. Then with a sign she sent off Zoé, who was arranging the bottles of medicine as an excuse for remaining in the room. And when they were alone, she drew him towards her, saying,

"What's the matter, darling? Your eyes are full of tears, I can see them. Come, speak; you have called to tell me something."

"No, no! I swear to you," he stammered.

But, choking with suffering, affected all the more by that sick-room in which he so unexpectedly found himself, he burst into sobs; he buried his face in the sheets, to stifle the explosion of his anguish. Nana understood. Rose had no doubt ended by sending the letter. She let him cry a while; the convulsions that had seized him were so violent, that they shook her in the bed. At length, with an accent of maternal compassion, she asked,

"You have some worry at home?"

He nodded his head. She paused again, then added very low, "So you know all?"

He nodded his head a second time. And silence again reigned, an oppressive silence, in that room of pain. It was the night before, on returning from a party at the Empress's, that he had received the letter written by Sabine to her lover. After a frightful night, passed in dreaming of vengeance, he had gone out early in the morning, to withstand a temptation to kill his wife. Outside in the open air, struck by the mildness of the beautiful June morning, he had been unable to collect his scattered ideas, and had come to Nana's as he always came when in trouble. There only he would abandon himself to his misery, with the cowardly joy of being consoled.

"Come, be calm," resumed the young woman affectionately. "I have known it for a long while; but I would never have opened your eyes. You recollect last year you had suspicions. Then, thanks to my prudence, things got all right again. In short, you had no proofs. Well! to-day, if you have any, it's certainly hard, as I can understand. Yet you must be reasonable. One's not dishonoured because of that."

He no longer wept. Shame had possession of him, though he had for a long time past talked with her about the most intimate details of his married life. She had to encourage him. Come, she was a woman, she could hear everything. But he muttered in a hollow voice,

"You're ill; I mustn't tire you! It was stupid of me to come. I am going."

"But no," said she, quickly. "Stay, I may be able to give you some good advice. Only, don't make me talk too much; the doctor has forbidden me to do so."

He had left his seat, and was walking about the room. Then she questioned him.

"What will you do now?"

"I will thrash the man, of course!"

She pouted disapprovingly. "That's not a very smart thing to do. And your wife?"

"I shall sue for a separation. I have a proof."

"My dear fellow, that's not smart at all; it's even absurd. You know I'll never let you do anything of the kind."

And, sedately, in her feeble voice, she pointed out to him the useless scandal of a duel and a lawsuit. For a week he would be the chief topic in all the papers. He would be playing with his entire existence, his peace of mind, his high position at court, the honour of his name; and why? to be laughed at.

"What does it matter?" cried he. "I shall be avenged!"

"Ducky," said she, "when a man doesn't avenge himself at once in such matters, he doesn't avenge himself at all."

The words he was about to utter died away on his lips. He was certainly no coward, but he felt that she was right. An uneasiness increased within him—something like a feeling of impoverishment and shamefulness had unmanned him, in the outburst of his wrath. Besides, she hit him another blow, with a frankness that decided on telling all.

"And would you like to know what it is that bothers you, darling? It is that you yourself deceive your wife. Eh! you don't stop out all night to say your prayers. Your wife must know the true reason. Then with what can you reproach her? She will say that you gave her the example, and that will shut you up. There, darling! that's why you're here stamping about instead of being there murdering them both."

Muffat had fallen into a chair, overwhelmed by that brutality of language. She remained silent awhile, regaining breath; then she faltered, in a very low voice,

"Oh! I'm sore all over. Help me to raise myself a little. I keep slipping down, my head is too low."

When he had assisted her, she sighed and felt better, and she returned to the grand sight of a trial for judicial separation. Could he not conceive the countess's counsel amusing all Paris in talking of Nana? Everything would be related—her fiasco at the Variety Theatre, her mansion, her life. Ah, no! she did not care for such an advertisement. Some dirty women might have urged him to be so foolish, so as to gain notoriety at his expense; but she desired his happiness before everything. She had drawn him towards her. She held him now, with his head on the pillow beside her own, and her arm round his neck, and she whispered gently,

"Listen, ducky; you must make it up with your wife."

He was indignant. Never! His heart was breaking; the shame was too great. She, however, tenderly insisted.

"You must make it up with your wife. Come, you don't want to hear everyone say that I estranged you from your family? It would give me too bad a reputation. What would everyone think of me? Only swear that you'll always love me; for, now that you're going to be another's—"

Her sobs were choking her. He interrupted her with kisses, saying,

"You are mad—it is impossible!"

"Yes, yes," resumed she; "you must do it. It's only right; and, after all, she's your wife. It's not as though you were unfaithful to me with the first woman you came across."

And she continued thus, giving him the best advice. She even talked of God. He seemed to be listening to M. Venot, when the old man used to sermonize him, to save him from sin. She, however, did not talk of breaking off. She preached complaisancy—the sharing of him by his wife and his mistress, a quiet life, without any bother for any one, something like a happy dozing through the inevitable nastinesses of life. It would change nothing in their existence. He would still be her best-loved ducky, only he would not come quite so frequently, and would devote to the countess the days he did not spend with her. Her strength was failing her; she concluded in a whisper,

"That way, I shall know that I have performed a good action. You will love me all the more."

Then there was silence. She closed her eyes, looking paler still on the pillow. He had listened to her, under the pretext of not wishing to tire her. At the end of a few minutes, she reopened her eyes, and murmured,

"And money, too? Where will you get money if you quarrel? Labordette came yesterday about the bill. I'm in want of everything; I've not a thing left to put on."

Then, closing her eyes again, she appeared as though dead. A shade of intense anguish overspread Muffat's face. In the blow that had come upon him, he had forgotten, ever since the night before, the monetary difficulties from which he no longer knew how to extricate himself. In spite of the most distinct promises, his note for a hundred thousand francs, already renewed once, had been put into circulation; and Labordette, affecting to be greatly vexed, made out it was all Francis's fault, and said that he would never again compromise himself in an affair with an uneducated man. It would have to be paid, the count would never let his note be protested. Then, besides Nana's innumerable claims, there was a most wasteful expenditure going on in his own home. On their return from Les Fondettes, the countess had suddenly developed a taste for luxury, an appetite for worldly enjoyments, which were rapidly devouring their fortune. People were beginning to talk of her ruinous caprices, a complete change of her household, five hundred thousand francs frittered away in transforming the old house in the Rue Miromesnil, and extravagant costumes, and large sums of money that had disappeared, melted, or been given away perhaps, without her troubling herself to render the least account. Twice Muffat had ventured to make some observations, being desirous of knowing; but she had looked at him so peculiarly, smiling the while, that he did not dare to ask any questions for fear of receiving too plain an answer. If he accepted Daguenet as a son-in-law from Nana, it was especially with the idea of being able to reduce Estelle's dowry to two hundred thousand francs, and of making arrangements respecting the balance with the young man, who would be only too delighted at such an unexpectedly good marriage.

However, during the last week, in view of the necessity of immediately finding the hundred thousand francs for the bill, Muffat had only been able to think of one expedient, from which he recoiled. It was to sell a magnificent estate called Les Bordes, estimated at half-a-million, and which the countess had recently inherited from an uncle. Only, he needed her assent, and she also, by her marriage contract, could not dispose of it without his. The night before he had made up his mind to ask his wife for her consent. But now his plans were all upset, he could never accept such a compromise knowing what he did. This thought made the blow he had received all the harder. He understood what it was that Nana wished; for, in the increasing constraint that prompted him to confide in her regarding everything, he had complained about the difficulty he was in, he had told her how anxious he was to get the countess's consent.

However, Nana did not appear to insist. She did not re-open her eyes. Seeing her so pale, he was frightened, and induced her to take a little ether. Then she sighed, and questioned him, but without naming Daguenet.

"When is the marriage coming off?"

"The contract is to be signed on Tuesday, in five days from now," he replied.

Then, with her eyes still closed, as though she was speaking in the night of her thoughts, she added, "Well, ducky, think what you had better do. For myself, I want everyone to be pleased."

He pacified her by taking her hand. Yes, he would think about it, the main thing was for her to rest. And his indignation left him; that sick-room, so warm and so still, smelling strongly of ether, had ended by lulling him in a blessed peacefulness. All his manliness, aroused by the injury, had disappeared on his contact with the warmth of that bed, beside that suffering woman, whom he nursed, under the excitement of his fever, and with the recollection of their voluptuous pleasures. He leant over her, he held her in his embrace; though her face did not move, on her lips hovered the keen smile of victory. At that moment Dr. Boutarel entered the room.

"Well! and how is this dear child?" said he familiarly to Muffat, whom he treated as the husband. "The deuce! she has been talking!"

The doctor was a handsome man, still young, and had a superb connection in the world of gallantry. Very gay, always laughing like a comrade with the ladies, but never departing from his professional position, he charged monstrous fees, which invariably had to be paid with great punctuality. He would trouble himself to call for the least thing. Nana often sent for him two or three times a week, always trembling at the thought of death, and anxiously telling him of every little ache and pain, which he cured whilst amusing her with gossip and funny stories. All the women adored him. But this time the complaint was serious.

Muffat withdrew, deeply affected. He had no other feeling but that of compassion, at seeing his poor Nana so weak. As he was leaving the room, she beckoned him back, and offered her forehead to be kissed; then, in a low voice, with a playfully menacing air, she whispered:

"You know what I told you you might do. Make it up with your wife, or I shall be angry!"

Countess Sabine had wished her daughter's marriage contract to be signed on a Tuesday, to inaugurate the restoration of her town-house, the paintings of which were scarcely dry, by a grand party. Five hundred invitations had been sent out, a few in all the different sets. On the morning itself, the upholsterers were still putting up some of the hangings; and, at the time of lighting the chandeliers, towards nine o'clock, the architect, accompanied by the countess who was enraptured, was giving his final instructions.

It was one of those charming spring parties. The warm June evening had enabled the two doors of the drawing-room to be thrown wide open, and the ball to be carried even on the gravel paths of the garden. When the first guests arrived they were fairly dazzled, as the count and countess greeted them at the door. It was difficult to recall the room of bygone days in which lingered the icy recollection of old Countess Muffat— that antique apartment, full of devout severity, with its solid mahogany furniture in the style of the Empire, its yellow velvet hangings, its greenish ceiling saturated with dampness. Now, in the entrance vestibule, mosaics set off with gold shone beneath the tall candelabra; whilst the marble staircase unrolled its finely-chiselled balustrade. Then the drawing-room was resplendent with Genoa velvet hangings, and a ceiling embellished with a vast painting by Boucher,* which the architect had purchased for one hundred thousand francs at the sale of the château of Dampierre. The crystal chandeliers and candelabra illuminated a profusion of mirrors and costly furniture. One could have said that Sabine's easy-chair—that solitary seat covered with crimson silk, and the softness of which used to seem so much out of place—had extended and multiplied until it filled the entire house with a voluptous indolence, a keen enjoyment, which burned with all the intensity of latent fires.

The dancing had commenced. The orchestra, placed in the garden in front of one of the open windows, was playing a waltz, the sprightly rhythm of which arrived softened and subdued from the open air. And the garden spread itself out in a transparent shadow, lighted up by Venetian lanterns, with a purple tent for refreshments erected at the edge of the lawn. This waltz—the saucy waltz of the "Blonde Venus," which resembled the laugh raised by some over-free piece of buffoonery—penetrated the old house with a sonorous swell, warming the walls with its tremor. It seemed like some breath of the flesh coming from the street, sweeping before it the whole of a defunct age in the haughty abode, carrying away the past of the Muffats, centuries of honour and of faith slumbering beneath the ceilings.

Close to the fire-place, however, the old friends of the

---

*François Boucher (1703–1770), French painter of pastoral and mythological scenes.

count's mother had taken refuge in their accustomed seats, feeling dazed and out of their element. They formed a little group in the midst of the gradually increasing crowd. Madame du Joncquoy, no longer recognising the place, had at first gone into the dining-room. Madame Chantereau looked with amazement at the garden, which seemed to her immense. Soon all sorts of bitter reflections were whispered in this corner.

"I say," murmured Madame Chantereau; "supposing the old countess were only to return. Just fancy her look on beholding all these people, and all this gold, and this hubbub. It is scandalous!"

"Sabine is mad," replied Madame du Joncquoy. "Did you notice her at the door? Look, you can see her from here. She has all her diamonds on."

They stood up for a moment to look at the count and countess in the distance. Sabine, in a white costume trimmed with some magnificent English lace, was triumphant with beauty—young, lively, and with a touch of intoxication in her continual smile. Muffat, beside her, looking aged and rather pale, smiled also in his calm, dignified manner.

"And to think that he was the master," resumed Madame Chantereau, "that not the smallest seat would have been admitted here without his permission! Ah, well! she has changed all that, he obeys her now. Do you recollect the time when she would not alter a thing in the drawing-room? The whole house is altered now."

But they ceased talking as Madame de Chezelles entered, followed by a troop of young men, all of them enraptured, and giving vent to their admiration in faint exclamations.

"Oh, delicious! exquisite! so full of taste!"

And she called back to them, "It's just as I said! There's nothing like these old buildings when one knows how to arrange them. They look so grand! Is it not quite worthy of Louis XIV.'s time. Now, at least, she can receive."

The two old ladies had sat down again, and lowering their voices, they talked of the marriage, which surprised many people. Estelle had just passed, in a pink silk dress, still flat and thin, with her expressionless virgin face. She had accepted Daguenet quietly; she showed neither joy nor sadness, but remained as cold and pale as on those winter nights when she used to put the logs of wood on the fire. All this entertainment given for her, these illuminations, these flowers, this music, left her cold.

"An adventurer!" Madame du Joncquoy was saying. "I have never seen him."

"Take care, here he comes," murmured Madame Chantereau.

Daguenet, who had caught sight of Madame Hugon with her sons, had hastened to offer her his arm, and he laughed; he showed her an amount of affectionate attention, as though she had had something to do with his stroke of fortune.

"Thank you," said she, seating herself by the fire-place. "This is my old corner."

"Do you know him?" asked Madame du Joncquoy, when Daguenet had gone off.

"Certainly, he is a charming young man. George likes him immensely. Oh! he comes of a most honourable family."

And the good lady defended him against a covert hostility which she felt existed. His father, who was greatly esteemed by Louis-Philippe, had occupied a prefect's post until his death. The young man had perhaps been rather dissipated. It was said that he was ruined. At any rate, one of his uncles, a rich landed proprietor, was going to bequeath his fortune to him. But the other ladies shook their heads, whilst Madame Hugon, feeling rather embarrassed, kept laying great stress on the honourable position of the family. She felt very tired and complained of her legs. For a month past she had been stopping at her house in the Rue Richelieu, for a host of business matters, so she said. A shade of sadness veiled her maternal smile.

"All the same," concluded Madame Chantereau, "Estelle might have made a far better match."

There was a flourish of music. It was the commencement of a quadrille. The crowd moved to the sides of the room to leave an open space. Light dresses passed, mixed with the dark dress suits; whilst the blaze of light shone on the sea of heads, illuminating the sparkling jewels, the waving white plumes, and

the bloom of lilac and roses. It was already very warm. A penetrating perfume rose from the light tulles, the satins, and the
silks, among which the bare shoulders paled, beneath the
lively notes of the orchestra. Through the open doors one
could see rows of women seated in the adjacent rooms, with a
discreet brightness in their smile, a sparkle in their eyes, a pout
on their lips, gently fanning themselves. And guests still continued to arrive. A footman announced their names, whilst
amidst the various groups gentlemen slowly tried to find places
for the ladies on their arms, standing on tiptoe in search of a
vacant chair. But the house was filling, the skirts were packing
closer together with a slight noise. There were places where a
mass of lace, bows, and flounces barred the way, the wearers
politely resigned, retaining all their grace, accustomed as they
were to such brilliant crushes. However, out in the garden, in
the roseate light of the Venetian lanterns, couples were wandering about, having escaped from the stifling atmosphere of
the great drawing-room. The shadows of dresses passed over
the lawn, as though keeping time to the music of the quadrille,
which sounded softer in the distance behind the trees.

Steiner, who was there, had just come across Foucarmont
and La Faloise partaking of champagne in the refreshment
tent.

"It's awfully swell," La Faloise was saying, while examining
the purple tent, and the gilded lances which supported it.
"One could almost think oneself at the gingerbread fair. Yes,
that's it! the gingerbread fair!"

He now affected to continually poke fun at everything, pos-
ing as a young man who was sick of the world, and who could
find nothing worthy of being looked at in a serious light.

"Wouldn't poor Vandeuvres be surprised if he returned
here?" murmured Foucarmont. "Don't you recollect when he
used to be bored to death over there, opposite the fire-place?
By Jove! no one laughed then."

"Vandeuvres! don't mention him, he's extinguished!" resumed La Faloise, disdainfully. "He was greatly mistaken if he
thought he was going to astonish us with his roasting! Not a
soul talks of it now. He's out of it, done for, scratched. Van-

deuvres! talk of another!" Then, as Steiner shook hands with them, he continued, "You know Nana's just arrived. Oh! such an entry, my boy! something prodigious! First of all, she embraced the countess; then, when the children drew near, she blessed them, saying to Daguenet, 'Listen, Paul; if you deceive her you'll have me after you.' What! didn't you see it? Oh! she was grand! such a success!"

The other two listened to him with their mouths open. At length they burst out laughing. He, delighted, thought himself very wonderful.

"Eh! you believed it all? Well, why not? It's Nana who arranged the marriage. Besides, she's one of the family."

The two Hugons passed just then, and Philippe made him desist. Then, as men, they talked of the marriage. George became very incensed with La Faloise, who related the story of it. Nana had indeed saddled Muffat with one of her former lovers for a son-in-law, only it was untrue that she had had Daguenet to see her the night before. Foucarmont incredulously shrugged his shoulders. Did any one ever know whom Nana had to see her of a night? But George angrily replied with a "Sir, I know!" which made them all laugh. Anyhow, as Steiner said, it was a very peculiar state of affairs.

Little by little the refreshment tent was becoming crowded. They moved away from the bar, without separating. La Faloise stared impudently at the women, as though he thought himself at Mabille. At the end of a path they were greatly surprised on beholding M. Venot engaged in a long conversation with Daguenet; and some very poor jokes amused them immensely. He was confessing him; he was giving him some advice for the first night. Then they went and stood in front of one of the open doors of the drawing-room, where some couples dancing a polka were steering their way amidst the men who remained standing. The candles were guttering from the breeze coming from outside. When a couple passed, keeping time to the music, it refreshed the heated atmosphere like a gentle puff of wind.

"By Jove! they can't be very cold in there!" murmured La Faloise.

Their eyes blinked on coming from out of the mysterious shadows of the garden; and they drew each other's attention to the Marquis de Chouard, who, standing all alone, and stretched to the full height of his tall figure, overlooked the bare shoulders around him. His pale face appeared very severe, and bore an expression of haughty dignity beneath his crown of scanty white locks. Scandalized by Count Muffat's conduct, he had publicly broken off all connection with him, and affected not to visit at the house. If he had consented to appear on this occasion, it was on account of the earnest entreaties of his grand-daughter, whose marriage, however, he disapproved of in indignant language against the disorganisation of the upper classes by the shameful compromises of modern debauchery.

"Ah! the end is at hand," Madame du Joncquoy, beside the fire-place, was whispering to Madame Chantereau. "That hussy has so bewitched the unhappy fellow. We who used to know him so staunch a believer—so noble!"

"It appears that he's ruining himself," continued Madame Chantereau. "My husband has had a note of his. He lives now altogether in that mansion of the Avenue de Villiers. All Paris is talking about him. Really! I cannot excuse Sabine either, though we must admit that he gives her a great many causes for complaint; and, well! if she also throws the money out of the window—"

"She does not only throw money," interrupted the other. "Well, as they are both at work, they will reach the end all the sooner. A regular drowning in the mire, my dear."

But a gentle voice interrupted them. It was M. Venot. He had come and seated himself behind them, as though desirous of being out of the way; and leaning towards them, he murmured,

"Why despair? God manifests Himself when all seems lost."

He was peacefully assisting at the downfall of that house which once upon a time he had governed. Ever since his sojourn at Les Fondettes, he had quietly allowed the undermining to go on, fully aware of how powerless he was to cope with it. He had accepted everything—the count's mad infatuation for Nana, Fauchery's close attendance on the countess, even Daguenet's marriage with Estelle. What mattered those things? And he showed himself more supple, more mysterious, entertaining the idea of influencing the young couple the same as he had the now disunited one, knowing that great disorders lead to great devotions. Providence would have its hour.

"Our friend," continued he in a low voice, "is still animated with the best religious sentiments. He has given me the sweetest proofs."

"Well, then!" said Madame du Joncquoy; "he should first of all make it up with his wife."

"No doubt. Just now I happen to have the hope that their reconciliation will not be long in coming about."

Then the two old ladies questioned him; but he became very humble again. They must let Heaven accomplish it in its own way. His sole desire in bringing the count and countess closer together was to avoid a public scandal. Religion tolerated many failings when appearances were kept up.

"At any rate," resumed Madame du Joncquoy, "you ought to have prevented this marriage with this adventurer."

"You are mistaken; M. Daguenet is a very worthy young man. I am acquainted with his ideas. He wishes to cause his youthful errors to be forgotten. Estelle will bring him into the right path, you may be sure."

"Oh, Estelle!" disdainfully murmured Madame Chantereau. "I think the dear child is quite without any will whatever. She is altogether so insignificant!"

This expression of opinion caused M. Venot to smile. However, he did not explain himself respecting the young bride. Closing his eyes, as though to withdraw from the conversation, he again hid himself in his corner behind the skirts. Madame Hugon, in the midst of her absent-minded weariness, had overheard a few words. She joined in, and as she addressed herself to the Marquis de Chouard, who had come to greet her, thus concluded with her tolerating air:

"You ladies are too severe. Existence is already so bad for everyone. Eh! my friend? we ought to forgive a great deal in others, when we wish to be ourselves worthy of pardon."

The marquis remained embarrassed for a few moments, fearing an allusion to himself. But the good lady had so sad a smile, that he soon regained his composure, and said,

"No, certain faults deserve no pardon. It is by such complaisances that society totters on its foundations."

The ball had become more animated than ever. Another quadrille gave a kind of gentle swing to the floor of the drawing-room, as though the old house had staggered beneath the commotion of the merry-making. Now and again, in the mixed paleness of the faces, there stood out a woman's countenance, carried away by the dance, with sparkling eyes and parted lips, and the full light of a chandelier shining on her white skin. Madame du Joncquoy declared that the count and countess must have been out of their senses. It was madness to squeeze five hundred people into a room that could scarcely hold two hundred. Why not have the contract signed on the Place du Carrousel at once? It was the result of new manners, Madame Chantereau said. In her younger days such solemnities took place in the bosom of one's family; now one must have a mob, the whole street being freely allowed to enter. Unless one had such a crush, the entertainment would be considered quiet and uneventful. One advertised one's luxury, one introduced into one's abode the very scum of Paris; and there was nothing more natural if such promiscuousness ended by corrupting the home. The two ladies complained that they did not know more than fifty of the persons present. How was it so? Young girls in low-neck dresses displayed their bare shoulders; a woman wore a golden dagger stuck in her chignon, whilst the body of her dress, embroidered with jet black beads, looked like a coat of mail; another was being smilingly followed about, her skirts so tight fitting that they gave her a most singular appearance. All the luxury of the close of the winter season was there, the world of pleasure with its tolerations, all that which the mistress of a house picks from her acquaintances of a day, a society where great names and great infamies elbowed each other in the same appetite for pleasure. The heat was increasing, the quadrille unrolled the cadenced symmetry of its figures amidst the overcrowded rooms.

"The countess is stunning!" resumed La Faloise at the garden door. "She looks ten years younger than her daughter. By the way, Foucarmont, you can give us some information. Vandeuvres used to bet that she had no thighs worth speaking of."

This affectation of cynicism bored the other gentlemen. Foucarmont contented himself with replying,

"Consult your cousin, my boy. He's just coming this way."

"Yes! that's an idea," cried La Faloise. "I'll bet ten louis that her thighs are good."

Fauchery was indeed just arriving. As an intimate friend of the house, he had passed through the dining-room so as to avoid the crush at the doors. Taken up again by Rose at the beginning of the winter, he now divided himself between the singer and the countess, feeling very wearied, not knowing how to break off with one of the two. Sabine flattered his vanity, but Rose amused him more. The latter, too, entertained a genuine affection for him, a tenderness of really conjugal fidelity, which grieved Mignon immensely.

"Listen, we want some information," said La Faloise, squeezing his cousin's arm. "You see that lady in white silk?"

Ever since his inheritance had given him an insolent assurance, he affected to poke fun at Fauchery, having an old spite to gratify, wishing to be revenged for the banterings of the time when he first arrived from the country.

"Yes, that lady who has a lot of lace about her."

The journalist stood on tiptoe, not yet understanding. "The countess?" he ended by saying.

"Just so, my boy. I've bet ten louis. Are her thighs good?"

And he burst out laughing, delighted at having succeeded in taking down a peg that fellow who had once amazed him so much when he asked him if the countess had a lover. But Fauchery, without showing the least surprise, looked him straight in the face.

"You idiot!" said he at last, shrugging his shoulders.

Then he shook hands with the other gentlemen, whilst La Faloise, quite put out of countenance, was no longer very sure of having said something funny. They stood conversing together. Ever since the races, the banker and Foucarmont had joined the set at the Avenue de Villiers. Nana was much better; the count called every evening to see how she was progressing. However, Fauchery, who merely listened, seemed preoccupied. That morning, during a quarrel, Rose had deliberately told him that she had sent the letter. Yes, he might go and call on his grand lady, he would be well received. After hesitating for a long time, he had courageously made up his mind to come. But La Faloise's stupid joke had upset him, in spite of his apparent serenity.

"What's the matter with you?" asked Philippe. "You don't seem well."

"I? oh! I'm all right. I've been working, that's why I'm so late." Then, coolly, with one of those unknown heroisms which unravel the common tragedies of life, he added, "With all that, I've not paid my respects to our hosts. One must be polite."

He even dared to joke, and turning to La Faloise, said, "Am I not right, idiot?"

And he made a passage for himself through the crowd. The footman was no longer bawling out the names. The count and countess, however, were still near the door, conversing with some ladies who had just entered. At length he reached the spot where they stood, whilst the gentlemen he had just left on the steps leading into the garden stood up on tiptoe to have a good view of the scene. Nana must have been gossiping.

"The count does not see him," murmured George. "Attention! he's turning round. There, now they're at it."

The orchestra was again playing the waltz of the "Blonde Venus." First of all, Fauchery bowed to the countess, who continued to smile, serenely delighted. Then he stood for a moment immovable, calmly waiting, behind the count's back. The count that night maintained his haughty gravity—the official bearing of a high dignitary. When at length he lowered his eyes towards the journalist, he exaggerated still more his majestic attitude. For some seconds the two men looked at each other; and it was Fauchery who first held out his hand. Muffat clasped it. Their hands were locked one in the other. Countess Sabine smiled in front of them, her eyes cast on the ground; whilst the waltz continued to unroll its saucy rhythm.

"But it's going splendidly!" said Steiner.

"Are their hands glued together?" asked Foucarmont, amazed at the length of time they remained clasped.

An invincible recollection brought a rosy blush to Fauchery's pale cheeks. He again beheld the property-room, with its greenish light and its odd assortment of things smothered with dust; and Muffat was there, holding the egg-cup, and taking advantage of his suspicions. Now, Muffat no longer had any doubts; it was a last shred of dignity collapsing. Fauchery, relieved of his fright, seeing the countess's evident gaiety, was seized with a desire to laugh. It seemed to him so comic.

"Ah! this time it is indeed she!" exclaimed La Faloise, who stuck to a joke when once he thought it a good one. "There's Nana over there. Look, she's entering the room!"

"Shut up, you idiot!" murmured Philippe.

"I tell you it is she! They're playing her waltz! She comes; and, besides, she's had a share in the reconciliation. Dash it all! What! you don't see her! She's pressing them all to her heart—my male cousin, my female cousin and her spouse—and calling them her little ducky darlings. They always upset me, these family scenes."

Estelle had drawn near. Fauchery complimented her, whilst she, looking very stiff in her pink dress, watched him with the surprised air of a silent child, glancing also at her father and mother. Daguenet, too, heartily shook hands with the journalist. They formed a smiling group; and M. Venot glided behind, looking tenderly on them, enveloping them all with his devout meekness, happy at beholding these last defections, which were preparing the ways of Providence.

But the waltz still continued its voluptuous whirl. It was an increase of the wave of pleasure, overtaking the old mansion like a rising tide. The orchestra swelled the trills of its little flutes, the rapturous sighs of its violins; beneath the Genoa velvet hangings, the gildings and the paintings, the chandeliers gave out a life-like warmth, a light as bright as sunshine; whilst the crowd of guests reflected in the mirrors, seemed to increase with the louder murmur of the voices. Around the drawing-room, the couples which passed with arms encircling waists, amidst the smiles of seated women, accentuated the shaking of the flooring. In the garden the ember-like glimmer of the Venetian lanterns lighted up the dark shadows of the promenaders seeking a breath of air along the walks, as though with the distant reflection of a fire. And this trembling of the walls, this ruddy cloud, was like the blazing of the end, in which the ancient family honour fell to pieces, burning at the four corners of the home. The timid gaieties, then scarcely beginning, which one April evening Fauchery had heard ring with a sound of breaking glass, had little by little become emboldened, maddened, to burst forth into the resplendency of that entertainment. Now, the crack increased; it attacked the house, and gave warning of its approaching destruction. Amongst the drunkards of the slums, it is by the blackest misery—the cupboard without bread, the craving for alcohol eating up the last sticks—that corrupted families reach their end. Here, over the downfall of these riches, heaped together and set fire to at one fell swoop, the waltz sounded the knell of an ancient race; whilst Nana, invisible, but hovering above the ball with her supple limbs, polluted all those people, penetrating them with the ferment of her odour floating in the warm air upon the wings of the saucy rhythm of the music.[4]

It was on the night of the wedding at the church that Count Muffat appeared in his wife's bed-room, which he had not entered for two years past. The countess, greatly surprised, drew back at first, but she preserved her smile—that smile of intoxication which now never left her. He, very much embarrassed, could only stutter a few words. Then she gave him a little lecture. But neither the one nor the other ventured on a complete explanation. It was religion that required this mutual forgiveness; and it was tacitly agreed between them that they should retain their liberty. Before going to bed, as the countess still seemed to hesitate, they discussed business matters. He, the first, talked of selling Les Bordes. She at once consented. They both had great want of money; they would share the proceeds. That completed the reconciliation. Muffat experienced a real relief in spite of his remorse.

That day, too, as Nana was dozing, towards two o'clock, Zoé

ventured to knock at the door of her bed-room. The curtains
were drawn, a warm breeze entered by one of the windows, in
the still freshness of the subdued light. The young woman got
up a little now, though still rather weak. She opened her eyes
and asked,

"Who is it?"

Zoé was about to reply, but Daguenet, forcing his way in, announced himself. On hearing him, she leant upon the pillow,
and, sending the maid away, said,

"What, it's you! on your wedding day! Whatever is the matter?"

He, not seeing clearly, remained standing in the middle of
the room. However, he soon got used to the obscurity, and advanced forward in his dress clothes, with a white tie and gloves;
and he kept saying,

"Well! yes, it's I. Don't you recollect?"

No, she remembered nothing. So he had to crudely refresh
her memory, in his jocular way.

"Why, your commission. I've brought you the handsel of my
innocence."

Then, as he was close to the bed, she seized hold of him with
her bare arms, shaking with laughter and, almost weeping, for
she thought it so nice of him.

"Ah! my Mimi, how funny he is! He has not forgotten it! and
I who no longer remembered! So you've given them the slip,
you've just come from the church? It's true—you've an odour
of incense about you. But kiss me—! oh! more than that, my
Mimi! It will perhaps be for the last time."

Their tender laugh expired in the darkened room, about
which there still hung a vague smell of ether. The close warmth
swelled the window curtains, children's voices sounded in the
Avenue. Then they made merry, though pressed for time.
Daguenet was to leave with his wife, directly after the wedding
breakfast.

CHAPTER XIII

Towards the end of September, Count Muffat, who was to dine at Nana's that evening, came at dusk to inform her of a sudden order he had received to be at the Tuileries. The house was not yet lighted up, the servants were laughing very loudly in the kitchen. He slowly ascended the staircase, the windows of which shone in the prevailing warm shadow. Upstairs, the parlour door made no noise as he opened it. A rosy daylight was fading from the ceiling of the room. The crimson hangings, the capacious sofas, the lacquer furniture, all that medley of embroidered stuffs, of bronzes and of china, was already disappearing beneath a slowly deepening veil of gloom, which penetrated the corners, hiding alike the brilliancy of the ivory and the glitter of the gold. And there, in this obscurity, by the aid alone of the light colour of her dress, he beheld Nana reclining in George's arms. All denial on their part was impossible. He uttered a suppressed cry, and stood as one lost.

Nana sprang to her feet and pushed him into the bedroom, to give the youngster time to get off.

"Come in here," she murmured, scarcely knowing what she said. "I will explain—"

She was exasperated at being caught like that. She had never before given way in such a manner at home, in that parlour with the doors unfastened. A number of things had tended to bring it about—a quarrel with George, who was madly jealous of Philippe. He sobbed so bitterly on her neck that she could not resist, scarcely knowing how to calm him, and pitying him in her heart. And, on the one occasion when she was so foolish as to forget herself thus—with a youngster who could not even bring her bunches of violets now, as his mother guarded him so strictly—the count must needs come and catch them. Really, she had no luck! That was all one got by being a good-natured girl!

However, the obscurity in the bed-room, where she had

pushed the count, was complete. Then, feeling her way, she went and rang furiously for a lamp. After all, it was that Julien's fault! If there had been a light in the parlour, nothing of all this would have happened. That stupid darkness which had come on had played the deuce with her heart.

"I beg of you, ducky, be reasonable," said she, when Zoé brought a light.

The count, sitting down, his hands on his knees, looked on the ground, overcome by what he had just seen. He could not utter a word of anger. He trembled, as though seized with a horror which froze him. This silent anguish deeply affected the young woman. She tried to console him.

"Well! yes, I was wrong. It was very naughty of me. You see, I am sorry for my fault. I am very grieved, as it annoys you so much. Come now; you, too, be nice, and forgive me."

She had sat down at his feet, and was seeking his glance with a look of submissive tenderness, to see if he was very angry with her. Then as, heaving a deep sigh, he recovered himself, she became more wheedling.

The count yielded to her entreaties. He merely insisted on George being sent away. But all illusion was gone; he could no longer believe in Nana's sworn fidelity. On the morrow Nana would deceive him again; and he remained in the torment of possessing her simply through cowardice—through his fright at the idea of living without her.

This was the epoch of her existence when Nana brightened Paris with an increase of splendour. She became more imposing still on the horizon of vice; she domineered over the city with the insolent display of her luxury, with her contempt for money, which caused her to publicly melt away fortunes. In her mansion there was like the glare of a furnace. Her continual desires fed it. The least breath from her lips would change the gold into fine ashes, which the wind swept away at every hour. Never before had such a mania for expense been seen. The house seemed built over an abyss, into which men with their wealth, their bodies, even their names, were precipitated, without leaving the trace of a little dust behind. This girl with the tastes of a parrot, nibbling radishes and burnt almonds, playing with her meat, had bills to the extent of five thousand francs a month for her table. In the servants' hall there was unbridled waste, a ferocious leakage, which emptied the casks of wine, and ran up bills increased by three or four hands through which they passed. Victorine and François reigned supreme in the kitchen, where they invited their friends, not to speak of a host of cousins whom they fed at their own homes with cold joints and meat soups. Julien exacted commissions from all the tradespeople. A glazier did not put in a thirty sou pane of glass but the butler had twenty added on for himself. Charles devoured the oats for the horses, ordering double the necessary supply, selling by a back door what came in by the front one; whilst in the midst of this universal pillage, of this sack of a town taken by assault, Zoé, by great art, succeeded in saving appearances, covering the thefts of all the others the better to hide and secure her own. But what was wasted was still worse—the food of the previous day thrown in the gutter, an incumbrance of victuals at which the servants turned up their noses, the glasses all sticky with sugar, gas-jets blazing away, turned on recklessly, sufficient to blow up the place; and negligences, and spitefulness, and accidents, all that can hasten ruin in an establishment devoured by so many mouths.

Then, upstairs in madame's rooms, the downfall was even greater still. Dresses costing ten thousand francs, worn only twice, and sold by Zoé; jewels which disappeared as though they had crumbled away at the bottoms of the drawers; idiotic purchases, novelties of the day, forgotten in a corner on the morrow, and swept into the street. She could never see anything costing a great deal without desiring it; she thus created around her a continual devastation of flowers and precious knick-knacks, being all the more delighted in proportion to the price paid for them. Nothing remained perfect in her hands; she broke everything, or it faded or became soiled between her little white fingers; a strewing of nameless remnants, of crumpled rags, of muddy tatters, followed in her wake. Then the heavy settlements burst out in the midst of this waste of pocket-money. Twenty thousand francs owing to the milliner, thirty thousand to the linendraper, twelve thousand to the bootmaker, her stable had swallowed fifty thousand, in six months her dressmaker's bill had run up to a hundred thousand francs. Without her having added to her household, which Labordette had estimated would cost on an average four hundred thousand francs yearly, she reached that year a million, amazed herself at the sum, and quite incapable of saying where all the money could possibly have gone to. Men piled up one upon the other, gold emptied out in barrowfuls, were unable to fill that chasm which was for ever opening deeper and deeper beneath the foundations of her house, in the disruption of her luxury.

Nana, however, still nursed a last caprice. Agitated once more with the idea of re-decorating her bed-room, she thought she had at last found something to suit her fancy—a room hung in tea-rose velvet, padded and reaching up to the ceiling, in the shape of a tent, ornamented with little silver buttons and with gold lace and cords. It seemed to her that this would look both rich and tender, a superb background to her fair skin. But the room, however, was merely to serve as a framework to the bed, a prodigy of dazzling brightness. Nana dreamed of a bed such as was never seen before—a throne, an altar, to which all Paris would come to adore her sovereign nudity. It was to be entirely of gold and silver, like an immense jewel, golden roses scattered over a silver network; at the head, a band of cupids amongst the flowers would be glancing down, with laughter on their faces, watching the voluptuous pleasures in the shadow of the curtains. She had consulted Labordette, who had brought two goldsmiths to see her. They were already preparing the drawings. The bed was to cost fifty thousand francs, and Muffat was to present her with it as a new year gift.

What surprised the young woman was that in this ever-flowing river of gold she was constantly without money. Some days she scarcely knew what to do for want of the most ridiculous sums, of a few louis. She had to borrow of Zoé, or else raise funds any way she could. But before resigning herself to extreme measures, she would sound her friends, getting out of the men whatever they had about them, even sous, in a jocular sort of way. For three months past she had especially been emptying Philippe's pockets in this manner. He now never called, whenever there was a crisis at hand, without leaving his purse behind him on leaving. Soon, becoming bolder, Nana had begun to ask him for loans—two hundred francs, three hundred francs, never more—for bills becoming due, or debts that could not remain longer unpaid; and Philippe, who, in July, had been made a captain, and pay-master of his regiment, would bring the money on the morrow, with the excuse that he was not rich, for good Madame Hugon now treated her sons with singular harshness. At the end of three months these little loans, often repeated, amounted to some ten thousand francs. The captain still laughed in his hearty, sonorous way, yet he was growing thin, appearing absent-minded at times, with a look of suffering on his face; but a glance from Nana transfigured him, in a sort of sensual ecstasy. She was very playful with him, intoxicating him with kisses behind doors, bewitching him with sudden abandonments of herself, which tied him to her petticoats the whole time he was off duty.

One night, Nana having mentioned that her name was also Thérèse, and that her saint's-day was on the 15th October, the gentlemen all sent her presents. Captain Philippe brought his—an old Saxon china comfit-box,* mounted with gold. He found her alone in her dressing-room, having just come out of her bath, clothed only in a loose scarlet and white flannel dressing-gown, and very busy examining the presents spread out on a table. She had already broken a scent bottle in rock crystal in trying to take the stopper out.

"Oh! you are too nice," said she. "Whatever is it? show me. What a child you are to spend your money in things like this!"

She scolded him, because he was not rich, although really very pleased to see him spend all he had on her, the only proof of love which ever touched her. However, she handled the comfit-box, wishing to see how it was made, opening and shutting it.

---

*Box for candy.

"Take care," he murmured; "it's not very strong."

But she shrugged her shoulders. Did he think she had the hands of a railway porter? And suddenly the hinge remained between her fingers, whilst the lid fell to the ground and broke. She stood lost in amazement, with her eyes fixed on the pieces.

"Oh! it's broken!" said she.

Then she began to laugh. The pieces on the floor looked funny to her. It was a nervous gaiety. She had the stupid and cruel laugh of a child who finds amusement in destruction. Philippe was seized for a moment with a feeling of indignation. The wretched woman did not know what agony that trifle had cost him. When she saw him looking so upset, she endeavoured to restrain herself.

"Anyhow, it wasn't my fault. It was cracked. Those old things never keep together. It was the lid! Did you see the stupid way in which it fell off?"

And she burst out laughing again. But as the young man's eyes filled with tears, in spite of his efforts to restrain them, she lovingly threw her arms round his neck.

"How silly you are! I love you all the same. If nothing was ever broken, the dealers would never sell anything. It's all made to be broken. Look at this fan! it isn't even stuck together!"

She seized hold of a fan and roughly pulled it open. The silk tore in two. That seemed to excite her. To show that she did not care anything for the other presents, as she had spoilt his, she regaled herself with a general massacre, knocking the different things about, proving, as she destroyed them all, there was not one of them that was solid. A glimmer lighted up her vacant eyes, a slight curl of her lips displayed her white teeth. Then when all the things were in pieces, she struck the table with her open hands, looking very red, and laughing louder than ever, and stammered forth in a childish voice,

"All gone! no more! no more!"

Then Philippe, yielding to the intoxication, cheered up, and pressing against her, kissed her on the neck and bosom. She abandoned herself to him, clinging to his shoulders, feeling so happy that she could not recollect having ever enjoyed herself so much before. And without leaving go of him, she caressingly said,

"I say, darling; you might manage to bring me ten louis tomorrow. It's an awful nuisance—a baker's bill which is worrying me."

He became very pale; then kissing her for a last time on the forehead, he merely said,

"I will do my best."

A pause ensued. She was dressing herself. He was pressing his face against the window pane. At the end of a minute he returned to where she stood, and said slowly,

"Nana, you ought to marry me."

The idea seemed so ludicrous to the young woman, that she could not finish fastening her petticoats.

"But, my poor fellow, you must be ill! Is it because I've asked you for ten louis that you offer me your hand? Never, I love you too much for that. What a stupid idea to get into your head!"

And, as Zoé entered the room to put madame's boots on, they dropped the subject. The maid had at once caught sight of the remnants of the presents scattered over the table. She asked if they were to be put anywhere; and madame having said that they could be thrown away, she gathered them up in her apron. Down in the kitchen, the servants quarrelled together as they shared madame's leavings.

That day George, in spite of having been forbidden by Nana to do so, had sneaked into the house. François had plainly enough seen him come in, but now the servants merely laughed among themselves over their mistress's embarrassments. He had crept into the parlour, when the sound of his brother's voice arrested his advance; and, with his ear at the key-hole, he had heard all that had taken place—the kisses, the offer of marriage. A feeling of horror froze him, he went off, idiotic and with a sensation of emptiness in his head. It was only when he reached the Rue Richelieu, in his room over his mother's, that his heart found relief in furious sobs. This time, doubt was impossible. An abominable vision kept appearing before his eyes—Nana in Philippe's arms; and it seemed to him an incest. When he thought himself calmed, memory returned, and in a fresh fit of jealous rage, he threw himself on his bed, biting the sheets and uttering horrible oaths, which increased his passion. The rest of the day passed thus. He complained of a headache, so as to be able to remain in his room. But the night was more terrible still: a murderous fever shook his frame in a continuous nightmare. If his brother had lived in the house, he would have gone and stabbed him with a knife. When day returned, he tried to reason with himself. It was he who ought to die, he would throw himself from the window as an omnibus passed. However, towards ten o'clock he went out; he wandered about Paris, rambled over the bridges, and then at last felt an invincible longing to see Nana. Perhaps with a word she would save him. And three o'clock was striking as he entered the house in the Avenue de Villiers.

Towards midday some shocking news had quite overwhelmed Madame Hugon. Philippe had been in prison since the previous evening, accused of having stolen twelve thousand francs from the regimental chest. For three months past he had been embezzling small sums, hoping to replace them, and hiding the deficit by means of false accounts; and this fraud had succeeded, thanks to the negligence of the managing council. The old lady, crushed by her child's crime, uttered at first a cry of rage against Nana. She knew of Philippe's intimacy with the young woman. Her sadness came from this misfortune, which was the cause of her remaining in Paris, through the fear of some catastrophe; but never had she dreaded such shame, and now she reproached herself for having refused him money, as though she had been an accomplice. Having sunk into an arm-chair, her legs, so to say, paralysed, she felt herself useless, incapable of doing anything, only fit to die; but the sudden thought of George consoled her. George was left her—he might do something, perhaps save them both. Then, without asking help from anyone, desirous of hiding all this amongst themselves, she dragged herself along and ascended the stairs, fortified by the thought that she still had one love remaining. But the room above was empty. The door-keeper told her that Monsieur George had gone out early. The signs of a second misfortune hovered about the room. The bed, with its torn and crumpled sheets, told an unmistakable tale of anguish; a chair knocked over on the ground amongst some clothes, seemed to forebode death. George was probably at that woman's, and Madame Hugon, with dry eyes and a firm step, descended the staircase. She wanted her sons, she was going to demand them.

Ever since the morning Nana had had nothing but worry. First of all there was that baker, who, as early as nine o'clock had called with his bill, a mere nothing—a hundred and thirty-three, francs' worth of bread, which she had been unable to settle for, in the midst of her regal style of living. He had called twenty times, exasperated at having lost the custom on the day he had declined to give further credit; and the servants espoused his cause. François said that madame would never pay him if he did not make a great fuss; Charles talked of going upstairs to get an old bill for straw settled; whilst Victorine advised them to wait till some gentleman called, and to get the money by going to the drawing-room when he was there. The servants' hall was deeply interested, all the tradespeople were kept informed of what was going on. There were gossipings of three and four hours' duration. Madame was disrobed, pulled to pieces, talked about, with the rancour of idle menials bursting with good living. Julien, the butler, alone pretended to take madame's part. She was, all the same, a fine woman; and when the others accused him of having enjoyed some of her favours, he laughed in a foppish sort of way, which put the cook beside herself, for she would have liked to have been a man to spit on such women, they disgusted her so much. François had maliciously left the baker waiting in the hall, without informing madame. As she came downstairs at lunchtime, she found herself face to face with him. She took his bill, and told him to call again about three o'clock. Then, muttering a number of filthy expressions, he went off, swearing to be punctual, and to pay himself some way or other.

Nana made a very poor lunch, being upset by this scene. This time she would have to satisfy the man. On ten different occasions at least, she had put the money for him on one side;

but somehow or other it had always dribbled away—one day
for flowers, or another day for a subscription for an old gen-
darme. She was, however, counting on Philippe, and was even
surprised that he had not already been with his two hundred
francs. It was awful ill-luck. Two days before she had again
rigged out Satin, a regular trousseau, spending nearly twelve
hundred francs in dresses and underclothing, and she had not
a louis left.

Towards two o'clock, as Nana was beginning to be anxious,
Labordette called. He brought the designs for the bedstead. It
was a diversion, and produced a fit of joy which caused the
young woman to forget everything else. She clapped her
hands, she danced; then, brimful of curiosity, leaning over a
table in the parlour, she examined the drawings, which Labordette explained to her.

"You see, this is the boat; in the centre a bunch of full-blown
roses, then a garland of flowers and buds; the leaves will be in
green gold and the roses in red gold. And this is the great design for the head—a troop of cupids dancing in a circle against
a silver trellis."

But Nana interrupted him, carried away by rapture.

"Oh! isn't he funny, the little one, the one in the corner,
turning a somersault? And look at his saucy laugh! They've all
got such wicked eyes! I say, my boy, I shall have to be careful of
what I do before them!"

She was in an extraordinary state of satisfied pride. The
goldsmiths had said that no queen ever slept on such a bedstead. Only there was a slight complication. Labordette
showed her two designs for the piece at the foot, the one which
reproduced the subject of the boat and cupids, the other
which was altogether a new design—a female figure representing Night enveloped in her veil, which a faun was drawing
aside, displaying her radiant nudity. He added that if she selected this second design, the goldsmiths intended to make
the figure representing Night like her. This idea, which was in
questionable taste, made her turn pale with pleasure. She saw
herself as a little silver statue, the symbol of the tepid, voluptuous pleasures of darkness,

"Of course, you will only sit for the head and shoulders," said Labordette.

"Why!" asked she, coolly looking him in the face. "As it is a question of a work of art, I sha'n't care a fig for the sculptor who copies me!"

So it was settled. She chose the second subject also; but he stopped her.

"Wait. It will cost six thousand francs more."

"Well! that's all the same to me!" cried she, bursting out laughing. "My little muff will pay!"

It was thus she called Count Muffat now amongst her intimate acquaintances; and the gentlemen never asked after him otherwise than as, "Did you see your little muff last night? Ah! I thought I should have found the little muff here!" A simple familiarity which, however, she did not as yet allow herself to make use of in his presence.

Labordette rolled up the drawings as he gave her some final information: the goldsmiths engaged to deliver the bedstead in two months' time, towards the 25th December; the very next week a sculptor would come to make the rough model for the figure of Night. As she walked with him to the stairs, Nana remembered the baker, and said suddenly,

"By the way, do you happen to have ten louis about you?"

One of Labordette's principles, and which he found invaluable, was never to lend money to women. He always gave the same answer,

"No, my girl; I'm quite stumped. But would you like me to call on your little muff?"

She refused; it was useless. Two days before she had got five thousand francs out of the count. Following Labordette, though it was scarcely half-past two when he called, the baker reappeared; and he roughly seated himself on a bench in the hall, swearing very loud. The young woman was listening to him up on the first floor. She turned pale; she suffered especially at hearing up there the secret joy of the servants. They were splitting their sides with laughing in the kitchen. The coachman looked on from the yard; François passed across the hall without any necessity, and then went and told the others

how things were progressing, after bestowing a chuckle of intelligence on the baker. They did not care a straw for madame;
the walls seemed bursting with the sounds of their mirth. She
felt herself all alone, despised by her servants, who spied on
her and bespattered her with their filthy jokes. Then as she
had had an idea of borrowing the hundred and thirty-three
francs from Zoé, she gave it up. She already owed her some
money; she was too proud to risk a refusal. So strong an emotion possessed her that she returned to her bed-room, saying
aloud,

"Never mind, my girl; only depend upon yourself. Your
body's your own, and it's best to make use of it rather than to
submit to an insult."

And without even ringing for Zoé, she hastily dressed herself to go to old Tricon's. It was her supreme resource in the
hours of great distress. Very much asked for, always required by
the old woman, she refused or accepted, according to her
wants; and the days, which were becoming more and more frequent, when she suffered from any embarrassment in her royal
career, she was always sure of finding twenty-five louis awaiting
her there. She would go to old Tricon's in the easy style gained
by habit, the same as poor people go to the pawn-shop.

But on leaving her bed-room, she ran up against George,
standing in the middle of the parlour. She did not notice his
wax-like paleness, the dull light in his wide open eyes. She uttered a sigh of relief.

"Ah! you've come from your brother?"

"No," said the youngster, turning paler still.

Then she made a gesture of despair. What did he want? Why
was he standing in front of her? Come, she was in a hurry; and
she passed him. Then retracing her steps, she asked,

"Have you any money with you?"

"No."

"It's true—how stupid of me! Never a thing, not even the six
sous for their omnibus. Mamma won't. What men!"

And she was hurrying off; but he stopped her. He wished to
speak to her. She, excited, kept saying that she had not time,
when with a word he made her leave off.

"Listen, I know you are going to marry my brother."

Well, that was comic. She dropped into a chair to laugh at her ease.

"Yes," continued the youngster; "and I will not have it. It is I whom you must marry. That is why I have come."

"Eh, what? you also?" she exclaimed. "Is it then a family complaint? But, never! What an idea! Did I ever ask you to do such a disgraceful thing? Neither the one nor the other— never!"

Then George's face brightened up. He might by chance have been mistaken. He resumed, "Then swear to me that you are not my brother's mistress."

"Ah! you're becoming a confounded nuisance!" said Nana, rising to her feet, impatient to be off. "It's funny for a minute, but I tell you I'm in a hurry! I'm your brother's mistress when I choose to be. Do you keep me—do you pay here, that you come and call me to account? Yes, I'm your brother's mistress."

He had seized her arm, and squeezed it almost enough to break it, as he stammered out, "Don't say that—don't say that—"

With a slap she freed herself.

"He's whipping me now! the young monkey! My little fellow, you must be off, and at once too. I've let you be here through kindness. It's just so, however wide you may open your eyes! You didn't expect, I suppose, to have me for your mamma until the day of my death. I've something better to do than to nurse brats."

He listened to her in an agony which stiffened his limbs and left him powerless. Each word stabbed him to the heart, with a blow so hard that he felt it was killing him. She, not even noticing his suffering, continued, happy at being able to vent herself on him for all her worries of the morning.

"It's just the same with your brother; he's a nice one, he is! He promised me two hundred francs. Ah, well! I may wait for ever for him. It's not that I care about his money! Not enough to pay for my pomades. But he's left me in a fix! Now would you like to know? Well, through your brother's fault, I'm going out to earn twenty-five louis from another man."

Then, in a state of bewilderment, he stood before the door; and he cried, and implored, clasping his hands together, and muttering, "Oh, no! oh, no!"

"Well, I'm willing," said she. "Have you the money?"

No, he had not got the money. He would have given his life to have had it. Never before had he felt so miserable, so useless, such a child. All his poor body, shaken with sobs, expressed a grief so great that she ended by seeing it and feeling for him. She pushed him gently on one side.

"Come, ducky, let me pass; you must. Be reasonable. You're a baby, and it was all very nice for a week; but to-day I must attend to my affairs. Think it over now. Your brother, too, is a man. I don't say with him—Ah! do me a kindness; don't mention to him anything of all this. He has no need to know where I'm going. I always say too much when I'm angry."

She laughed. Then, putting her arms round him and kissing him on the forehead, she added,

"Good-bye, baby; it's over, all over, you understand. Now, I'm off."

And she left him. He was standing in the centre of the parlour. The last words sounded like a knell in his ears, "It is over, all over"; and the ground seemed to open beneath his feet. In the vacuum of his brain, the man who was awaiting Nana had disappeared; Philippe alone remained, continually in the woman's bare arms. She did not deny it; she certainly loved him, as she wished to spare him the grief of knowing her to be unfaithful. It was over, all over. He drew a long breath, he gazed around the room, choked by a weight that was crushing him. Recollections returned to him one by one—the merry nights at La Mignotte, hours of love during which he thought himself her child, the voluptuous pleasures snatched in that very room. And never, never more! He was too little, he had not grown quick enough; Philippe had taken his place, because he had a beard. So, it was the end, he could no longer live. His vice had become full of an infinite tenderness, of a sensual adoration, in which his whole being was centred. Then, how could he forget, when his brother would remain there—his brother, who was of the same blood, another self whose pleasure drove him mad with jealousy? It was the end, he wished to die.

All the doors were left open as the servants noisily scuttled about, they having seen madame go out on foot. Downstairs, on the bench in the hall, the baker was laughing with Charles and François. As Zoé crossed the parlour at a run, she appeared surprised at seeing George, and asked him if he was waiting for madame. Yes, he was waiting for her, he had forgotten to tell her something. And, when he was again alone, he ferreted about. Finding nothing better, he took from the dressing-room a pair of sharply pointed scissors, which Nana was continually using, cutting her hangnails and little hairs with them.

Then, for an hour, he waited patiently, his hand in his pocket, his fingers nervously clutching the scissors.

"Here's madame," said Zoé, coming back; she had probably been watching for her out of the bed-room window.

More scuttling about was heard in the house, and sounds of laughter died away as doors were closed. George heard Nana pay the baker and utter a few brief words. Then she came up the stairs.

"What! you're still here!" said she, as she caught sight of him. "Ah! we shall have a row, my little man!"

He followed her whilst she moved towards the bed-room.

"Nana, will you marry me?"

But she shrugged her shoulders. It was too absurd, she did not answer. Her idea was to bang the door in his face.

"Nana, will you marry me?"

She slammed the door. With one hand he opened it, whilst he withdrew the other hand holding the scissors from his pocket. And, simply, with one violent blow, he thrust them into his chest.

Nana, however, had had a feeling that something terrible was going to happen. She turned round. When she saw him strike himself, she was seized with indignation.

"But he's cracked! he's cracked! And with my scissors too! Will you leave off, you wicked child! Ah! good heavens!—ah! good heavens!"

She was seized with fear. The youngster, fallen on his knees, had struck himself a second blow, which had laid him flat on the carpet. He blocked the threshold of the bed-room. Then she became quite bewildered; she shouted with all her might, not daring to step over that body, which shut her in and prevented her running for help.

"Zoé! Zoé! come quick. Make him leave off. It's absurd, a child like that! He's killing himself now! and in my house, too! Did anyone ever see such a thing?"

He frightened her. He was all white, and his eyes were closed. The wound scarcely bled at all, there was only a little blood which trickled from under the waistcoat. She had nerved herself to pass over the body, when an apparition caused her to draw back. Opposite to her, by the open door of the parlour, she beheld an old lady advancing, and she recognised Madame Hugon, terrified, unable to account for her presence. She continued to step back; she still wore her bonnet and gloves. Her terror became such that she attempted to defend herself in a hesitating voice.

"Madame, it was not I, I swear to you. He wanted to marry me, I said 'no,' and he's killed himself."

Madame Hugon slowly approached, dressed in black, with her pale face and white hair. In the carriage the thought of George had left her, and Philippe's sin had alone occupied her mind. Perhaps that woman could give some explanations to the judges which might cause them to be more lenient; and her intention was to implore her to bear witness in her son's favour. Downstairs the doors of the mansion were wide open. She hesitated at the staircase, with her poor legs, when, suddenly, shouts of fear had directed her steps. Then, upstairs, she beheld a man lying on the floor, his shirt stained with blood. It was George—it was her other child.

Nana kept repeating, in an idiotic way: "He wanted to marry me. I said 'no,' and he's killed himself."

Without a cry, Madame Hugon stooped down. Yes, it was the other one, it was George. The one dishonoured, the other dead. It did not surprise her, in the downfall of her whole existence. Kneeling on the carpet, ignoring the place where she was, noticing no one, she looked fixedly in George's face, she listened with a hand upon his heart. Suddenly she uttered a faint sigh. She had felt his heart beat. Then she raised her head, examined the room and the woman, and seemed to recollect. A fire lighted up her vacant eyes. She was so grand and so terrible that Nana trembled as she continued to defend herself, over that corpse which separated them.

"I swear to you, madame—if his brother was here, he could explain."

"His brother is a thief, he is in prison," said the mother harshly.

Nana remained transfixed, gasping for breath. But why all that? The other had robbed—they were mad then, in that family! She ceased struggling, no longer seeming to be in her own house, but leaving Madame Hugon to give her own orders. Some of the servants had at last hastened to the spot; the old lady insisted on having George, insensible as he was, taken to her carriage. She would remove him from that house, though it killed him. Nana, with a stupefied gaze, watched the servants carrying that poor Zizi by his legs and shoulders. The mother followed behind, quite exhausted now, leaning on the furniture, as though sunk into the nothingness of all she loved. On the landing she sighed and turning round, said twice,

"Ah! you have done us much harm! You have done us much harm!"

That was all. Nana seated herself, in her stupor, with her gloves still on her hands, and her bonnet on her head. The house relapsed into a dull silence, the carriage had just gone off; and she remained immovable, without an idea, her head all buzzing with what had just transpired. A quarter of an hour later, Count Muffat found her in the same place. But then she eased herself with a great flow of words, telling him of the misfortune, repeating twenty times the same details, picking up the scissors smeared with blood, to imitate Zizi's gesture when he stabbed himself. And she seemed especially anxious to prove her innocence.

"Come now, darling, was it my fault? If you were Justice, would you condemn me? I never told Philippe to steal, that's very certain, any more than I drove this poor fellow to kill himself. In all this, I'm the most miserable. They come and make fools of themselves here; they cause me a great deal of pain; I'm treated like a wretch of a woman."

And she burst out crying. Her nerves were highly unstrung, which rendered her weak and doleful, and deeply moved with an immense sorrow.

"You, too, you don't seem very pleased. Ask Zoé, now, if I'm at all to blame. Zoé, speak; explain to the count—"

For some few minutes the maid, having fetched from the dressing-room a towel and a basin of water, had been rubbing the carpet to get rid of a stain of blood, whilst it was still wet.

"Oh, sir!" she declared; "madame is quite broken-hearted!"

Muffat was greatly affected, feeling stunned by the drama, his thoughts full of that mother weeping for her two children. He knew her great heart; he saw her in her widow's weeds, pining away all alone at Les Fondettes. But Nana's despair increased. Now, the picture of Zizi, lying on the floor, with a red spot on his shirt, put her quite beside herself.

"He was so pretty, so gentle, so caressing! Ah! you know, ducky, it's so much the worse if you don't like it. I loved him, the baby! I can't control myself; it's stronger than I am. And then it can't matter to you now. He is no longer here. You have what you wanted; you may be quite sure of never catching us together again."

This last idea overwhelmed him with such regret that he ended by trying to console her. She must bear up. She was right; it was not her fault. But she stopped him to say,

"Listen, you must run and bring me news of him. At once! I insist!"

He took his hat and went off to obtain news of George. When he returned, at the end of three quarters of an hour, he beheld Nana leaning out of the window anxiously awaiting him; and he called to her from the pavement that the little fellow was not dead, and that they even hoped to save his life. Then she changed at once to a great joy. She sang, danced, and thought life beautiful. Zoé, however, was not satisfied with her cleansing. She kept looking at the stain, and saying each time she passed,

"You know, madame, it hasn't gone away."

And in fact, as it dried, the stain appeared a pale red on one of the white ornaments of the carpet. It was on the very threshold of the room, like a line of blood barring the way.

"Bah!" said Nana, happy once more, "the footsteps will wear it away."

By the morrow Count Muffat had also forgotten the incident. When in the cab on the way to the Rue Richelieu, he had sworn never to return to that woman. Heaven gave him a warning. He looked on Philippe's and George's calamity as foreboding his own ruin. But neither the spectacle of Madame Hugon in tears, nor the sight of the youth consumed with fever, had had the power to make him keep his oath; and from the short moment of emotion caused by the drama, all that remained to him was the secret joy of being rid of a rival, whose charming youth had always exasperated him. He now experienced an exclusive passion, one of those passions of men who have had no youth. He loved Nana with a necessity always to know that she was his alone—to hear her, to touch her, to be under the influence of her breath. It was an attachment which had got beyond the mere gratification of his senses, and had reached the purer feeling—an anxious affection, jealous of the past, dreaming at times of redemption, of pardon bestowed, both of them kneeling before God the Father. Each day religion regained some of its ascendeney over him. He again practised going to confession and communicating, struggling unceasingly, mingling his remorse with the joys of sin and of penitence. Then, his spiritual director having permitted him to wear out his passion, he had made a habit of that daily damnation, which he redeemed by bursts of faith, full of a devout humility. He very naïvely offered to heaven, as an expiatory suffering, the abominable torment he endured. This torment continued to increase. It raised his calvary of a believer, of a grave and profound heart, fallen into the mad sensuality of a courtesan. What caused him the most agony were the continual infidelities of that woman, for he could not accustom himself to share with others, failing to understand her stupid infatuations. He longed for an eternal love, ever the same. Yet, she had sworn to be faithful, and he paid her for that; but he felt that she lied, unable to guard herself, giving herself to her friends and the passersby, like some good animal born to live in a state of nakedness.

One morning that he observed Foucarmont leaving her house at a rather peculiar hour, he sought an explanation. She at once flew into a passion, tired of his jealousy. She had already, on several occasions, been very nice. For instance, the night when he had caught her with George she had been the first to make it up, admitting her fault, loading him with caresses and pretty words, to help him get over it; but at length he bored her with his obstinacy in not understanding women, and she roughly said,

"Well! yes, I've been Foucarmont's mistress. What next? Eh! that puts your hair out of curl, my little muff!"

It was the first time she called him "little muff" to his face. He remained bursting with rage at the brazenness of her avowal; and, as he clinched his fists, she walked towards him, and looked him straight in the face.

"Now, that's enough, do you hear? If it doesn't please you, just oblige me by going off. I won't have you kicking up a row in my house. Understand that I intend to be free to do as I like. When a man pleases me, I'll have him here. Exactly, that's what I mean. And you must make up your mind at once: yes or no, the door is open."

She had gone and opened the door. He did not go. So now it became her way of attaching him to her all the more; for nothing at all, at the least quarrel, she gave him his choice, accompanied by some of the most abominable reflections. Ah, well! she would always be able to find some one better than he, she had only too many people to choose from; one could pick up men outside, as many as one wanted, and fellows who were not such ninnies as he, whose blood boiled in their veins. He bowed his head, he waited for better times, when she would be in want of money; then she became caressing, and he forgot everything—a night of love compensated for the tortures of a week. His reconciliation with his wife had made his home unbearable. The countess, cast off by Fauchery, who was once more completely under Rose's influence, sought forgetfulness in other amours, in the attack of the feverish anxiety of her forty years, ever nervous, and filling the house with the exasperating commotion of her mode of living. Since her marriage, Estelle no longer saw her father. This skinny and insignificant looking girl had suddenly developed into a woman with an iron will so absolute that Daguenet trembled before her; now he accompanied her to church, converted, and furious with his father-in-law, who was ruining them with an abandoned female. M. Venot alone remained affectionate towards the count, whilst biding his time. He had even succeeded in gaining access to Nana; he frequented the two houses, where one often came across his continual smile behind the doors. And Muffat, miserable in his own home, driven from thence by dulness and shame, preferred rather to live amidst the insults of the Avenue de Villiers.

Soon, only one question remained between Nana and the count; that of money. One day, after formally promising to bring ten thousand francs, he had dared to present himself at the appointed time empty-handed. For the previous two days, she had been exciting him with endless caresses. Such a breaking of his word, so many endearing little ways wasted, threw her into an abusive rage. She became quite white.

"Eh! you've no money? Then, my little muff, return to whence you came, and quicker than that too! What a sordid wretch! and he was going to kiss me! No money, no anything! you understand!"

He entered into some explanations. He would have the money the day after the morrow. But she interrupted him violently.

"And my bills that are coming due! They'll seize my goods, whilst his lordship comes here on tick. Now, just look at yourself! Do you think I love you for yourself? When one has a mug like yours, one pays the women who are willing to put up with you. Damnation! if you don't bring me the ten thousand francs

to-night, you sha'n't even so much as suck the tip of my little
finger. Really! I must send you back to your wife!"

That night he brought the ten thousand francs. Nana held
out her lips. He took a long kiss, which consoled him for all his
day of agony. What annoyed the young woman was always having him attached to her skirts. She complained to M. Venot,
imploring him to take her little muff to the countess. Their
reconciliation did not appear to have been of much use and
she regretted having had anything to do with it, as he was for
ever at her back. The days when, blinded by anger, she forgot
her interests, she swore to play him such a dirty trick that he
would never again be able to come near her. But while she
blackguarded him, slapping her thighs meanwhile—she might
even have spat in his face—he would have remained and
thanked her. Then they had continual quarrels about money.
She roughly demanded it. She abused him in regard to the
most miserable sums, odiously greedy every minute, delighting
in cruelly telling him that she only tolerated him for his money
and for nothing else, that she didn't care for him, that she
loved another, and that she was very unfortunate in having to
do with such an idiot as he! They did not even want to have
him any longer at court, where there was a talk of requesting
him to send in his resignation. The Empress had said, "He is
too disgusting." That was very true. And Nana always repeated
the words as a parting shot in their quarrels.

"Really! you are too disgusting!"

She no longer put the least constraint upon herself now, she
had regained complete liberty. Every day she took her drive in
the Bois round the lake, forming acquaintances there which
became more intimate elsewhere. It was the great angling
match for men, the baiting in the full light of day, the hooking
by illustrious harlots, beneath the smile of toleration and the
dazzling luxury of Paris. Duchesses drew each other's attention
to her, the wives of wealthy tradesmen copied her bonnets; at
times her landau, when striving to pass, would arrest a long
string of grand equipages, containing financiers holding all
Europe in their cash-boxes, and ministers whose big fingers
were half throttling France; and she formed a part of this

world of the Bois. She occupied an important position there, known by the people of every capital, greatly in demand with all foreigners, adding the mad fit of her debauchery to the splendours of that crowd like the very glory and keen enjoyment of a nation. Then the intimacies of a night—mere birds of passage, of which she herself lost all recollection on the morrow—would take her to the grand restaurants, often to the Café de Madrid, when the weather was fine. All the staff of the embassies defiled there; she dined with Lucy Stewart, who murdered the French language, and who paid to be amused, taking the girls at so much an evening, with instructions to them to be funny, while they themselves were so sick of everything and so worn out that they never even touched them. And the girls called it going on the spree. They returned home delighted at having been treated with such disdain, and finished the night with some lover of their choice.

Count Muffat pretended to be ignorant of these goings on, when Nana did not tell him of them herself. He suffered, too, a great deal from the disgraces of his daily existence. The mansion in the Avenue de Villiers was becoming a regular hell, a mad-house in which sudden crazes at all hours of the day led to the most odious scenes. Nana had arrived at the point of battling with her servants. At one time she was especially good to Charles, the coachman. Whenever she stopped at a restaurant, she sent him out refreshments by the waiters; she would talk to him from inside her landau, highly amused, thinking him very funny as he roundly abused the other drivers whenever there was a block in the street. Then, without rhyme or reason, she completely changed and treated him as a fool. She was always wrangling about the straw, the bran, and the oats; in spite of her love for animals, she considered that her horses ate too much. So at length, one settling day, as she accused him of robbing her, Charles flew into a passion, and bluntly called her a strumpet; her horses, anyhow, were worth more than she, they did not let everyone muck them about. She retorted in a similar style, and the count was obliged to separate them and turn the coachman off the premises.

But this was only the beginning of a general stampede of the

servants. Victorine and François went off, after the discovery of
a robbery of diamonds. Even Julien disappeared, and a story
was circulated that the count had implored him to go, giving
him at the same time a large sum of money, because madame
had taken a great fancy to him. Every week fresh faces were
seen in the servants' hall. Never had there been such waste;
the house was like a passage through which the scum of the
servants' registry-offices defiled in a massacring gallop. Zoé
alone kept her place, with her neat look and her only anxiety
of organising the disorder, so long as she had not saved sufficient to settle down on her own account, a plan which she had
been working at for a long time past.

And yet those were only the avowable cares. The count bore
with Madame Maloir's stupidity, playing at bézique with her, in
spite of her rank odour. He put up with Madame Lerat and her
cackling, and with little Louis and his doleful complaints of a
child devoured by disease—some putrefaction bequeathed by
an unknown father. But he had to endure other things far
worse. One night, behind a door, he had heard Nana furiously
telling her maid that a pretended rich man had just taken her
in. Yes, a handsome fellow, who said he was American, and
owned gold mines in his own country—a mean vagabond who
had gone off whilst she was asleep, without leaving a sou behind, and even taking a packet of cigarette papers away with
him; and the count, very pale, had crept downstairs again on
tiptoe, so that he might feign ignorance of the occurrence. On
another occasion he was obliged to be aware of everything.
Nana, infatuated with a singer at a music-hall, and forsaken by
him, wanted to commit suicide in a fit of gloomy sentimental-
ity. She swallowed a glass of water in which she had soaked a
handful of matches, and was horribly ill in consequence, but
did not die. The count had to nurse her and listen to the story
of her passion intermingled with tears and oaths never to care
for men again. In her contempt for the pigs, as she called
them, she could not, however, keep her heart free, having always some sweetheart about her skirts, and indulging in the
most inexplicable caprices, through the depraved tastes of her
wearied body.

Since Zoé relaxed her supervision to meet her own ends, the good management of the household had disappeared to the extent that Muffat dared not open a door, draw a curtain, or look into a cupboard. The machinery no longer worked. Gentlemen were hanging about everywhere; at every minute they were knocking up against each other. Now, he invariably coughed before entering a room, having almost found the young woman with her arms round Francis's neck one evening that he had left the dressing-room for a couple of minutes to order the carriage, whilst the hairdresser was giving a few finishing touches to madame's hair. It was for ever sudden abandonments behind his back—pleasures snatched in odd corners, quickly, and in her chemise or in her most gorgeous costumes, with whoever happened to be with her. Then delighted with her robbery, she would rejoin him, looking very red in the face. With him there would have been no pleasure; he was such an abominable nuisance!

In the agony of his jealousy, the unhappy man had reached the state of feeling easy whenever he left Nana and Satin alone together. He would have encouraged her in this connection for the sake of keeping the men away. But on this side also everything went wrong. Nana deceived Satin, the same as she deceived the count, having a rage for the most monstrous crazes, picking up girls from the street corners. When returning home in her carriage, she would at times become enamoured of some strumpet caught sight of on the pavement, her senses inflamed, her imagination kindled; and she would take the woman with her, then pay her and send her away. At other times, disguised as a man, she would frequent houses of ill repute, and witness spectacles of debauchery, which helped her to forget her weariness; and Satin, annoyed at being continually forsaken, would disturb the house with the most atrocious scenes. She had ended by gaining complete mastery over Nana, who respected her. Muffat even thought of allying himself with her. When he did not dare to do anything himself, he would set Satin to work. Twice she had made her darling take him back; whilst he showed himself very obliging, giving her a word of warning or making himself scarce at the least sign.

Only the understanding did not last long; for Satin too was cracked. On certain days she would smash everything, feeling half dead, ruining what little health she had left in excesses of anger or of dissipation, looking pretty though, in spite of all. Zoé probably set her off; for she took her into corners, as though she wished to gain her over in the interests of that grand business of hers, that plan of which she had never yet spoken to anyone.

Singular fits of revolt, however, still took possession of Count Muffat. He who had tolerated Satin for months past, who had ended by accepting strangers, all that troop of men galloping through Nana's bedroom, became enraged at the idea of being deceived by any of his friends, or even acquaintances. When she owned to him her intimacy with Foucarmont, he suffered so much, he considered the young man's treachery so abominable, that he wished to provoke him to a duel. As he did not know whom to ask to be his seconds in such an affair, he consulted Labordette. The latter was so astounded, that he could not refrain from laughing.

"A duel about Nana! But, dear sir, all Paris would laugh at you. No one could fight for Nana; it would be too ridiculous."

The count became very pale. He made a violent gesture. "Then I will strike him, in the street before every one."

For an hour Labordette had to reason with him. A blow would make the story odious; by the evening every one would know the real cause of the meeting—he would be the laughing-stock of the newspapers. And Labordette kept returning to this conclusion.

"Impossible, it would be too ridiculous!"

Each time these words fell upon Muffat sharp and clean like the blow of a knife. He could not even fight for the woman he loved; every one would split their sides with laughing. Never before had he so painfully felt the misery of his love, that solemn feeling of his heart lost in that fooling of pleasure. This was his last revolt; he let himself be convinced. From that time he assisted at the procession of his friends, of all the men who lived there in the privacy of the mansion.

In a few months Nana devoured them greedily, one after the

other. The increasing requirements of her luxury whetted her appetite, she cleaned a man out with the craunch* of her teeth. First, she had Foucarmont, who did not last a fortnight. He had dreamed of leaving the navy. In ten years of a seafaring life he had saved some thirty thousand francs, which he wanted to risk in the United States; and his prudent and even miserly instincts were silenced—he gave all, even his signature to accommodation bills, thus affecting his future. When Nana turned him adrift, he was penniless. However, she showed herself very kind-hearted—she advised him to return to his ship. What was the use of being obstinate? As he had no money left, he could not possibly remain with her. He ought to understand that and be reasonable. A ruined man fell from her hands like ripe fruit, to rot on the earth all by himself.

Next, Nana tackled Steiner without disgust, but also without love. She called him a dirty Jew. She seemed to be gratifying an old hatred which she could not very well explain to herself. He was fat, he was stupid, and she turned him about, taking double mouthfuls, wishing to have done with the Prussian all the quicker. He had given up Simone. His Bosphorus speculation was already in jeopardy. Nana hastened his downfall by the most lavish expenditure. For a month still he struggled, performing miracles. He covered Europe with a colossal publicity—posters, advertisements, prospectuses—and extracted money from the most distant countries. All those savings, the louis of the speculators the same as the sous of the poor people, were swallowed up in the Avenue de Villiers. He had also gone into partnership with an iron-founder in Alsace. There were there, in a corner of the country, workmen black with coal dust, bathed with perspiration, who, night and day, tightened their muscles and heard their bones crack, to supply the means for Nana's pleasures. She devoured all like a great fire—the thefts at the Bourse, the earnings of labour.

This time she finished Steiner. She returned him to the pavement, sucked to the bone, so emptied that he remained

---

*Archaic form of "crunch."

even incapable of inventing a fresh roguery. In the collapse of
his banking establishment he went crazy; he trembled at the
name of the police. He was made a bankrupt; and the mere
word "money" bewildered him, threw him into a childish state
of embarrassment—he who had handled millions. One
evening when with her, he burst out crying. He asked her to
lend him a hundred francs to pay his servant; and Nana, affected and amused by this ending of the terrible old man who
for twenty years past had been skimming the Paris market,
brought him the money, saying,

"You know, I give 'em you because it's funny; but listen, my
little man, you're not of an age for me to keep you. You must
seek some other occupation."

Then Nana at once started on La Faloise. He had for a long
time been soliciting the honour of being ruined by her, so as
to be a perfect swell. That was what he was in want of; he must
have a woman to bring him out. In two months Paris would
know him, and he would read his own name in all the newspapers. Six weeks sufficed. His inheritance consisted of landed
estates, fields, pastures, woods, and farms. He had to sell them
rapidly, one after the other. At every bite Nana devoured an
acre. The foliage frizzling beneath the sun, the rich ripe corn,
the golden vines in September, the tall grass in which the cows
buried themselves up to their shoulders—all went as though
engulfed in some abyss; and there were also a stream, a lime
quarry, and three windmills which disappeared. Nana passed
like an invading army—like one of those clouds of locusts
whose flight destroys a whole province similar to a flame of
fire. She burnt the earth wherever she placed her tiny foot.
Farm after farm, meadow after meadow, she nibbled up the inheritance in her pretty way, without even noticing what she was
about, just the same as she would craunch up a bag of burnt almonds, placed on her knees, between her meals. It was a matter of no consequence; they were merely sweeties. But one
night there only remained a small wood. She swallowed it with
a disdainful air, for it was really not worth the trouble of opening one's mouth for.

La Faloise laughed in an idiotic way as he sucked the knob

of his walking-stick. Debts were crushing him down; he no longer possessed a hundred francs of income. He saw himself obliged to go back to the country and live with a maniacal uncle. But that did not matter; he was a swell. The "Figaro" had twice printed his name; and with his skinny neck rising out of his collar slightly turned down in front, his waist encased in a waistcoat a great deal too tight, he swaggered about, uttering exclamations like a parrot, and affecting the languors of a wooden puppet that has never had an emotion. Nana, whom he irritated immensely, ended by beating him.

Fauchery, however, had returned, brought by his cousin. The unfortunate Fauchery at this time had become quite a family man. After breaking off with the countess, he found himself in the hands of Rose, who treated him as a real husband. Mignon simply remained madame's major-domo. Installed as master, the journalist used to lie to Rose, and, whenever he deceived her, had to take all sorts of precautions, full of the scruples of a good spouse desirous of at length settling down. Nana's triumph was to hook him and to devour a newspaper he had started with the money of one of his friends. She did not openly go about with him. She took a delight, on the contrary, in treating him as a gentleman who must conceal his movements; and whenever she spoke of Rose, she would say "that poor Rose." The newspaper supplied her with flowers for a couple of months. She had subscribers in the country. She took everything, from the leading article to the theatrical notes. Then, after wearing out the editors, dislocating the management, she satisfied one of her big caprices—a winter garden in a corner of her mansion—which carried off the printing establishment.

It was merely by way of amusement, however. When Mignon, delighted with what was taking place, hastened to see if he could not fix Fauchery on her for good, she asked him if he was poking fun at her—a fellow without a sou, living on his articles and his plays; not if she knew it! Such stupidity was only worthy of a woman of talent like that poor Rose; and, full of mistrust, fearing some underhand dealing on Mignon's part, who was quite capable of denouncing them to his wife, she dismissed Fauchery, who for some time had only been paying her in advertisements.

But she remembered him with pleasure; they had amused themselves so much together with that idiot La Faloise. They would never perhaps have thought of being together again, if the pleasure of humbugging such a fool had not excited them. It seemed to them so funny. They would embrace each other under his nose, they lived the merriest possible life at his expense, they would send him on some errand to the other end of Paris, whenever they wanted to be alone together; then, when he returned, they would make jokes and allusions that he was unable to understand. One day, incited by the journalist, she bet that she would give La Faloise a slap in the face; that very evening she did so, then continued to beat him, finding it amusing, and delighted at being able to show what cowards men were. She called him her slapping machine, told him to come up and receive his slaps, slaps which made her hand quite red, because she was not yet accustomed to the exercise. La Faloise laughed in his idiotic way, with his eyes full of tears. This familiarity delighted him; he thought it grand.

"You don't know," said he one night, very excited after receiving a shower of blows, "you ought to marry me. Eh! shouldn't we make a jolly couple?"

It was not an empty remark. He had slyly projected this marriage, seized with a mania for astonishing Paris. Nana's husband—eh! what an effect! A rather grand apotheosis! But Nana snuffed him out in fine style.

"I marry you! Well! if I'd been worried with any such idea I could long ago have found a husband! And a man who would be worth twenty such as you, my little fellow. I have received no end of proposals. Come reckon them up with me: Philippe, George, Foucarmont, Steiner, there's four, without counting the others whom you don't know. They all sing the same chorus. I can't be nice with them without they at once start off singing: 'Will you marry me? will you marry me?' " She was becoming excited. Then she burst out indignantly, "Well! no, I won't! Was I ever made for such a life as that? Look at me. I

should no longer be Nana if I saddled myself with a husband.
And, besides, it's too disgusting."

And she spat on the ground, she hiccoughed with disgust,
as though she saw all the filth of the earth spreading beneath
her.

One night La Faloise disappeared. A week later it was stated
that he was in the country with his uncle, who had a mania for
botanising; he mounted his specimens, and stood a chance of
marrying a cousin who was very ugly and extremely devout.
Nana did not weep for him much. She merely said to the
count,

"Well, my little muff! that's another rival the less. You're in
high feather to-day. But he was becoming serious; he wanted to
marry me."

As he turned pale, she laughingly put her arms round his
neck, thrusting each of her cruelties into him with a caress.

"And it's that which bothers you, isn't it? You can't marry
Nana. Whilst they're all trying to get me to marry them, you're
chafing all alone in your corner. It's not possible, you must wait
till your wife croaks. Ah! if your wife was to croak, wouldn't you
just hasten to me—wouldn't you just throw yourself at my feet
and offer me everything, all the usual style, with sighs, and
tears, and protestations? Eh, darling! it would be so nice!"

Her voice had become soft, she fooled him with an air of ferocious cajolery. He, deeply moved, blushed as he returned
her embraces. Then she cried,

"Damn it all! to think that I guessed right! He has thought
of it, he's waiting till his wife croaks. Ah, well! this is too
much—he's a bigger scamp than the others!"

Muffat had accepted the others. Now he made it a last point
of dignity to remain the "master" with the servants and the frequenters of the house—the man who, giving the most, was the
official lover. And his passion became madder than ever. He
kept his place by paying, buying even smiles at fabulous prices,
often robbed and never receiving his money's worth; but it was
like a disease that was devouring him, he could not help suffering from it. When he entered Nana's bed-room, he contented himself with opening the windows for a minute, so as to

get rid of the odours left by the others—the effluvia of both
dark and fair, the cigar smoke, the staleness of which nearly
suffocated him. The room was becoming a public square;
boots of all kinds were continually being wiped on the threshold, and not one was arrested by that bloody mark which
barred the entry. Zoé was greatly worried by that stain, merely
a tidy girl's mania. She was annoyed at always seeing it there;
her eyes were attracted to it in spite of herself. She never entered madame's room without saying,

"It's funny it doesn't go away; yet a great many people come
here."

Nana, who had been receiving better news of George, then
in a state of convalescence at Les Fondettes with his mother,
each time made the same reply:

"Ah, well! you must give it time. It's gradually becoming
paler beneath the footsteps."

And, indeed, each one of the gentlemen—Foucarmont,
Steiner, La Faloise, Fauchery, and the others—had carried
away a little of the stain on the soles of their boots. And Muffat, who was worried as much as Zoé by the mark of blood,
studied it in spite of himself, to read, as it were, in its rosier and
rosier effacement, the number of men who passed there. He
had a secret dread of it, always stepping over it through a sudden fear of crushing something living—a naked limb lying on
the floor.

Then in that room an unconquerable feeling intoxicated
him. He forgot all—the mob of other men who passed
through it, the mourning that barred the door. Outside, at
times, in the open air of the street, he would shed tears of
shame and indignation, and swear never to return there; and
the moment he had passed the threshold, he was recaptured.
He felt his will give way in the warmth of the apartment; his
flesh penetrated with a perfume, overpowered by a voluptuous
desire of annihilation. He, devout and used to the rapturous
feelings enkindled by the contemplation of gorgeous shrines,
experienced exactly the same sensations of a believer, as when,
kneeling in some church, he became entranced by the sounds
of the organ and the perfume of the incense. The woman

ruled him with the jealous despotism of a god of anger, terri-
fying him, giving him seconds of joy, acute as spasms, for hours
of frightful torments, of visions of hell and everlasting damnation. It was always the same stutterings, the same prayers, and
the same despondencies, especially the same humilities of an
accursed creature crushed beneath the mud of his origin. The
desires of his flesh, the requirements of his soul, mingled and
seemed to rise from the obscure depths of his being, like a single blossom of the tree of life. He abandoned himself to the
power of love and faith, whose double lever animates the
world. And always, in spite of the struggles of his reason,
Nana's room filled him with madness. He shiveringly succumbed to the all-powerfulness of her sex, the same as he felt
lost before the vast unknown of heaven.

Then when she found him so humble, Nana's triumph became tyrannical. She instinctively had a rage for debasing
everything. It was not sufficient for her to destroy things; she
polluted them. Her delicate hands left abominable traces behind them; they decomposed by their mere touch all that they
had broken. And he, idiot that he was, lent himself to this
sport, with the vague remembrance of saints devoured by lice,
and who eat what they had voided. When she had him in her
room, with the doors fastened, she would feast herself with the
sight of man's infamy. At first it was merely fun. She would give
him little slaps and make him do comical things, such as lisping like a child, repeating ends of sentences.

"Say it like me, 'And dash it all! Coco doesn't care!'"

He would be obedient even to imitating her accent.

"And dash it all! Coco doesn't care!"

Or she would do the woolly bear, on all fours on the fur
rugs, in her chemise, and turning round and round and grunting, as though she meant to eat him up; and she would even
bite his calves, just for fun. Then she would get up and say,

"Now it's your turn. I bet you won't do the woolly bear as
well as me."

It was charming. She amused him as a bear, with her white
skin and her golden mane. He laughed, he also went on all

fours, he grunted and bit her calves, whilst she hopped about, pretending to be greatly frightened.

"Aren't we stupid, eh?" she would end by saying. "You've no idea how ugly you look, my dear! Ah, well! if they could only see you now, at the Tuileries!"

But these little games soon took an ugly turn. It wasn't through cruelty on her part, for she still remained a good-natured girl; it was like a breath of madness, which passed and increased little by little in the closed room. A lewdness seemed to possess them, and inspire them with the delirious imaginations of the flesh. The old devout frights of their night of wakefulness had now turned into a thirst for bestiality, a mania for going on all fours, for grunting and biting. Then one day, as he was doing the woolly bear, she pushed him so roughly that he fell against a piece of furniture; and she broke out into an involuntary laugh as she saw a bump on his forehead. From that time, having already acquired a taste for it by her experiment on La Faloise, she treated him as an animal, goaded him and pursued him with kicks.

"Gee up! gee up! you're the horse. Haw, gee! dirty jade! move along quicker than that!"

At other times he was a dog. She would throw her scented handkerchief to the other end of the room, and he had to go and pick it up with his teeth, crawling along on his hands and knees.

"Fetch it, Cæsar! I'll give you the stick if you're not quick! Good dog, Cæsar! pretty, obedient fellow! Now, beg!"

And he delighted in his baseness, and relished the enjoyment of being a brute. He aspired at falling still lower—he would cry out,

"Hit harder! Bow wow! I'm mad, hit away!"

She was seized with a caprice. She insisted on his coming one evening arrayed in his gorgeous chamberlain's costume. Then she laughed and ridiculed him when she had him in his court dress, with the sword, and the hat, and the white breeches, and the scarlet cloth dress coat bedizened with gold, and the symbolical key hanging over the left-hand tail. This key especially amused her, and filled her with a mad fancy for filthy

explanations. Always laughing, and carried away by a disre-
spect for greatness, and by the delight of vilifying it beneath
the official pomp of that costume, she shook him and pinched
him, and kept exclaiming, "Eh! get along, you chamberlain!"
ending by accompanying her words with kicks behind; and she
heartily meant those kicks for the Tuileries, for the majesty of
the imperial court, throning herself on high, over the fear and
the prostration of all. That was what she thought of society! It
was her revenge—an unconscious family grudge, bequeathed
with the blood. Then, the chamberlain having undressed, his
coat spread out on the floor, she cried to him to jump, and he
jumped; she cried to him to spit, and he spat; she cried to him
to walk over the gold, over the eagles, over the decorations,
and he walked. Slap! bang! there was nothing left—all had col-
lapsed. She demolished a chamberlain as easily as she broke a
scent-bottle or a comfit-box, and she turned him into a lump
of filth—a heap of mud at a street corner.

The goldsmiths, however, had not kept their word. The bedstead was not delivered until towards the middle of January.
Muffat at the time was in Normandy, where he had gone to sell
a last remnant of the wreck. He was not expected back until
two days later; but, having settled his business, he hastened his
return, and without even calling at the Rue Miromesnil, he
went to the Avenue de Villiers. Ten o'clock was striking. As he
had the key of a little door opening on to the Rue Cardinet,
he entered without being noticed. Upstairs, in the parlour,
Zoé, who was dusting some bronzes, was struck with amazement; and, not knowing how to detain him, began telling him
a long story about M. Venot, who, in a most agitated state of
mind, had been seeking him since the day before; that he had
already called there twice, and implored her to send the count
at once to him if he came to madame's first. Muffat listened to
her without understanding anything of the rigmarole; then he
noticed her confusion, and seized suddenly with a jealous
rage, of which he no longer thought himself capable, he
rushed against the door of the bed-room, from whence issued
sounds of laughter. The door gave way and flew open, whilst
Zoé retired shrugging her shoulders. So much the worse! As

madame was going mad, madame must get out of the mess by herself.

And Muffat, on the threshold, uttered a cry at the sight before him.

"My God! my God!"

The newly decorated room was resplendent in its regal luxury. Silver buttons strewed the tea rose velvet hangings with shining stars. It was the rosy colour of flesh which illuminates the sky on fine nights, when Venus sparkles at the horizon on the light background of the expiring day; whilst the cords of gold hanging down at the corners, the gold lace framing the panels, were like bright flames, or loose switches of red hair, half covering the great nudity of the room, the voluptuous paleness of which they enriched. Then, opposite, was the gold and silver bedstead, which shone with the new brightness of its chasings—a throne large enough for Nana to stretch the royalty of her naked limbs—an altar of a Byzantine richness, worthy of the all-powerfulness of her sex, and on which at this very moment she displayed it, uncovered, and in the religious immodesty of a dreaded idol. And, near her, beneath the snowy reflection of her bosom, in the midst of her goddess-like triumph, sprawled a shameful and decrepit object, a comical and lamentable ruin, the Marquis de Chouard in his night-shirt.

The count joined his hands. Seized with a great fit of trembling, he repeated, "My God! my God!"

It was for the Marquis de Chouard that the golden roses of the boat flowered—bunches of golden roses blooming amidst the golden foliage; it was for him that the cupids, dancing in a circle against the silver trellis, leant forward with a laugh of amorous sauciness; and it was for him that the faun at his feet uncovered the sleeping nymph, wearied with voluptuousness—that figure of Night, copied from Nana's celebrated nudity, even to the too amply developed thighs, which would cause everyone to recognise her. Thrown there like a piece of human rubbish, corrupted and shattered by sixty years of debauchery, the marquis appeared as a corner of a charnelhouse, surrounded by the glory of the woman's dazzling flesh. When he saw the door open he raised himself up, seized with

the fright of a paralytic old man. This last night of licentious-
ness had smitten him with imbecility, he had fallen into his second childhood; and, no longer able to find his words—half
paralysed, stuttering, shivering—he remained in an attitude of
flight, his night-shirt rucked up over his skeleton of a body,
one leg outside the clothes—a poor, livid leg covered with grey
hairs. Nana, in spite of her annoyance, could not help laughing.

"Lie down—get under the clothes," said she, pushing him
back and covering him with the sheet, like some bit of dirt one
does not wish to be seen.

And she ran to close the door. She had really no luck with
her little muff!—he was always putting in an appearance at an
awkward moment. And why, too, did he go off to seek for
money in Normandy? The old fellow had brought her four
thousand francs, and she had let him have his way. She pushed
the door to again, and cried,

"So much the worse! it's all your fault. That's not the way to
enter a room! There, that'll do. Good-bye!"

Muffat stood in front of that closed door, utterly crushed by
what he had just seen. His fit of trembling increased—a trembling which ascended from his legs to his chest and to his
head. Then, like a tree caught in the hurricane, he staggered
and fell on his knees, cracking in all his limbs; and, despair-
ingly holding out his hands, he muttered,

"It is too much. Oh, God! it is too much!"

He had accepted everything, but he could no longer bear it.
He felt himself without strength, in that darkness where man
succumbs with his reason. With an extraordinary outburst,
holding high his joined hands, he sought Heaven, he called on
God.

"Oh, no! I will not! Oh! come to me, my God! help me, or
rather let me die! Oh, no! not that man, my God! it is ended—
take me, carry me off, that I may no longer see, that I may no
longer feel. Oh! I belong to Thee, my God! Our Father which
art in Heaven—"

And he continued, burning with faith, and an ardent prayer
came from his lips. But someone touched him on the shoul-

der. He raised his eyes: it was M. Venot, surprised at finding
him praying before that closed door. Then, as though God
Himself had replied to his appeal, he threw himself into the little old man's arms. At last he could weep: he sobbed, and kept
repeating,

"My brother, my brother—"

All his suffering humanity found relief in this cry. He bathed
M. Venot's face with his tears, he kissed him, uttering disconnected sentences.

"Oh, my brother, how I suffer! You alone are left to me, my
brother. Take me away for ever, oh! for mercy's sake, take me
away."

Then M. Venot pressed him to his bosom. He called him his
brother also. But he had another blow to deal him. Since the
previous day he had been seeking him to tell him that Countess Sabine had crowned her follies by eloping with a young
man employed at a large linen-draper's—a frightful scandal, of
which all Paris was already gossiping. Seeing him under the influence of such a religious exaltation, he thought the moment
a favourable one, and told him at once what had occurred,
that flatly tragical end in which his house was foundering. The
count was not affected in the least; his wife had gone off, that
was nothing to him, he would see about it later on. And, again
giving way to his anguish, looking at the door, the walls, the
ceiling, in a terrified manner, he could do no more than utter
these imploring words:

"Take me away, I can bear it no longer; take me away."

M. Venot took him off like a child. From that time he was his
entirely. Muffat once more returned to the strict duties of religion. His life was blasted. He had resigned his chamberlain's
office in accordance with the desire of the offended modesty
of the Tuileries. His daughter Estelle had commenced an action against him to recover a sum of sixty thousand francs left
her by an aunt, and which she ought to have received at the
time of her marriage. Ruined, and living very moderately with
the remnants of his great fortune, he allowed himself to be finished little by little by the countess, who devoured the leavings
Nana had disdained. Sabine, corrupted by that woman's

promiscuousness, incited to extremes, became the final sapper, the very canker of the home. After various adventures she had returned, and he had taken her back in the resignation of Christian pardon. She accompanied him like his living shame. But he, becoming more and more indifferent, ended by no longer suffering from such things. Heaven had rescued him from the arms of woman to place him again in the very arms of God. It was a religious prolongation of Nana's voluptuous pleasures, with the stutterings, the prayers, and the despondencies—the humilities of an accursed creature crushed beneath the mud of his origin. In the dark corners of churches, his knees chilled by the cold stones, he found again his enjoyments of former days, the spasms of his muscles and the delicious perturbations of his intelligence, in the same atonement of the obscure requirements of his being.

The night of the rupture Mignon called at the Avenue de Villiers. He had got accustomed to Fauchery, he had ended by discovering a thousand advantages in the presence of a husband at his wife's. He left to him all the little cares of the home, relied on him for an active supervision, and used the money that came from his dramatic successes for the daily expenses of the household; and as, on the other hand, Fauchery behaved very reasonably—never indulging in any ridiculous jealousy, but being as accommodating as Mignon himself with regard to the opportunities Rose had—the two men got on together better than ever, delighted with their association, so fertile in every kind of happiness, and each one making his nest beside the other, in a home where neither of them any longer stood on ceremony. It was regulated, it worked very well, they rivalled each other in their exertions for the common felicity. It just happened that Mignon had called, by Fauchery's advice, to see if he could not entice away Nana's maid, whose wonderful intelligence the journalist had fully appreciated. Rose was in great distress. For a month past she had had to put up with inexperienced girls, who caused her continual embarrassments.

As Zoé admitted him, he pushed her at once into the dining-room. At the first word she smiled. It was impossible. She was leaving madame, she was about to set up in business on her own account; and she added, with an air of discreet vanity, that every day she was receiving proposals—all the ladies wanted her. Madame Blanche had offered her a bridge of gold to get her back. Zoé was going to acquire old Tricon's business, an old project which she had nursed for a long while, an ambition to realise a fortune, in which she was about to invest her savings. She was full of great ideas. She dreamed of enlarging the concern, of taking a mansion, and collecting in it every pleasure. It was for this that she had even tried to get hold of Satin, a little blockhead who was now dying in the hospital, she had so ruined her health.

Mignon having persisted in his offer, mentioning the risks one runs in business, Zoé, without explaining herself as to the nature of her projected establishment, contented herself with saying, with a self-satisfied smile, just as though she had taken a confectioner's shop,

"Oh! affairs of luxury always succeed. You see I have been so long with the others that now I wish the others to be with me."

And a ferocious feeling made her curl her lip. She would at last be "madame." She would have at her feet, for the sum of a few louis, those women whose slops she had been emptying for fifteen years past.

Mignon wished to see Nana, and Zoé left him for a minute, after saying that madame had passed a very unpleasant day. He had only called there once, he did not know the house at all. The dining-room, with its Gobelin tapestry, its sideboard, and its silver plate, amazed him. He familiarly opened the doors, and visited the drawing-room and the winter garden, and then returned to the hall; and this excessive luxury—the gilded furniture, the silks, and the velvets—filled him little by little with an admiration which caused his heart to bump. When Zoé came downstairs to fetch him, she offered to show him the other rooms—the bed-room, the dressing-room. Then, in the bed-room, Mignon's heart almost burst. He was excited to the highest point of enthusiasm. That confounded Nana astounded him, he who was not easily surprised at anything. In the midst of the downfall of the establishment, of the waste and the massacring gallop of the servants, there was a pile of riches which stopped up the holes and covered the ruins.

And Mignon, in the face of that magisterial monument, re-called many great works he had seen. Near Marseilles he had been shown an aqueduct, the stone arches of which spanned an abyss—a Cyclopean work which had cost millions and ten years of struggle. At Cherbourg he had seen the new harbour in course of construction—a gigantic undertaking, hundreds of men sweating in the sunshine, machines filling the sea with huge masses of rock, erecting a wall where at times workmen were squashed to a bloody pulp. But all that seemed small to him now. Nana exalted him far more; and in contemplating her work, he experienced once again that sensation of respect experienced by him one night at an entertainment in a château which a sugar refiner had had built—a palace the royal splendour of which had been paid for by one single thing, sugar. She had paid with something different, a bit of fun at which one laughed—a little of her delicate nudity. It was with this shameful and yet so mighty a nothing, the power of which excited the world, that all alone, without workmen, with-out machinery invented by engineers, she had shaken Paris and built up that fortune beneath which dead bodies were slumbering.

"Ah! damn it all! what a tool!" exclaimed Mignon enrap-tured, and with a return of personal gratitude.

Nana little by little had become very sorrowful. At first the meeting of the marquis and the count had thrown her into a nervous fever, accompanied by a slight touch of gaiety. Then, the thought of the old fellow who had gone off in a cab, half dead, and of her poor muff whom she would never see again, after having so often vexed him, brought about the beginning of a sentimental melancholy. After this she had got quite angry on hearing of Satin's illness. The girl had disappeared a fort-night before, and was now gradually dying at the Lariboisière Hospital, Madame Robert having put her into such a frightful state. As she was ordering the carriage to go and see the little baggage once more, Zoé had quietly given her a week's notice to leave. That threw her into despair. It seemed as though she was losing one of her family; and she implored Zoé to remain. The latter, highly flattered by madame's grief, ended by kissing her, to show that there was no ill-feeling at parting. She was obliged to go; the heart was silent when business was in question. But that was a day of worries. Nana, thoroughly disgusted, no longer thinking of going out, was wandering about her parlour, when Labordette, who had come to tell her of some magnificent lace to be had at a bargain, mentioned between two other phrases about nothing at all that George was dead. She turned icy cold.

"Zizi! dead!" she cried.

And her glance, by an involuntary movement, sought the pink stain on the carpet. But it had vanished at last; the footsteps had worn it away. Labordette, however, gave her some particulars. One did not know exactly how it had happened: some talked of a wound having opened, others told the story of a suicide—a plunge into one of the fountains at Les Fondettes. Nana kept repeating,

"Dead! dead!"

Then she burst into sobs, and relieved her feelings pent up since the morning. It was an infinite sadness—something profound and immense which overwhelmed her. Labordette having tried to console her about George, she waved her hand to make him desist, and said in broken tones,

"It's not only him, it's all, it's everything. I'm very unhappy, Oh! I know! they'll again say that I'm an abominable woman. That mother who is weeping there, and that poor man who was moaning this morning at my door, and the others who are all ruined, after having squandered their sous with me. That's right, give it to Nana, give it to the beast! Oh! I've a broad back, I can hear them as though I was there. That dirty strumpet who entices everyone; who clears out some, and kills the others; who causes pain to no end of people—"

She was forced to interrupt herself; suffocated by her tears, she had fallen in her anguish across a sofa, with her head buried in a cushion. The misfortunes she felt around her, those miseries that she had caused, enveloped her in a warm and continuous flow of sensibility; and her voice became lost in the plaintive accents of a little girl.

"Oh! I suffer—oh! I suffer. I cannot, it's stifling me. It's too hard not to be understood, to see everyone put themselves against you, because they're the strongest. Yet, when one has nothing to reproach oneself with, when one has a free conscience—well, no! well, no—"

Her anger changed to indignation. She got up, wiped her eyes; and paced agitatedly about the room.

"Well, no! they may say what they like, it isn't my fault! Am I cruel? I give all I have—I wouldn't hurt a fly. It's they; yes, it's they! I never wanted to be unpleasant to any of them. And they were always hanging about my skirts, and now they croak, or beg, and all pretend to be in despair."

Then, stopping in front of Labordette, and tapping him on the shoulders, she continued,

"Come now, you were there, speak the truth. Was it I who led them on? Weren't there always a dozen exerting themselves to invent something more abominable than the others? They disgusted me! I held myself aloof so as not to follow in their wake, I was afraid. Here's an instance—they all wanted to marry me. A nice idea! Eh! yes, my dear fellow, I might have been twenty times a baroness or a countess if I had consented. Well! I refused, because I was reasonable. Ah! I preserved them from many detestable actions and many crimes! They would have stolen, murdered, killed father and mother. I had but to say a word, and I didn't say it. To-day, you see my reward. It's like that Daguenet whom I got married—a half-starved wretch whose position I made, after keeping him for nothing for weeks together. Yesterday, I met him; he turned away his head. Well! go to the devil, pig! I'm not so foul as you are!"

She was walking about again; she violently banged her fist down on a small round table.

"Damn it all! it's not just! Society is badly constructed. The women are abused, when it's the men who are entirely to blame, they expect such things. Listen! I can tell you now—in all I've ever had to do with men, well! I never had the least pleasure—no, not the least. They always bored me, on my word of honour! So, I ask you now if there's any fault of mine in all this? Ah, yes! they almost badgered me out of my life! Without them, my dear fellow, and what they've made me, I should be now in a convent praying, for I've always been religious. And, hang 'em! after all, if they have left their money and their skin, it's their own fault! I've nothing to do with it!"

"Of course," said Labordette, convinced.

Zoé ushered in Mignon. Nana received him smiling; she had had a good cry, but now it was over. He complimented her on her abode, still warmed with enthusiasm; but she soon let him see that she had had enough of her mansion. Now she was dreaming of something else—she would get rid of it all, one fine day. Then, as he mentioned as a pretext for his visit a benefit performance to be given for old Bosc, who was tied to his chair by an attack of paralysis, she expressed a great deal of sorrow, and took two boxes. Zoé, however, having said that the carriage was waiting, she asked for her bonnet; and as she tied the strings, she related the story of poor Satin's mishap, then added:

"I'm off to the hospital. No one ever loved me as she did. Ah! one is quite right in accusing men of having no hearts! Who knows? she's perhaps dead already. All the same, I shall ask to see her. I must kiss her once more."

Labordette and Mignon smiled. She was no longer sad, she smiled also, for those two did not count, they could understand. And they both admired her, in a thoughtful silence, as she finished buttoning her gloves. She alone stood erect, in the midst of the piled-up wealth of her mansion, with a crowd of men trampled beneath her feet. Like those antique monsters whose dreaded domain was covered with bones, she trod on skulls, and catastrophe surrounded her: Vandeuvres's furious conflagration; the melancholy of Foucarmont, drowned in the China seas; the collapse of Steiner, now forced to live as an honest man; the satisfied imbecility of La Faloise, and the tragical downfall of the Muffats; and George's white corpse watched over by Philippe, discharged from prison the day before. Her work of ruin and death was accomplished, the fly that had taken its flight from the filth of the slums, carrying with it the ferment of social decay, had poisoned those men merely by touching them. It was good, it was just; she had avenged her people, the rogues and the vagabonds from whom she sprang. And whilst in a halo her sex ascended and shone on her scattered victims like a rising sun lighting up a field of carnage, she retained her unconsciousness of a superb beast, ignorant of her work, always good-natured. She remained big and plump, with beautiful health and unalloyed gaiety. But all that no longer counted. Her mansion seemed to her idiotic—it was so small, and full of a heap of furniture which was always in her way. A mere nothing, she only wanted to commence again. She dreamed, too, of something better; and she went off in a gorgeous costume to kiss Satin a last time—clean, solid, looking quite new, as though she had never been in use.

CHAPTER XIV

Nana abruptly disappeared—another plunge, a wild prank, a flight into strange lands. Before her departure she procured herself the emotion of a sale by auction, sweeping everything off—the mansion, the furniture, the jewellery, and even the dresses and the linen. Figures were quoted. The five days produced more than six hundred thousand francs. For a last time Paris had seen her in a fairy piece, "Mélusine," at the Gaiety Theatre, that Bordenave had audaciously taken without a sou. She was there with Prullière and Fontan. Her part was a dumb one, all show, but a real hit—three plastic postures of a powerful and silent fairy. Then in the midst of this great success, when Bordenave, advertising-mad, was covering Paris with colossal posters, it was stated one fine morning that the night before she had left for Cairo—a simple discussion with her manager, a word that had not pleased her, the caprice of a woman too rich to allow herself to be annoyed. Besides, it was a fad of hers. For a long time past she had longed to go and see the Turks.

Months passed by. She was forgotten. Whenever her name was mentioned amongst her friends, the strangest stories circulated. Each gave contrary and prodigious information. She had captivated the viceroy; she reigned in the innermost recesses of a palace, over two hundred slaves, whose heads she cut off to make her laugh. Not at all. She had ruined herself with a big negro—a filthy infatuation which had left her without a chemise, in the midst of the crapulous debauchery of Cairo. A fortnight later there was universal astonishment. Some one swore he had met her in Russia. A legend gradually developed. She was the mistress of a prince; her diamonds were talked about. All the women were soon acquainted with them, through the descriptions that were current, without any one being able to give their source—rings, bracelets, earrings, a diamond necklace as broad as two fingers, and a queenly diadem surmounted by a central brilliant as big as one's thumb.

In the unknown of these far-oft lands, she assumed the mysterious radiance of an idol covered with precious stones. Now, she was only mentioned gravely, with the pensive respect for that fortune made amongst the barbarians.

One July evening towards eight o'clock, Lucy, who was driving down the Rue du Faubourg-Saint-Honoré, caught sight of Caroline Héquet, who had gone out on foot to give an order to a tradesman of the neighbourhood. She called to her, and at once said,

"Have you dined? are you free? Oh, then, my dear! come with me. Nana has returned!"

The other, on hearing this, at once got into the carriage, and Lucy continued,

"And you know, my dear, she is perhaps dead whilst we are talking."

"Dead! what an idea!" cried Caroline in amazement. "And where? and of what?"

"At the Grand Hotel, of the small-pox—oh! quite a story!"

Lucy had told her coachman to drive quick. So, as the horses rapidly trotted along the Rue Royale and the Boulevards, she related the story of Nana's adventure, in broken sentences, and without once taking breath.

"You can't imagine. Nana arrives from Russia, I forget why—a row with her prince. She leaves her luggage at the station and goes off to her aunt. You recollect that old woman? Good! She finds her baby ill with the small-pox. The baby dies on the morrow, and she has a row with the aunt about the money she ought to have sent, and which the other had never seen a sou of. It seems the child died of that—in short, the child was not well fed or looked after. Very well, Nana goes off, puts up at a hotel, then meets Mignon, just as she was thinking of fetching her luggage. She becomes very peculiar, she has the shivers, wants to be sick, and Mignon takes her to her room, promising to look after her affairs. Eh! isn't it funny, isn't it strange? But here's the best part. Rose hears of Nana's illness, is indignant at learning that she's all alone in an out-of-the-way place, and weepingly hastens to nurse her. You recollect how they detested each other? a couple of furies! Well! my dear, Rose had

Nana removed to the Grand Hotel, so that she might at least die in a swell place; and she's already passed three nights with her, and may very likely die of it afterwards. It's Labordette who told me all this, so I wanted to see—"

"Yes, yes," interrupted Caroline, greatly excited. "We will go."

They had arrived. On the Boulevard the coachman had been obliged to pull up in the midst of a block of vehicles and foot passengers. During the day the Corps Législatif had voted for a declaration of war.[5] A crowd poured down from all the side streets and covered the footpaths and the roadway. At the Madeleine end the sun had set behind a bloodred cloud, the fiery reflection of which illuminated the tall windows. Twilight was coming on, a dull and melancholy hour, with the darkening avenues, which the gas-lamps had not yet lit up with their bright specks. And amongst this mass of people on the march distant voices became louder, pale faces sparkled with animated glances, whilst a deep breath of anguish and of spreading stupor turned all heads.

"There's Mignon," said Lucy. "He will give us some news."

Mignon was standing under the vast portico of the Grand Hotel, with a nervous air about him as he watched the crowd. At the first questions Lucy put to him, he flew into a passion, exclaiming,

"I don't know! For the last two days I've not been able to get Rose away from up there. It's idiotic for her to risk her skin like that! She'll look nice, if she catches it, with scars all over her face! It will suit us nicely."

The idea that Rose might lose her beauty exasperated him. He would leave Nana just as she was, not understanding those silly devotions which women went in for. But here Faucherey crossed the Boulevard, and when he had joined the others, he also anxiously asked for news, and then the two men tried to incite each other to go up. They were most affectionate to one another now.

"Always the same, little 'un," observed Mignon. "You ought to go up and force her to come away."

"Really! You're kind, you are!" said the journalist. "Why don't you go up yourself?"

Then, as Lucy inquired the number of the room, they both implored her to induce Rose to come down; otherwise it would end by their getting angry. Lucy and Caroline, however, did not go up at once. They had caught sight of Fontan strolling along with his hands in his pockets, highly amused by the different faces in the crowd. When he learnt that Nana was upstairs ill, he remarked with a great display of feeling,

"Poor girl! I will go and shake hands with her. What's the matter with her?"

"Small-pox," replied Mignon.

The actor had already taken a step in the direction of the courtyard, but he retraced it, and with a shiver simply murmured, "Ah, the deuce!"

It was no joke catching small-pox. Fontan had nearly had it when he was five years old. Mignon related the story of one of his nieces who had died of it. As for Fauchery, he could talk of it, for he still bore the marks—three spots, which he showed to the others, close to his nose; and as Mignon pressed him again to go up, on the pretext that people never had it twice, he violently disputed that theory. He instanced cases, and called the doctors fools. But Lucy and Caroline, surprised at the vast increase of the crowd, interrupted them.

"Look there! look there! What a mob of people!"

The night was advancing, the lamps in the distance were being lighted one by one. One could, however, distinguish spectators at the windows; whilst under the trees the human tide swelled every minute, in one long stream, from the Madeleine to the Bastille. The vehicles rolled slowly along. A kind of buzz arose from that compact mass, dumb as yet, assembled together in the idle desire of forming a crowd, stamping, and excited with the same fever. But a huge commotion caused the crowd to fall back. In the midst of all the jostling, passing through the groups that made way for them, a band of men in caps and white blouses appeared, uttering this cry, to the time of hammers beating on the anvil,

"To Berlin! to Berlin! to Berlin!"

And the crowd looked on with a gloomy distrust, already attracted, nevertheless, and stirred with visions of heroic deeds, the same as when a military band passes by.

"Yes, yes; go and get your heads broken!" murmured Mignon, seized with a philosophic fit.

But Fontan thought it very grand. He talked of enlisting. When the enemy was at the frontier all citizens ought to rise in arms to defend the fatherland, and he assumed a posture worthy of Bonaparte at Austerlitz.

"Well, are you going up with us?" asked Lucy of him.

"Ah, no!" said he, "not to get ill!"

On one of the seats in front of the Grand Hotel sat a man, hiding his face in his handkerchief. Fauchery, on arriving, had drawn Mignon's attention to him with a wink. So he was always there? Yes, he was always there; and the journalist stopped the two women to point him out to them. As he raised his head they recognised him, and uttered a slight exclamation. It was Count Muffat, who glanced upwards at one of the windows.

"You know he's been there ever since this morning," related Mignon. "I saw him at six o'clock, he has scarcely moved since. At the first words Labordette uttered, he came and posted himself there, with his handkerchief over his face. Every half hour he crawls as far as here, to inquire if the person upstairs is better, and then returns to his seat. Well! you know, it's not healthy, that room. One may love people without wishing to croak."

The count, with upturned eyes, did not appear to be aware of what was going on around him. No doubt he was ignorant of the declaration of war—he neither felt nor heard the crowd.

"Look!" said Fauchery, "here he comes; now just watch him."

The count had indeed quitted his seat, and had entered under the lofty doorway; but the doorkeeper, who by this time had become accustomed to him, did not give him time to repeat his question. He said abruptly,

"Sir, she died just a minute ago."

Nana dead! It was a blow for all of them. Muffat, without a word, returned to the seat, his face buried in his handkerchief.

The others cried out, but their voices were abruptly drowned, as another crowd passed along yelling,

"To Berlin! to Berlin! to Berlin!"

Nana dead! Was it possible? such a fine girl! Mignon sighed with relief; Rose would at last come down. There ensued a coolness. Fontan, who was longing for a tragic part, assumed an expression of grief, his mouth drawn down, his eyes turned up to the lids; whilst Fauchery, really affected in spite of his journalistic affectation of ridiculing everything, nervously champed his cigar. The two women, however, could not suppress their exclamations. The last time that Lucy had seen her was at the Gaiety Theatre, Blanche also, in "Mélusine." Oh! she was grand, my dear, when she appeared in the midst of the crystal grotto! The gentlemen recollected very well. Fontan played Prince Cocorico. And, their memories awakened, they launched forth into interminable details. Eh! in the crystal grotto, was she not just fine with her rich nature? She did not say a word; the authors had even struck out a cue, because it interfered. No, nothing at all, it was far grander; and she electrified the audience merely by showing herself. A form such as one will never see again—such shoulders, such legs and such a waist! How queer that she should be dead! You know that over her tights she simply wore a golden sash round the hips, which was scarcely sufficient. Around her, the grotto, all in glass, sparkled; there were cascades of diamonds, and strings of pearls trickled down amongst the stalactites of the roof; and in that transparency, in that pellucid spring, intersected by a broad ray of electric light, she appeared like a sun, with her skin and her hair of fire. Paris would ever see her thus, beaming in the midst of the crystal, poised in the air like a goddess. No, it was too stupid to allow oneself to die in such a position! Now, she must be a pretty sight up there!

"And what pleasure wasted!" said Mignon in the melancholy voice of a man who does not like to see good and useful things cast away.

He sounded Lucy and Caroline to know if they still had the intention of going upstairs. Most certainly they were going up; their curiosity had increased. Just then Blanche arrived all out of breath, and exasperated with the crowd which blocked all the footpaths; and when she learnt the news, the exclamations recommenced. The ladies moved towards the staircase, making a great noise with their skirts. Mignon followed them, calling out,

"Tell Rose I'm waiting for her. At once, please."

"One doesn't know for certain whether the contagion is most to be feared at the commencement or towards the end," Fontan was explaining to Faucherery. "A house-surgeon I know even assured me that the hours which follow death are most especially dangerous. Miasmata are expelled from the corpse. Ah! I regret this sudden end. I should have been so glad to have shaken her hand a last time."

"What good would it do now?" asked the journalist.

"Yes, what good?" repeated the other two.

The crowd continued to increase. In the flood of light from the shops, beneath the dancing sheets of flaring gas, one could distinguish a sea of hats drifting in a double current along the footpaths. At this time the fever was passing from one to another. People joined the bands in blouses; a continuous pushing swept the roadway; and the cry returned, issuing from every throat, jerky and obstinate,

"To Berlin! to Berlin! to Berlin!"

Upstairs, on the fourth floor, the room cost twelve francs a day, Rose having desired something decent, without being luxurious, however; for one does not want luxury when suffering. Hung in Louis XIII. cretonne, with large flowers, the room contained the mahogany furniture peculiar to all hotels, and a red carpet sprinkled with black foliage. A heavy silence reigned there, broken only by a whisper, when voices resounded in the corridor.

"I tell you we've lost our way. The waiter told us to turn to the right. What a barrack!"

"Wait a minute—Let's see. Room 401, room 401—"

"Here! this way—405, 403. This must be it. Ah! at last, 401! Come, hush! hush!"

The voices ceased. There was a slight coughing, then a momentary pause, and the door opened slowly, admitting Lucy, followed by Caroline and Blanche. But they halted; there were already five women in the room. Gaga was stretched out in the only easy-chair—one in red velvet. Simone and Clarisse, standing in front of the fire-place, were conversing with Léa de Horn, seated on a chair; whilst before the bed, to the left of the door, Rose Mignon, leaning against the woodwork of the foot, was looking fixedly at the corpse, lost in the shadow of the curtains. All the others had their bonnets and gloves on, like ladies out visiting; she only had bare hands, and her hair in disorder, her face pale with the fatigue of three nights of nursing. And there she stood, feeling stupid, with her features swollen from weeping, in the presence of that so sudden death. On the corner of the chest of drawers, a lamp with a shade lighted up Gaga with a brilliant flood of light.

"Ah! what a misfortune!" murmured Lucy, as she squeezed Rose's hand. "We wanted to bid her good-bye."

And she turned her head to catch a glimpse of Nana, but the lamp was too far off, and she did not like to move it nearer. On the bed a grey mass lay stretched out—one could only distinguish the golden chignon, and a palish-looking spot which was probably the face. Lucy added:

"I have never seen her since she was at the Gaiety Theatre, in the grotto."

Then Rose, shaking off her torpor, smiled and said, "Ah she is altered—she is altered!"

And she returned to her contemplation, without a gesture, without a word. Perhaps they would be able to look at her by-and-by; and the three women joined the others in front of the fire-place. Simone and Clarisse were talking, in an under-tone, about the deceased's diamonds. Now, did they really exist, those diamonds? No one had seen them, it was probably all bosh. But Léa de Horn knew someone who was acquainted with them; oh! some monstrous stones! Besides, that wasn't all, she had brought heaps of other riches from Russia—embroidered stuffs, precious knick-knacks, a service of gold plate, and even furniture; yes, my dear, fifty-two articles, some enormous cases, sufficient to load three luggage vans. It was all at the station. Ah! she had no luck, to die without even having time to unpack her things; and bear in mind that she had also some sous besides all these, something like a million. Lucy inquired who would inherit it all. Some distant relatives, the aunt very likely. A fine windfall for that old woman. She knew nothing yet; the invalid obstinately refused to have her informed, bearing her some ill-will for the death of her youngster. Then they all pitied the little fellow, as they recollected having seen him at the races—a baby full of disease, and who looked so sad and so old; in short, one of those poor brats who never wanted to be born.

"He is far happier in his grave," said Blanche.

"Bah! and she also," added Caroline. "Life isn't so pleasant after all."

Gloomy ideas possessed them, in the severity of that chamber of death. They were afraid, it was stupid to remain talking there so long; but a desire to see kept them rooted to the carpet. It was very warm, the lamp-glass shone on the ceiling like a moon, in the damp shadow which filled the apartment. Under the bed a soup plate full of some disinfectant exhaled a most unsavoury odour. And now and again a slight breath of air swelled the curtains of the window, opened on to the Boulevard, from whence arose a dull murmuring sound.

"Did she suffer much?" asked Lucy, who had been absorbed in the group above the clock—the three Graces, naked, and smiling like opera dancers. Gaga appeared to wake up.

"Ah! yes, she did! I was there when she passed away. I can tell you that there is nothing beautiful in it. She was seized with a shivering fit—"

But she could not continue her explanation. A cry arose— "To Berlin! to Berlin! to Berlin!"

And Lucy, who was stifling, opened the window wide, and leant out on the balustrade. There it was pleasant. A delightful coolness came from the starry sky. On the opposite side of the way, windows were ablaze with light, whilst the reflections of the gas danced among the gilded letters of the signs. Then down the street it was very amusing. One could see the currents of the crowd roll like a torrent along the footpaths and the roadway, in the midst of a block of vehicles and large moving shadows, among which the lights of the shops and of the street lamps sparkled. But the band, that now approached with loud shouts, carried torches. A ray of red light came from the direction of the Madeleine, dividing the mob with a trail of fire, spreading afar over the heads like the reflection of a conflagration. Lucy, forgetting where she was, called to Blanche and Caroline, exclaiming,

"Come quick! You can see very well from here."

All three leant out, greatly interested. The trees interfered with their view. At times the torches disappeared beneath the foliage. They tried to catch a glimpse of the gentlemen waiting below, but the projection of a balcony hid the hotel entrance, and they could only distinguish Count Muffat, still huddled up on the seat like a dark bundle, his face buried in his handkerchief. A carriage had stopped, and Lucy recognised Maria Blond, another one who was hastening there. She was not alone, a stout man got out after her.

"Why, it's that thief Steiner," said Caroline. "What! hasn't he been packed back to Cologne yet? I shall like to see how he looks when he comes in."

They turned round, but at the expiration of ten minutes, when Maria Blond appeared, after having twice mistaken the staircase, she was alone; and as Lucy questioned her with surprise, she exclaimed,

"He! ah, my dear! you made a mistake if you thought he was coming up! It's even wonderful for him that he came as far as the door with me. There's about a dozen of them downstairs, all smoking cigars."

In truth, all those gentlemen were there. Come for a stroll, just to see what was going on on the Boulevards, they had met together, and launched forth exclamations on the poor girl's death. Then they lapsed into politics and strategy. Bordenave, Daguenet, Labordette, Prullière, and others had swelled the group; and they were listening to Fontan, who was explaining his plan of campaign for capturing Berlin in five days.

However, Maria Blond, seized with compassion before the

bed, was murmuring as the others had done, "Poor dear! the last time I saw her was at the Gaiety Theatre, in the grotto."

"Ah! she is altered—she is altered!" repeated Rose Mignon, with her smile of dull grief.

Two more women arrived: Tatan Néné and Louise Violaine. They had been wandering about the hotel for quite twenty minutes, sent from waiter to waiter. They had gone up and down more than thirty flights of stairs, in the midst of a host of travellers who were flying from Paris, in the panic caused by the declaration of war and the commotion on the Boulevards. So, immediately on entering the room they sank into some chairs, too fatigued to think of the deceased. Just then, a great noise was heard in the next apartment; there was a moving of trunks, a knocking about of furniture, mingled with a sound of voices uttering barbarous accents. The room was occupied by a young Austrian couple. Gaga related that, during the death agony, the pair had played at running after each other; and as there was a door between the two rooms, one could hear them laughing and kissing, each time one of them was caught.

"Well, I must be off," said Clarisse. "We can't bring her to life again. Are you coming, Simone?"

They all glanced at the bed, without stirring. Yet they were getting ready to leave, they gently smoothed down their skirts. At the window Lucy was again leaning out, but alone. A sadness brought a lump to her throat, as though a profound melancholy arose from that yelling mob beneath. Torches continued to pass, casting flakes of fire around; in the distance the various bands, huddled together in the darkness, looked like flocks of sheep driven at night-time to the slaughter-house; and all that giddiness, those confused masses surging like the ocean, exhaled a terror, a great pity for coming massacres. They banished dull care, their shouts burst out in the intoxication of their fever rushing against the unknown, far away in the distance, behind the dark boundary of the horizon.

"To Berlin! to Berlin! to Berlin!"

Lucy turned round, her back against the balustrade of the window, and looking very pale, exclaimed, "Good heavens! what will become of us?"

The other women shook their heads. They were very grave, and full of anxiety about what was happening.

"I," said Caroline Héquet in her sedate way; "I'm off to London the day after to-morrow. Mamma is already there preparing a house for me. I'm certainly not going to stop in Paris to be massacred."

Her mother, like a prudent woman, had invested all her money abroad. One never knows how a war may end. But Maria Blond flew into a passion. She was patriotic; she talked of following the army.

"There's a runaway for you! Yes, if they would let me, I would dress up as a man and go and shoot those Prussian pigs! And if we were all to croak, what next? A pretty thing our bodies are!"

Blanche de Sivry was exasperated.

"Don't speak against the Prussians! They are men like the others, and are not for ever bothering women like your Frenchmen. They've just expelled the little Prussian who was with me—a fellow awfully rich and gentle as a lamb—incapable of hurting any one. It's a disgrace; it'll ruin me. And, do you know, if I'm bothered too much, I'll go and join him in Germany!"

Then, whilst each had her say, Gaga murmured in a doleful voice,

"It's the end; I've no luck. Only a week ago, I paid the last instalment for my little house at Juvisy. Ah! heaven knows what trouble it cost me! Lili had to help me. And now war's declared. The Prussians will come; they'll burn everything. How can I commence all over again at my age?"

"Of course," added Simone. "It will be funny. Perhaps on the contrary, we shall do—"

And she completed her thought with a smile. Tatan Néné and Louise Violaine were of the same opinion. The first one related that she had had some jolly times with soldiers—oh! delightful fellows who would do anything for a woman. But having raised their voices too high, Rose Mignon, still leaning against the woodwork at the foot of the bed, made them leave off with a gentle "hush!" They were startled, and glanced sideways towards the corpse, as though that request for silence had issued from the very shadow of the curtains; and in the heavy quiet that prevailed—that quiet of nothingness in which they were conscious of the rigidity of the corpse stretched out near them—the shouts of the mob burst out again,

"To Berlin! to Berlin! to Berlin!"

But they soon forgot their fright. Léa de Horn, who had a political salon, where some of Louis-Philippe's ex-ministers indulged in smart epigrams, resumed in a low voice, as she shrugged her shoulders,

"What a mistake, this war! what awful stupidity!"

Then Lucy at once defended the empire. She had been kept by one of the imperial princes; for her it was a family matter.

"Nonsense, my dear; we couldn't allow ourselves to be insulted any longer. This war is the honour of France. Oh! you know, I don't say that because of the prince. He was so stingy! Just fancy, every night he hid his louis in his boots, and whenever we played at bézique he used beans, because one day I seized the stakes, just for a joke. But that doesn't prevent my being just. The Emperor was in the right."

Léa wagged her head with an air of superiority, like a woman who repeats the opinions of eminent personages. And, raising her voice, she added:

"It's the end. They're all mad at the Tuileries. France ought to have sent them to the right about yesterday rather than—"

The others violently interrupted her. She was cracked. What was the matter with her? What had the Emperor ever done to her? Wasn't everyone happy? Wasn't business in a flourishing state? Paris could never be livelier. Gaga flew into a passion, roused with indignation.

"Shut up! it's idiotic! you don't know what you're saying! I lived in Louis-Philippe's time, an epoch of toast and water and sordidness, my dear. And then came '48. Ah! a fine thing, a disgusting time, their Republic! After February I was actually starving, I tell you! But if you had passed through all that, you would fall on your knees before the Emperor, for he's been our father, yes, our father."

They had to calm her. Then she resumed in a religious outburst, "O God! give the Emperor the victory. Preserve us the Empire!"

All repeated the prayer. Blanche admitted that she burnt candles for the Emperor. Caroline, full of a religious feeling, had for two months past gone everywhere that she was likely to come across him, without succeeding in attracting his notice. And the others broke out into furious tirades against the Republicans, talked of expelling them beyond the frontier, so that Napoleon III., after vanquishing the enemy, might reign peacefully, in the midst of the universal joy.

"That beast Bismarck—there's a scoundrel for you!" observed Maria Blond.

"To think that I once knew him!" cried Simone. "If I had only known, I would have put some poison in his glass."

But Blanche, still feeling aggrieved at the expulsion of her Prussian, dared to take Bismarck's part. He wasn't a bit wicked. Each one had his own duties. She added,

"You know, he adores women."

"What's that to us?" said Clarisse. "You don't think we want him, do you?"

"There are always too many men like him," gravely declared Louise Violaine. "We had better do without them altogether than have any acquaintance with such monsters."

And the discussion continued. They pulled Bismarck to pieces, each one gave him a kick in her Bonapartist zeal, whilst Tatan Néné said in a vexed manner,

"Bismarck! How they used to tease me about him! Oh! I owe him a grudge. I had never heard of him, that Bismarck! One can't know every one."

"All the same," said Léa de Horn conclusively, "that Bismarck's going to give us a good hiding—"

She was unable to continue. The other women all flew at her. Eh? what?—a hiding? It was Bismarck who was going to be sent back home, with kicks behind. She had better shut up, she was unworthy to be a Frenchwoman!

"Hush!" whispered Rose Mignon, feeling hurt at such a noise.

The frigidity of the corpse again impressed them. They all

ceased talking, uneasy and brought anew face to face with death, with the secret dread of evil. On the Boulevard the cry passed, hoarse and rending,

"To Berlin! to Berlin! to Berlin!"

Then, just as they were making up their minds to leave, a voice called from the corridor,

"Rose! Rose!"

Gaga, surprised, opened the door and disappeared for a moment. Then, when she returned, she said,

"My dear, it's Fauchery who is there at the end of the passage. He won't come any nearer. He is in an awful state because you persist in remaining here with the body."

Mignon had succeeded in inciting the journalist. Lucy, still at the window, leant out; and she caught sight of the gentlemen waiting on the pavement, looking up and making signs to her. Mignon, exasperated, was holding up his fists. Steiner, Fontan, Bordenave, and the others were opening their arms in an anxious and reproachful way; whilst Daguenet, so as not to compromise himself, was quietly smoking his cigar, his hands behind his back.

"I was forgetting, my dear," said Lucy, leaving the window open. "I promised to make you go down. They're all beckoning for us."

Rose moved away painfully from the foot of the bedstead. She murmured, "I will go down; I will go down. She no longer wants me now. We will send for a sister of charity."

And she looked about without being able to find her bonnet and shawl. She mechanically filled a basin with water at the wash-stand and washed her hands and face, as she continued.

"I don't know how it is, but it's been a great shock to me. We were not very nice to each other. Well! now I feel quite stupid. Oh! I've all sorts of ideas—a longing to die myself—the end of the world. Yes, I want some fresh air."

The dead body was beginning to fill the room with a fearful stench. There was quite a panic after such a long period of unconcern.

"Let's be off! let's be off, my dears!" repeated Gaga. "It isn't healthy."

They left the room quickly, throwing another glance towards the bed; but as Lucy, Blanche, and Caroline were still there, Rose gave a last look round to see that all was tidy. She drew the curtain before the window. Then she thought that the lamp was not proper, there ought to be a candle; and, after taking one of the brass candlesticks from the mantelpiece, she lit the candle, and placed it on the night-table beside the corpse. A bright light suddenly illuminated the face of the deceased. It was horrible. They shuddered, and hastened away.

"Ah! she is altered—she is altered!" murmured Rose Mignon, who was the last to leave the room.

She went off and closed the door. Nana was left alone, her face turned upwards in the candle-light. It was a charnel-house, a mass of matter and blood, a shovelful of putrid flesh, thrown there on the cushion. The pustules had invaded the entire face, one touching the other; and, faded, sunk in, with the greyish aspect of mud, they already seemed like a mouldiness of the earth on that shapeless pulp, in which the features were no longer recognisable. One of the eyes, the left one, had completely disappeared amidst the eruption of the purulence; the other, half open, looked like a black and tainted hole. The nose still continued to suppurate. A reddish crust starting from one of the cheeks, invaded the mouth, which it distorted in an abominable laugh; and on this horrible and grotesque mask of nothingness, the hair, that beautiful hair, retaining its sun-like fire, fell in a stream of gold. Venus was decomposing. It seemed as if the virus gathered by her in the gutters, from the tolerated carrion—that ferment with which she had poisoned a people—had ascended to her face and rotted it.

The room was deserted. A strong breath of despair mounted from the Boulevard, and swelled the curtain.

"To Berlin! to Berlin! to Berlin!"

Endnotes

1. (p. 195) *Galerie Montmartre . . . Galerie des Variétés . . . Galerie Saint-Marc:* These arcades, along with the Passage des Panoramas mentioned on page 33 and the Galerie Feydeau, on page 197, were pedestrian streets with glass roofs, lined with shops—the distant ancestors of today's shopping malls. The German critic and philosopher Walter Benjamin considered them to be the emblematic feature of nineteenth-century Paris and compiled and wrote an immense, unfinished book, *The Arcades Project* (1927–1940), that springs from a contemplation of their role in society. Although many arcades of the period have been demolished, these five, which are interconnected, still stand.

2. (p. 205) *Fauchery's article, entitled the "Golden Fly" . . . which it entered by the windows:* This article, entirely Zola's invention, constitutes his thesis statement, baldly put forth, the least subtle detail in a book that manages to be at once deft and broad. The reference to the girl having been "born from four or five generations of drunkards" is the only direct allusion in *Nana* to its predecessor, *L'Assommoir* (published in English as *The Drinking Den, The Dram Shop,* or *The Drunkard*). The genetic notions advanced here have long been discredited, although we know that behavior is often handed down through the generations by example.

3. (p. 320) *Then the conversation having turned . . . "may God preserve the Emperor as long as possible!":* This is another instance of Zola's unsubtle message-bearing. We are meant to remark upon the irony of Nana—descendant of generations of alcoholics—denouncing the Republicans as drunkards, assisted, of course, by the propaganda that the right-wing *Figaro* fed to its readers. That newspaper called Zola a "socialist"—a contentious word—in its review of *Nana*, but also ran a page of illustrations of the book's characters.

4. (p. 387) *But the waltz still continued its voluptuous whirl . . . saucy rhythm of the music:* In its foreshadowing of the events of the following two years—the Siege of Paris during the Franco-Prussian War and the subsequent Commune (an insurrection against the French government in the spring of 1871), and the burning of many official edifices and homes of the rich during the week of the Commune's suppression—this passage harks back to much

of the literature evoking the dawn of the Revolution, seen by many in the following century as having been a sort of divine punishment for the decadence of the aristocracy. Nana appears here as the agent of that wrath, and we are perhaps meant to see her as a harbinger of the *pétroleuses*, the women who were alleged to have started the fires in Paris in May 1871.

5. (p. 436) *During the day the Corps Législatif had voted for a declaration of war:* This dates the scene exactly, to July 19, 1870. Prussian Chancellor Otto von Bismarck, who was then in the process of uniting the disparate duchies and principalities of Germany into a single state, actively welcomed war with France, both to exhaust his country's nearest rival and to annex the German-speaking French provinces Alsace and Lorraine. He was too smart to declare war himself, however. When a member of the Hohenzollern family—a relative of the German emperor—was proposed as king of Spain, France took the fatal step. One military defeat followed another in quick succession, and the war was over by January, with France decisively trounced.

Inspired by
Nana

One of the most ambitious projects in Western literature, Émile Zola's *Les Rougon-Macquart*, a cycle of twenty novels, was published between 1871 and 1893. *Nana* is the ninth novel in the sequence, which is subtitled *The Natural and Social History of a Family Under the Second Empire*. The first book, *Les Fortune des Rougon* (1871; *The Fortune of the Rougons* or *The Rougon Family Fortune*), introduces the powerful Rougons and the lower-class Macquarts. Zola was deeply fascinated and philosophically driven by social determinism; he believed that human character was shaped by heredity, environment, and the cultural moment. He coined the term "naturalism" to describe this approach to literature, and it quickly became a movement of which Zola was the acknowledged leader.

In the Rougon-Macquart books, Zola places his characters in different socio-economic and professional contexts—including the Provençal countryside, a laundress's working-class neighborhood, the Parisian art scene, and the bleak battlefield at Sedan in 1870—and documents their behavior and development. Though the results are deeply imaginative, Zola regarded his novels as "experiments." Rather than a creative excursion, each book is akin to a study in which the author records his observations with strict, even scientific, exactitude. Zola's cycle pays homage to French fiction writer Honoré de Balzac (1799–1850), who is widely credited with introducing realism to literature. Balzac's titanic series *La Comédie humaine* (*The Human Comedy*) comprises roughly ninety novels and novellas. Conversely, Zola's almost detached approach to his fiction runs counter to that of Marcel Proust (1871–1922) in his seven-part cycle *À la recherche du temps perdu* (*Remembrance of Things Past*), in which the narrator's subjectivity determines the course of the honeycombed narrative.

The novels of Zola's Rougon-Macquart cycle, in order of their appearance, are:

La Fortune des Rougon (1871; *The Fortune of the Rougons* or *The Rougon Family*)

La Curée (1872; *The Kill*)

Le Ventre de Paris (1873; *The Belly of Paris* or *Savage Paris*)

La Conquête de Plassans (1874; *The Conquest of Plassans*)

La Faute de l'abbé Mouret (1875; *The Sin of Father Mouret*)

Son Excellence Eugène Rougon (1876; *His Excellency Eugène Rougon*)

L'Assommoir (1877; *The Drinking Den, The Dram Shop*, or *The Drunkard*)

Une Page d'amour (1878; *A Page of Love* or *A Love Affair*)

Nana (1880)

Pot-Bouille (1882; *Restless House*)

Au Bonheur des dames (1883; *Ladies' Delight* or *A Ladies' Paradise*)

La Joie de vivre (1884; *The Joy of Life* or *Zest for Life*)

Germinal (1885)

L'Oeuvre (1886; *The Masterpiece*)

La Terre (1887; *Earth* or *The Soil*)

La Rêve (1888; *The Dream*)

La Bête humaine (1890; *The Human Beast* or *The Beast in Man*)

L'Argent (1891; *Money*)

La Débâcle (1892; *The Debacle* or *The Collapse*)

Le Docteur Pascal (1893; *Doctor Pascal*)

After the Rougon-Macquart cycle, Zola wrote two shorter series: *Les Trois Villes* (*Three Cities: Lourdes*, 1894; *Rome*, 1896; *Paris*, 1898), the first two comprising a scathing attack on the Catholic Church; and *Les Quatre Évangiles* (1899–1903; *The Four Gospels*), the last volume of which was left unfinished at Zola's death.

Comments & Questions

In this section, we aim to provide the reader with an array of perspectives on the text, as well as questions that challenge those perspectives. The commentary has been culled from sources as diverse as reviews contemporaneous with the work, letters written by the author, literary criticism of later generations, and appreciations written throughout the work's history. Following the commentary, a series of questions seeks to filter Émile Zola's Nana *through a variety of points of view and bring about a richer understanding of this enduring work.*

COMMENTS

The Nation

So far 'Nana' is indisputably M. Zola's worst book. Curiously enough, the impression that it must leave upon every reader, whether blasé or inexperienced, is that it is unreal and amateurish. This is unfortunate, for M. Zola has certainly never chosen a theme better capable of illustrating his great theory that there is no sunshine anywhere in life, and it cannot fail to be disappointing to so distinguished a moralist to make so slight an impression with so potent a subject. Compared with the conviction conveyed in such a sentence as "He knows not that the dead are there, and that her guests are in the depths of hell," 'Nana' seems trivial. There are some "facts of life" which can be estimated quite accurately without experience of them, and it might be objected to this book that the misery of the life of a "Nana" is one; but it is a sufficient objection to it that, judged by M. Zola's own standard, it fails in verisimilitude.

—February 19, 1880

Henry James

Does [M. Zola] call that vision of things of which *Nana* is a representation, *nature?* The mighty mother, in her blooming richness, seems to blush from brow to chin at the insult! On what authority does M. Zola represent nature to us as a combination

of the cesspool and the house of prostitution? On what authority does he represent foulness rather than fairness as the sign
that we are to know her by? On the authority of predilections
alone; and this is his great trouble and the weak point of his in-
contestably remarkable talent. . . . Reality is the object of M.
Zola's efforts, and it is because we agree with him in appreciat-
ing it highly that we protest against its being discredited. In a
time when literary taste has turned, to a regrettable degree, to
the vulgar and the insipid, it is of high importance that realism
should not be compromised. Nothing tends more to compromise it than to represent it as necessarily allied to the impure.
That the pure and impure are for M. Zola, as conditions of taste,
vain words, and exploded ideas, only proves that his advocacy
does more to injure an excellent cause than to serve it. It takes
a very good cause to carry a *Nana* on its back, and if realism
breaks down, and the conventional comes in again with a rush,
we may know the reason why. . . . Taste, in its intellectual appli-
cations, is the most human faculty we possess, and as the novel
may be said to be the most human form of art, it is a poor speculation to put the two things out of conceit of each other. Calling it naturalism will never make it profitable. It is perfectly easy
to agree with M. Zola, who has taken his stand with more em-
phasis than necessary; for the matter reduces itself to a question
of application. It is impossible to see why the question of application is less urgent in naturalism than at any other point of the
scale, or why, if naturalism is, as M. Zola claims, a method of observation, it can be followed without delicacy or tact. There are
all sorts of things to be said about it; it costs us no effort whatever to admit in the briefest terms that it is an admirable invention, and full of promise; but we stand aghast at the want of tact
it has taken to make so unreadable a book as *Nana.*

> —from an unsigned review in *The Parisian*
> (February 26, 1880)

Gustave Flaubert
In my opinion *Nana* contains wonderful things: Bordenave,
Mignon, etc., and the end, which is epic. It is a colossus with
dirty feet, but it is a colossus.

Many things in it shock me, but no matter! One must be able to admire things one doesn't love.

> —from a letter to Mme. Roger des Genettes,
> translated by Francis Steegmuller (April 18, 1880)

A. K. Fiske

Critics have had their say regarding the latest product of that genius of the muck-rake, Emile Zola. Many of them have endeavored to find a justification for his opening of the sewers of human society into the gardens of literature. Much ability is displayed in this offensive work of engineering skill, and people are asked to pardon the foul sights and odors because of the consummate art with which they are presented. But intellectual power and literary workmanship are neither to be admired nor commended of themselves. They are to be judged by their fruits, and are no more to be justified in producing that which is repulsive or unwholesome than a manufactory whose sole purpose is to create and disseminate bad smells and noxious vapors. Such an unsavory establishment might do its work with a wonderful display of skill and most potent results, but the health authorities of society would have ample occasion for taking measures against its obnoxious business, while those who encouraged the introduction of its products into their households would be guilty of inconceivable folly, besides exhibiting a morbid liking for filthy exhalations.

But it is not alone in M. Zola's literary talent that excuse is found for his work. It is said to lay bare a phase of human life whose existence is actual, and knowledge of which affords security and perhaps suggests remedies for its evils. The phase of life with which he deals in "Nana" is undoubtedly real, but is, unfortunately, not so far a realm of the unknown that an accurate exploration or a vivid portrayal of its characters and scenes is at all necessary or desirable. Those who are likely to make a salutary use of a knowledge of its secrets have no difficulty in obtaining it, and there is no reason for bringing its revelations into the family circle or the chamber of the schoolgirl. The life of the fallen among women is no deep mystery. It is well enough known in its glare and glitter, in its allurement and revelry, in its Circean fascinations and their besotting effects, in its coarse vulgarity and in its bestial pollutions. The whole Avernian descent from gay hilarity and defiance of doom to putridity and despair is a reality of the world's everyday experience. . . .

But, though these things are real, M. Zola's delineations of them are not truthful. His work has been called "realistic," and that has been paraded as a merit; but what is meant by this word upon which a new meaning is thrust to serve the purposes of criticism? People averse to analyzing take it to mean that the work in question portrays life and character precisely as they exist, without the color or the glamour which fiction is supposed generally to throw over its descriptions. But as applied to Zola's work it means nothing of the kind. It means that he drags into literature what others would not touch because of its coarseness or its foulness. He displays no extraordinary power in painting scenes of actual life, in portraying human character or in fathoming the feelings or the motives of men. . . . M. Zola may know more of the life that he undertakes to portray than decent readers care to know, but men who go through the world with their eyes open, and are capable of making those inferences in regard to character and experience which surface indications suggest, know that this book is replete with exaggeration. It does not describe the real life of the class whose type is its central figure, with the sharp lines of truth. The picture is colossal in proportions and flaring in colors. It is no more in the tone of every-day reality than "King Lear" or "The Bride of Lammermoor." This huge, fleshy Venus, with gross attractions of person and no touch of mental or moral charm, exercising a relentless dominion of lust over the rich and proud, the stupid and the brilliant, the unsophisticated and the experienced, is a daring figment of the imagination, as much so as the witch that lured the companions of Ulysses to their swinish fate.

—from a review of *Nana* published in the
North American Review (July 1880)

Harper's Weekly

A book not worth the reading, and in all respects not worth the writing, is Zola's *Nana*, which the Austrian has forbidden the sale of, on account of a conviction that it is an outrage upon morality.

—August 9, 1884

Havelock Ellis

The chief service which Zola has rendered to his fellow-artists and successors, the reason of the immense stimulus he supplies, seems to lie in the proofs he has brought of the latent artistic uses of the rough, neglected details of life. The Rougon-Macquart series has been to his weaker brethren like that great sheet knit at the four corners, let down from Heaven full of four-footed beasts and creeping things and fowls in the air, and bearing in it the demonstration that to the artist as to the moralist nothing can be called common or unclean. It has henceforth been possible for other novelists to find inspiration where before they could never have turned, to touch life with a vigour and audacity of phrase which, without Zola's example, they would have trembled to use, while they still remain free to bring to their work the simplicity, precision, and inner experience which he has never possessed. Zola has enlarged the field of the novel.

—from *Affirmations* (1898)

Ben Ray Redman

"Nana" is, I firmly believe, a very bad novel. The real tragedy of the book, though not the one the author intended, is the transformation of a woman into a symbol. At the outset Nana is a perfectly credible trull, unscrupulous, voluptuous, shameless, and vigorous; but her life, for the reader, has scarcely commenced before she starts to change slowly from a full-blooded animal into a symbol of evil. . . . "Nana" could never have been written by a man who possessed a shred of humor: it is grotesque.

—from *The Nation* (August 1, 1923)

Roland Barthes

Nana is truly an epic book; not only because of the admirable excess of the descriptions, but also because of the very tempo of the work, the familiar tempo of catastrophes. Zola wishes to describe a degradation, a collapse, and the whole movement of his narrative bows to that intention.

—from the *Bulletin Mensuel* (June 1955)

QUESTIONS

1. Does the character Nana seem convincing to you? Is she "realistic"? One critic says that early on she "starts to change slowly from a full-blooded animal into a symbol of evil." What do you think?

2. A critic for *Harper's Weekly* described *Nana* as "an outrage upon morality." But one can imagine another critic finding fault with it for being just the opposite—too moralistic. Zola himself made claims of scientific objectivity. Do any of these positions do justice to the novel? Could it be that all of them—scientific, amoral, moral—apply, but only to separate passages?

3. Which, in this novel, is the most powerful shaper of human character: heredity, the environment, or the historical moment?

For Further Reading

OTHER WORKS BY ÉMILE ZOLA

L' Assommoir. 1877. Translated by Margaret Mauldon. Oxford and New York: Oxford University Press, 1998. Zola's novel appears in other editions with the title translated as *The Drinking Den, The Dram Shop,* and *The Drunkard.*

Germinal. 1885. Translated by Havelock Ellis; introduction and notes by Dominique Julien. New York: Barnes & Noble Classics, 2005.

The Dreyfus Affair: "J'Accuse" and Other Writings. Edited by Alain Pagés; translated by Eleanor Levieux. New Haven, CT: Yale University Press, 1998.

Zola—Photographer. Compiled and edited by François Émile-Zola and Massin; translated by Liliane Emery Tuck. New York: Seaver Books, 1988.

BIOGRAPHIES

Brown, Frederick. *Zola: A Life.* New York: Farrar, Straus and Giroux, 1995. The best and most up-to-date life in English.

Hemmings, F. W. J. *The Life and Times of Émile Zola.* New York: Scribner, 1977.

Josephson, Matthew. *Zola and His Time.* London: Victor Gollancz, 1929.

Schom, Alan. *Émile Zola: A Biography.* New York: Henry Holt, 1988.

Vizetelly, Ernest. *Émile Zola: Novelist and Reformer.* 1904. Freeport, NY: Books for Libraries Press, 1971.

BIO-CRITICAL WORKS

Bédé, Jean Albert. *Émile Zola.* New York: Columbia University Press, 1974.

Berg, William J., and Laurey K. Martin. *Émile Zola Revisited.* Twayne's World Author Series. New York: Twayne, 1992.

Bloom, Harold, ed. *Émile Zola: Modern Critical Views.* Philadelphia, PA: Chelsea House, 2004.

Friedman, Lee Max. 1937. *Zola & the Dreyfus Case: His Defense of Liberty and Its Enduring Significance.* New York: Gordon Press, 1973.

Howells, William Dean. *Émile Zola.* Digireads.com, 2004.

Knapp, Bettina L. *Émile Zola.* New York: Frederick Ungar, 1980.

Walker, Philip D. *Émile Zola.* New York: Humanities Press, 1968.

Wilson, Angus. *Émile Zola: An Introductory Study of His Novels.* New York: William Morrow, 1952.

CRITICAL WORKS

Berg, William J. *The Visual Novel: Émile Zola and the Art of His Times.* University Park: Pennsylvania State University Press, 1992.

Carter, Lawson A. *Zola and the Theater.* 1963. Westport, CT: Greenwood Press, 1977.

Gural-Migdal, Anna, and Robert Singer, eds. *Zola and Film: Essays in the Art of Adaptation.* Jefferson, NC: McFarland, 2005.

Petrey, Sandy. *Realism and Revolution: Balzac, Stendhal, Zola, and the Performances of History.* Ithaca, NY: Cornell University Press, 1988.

WORK CITED IN THE INTRODUCTION

Mitterand, Henri, and Jean Vidal, eds. *Album Zola.* Paris: Gallimard, 1963.

Look for the following titles, available now and forthcoming from
BARNES & NOBLE CLASSICS.

Title	Author	ISBN	Price
Aesop's Fables	Aesop	1-59308-062-X	$5.95
The Age of Innocence	Edith Wharton	1-59308-143-X	$5.95
Agnes Grey	Anne Brontë	1-59308-323-8	$5.95
Alice's Adventures in Wonderland and Through the Looking-Glass	Lewis Carroll	1-59308-015-8	$5.95
Anna Karenina	Leo Tolstoy	1-59308-027-1	$8.95
The Art of War	Sun Tzu	1-59308-017-4	$7.95
The Awakening and Selected Short Fiction	Kate Chopin	1-59308-113-8	$6.95
Babbitt	Sinclair Lewis	1-59308-267-3	$7.95
Barchester Towers	Anthony Trollope	1-59308-337-8	$7.95
The Beautiful and Damned	F. Scott Fitzgerald	1-59308-245-2	$7.95
Beowulf	Anonymous	1-59308-266-5	$4.95
Bleak House	Charles Dickens	1-59308-311-4	$9.95
The Bostonians	Henry James	1-59308-297-5	$7.95
The Brothers Karamazov	Fyodor Dostoevsky	1-59308-045-X	$9.95
The Call of the Wild and White Fang	Jack London	1-59308-200-2	$5.95
Candide	Voltaire	1-59308-028-X	$4.95
A Christmas Carol, The Chimes and The Cricket on the Hearth	Charles Dickens	1-59308-033-6	$5.95
The Collected Poems of Emily Dickinson	Emily Dickinson	1-59308-050-6	$5.95
Common Sense and Other Writings	Thomas Paine	1-59308-209-6	$6.95
The Communist Manifesto and Other Writings	Karl Marx and Friedrich Engels	1-59308-100-6	$5.95
The Complete Sherlock Holmes, Vol. I	Sir Arthur Conan Doyle	1-59308-034-4	$7.95
The Complete Sherlock Holmes, Vol. II	Sir Arthur Conan Doyle	1-59308-040-9	$7.95
A Connecticut Yankee in King Arthur's Court	Mark Twain	1-59308-210-X	$7.95
The Count of Monte Cristo	Alexandre Dumas	1-59308-151-0	$7.95
The Country of the Pointed Firs and Selected Short Fiction	Sarah Orne Jewett	1-59308-262-2	$6.95
Daisy Miller and Washington Square	Henry James	1-59308-105-7	$4.95
Daniel Deronda	George Eliot	1-59308-290-8	$8.95
David Copperfield	Charles Dickens	1-59308-063-8	$7.95
Dead Souls	Nikolai Gogol	1-59308-092-1	$7.95
The Death of Ivan Ilych and Other Stories	Leo Tolstoy	1-59308-069-7	$7.95
The Deerslayer	James Fenimore Cooper	1-59308-211-8	$7.95
Don Quixote	Miguel de Cervantes	1-59308-046-8	$9.95
Dracula	Bram Stoker	1-59308-114-6	$6.95
Emma	Jane Austen	1-59308-152-9	$6.95
The Enchanted Castle and Five Children and It	Edith Nesbit	1-59308-274-6	$6.95
Essays and Poems by Ralph Waldo Emerson		1-59308-076-X	$6.95
Essential Dialogues of Plato		1-59308-269-X	$9.95
The Essential Tales and Poems of Edgar Allan Poe		1-59308-064-6	$7.95
Ethan Frome and Selected Stories	Edith Wharton	1-59308-090-5	$5.95

(continued)

Middlemarch	George Eliot	1-59308-023-9	$8.95
Moby-Dick	Herman Melville	1-59308-018-2	$9.95
Moll Flanders	Daniel Defoe	1-59308-216-9	$5.95
The Moonstone	Wilkie Collins	1-59308-322-X	$7.95
My Ántonia	Willa Cather	1-59308-202-9	$5.95
My Bondage and My Freedom	Frederick Douglass	1-59308-301-7	$6.95
Nana	Émile Zola	1-59308-292-4	$6.95
Narrative of Sojourner Truth		1-59308-293-2	$6.95
Narrative of the Life of Frederick Douglass, an American Slave		1-59308-041-7	$4.95
Nicholas Nickleby	Charles Dickens	1-59308-300-9	$8.95
Night and Day	Virginia Woolf	1-59308-212-6	$7.95
Northanger Abbey	Jane Austen	1-59308-264-9	$5.95
Nostromo	Joseph Conrad	1-59308-193-6	$7.95
O Pioneers!	Willa Cather	1-59308-205-3	$5.95
The Odyssey	Homer	1-59308-009-3	$5.95
Oliver Twist	Charles Dickens	1-59308-206-1	$6.95
The Origin of Species	Charles Darwin	1-59308-077-8	$7.95
Paradise Lost	John Milton	1-59308-095-6	$7.95
Père Goriot	Honoré de Balzac	1-59308-285-1	$7.95
Persuasion	Jane Austen	1-59308-130-8	$5.95
Peter Pan	J. M. Barrie	1-59308-213-4	$4.95
The Picture of Dorian Gray	Oscar Wilde	1-59308-025-5	$4.95
The Pilgrim's Progress	John Bunyan	1-59308-254-1	$7.95
Poetics and Rhetoric	Aristotle	1-59308-307-6	$9.95
The Portrait of a Lady	Henry James	1-59308-096-4	$7.95
A Portrait of the Artist as a Young Man and Dubliners	James Joyce	1-59308-031-X	$6.95
The Possessed	Fyodor Dostoevsky	1-59308-250-9	$9.95
Pride and Prejudice	Jane Austen	1-59308-201-0	$5.95
The Prince and Other Writings	Niccolò Machiavelli	1-59308-060-3	$5.95
The Prince and the Pauper	Mark Twain	1-59308-218-5	$4.95
Pudd'nhead Wilson and Those Extraordinary Twins	Mark Twain	1-59308-255-X	$5.95
The Purgatorio	Dante Alighieri	1-59308-219-3	$7.95
Pygmalion and Three Other Plays	George Bernard Shaw	1-59308-078-6	$7.95
The Red and the Black	Stendhal	1-59308-286-X	$7.95
The Red Badge of Courage and Selected Short Fiction	Stephen Crane	1-59308-119-7	$4.95
Republic	Plato	1-59308-097-2	$6.95
The Return of the Native	Thomas Hardy	1-59308-220-7	$7.95
Robinson Crusoe	Daniel Defoe	1-59308-360-2	$5.95
A Room with a View	E. M. Forster	1-59308-288-6	$5.95
Sailing Alone Around the World	Joshua Slocum	1-59308-303-3	$6.95
Scaramouche	Rafael Sabatini	1-59308-242-8	$6.95
The Scarlet Letter	Nathaniel Hawthorne	1-59308-207-X	$4.95
The Scarlet Pimpernel	Baroness Orczy	1-59308-234-7	$5.95
The Secret Garden	Frances Hodgson Burnett	1-59308-277-0	$5.95
Selected Stories of O. Henry		1-59308-042-5	$5.95
Sense and Sensibility	Jane Austen	1-59308-125-1	$5.95
Sentimental Education	Gustave Flaubert	1-59308-306-8	$6.95
Silas Marner and Two Short Stories	George Eliot	1-59308-251-7	$6.95

(continued)

Sister Carrie	Theodore Dreiser	1-59308-226-6	$7.95
Six Plays by Henrik Ibsen		1-59308-061-1	$8.95
Sons and Lovers	D. H. Lawrence	1-59308-013-1	$7.95
The Souls of Black Folk	W. E. B. Du Bois	1-59308-014-X	$5.95
The Strange Case of Dr. Jekyll and Mr. Hyde and Other Stories	Robert Louis Stevenson	1-59308-131-6	$4.95
Swann's Way	Marcel Proust	1-59308-295-9	$8.95
A Tale of Two Cities	Charles Dickens	1-59308-138-3	$5.95
Tao Te Ching	Lao Tzu	1-59308-256-8	$5.95
Tess of d'Urbervilles	Thomas Hardy	1-59308-228-2	$7.95
This Side of Paradise	F. Scott Fitzgerald	1-59308-243-6	$6.95
Three Lives	Gertrude Stein	1-59308-320-3	$6.95
The Three Musketeers	Alexandre Dumas	1-59308-148-0	$8.95
Thus Spoke Zarathustra	Friedrich Nietzsche	1-59308-278-9	$7.95
Tom Jones	Henry Fielding	1-59308-070-0	$8.95
Treasure Island	Robert Louis Stevenson	1-59308-247-9	$4.95
The Turn of the Screw, The Aspern Papers and Two Stories	Henry James	1-59308-043-3	$5.95
Twenty Thousand Leagues Under the Sea	Jules Verne	1-59308-302-5	$5.95
Uncle Tom's Cabin	Harriet Beecher Stowe	1-59308-121-9	$7.95
Utopia	Sir Thomas More	1-59308-244-4	$5.95
Vanity Fair	William Makepeace Thackeray	1-59308-071-9	$7.95
The Varieties of Religious Experience	William James	1-59308-072-7	$7.95
Villette	Charlotte Brontë	1-59308-316-5	$7.95
The Virginian	Owen Wister	1-59308-236-3	$7.95
The Voyage Out	Virginia Woolf	1-59308-229-0	$6.95
Walden and Civil Disobedience	Henry David Thoreau	1-59308-208-8	$5.95
War and Peace	Leo Tolstoy	1-59308-073-5	$12.95
Ward No. 6 and Other Stories	Anton Chekhov	1-59308-003-4	$7.95
The Waste Land and Other Poems	T. S. Eliot	1-59308-279-7	$4.95
The Way We Live Now	Anthony Trollope	1-59308-304-1	$9.95
The Wind in the Willows	Kenneth Grahame	1-59308-265-7	$4.95
The Wings of the Dove	Henry James	1-59308-296-7	$7.95
Wives and Daughters	Elizabeth Gaskell	1-59308-257-6	$7.95
The Woman in White	Wilkie Collins	1-59308-280-0	$7.95
Women in Love	D. H. Lawrence	1-59308-258-4	$8.95
The Wonderful Wizard of Oz	L. Frank Baum	1-59308-221-5	$6.95
Wuthering Heights	Emily Brontë	1-59308-128-6	$5.95

BARNES & NOBLE CLASSICS

If you are an educator and would like to receive an
Examination or Desk Copy of a Barnes & Noble Classic edition,
please refer to Academic Resources on our website at
WWW.BN.COM/CLASSICS
or contact us at
B&NCLASSICS@BN.COM.

All prices are subject to change.